Published by First Second
First Second is an imprint of Roaring Brook Press,
a division of Holtzbrinck Publishing Holdings Limited Partnership
120 Broadway, New York, NY 10271
firstsecondbooks.com
mackids.com

Library of Congress Control Number: 2022905669

Our books may be purchased in bulk for promotional, educational,
or business use. Please contact your local bookseller or the Macmillan Corporate
and Premium Sales Department at (800) 221-7945 ext. 5442 or by email
at MacmillanSpecialMarkets@macmillan.com.

First edition, 2023
Edited by Robyn Chapman and Michael Moccio
Cover design and interior book design by Molly Johanson
Production editing by Kat Kopit
Authenticity readers: Francesca Lyn and Noemi Martinez
Thanks to Dennis Pacheco for help with the Spanish dialogue

Drawn and colored in Procreate with a pencil-style digital nib and inked with a
brush-style digital nib. Dialogue, word balloons, and other finishing touches were
added in Photoshop. The lettering is a mix of hand lettering and a custom font
composed of the artist's handwriting.

Printed in China by 1010 Printing International Limited, Kwun Tong, Hong Kong

ISBN 978-1-250-80140-1 (hardcover)
10 9 8 7 6 5 4 3 2 1

Don't miss your next favorite book from First Second! For the latest updates go
to firstsecondnewsletter.com and sign up for our enewsletter.

TRAVIS DAVENTHORPE
FOR THE WIN!

BY
WES MOLEBASH

:01
First Second
NEW YORK

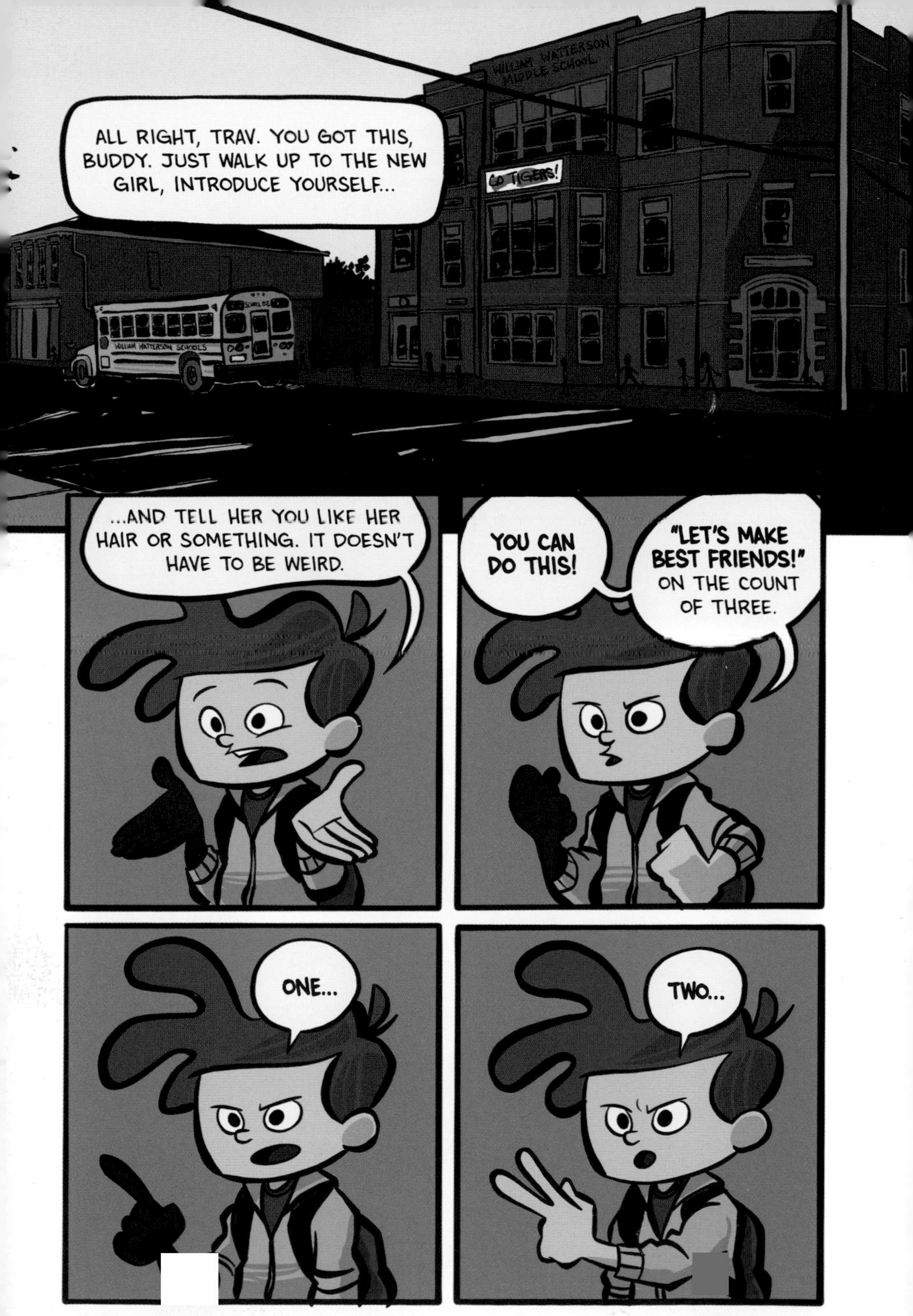
WILLIAM WATTERSON MIDDLE SCHOOL
GO TIGERS!
ALL RIGHT, TRAV. YOU GOT THIS, BUDDY. JUST WALK UP TO THE NEW GIRL, INTRODUCE YOURSELF...
WILLIAM WATTERSON SCHOOLS
...AND TELL HER YOU LIKE HER HAIR OR SOMETHING. IT DOESN'T HAVE TO BE WEIRD.
YOU CAN DO THIS!
"LET'S MAKE BEST FRIENDS!" ON THE COUNT OF THREE.
ONE...
TWO...

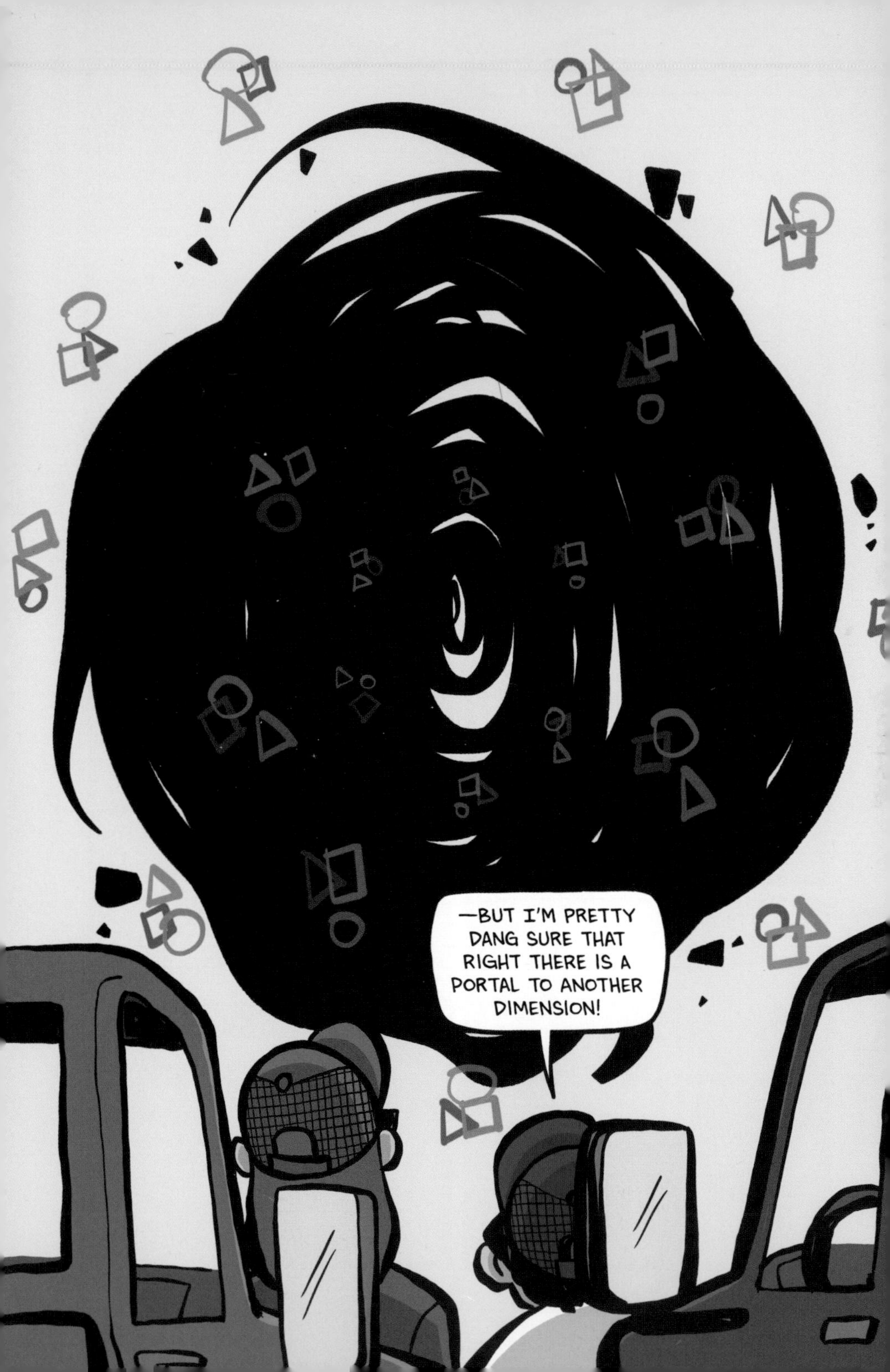
—BUT I'M PRETTY DANG SURE THAT RIGHT THERE IS A PORTAL TO ANOTHER DIMENSION!

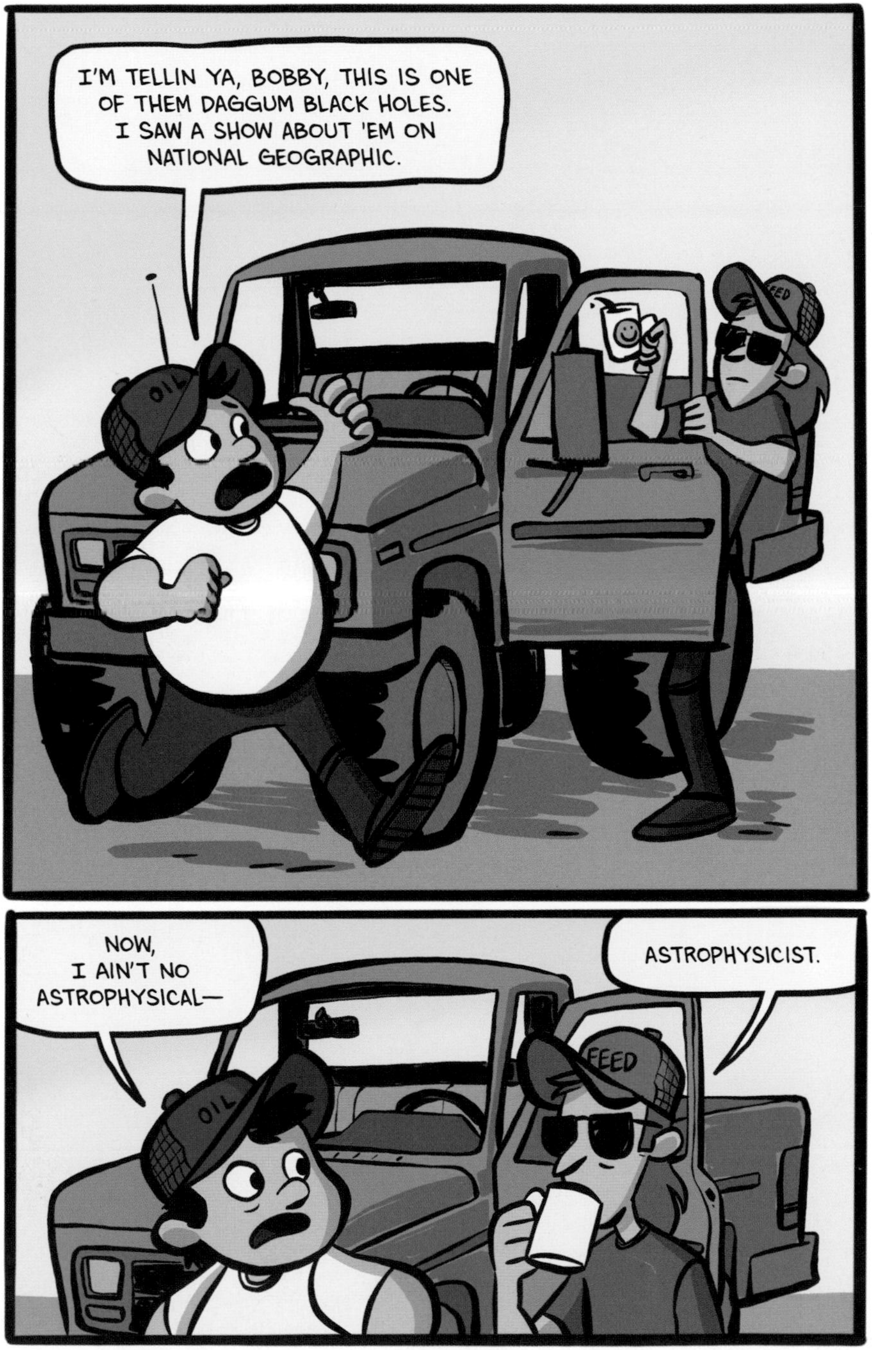
I'M TELLIN YA, BOBBY, THIS IS ONE OF THEM DAGGUM BLACK HOLES. I SAW A SHOW ABOUT 'EM ON NATIONAL GEOGRAPHIC.
OIL
FEED
NOW, I AIN'T NO ASTROPHYSICAL—
ASTROPHYSICIST.
OIL
FEED

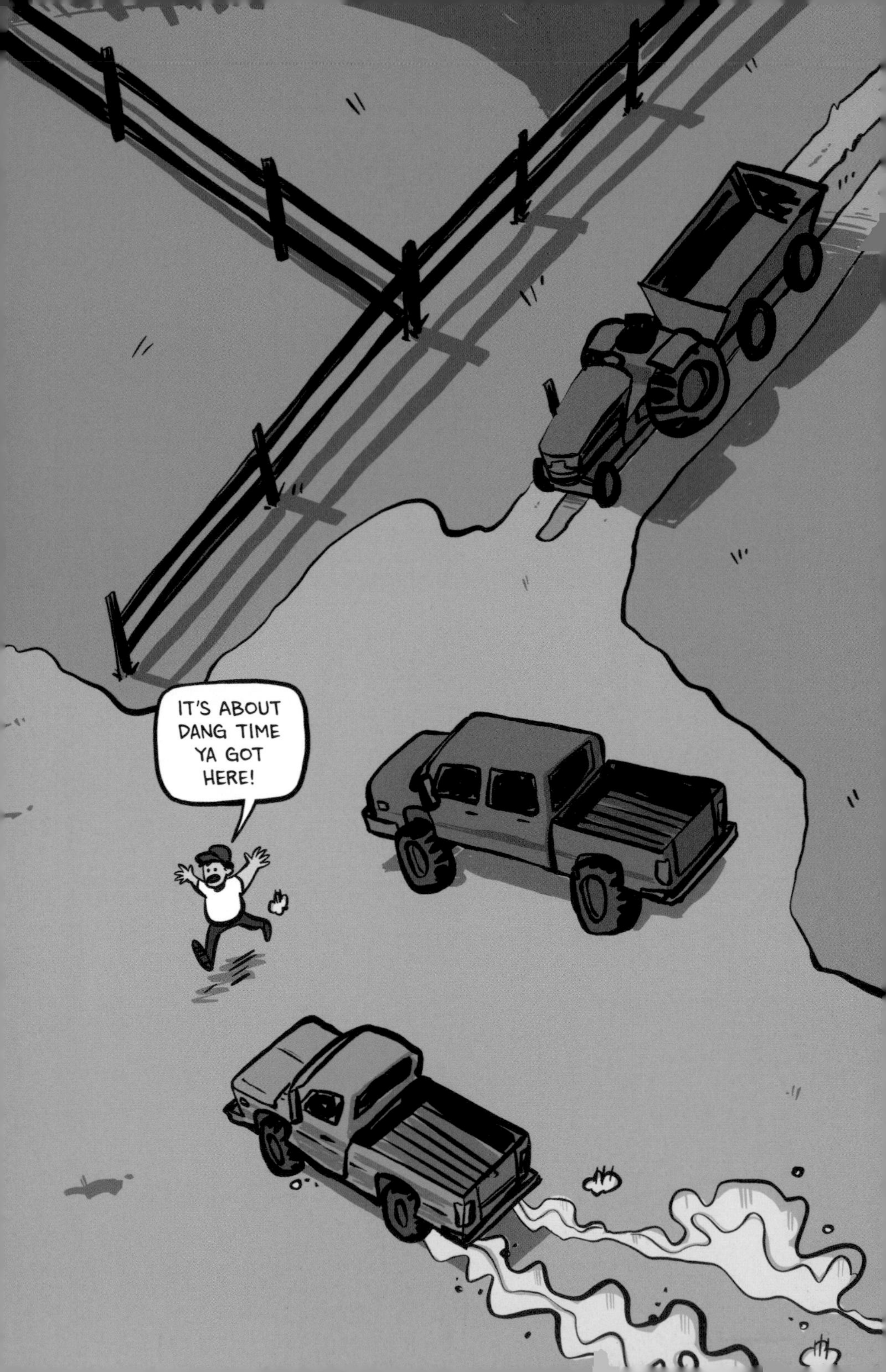
IT'S ABOUT DANG TIME YA GOT HERE!

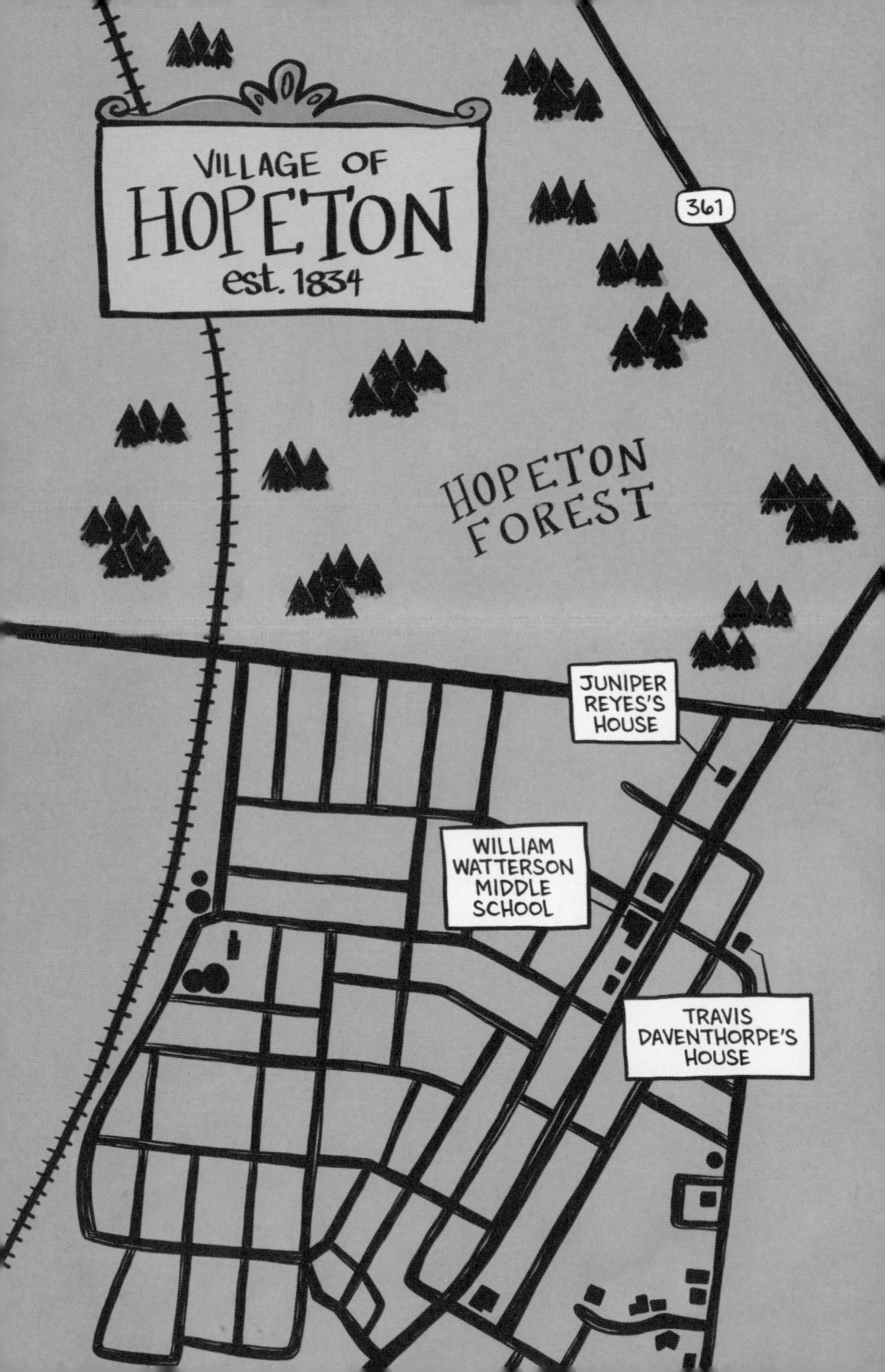
VILLAGE OF
HOPETON
est. 1834
361
HOPETON
FOREST
JUNIPER
REYES'S
HOUSE
WILLIAM
WATTERSON
MIDDLE
SCHOOL
TRAVIS
DAVENTHORPE'S
HOUSE

FOR KARI:
YOU'RE MY FAVORITE PERSON IN THE
WHOLE WIDE WORLD.

FOR PARKER AND CONNOR:
THIS BOOK WAS MADE WITH YOU IN
MIND. I HOPE YOU LIKE IT.

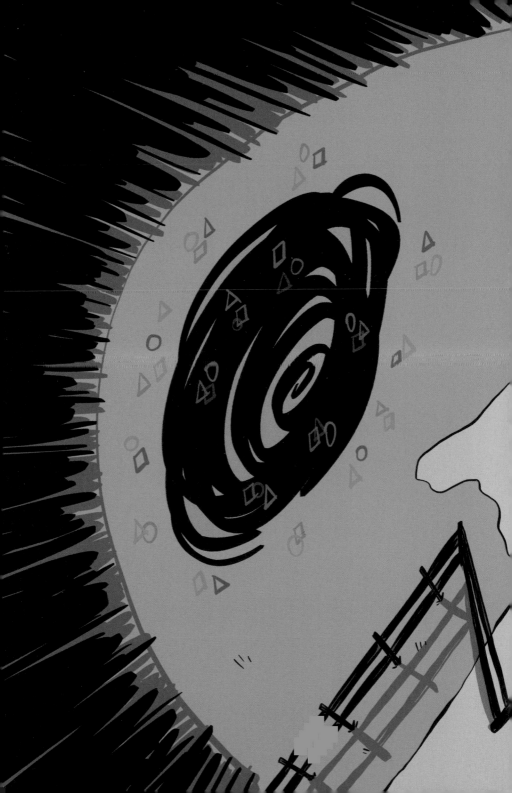

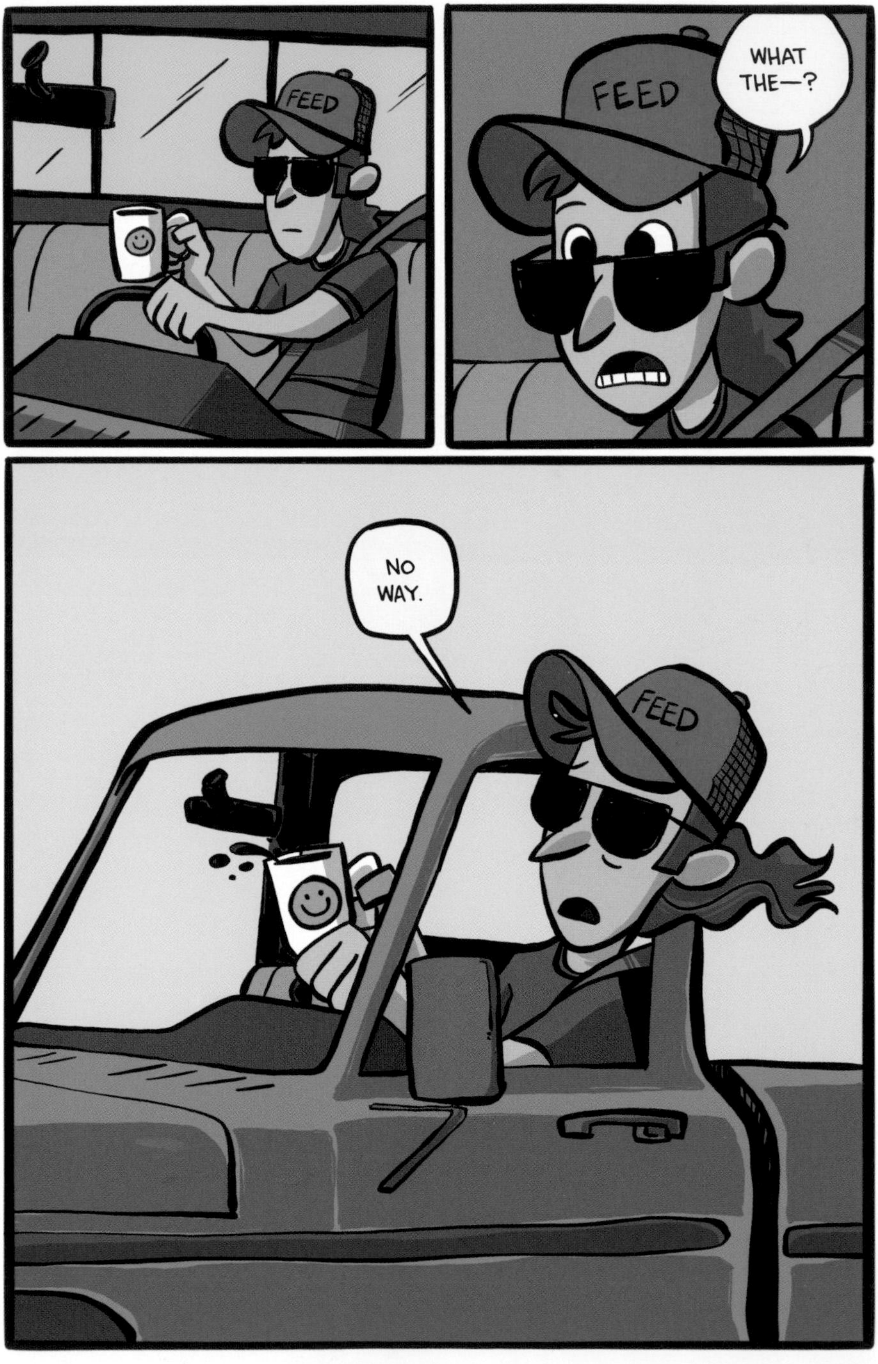
FEED
FEED
WHAT THE—?
NO WAY.
FEED

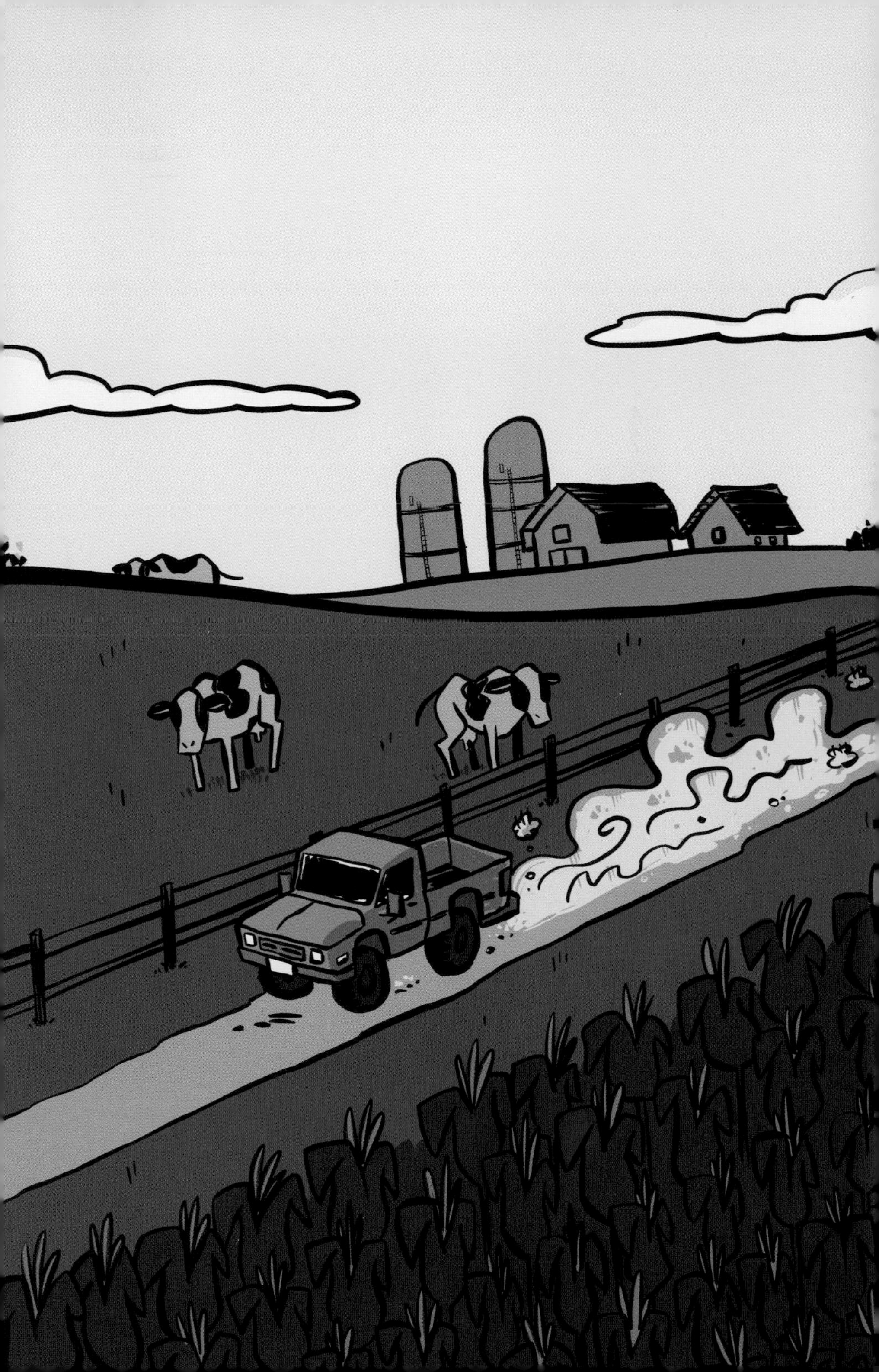

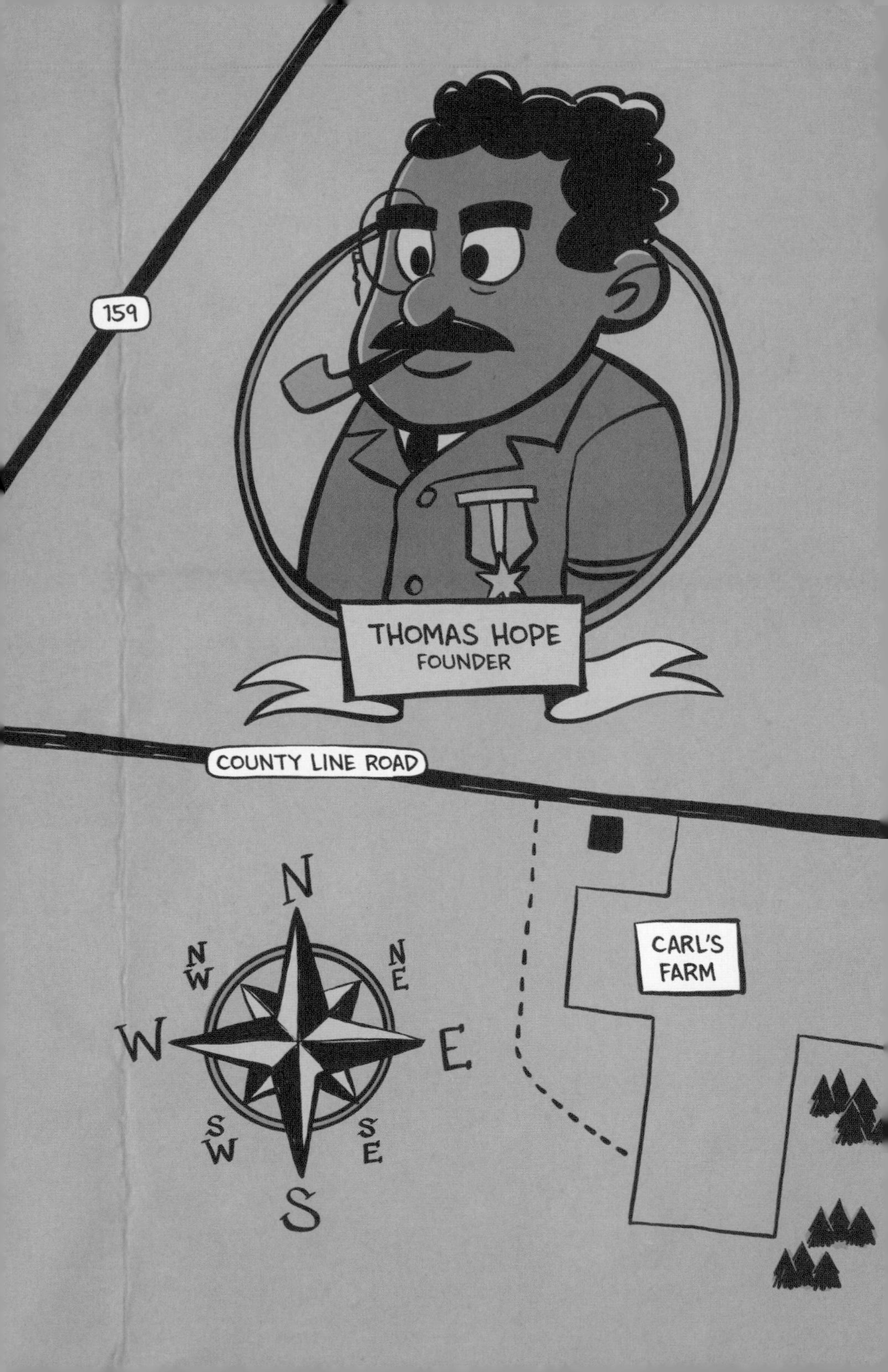
159
THOMAS HOPE
FOUNDER
COUNTY LINE ROAD
CARL'S FARM
N
NE
E
SE
S
SW
W
NW

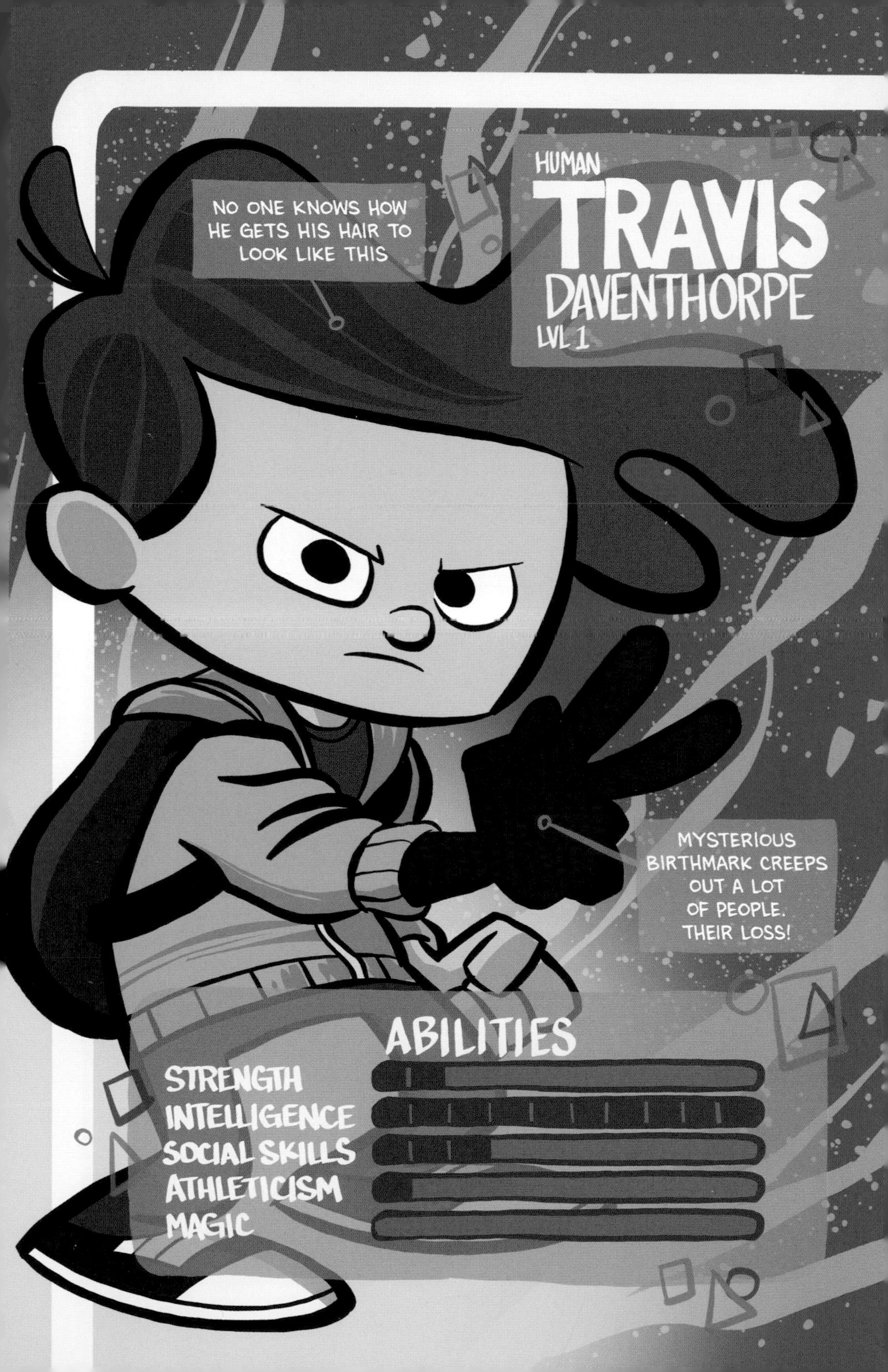
HUMAN
TRAVIS
DAVENTHORPE
LVL 1
NO ONE KNOWS HOW HE GETS HIS HAIR TO LOOK LIKE THIS
MYSTERIOUS BIRTHMARK CREEPS OUT A LOT OF PEOPLE. THEIR LOSS!
ABILITIES
STRENGTH
INTELLIGENCE
SOCIAL SKILLS
ATHLETICISM
MAGIC

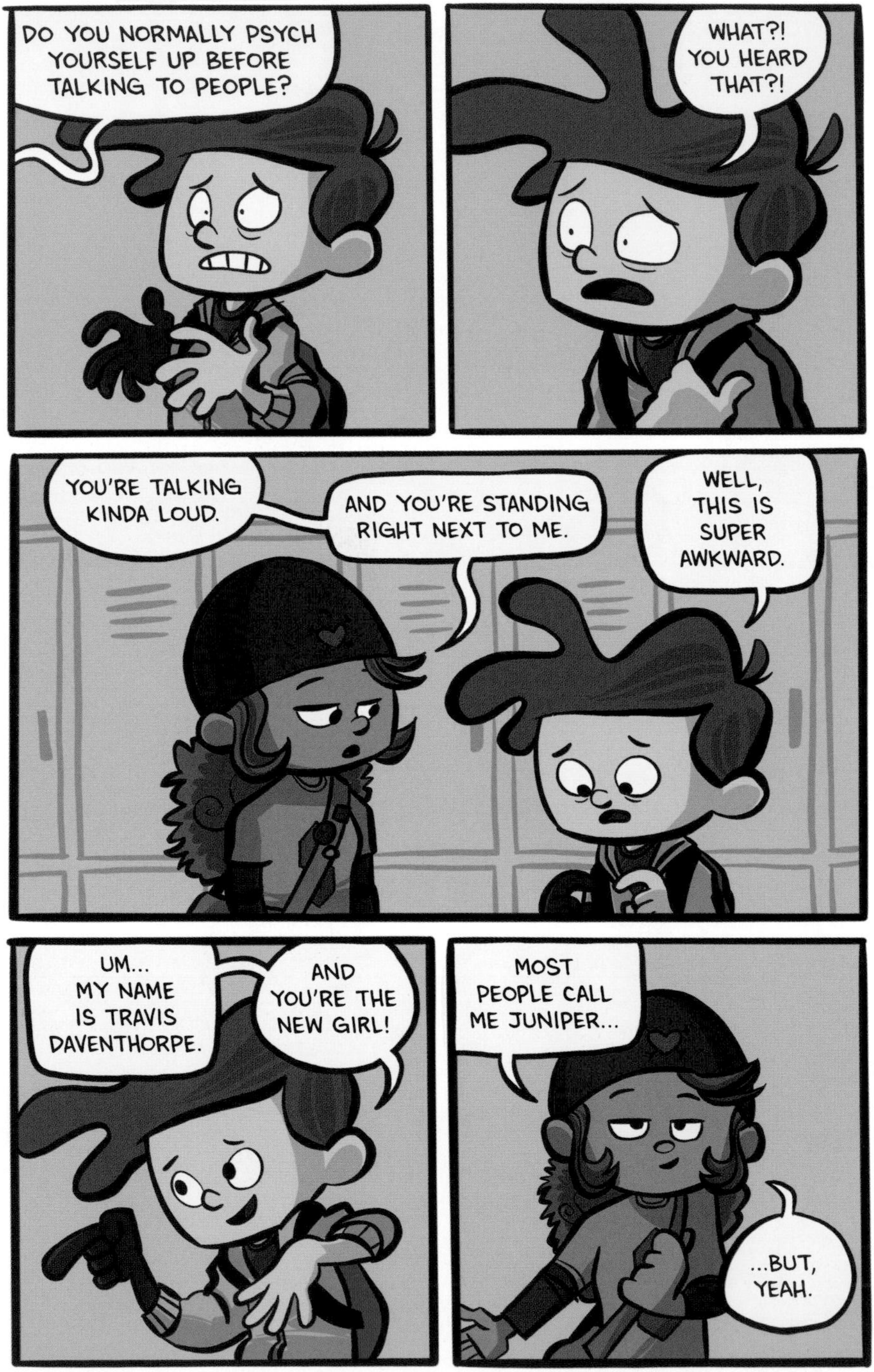
DO YOU NORMALLY PSYCH YOURSELF UP BEFORE TALKING TO PEOPLE?
WHAT?! YOU HEARD THAT?!
YOU'RE TALKING KINDA LOUD.
AND YOU'RE STANDING RIGHT NEXT TO ME.
WELL, THIS IS SUPER AWKWARD.
UM... MY NAME IS TRAVIS DAVENTHORPE.
AND YOU'RE THE NEW GIRL!
MOST PEOPLE CALL ME JUNIPER...
...BUT, YEAH.

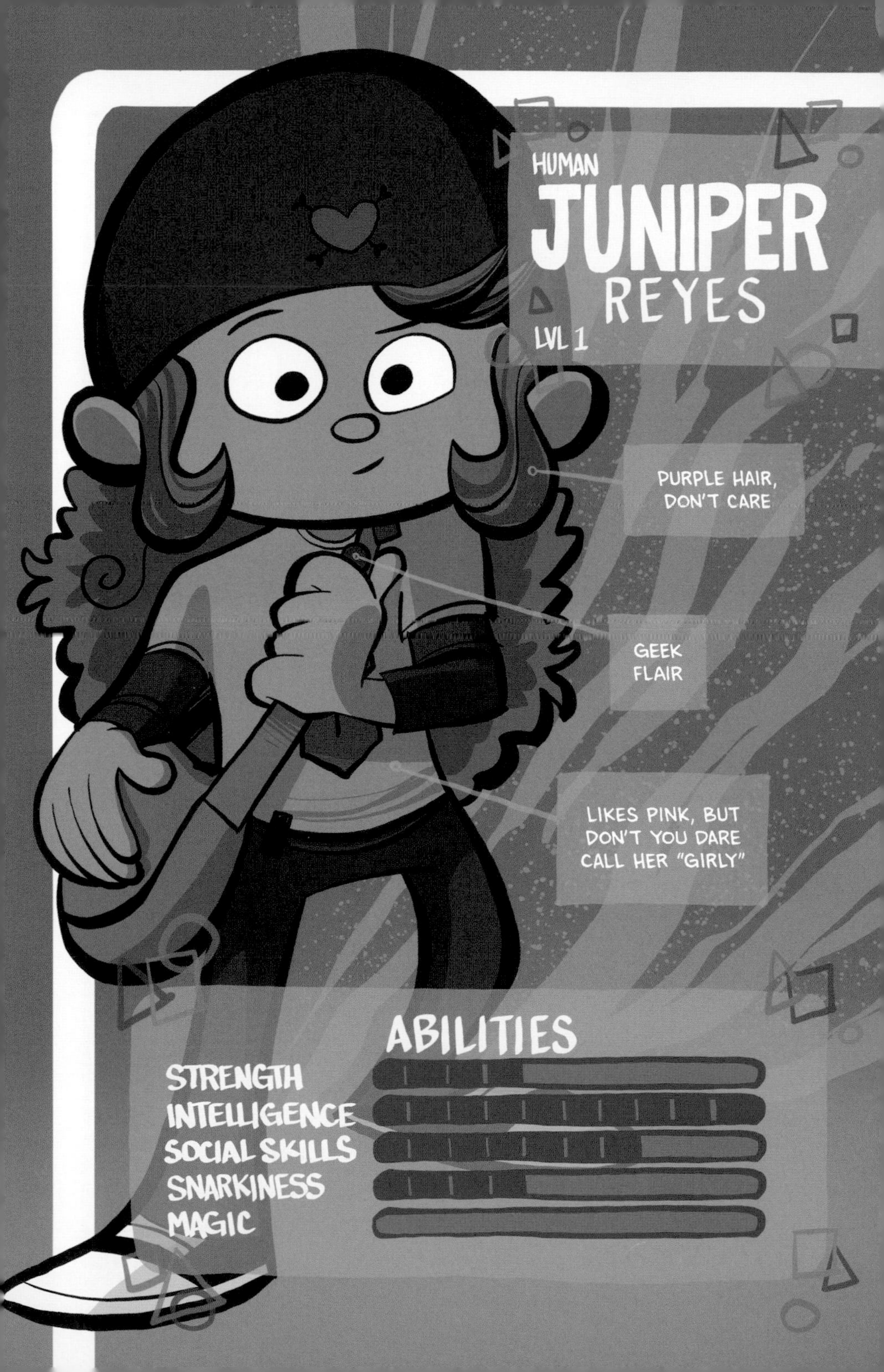
HUMAN
JUNIPER
REYES
LVL 1
PURPLE HAIR, DON'T CARE
GEEK FLAIR
LIKES PINK, BUT DON'T YOU DARE CALL HER "GIRLY"
ABILITIES
STRENGTH
INTELLIGENCE
SOCIAL SKILLS
SNARKINESS
MAGIC

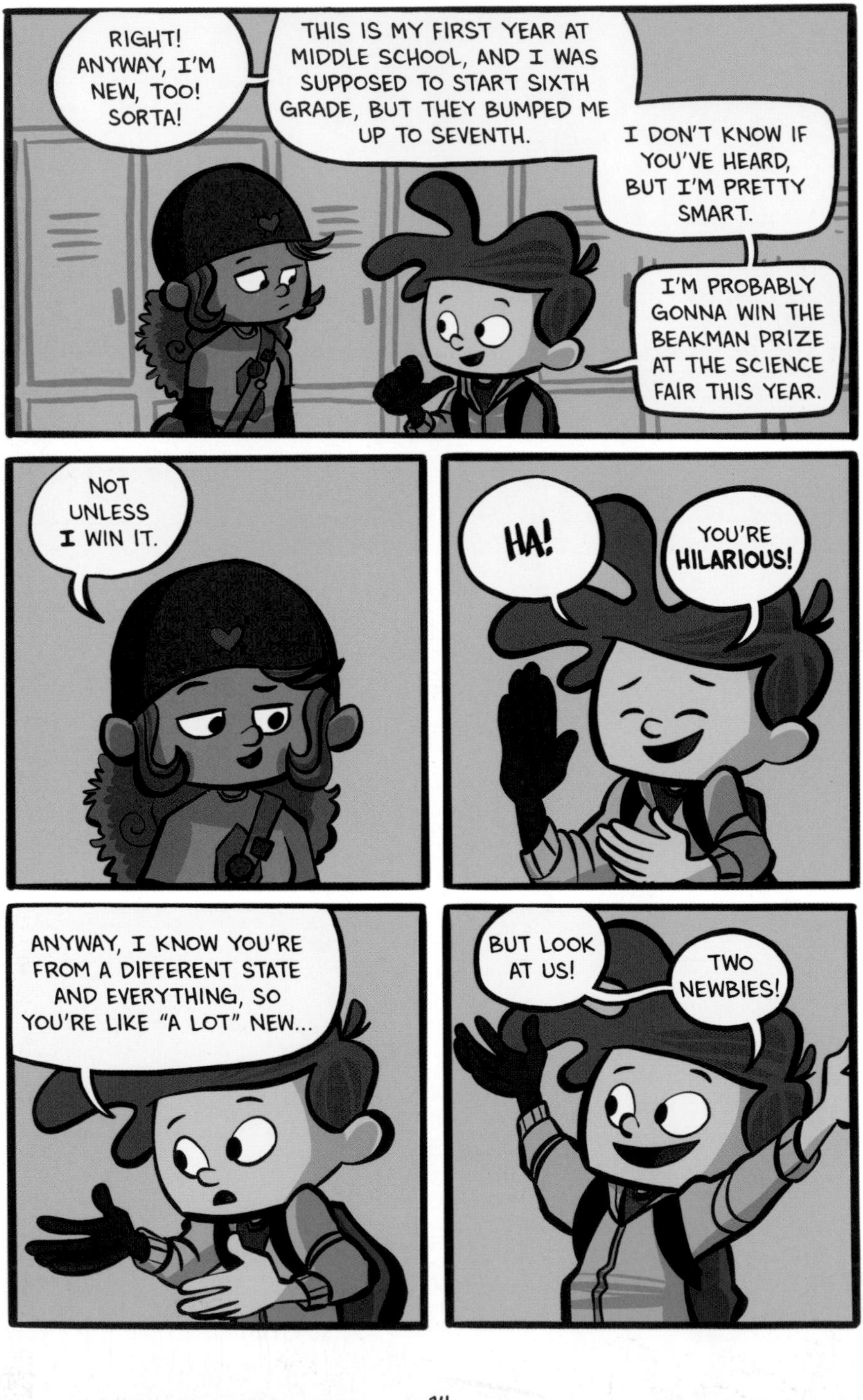
RIGHT! ANYWAY, I'M NEW, TOO! SORTA!
THIS IS MY FIRST YEAR AT MIDDLE SCHOOL, AND I WAS SUPPOSED TO START SIXTH GRADE, BUT THEY BUMPED ME UP TO SEVENTH.
I DON'T KNOW IF YOU'VE HEARD, BUT I'M PRETTY SMART.
I'M PROBABLY GONNA WIN THE BEAKMAN PRIZE AT THE SCIENCE FAIR THIS YEAR.
NOT UNLESS **I** WIN IT.
HA!
YOU'RE **HILARIOUS!**
ANYWAY, I KNOW YOU'RE FROM A DIFFERENT STATE AND EVERYTHING, SO YOU'RE LIKE "A LOT" NEW...
BUT LOOK AT US!
TWO NEWBIES!

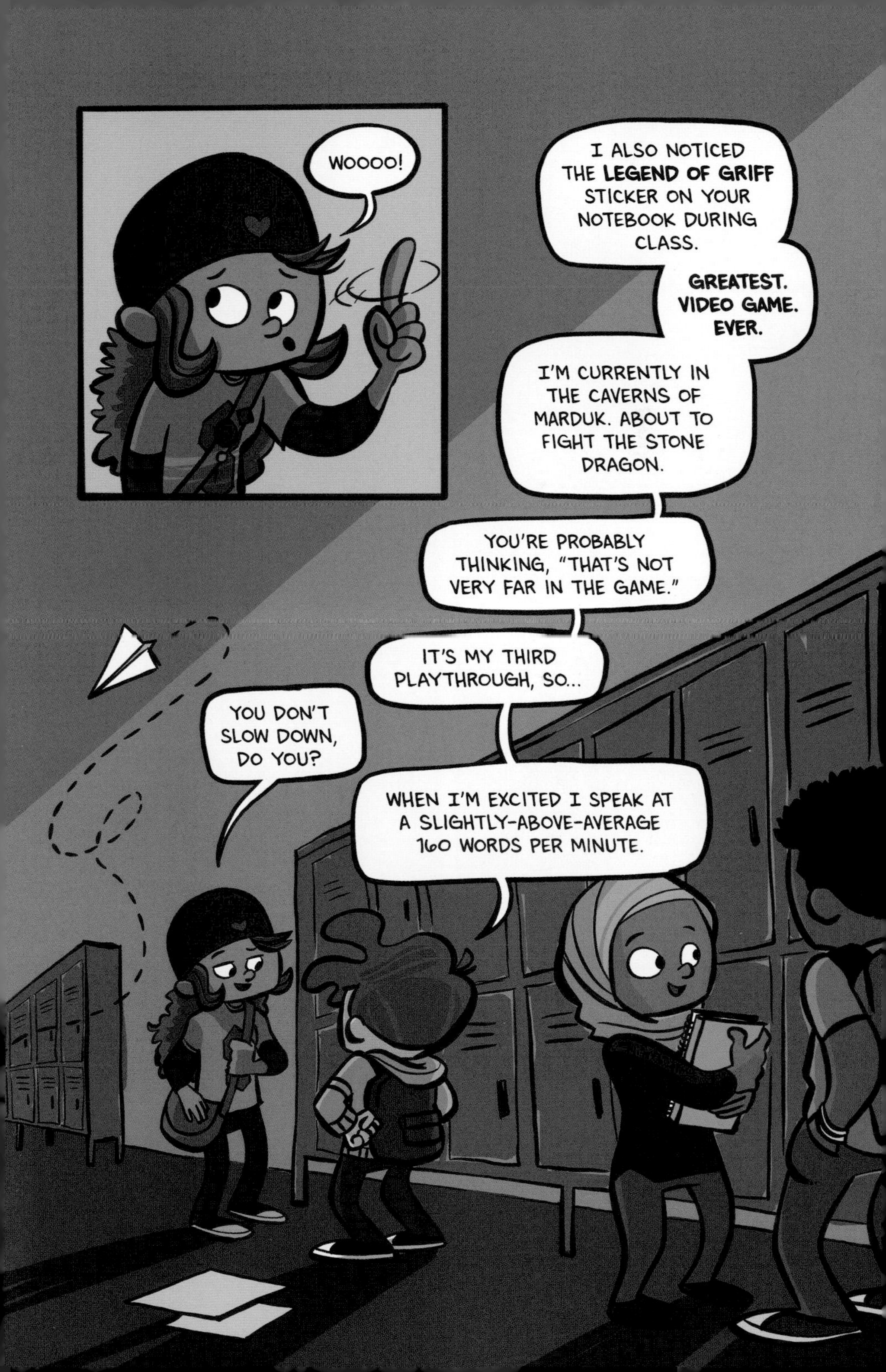
WOOOO!
I ALSO NOTICED THE **LEGEND OF GRIFF** STICKER ON YOUR NOTEBOOK DURING CLASS.
GREATEST. VIDEO GAME. EVER.
I'M CURRENTLY IN THE CAVERNS OF MARDUK. ABOUT TO FIGHT THE STONE DRAGON.
YOU'RE PROBABLY THINKING, "THAT'S NOT VERY FAR IN THE GAME."
IT'S MY THIRD PLAYTHROUGH, SO...
YOU DON'T SLOW DOWN, DO YOU?
WHEN I'M EXCITED I SPEAK AT A SLIGHTLY-ABOVE-AVERAGE 160 WORDS PER MINUTE.

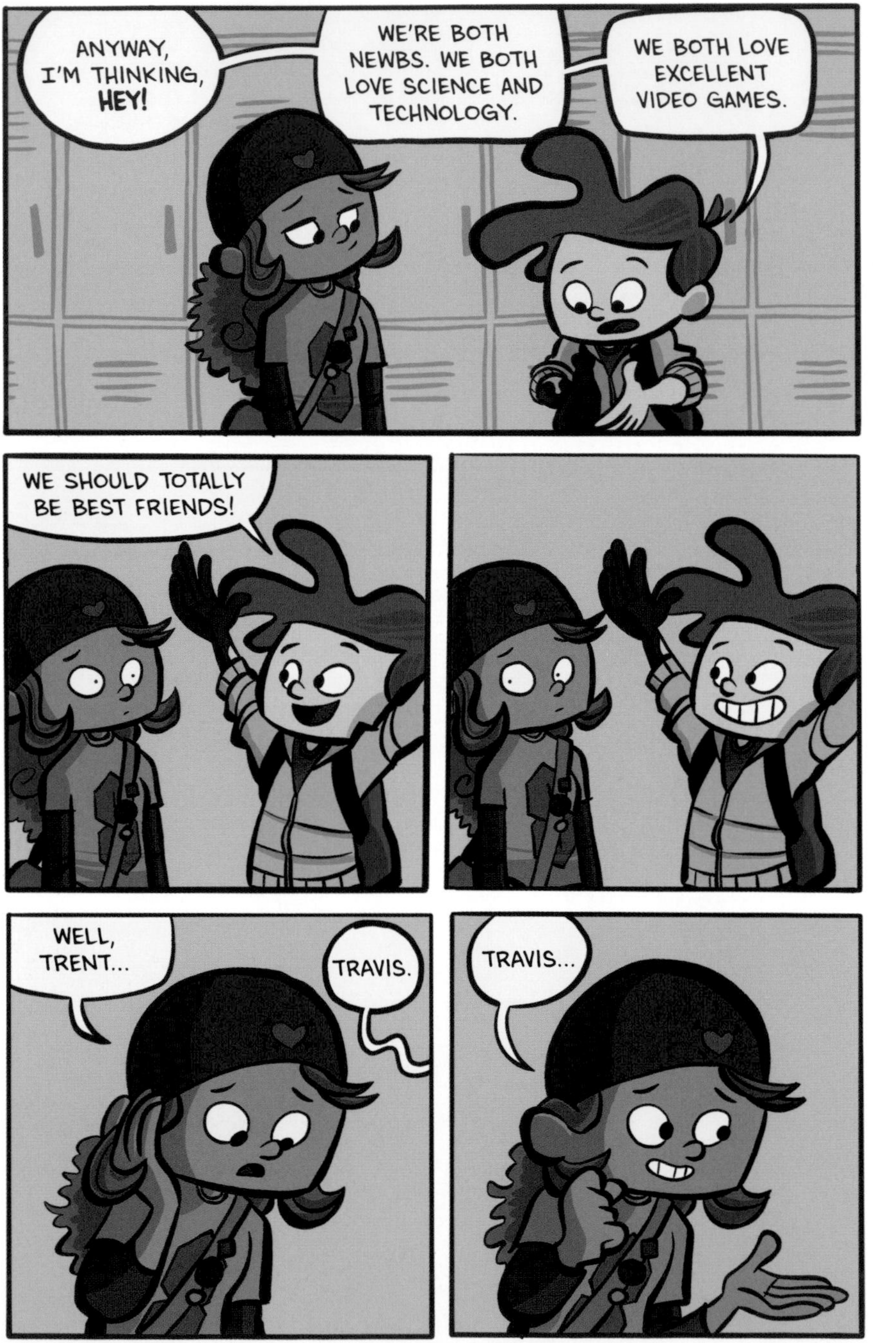
ANYWAY, I'M THINKING, HEY!
WE'RE BOTH NEWBS. WE BOTH LOVE SCIENCE AND TECHNOLOGY.
WE BOTH LOVE EXCELLENT VIDEO GAMES.
WE SHOULD TOTALLY BE BEST FRIENDS!
WELL, TRENT...
TRAVIS.
TRAVIS...

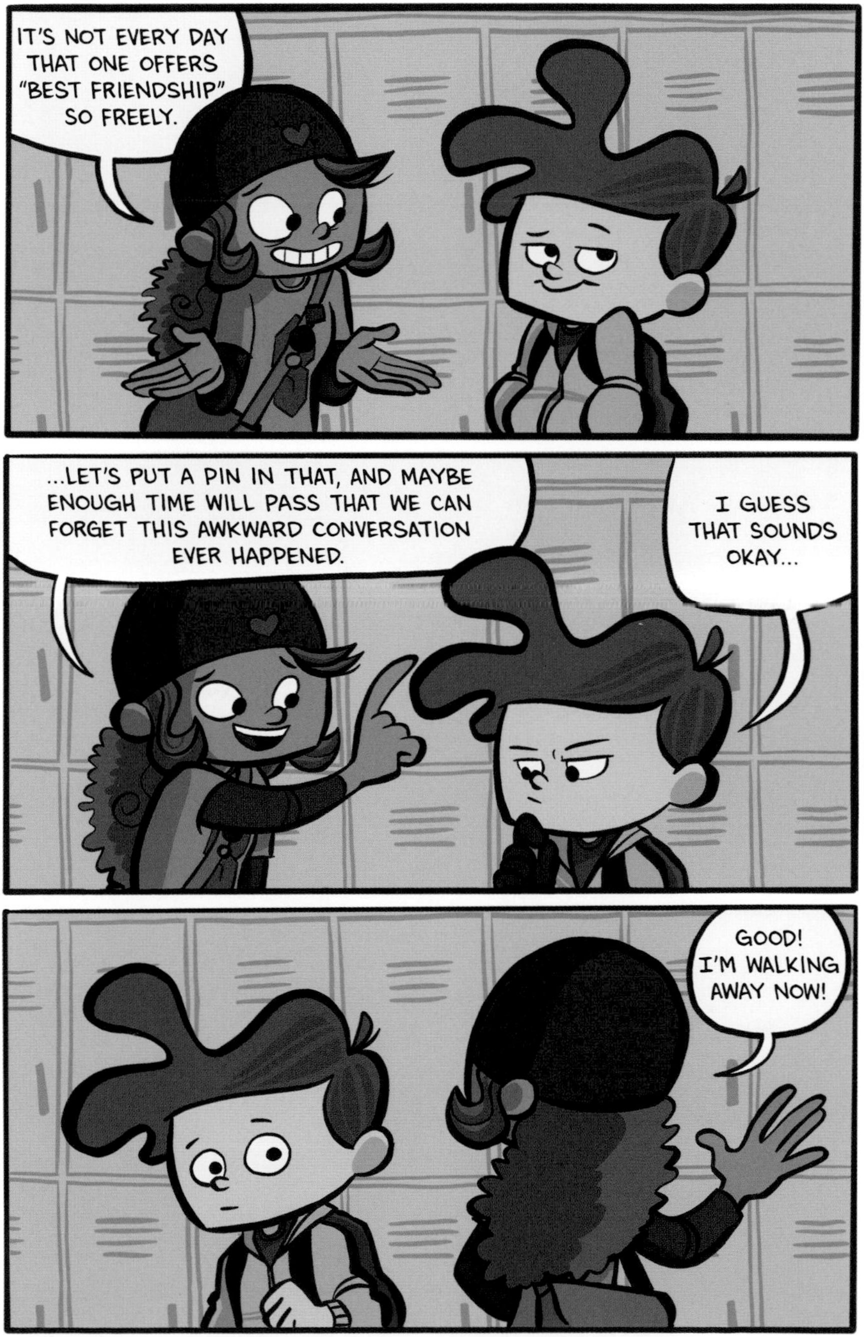
IT'S NOT EVERY DAY THAT ONE OFFERS "BEST FRIENDSHIP" SO FREELY.
...LET'S PUT A PIN IN THAT, AND MAYBE ENOUGH TIME WILL PASS THAT WE CAN FORGET THIS AWKWARD CONVERSATION EVER HAPPENED.
I GUESS THAT SOUNDS OKAY...
GOOD! I'M WALKING AWAY NOW!

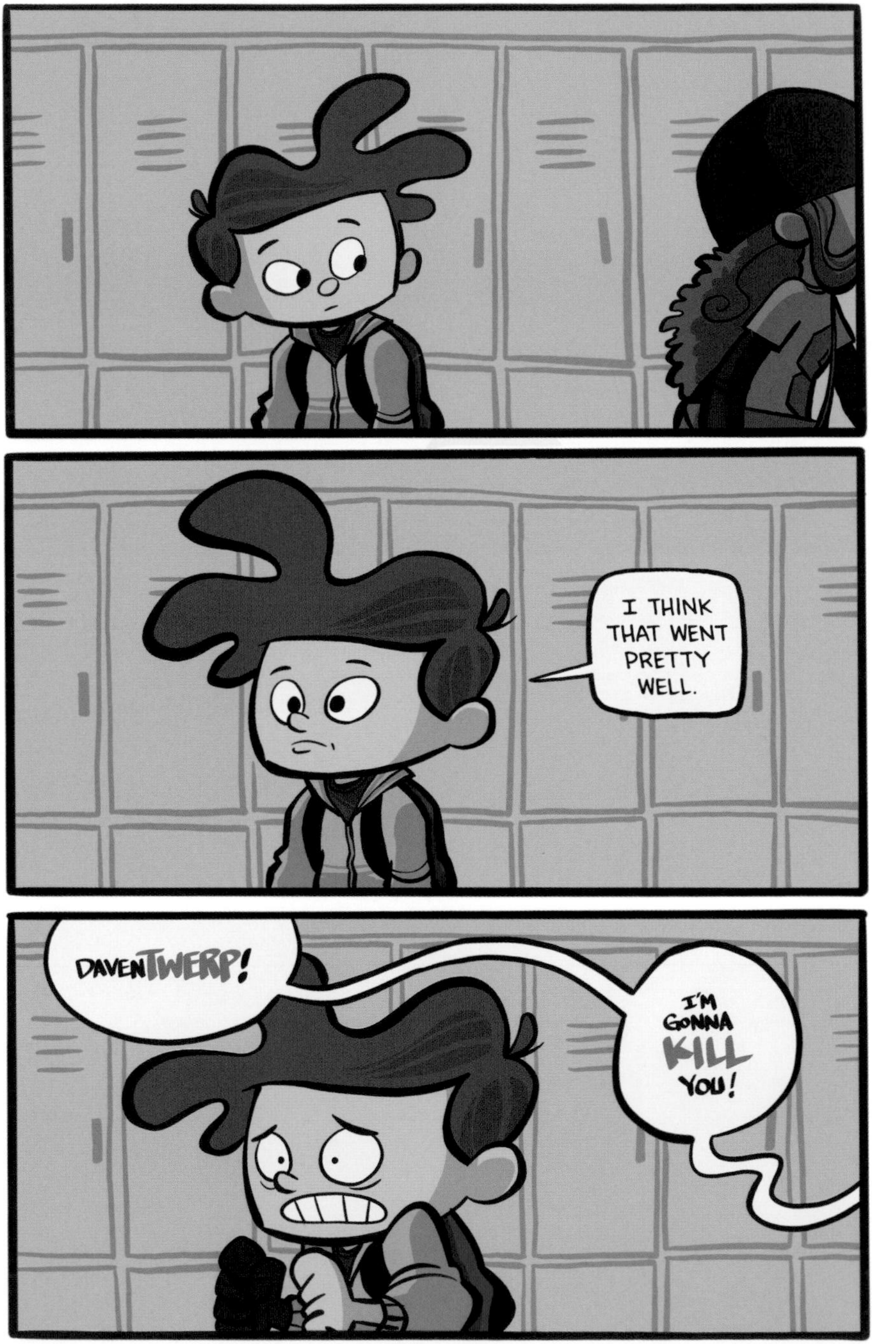
I THINK THAT WENT PRETTY WELL.
DAVENTWERP!
I'M GONNA KILL YOU!

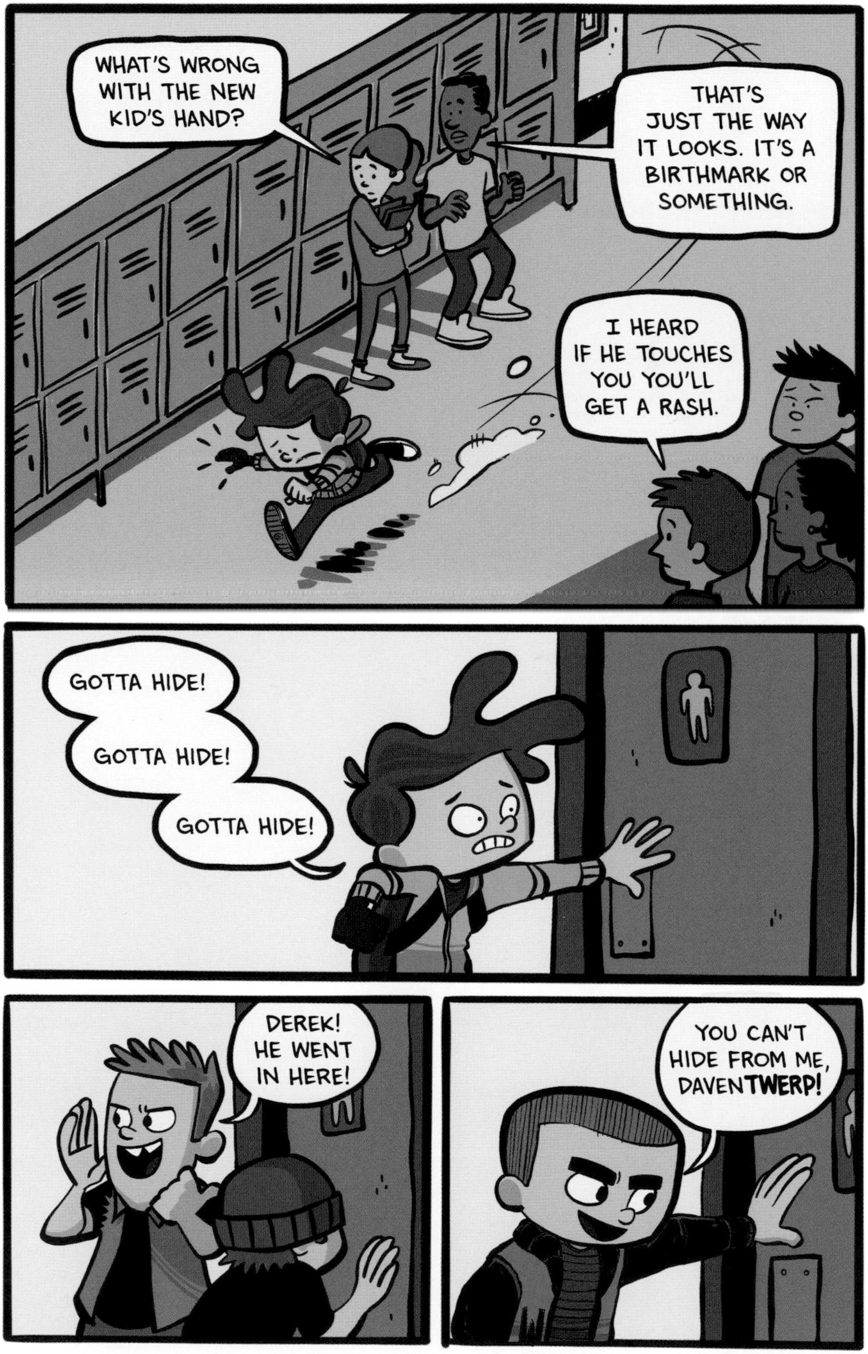
WHAT'S WRONG WITH THE NEW KID'S HAND?
THAT'S JUST THE WAY IT LOOKS. IT'S A BIRTHMARK OR SOMETHING.
I HEARD IF HE TOUCHES YOU YOU'LL GET A RASH.
GOTTA HIDE!
GOTTA HIDE!
GOTTA HIDE!
DEREK! HE WENT IN HERE!
YOU CAN'T HIDE FROM ME, DAVEN**TWERP!**

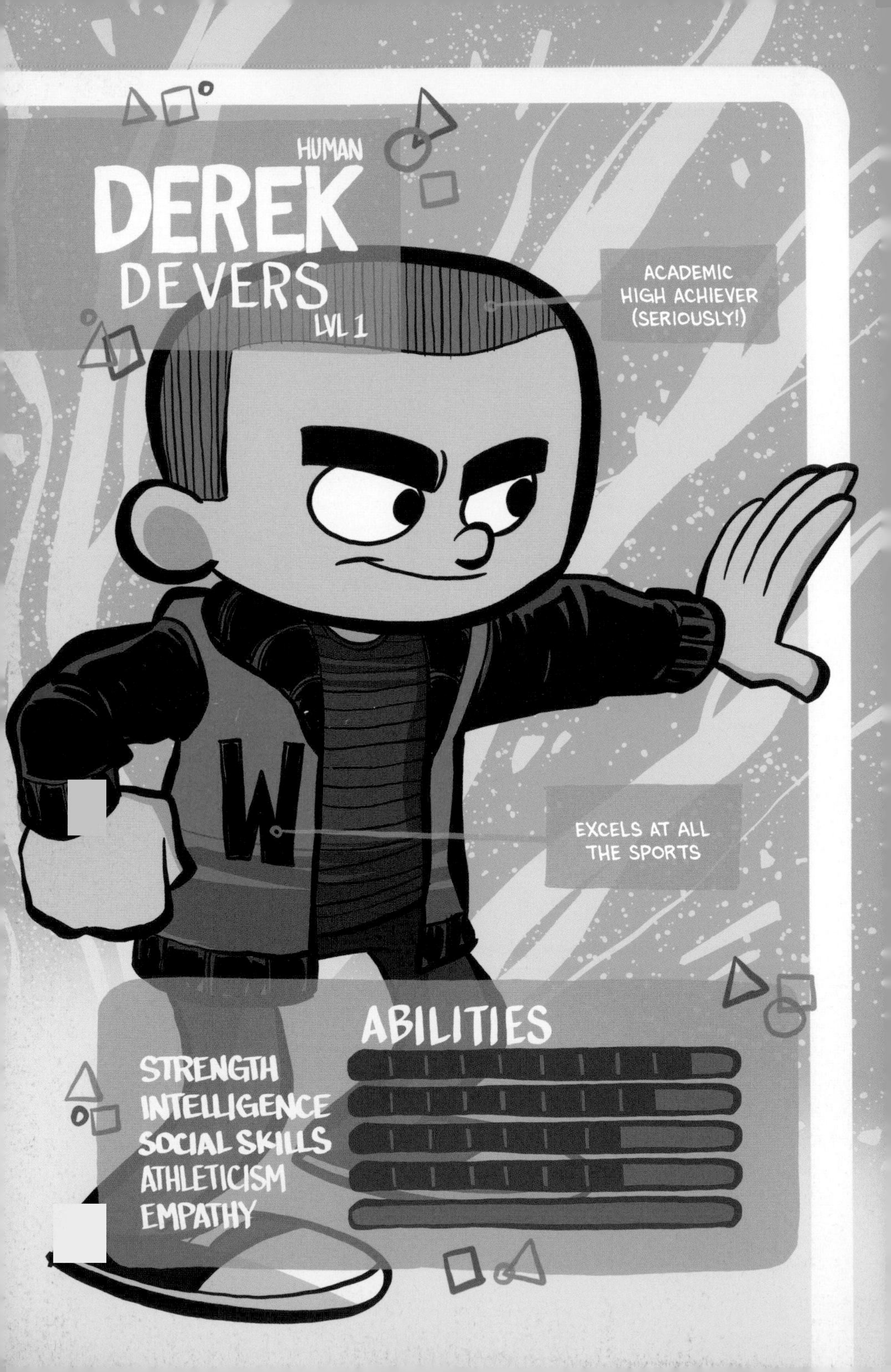
HUMAN
DEREK
DEVERS
LVL 1
ACADEMIC
HIGH ACHIEVER
(SERIOUSLY!)
EXCELS AT ALL
THE SPORTS
ABILITIES
STRENGTH
INTELLIGENCE
SOCIAL SKILLS
ATHLETICISM
EMPATHY

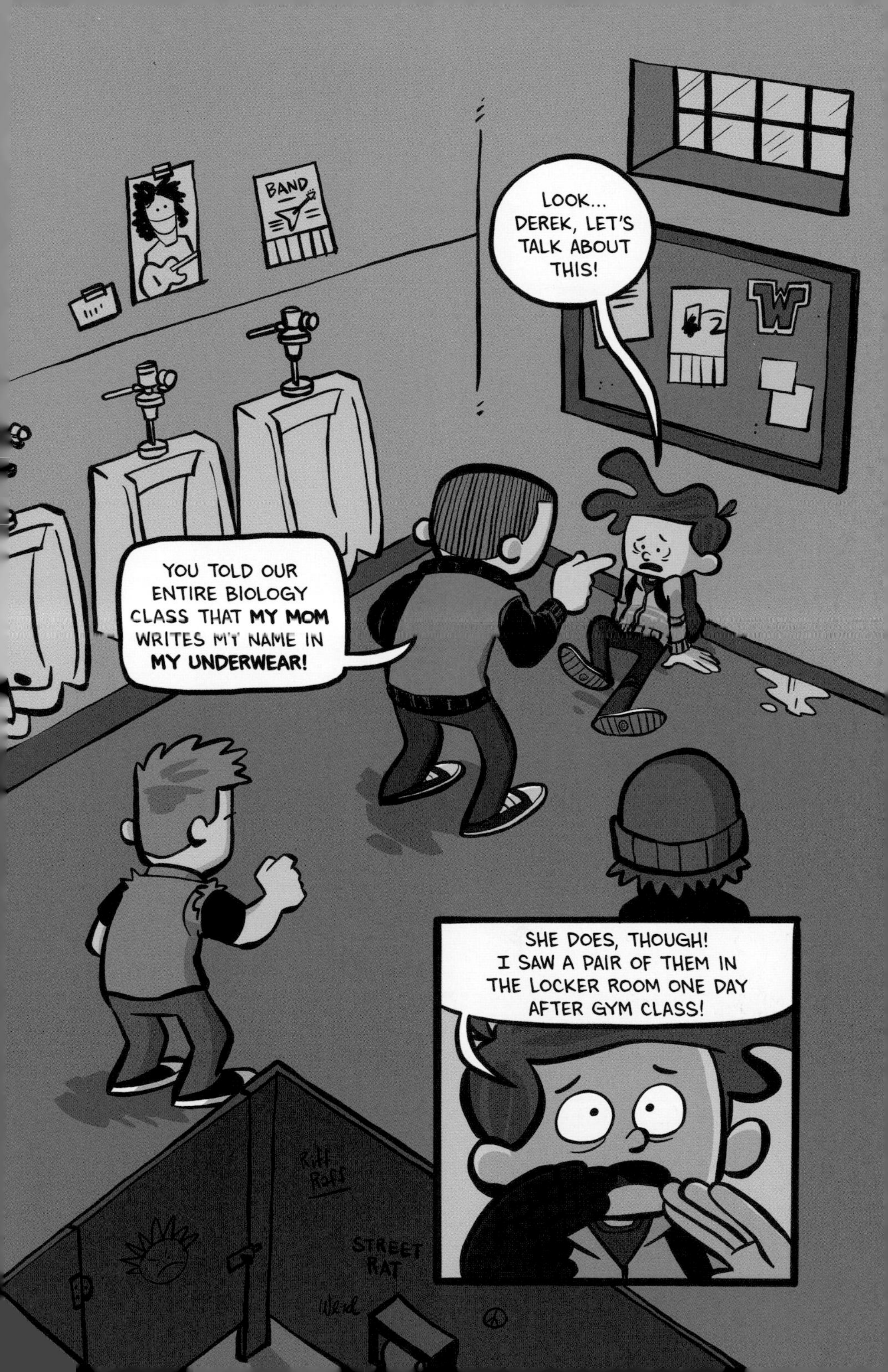

BAND
LOOK... DEREK, LET'S TALK ABOUT THIS!
YOU TOLD OUR ENTIRE BIOLOGY CLASS THAT **MY MOM** WRITES MY NAME IN **MY UNDERWEAR!**
SHE DOES, THOUGH! I SAW A PAIR OF THEM IN THE LOCKER ROOM ONE DAY AFTER GYM CLASS!
Riff Raff
STREET RAT

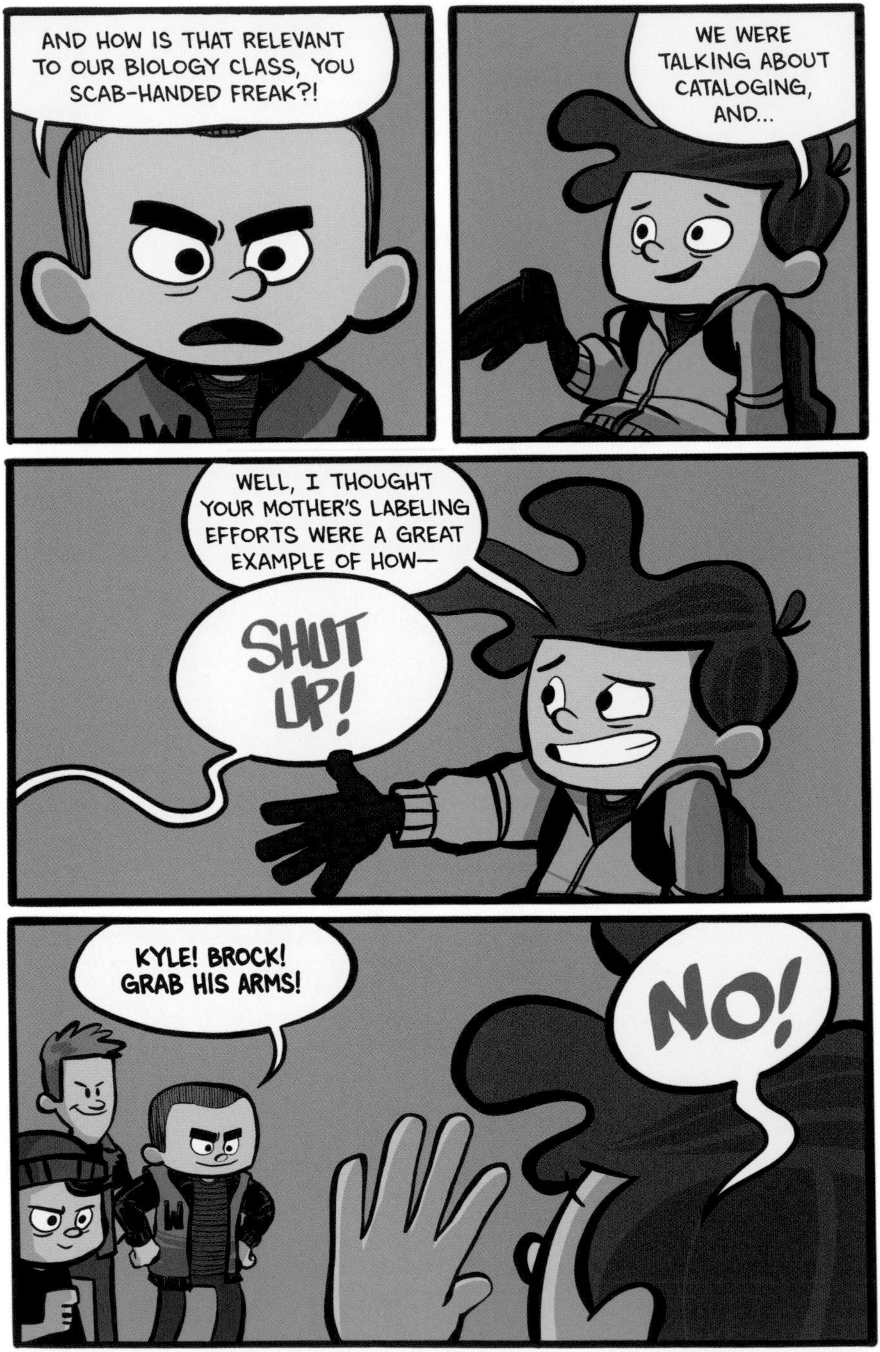
AND HOW IS THAT RELEVANT TO OUR BIOLOGY CLASS, YOU SCAB-HANDED FREAK?!
WE WERE TALKING ABOUT CATALOGING, AND...
WELL, I THOUGHT YOUR MOTHER'S LABELING EFFORTS WERE A GREAT EXAMPLE OF HOW—
SHUT UP!
KYLE! BROCK! GRAB HIS ARMS!
NO!

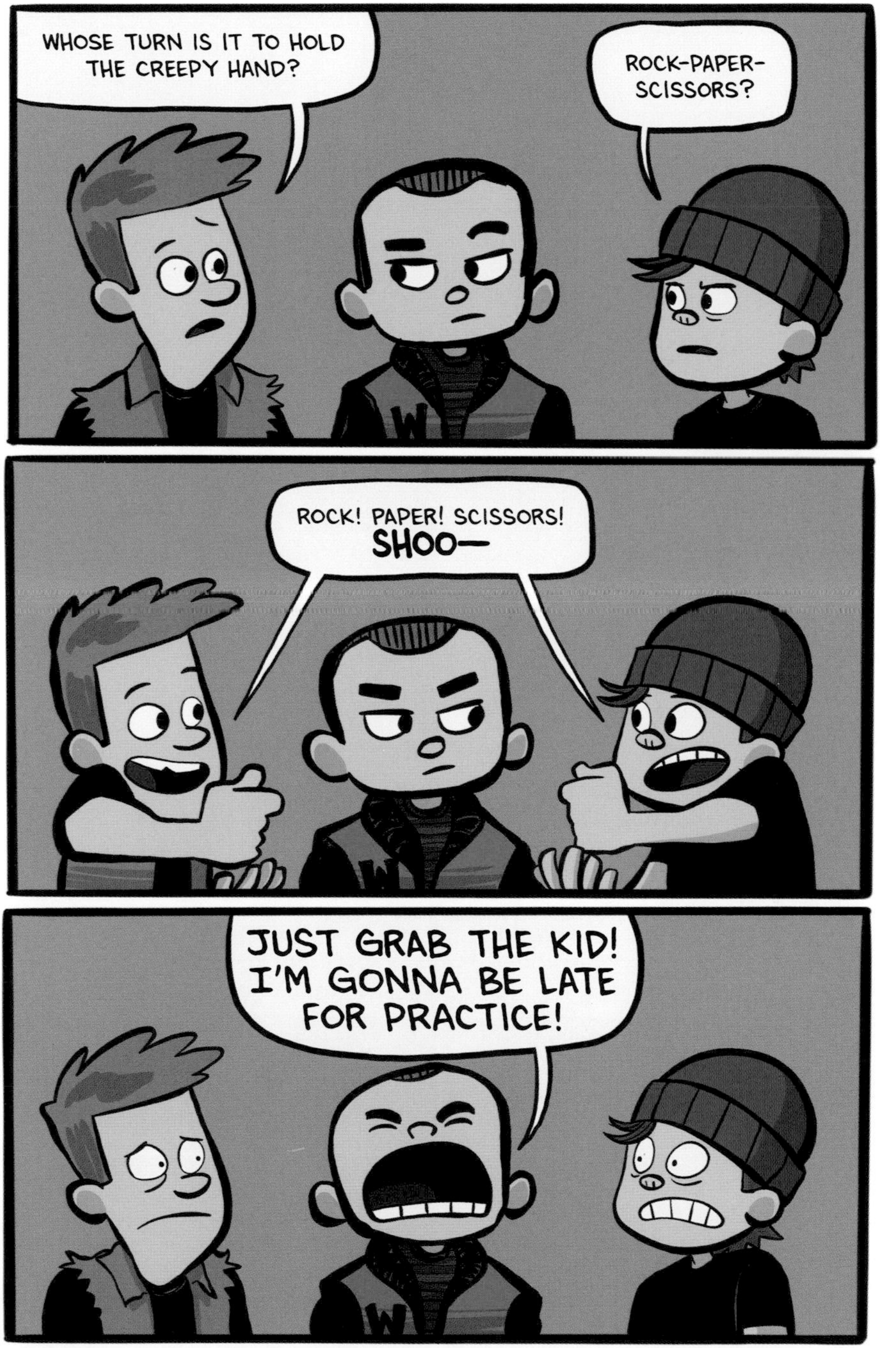
WHOSE TURN IS IT TO HOLD THE CREEPY HAND?
ROCK-PAPER-SCISSORS?
ROCK! PAPER! SCISSORS! SHOO—
JUST GRAB THE KID! I'M GONNA BE LATE FOR PRACTICE!

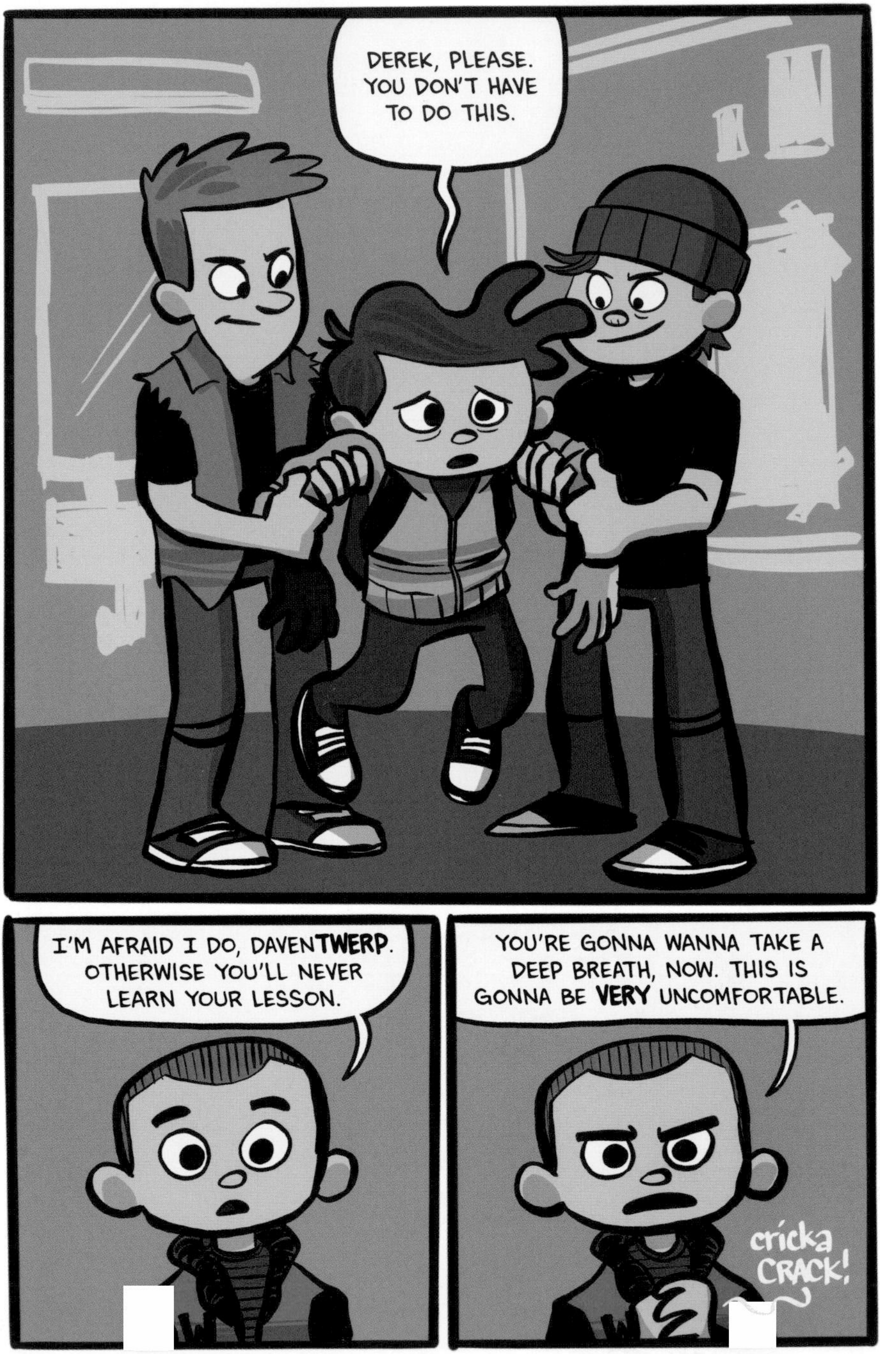
DEREK, PLEASE. YOU DON'T HAVE TO DO THIS.
I'M AFRAID I DO, DAVENTWERP. OTHERWISE YOU'LL NEVER LEARN YOUR LESSON.
YOU'RE GONNA WANNA TAKE A DEEP BREATH, NOW. THIS IS GONNA BE VERY UNCOMFORTABLE.
cricka CRACK!

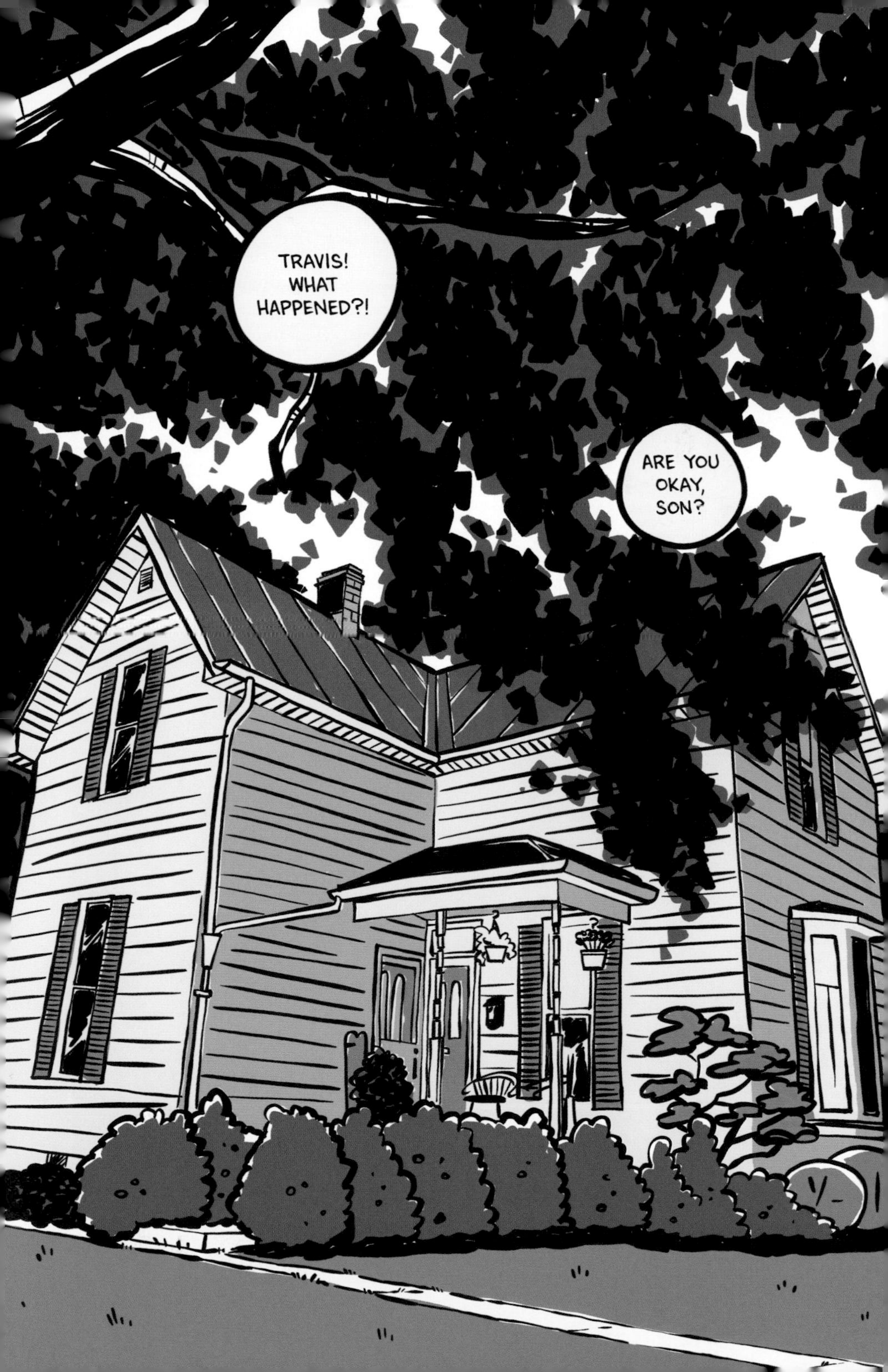
TRAVIS! WHAT HAPPENED?!
ARE YOU OKAY, SON?

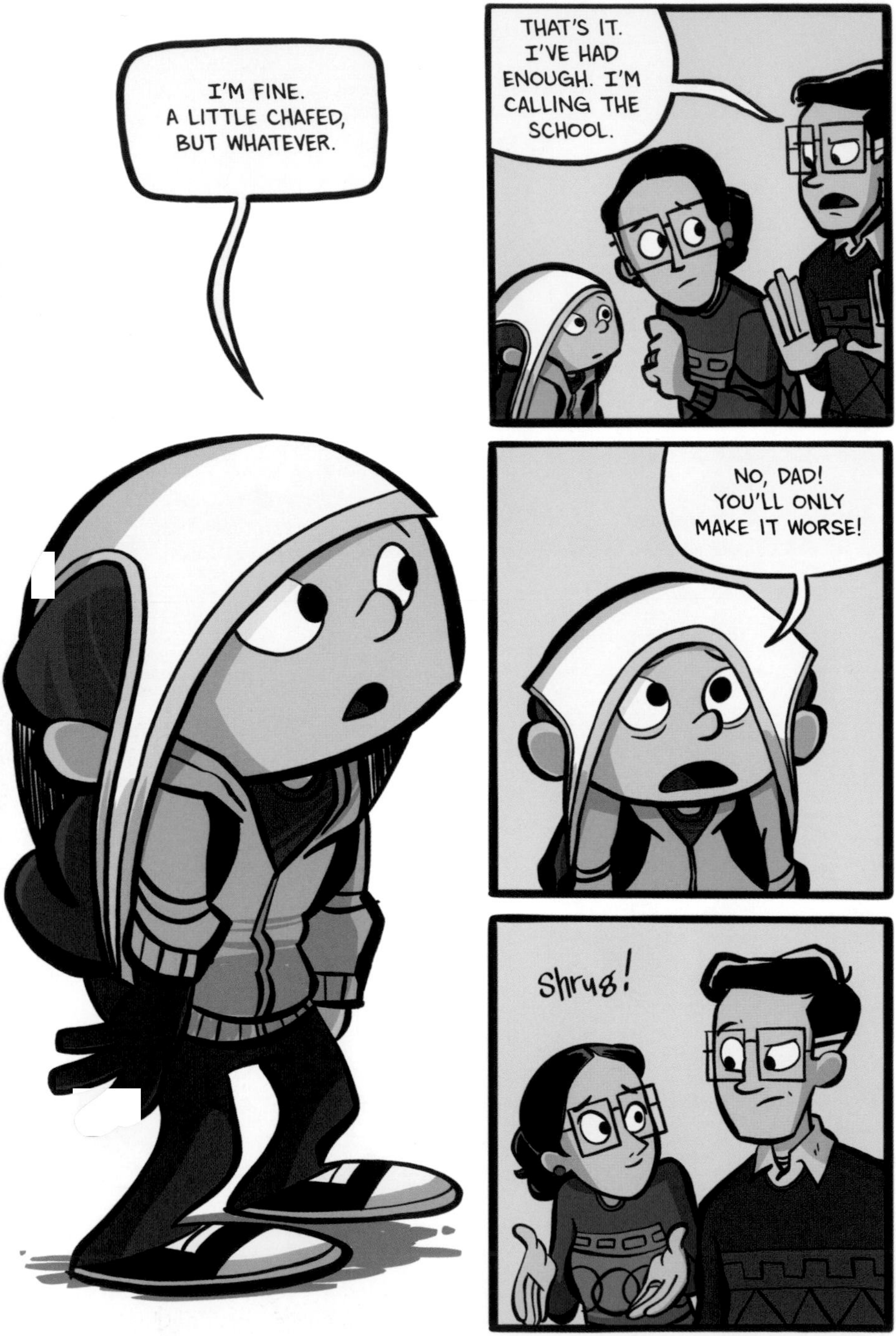
I'M FINE. A LITTLE CHAFED, BUT WHATEVER.
THAT'S IT. I'VE HAD ENOUGH. I'M CALLING THE SCHOOL.
NO, DAD! YOU'LL ONLY MAKE IT WORSE!
Shrug!

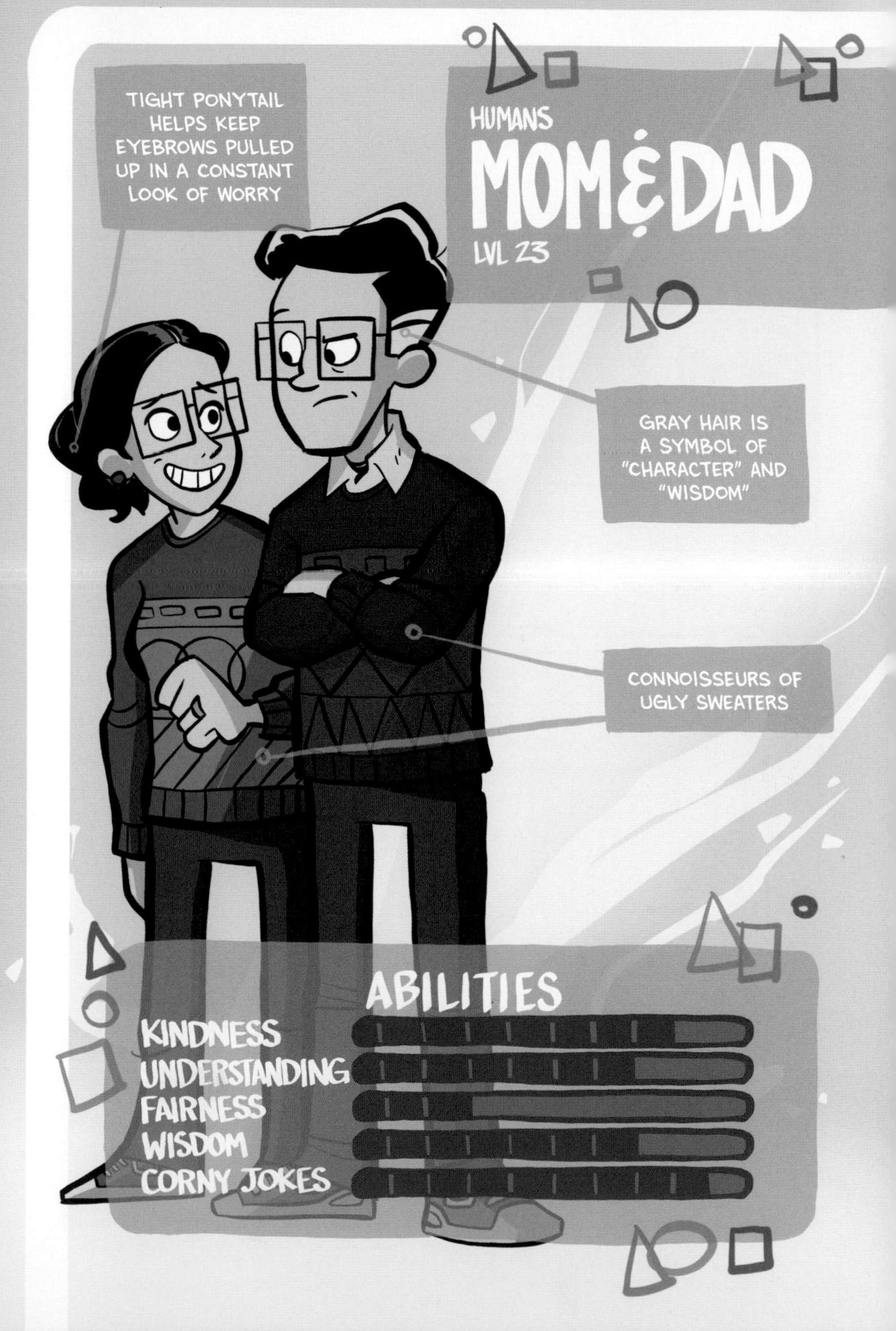
TIGHT PONYTAIL HELPS KEEP EYEBROWS PULLED UP IN A CONSTANT LOOK OF WORRY
HUMANS
MOM & DAD
LVL 23
GRAY HAIR IS A SYMBOL OF "CHARACTER" AND "WISDOM"
CONNOISSEURS OF UGLY SWEATERS
ABILITIES
KINDNESS
UNDERSTANDING
FAIRNESS
WISDOM
CORNY JOKES

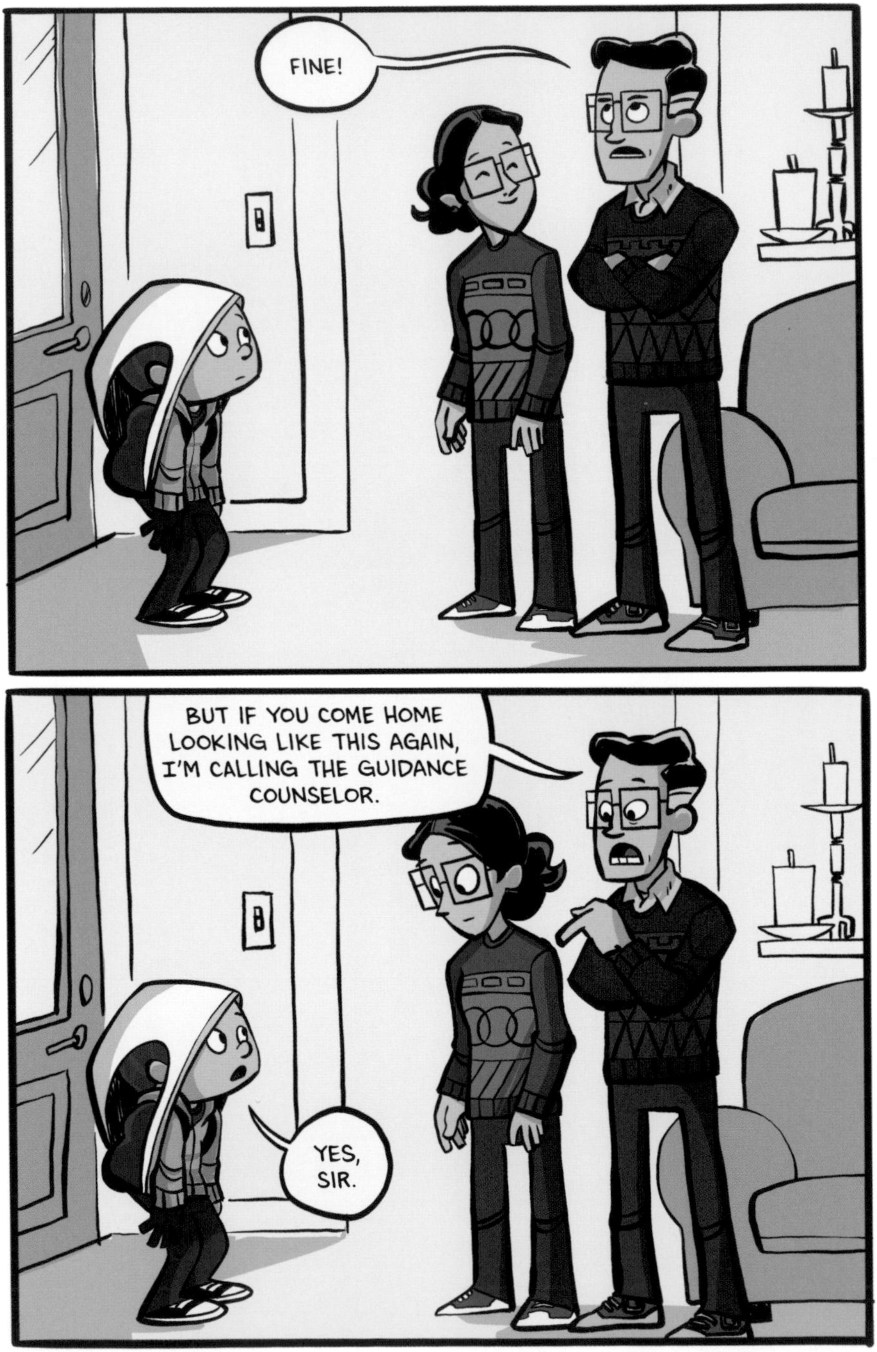
FINE!
BUT IF YOU COME HOME LOOKING LIKE THIS AGAIN, I'M CALLING THE GUIDANCE COUNSELOR.
YES, SIR.

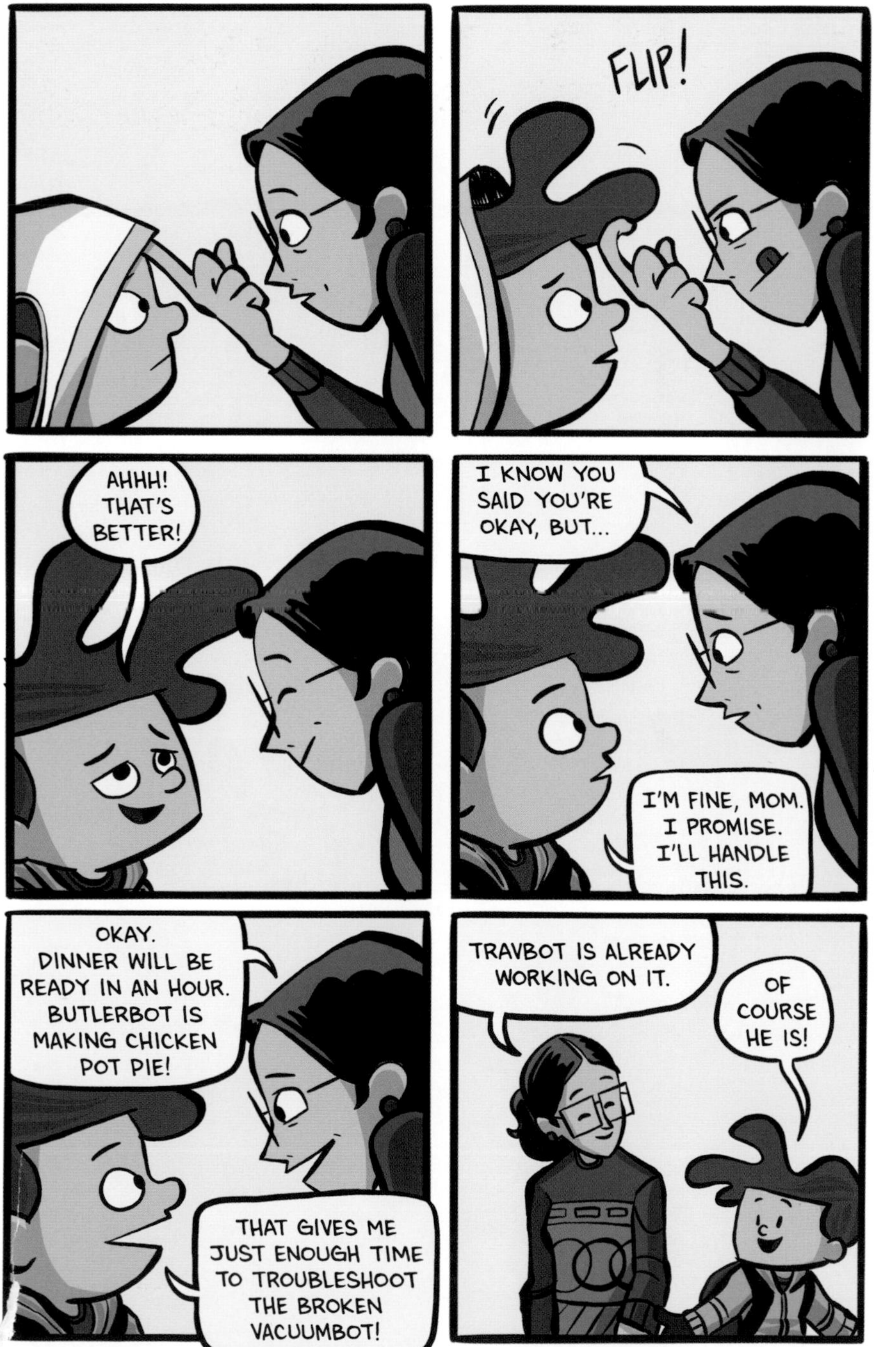
FLIP!
AHHH! THAT'S BETTER!
I KNOW YOU SAID YOU'RE OKAY, BUT...
I'M FINE, MOM. I PROMISE. I'LL HANDLE THIS.
OKAY. DINNER WILL BE READY IN AN HOUR. BUTLERBOT IS MAKING CHICKEN POT PIE!
THAT GIVES ME JUST ENOUGH TIME TO TROUBLESHOOT THE BROKEN VACUUMBOT!
TRAVBOT IS ALREADY WORKING ON IT.
OF COURSE HE IS!

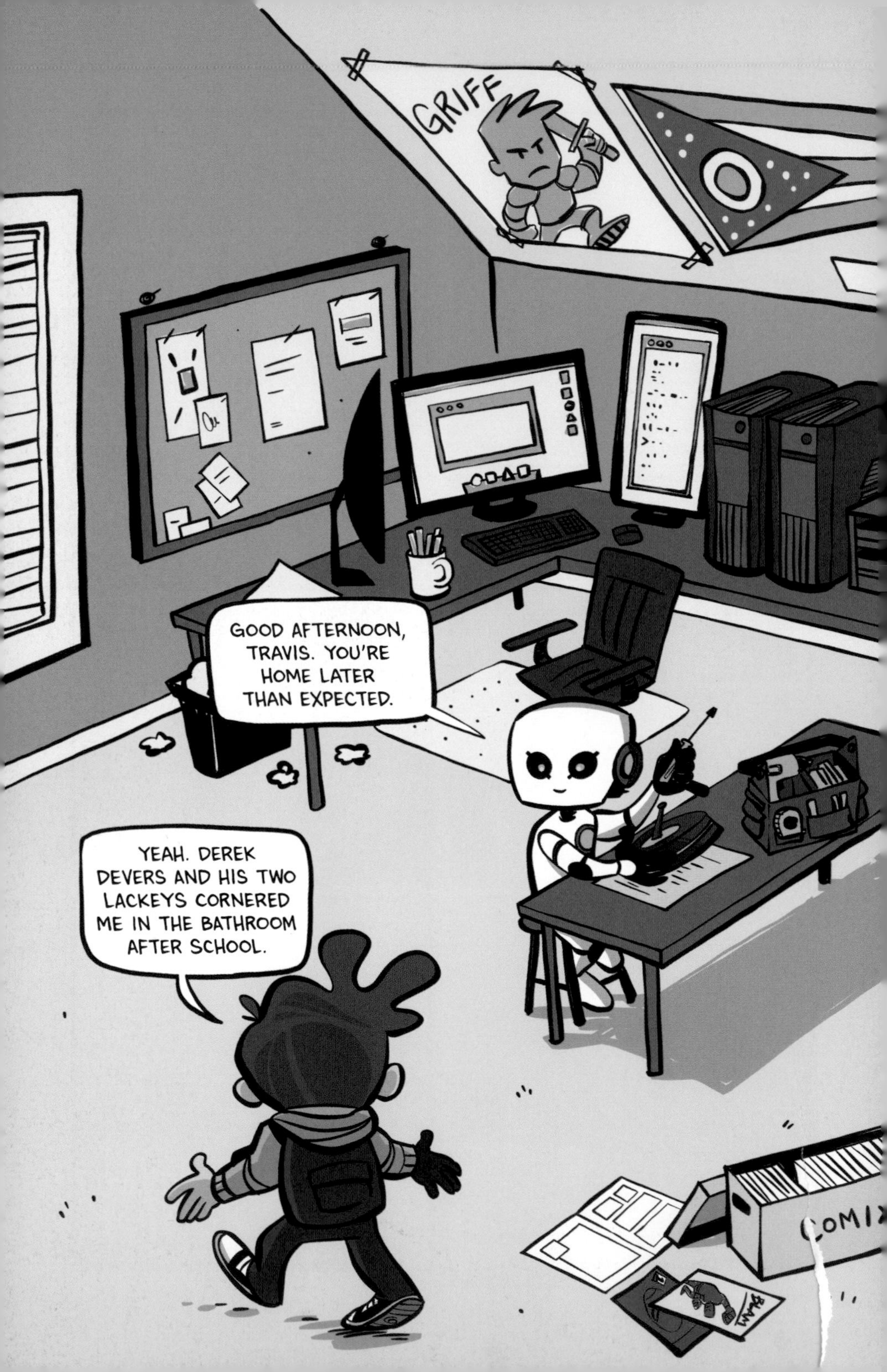
GRIFF
GOOD AFTERNOON, TRAVIS. YOU'RE HOME LATER THAN EXPECTED.
YEAH. DEREK DEVERS AND HIS TWO LACKEYS CORNERED ME IN THE BATHROOM AFTER SCHOOL.
COMIX

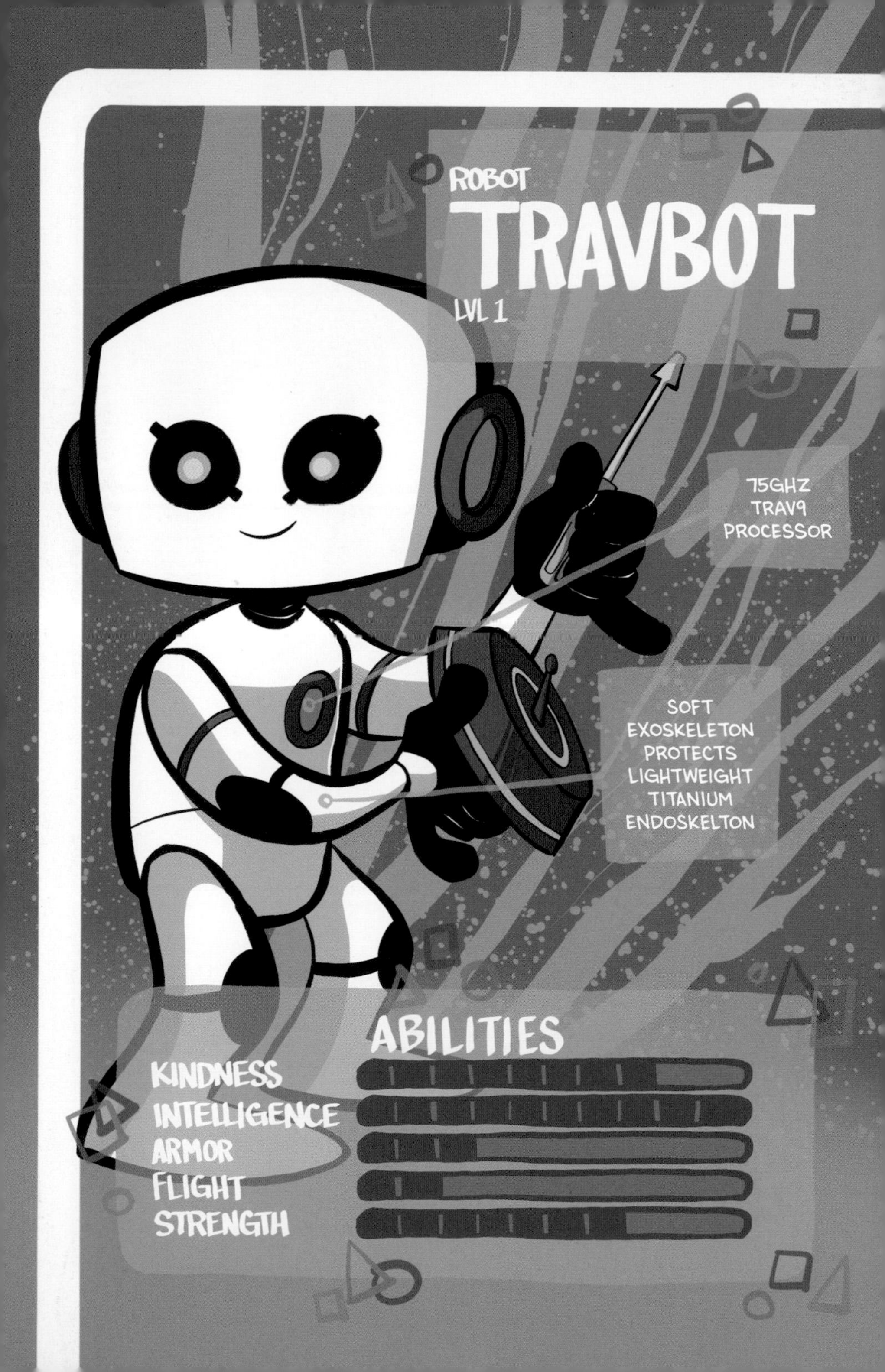
ROBOT
TRAVBOT
LVL 1
75GHZ
TRAV9
PROCESSOR
SOFT
EXOSKELETON
PROTECTS
LIGHTWEIGHT
TITANIUM
ENDOSKELTON
ABILITIES
KINDNESS
INTELLIGENCE
ARMOR
FLIGHT
STRENGTH

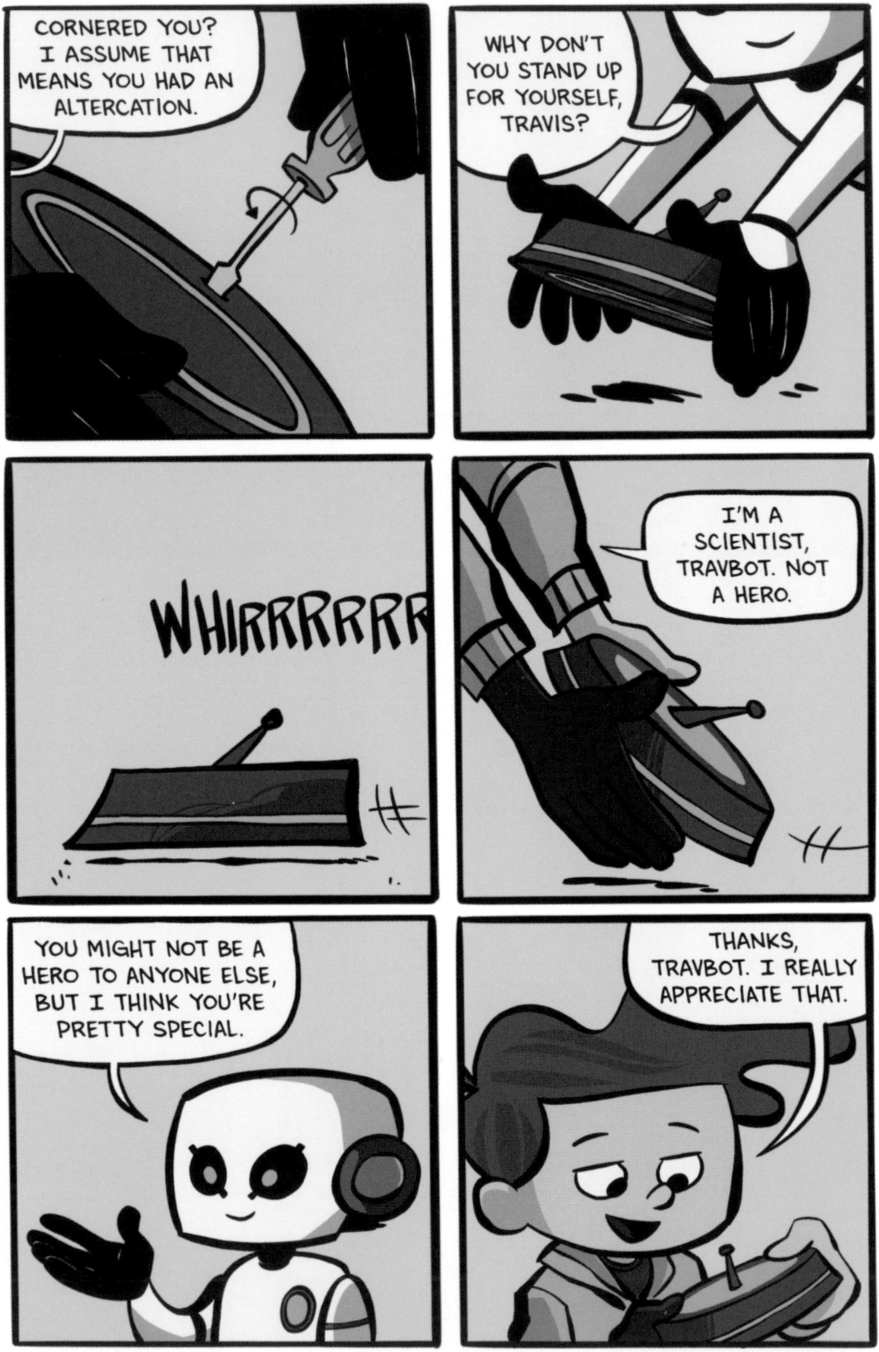
CORNERED YOU? I ASSUME THAT MEANS YOU HAD AN ALTERCATION.
WHY DON'T YOU STAND UP FOR YOURSELF, TRAVIS?
WHIRRRRRR
I'M A SCIENTIST, TRAVBOT. NOT A HERO.
YOU MIGHT NOT BE A HERO TO ANYONE ELSE, BUT I THINK YOU'RE PRETTY SPECIAL.
THANKS, TRAVBOT. I REALLY APPRECIATE THAT.

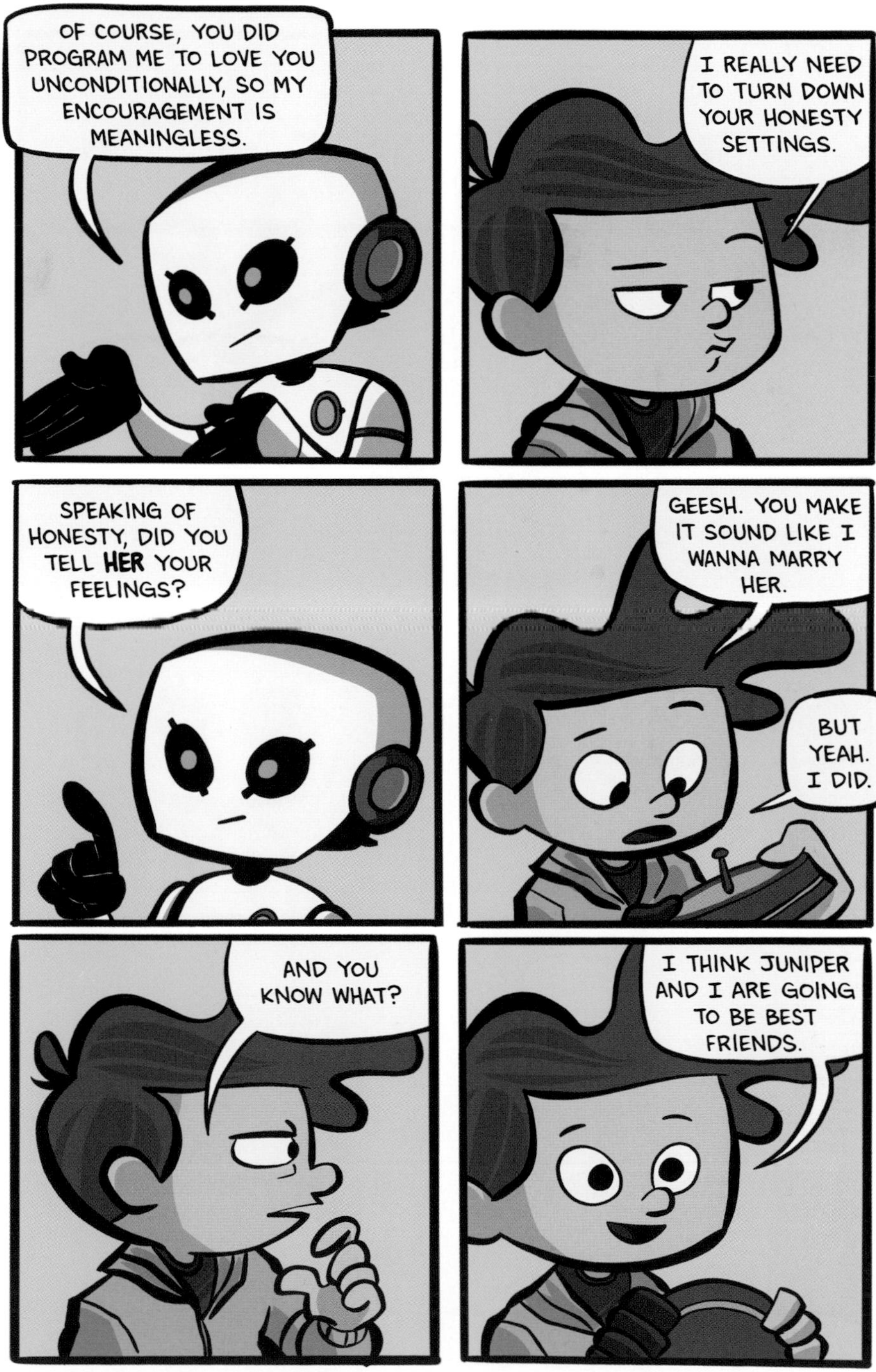
OF COURSE, YOU DID PROGRAM ME TO LOVE YOU UNCONDITIONALLY, SO MY ENCOURAGEMENT IS MEANINGLESS.
I REALLY NEED TO TURN DOWN YOUR HONESTY SETTINGS.
SPEAKING OF HONESTY, DID YOU TELL **HER** YOUR FEELINGS?
GEESH. YOU MAKE IT SOUND LIKE I WANNA MARRY HER.
BUT YEAH. I DID.
AND YOU KNOW WHAT?
I THINK JUNIPER AND I ARE GOING TO BE BEST FRIENDS.

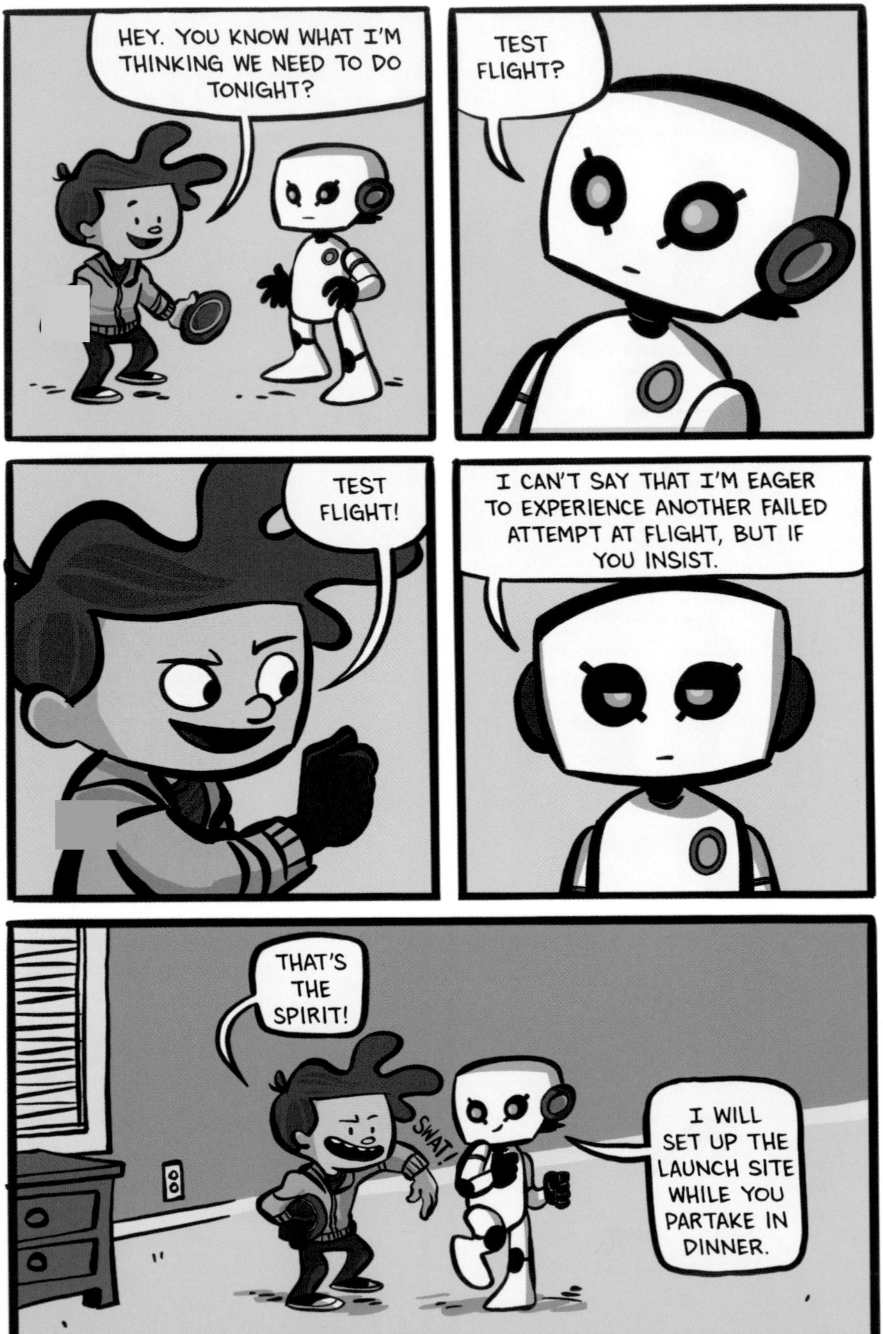
HEY. YOU KNOW WHAT I'M THINKING WE NEED TO DO TONIGHT?
TEST FLIGHT?
TEST FLIGHT!
I CAN'T SAY THAT I'M EAGER TO EXPERIENCE ANOTHER FAILED ATTEMPT AT FLIGHT, BUT IF YOU INSIST.
THAT'S THE SPIRIT!
SWAT!
I WILL SET UP THE LAUNCH SITE WHILE YOU PARTAKE IN DINNER.

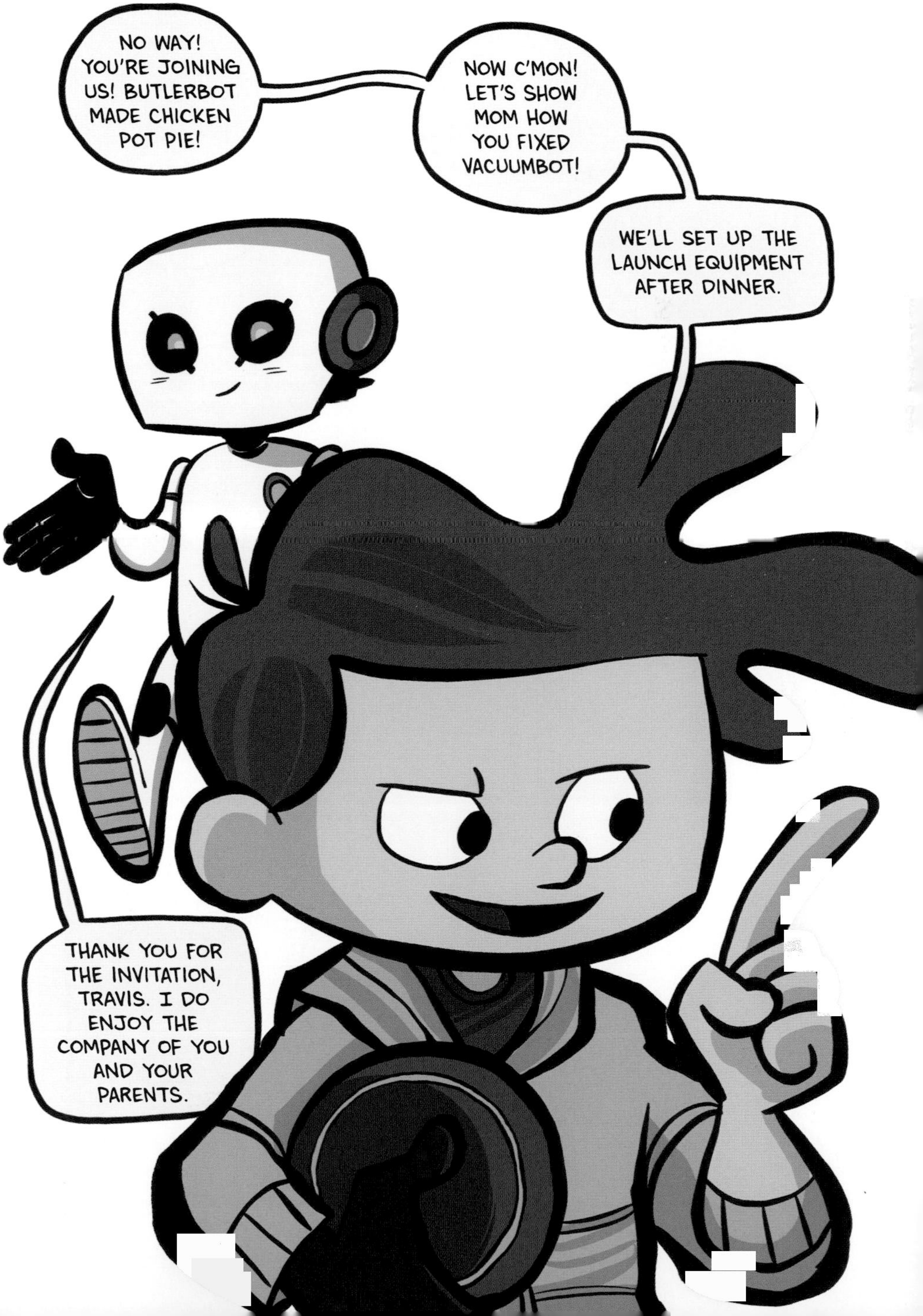
NO WAY! YOU'RE JOINING US! BUTLERBOT MADE CHICKEN POT PIE!
NOW C'MON! LET'S SHOW MOM HOW YOU FIXED VACUUMBOT!
WE'LL SET UP THE LAUNCH EQUIPMENT AFTER DINNER.
THANK YOU FOR THE INVITATION, TRAVIS. I DO ENJOY THE COMPANY OF YOU AND YOUR PARENTS.

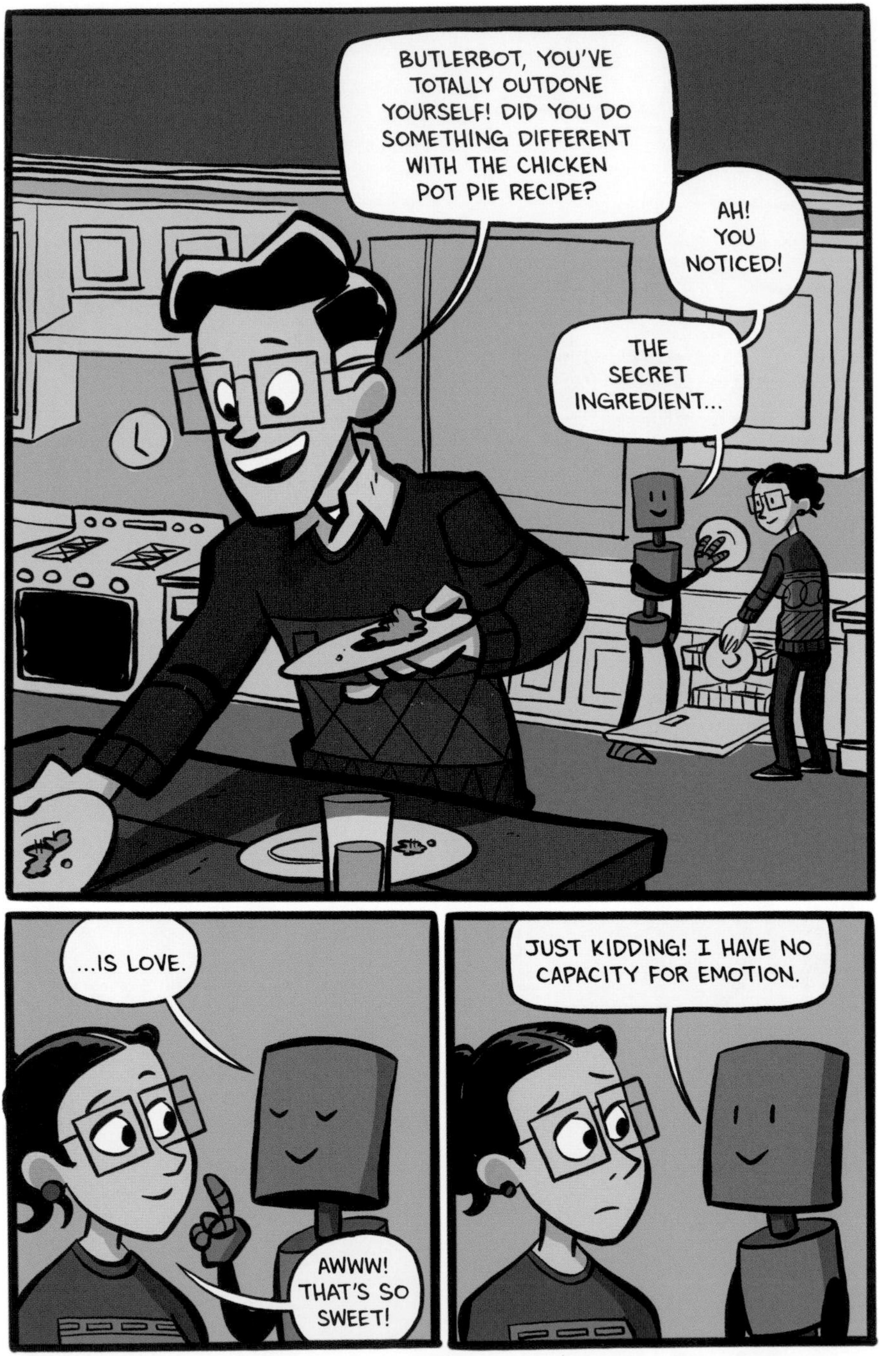
BUTLERBOT, YOU'VE TOTALLY OUTDONE YOURSELF! DID YOU DO SOMETHING DIFFERENT WITH THE CHICKEN POT PIE RECIPE?
AH! YOU NOTICED!
THE SECRET INGREDIENT...
...IS LOVE.
AWWW! THAT'S SO SWEET!
JUST KIDDING! I HAVE NO CAPACITY FOR EMOTION.

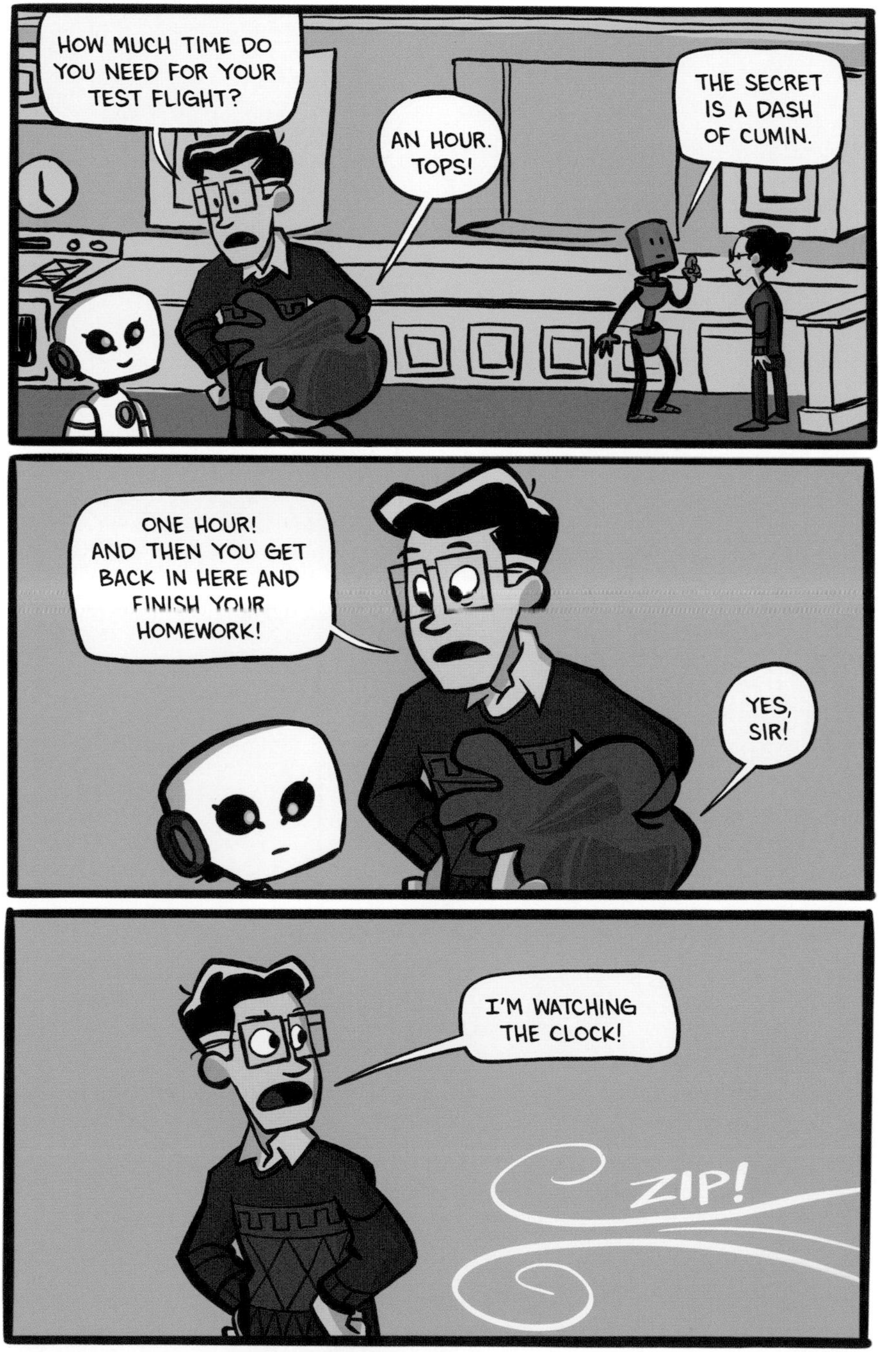
HOW MUCH TIME DO YOU NEED FOR YOUR TEST FLIGHT?
AN HOUR. TOPS!
THE SECRET IS A DASH OF CUMIN.
ONE HOUR! AND THEN YOU GET BACK IN HERE AND FINISH YOUR HOMEWORK!
YES, SIR!
I'M WATCHING THE CLOCK!
ZIP!

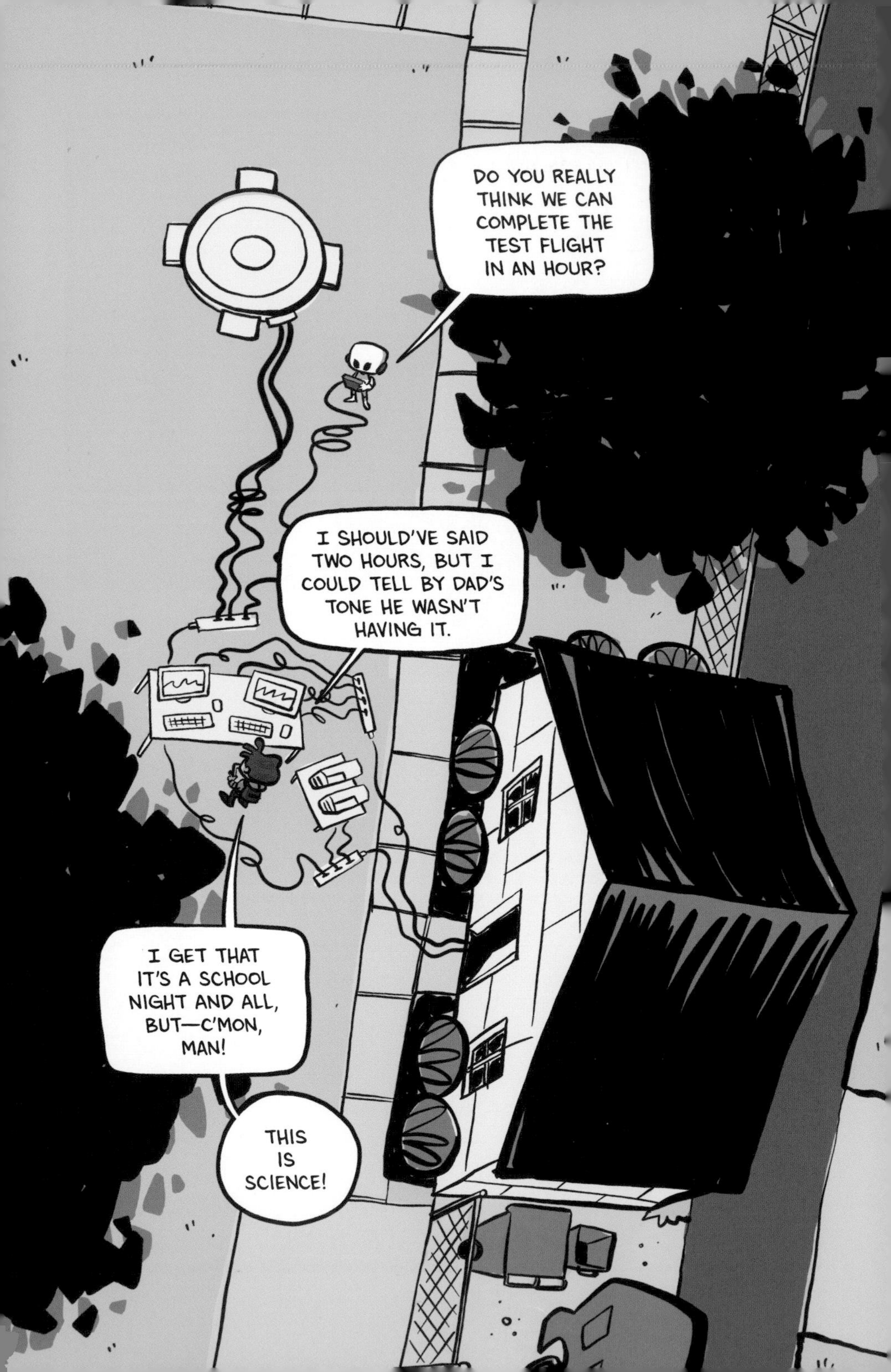
DO YOU REALLY THINK WE CAN COMPLETE THE TEST FLIGHT IN AN HOUR?
I SHOULD'VE SAID TWO HOURS, BUT I COULD TELL BY DAD'S TONE HE WASN'T HAVING IT.
I GET THAT IT'S A SCHOOL NIGHT AND ALL, BUT—C'MON, MAN!
THIS IS SCIENCE!

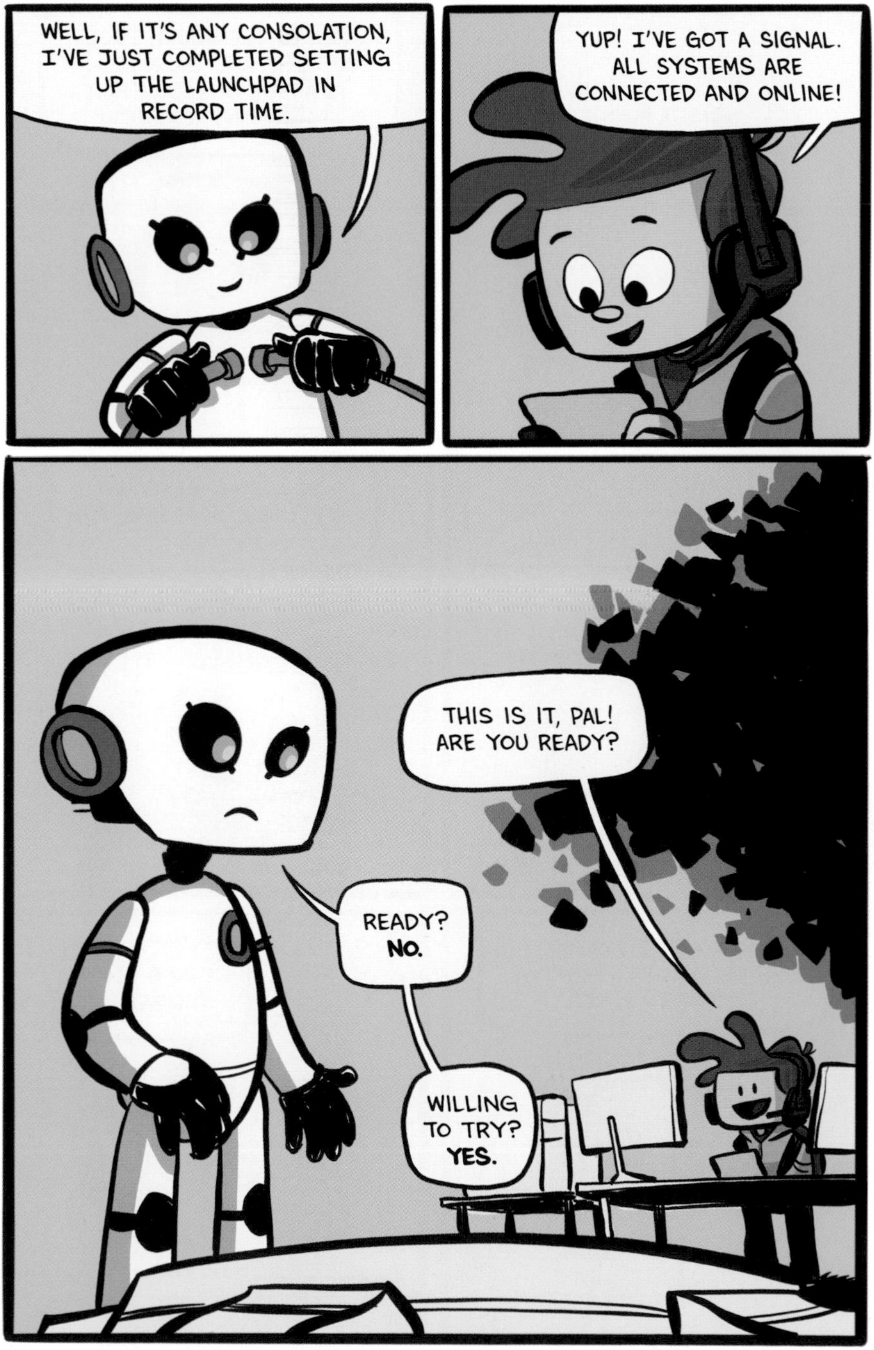
WELL, IF IT'S ANY CONSOLATION, I'VE JUST COMPLETED SETTING UP THE LAUNCHPAD IN RECORD TIME.
YUP! I'VE GOT A SIGNAL. ALL SYSTEMS ARE CONNECTED AND ONLINE!
THIS IS IT, PAL! ARE YOU READY?
READY? **NO.**
WILLING TO TRY? **YES.**

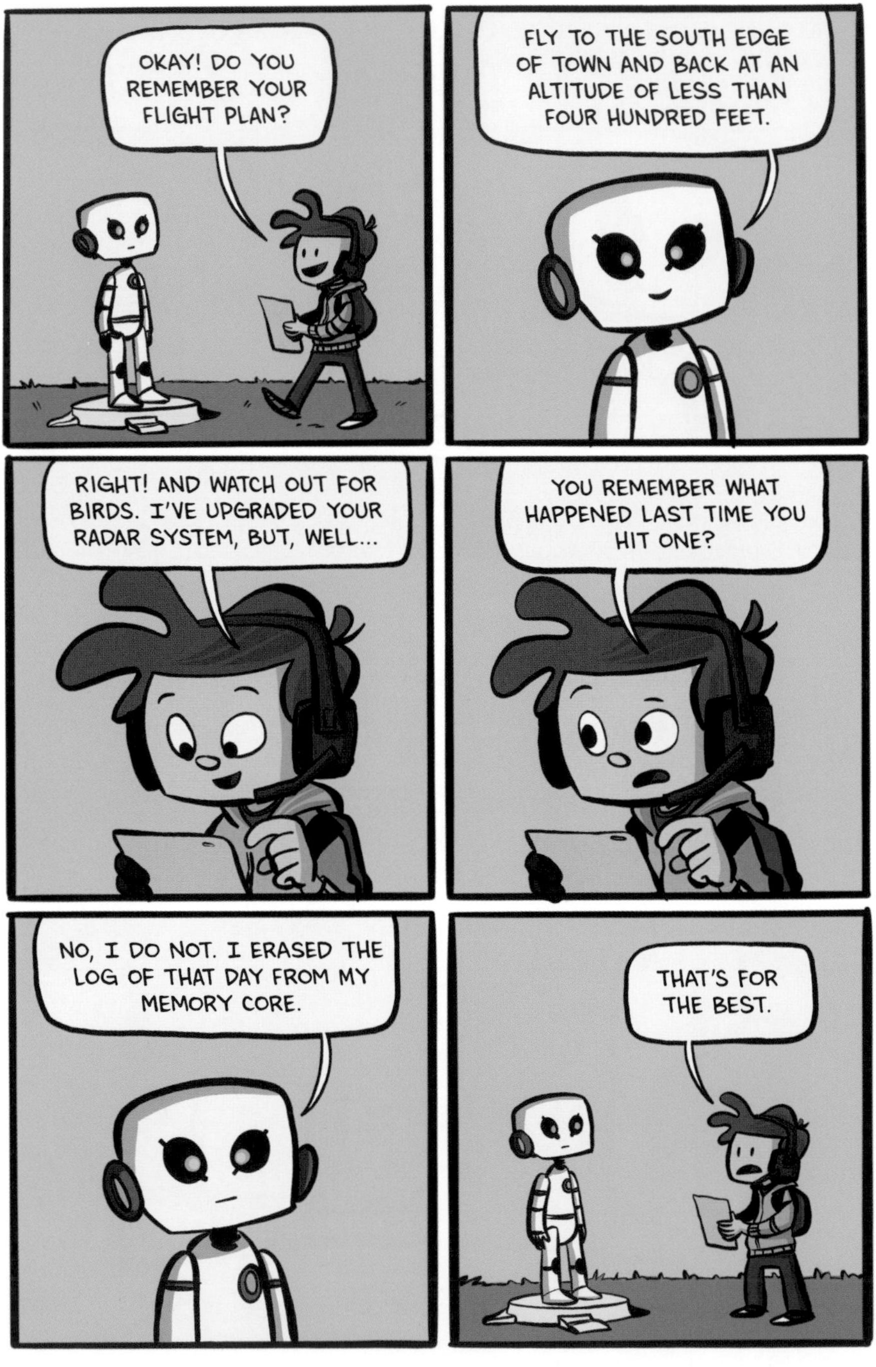
OKAY! DO YOU REMEMBER YOUR FLIGHT PLAN?
FLY TO THE SOUTH EDGE OF TOWN AND BACK AT AN ALTITUDE OF LESS THAN FOUR HUNDRED FEET.
RIGHT! AND WATCH OUT FOR BIRDS. I'VE UPGRADED YOUR RADAR SYSTEM, BUT, WELL...
YOU REMEMBER WHAT HAPPENED LAST TIME YOU HIT ONE?
NO, I DO NOT. I ERASED THE LOG OF THAT DAY FROM MY MEMORY CORE.
THAT'S FOR THE BEST.

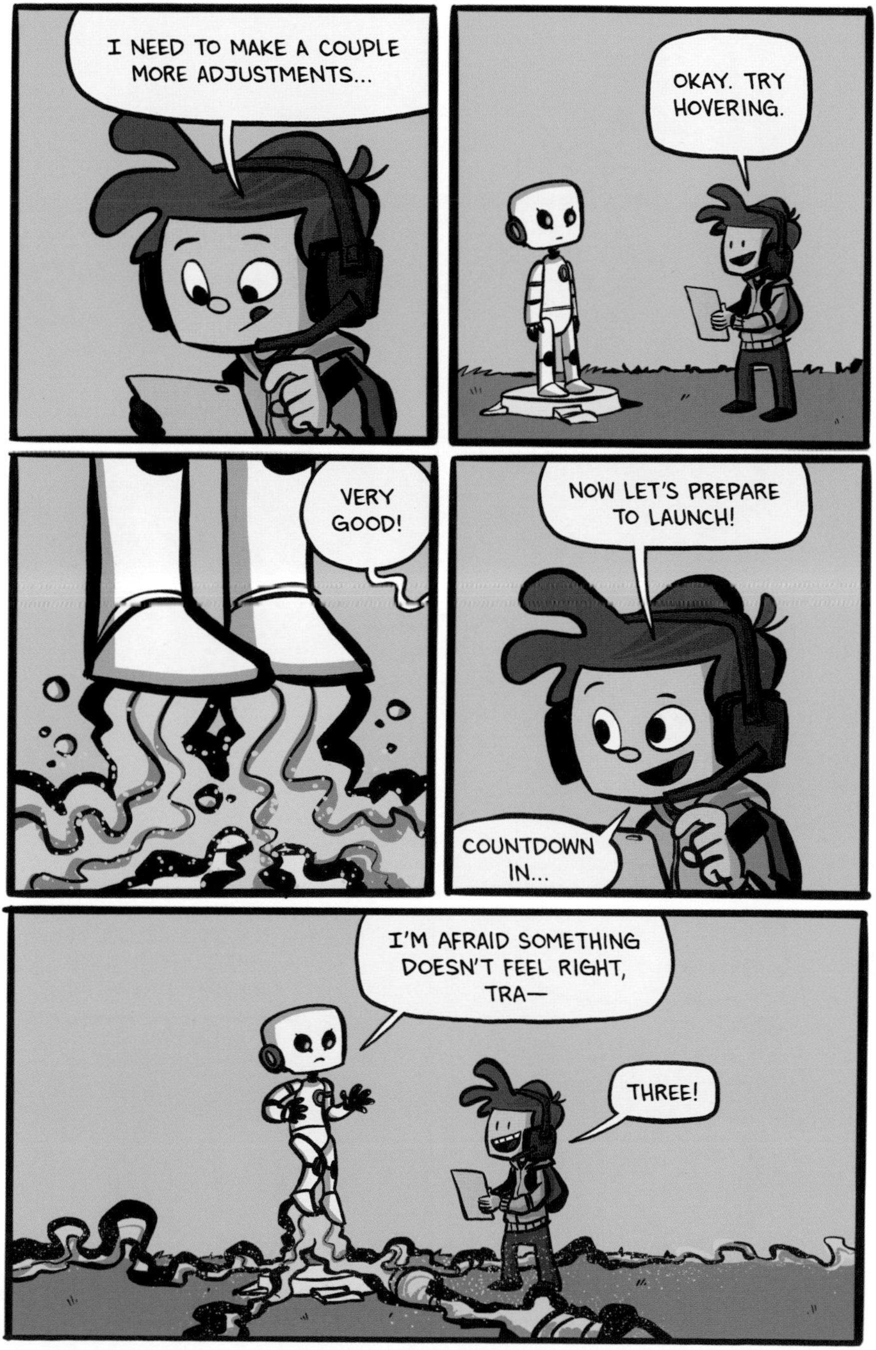
I NEED TO MAKE A COUPLE MORE ADJUSTMENTS...
OKAY. TRY HOVERING.
VERY GOOD!
NOW LET'S PREPARE TO LAUNCH!
COUNTDOWN IN...
I'M AFRAID SOMETHING DOESN'T FEEL RIGHT, TRA—
THREE!

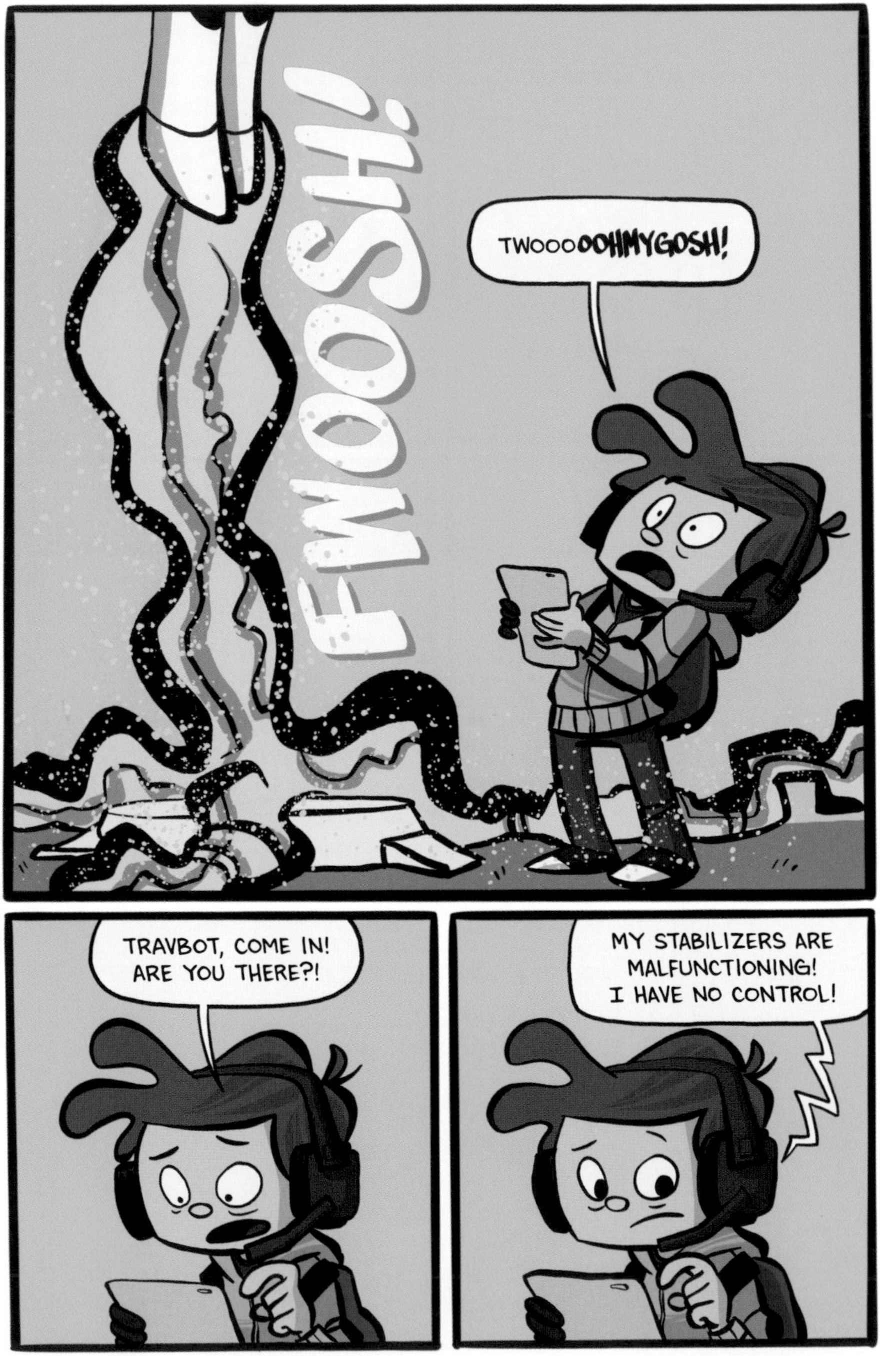
FWOOSH!
TWOOOOOHMYGOSH!
TRAVBOT, COME IN! ARE YOU THERE?!
MY STABILIZERS ARE MALFUNCTIONING! I HAVE NO CONTROL!

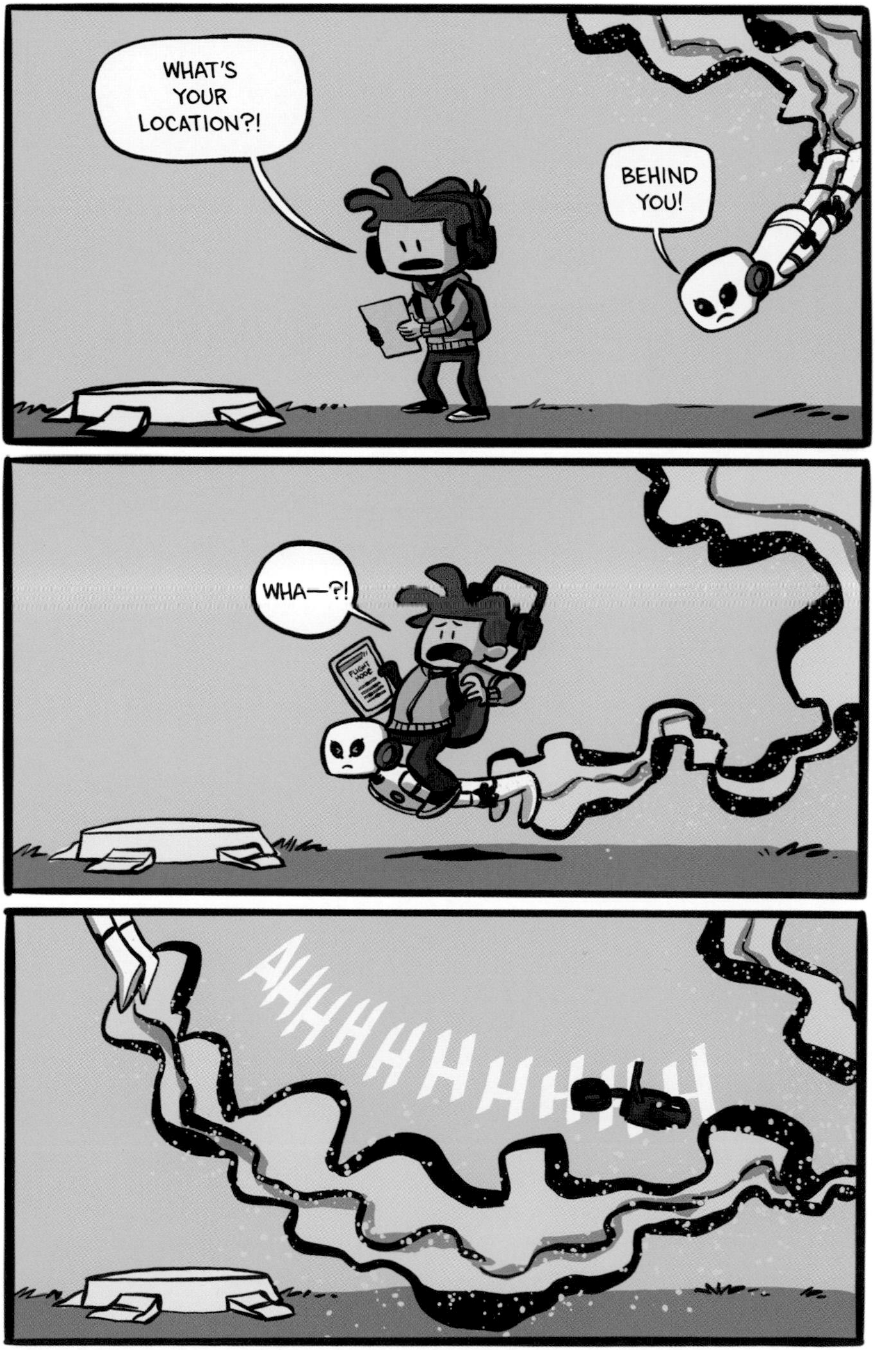
WHAT'S YOUR LOCATION?!
BEHIND YOU!
WHA—?!
FLIGHT MODE
AHHHHHHHHHH

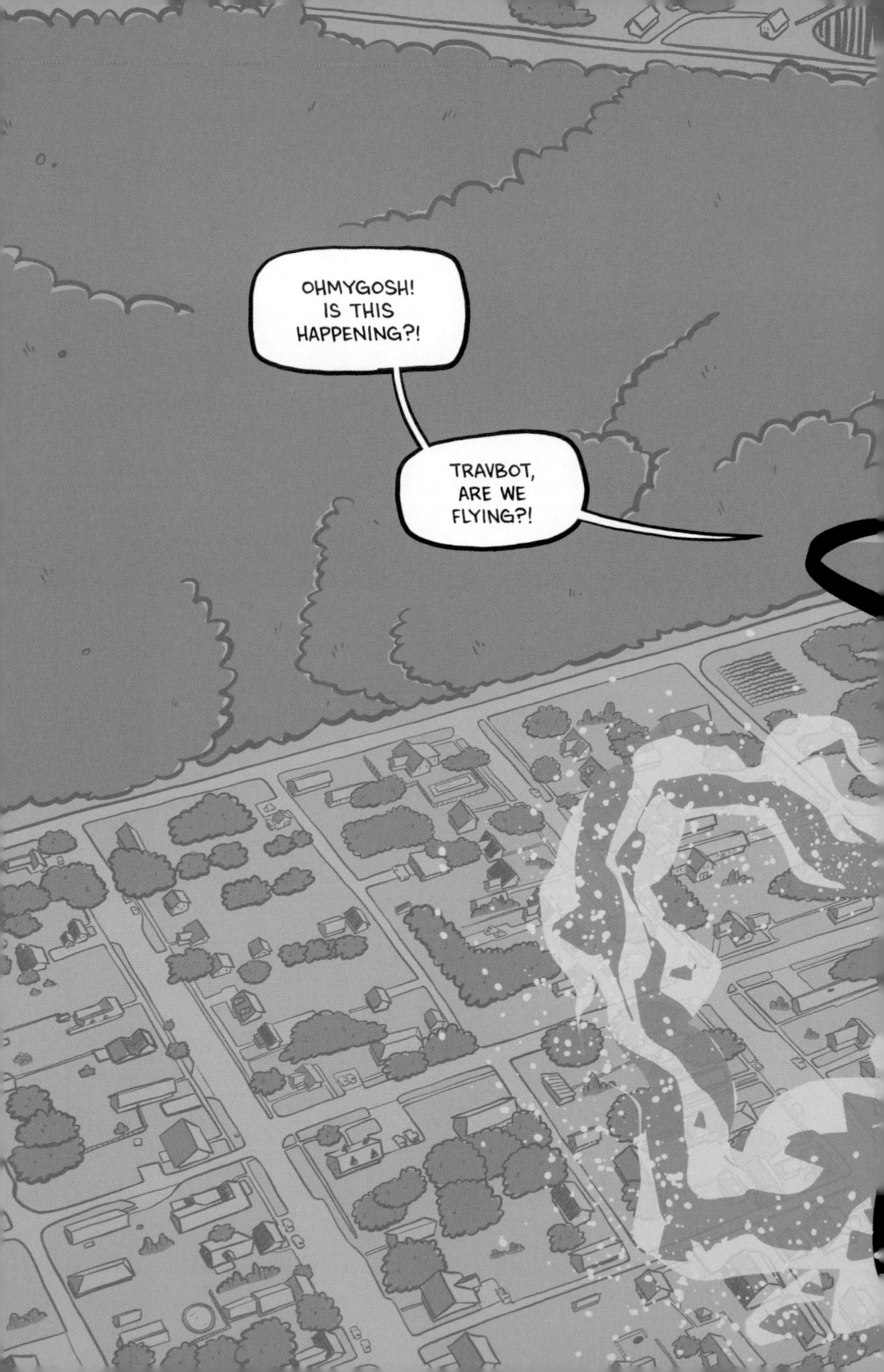
OHMYGOSH! IS THIS HAPPENING?!
TRAVBOT, ARE WE FLYING?!

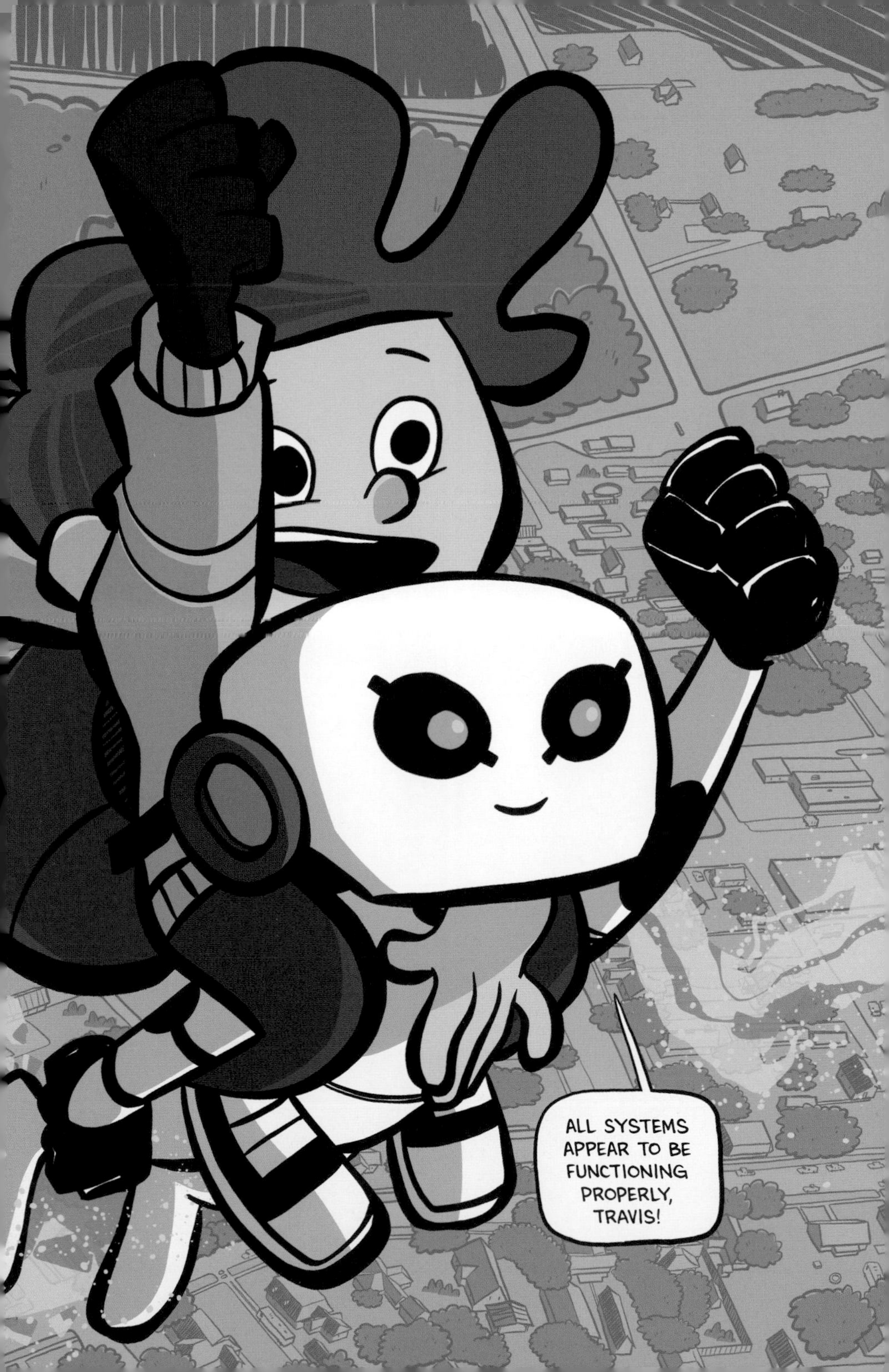
ALL SYSTEMS APPEAR TO BE FUNCTIONING PROPERLY, TRAVIS!

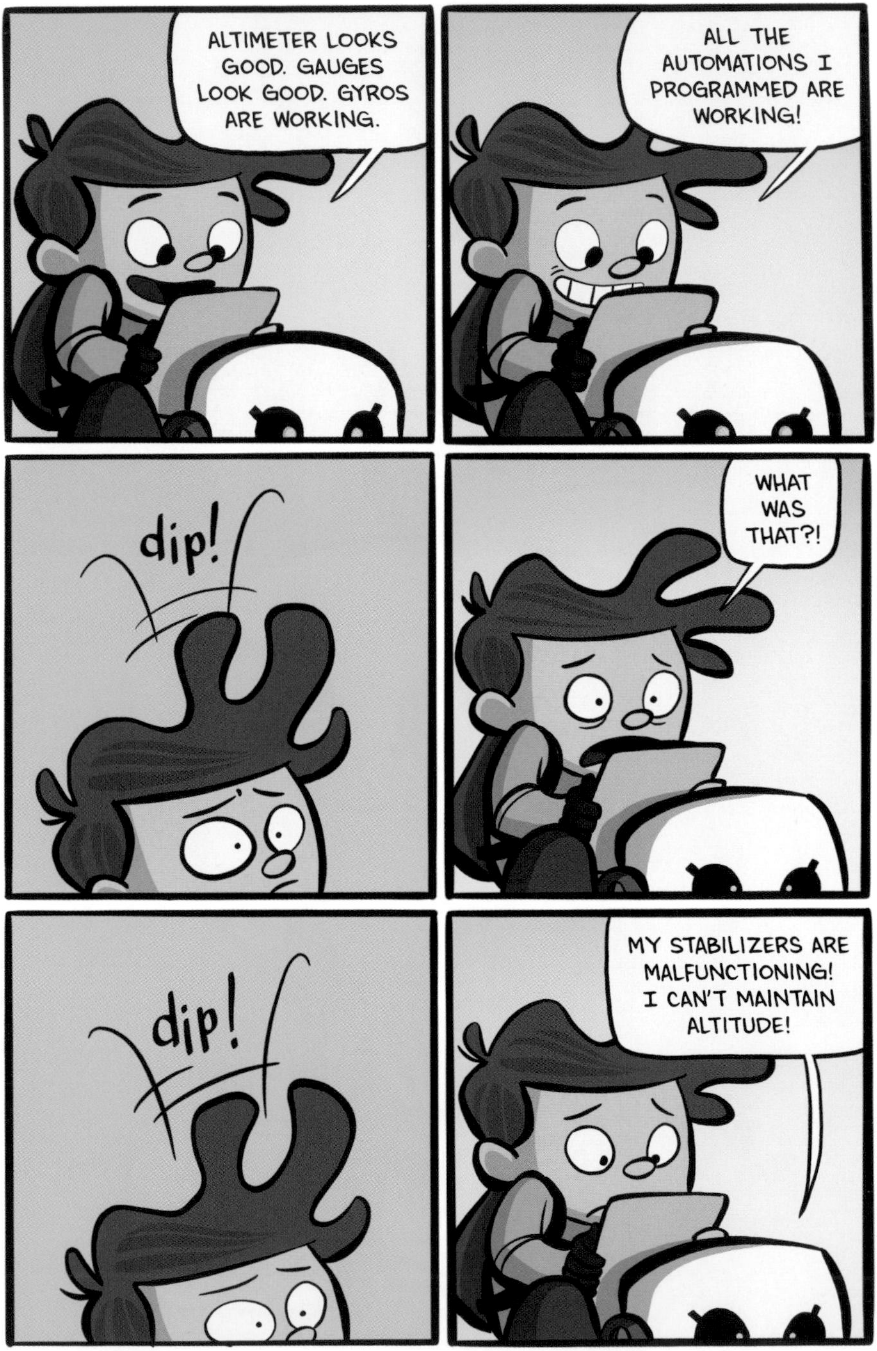
ALTIMETER LOOKS GOOD. GAUGES LOOK GOOD. GYROS ARE WORKING.
ALL THE AUTOMATIONS I PROGRAMMED ARE WORKING!
dip!
WHAT WAS THAT?!
dip!
MY STABILIZERS ARE MALFUNCTIONING! I CAN'T MAINTAIN ALTITUDE!

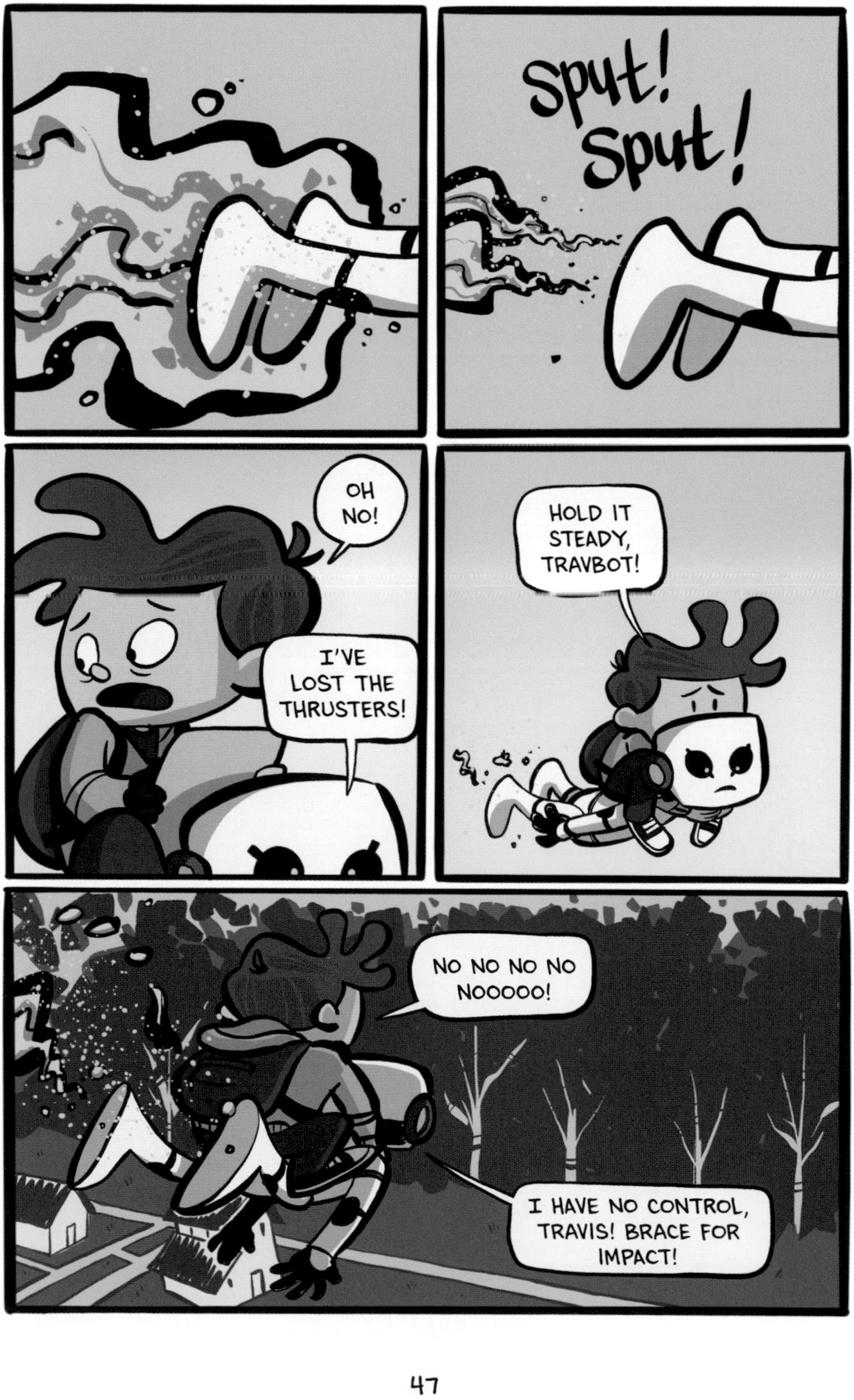
Sput! Sput!
OH NO!
I'VE LOST THE THRUSTERS!
HOLD IT STEADY, TRAVBOT!
NO NO NO NO NOOOOO!
I HAVE NO CONTROL, TRAVIS! BRACE FOR IMPACT!

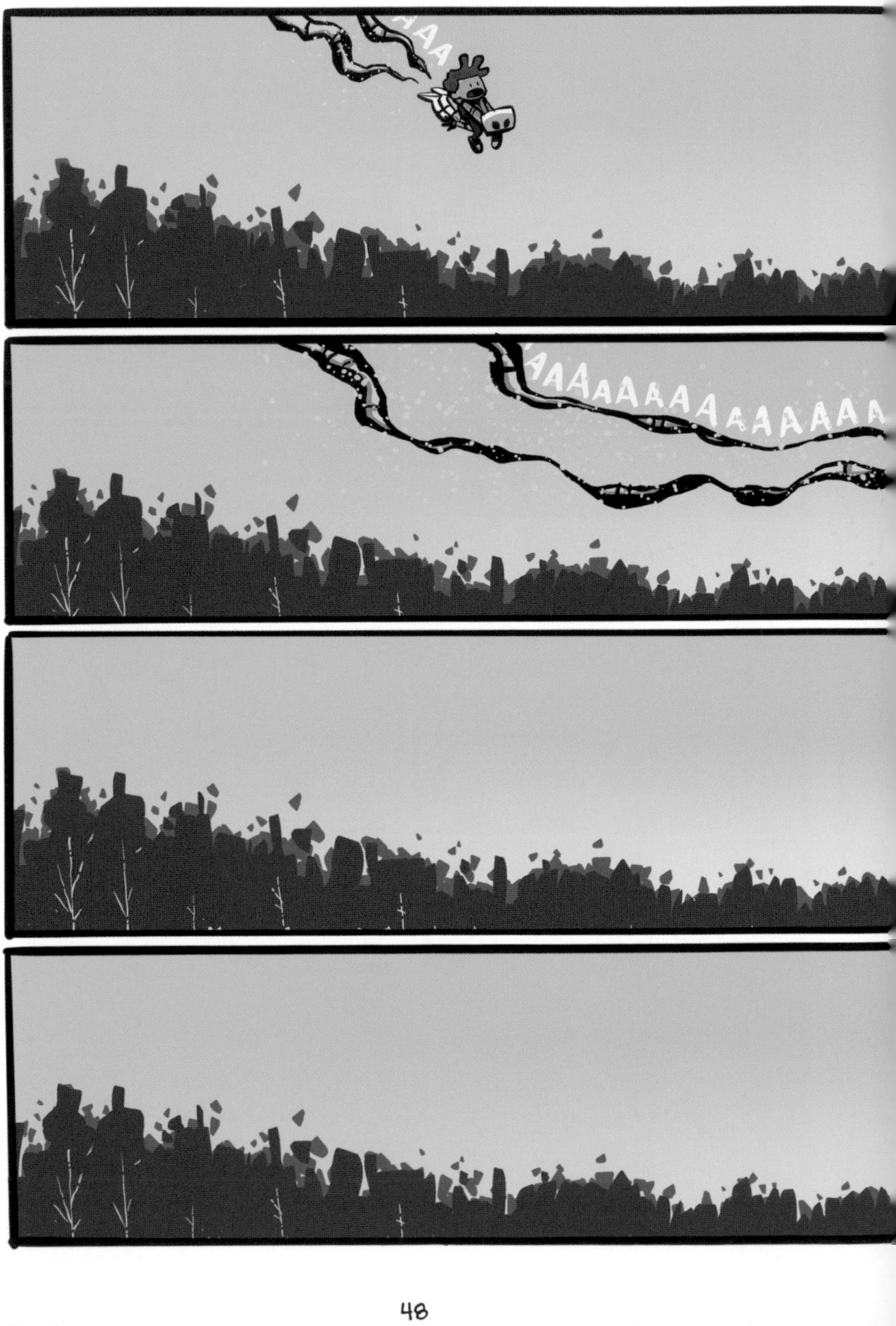
AAAA
AAAAAAAAAAAAAAA

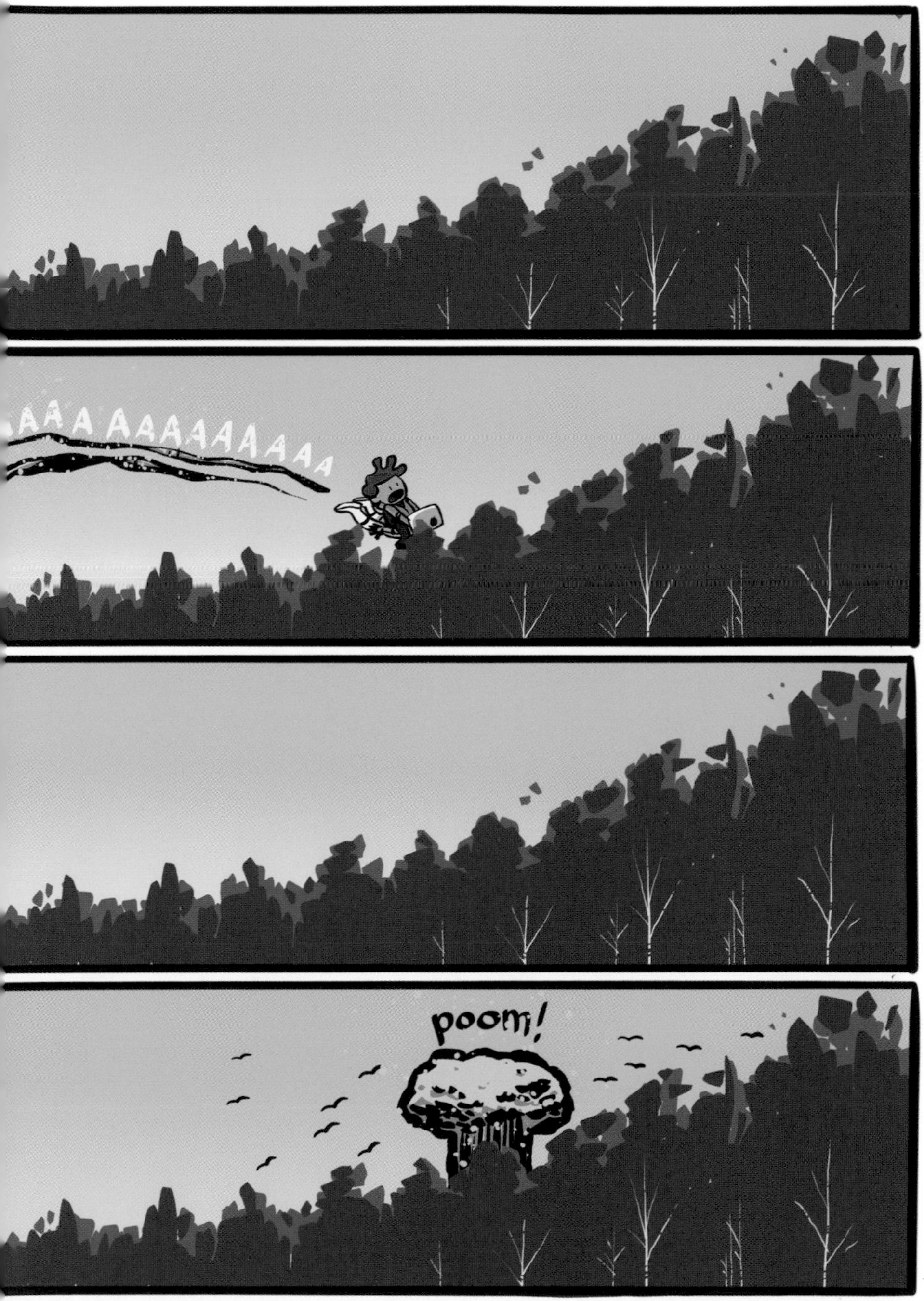
AAAA AAAAAAAAAA
poom!

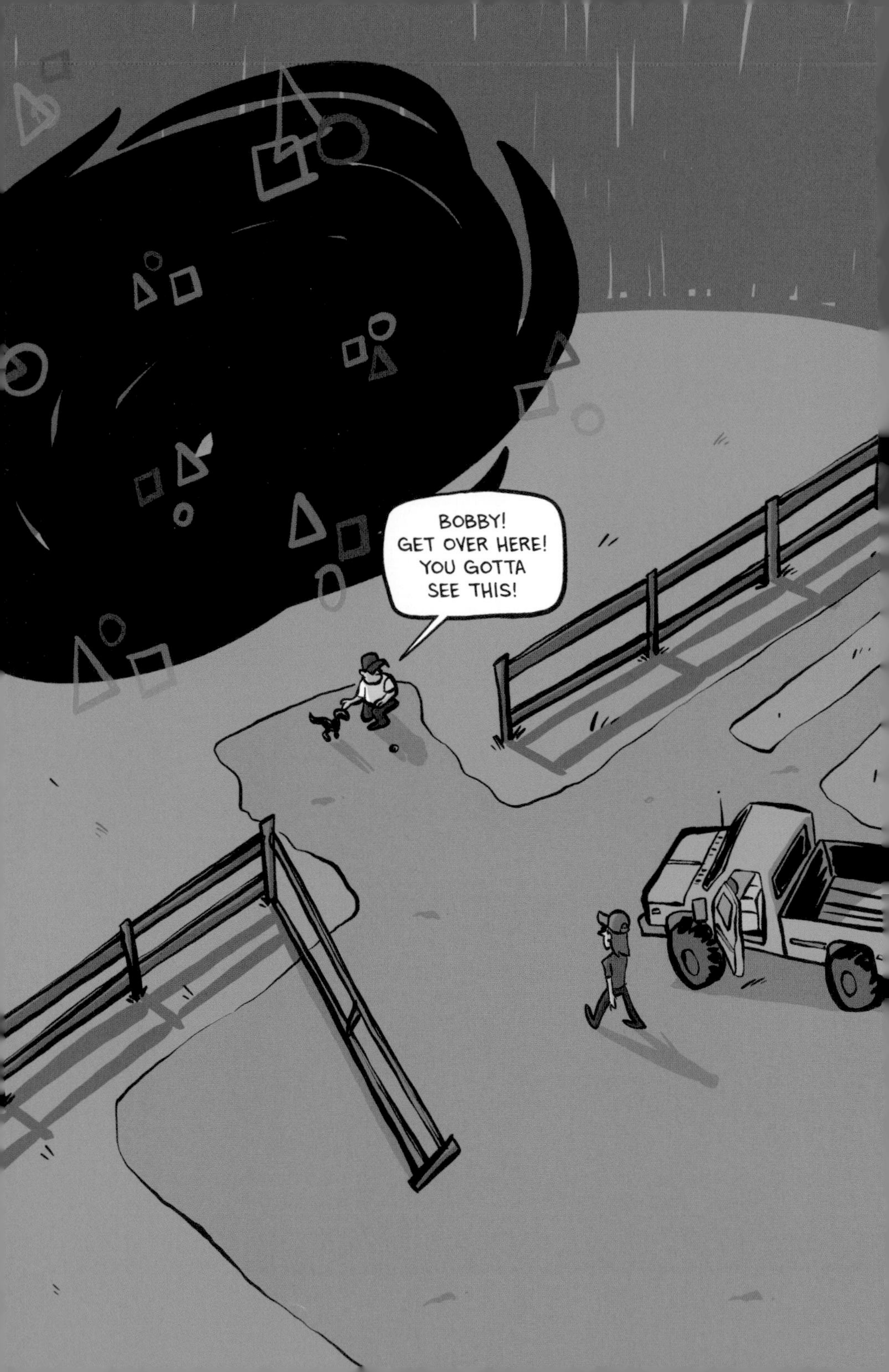
BOBBY! GET OVER HERE! YOU GOTTA SEE THIS!

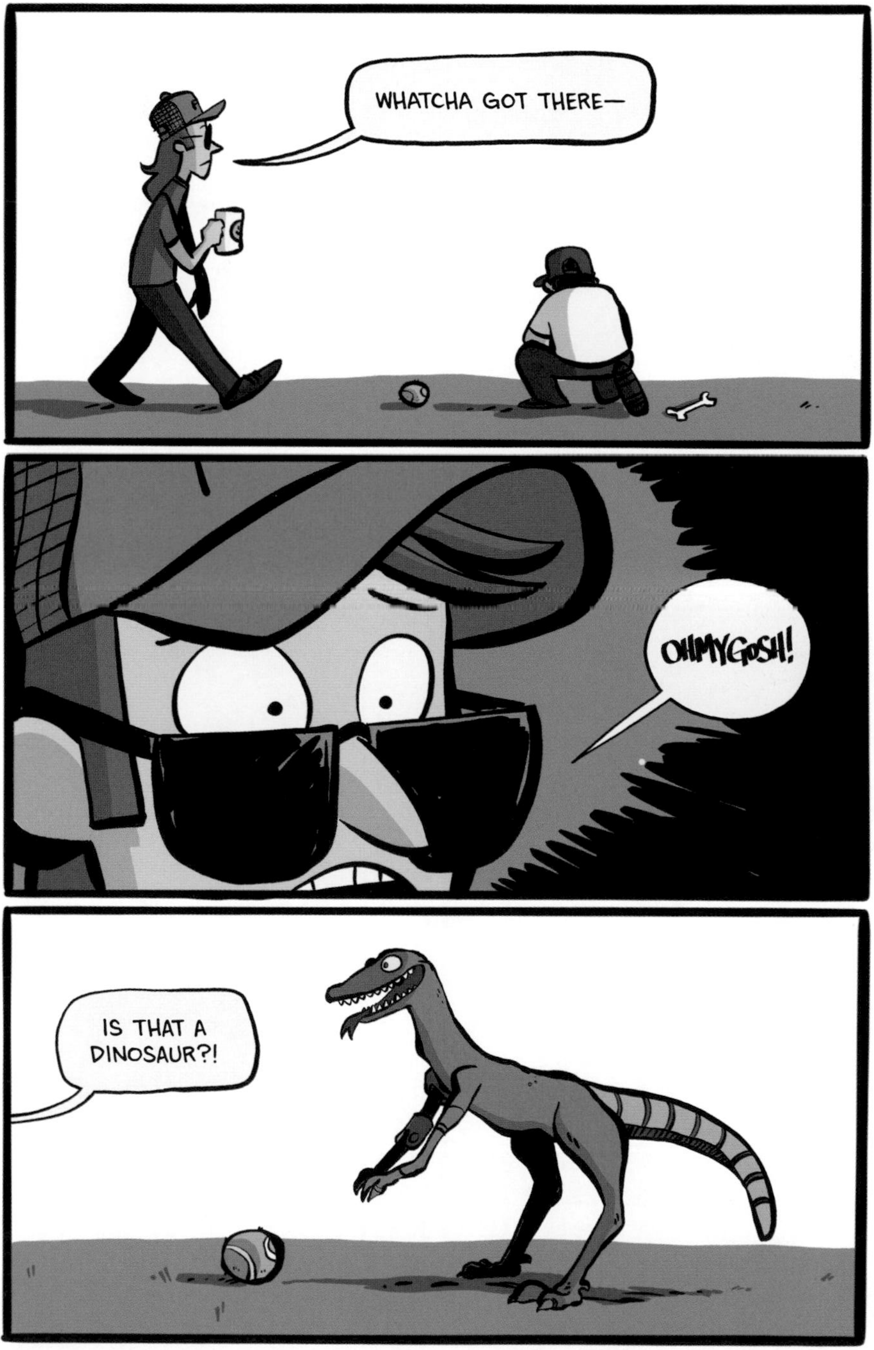
WHATCHA GOT THERE—
OHMYGOSH!
IS THAT A DINOSAUR?!

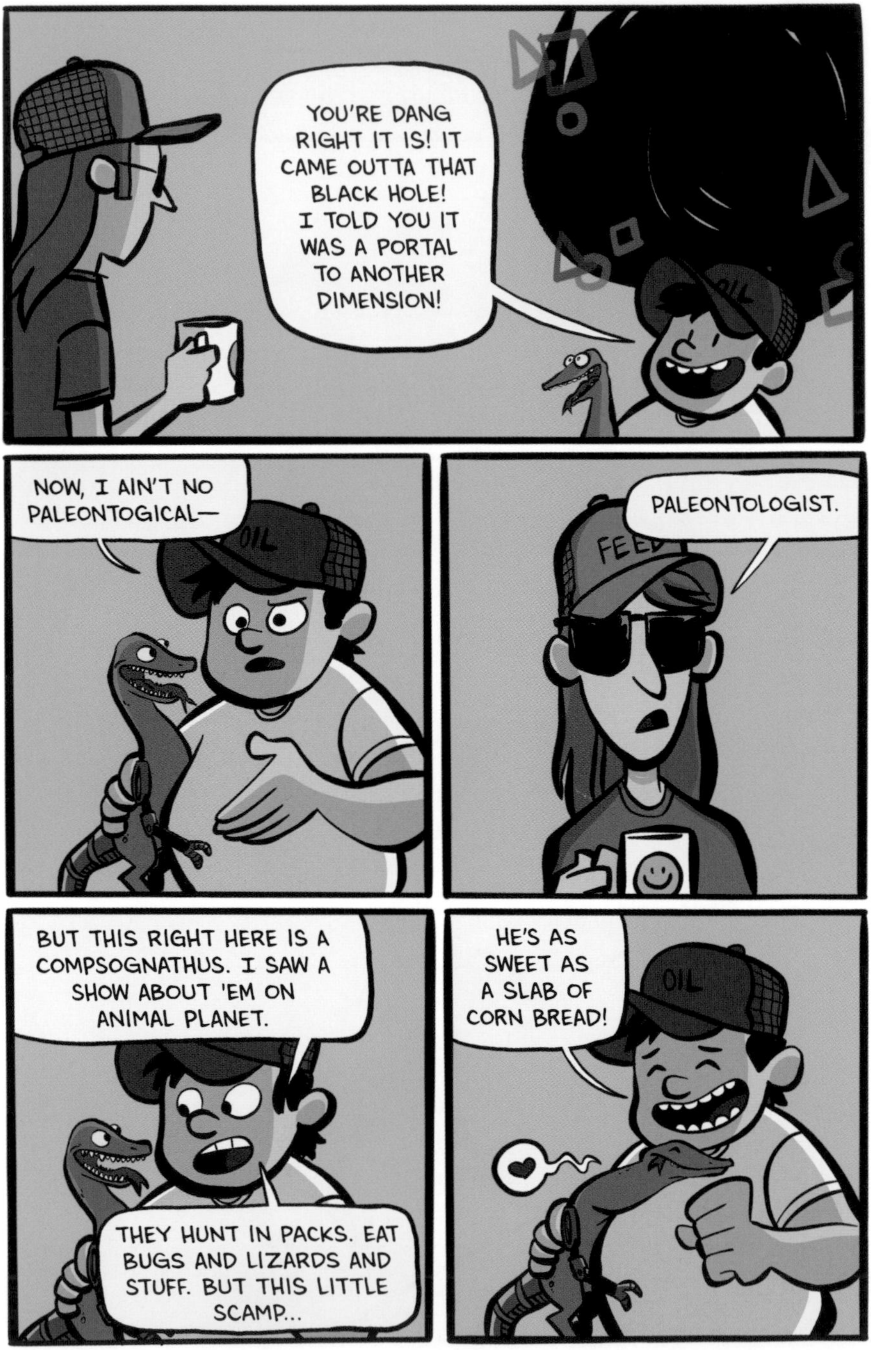
YOU'RE DANG RIGHT IT IS! IT CAME OUTTA THAT BLACK HOLE! I TOLD YOU IT WAS A PORTAL TO ANOTHER DIMENSION!
OIL
NOW, I AIN'T NO PALEONTOGICAL—
OIL
PALEONTOLOGIST.
BUT THIS RIGHT HERE IS A COMPSOGNATHUS. I SAW A SHOW ABOUT 'EM ON ANIMAL PLANET.
THEY HUNT IN PACKS. EAT BUGS AND LIZARDS AND STUFF. BUT THIS LITTLE SCAMP...
HE'S AS SWEET AS A SLAB OF CORN BREAD!
OIL

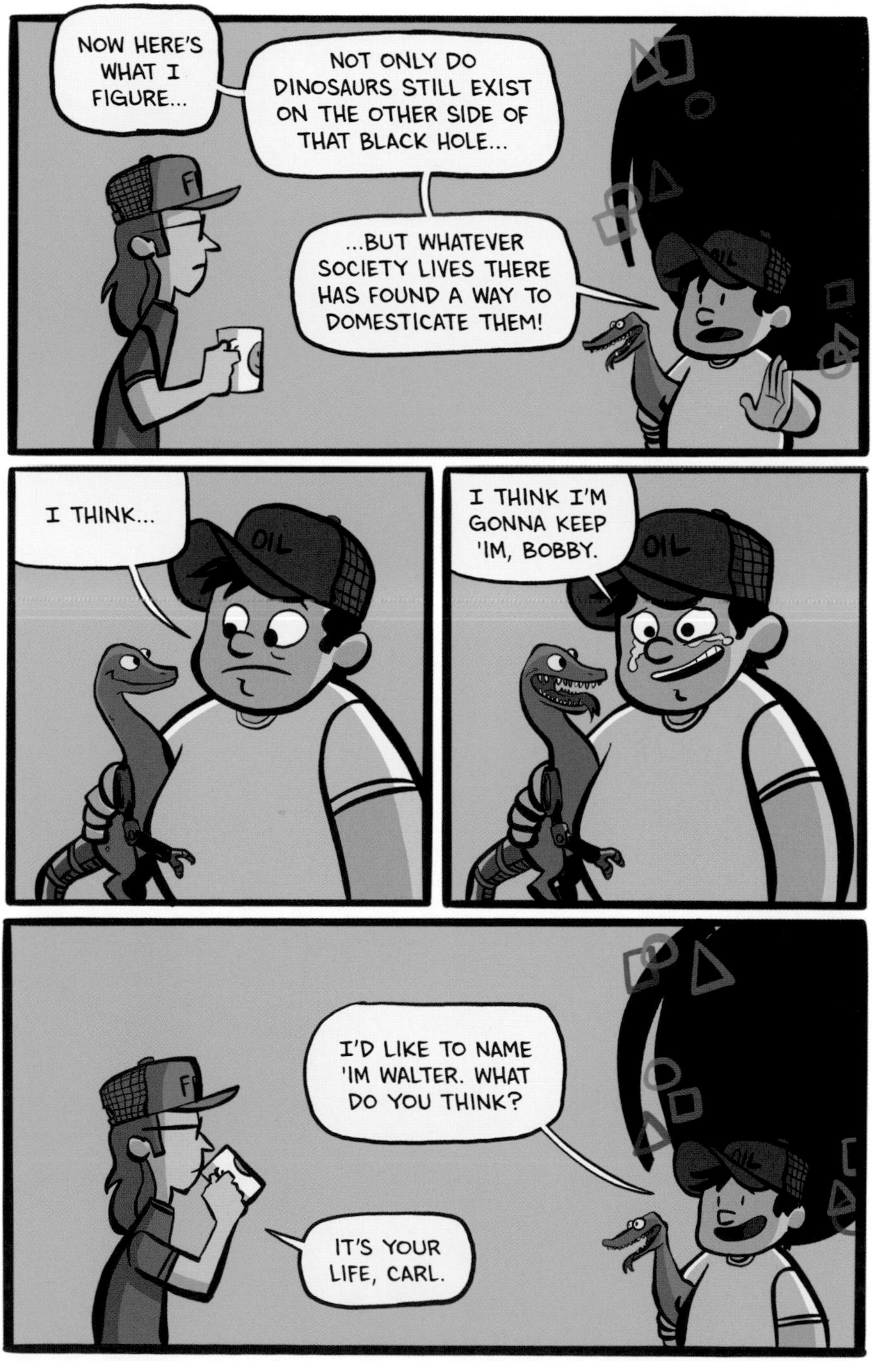
NOW HERE'S WHAT I FIGURE...
NOT ONLY DO DINOSAURS STILL EXIST ON THE OTHER SIDE OF THAT BLACK HOLE...
...BUT WHATEVER SOCIETY LIVES THERE HAS FOUND A WAY TO DOMESTICATE THEM!
I THINK...
I THINK I'M GONNA KEEP 'IM, BOBBY.
I'D LIKE TO NAME 'IM WALTER. WHAT DO YOU THINK?
IT'S YOUR LIFE, CARL.

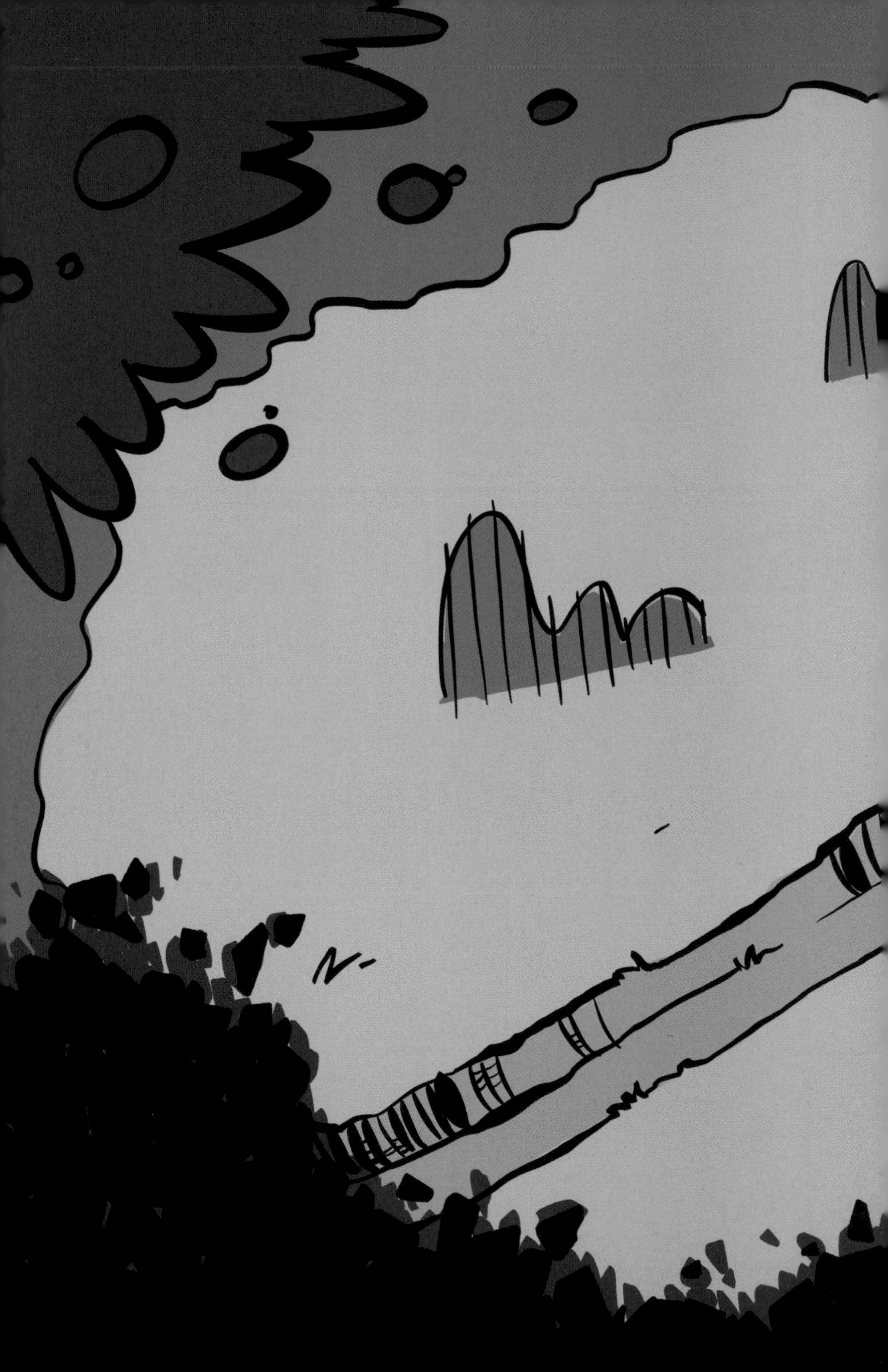

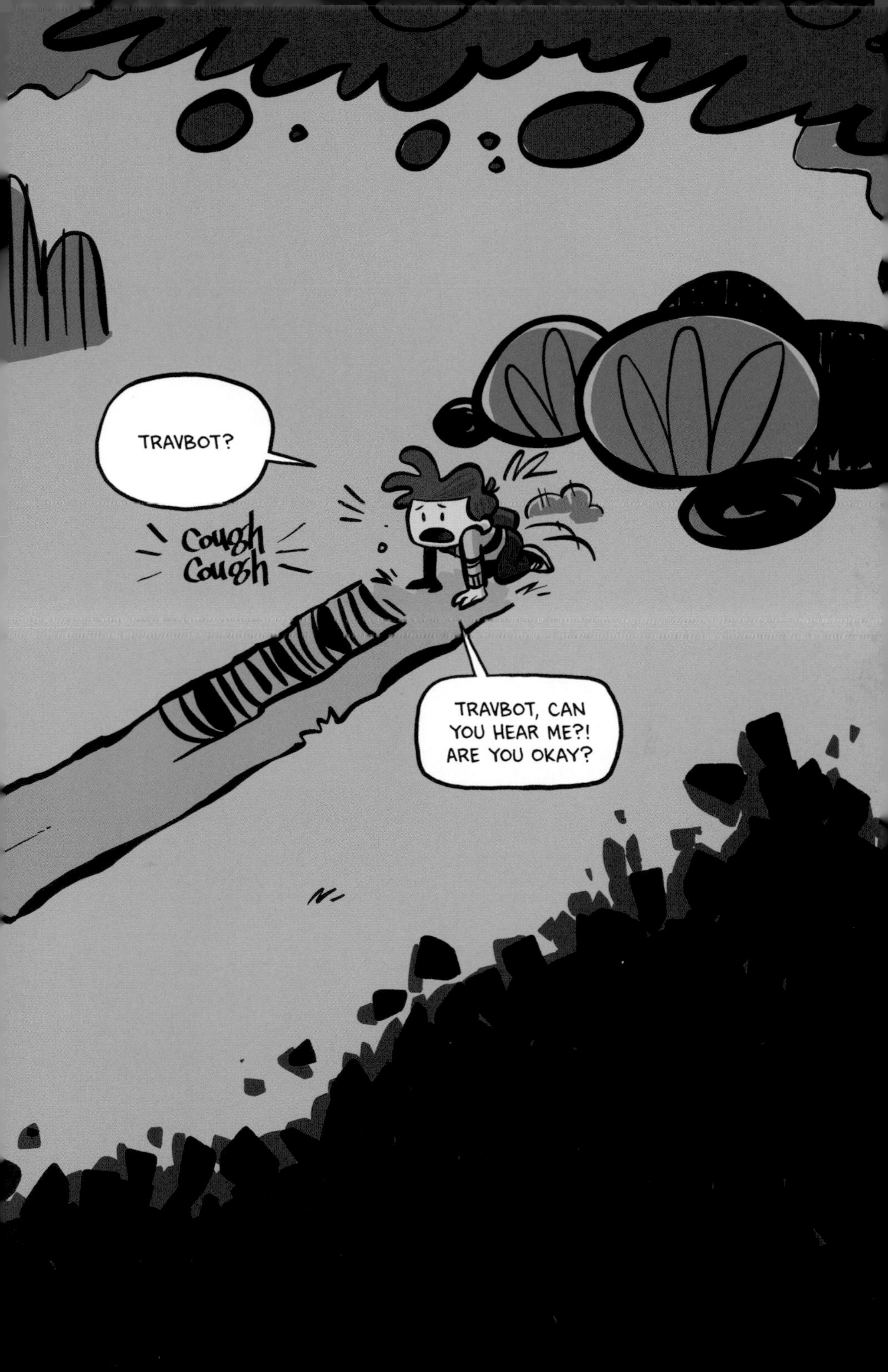
TRAVBOT?
Cough
Cough
TRAVBOT, CAN YOU HEAR ME?! ARE YOU OKAY?

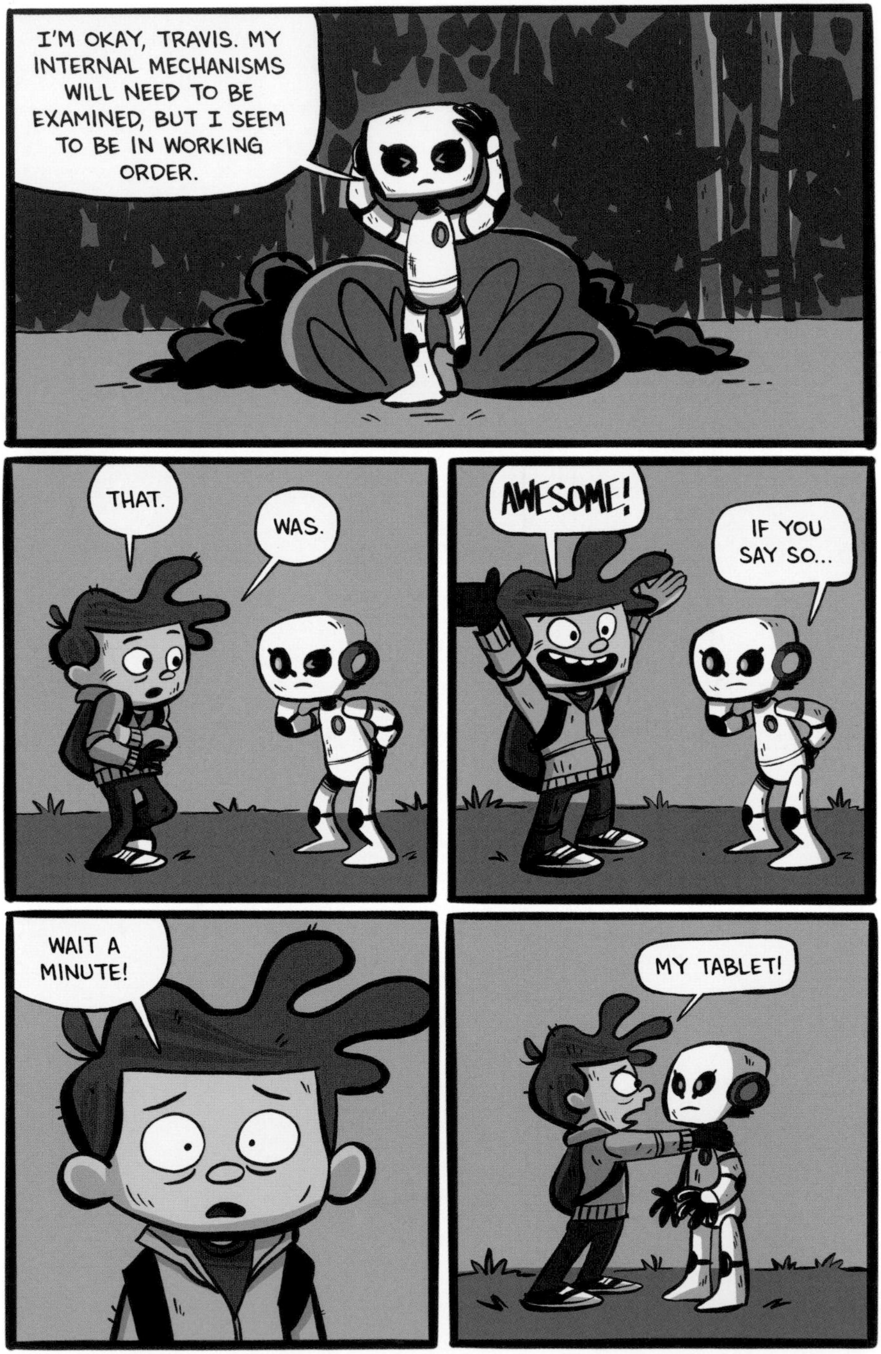
I'M OKAY, TRAVIS. MY INTERNAL MECHANISMS WILL NEED TO BE EXAMINED, BUT I SEEM TO BE IN WORKING ORDER.
THAT.
WAS.
AWESOME!
IF YOU SAY SO...
WAIT A MINUTE!
MY TABLET!

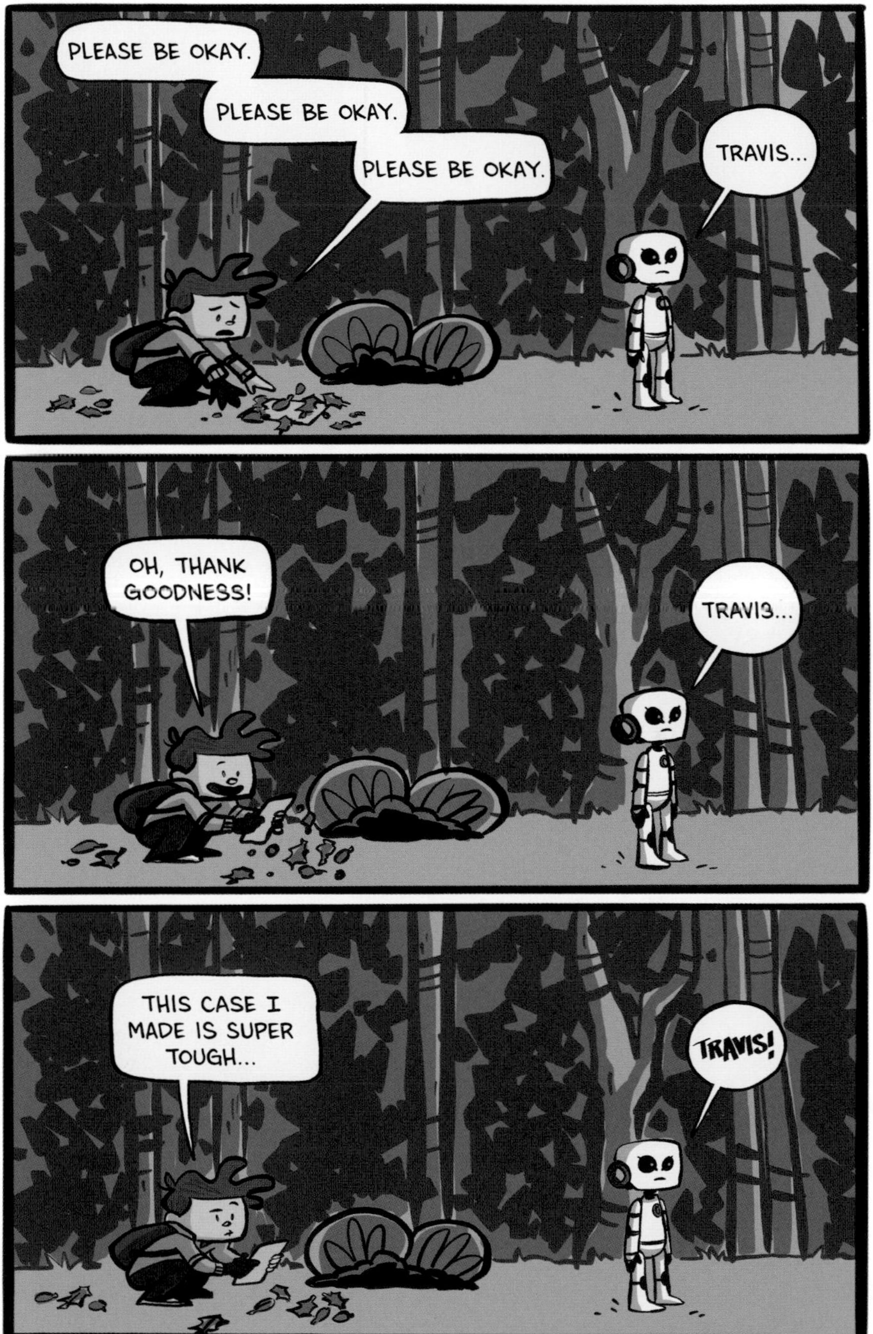
PLEASE BE OKAY.
PLEASE BE OKAY.
PLEASE BE OKAY.
TRAVIS...
OH, THANK GOODNESS!
TRAVIS...
THIS CASE I MADE IS SUPER TOUGH...
TRAVIS!

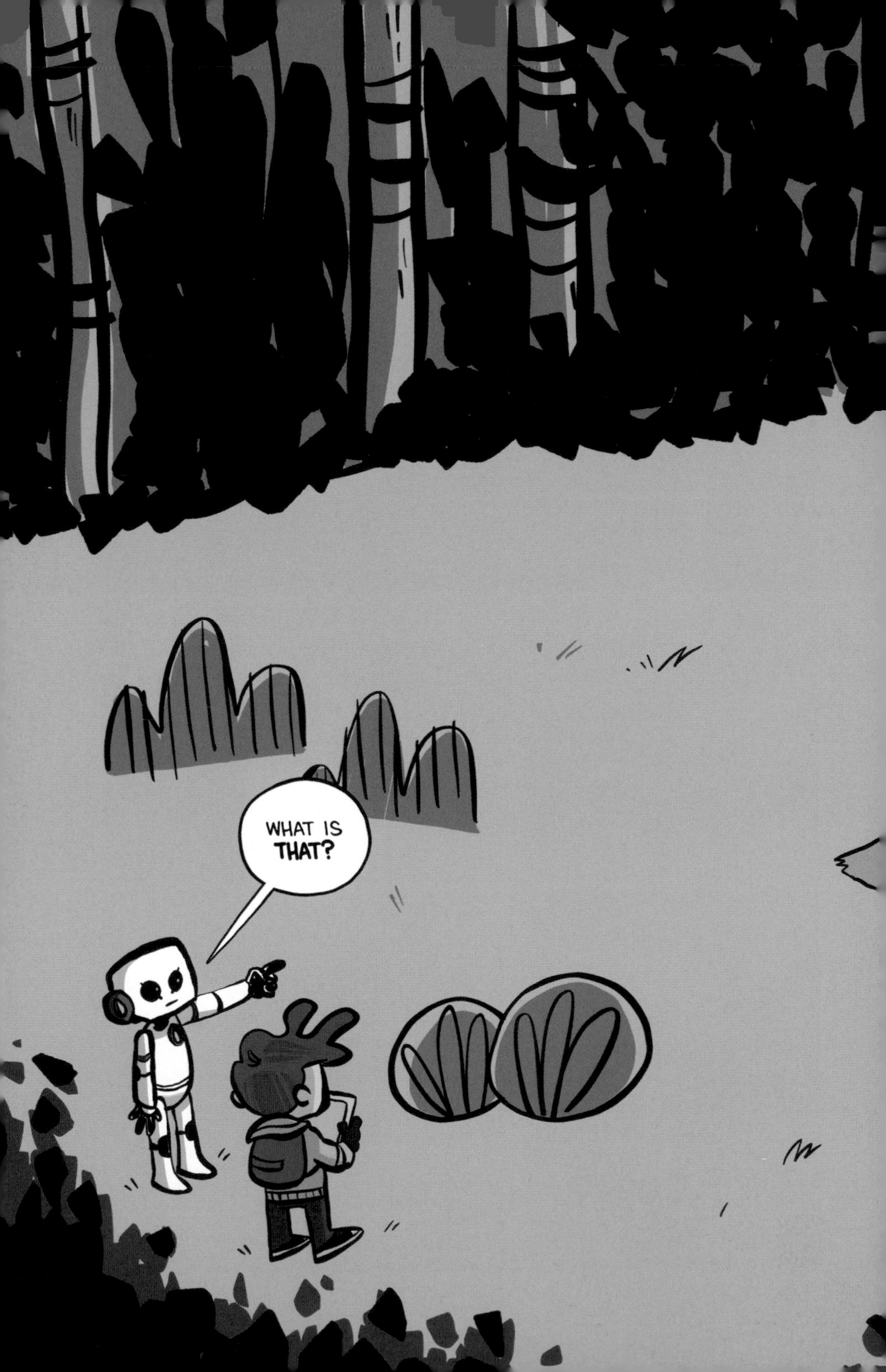
WHAT IS **THAT?**

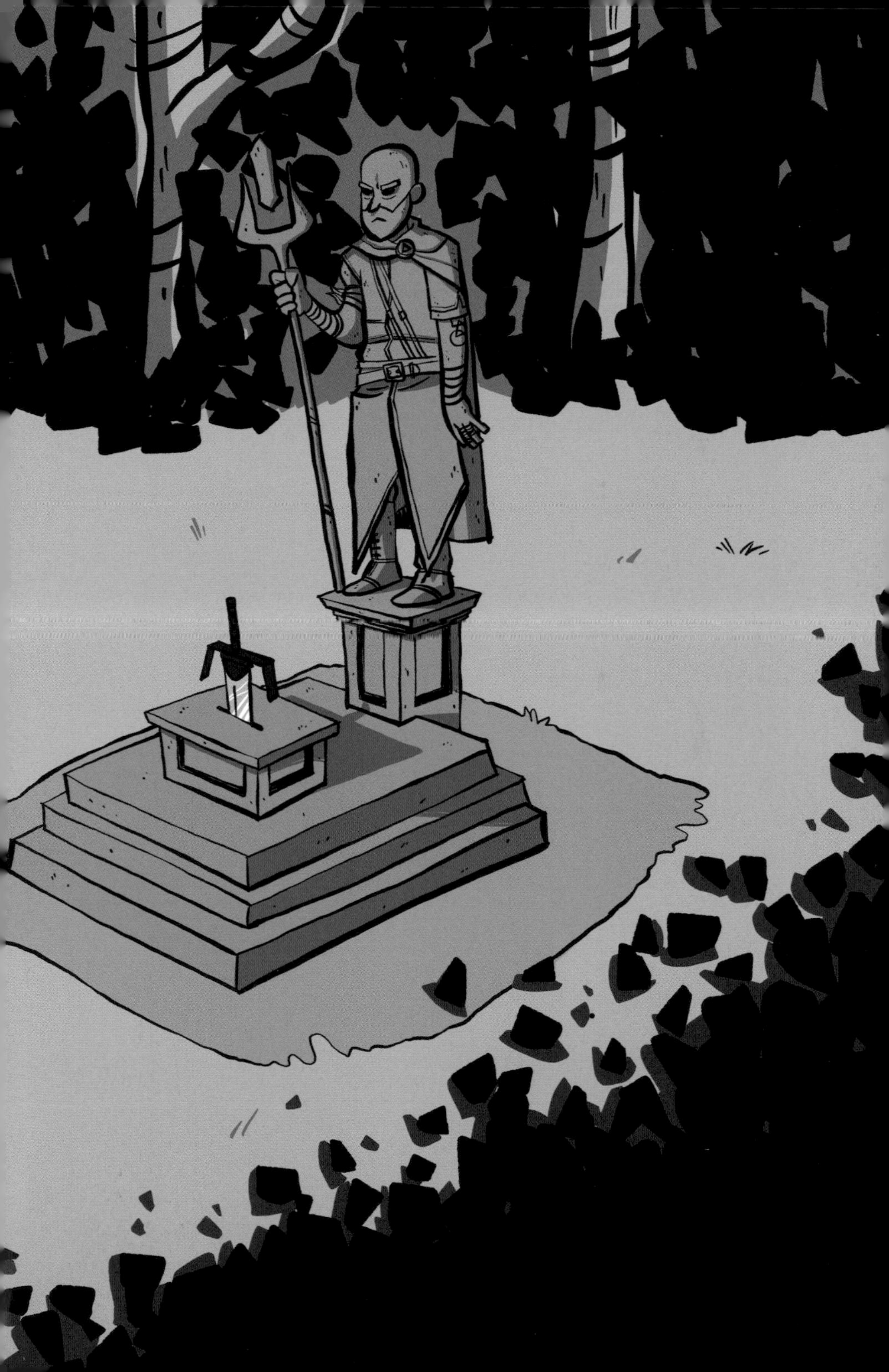

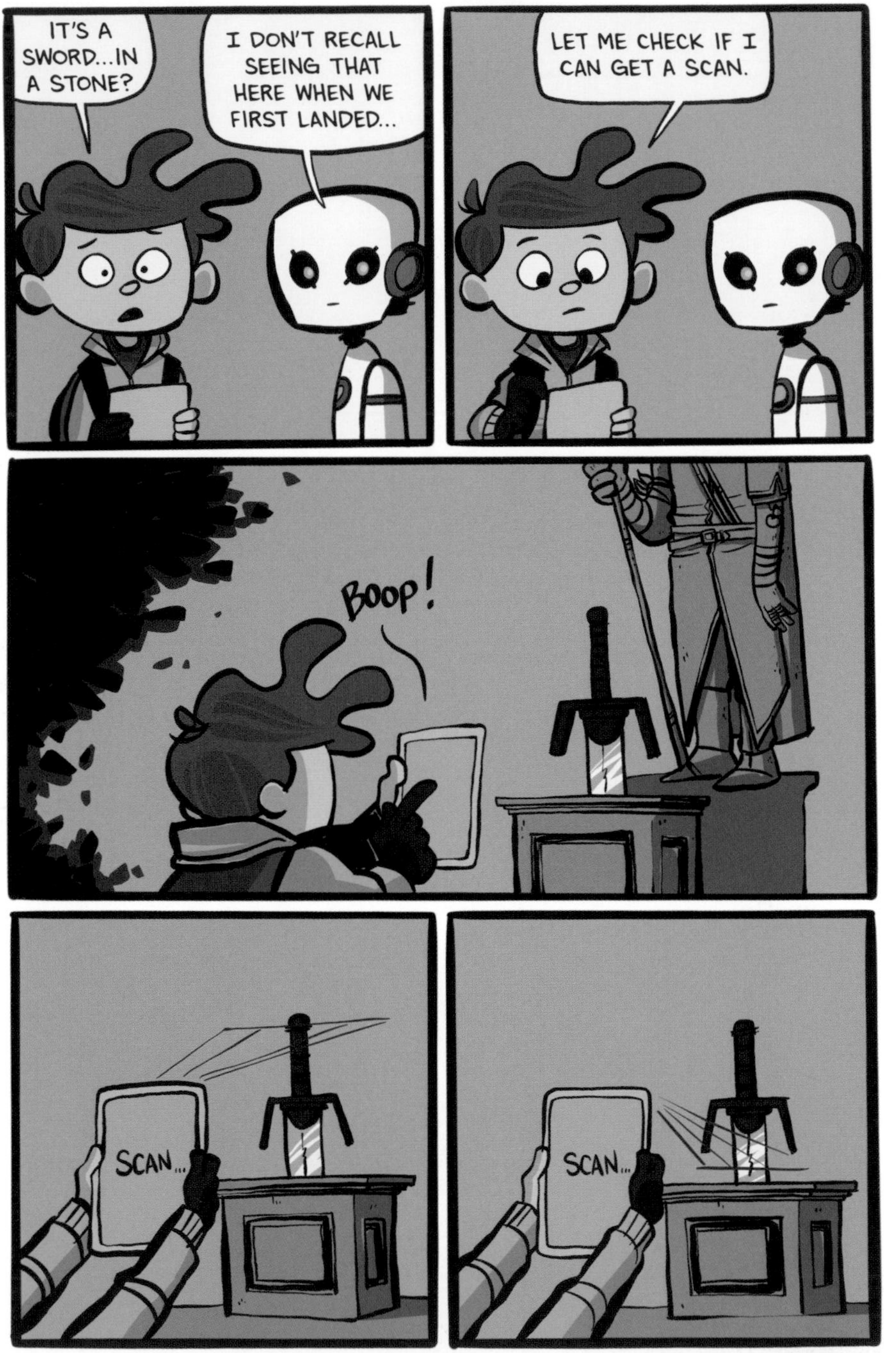
IT'S A SWORD...IN A STONE?
I DON'T RECALL SEEING THAT HERE WHEN WE FIRST LANDED...
LET ME CHECK IF I CAN GET A SCAN.
BOOP!
SCAN...
SCAN...

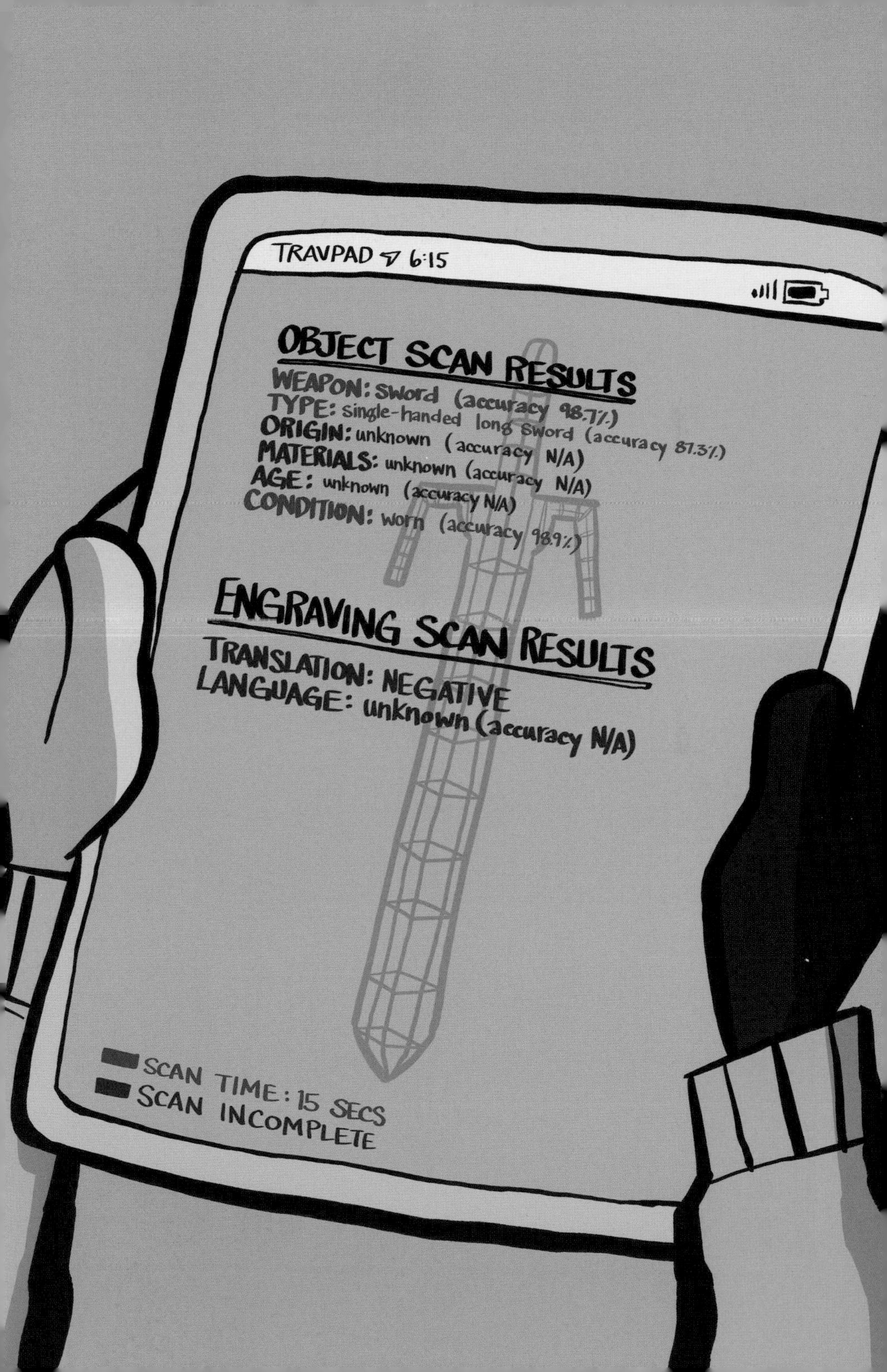

TRAVPAD 6:15
OBJECT SCAN RESULTS
WEAPON: sword (accuracy 98.7%)
TYPE: single-handed long sword (accuracy 87.3%)
ORIGIN: unknown (accuracy N/A)
MATERIALS: unknown (accuracy N/A)
AGE: unknown (accuracy N/A)
CONDITION: worn (accuracy 98.9%)
ENGRAVING SCAN RESULTS
TRANSLATION: NEGATIVE
LANGUAGE: unknown (accuracy N/A)
SCAN TIME: 15 SECS
SCAN INCOMPLETE

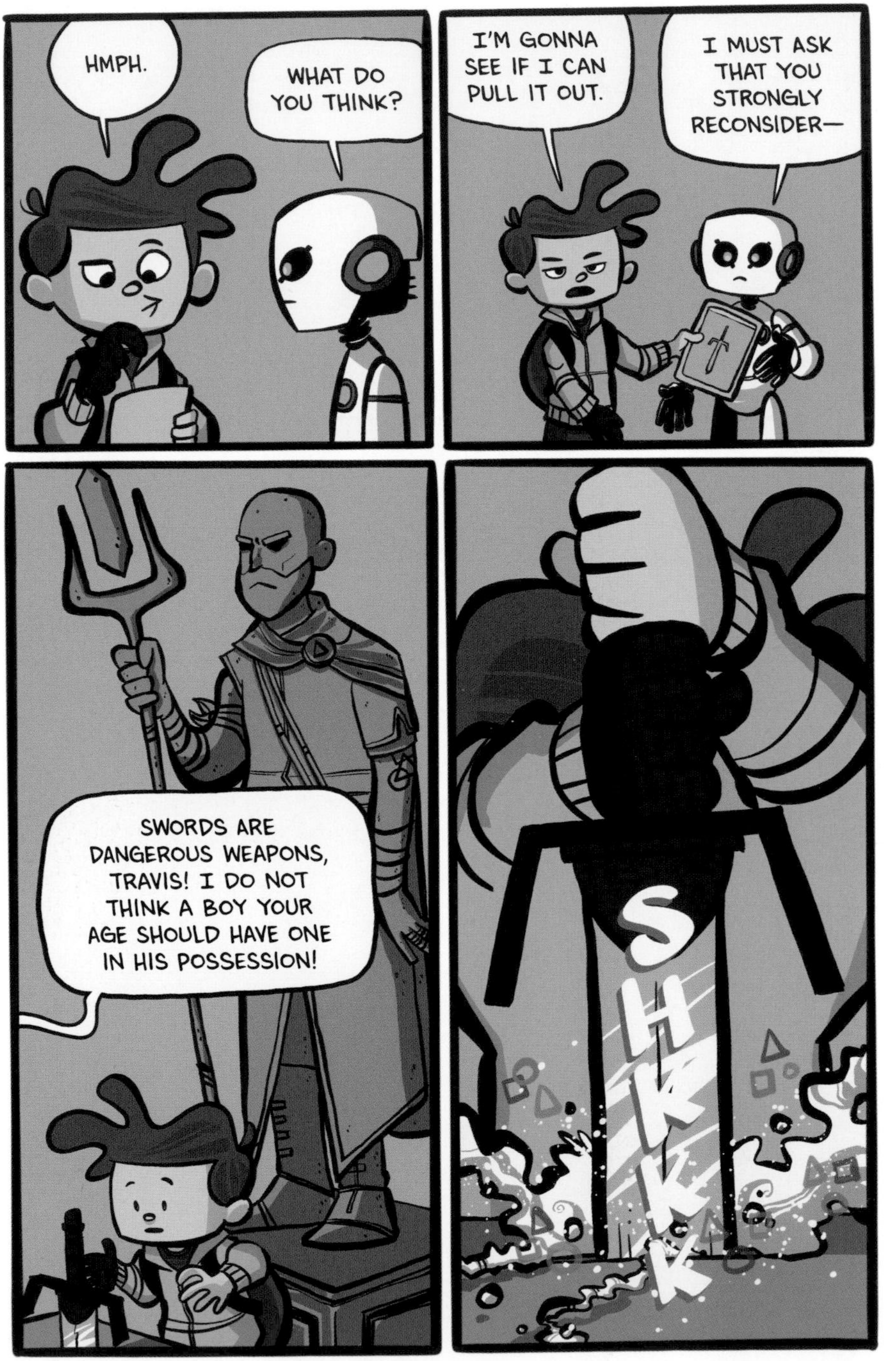
HMPH.
WHAT DO YOU THINK?
I'M GONNA SEE IF I CAN PULL IT OUT.
I MUST ASK THAT YOU STRONGLY RECONSIDER—
SWORDS ARE DANGEROUS WEAPONS, TRAVIS! I DO NOT THINK A BOY YOUR AGE SHOULD HAVE ONE IN HIS POSSESSION!
SHKKK

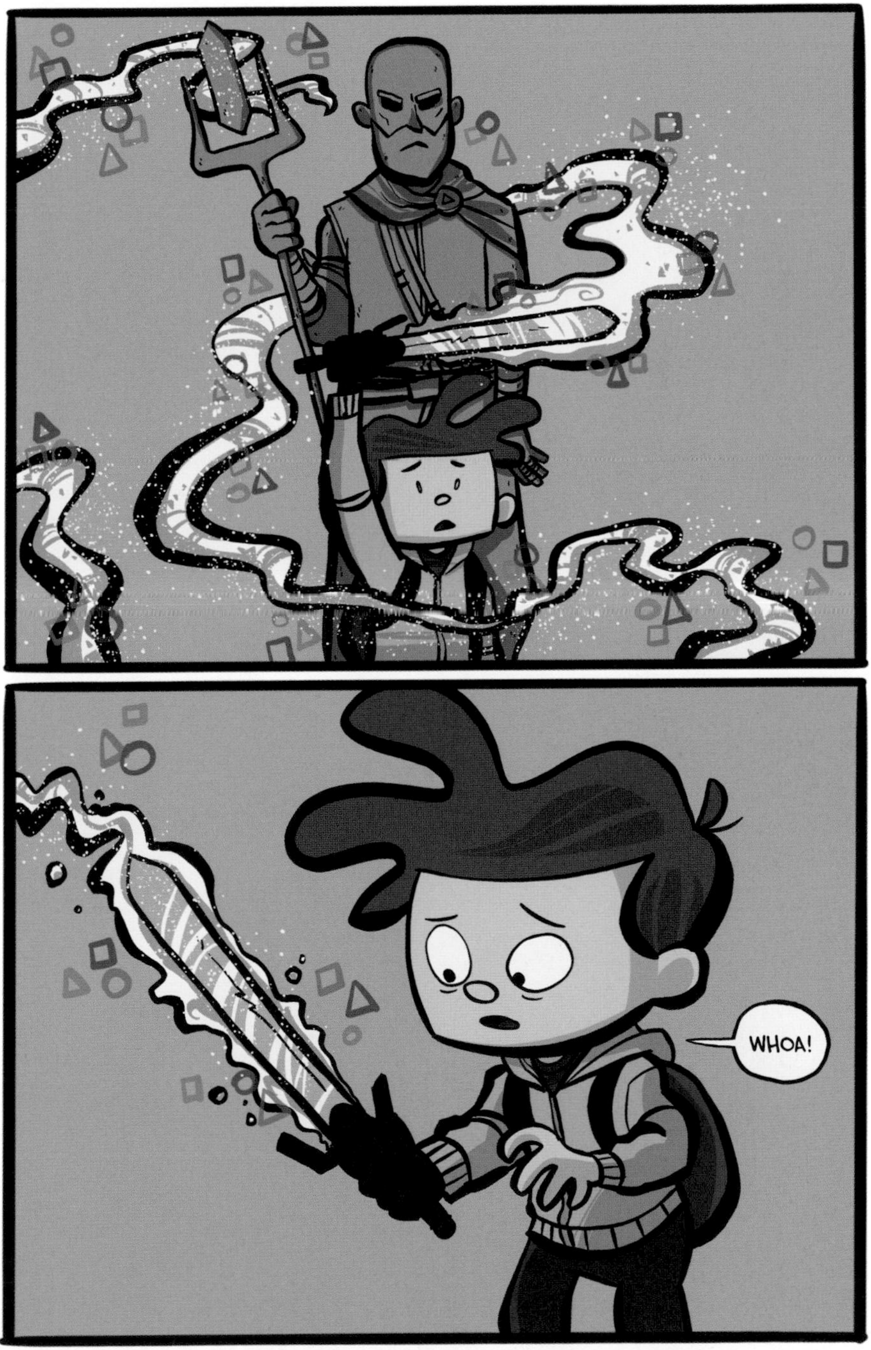
WHOA!

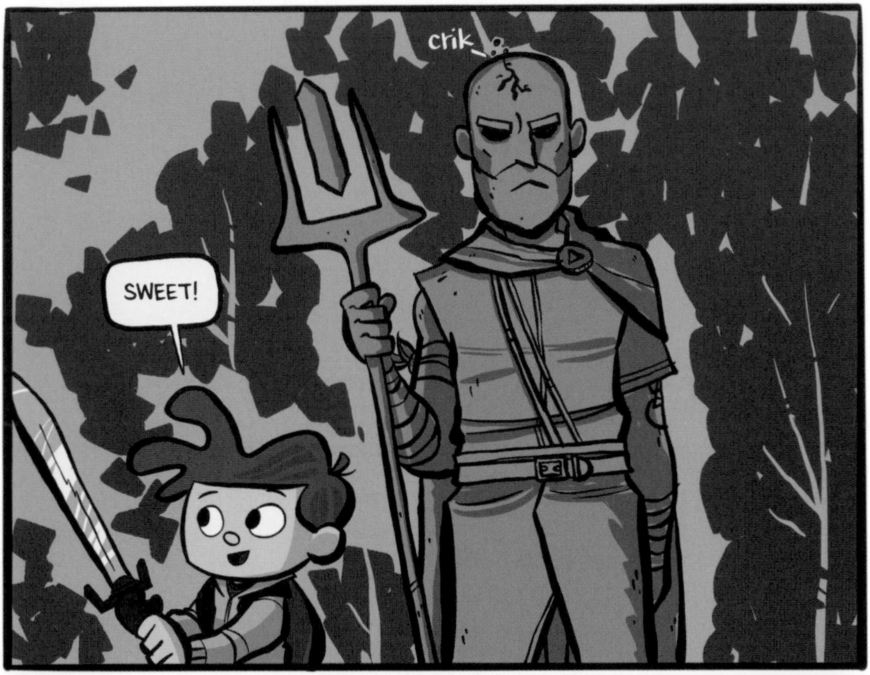
crik
SWEET!

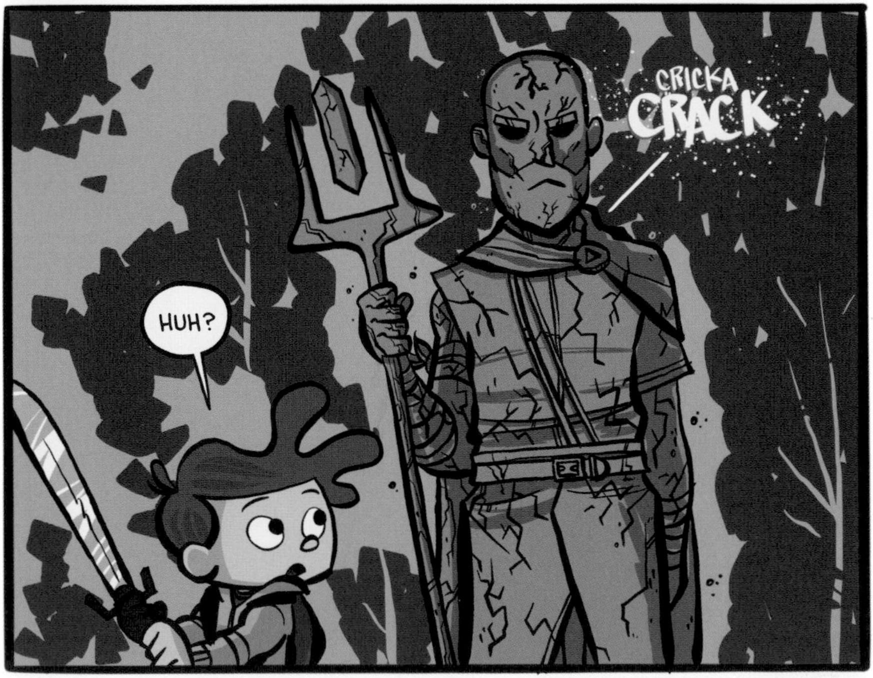
CRICKA CRACK
HUH?

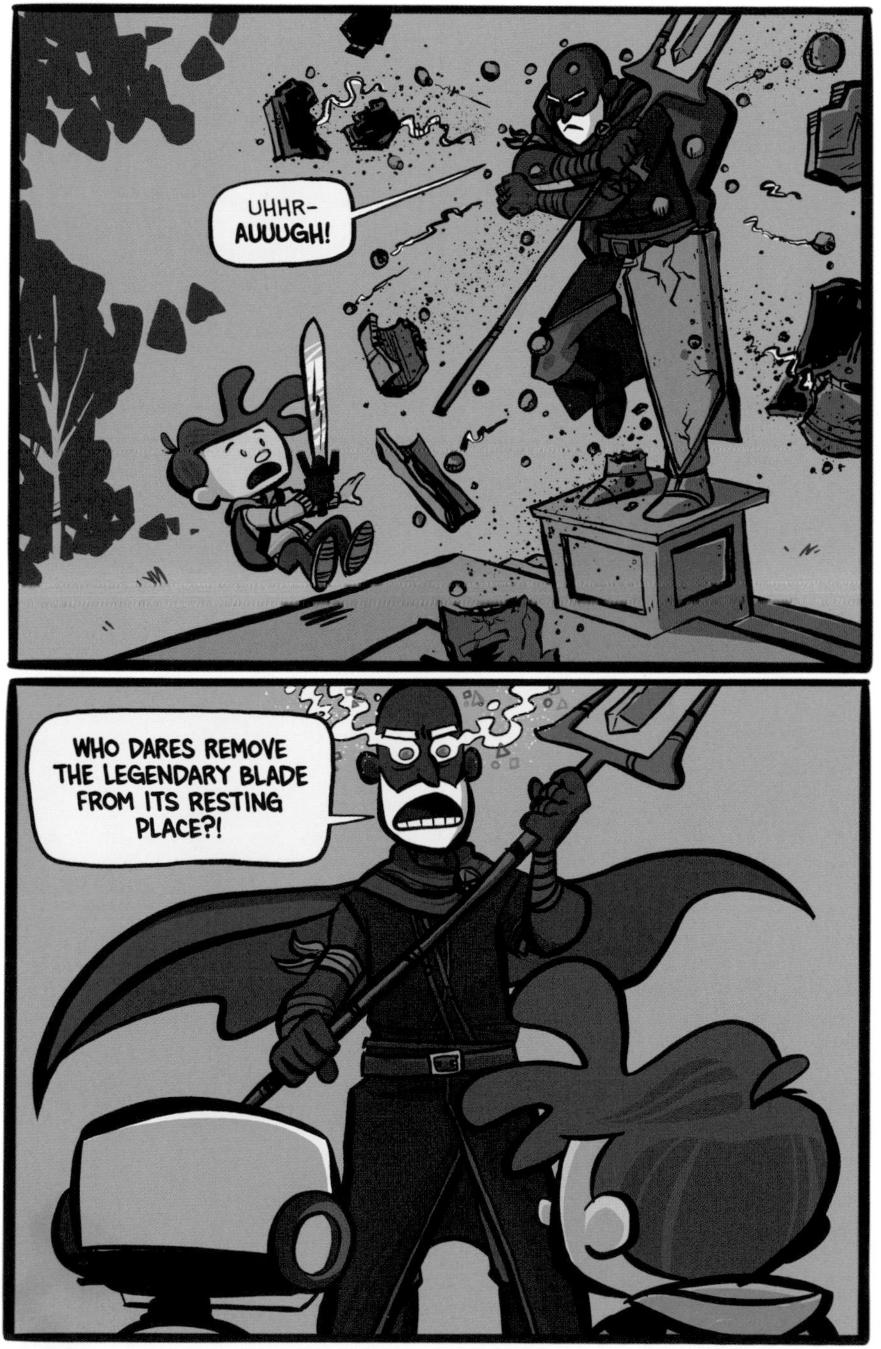
UHHR-
AUUUGH!
WHO DARES REMOVE THE LEGENDARY BLADE FROM ITS RESTING PLACE?!

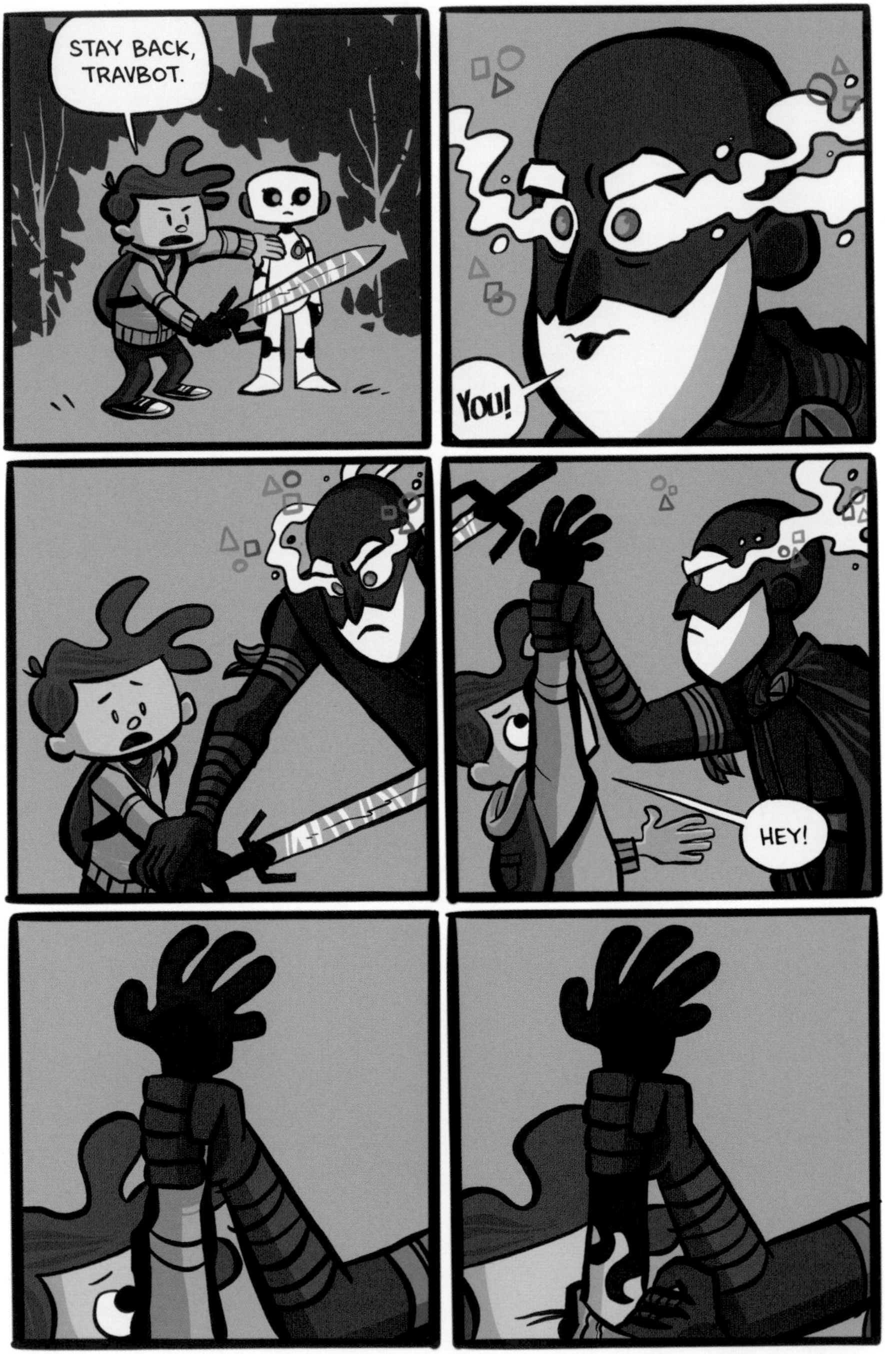
STAY BACK, TRAVBOT.
YOU!
HEY!

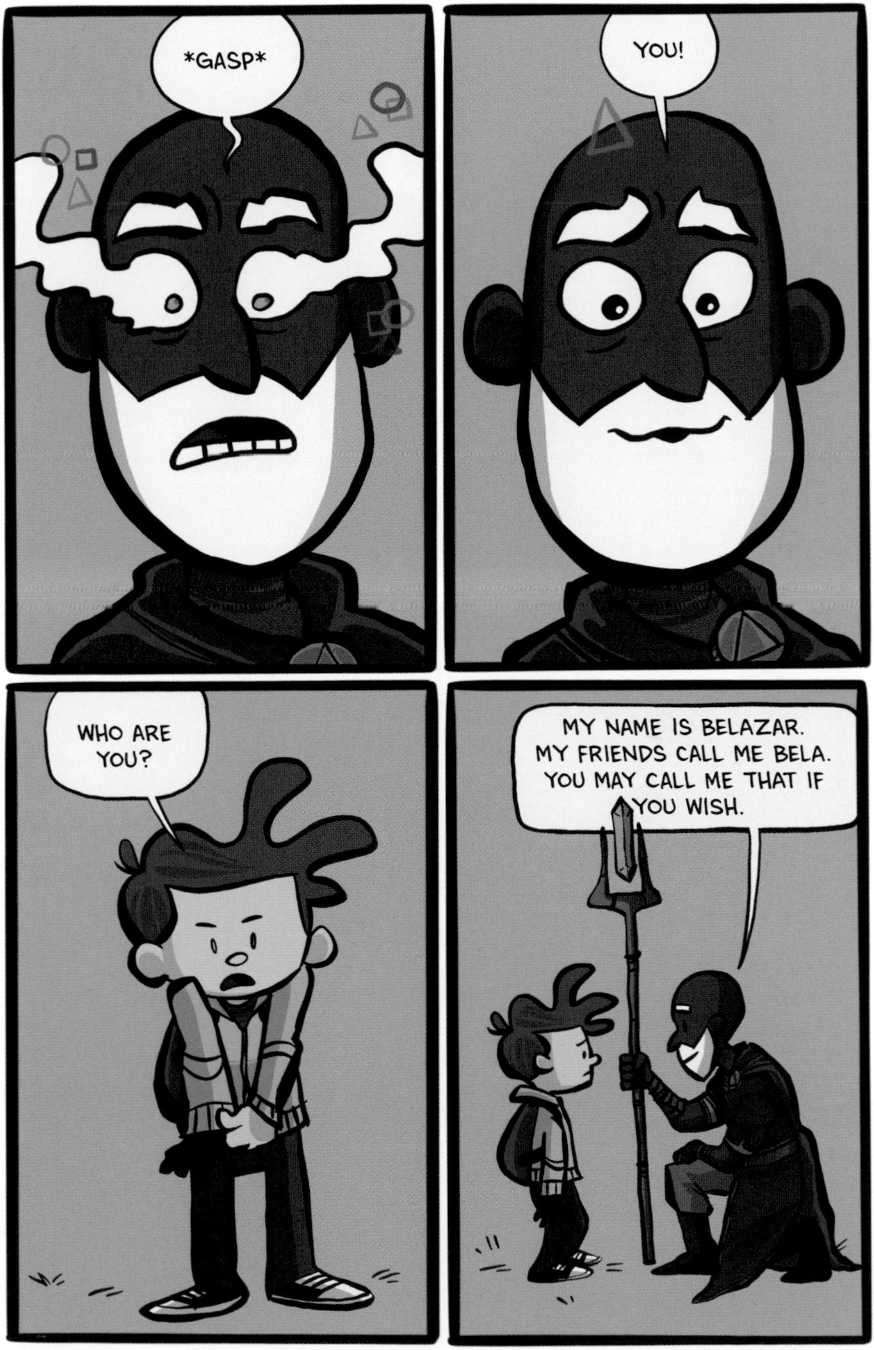
GASP
YOU!
WHO ARE YOU?
MY NAME IS BELAZAR. MY FRIENDS CALL ME BELA. YOU MAY CALL ME THAT IF YOU WISH.

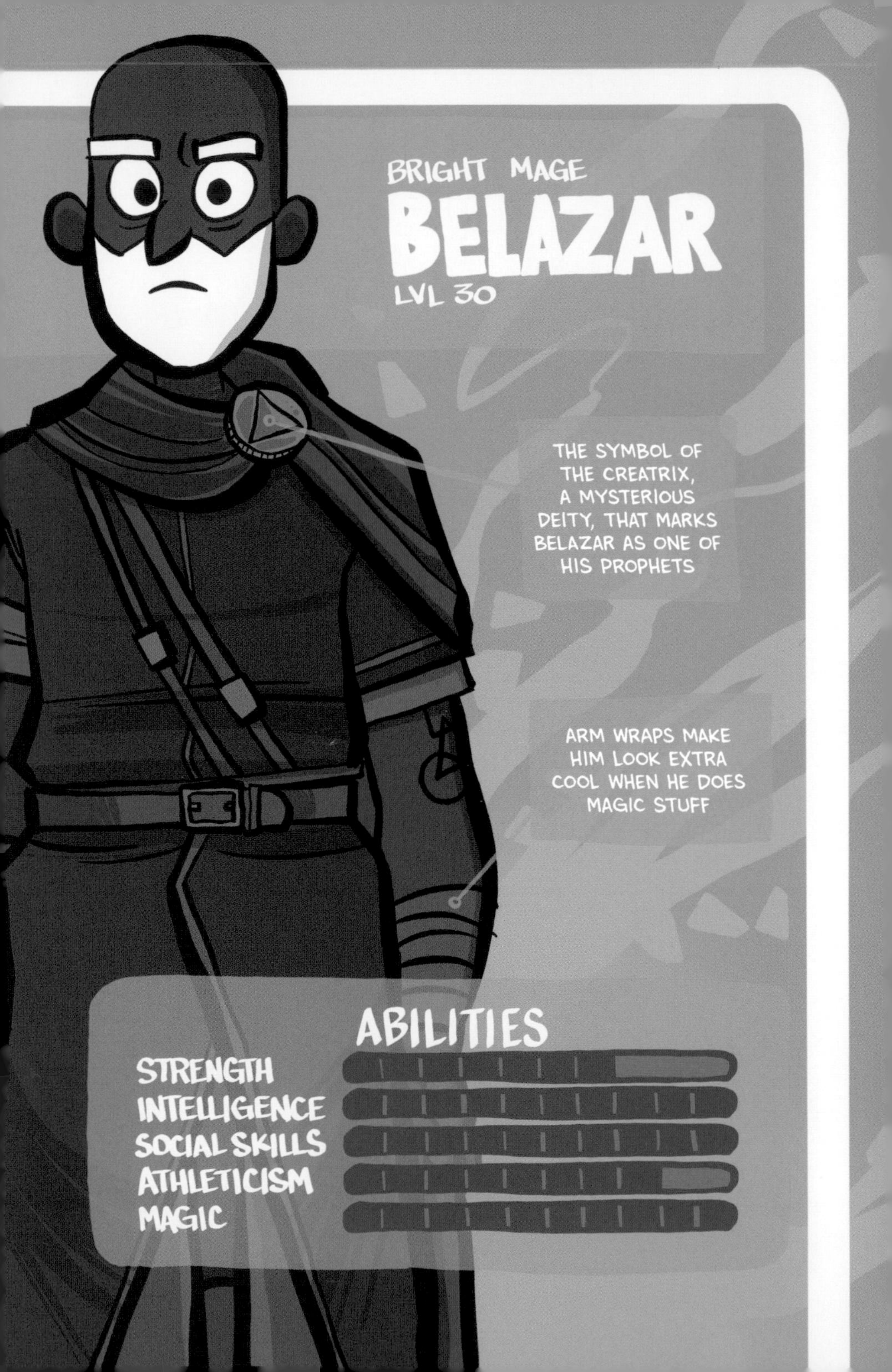
BRIGHT MAGE
BELAZAR
LVL 30
THE SYMBOL OF THE CREATRIX, A MYSTERIOUS DEITY, THAT MARKS BELAZAR AS ONE OF HIS PROPHETS
ARM WRAPS MAKE HIM LOOK EXTRA COOL WHEN HE DOES MAGIC STUFF
ABILITIES
STRENGTH
INTELLIGENCE
SOCIAL SKILLS
ATHLETICISM
MAGIC

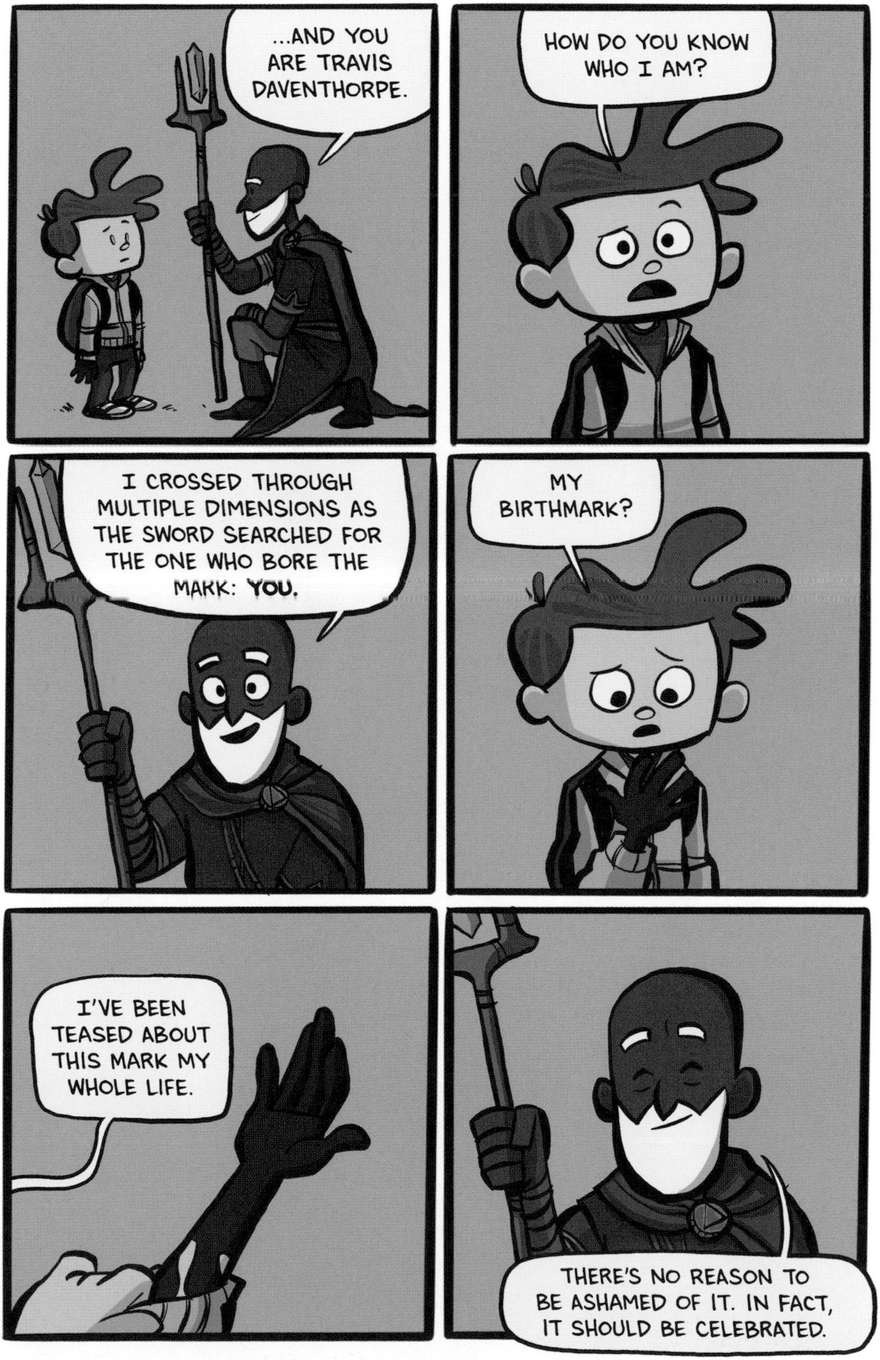
...AND YOU ARE TRAVIS DAVENTHORPE.
HOW DO YOU KNOW WHO I AM?
I CROSSED THROUGH MULTIPLE DIMENSIONS AS THE SWORD SEARCHED FOR THE ONE WHO BORE THE MARK: YOU.
MY BIRTHMARK?
I'VE BEEN TEASED ABOUT THIS MARK MY WHOLE LIFE.
THERE'S NO REASON TO BE ASHAMED OF IT. IN FACT, IT SHOULD BE CELEBRATED.

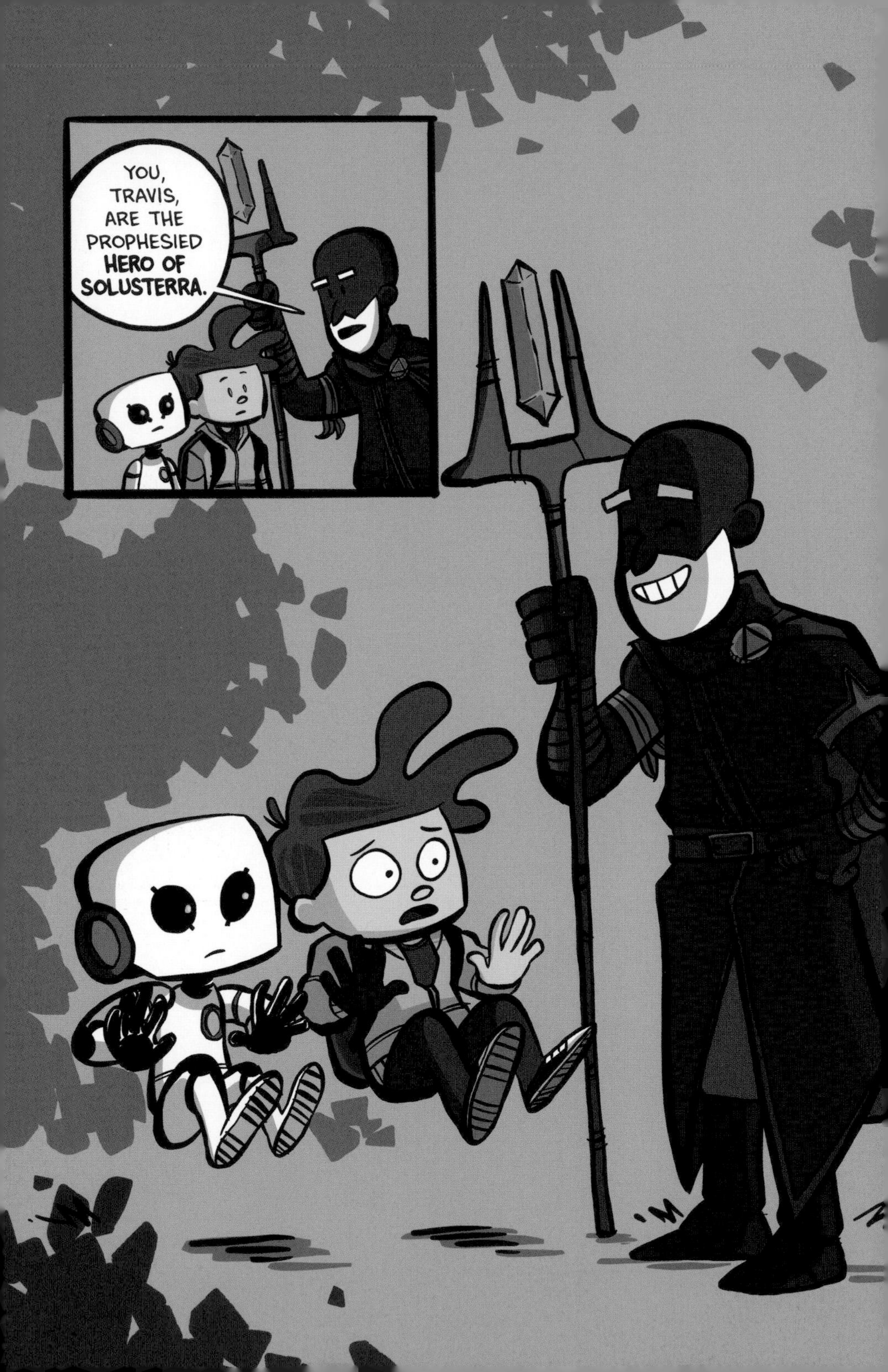
YOU, TRAVIS, ARE THE PROPHESIED **HERO OF SOLUSTERRA.**

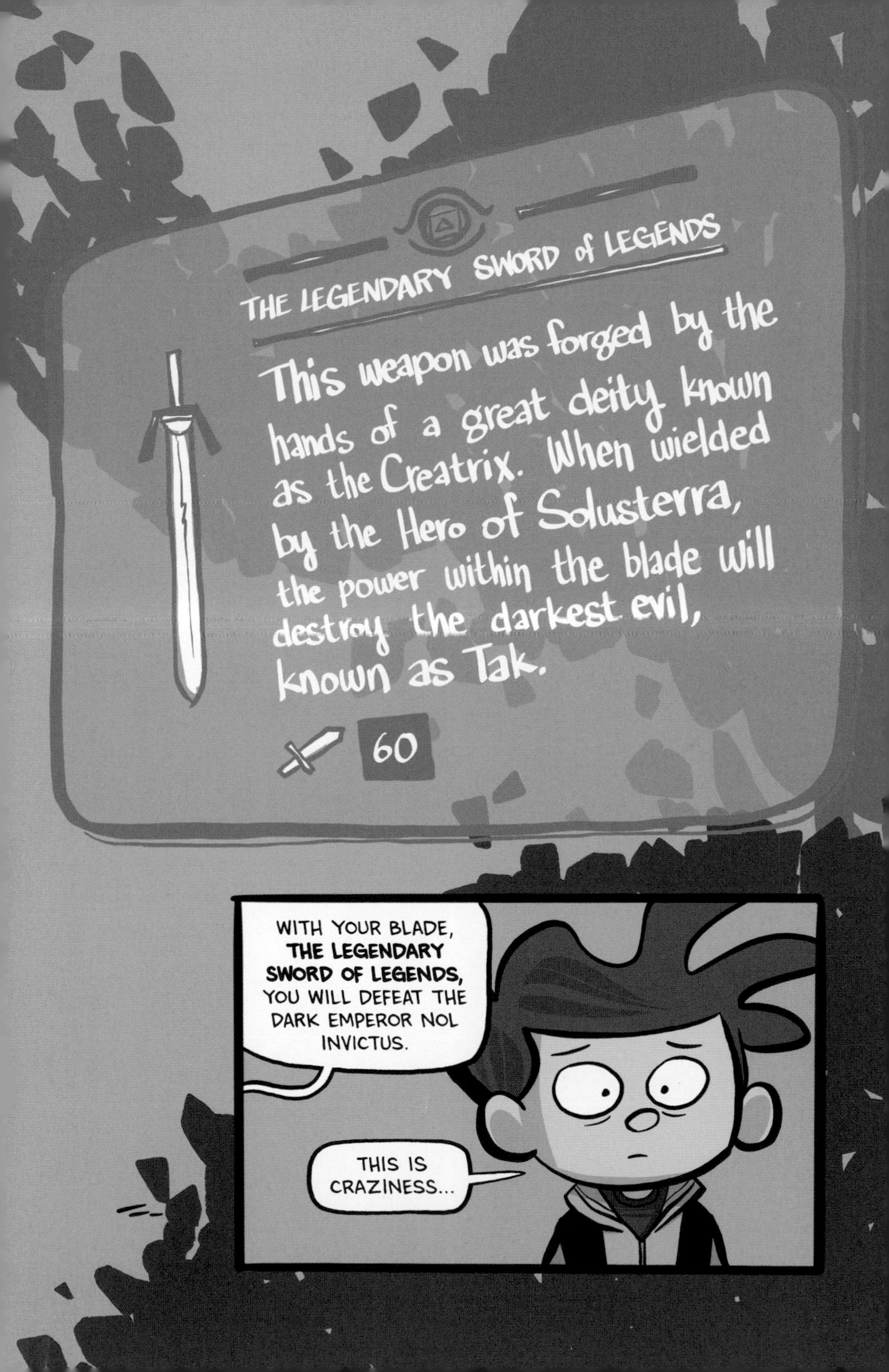
THE LEGENDARY SWORD of LEGENDS
This weapon was forged by the hands of a great deity known as the Creatrix. When wielded by the Hero of Solusterra, the power within the blade will destroy the darkest evil, known as Tak.
60
WITH YOUR BLADE, THE LEGENDARY SWORD OF LEGENDS, YOU WILL DEFEAT THE DARK EMPEROR NOL INVICTUS.
THIS IS CRAZINESS...

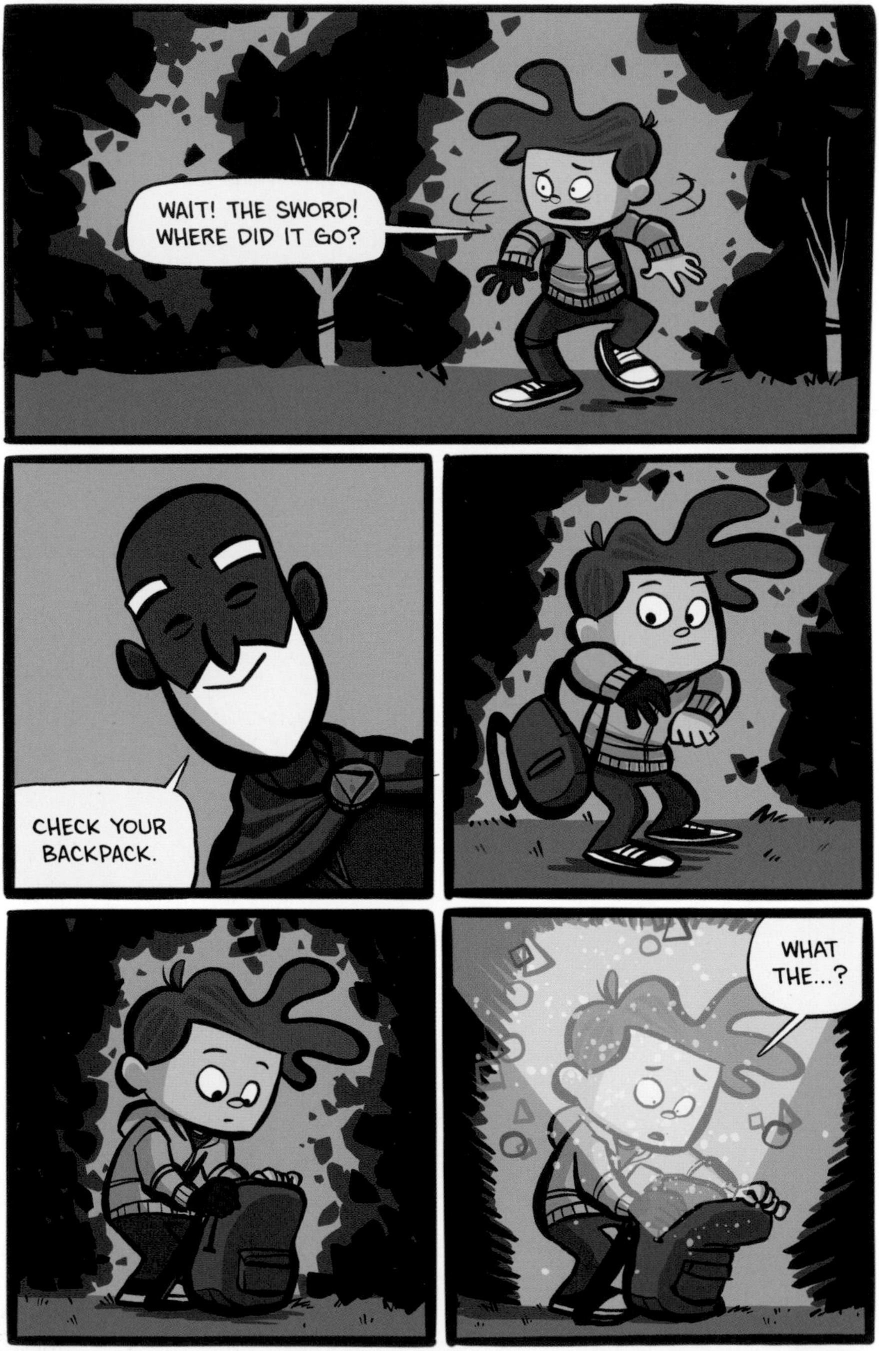
WAIT! THE SWORD! WHERE DID IT GO?
CHECK YOUR BACKPACK.
WHAT THE...?

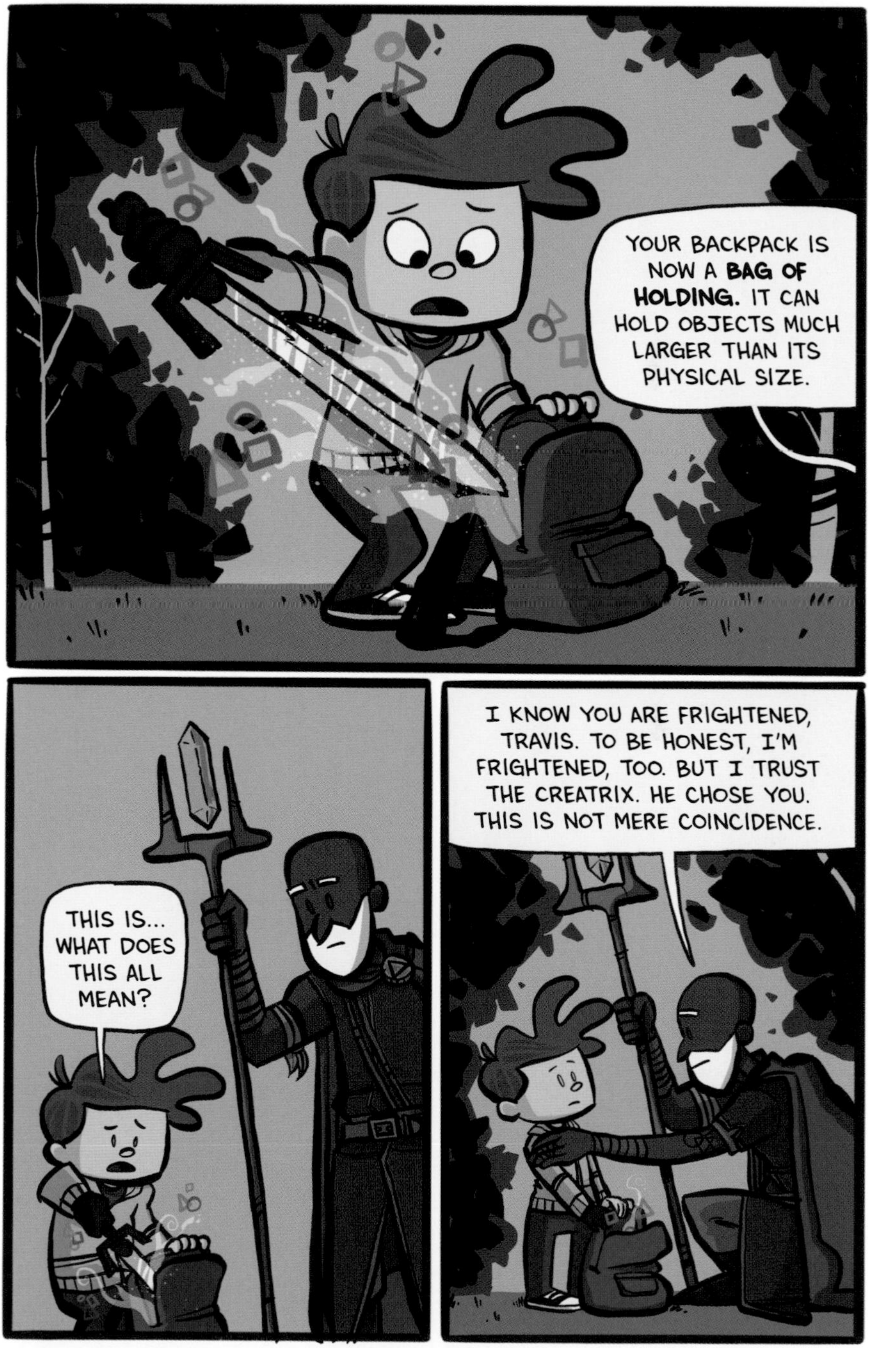
YOUR BACKPACK IS NOW A **BAG OF HOLDING.** IT CAN HOLD OBJECTS MUCH LARGER THAN ITS PHYSICAL SIZE.
THIS IS... WHAT DOES THIS ALL MEAN?
I KNOW YOU ARE FRIGHTENED, TRAVIS. TO BE HONEST, I'M FRIGHTENED, TOO. BUT I TRUST THE CREATRIX. HE CHOSE YOU. THIS IS NOT MERE COINCIDENCE.

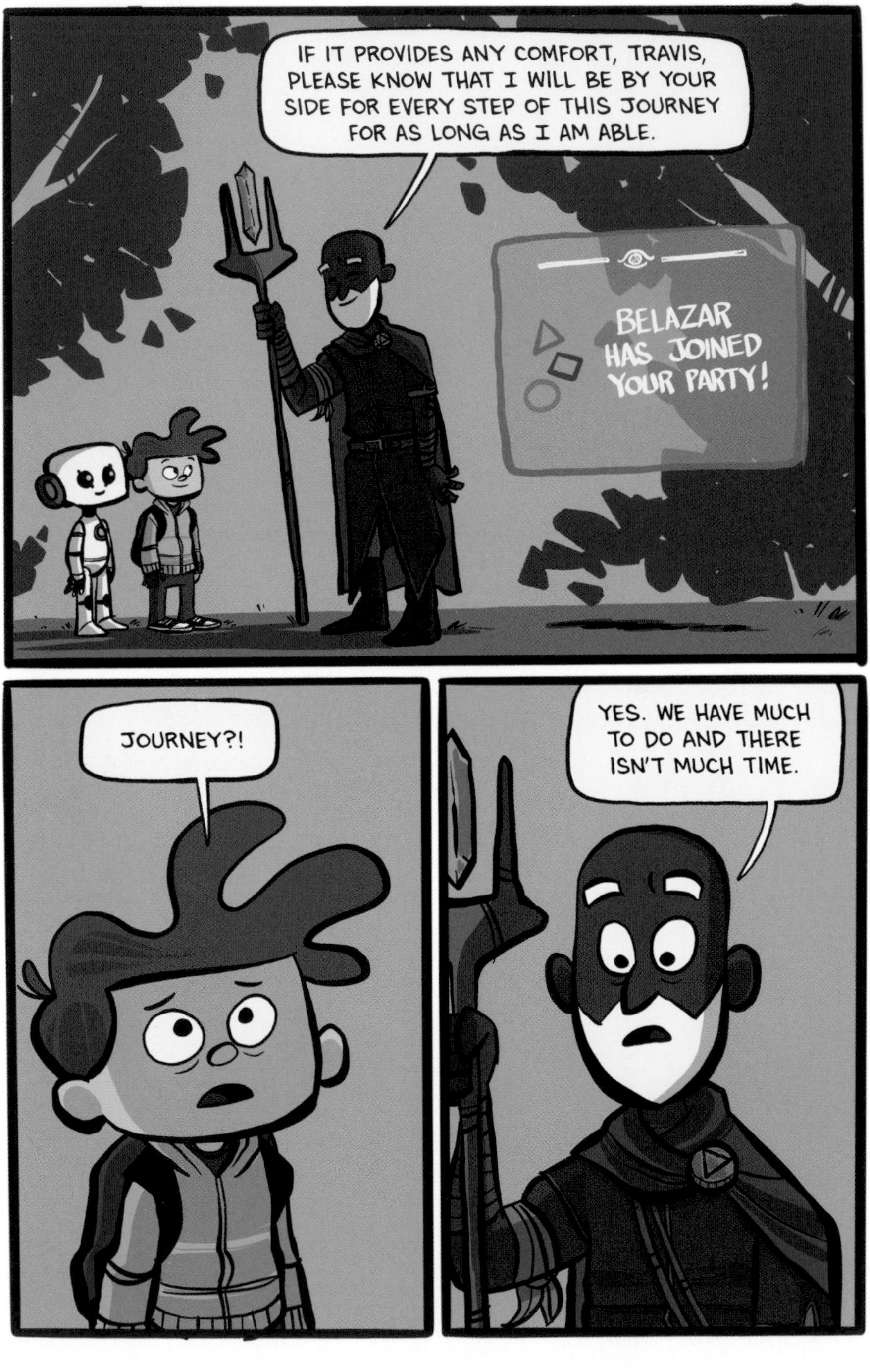
IF IT PROVIDES ANY COMFORT, TRAVIS, PLEASE KNOW THAT I WILL BE BY YOUR SIDE FOR EVERY STEP OF THIS JOURNEY FOR AS LONG AS I AM ABLE.
BELAZAR HAS JOINED YOUR PARTY!
JOURNEY?!
YES. WE HAVE MUCH TO DO AND THERE ISN'T MUCH TIME.

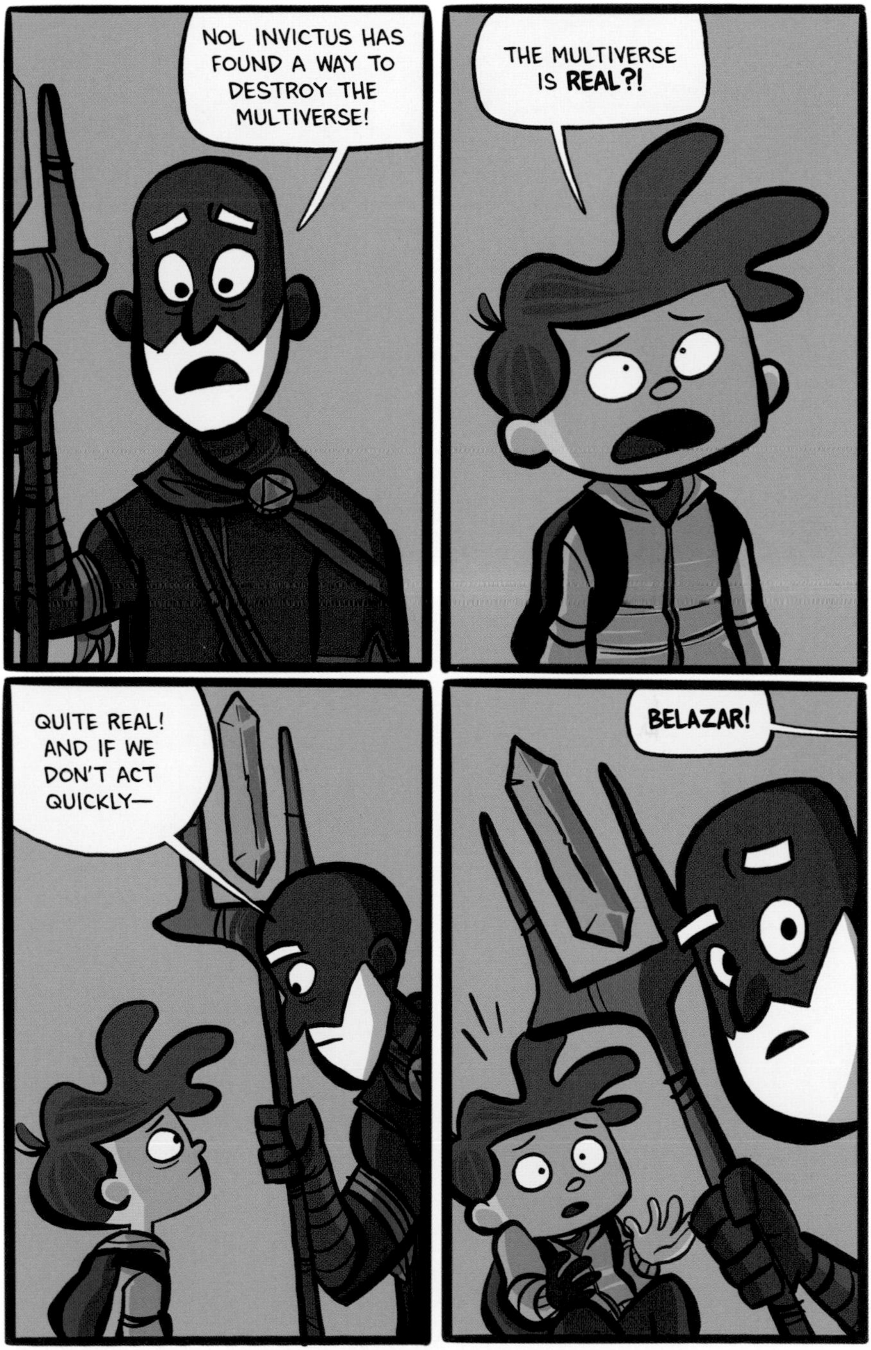
NOL INVICTUS HAS FOUND A WAY TO DESTROY THE MULTIVERSE!
THE MULTIVERSE IS **REAL?!**
QUITE REAL! AND IF WE DON'T ACT QUICKLY—
BELAZAR!

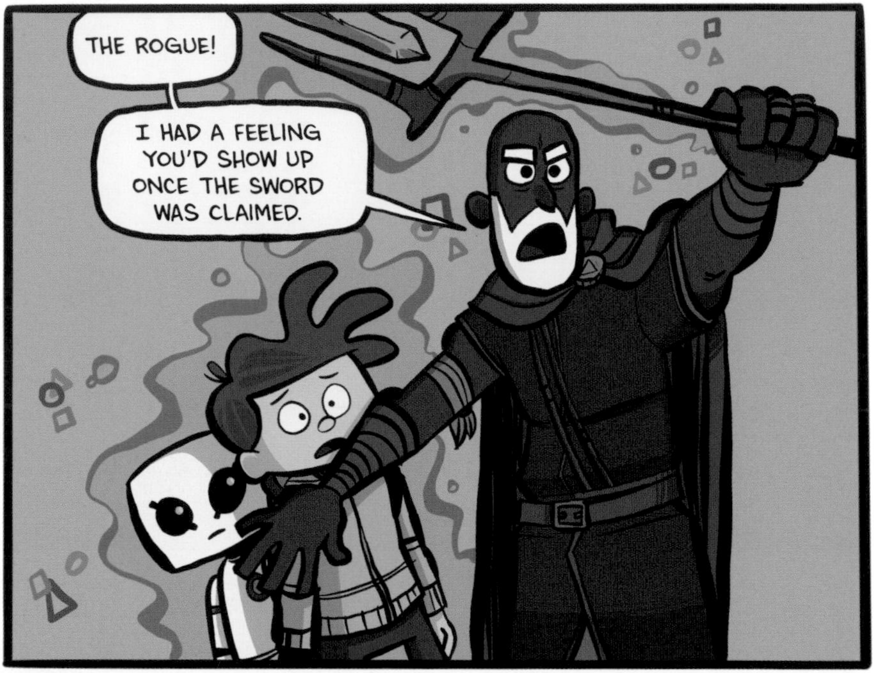
THE ROGUE!
I HAD A FEELING YOU'D SHOW UP ONCE THE SWORD WAS CLAIMED.

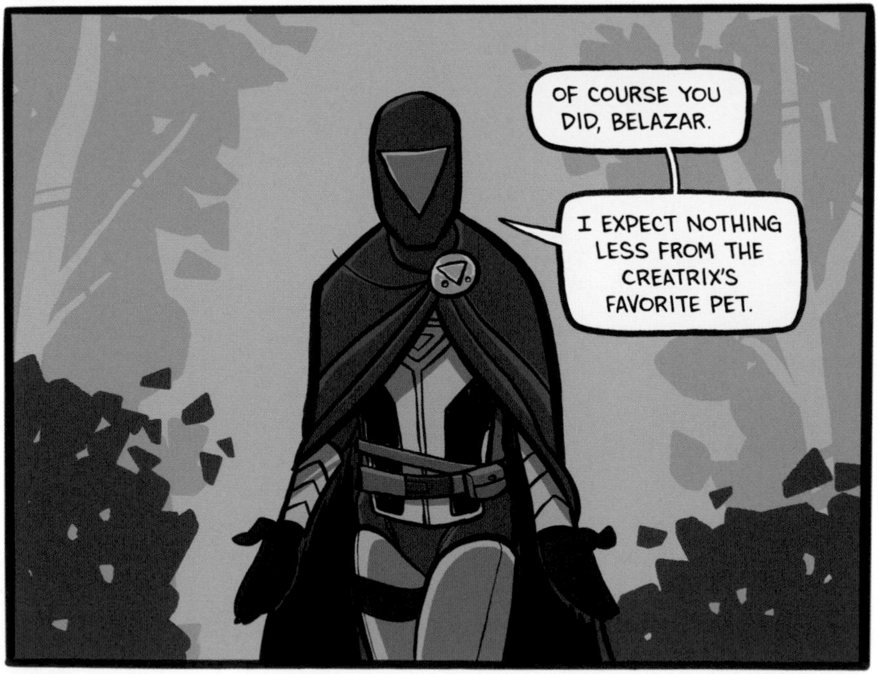
OF COURSE YOU DID, BELAZAR.
I EXPECT NOTHING LESS FROM THE CREATRIX'S FAVORITE PET.

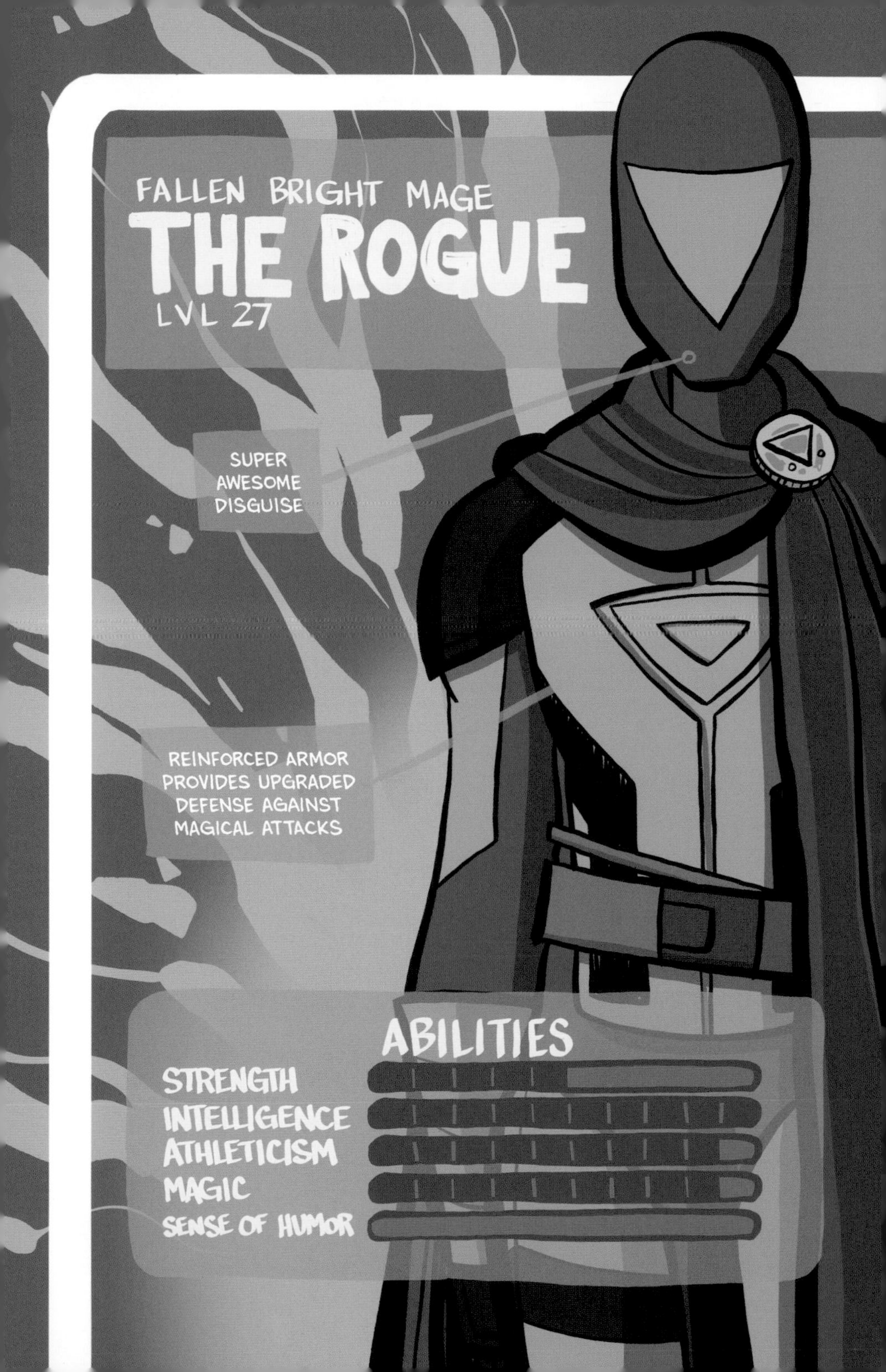
FALLEN BRIGHT MAGE
THE ROGUE
LVL 27
SUPER AWESOME DISGUISE
REINFORCED ARMOR PROVIDES UPGRADED DEFENSE AGAINST MAGICAL ATTACKS
ABILITIES
STRENGTH
INTELLIGENCE
ATHLETICISM
MAGIC
SENSE OF HUMOR

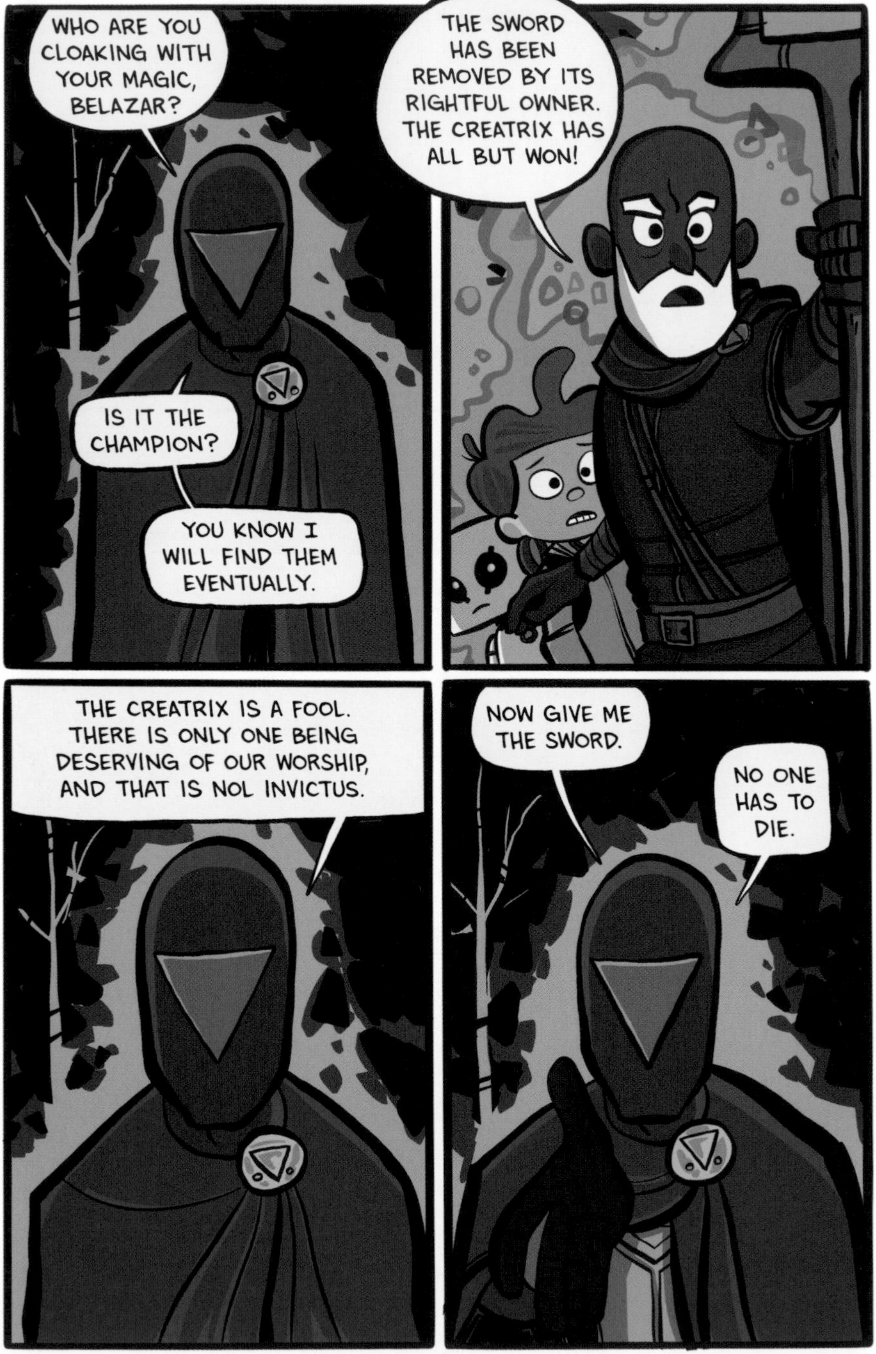
WHO ARE YOU CLOAKING WITH YOUR MAGIC, BELAZAR?
IS IT THE CHAMPION?
YOU KNOW I WILL FIND THEM EVENTUALLY.
THE SWORD HAS BEEN REMOVED BY ITS RIGHTFUL OWNER. THE CREATRIX HAS ALL BUT WON!
THE CREATRIX IS A FOOL. THERE IS ONLY ONE BEING DESERVING OF OUR WORSHIP, AND THAT IS NOL INVICTUS.
NOW GIVE ME THE SWORD.
NO ONE HAS TO DIE.

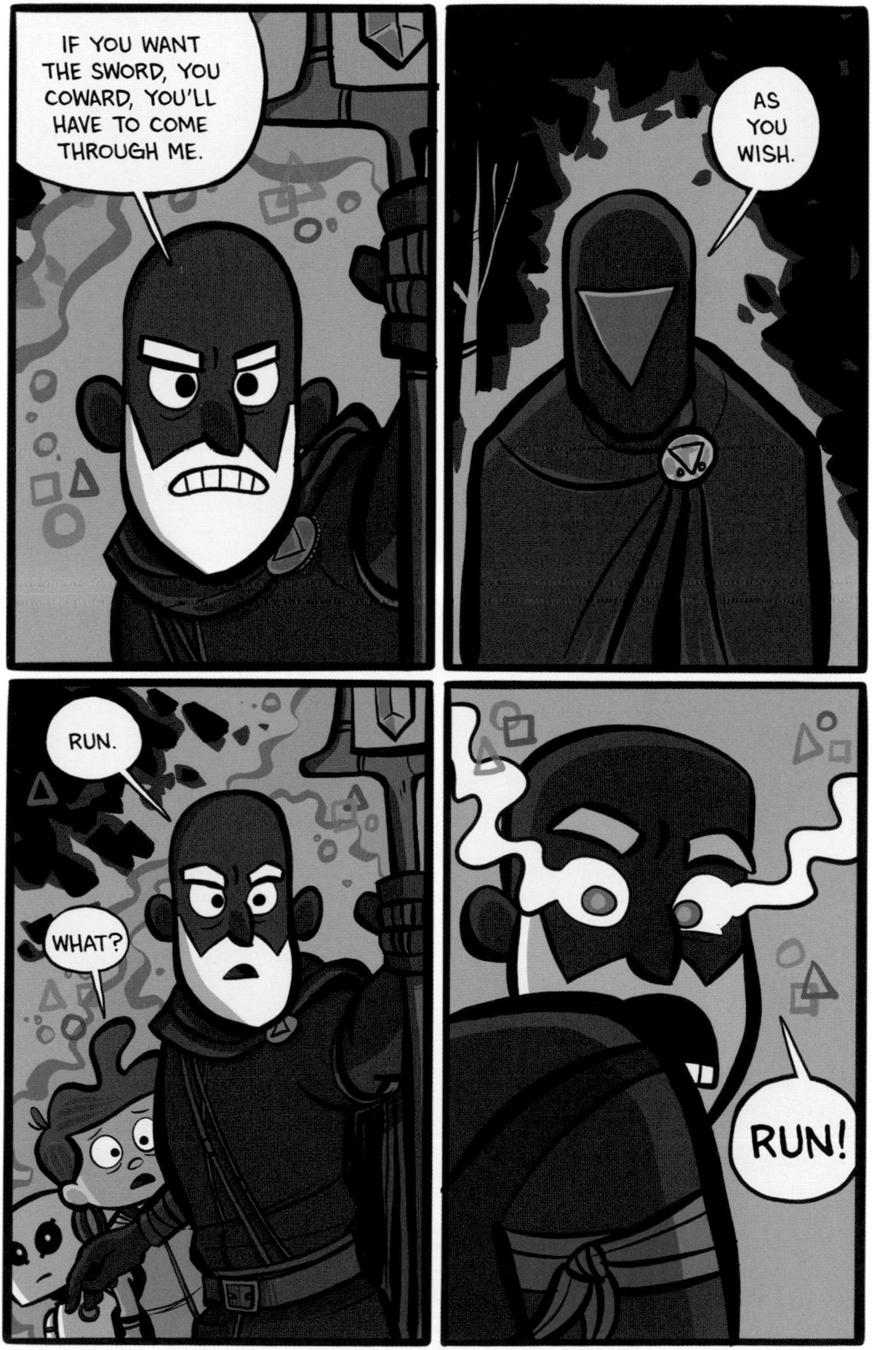
IF YOU WANT THE SWORD, YOU COWARD, YOU'LL HAVE TO COME THROUGH ME.
AS YOU WISH.
RUN.
WHAT?
RUN!

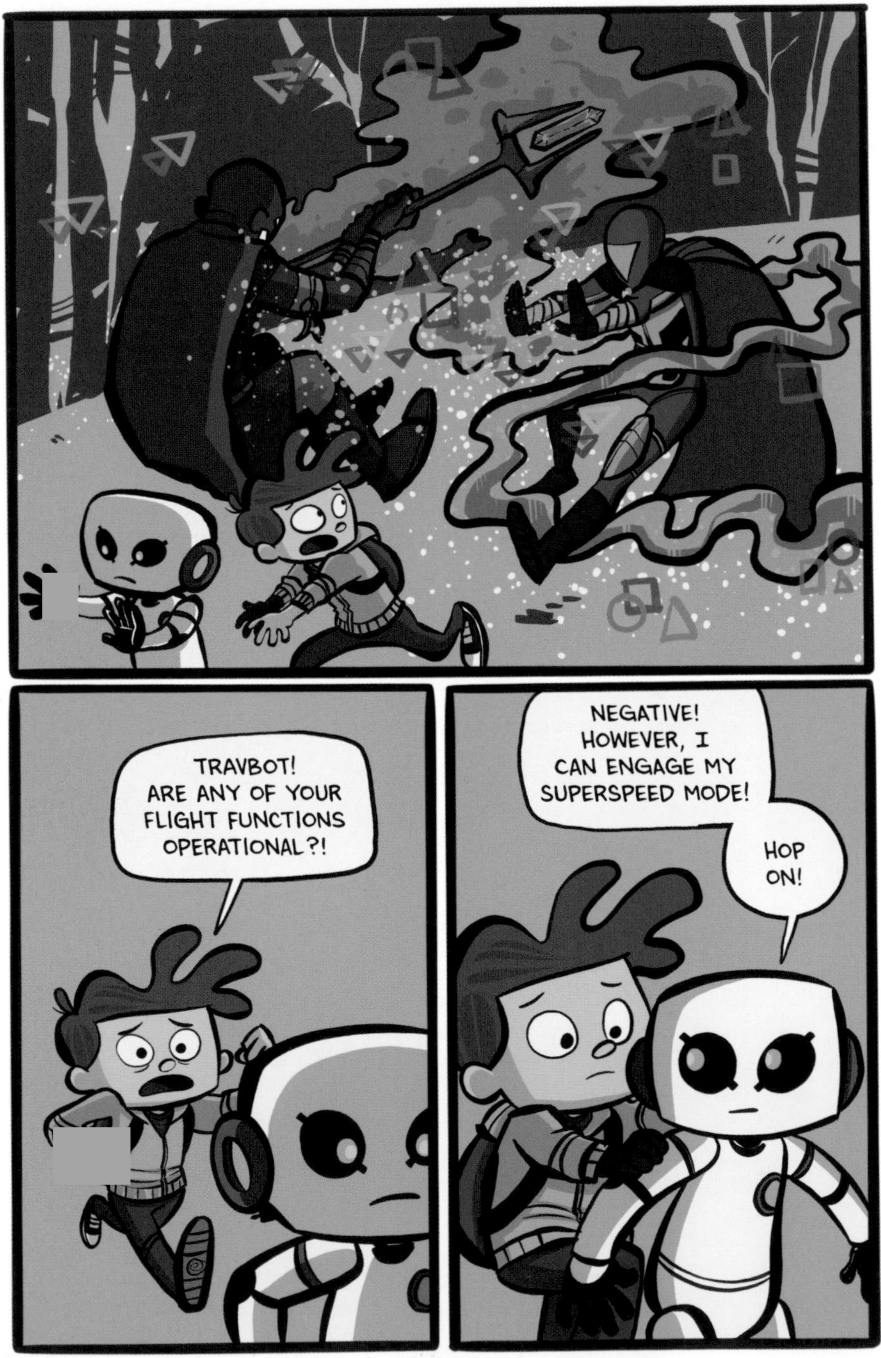
TRAVBOT!
ARE ANY OF YOUR
FLIGHT FUNCTIONS
OPERATIONAL?!
NEGATIVE!
HOWEVER, I
CAN ENGAGE MY
SUPERSPEED MODE!
HOP
ON!

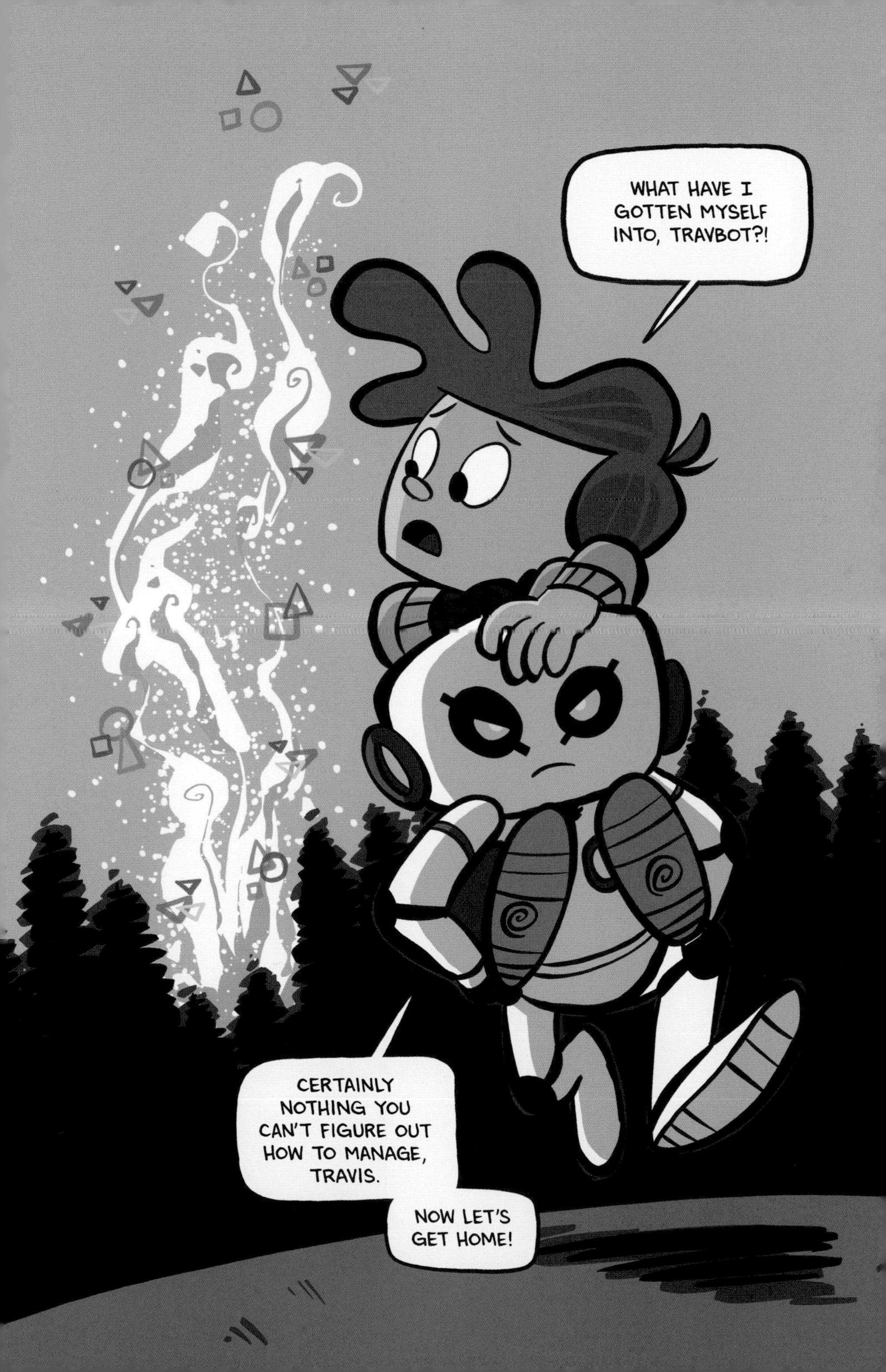
WHAT HAVE I GOTTEN MYSELF INTO, TRAVBOT?!
CERTAINLY NOTHING YOU CAN'T FIGURE OUT HOW TO MANAGE, TRAVIS.
NOW LET'S GET HOME!

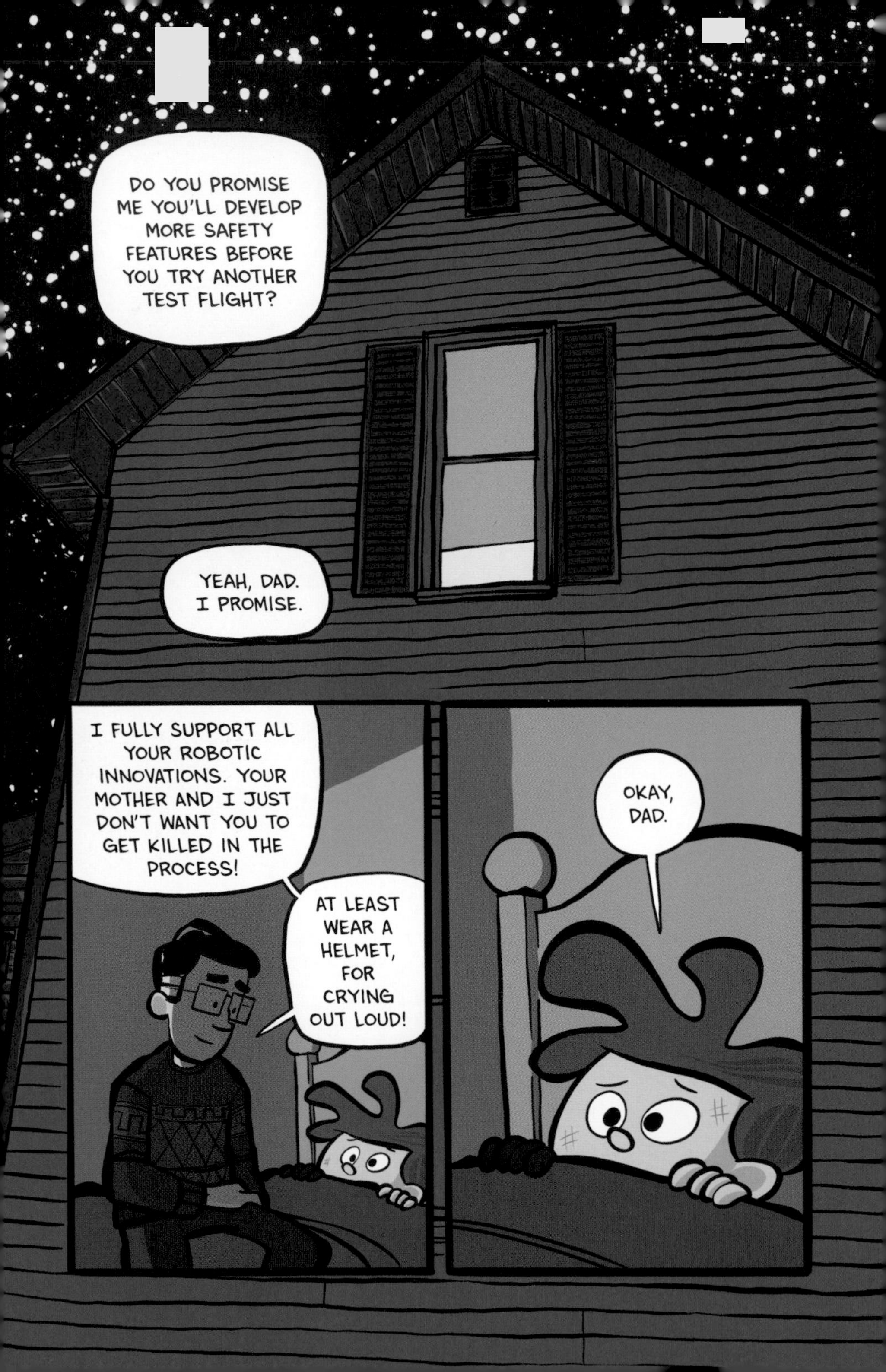
DO YOU PROMISE ME YOU'LL DEVELOP MORE SAFETY FEATURES BEFORE YOU TRY ANOTHER TEST FLIGHT?
YEAH, DAD. I PROMISE.
I FULLY SUPPORT ALL YOUR ROBOTIC INNOVATIONS. YOUR MOTHER AND I JUST DON'T WANT YOU TO GET KILLED IN THE PROCESS!
AT LEAST WEAR A HELMET, FOR CRYING OUT LOUD!
OKAY, DAD.

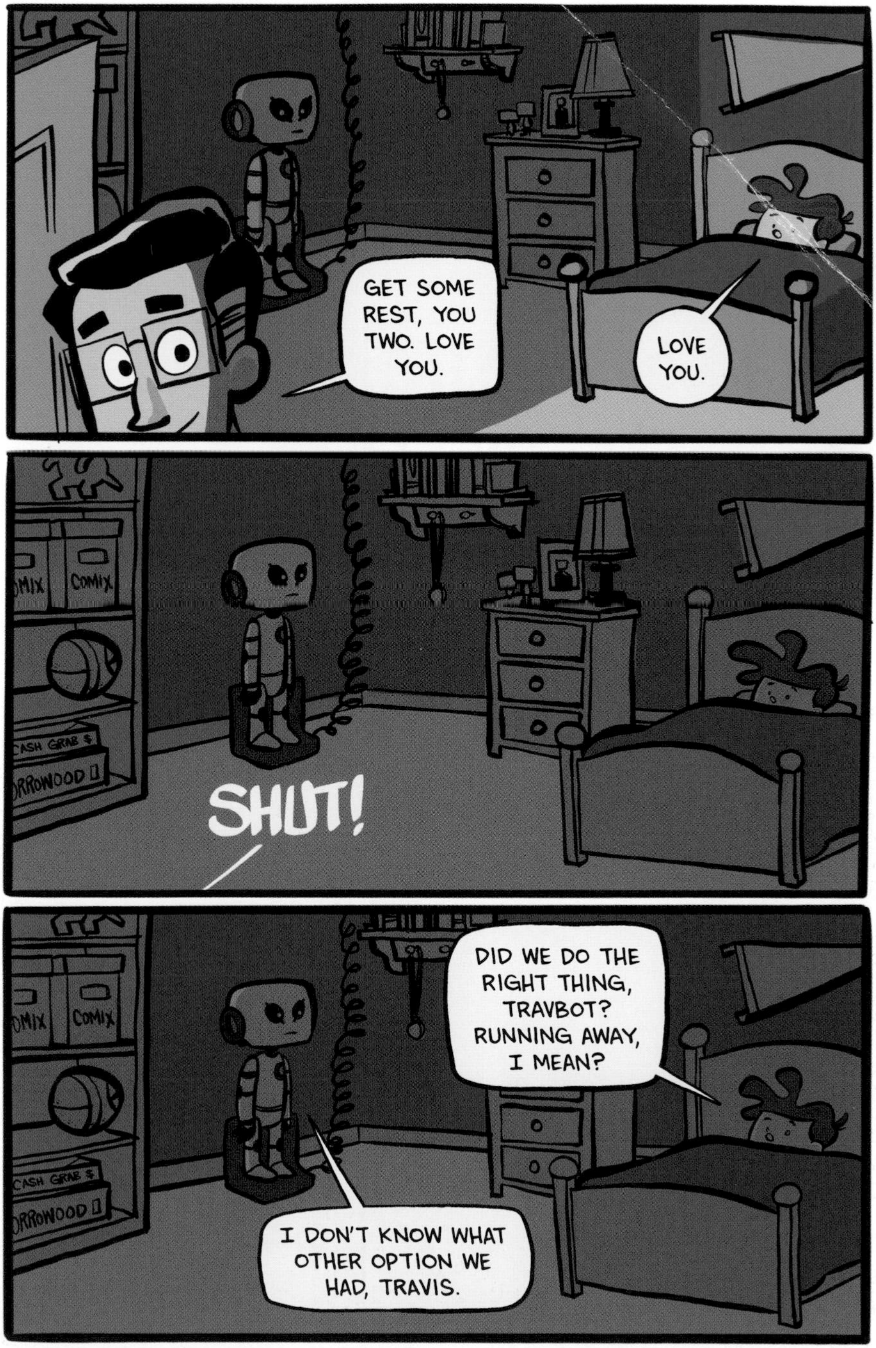
GET SOME REST, YOU TWO. LOVE YOU.
LOVE YOU.
SHUT!
DID WE DO THE RIGHT THING, TRAVBOT? RUNNING AWAY, I MEAN?
I DON'T KNOW WHAT OTHER OPTION WE HAD, TRAVIS.

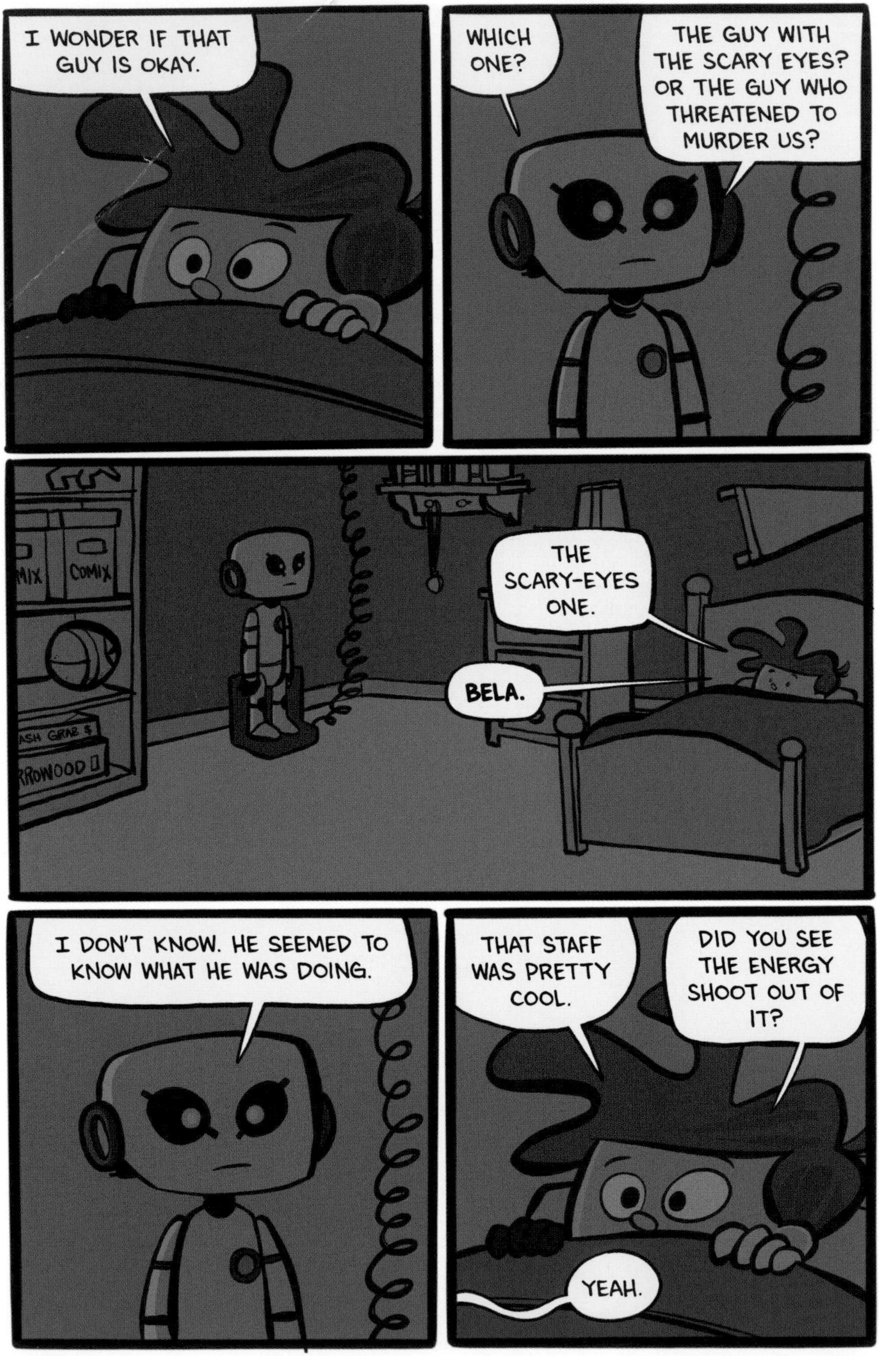
I WONDER IF THAT GUY IS OKAY.
WHICH ONE?
THE GUY WITH THE SCARY EYES? OR THE GUY WHO THREATENED TO MURDER US?
COMIX
THE SCARY-EYES ONE.
BELA.
I DON'T KNOW. HE SEEMED TO KNOW WHAT HE WAS DOING.
THAT STAFF WAS PRETTY COOL.
DID YOU SEE THE ENERGY SHOOT OUT OF IT?
YEAH.

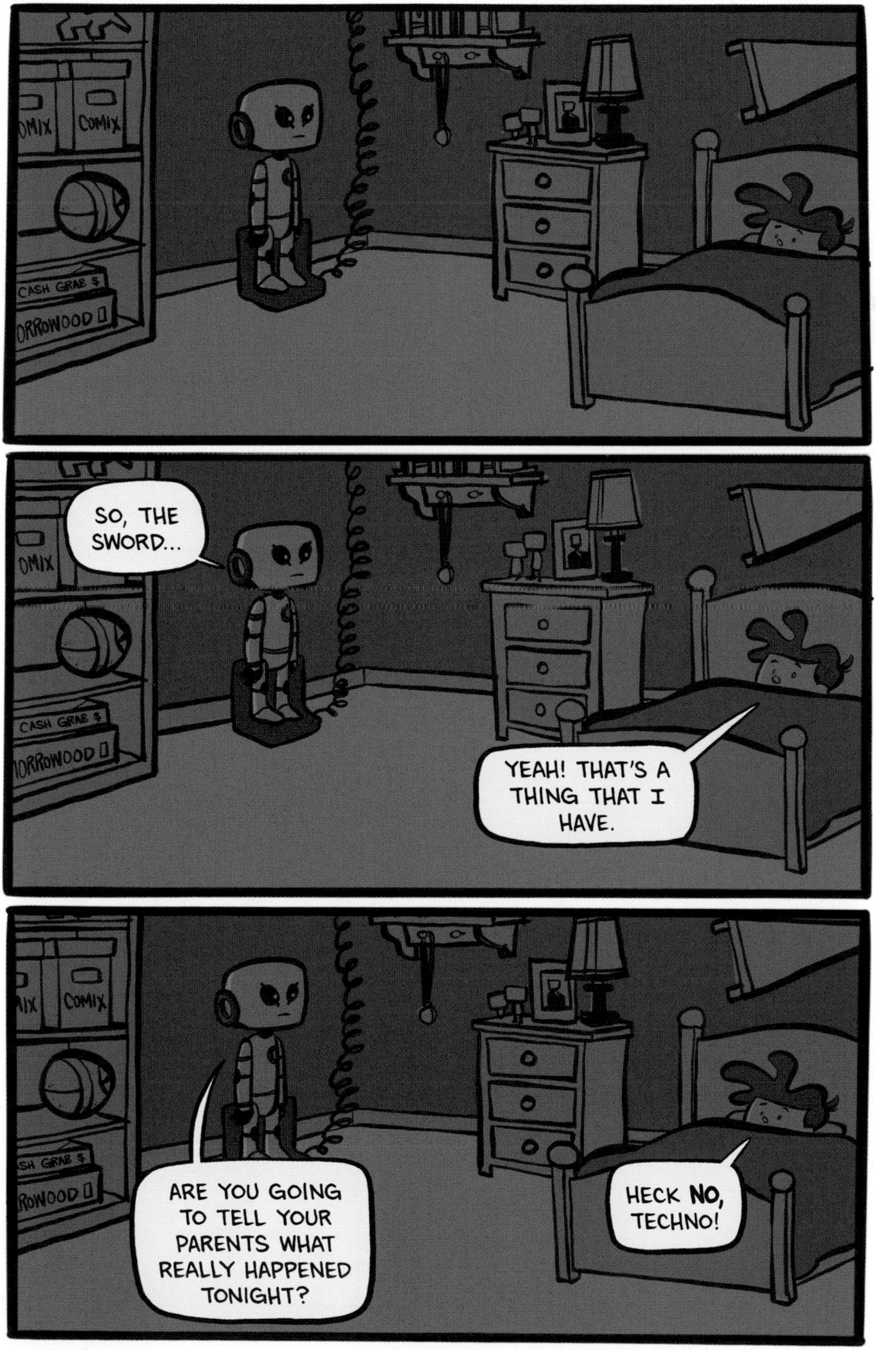
COMIX
COMIX
CASH GRAB $
ORROWOOD
SO, THE SWORD...
YEAH! THAT'S A THING THAT I HAVE.
ARE YOU GOING TO TELL YOUR PARENTS WHAT REALLY HAPPENED TONIGHT?
HECK **NO**, TECHNO!

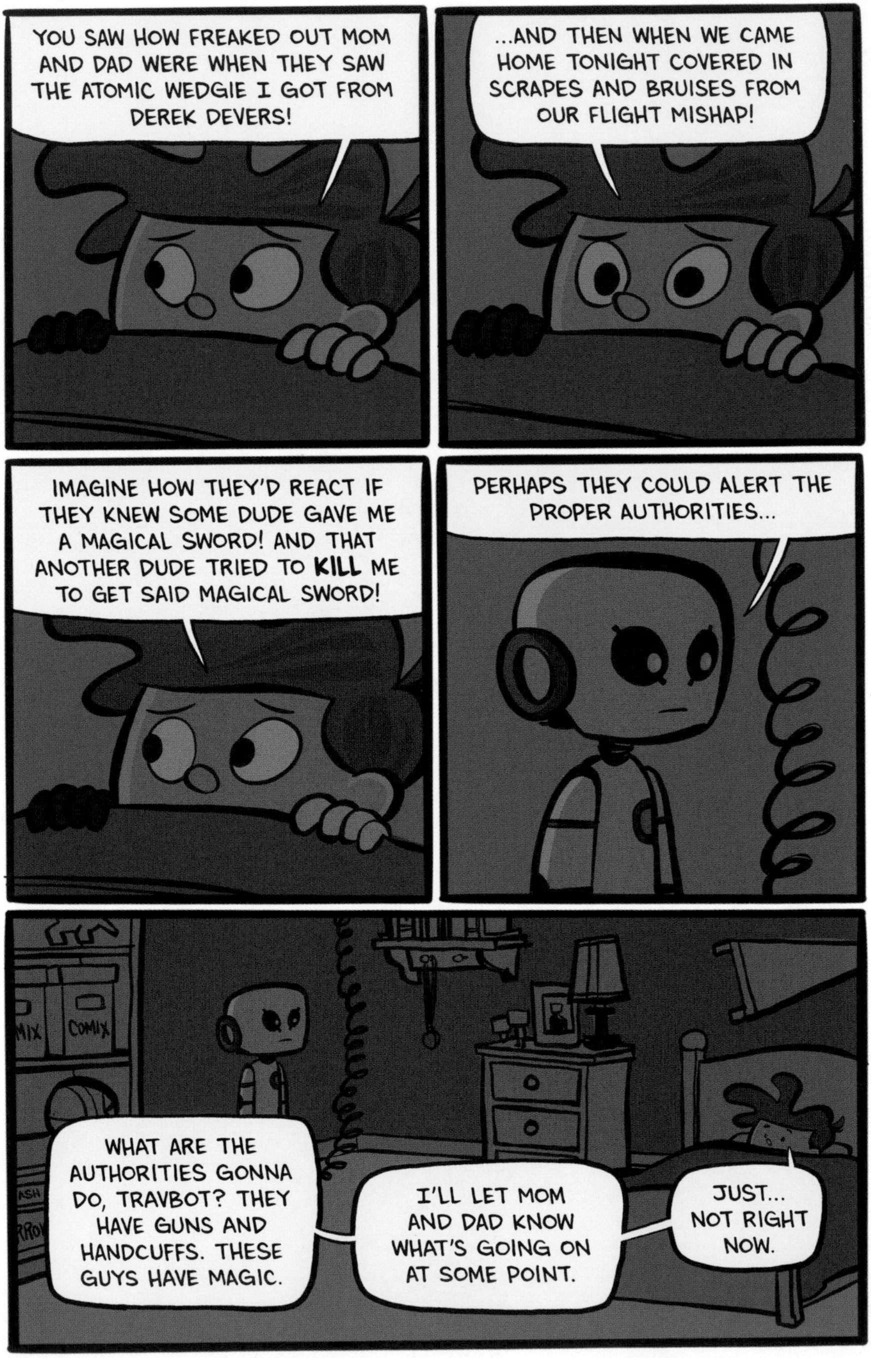
YOU SAW HOW FREAKED OUT MOM AND DAD WERE WHEN THEY SAW THE ATOMIC WEDGIE I GOT FROM DEREK DEVERS!
...AND THEN WHEN WE CAME HOME TONIGHT COVERED IN SCRAPES AND BRUISES FROM OUR FLIGHT MISHAP!
IMAGINE HOW THEY'D REACT IF THEY KNEW SOME DUDE GAVE ME A MAGICAL SWORD! AND THAT ANOTHER DUDE TRIED TO **KILL** ME TO GET SAID MAGICAL SWORD!
PERHAPS THEY COULD ALERT THE PROPER AUTHORITIES...
COMIX
COMIX
WHAT ARE THE AUTHORITIES GONNA DO, TRAVBOT? THEY HAVE GUNS AND HANDCUFFS. THESE GUYS HAVE MAGIC.
I'LL LET MOM AND DAD KNOW WHAT'S GOING ON AT SOME POINT.
JUST... NOT RIGHT NOW.

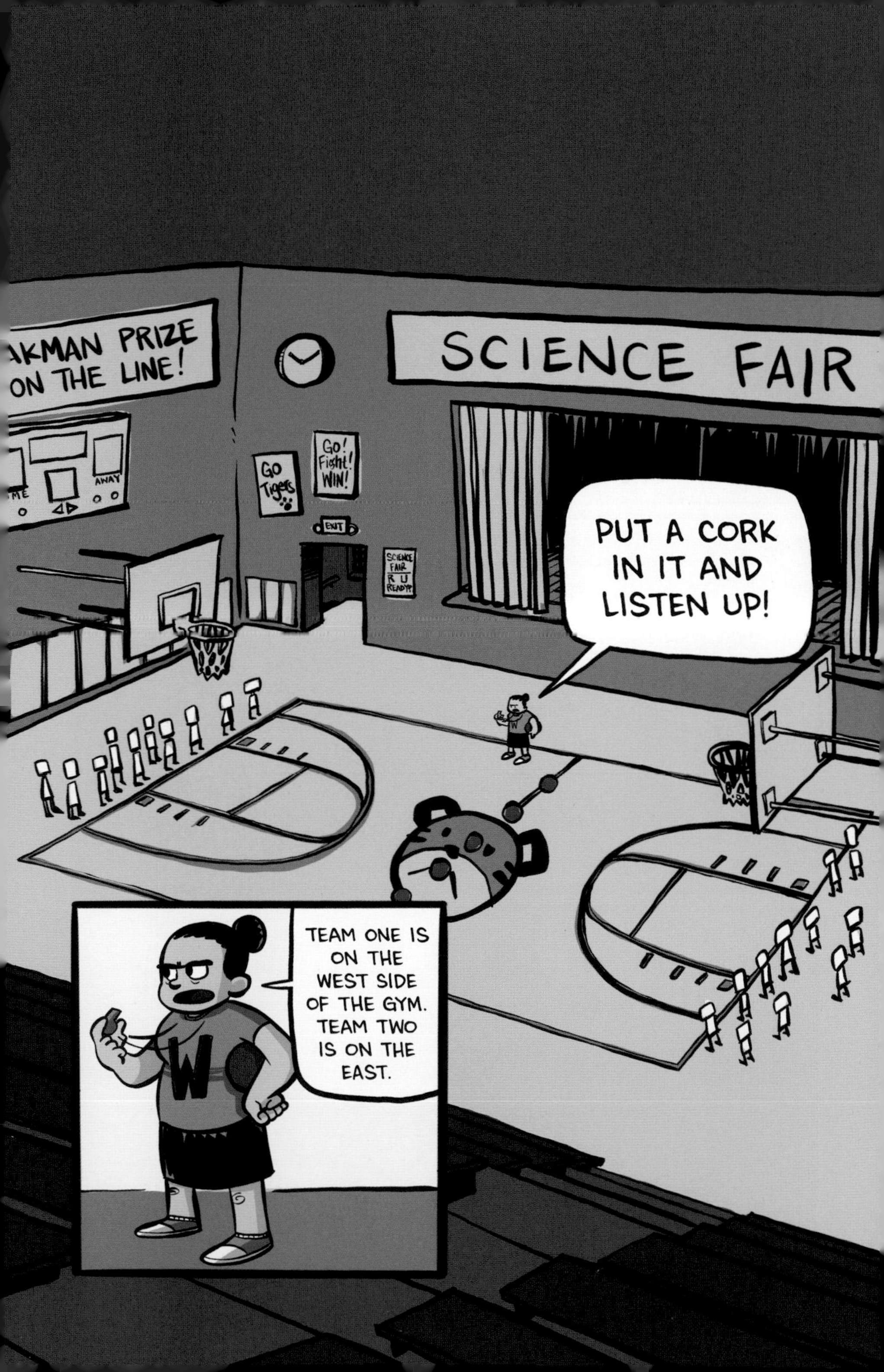
AKMAN PRIZE
ON THE LINE!
SCIENCE FAIR
Go Tigers
Go! Fight! WIN!
EXIT
SCIENCE FAIR R U READY?
AWAY
PUT A CORK IN IT AND LISTEN UP!
TEAM ONE IS ON THE WEST SIDE OF THE GYM. TEAM TWO IS ON THE EAST.

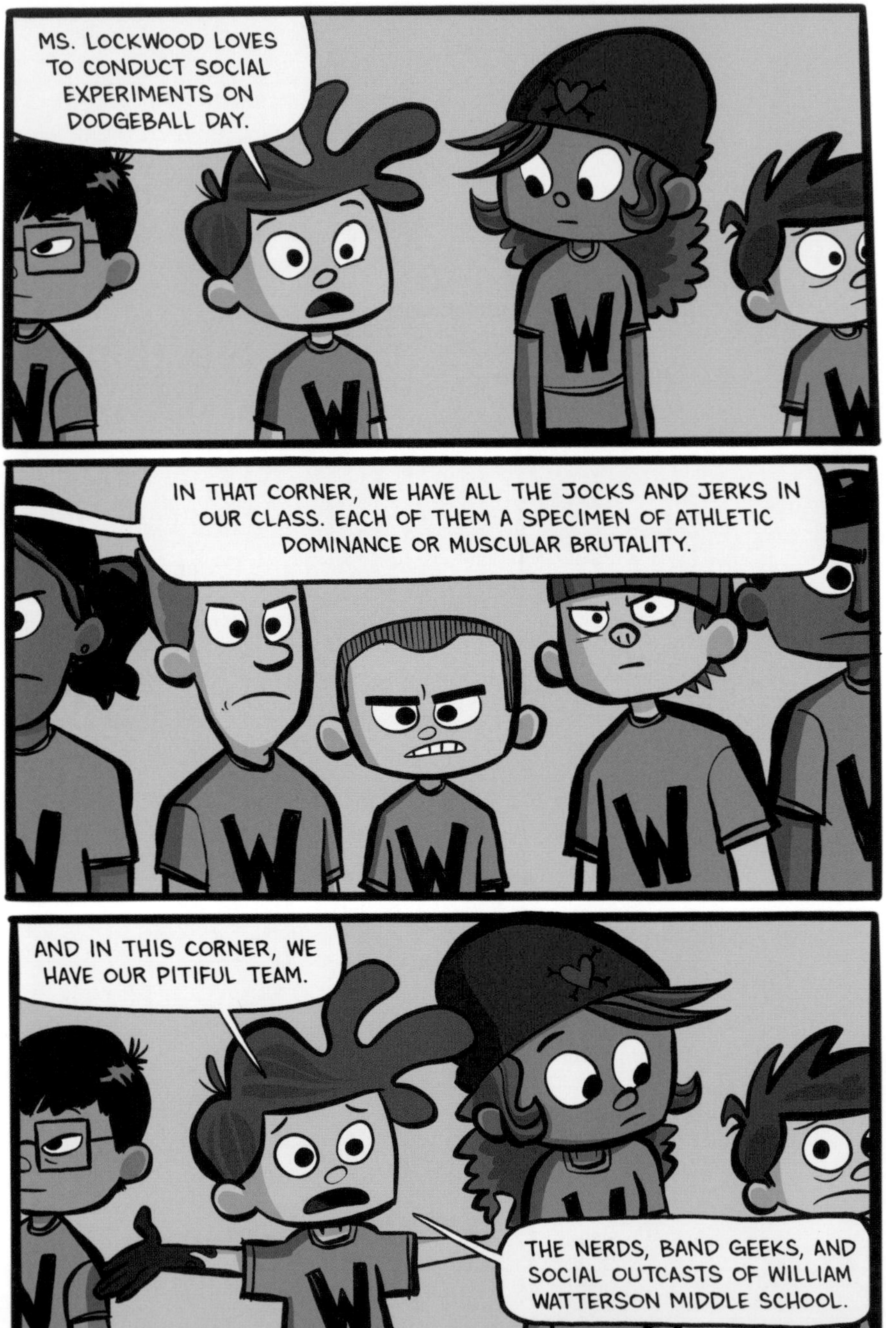
MS. LOCKWOOD LOVES TO CONDUCT SOCIAL EXPERIMENTS ON DODGEBALL DAY.
IN THAT CORNER, WE HAVE ALL THE JOCKS AND JERKS IN OUR CLASS. EACH OF THEM A SPECIMEN OF ATHLETIC DOMINANCE OR MUSCULAR BRUTALITY.
AND IN THIS CORNER, WE HAVE OUR PITIFUL TEAM.
THE NERDS, BAND GEEKS, AND SOCIAL OUTCASTS OF WILLIAM WATTERSON MIDDLE SCHOOL.

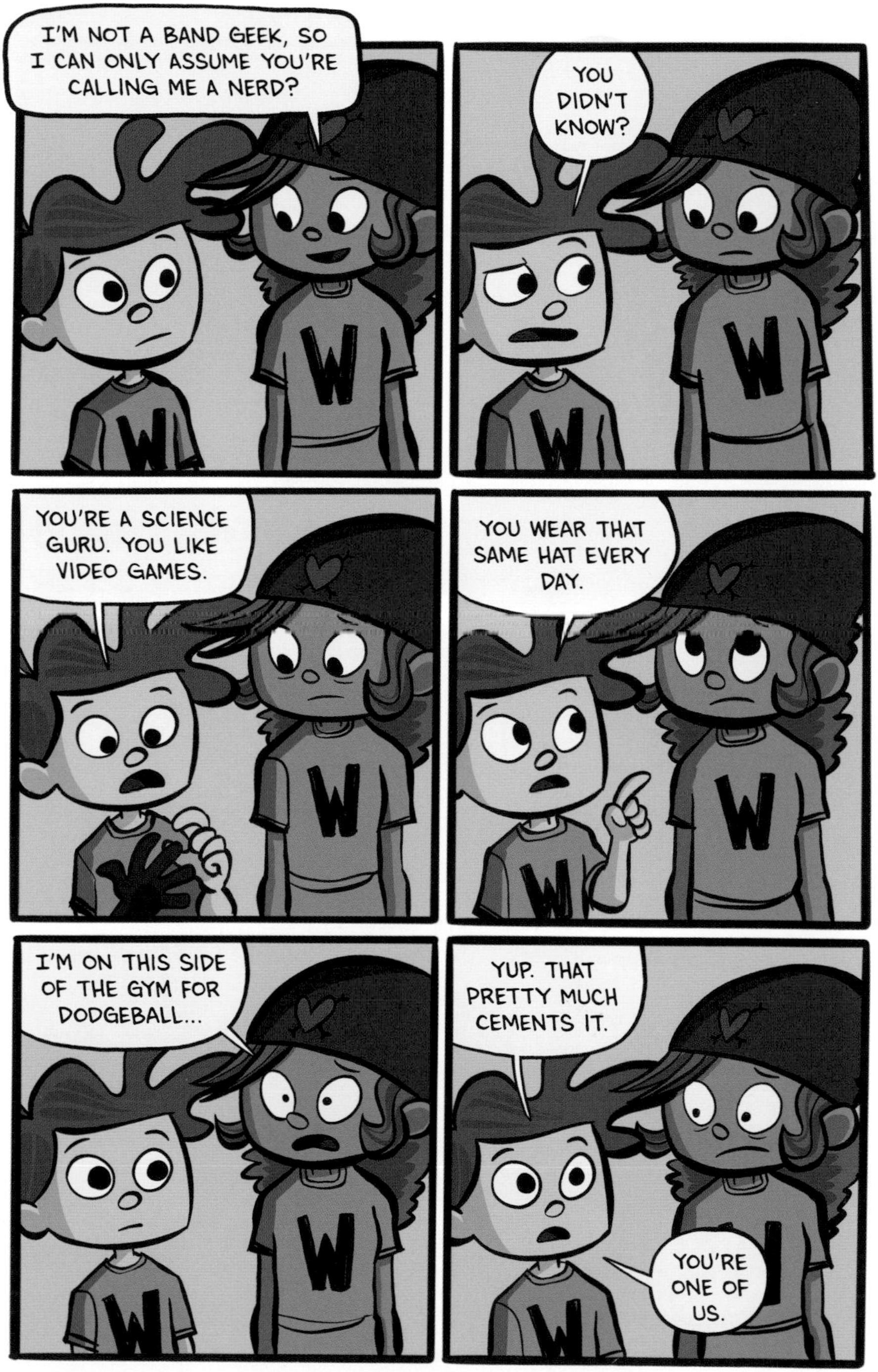
I'M NOT A BAND GEEK, SO I CAN ONLY ASSUME YOU'RE CALLING ME A NERD?
YOU DIDN'T KNOW?
YOU'RE A SCIENCE GURU. YOU LIKE VIDEO GAMES.
YOU WEAR THAT SAME HAT EVERY DAY.
I'M ON THIS SIDE OF THE GYM FOR DODGEBALL...
YUP. THAT PRETTY MUCH CEMENTS IT.
YOU'RE ONE OF US.

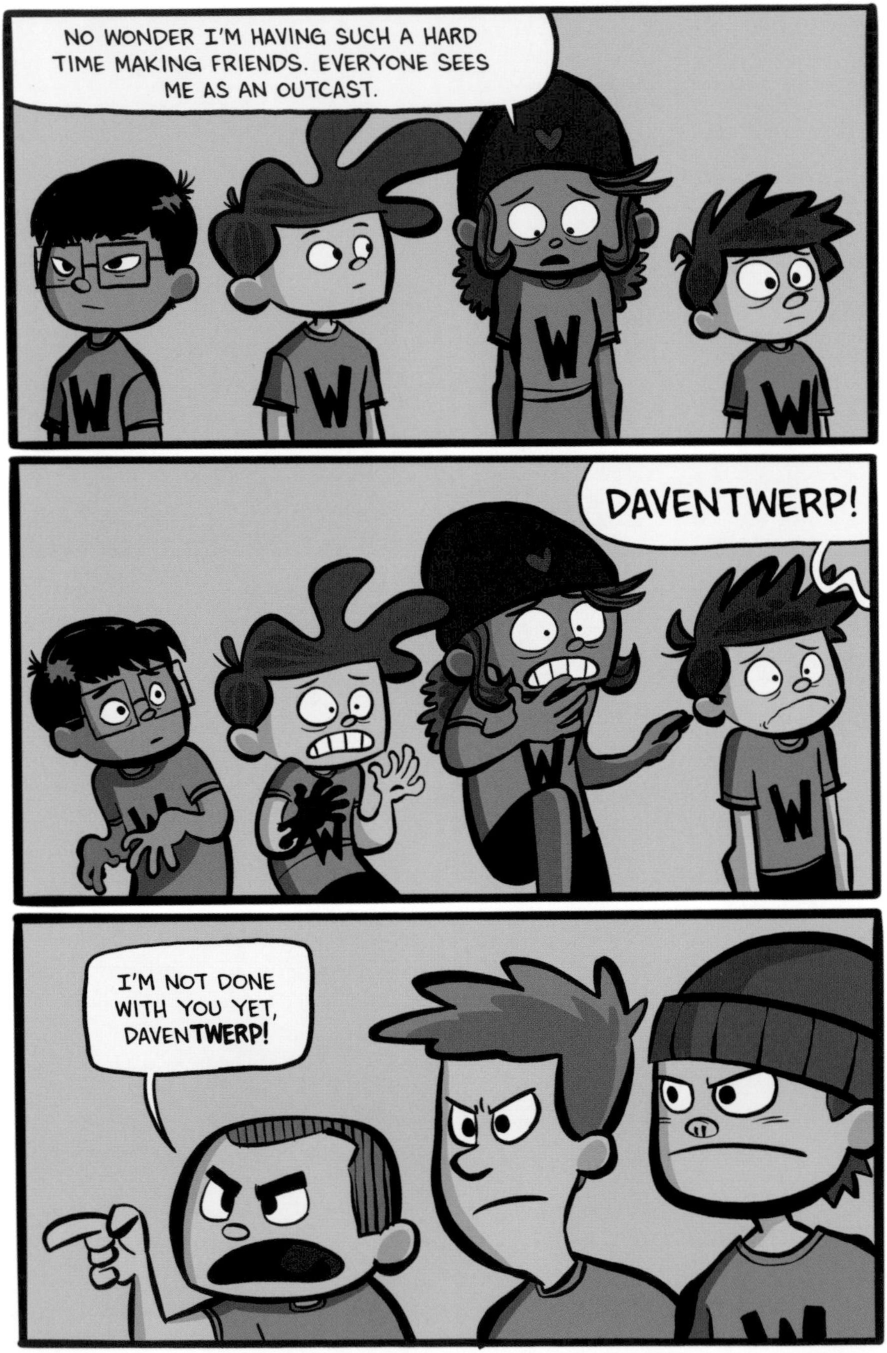
NO WONDER I'M HAVING SUCH A HARD TIME MAKING FRIENDS. EVERYONE SEES ME AS AN OUTCAST.
DAVENTWERP!
I'M NOT DONE WITH YOU YET, DAVEN**TWERP**!

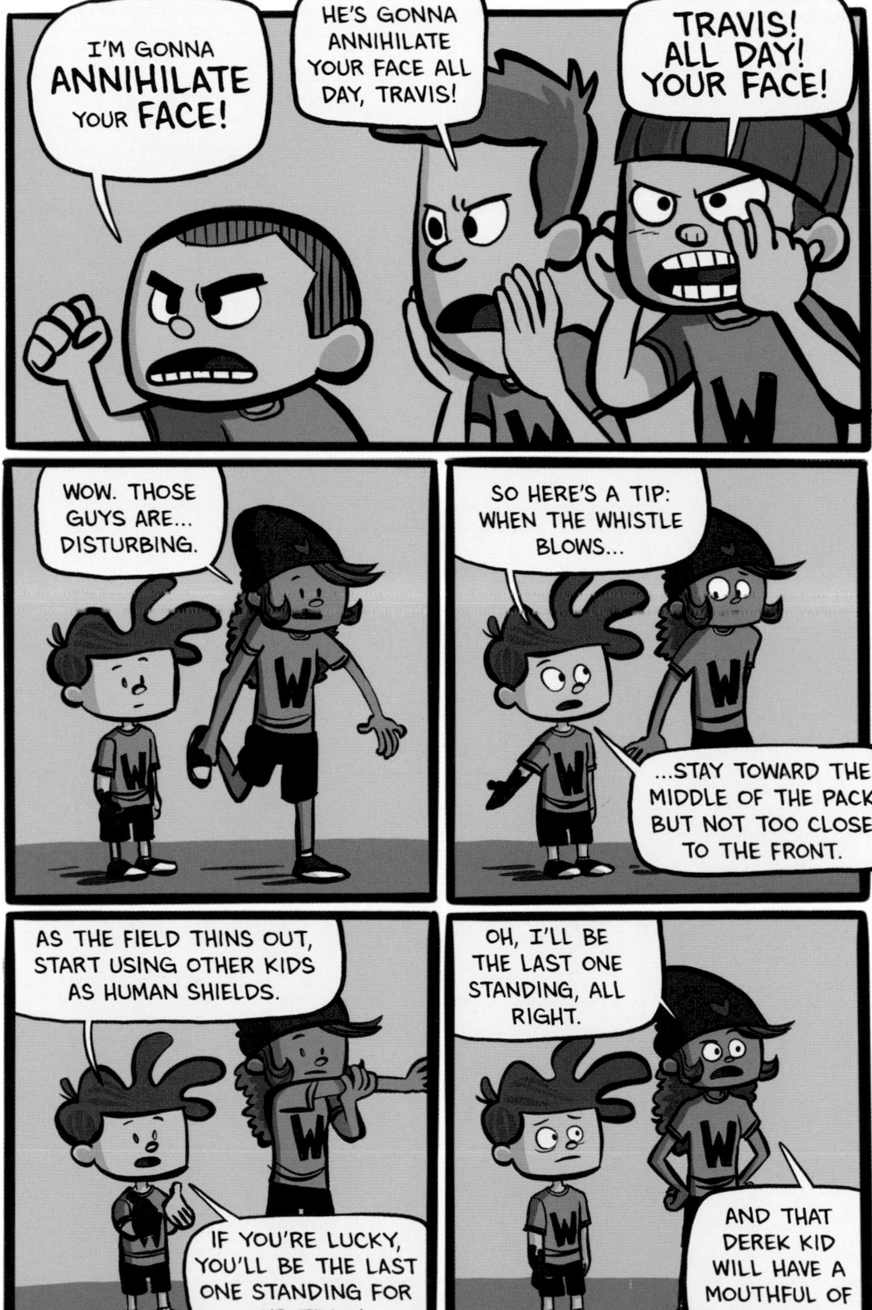
I'M GONNA ANNIHILATE YOUR FACE!
HE'S GONNA ANNIHILATE YOUR FACE ALL DAY, TRAVIS!
TRAVIS! ALL DAY! YOUR FACE!
WOW. THOSE GUYS ARE... DISTURBING.
SO HERE'S A TIP: WHEN THE WHISTLE BLOWS...
...STAY TOWARD THE MIDDLE OF THE PACK BUT NOT TOO CLOSE TO THE FRONT.
AS THE FIELD THINS OUT, START USING OTHER KIDS AS HUMAN SHIELDS.
IF YOU'RE LUCKY, YOU'LL BE THE LAST ONE STANDING FOR OUR TEAM!
OH, I'LL BE THE LAST ONE STANDING, ALL RIGHT.
AND THAT DEREK KID WILL HAVE A MOUTHFUL OF RUBBER.

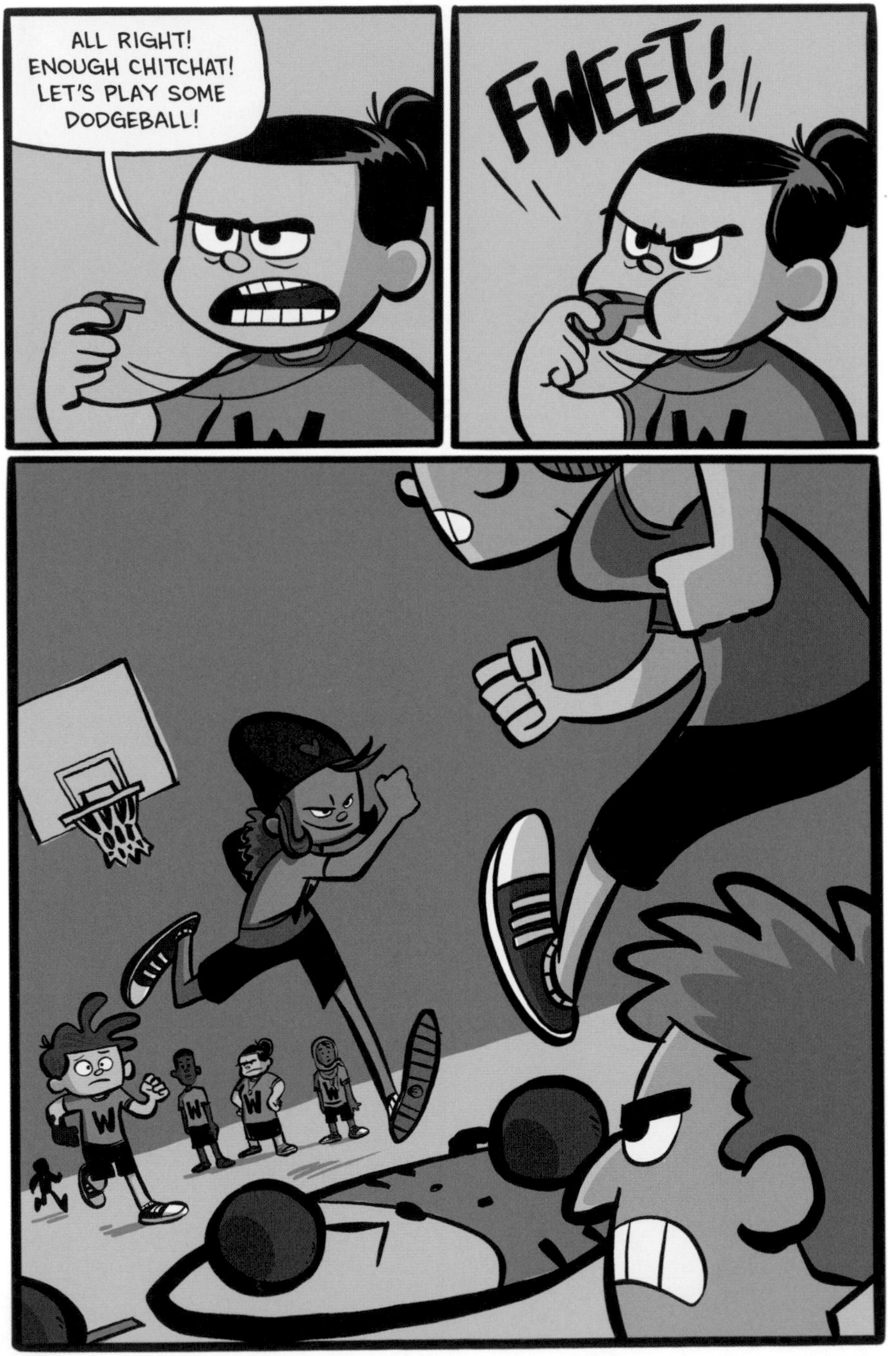
ALL RIGHT! ENOUGH CHITCHAT! LET'S PLAY SOME DODGEBALL!
FWEET!

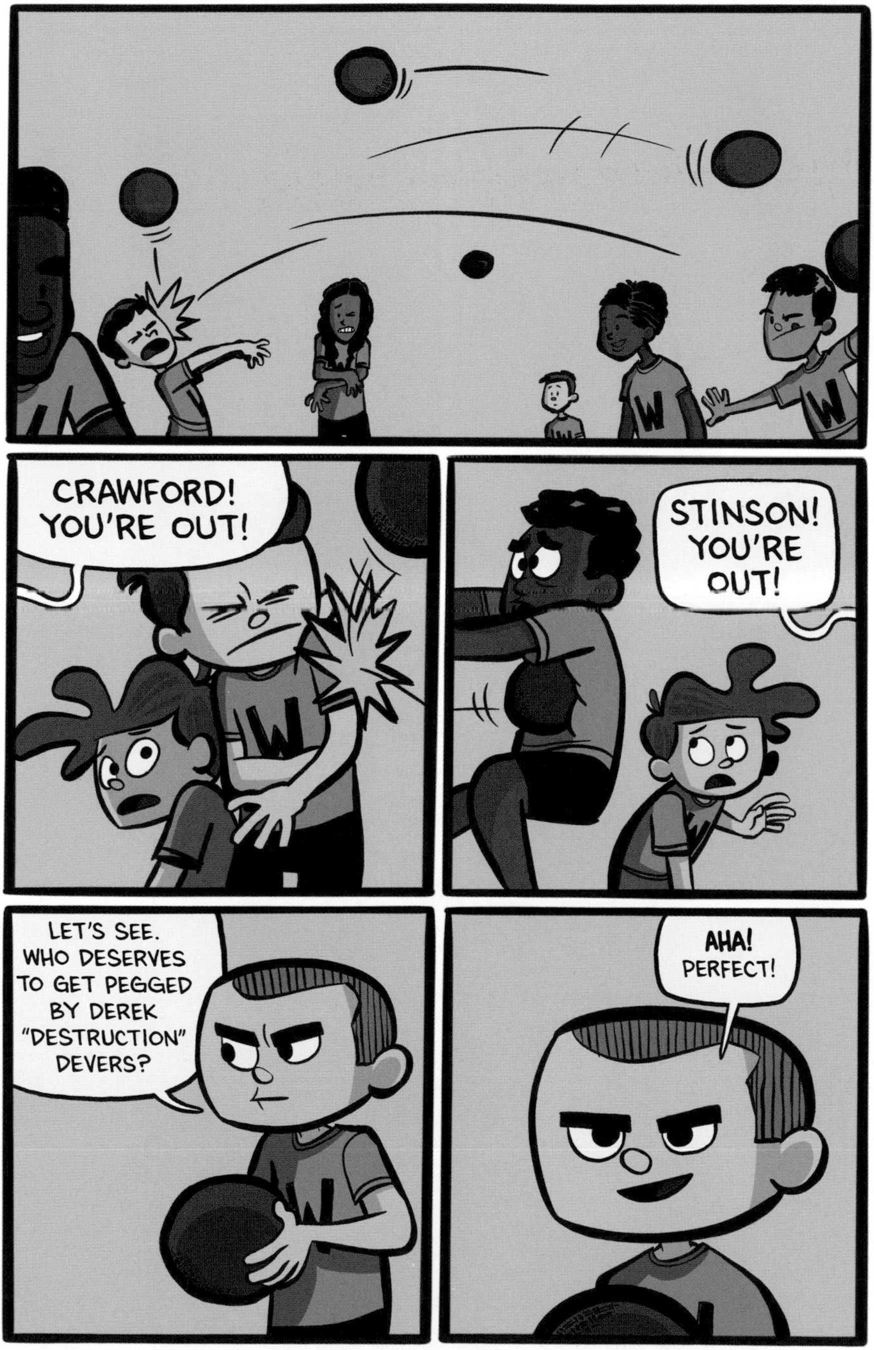
CRAWFORD! YOU'RE OUT!
STINSON! YOU'RE OUT!
LET'S SEE. WHO DESERVES TO GET PEGGED BY DEREK "DESTRUCTION" DEVERS?
AHA! PERFECT!

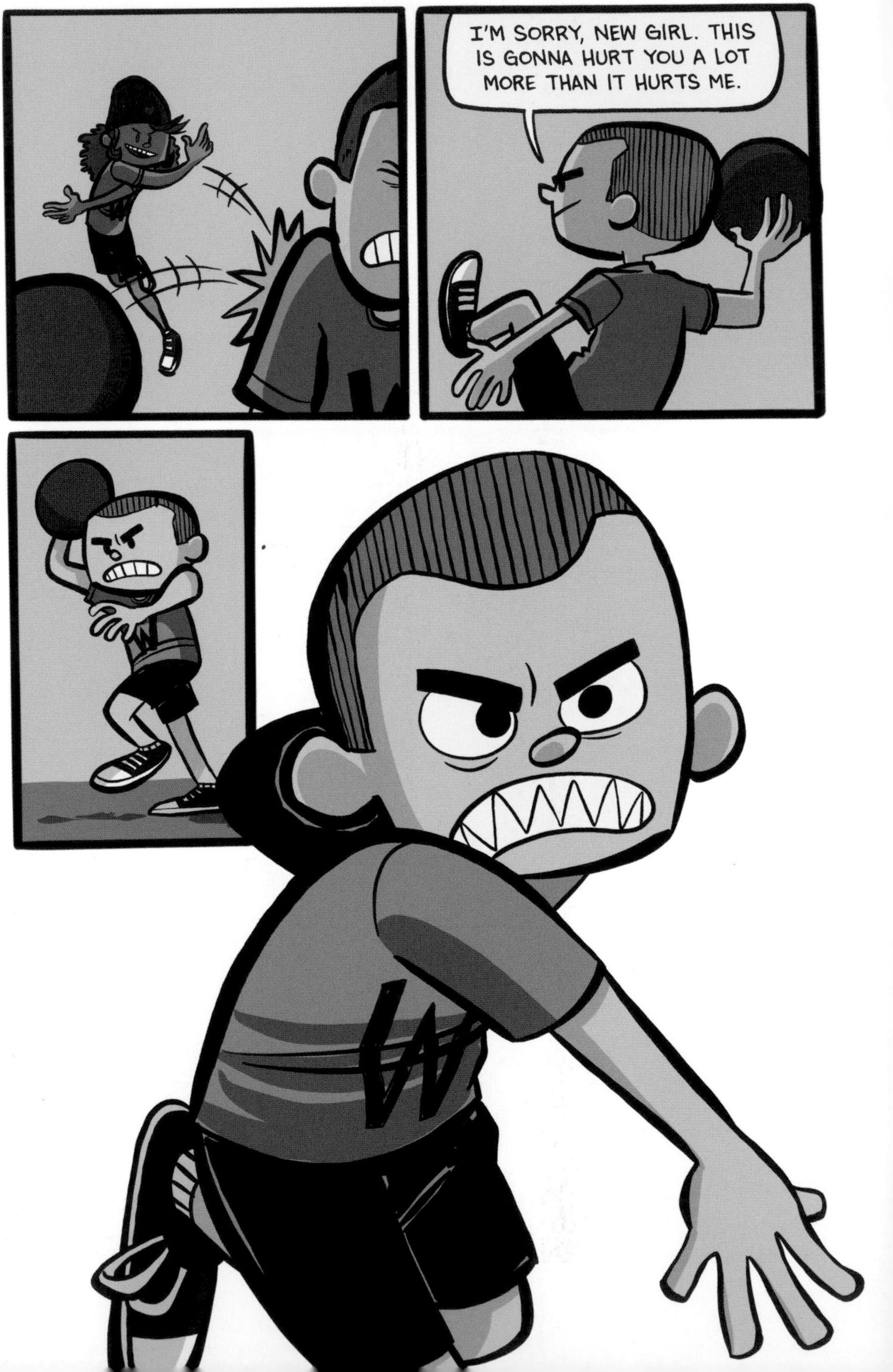
I'M SORRY, NEW GIRL. THIS IS GONNA HURT YOU A LOT MORE THAN IT HURTS ME.

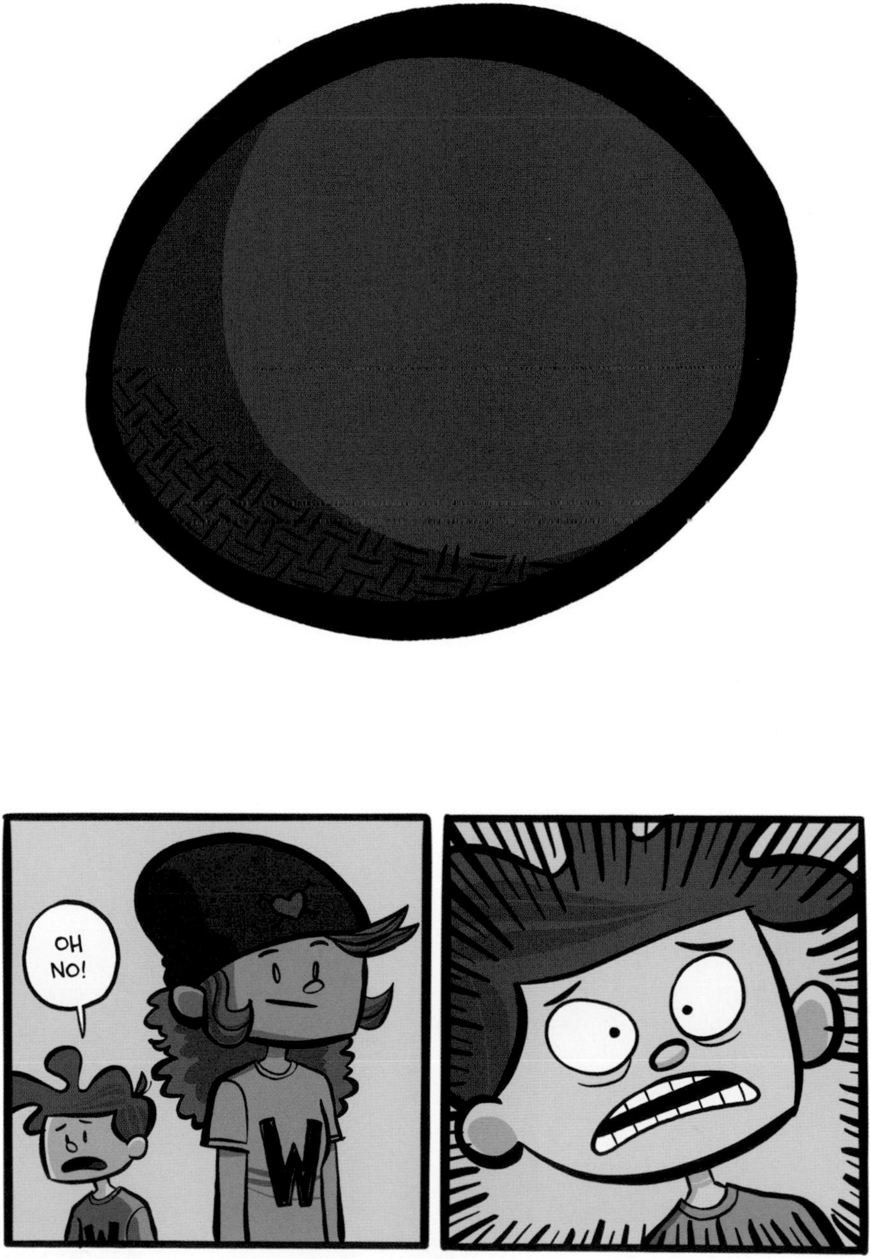
OH NO!

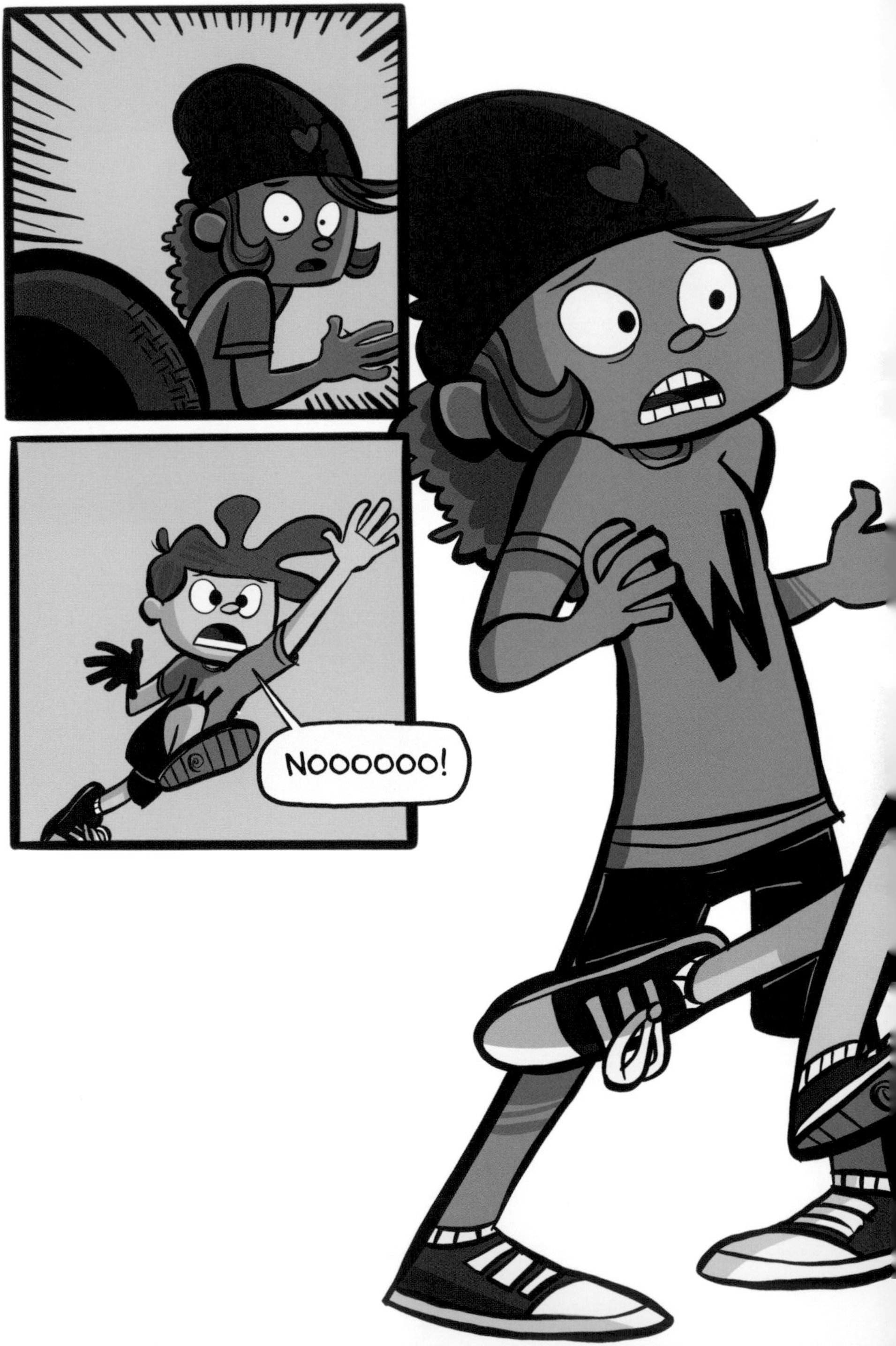
NOOOOOO!

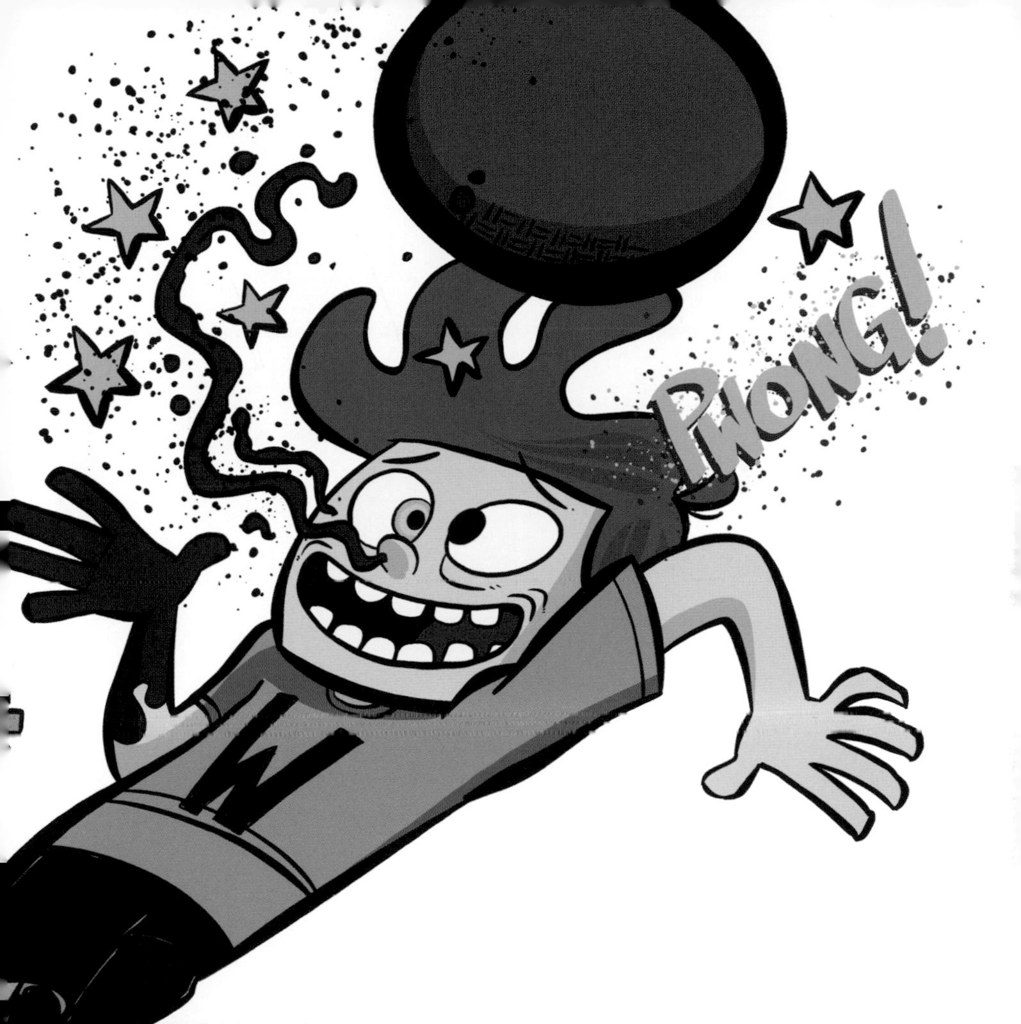
PWONG!

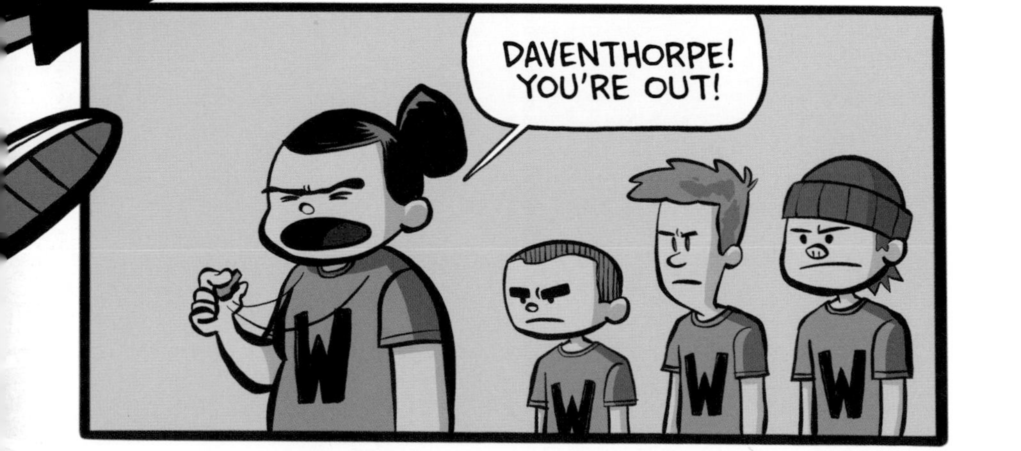
DAVENTHORPE! YOU'RE OUT!

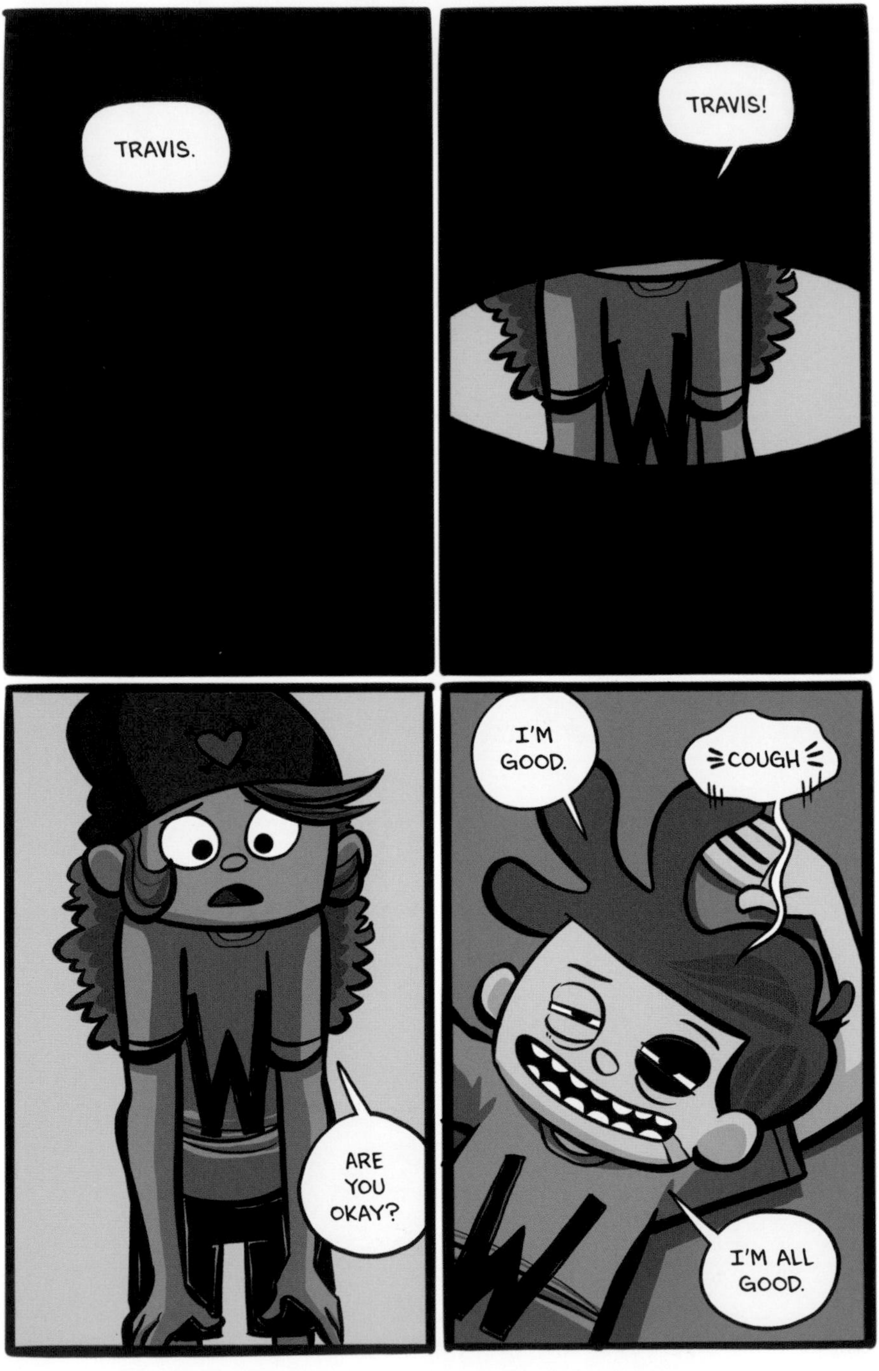
TRAVIS.
TRAVIS!
ARE YOU OKAY?
I'M GOOD.
COUGH
I'M ALL GOOD.

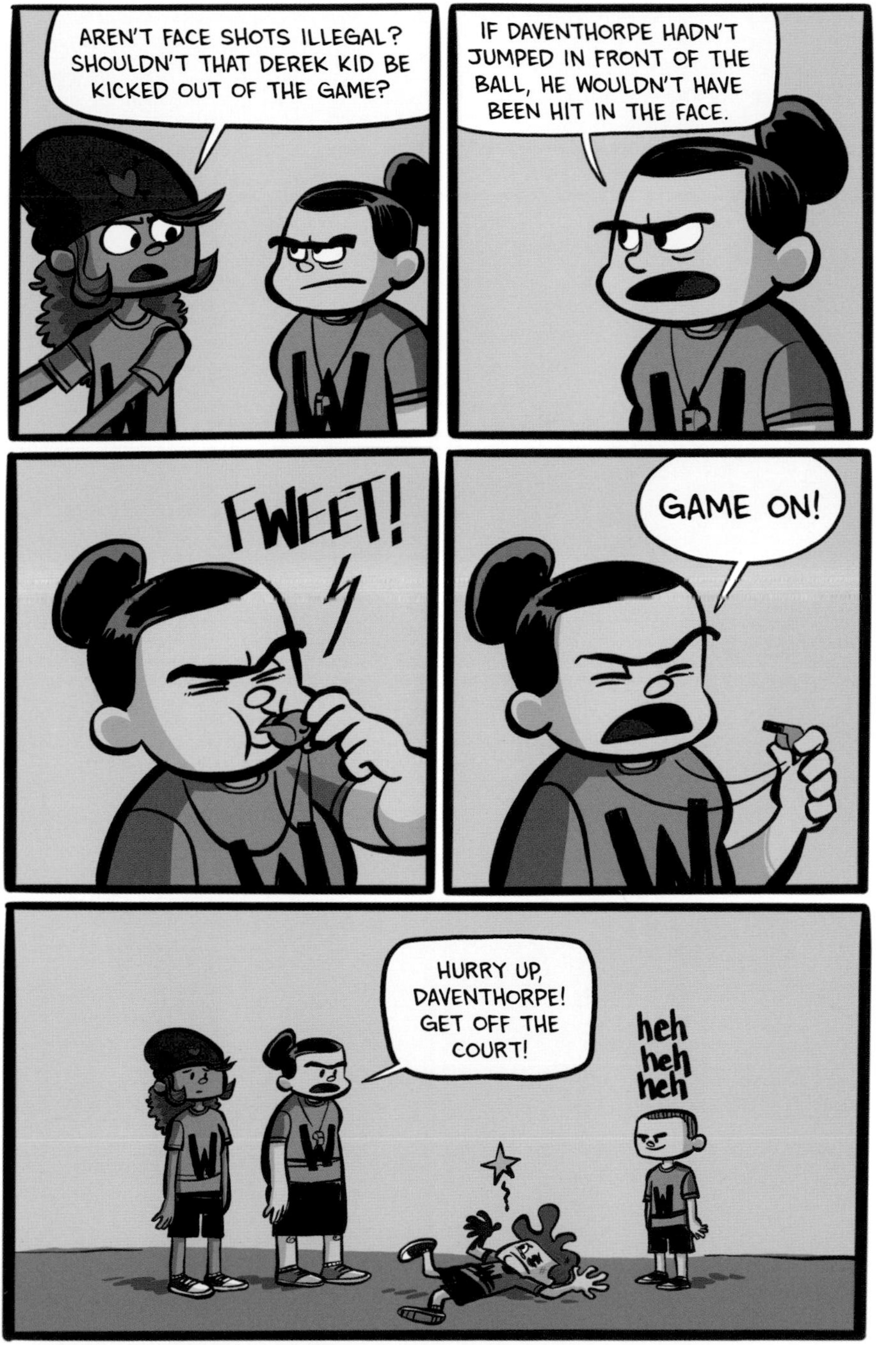
AREN'T FACE SHOTS ILLEGAL? SHOULDN'T THAT DEREK KID BE KICKED OUT OF THE GAME?
IF DAVENTHORPE HADN'T JUMPED IN FRONT OF THE BALL, HE WOULDN'T HAVE BEEN HIT IN THE FACE.
FWEET!
GAME ON!
HURRY UP, DAVENTHORPE! GET OFF THE COURT!
heh heh heh

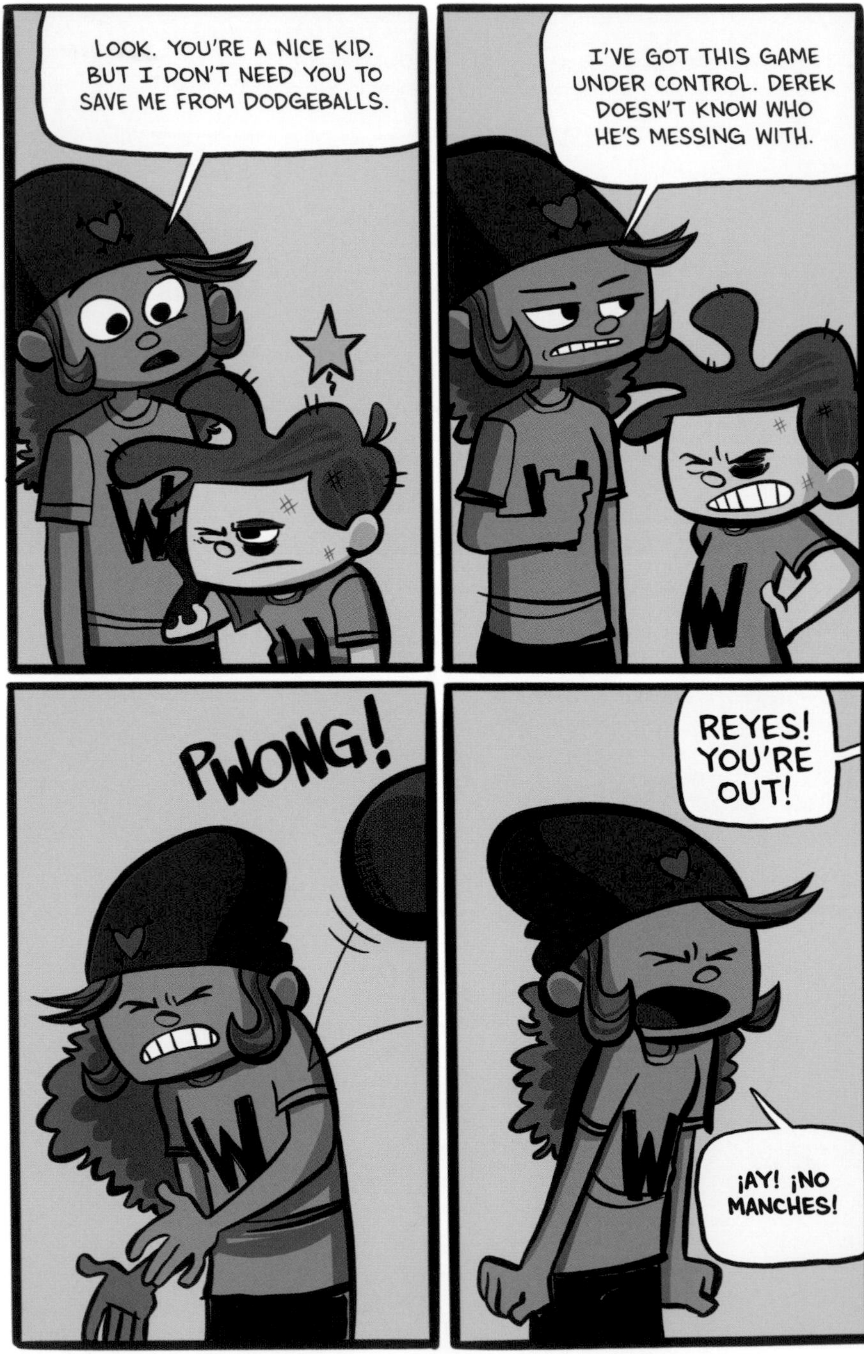
LOOK. YOU'RE A NICE KID. BUT I DON'T NEED YOU TO SAVE ME FROM DODGEBALLS.
I'VE GOT THIS GAME UNDER CONTROL. DEREK DOESN'T KNOW WHO HE'S MESSING WITH.
PWONG!
REYES! YOU'RE OUT!
¡AY! ¡NO MANCHES!

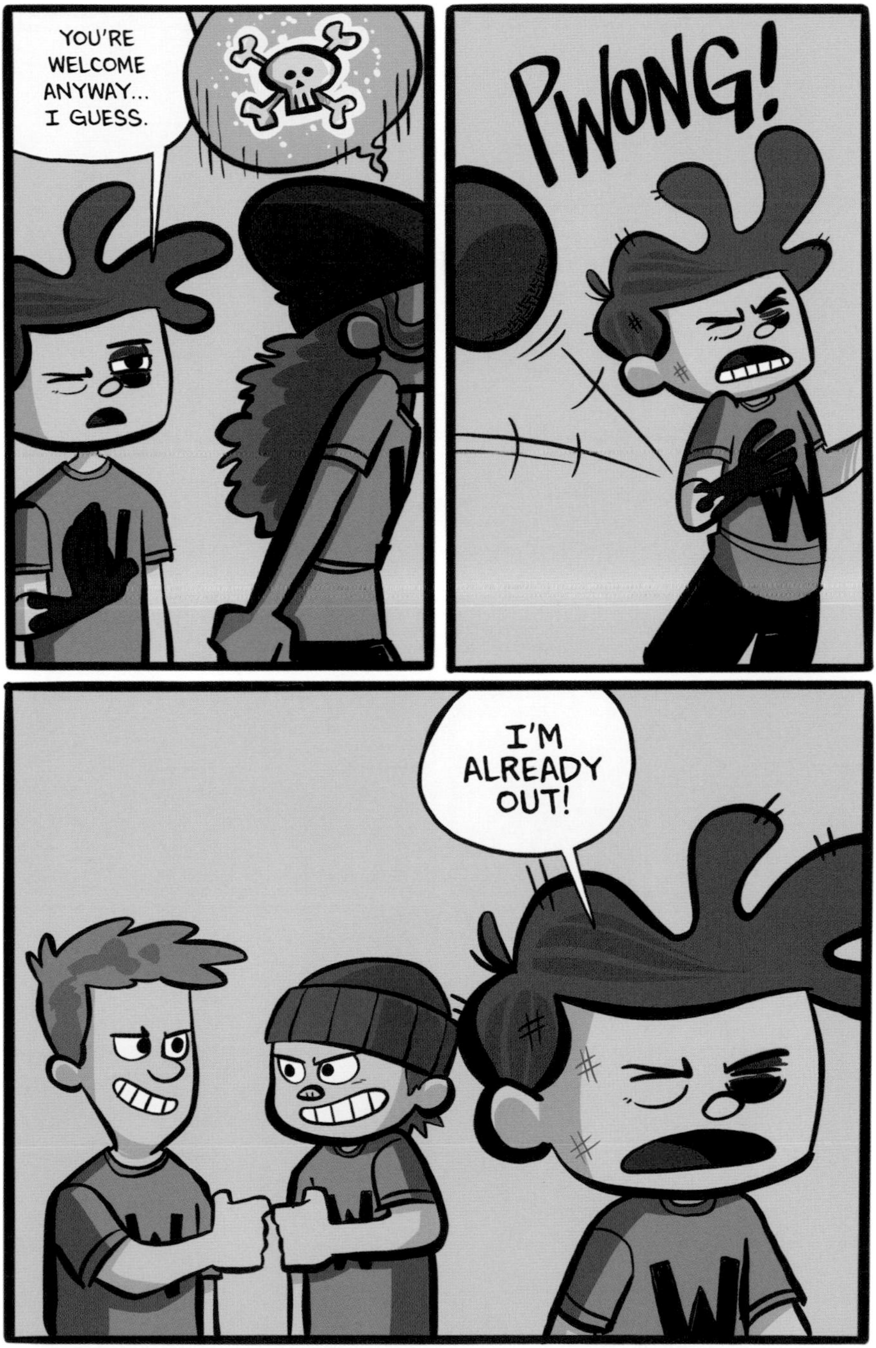
YOU'RE WELCOME ANYWAY... I GUESS.
PWONG!
I'M ALREADY OUT!

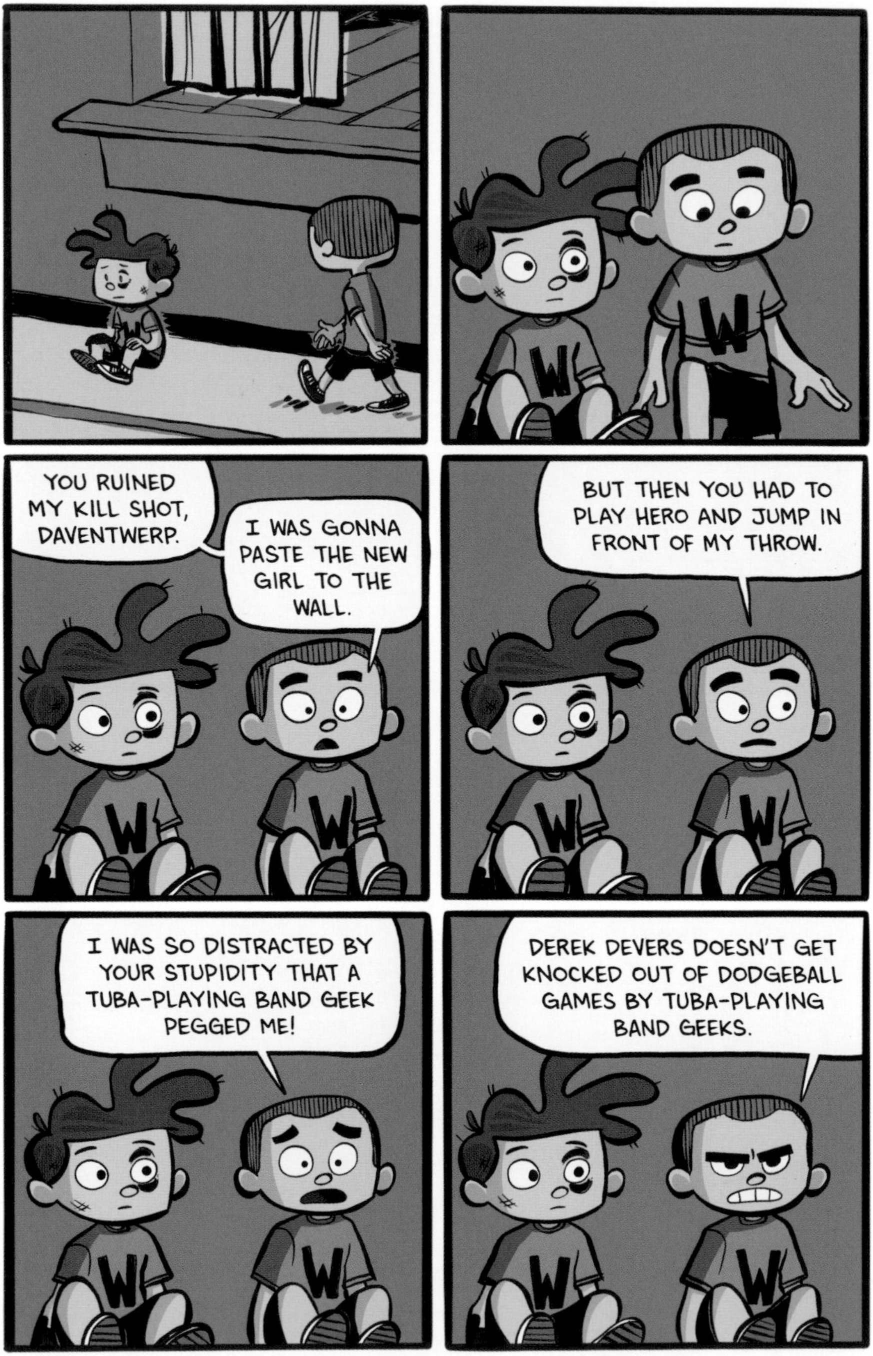
YOU RUINED MY KILL SHOT, DAVENTWERP.
I WAS GONNA PASTE THE NEW GIRL TO THE WALL.
BUT THEN YOU HAD TO PLAY HERO AND JUMP IN FRONT OF MY THROW.
I WAS SO DISTRACTED BY YOUR STUPIDITY THAT A TUBA-PLAYING BAND GEEK PEGGED ME!
DEREK DEVERS DOESN'T GET KNOCKED OUT OF DODGEBALL GAMES BY TUBA-PLAYING BAND GEEKS.

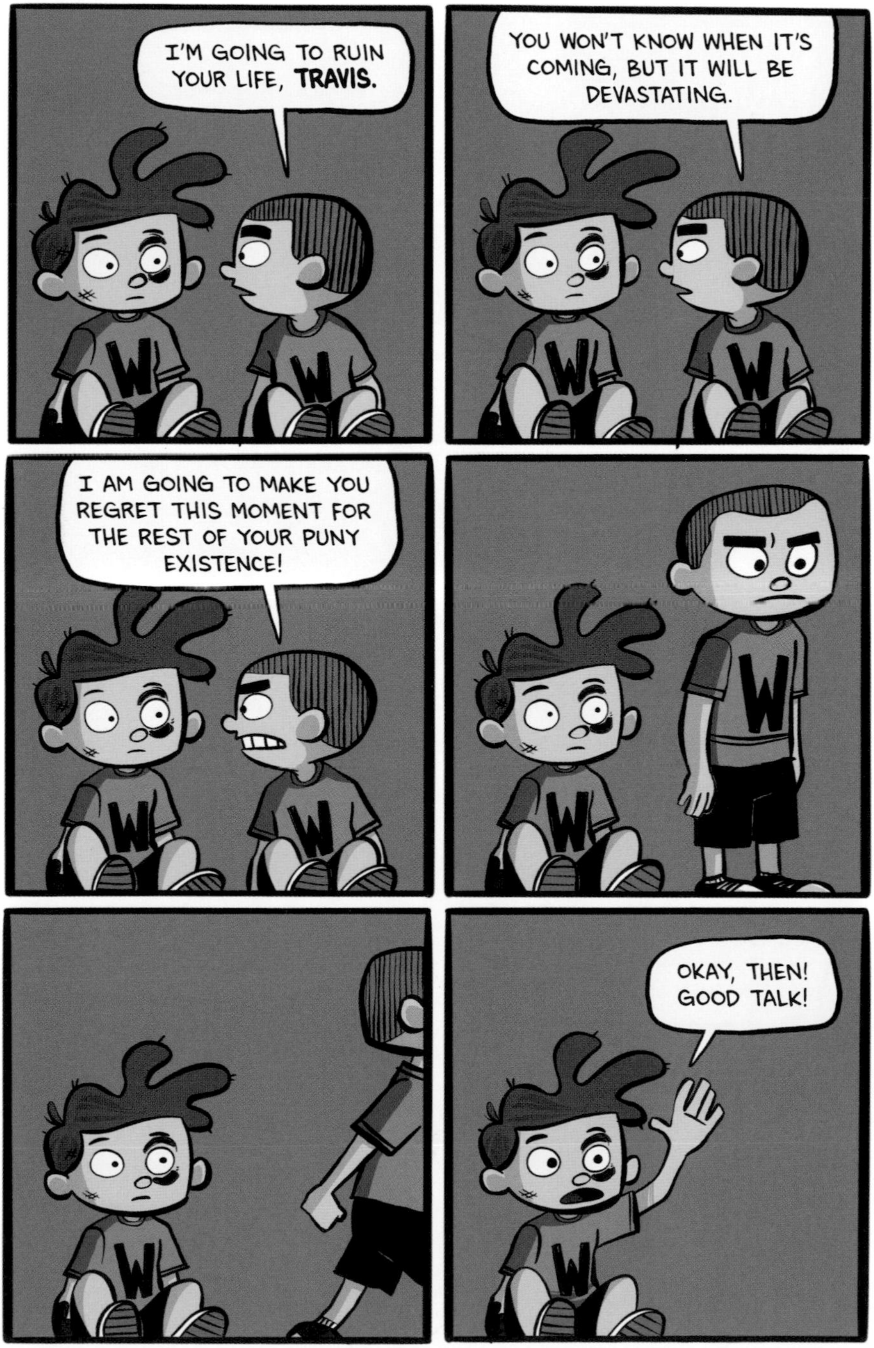
I'M GOING TO RUIN YOUR LIFE, **TRAVIS.**
YOU WON'T KNOW WHEN IT'S COMING, BUT IT WILL BE DEVASTATING.
I AM GOING TO MAKE YOU REGRET THIS MOMENT FOR THE REST OF YOUR PUNY EXISTENCE!
OKAY, THEN! GOOD TALK!

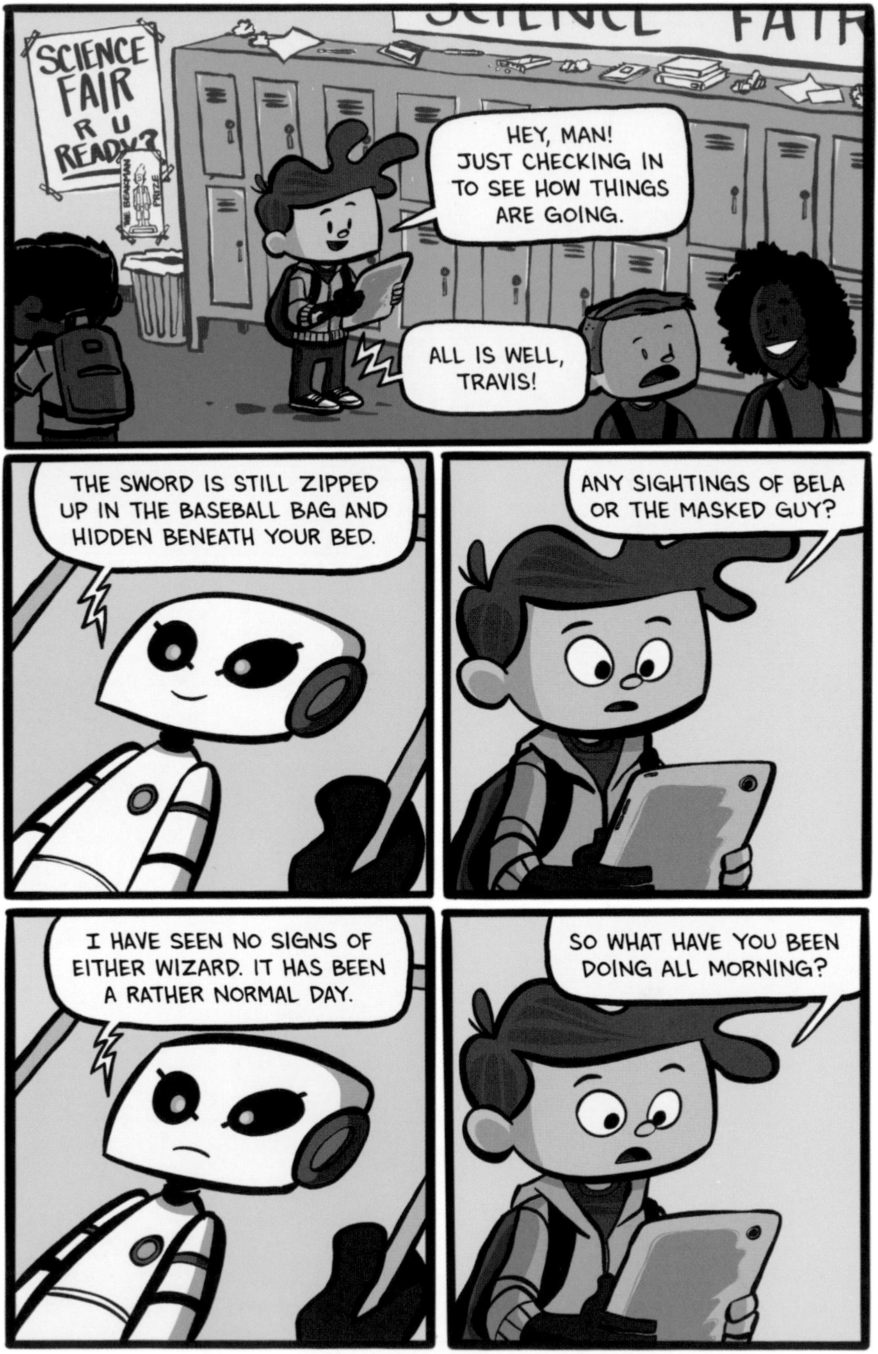
SCIENCE FAIR
SCIENCE FAIR R U READY?
THE BEARMAN PRIZE
HEY, MAN! JUST CHECKING IN TO SEE HOW THINGS ARE GOING.
ALL IS WELL, TRAVIS!
THE SWORD IS STILL ZIPPED UP IN THE BASEBALL BAG AND HIDDEN BENEATH YOUR BED.
ANY SIGHTINGS OF BELA OR THE MASKED GUY?
I HAVE SEEN NO SIGNS OF EITHER WIZARD. IT HAS BEEN A RATHER NORMAL DAY.
SO WHAT HAVE YOU BEEN DOING ALL MORNING?

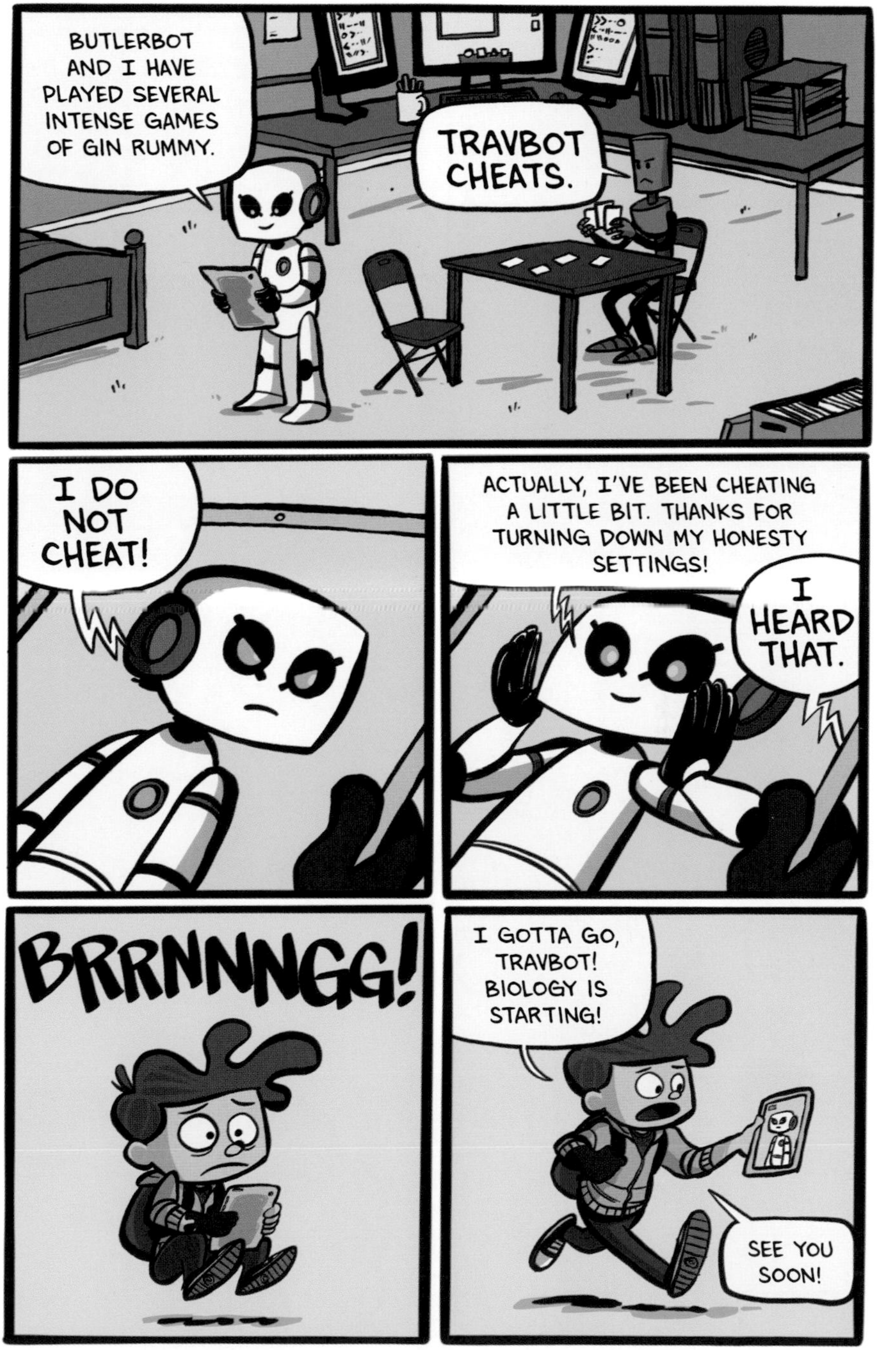
BUTLERBOT AND I HAVE PLAYED SEVERAL INTENSE GAMES OF GIN RUMMY.
TRAVBOT CHEATS.
I DO NOT CHEAT!
ACTUALLY, I'VE BEEN CHEATING A LITTLE BIT. THANKS FOR TURNING DOWN MY HONESTY SETTINGS!
I HEARD THAT.
BRRNNNGG!
I GOTTA GO, TRAVBOT! BIOLOGY IS STARTING!
SEE YOU SOON!

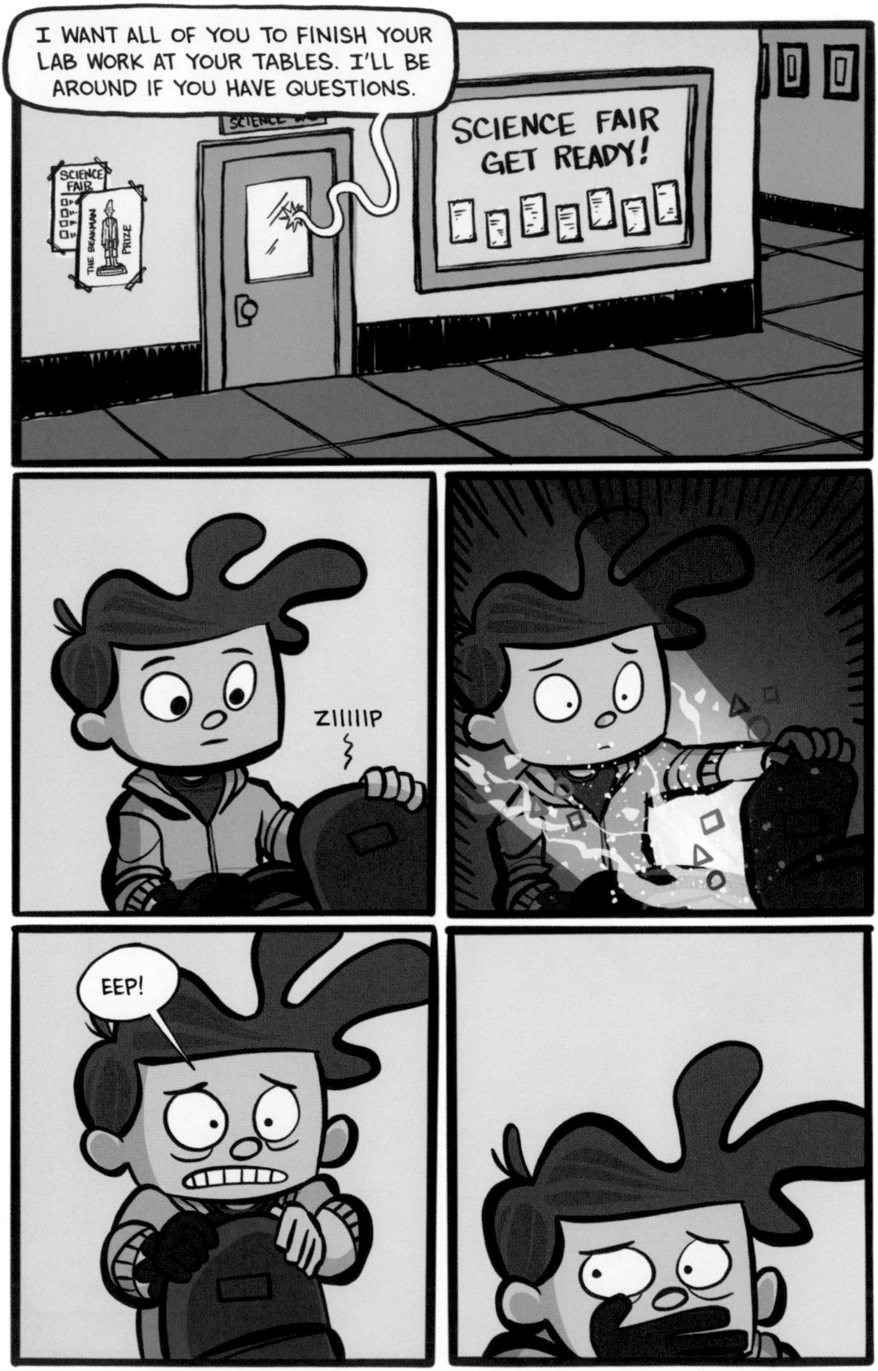
I WANT ALL OF YOU TO FINISH YOUR LAB WORK AT YOUR TABLES. I'LL BE AROUND IF YOU HAVE QUESTIONS.
SCIENCE FAIR
THE BEAKMAN PRIZE
SCIENCE FAIR GET READY!
ZIIIIIP
EEP!

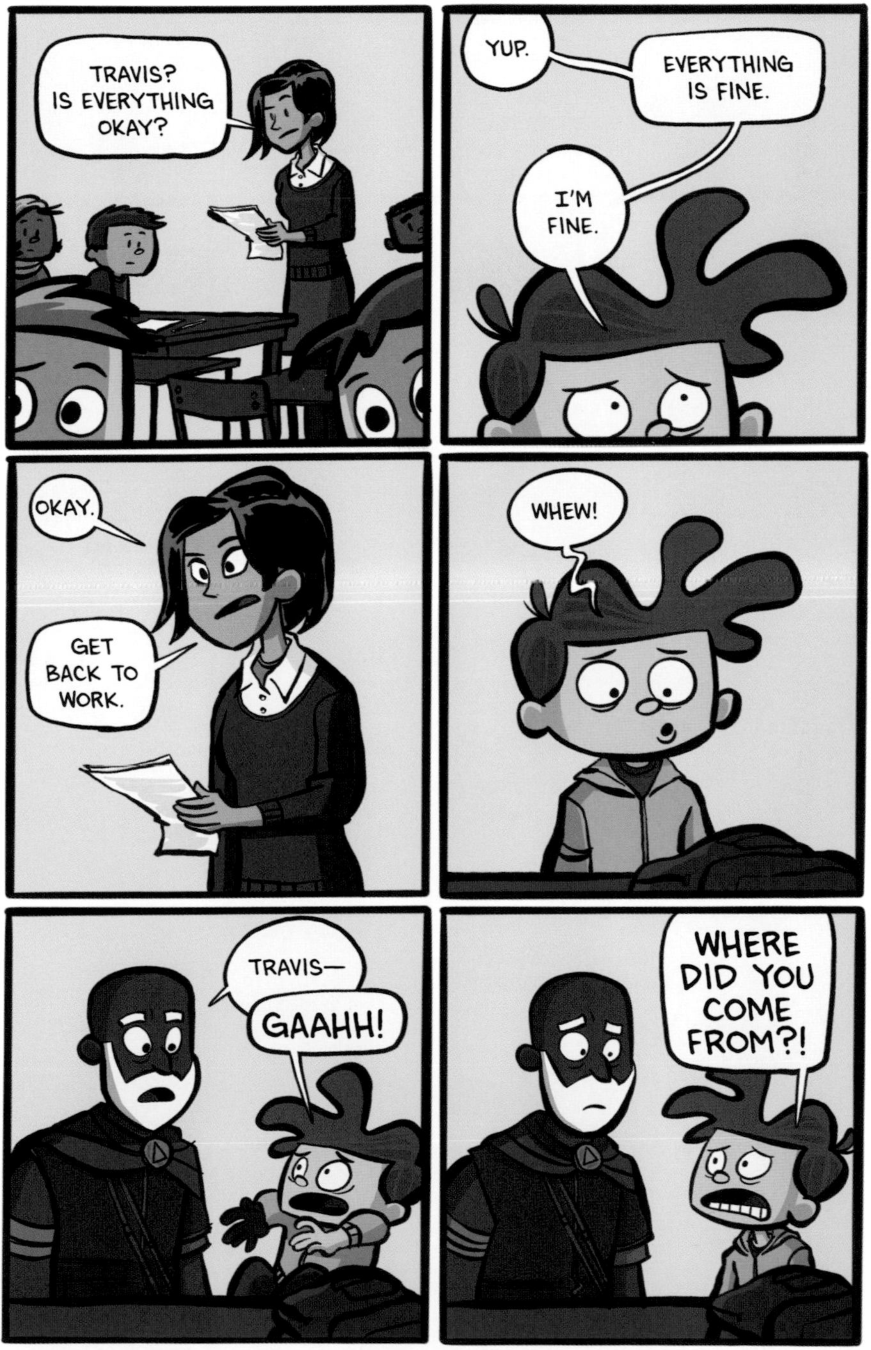
TRAVIS? IS EVERYTHING OKAY?
YUP.
EVERYTHING IS FINE.
I'M FINE.
OKAY.
GET BACK TO WORK.
WHEW!
TRAVIS—
GAAHH!
WHERE DID YOU COME FROM?!

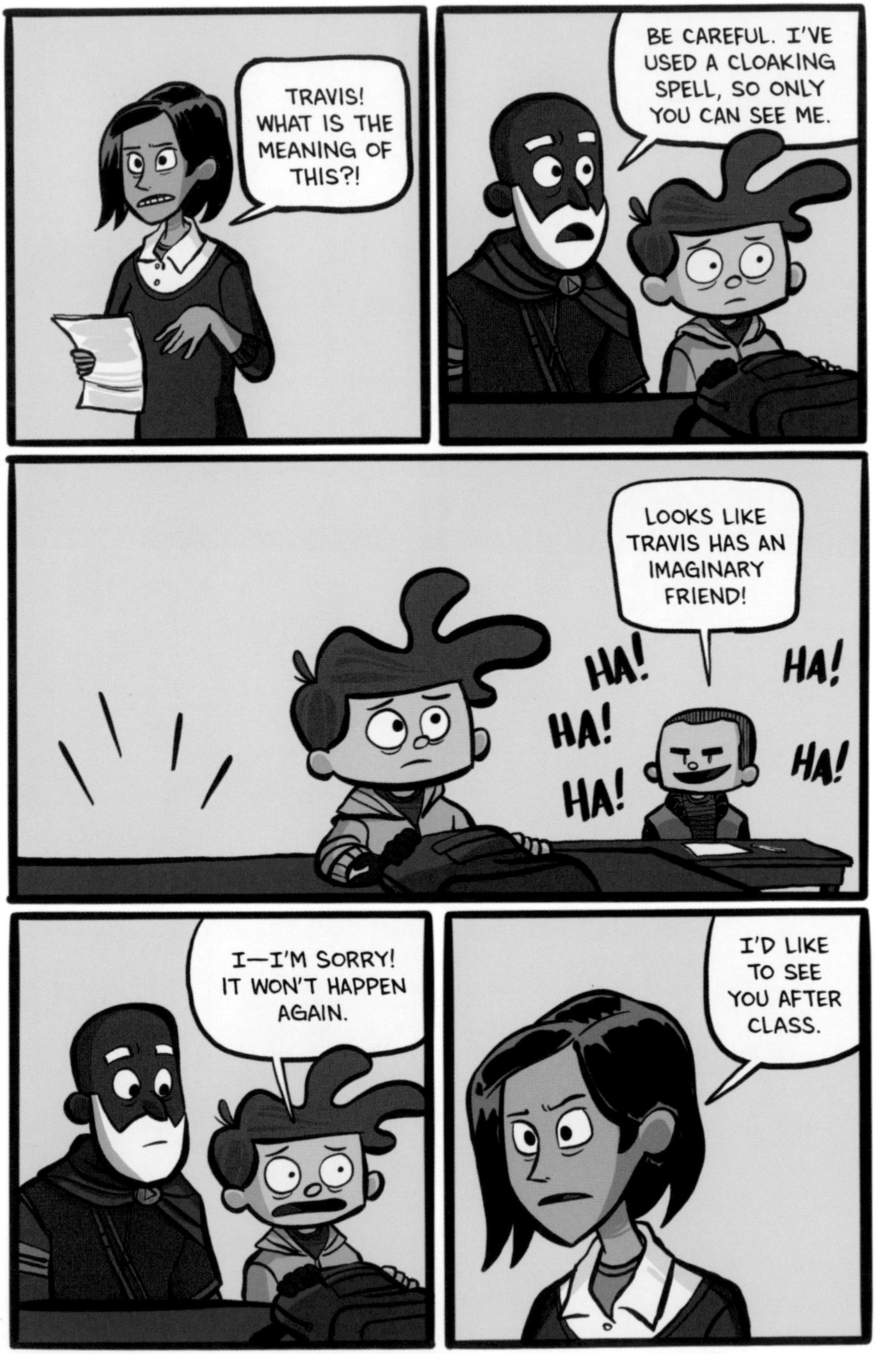
TRAVIS! WHAT IS THE MEANING OF THIS?!
BE CAREFUL. I'VE USED A CLOAKING SPELL, SO ONLY YOU CAN SEE ME.
LOOKS LIKE TRAVIS HAS AN IMAGINARY FRIEND!
HA! HA! HA! HA! HA!
I—I'M SORRY! IT WON'T HAPPEN AGAIN.
I'D LIKE TO SEE YOU AFTER CLASS.

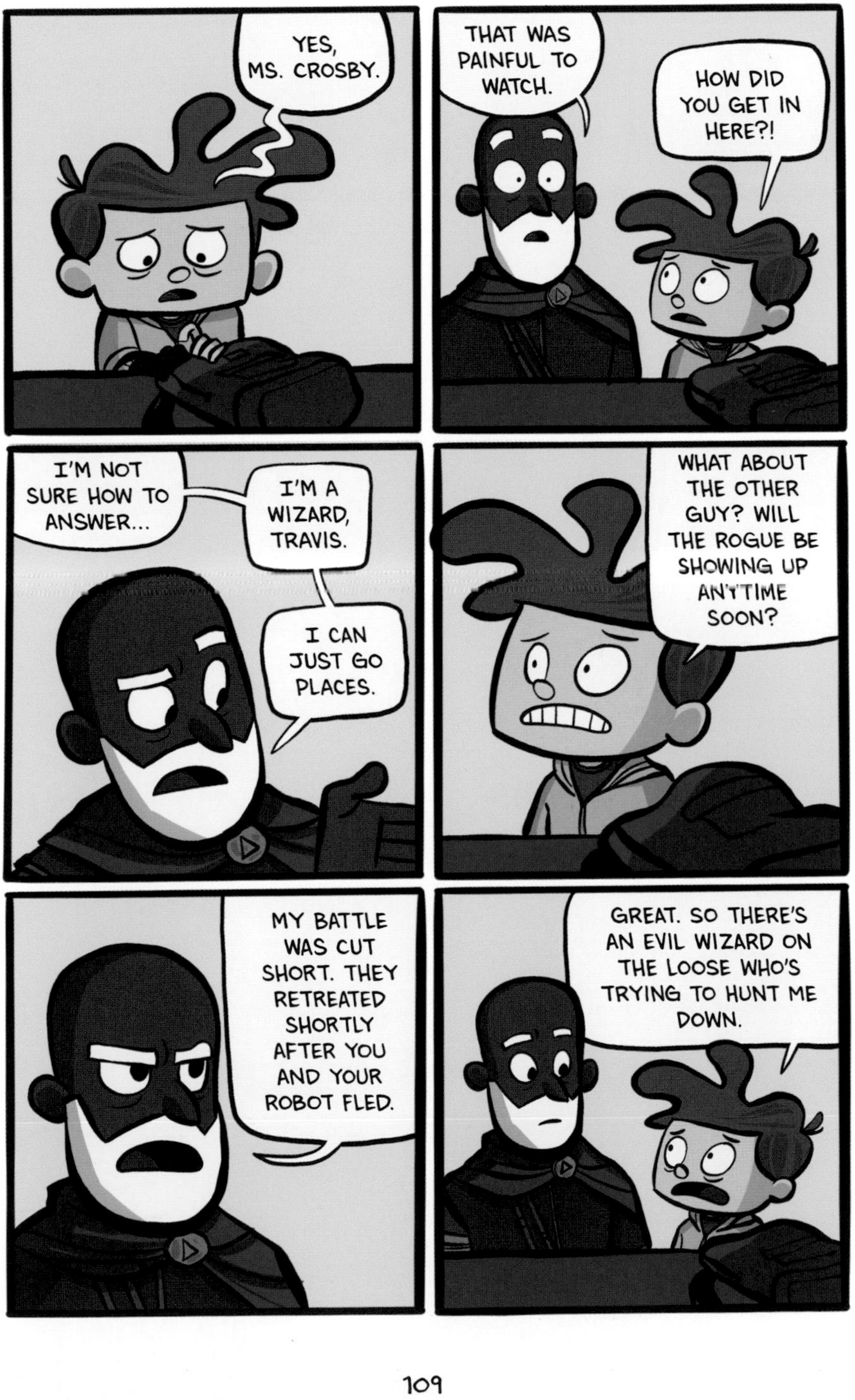
YES, MS. CROSBY.
THAT WAS PAINFUL TO WATCH.
HOW DID YOU GET IN HERE?!
I'M NOT SURE HOW TO ANSWER...
I'M A WIZARD, TRAVIS.
I CAN JUST GO PLACES.
WHAT ABOUT THE OTHER GUY? WILL THE ROGUE BE SHOWING UP ANYTIME SOON?
MY BATTLE WAS CUT SHORT. THEY RETREATED SHORTLY AFTER YOU AND YOUR ROBOT FLED.
GREAT. SO THERE'S AN EVIL WIZARD ON THE LOOSE WHO'S TRYING TO HUNT ME DOWN.

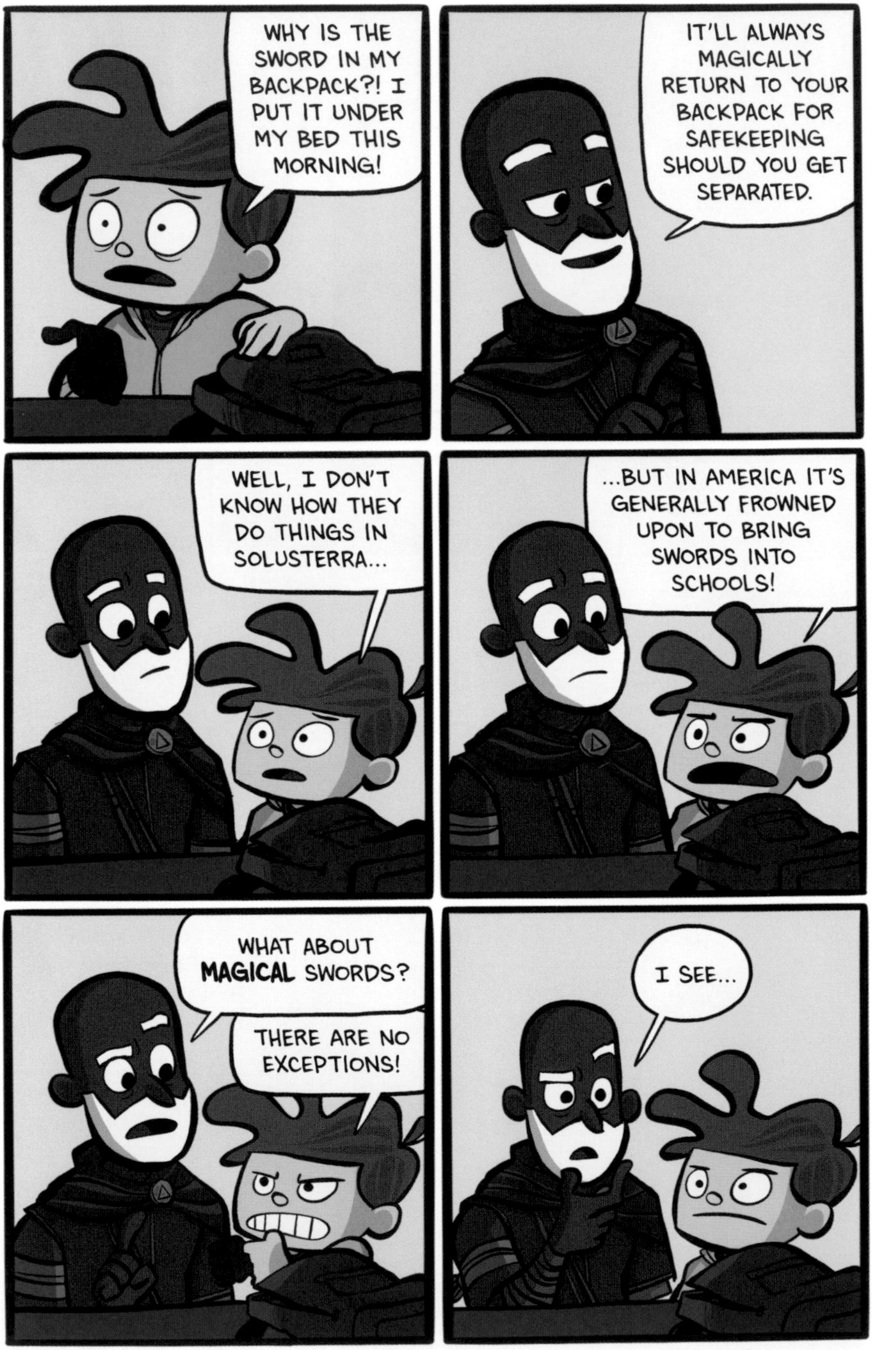
WHY IS THE SWORD IN MY BACKPACK?! I PUT IT UNDER MY BED THIS MORNING!
IT'LL ALWAYS MAGICALLY RETURN TO YOUR BACKPACK FOR SAFEKEEPING SHOULD YOU GET SEPARATED.
WELL, I DON'T KNOW HOW THEY DO THINGS IN SOLUSTERRA...
...BUT IN AMERICA IT'S GENERALLY FROWNED UPON TO BRING SWORDS INTO SCHOOLS!
WHAT ABOUT **MAGICAL** SWORDS?
THERE ARE NO EXCEPTIONS!
I SEE...

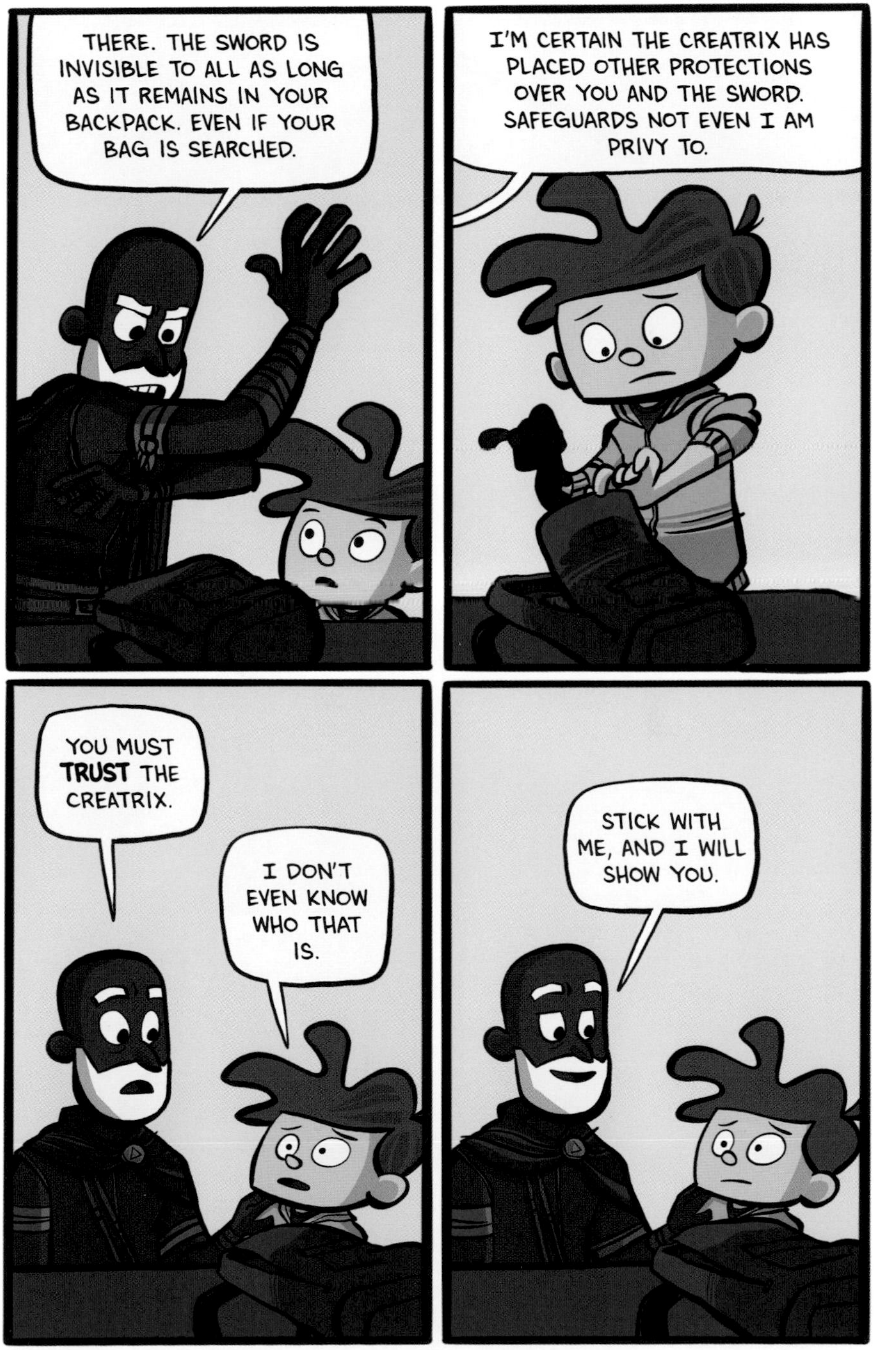
THERE. THE SWORD IS INVISIBLE TO ALL AS LONG AS IT REMAINS IN YOUR BACKPACK. EVEN IF YOUR BAG IS SEARCHED.
I'M CERTAIN THE CREATRIX HAS PLACED OTHER PROTECTIONS OVER YOU AND THE SWORD. SAFEGUARDS NOT EVEN I AM PRIVY TO.
YOU MUST **TRUST** THE CREATRIX.
I DON'T EVEN KNOW WHO THAT IS.
STICK WITH ME, AND I WILL SHOW YOU.

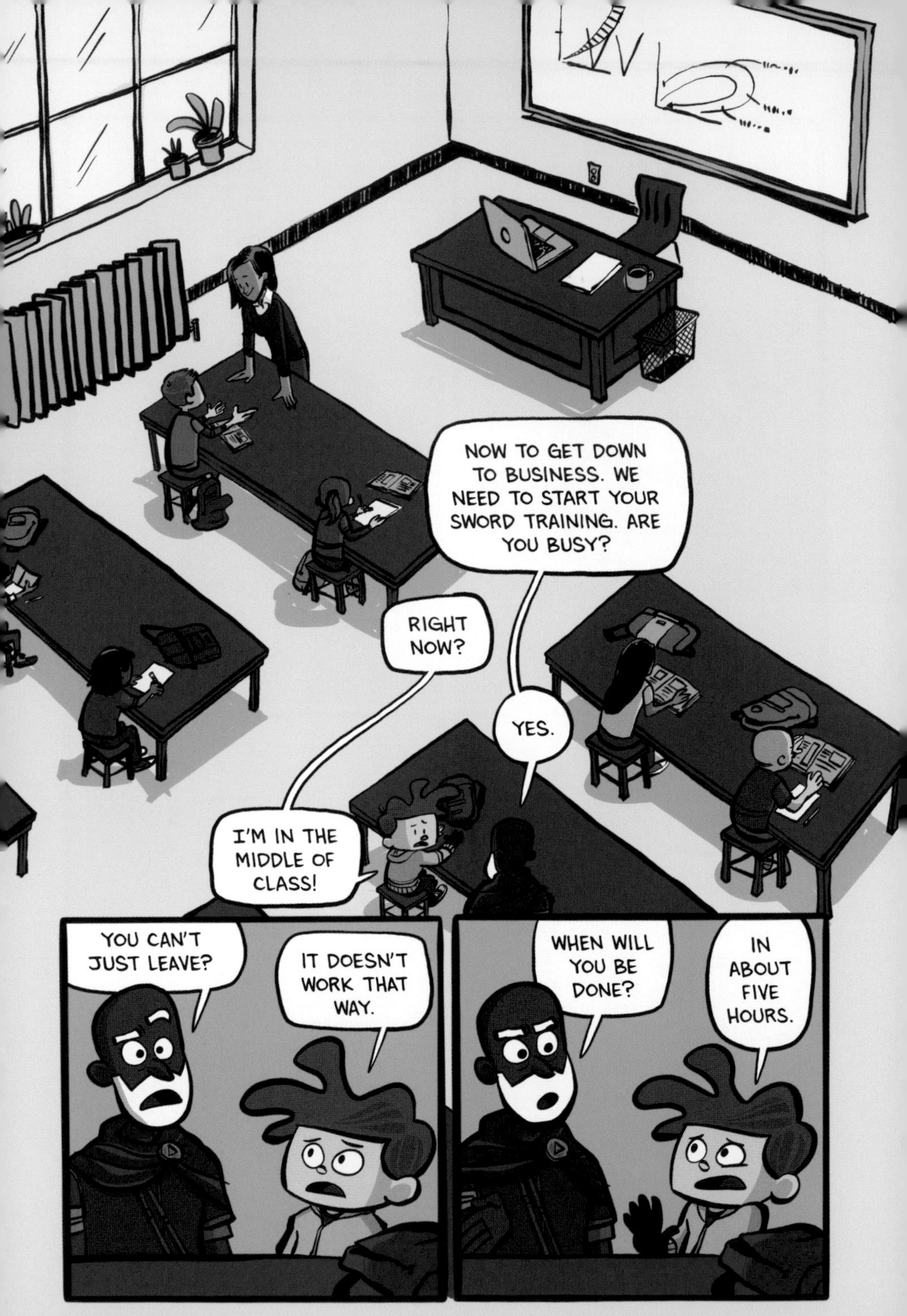
NOW TO GET DOWN TO BUSINESS. WE NEED TO START YOUR SWORD TRAINING. ARE YOU BUSY?
RIGHT NOW?
YES.
I'M IN THE MIDDLE OF CLASS!
YOU CAN'T JUST LEAVE?
IT DOESN'T WORK THAT WAY.
WHEN WILL YOU BE DONE?
IN ABOUT FIVE HOURS.

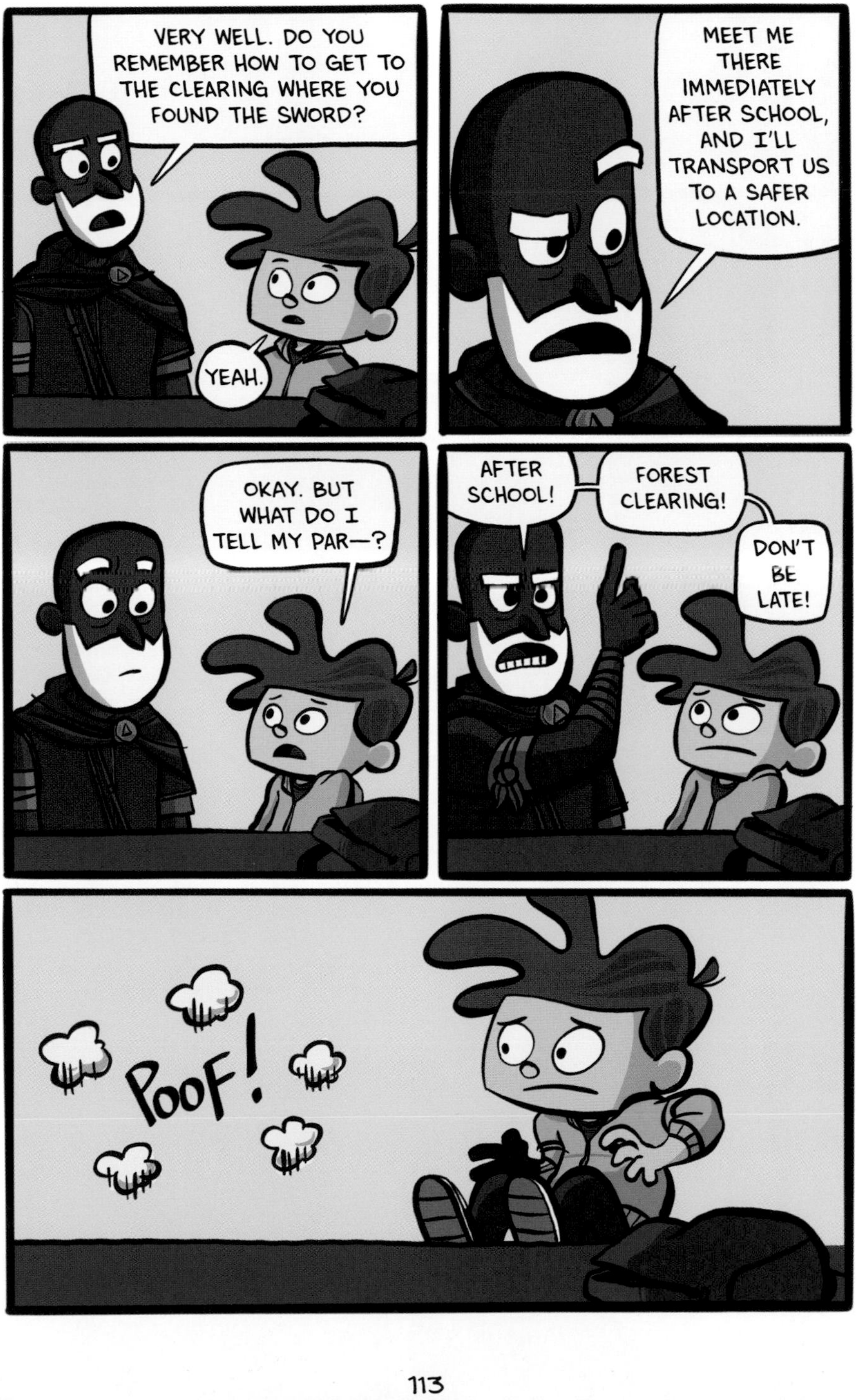
VERY WELL. DO YOU REMEMBER HOW TO GET TO THE CLEARING WHERE YOU FOUND THE SWORD?
YEAH.
MEET ME THERE IMMEDIATELY AFTER SCHOOL, AND I'LL TRANSPORT US TO A SAFER LOCATION.
OKAY. BUT WHAT DO I TELL MY PAR—?
AFTER SCHOOL!
FOREST CLEARING!
DON'T BE LATE!
POOF!

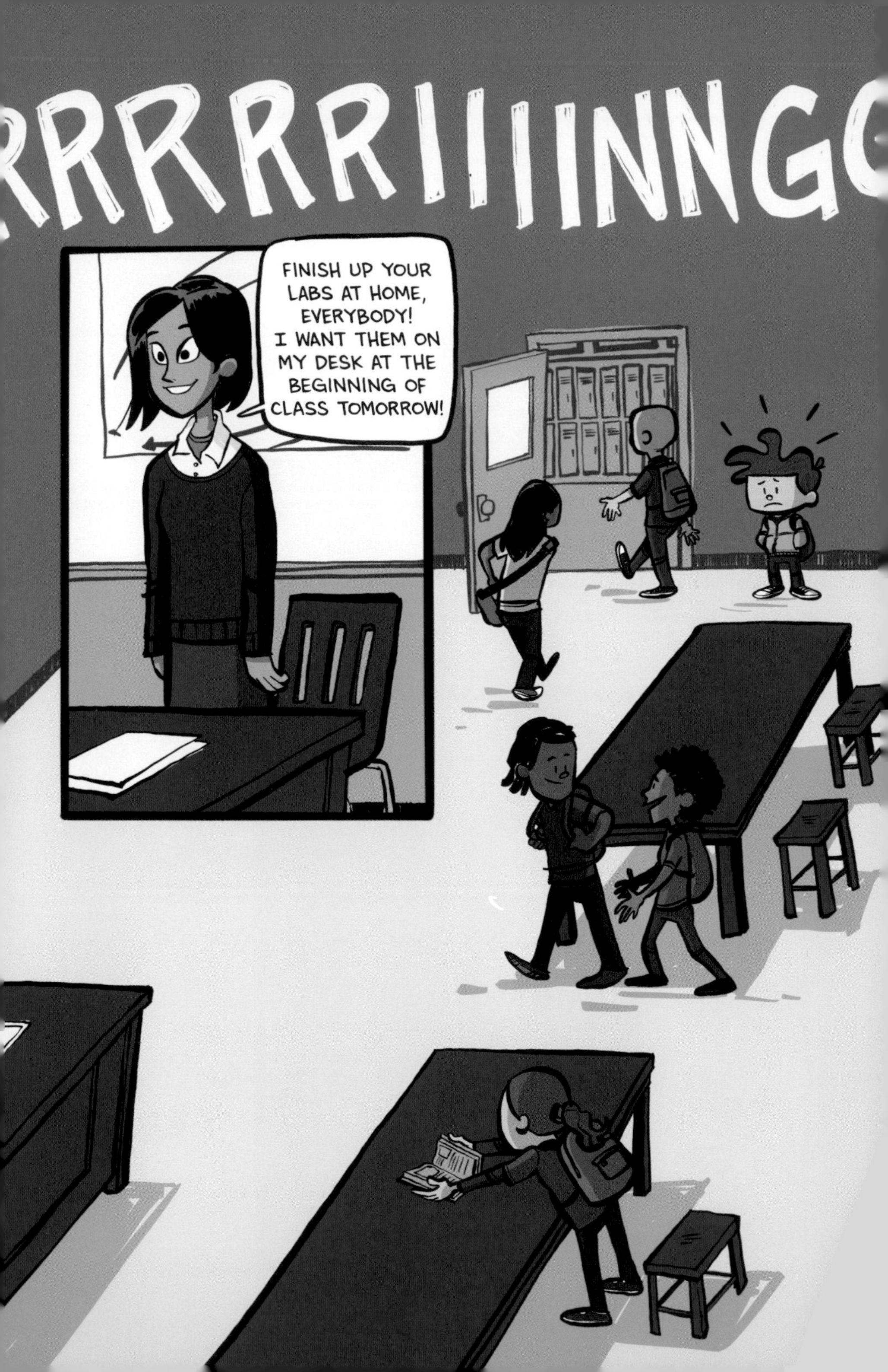
RRRRRRIIIINNG
FINISH UP YOUR LABS AT HOME, EVERYBODY! I WANT THEM ON MY DESK AT THE BEGINNING OF CLASS TOMORROW!

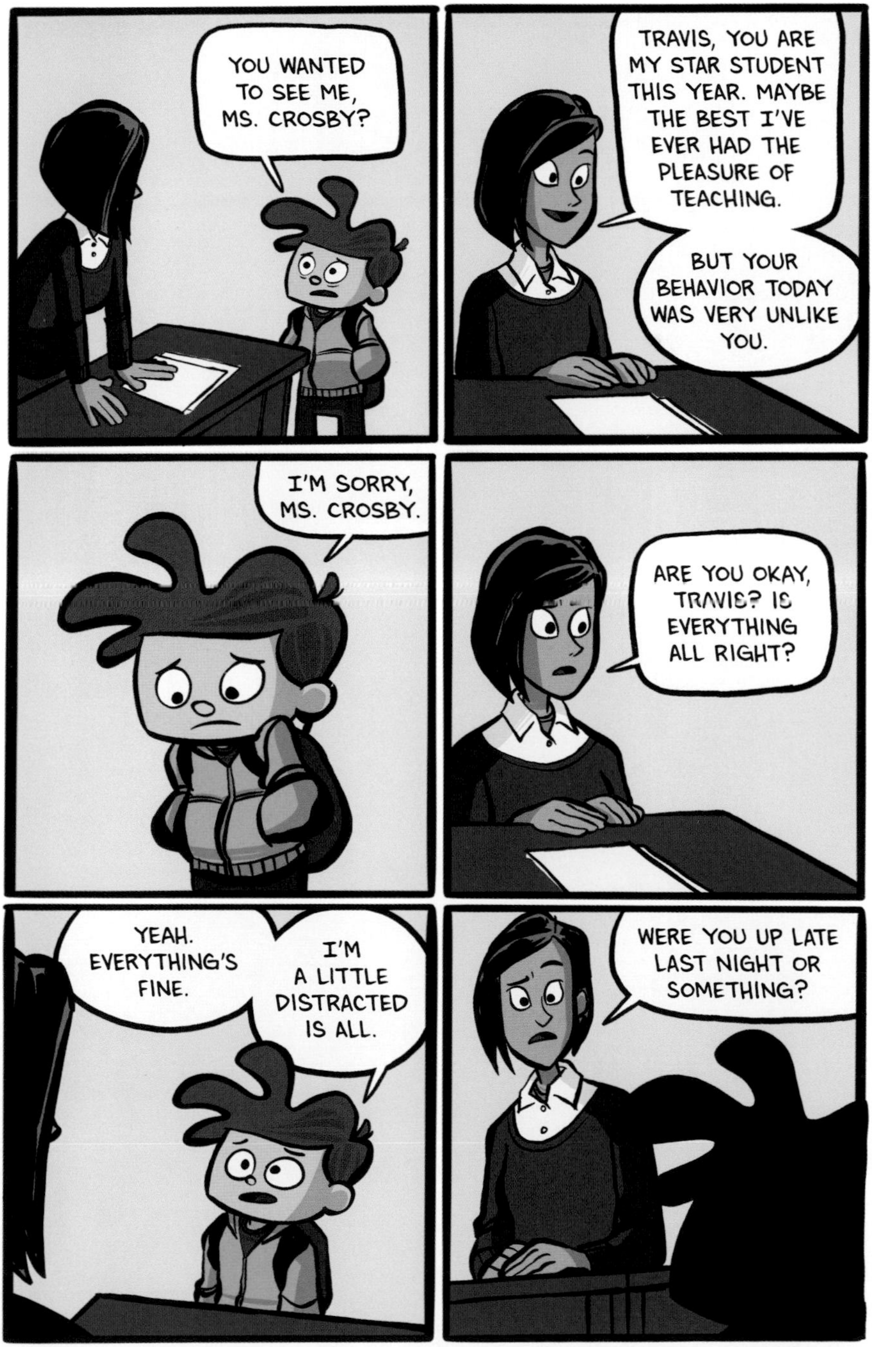
YOU WANTED TO SEE ME, MS. CROSBY?
TRAVIS, YOU ARE MY STAR STUDENT THIS YEAR. MAYBE THE BEST I'VE EVER HAD THE PLEASURE OF TEACHING.
BUT YOUR BEHAVIOR TODAY WAS VERY UNLIKE YOU.
I'M SORRY, MS. CROSBY.
ARE YOU OKAY, TRAVIS? IS EVERYTHING ALL RIGHT?
YEAH. EVERYTHING'S FINE.
I'M A LITTLE DISTRACTED IS ALL.
WERE YOU UP LATE LAST NIGHT OR SOMETHING?

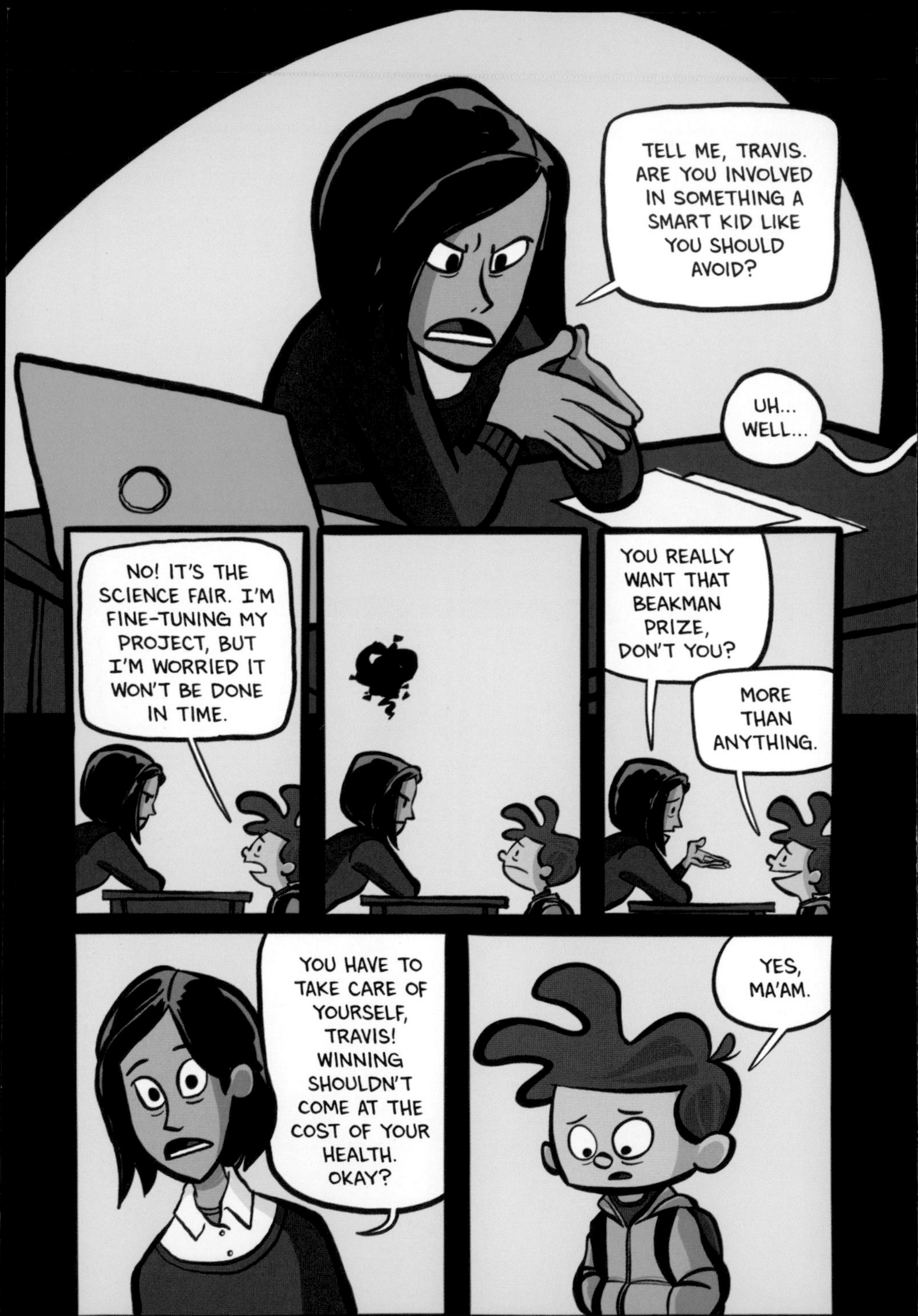
TELL ME, TRAVIS. ARE YOU INVOLVED IN SOMETHING A SMART KID LIKE YOU SHOULD AVOID?
UH... WELL...
NO! IT'S THE SCIENCE FAIR. I'M FINE-TUNING MY PROJECT, BUT I'M WORRIED IT WON'T BE DONE IN TIME.
YOU REALLY WANT THAT BEAKMAN PRIZE, DON'T YOU?
MORE THAN ANYTHING.
YOU HAVE TO TAKE CARE OF YOURSELF, TRAVIS! WINNING SHOULDN'T COME AT THE COST OF YOUR HEALTH. OKAY?
YES, MA'AM.

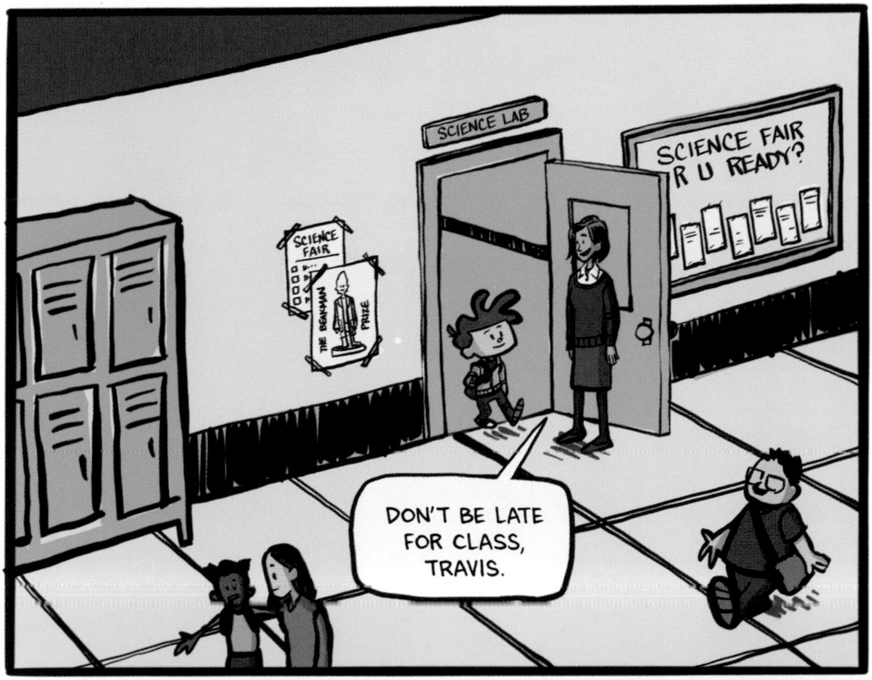
SCIENCE LAB
SCIENCE FAIR R U READY?
SCIENCE FAIR
THE BEAKMAN PRIZE
DON'T BE LATE FOR CLASS, TRAVIS.

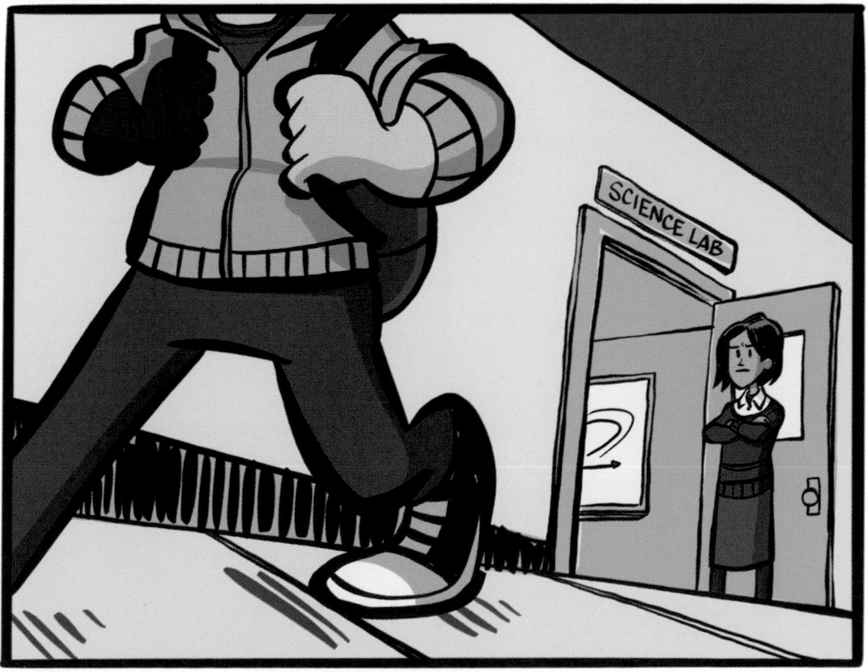
SCIENCE LAB

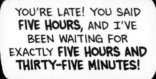

YOU'RE LATE! YOU SAID **FIVE HOURS,** AND I'VE BEEN WAITING FOR EXACTLY **FIVE HOURS AND THIRTY-FIVE MINUTES!**

I RAN HOME AFTER SCHOOL BECAUSE I WANTED TO GET TRAVBOT. AND ALSO I WANTED A SNACK.

OBVIOUSLY, YOU DON'T UNDERSTAND THE URGENCY OF OUR SITUATION. THAT'S MY FAULT.

EVERYONE HOLD HANDS. I'LL EXPLAIN MORE AS WE TRAVEL TO OUR DESTINATION.

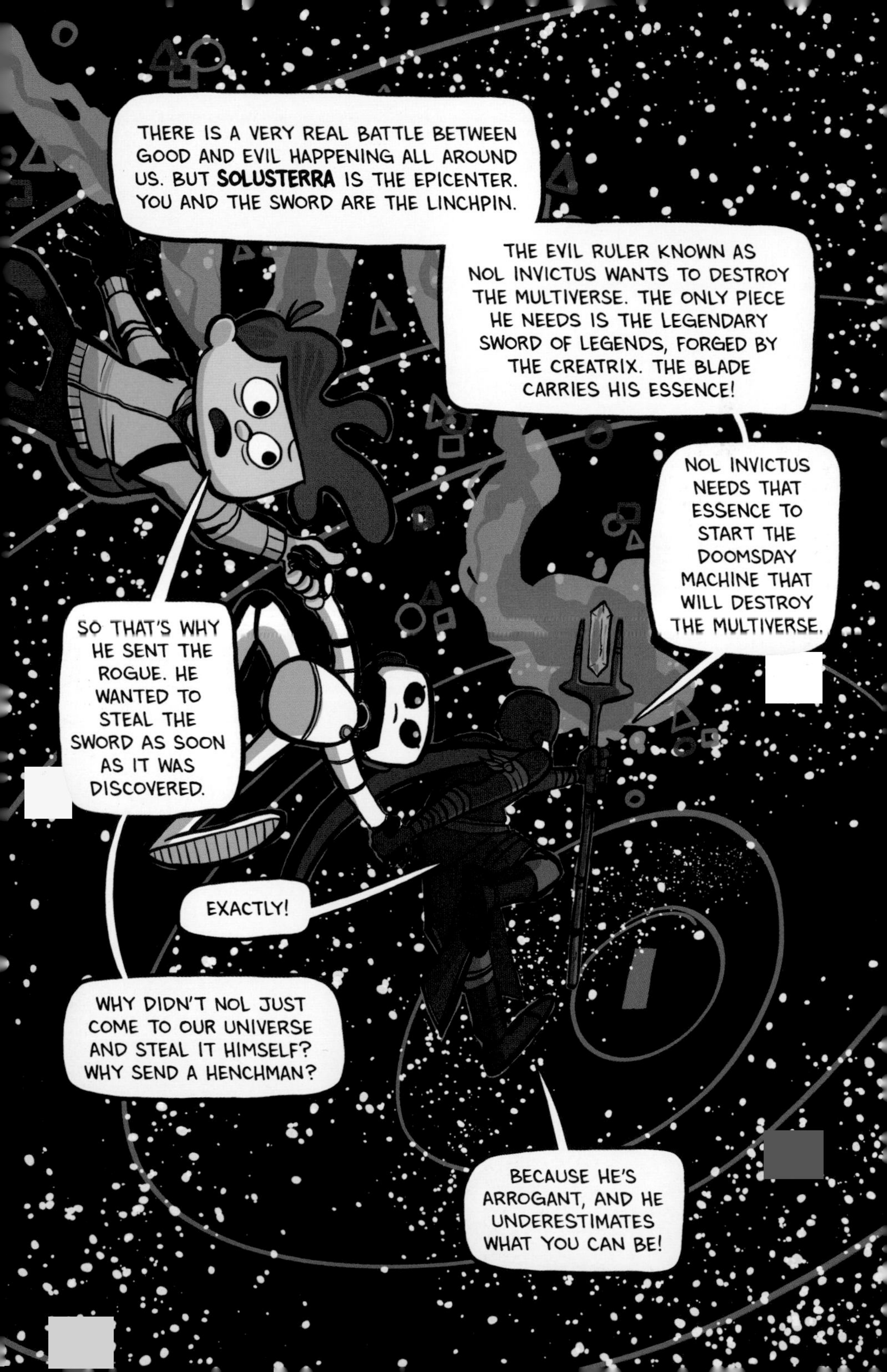
THERE IS A VERY REAL BATTLE BETWEEN GOOD AND EVIL HAPPENING ALL AROUND US. BUT **SOLUSTERRA** IS THE EPICENTER. YOU AND THE SWORD ARE THE LINCHPIN.
THE EVIL RULER KNOWN AS NOL INVICTUS WANTS TO DESTROY THE MULTIVERSE. THE ONLY PIECE HE NEEDS IS THE LEGENDARY SWORD OF LEGENDS, FORGED BY THE CREATRIX. THE BLADE CARRIES HIS ESSENCE!
NOL INVICTUS NEEDS THAT ESSENCE TO START THE DOOMSDAY MACHINE THAT WILL DESTROY THE MULTIVERSE.
SO THAT'S WHY HE SENT THE ROGUE. HE WANTED TO STEAL THE SWORD AS SOON AS IT WAS DISCOVERED.
EXACTLY!
WHY DIDN'T NOL JUST COME TO OUR UNIVERSE AND STEAL IT HIMSELF? WHY SEND A HENCHMAN?
BECAUSE HE'S ARROGANT, AND HE UNDERESTIMATES WHAT YOU CAN BE!

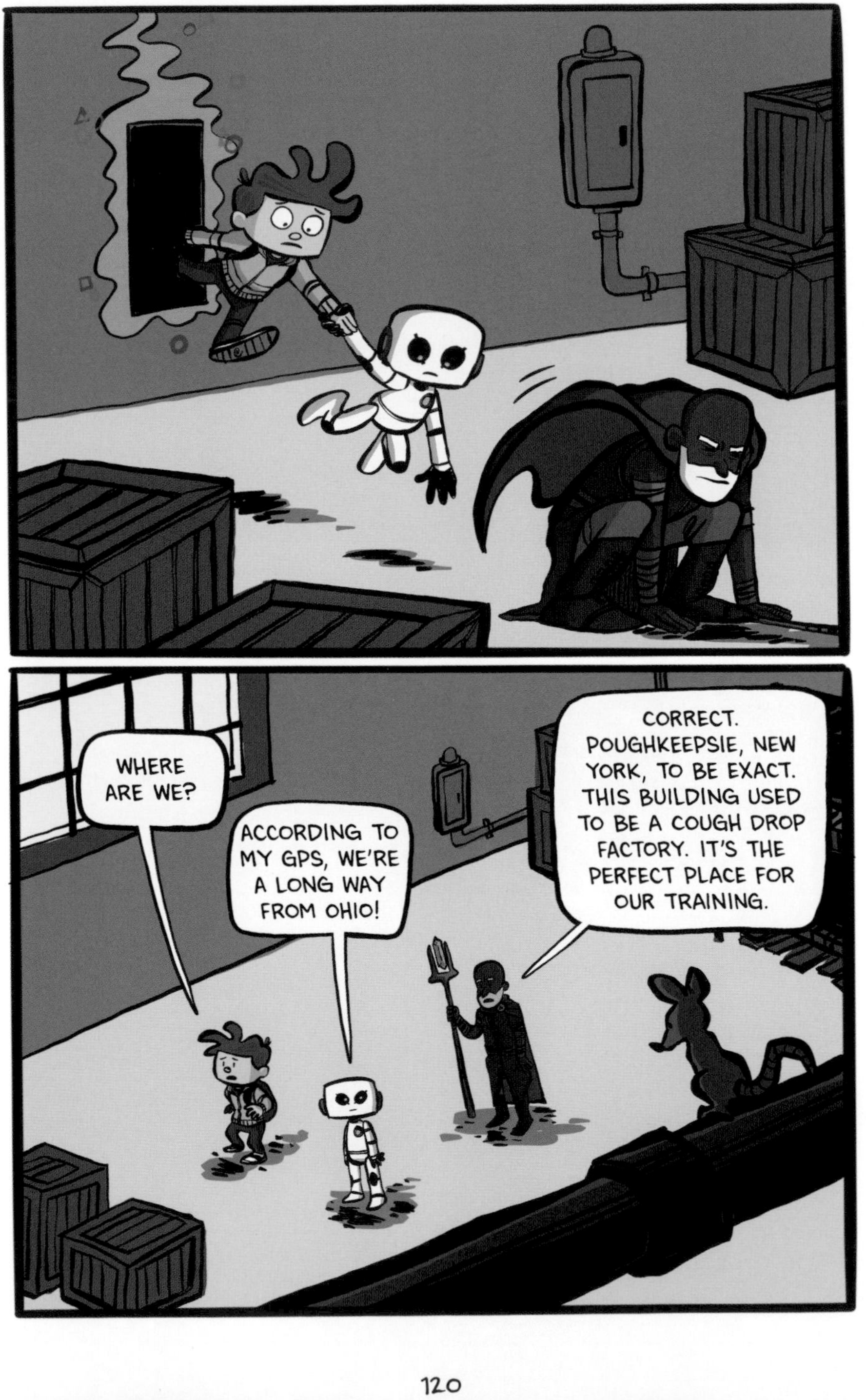
WHERE ARE WE?
ACCORDING TO MY GPS, WE'RE A LONG WAY FROM OHIO!
CORRECT. POUGHKEEPSIE, NEW YORK, TO BE EXACT. THIS BUILDING USED TO BE A COUGH DROP FACTORY. IT'S THE PERFECT PLACE FOR OUR TRAINING.

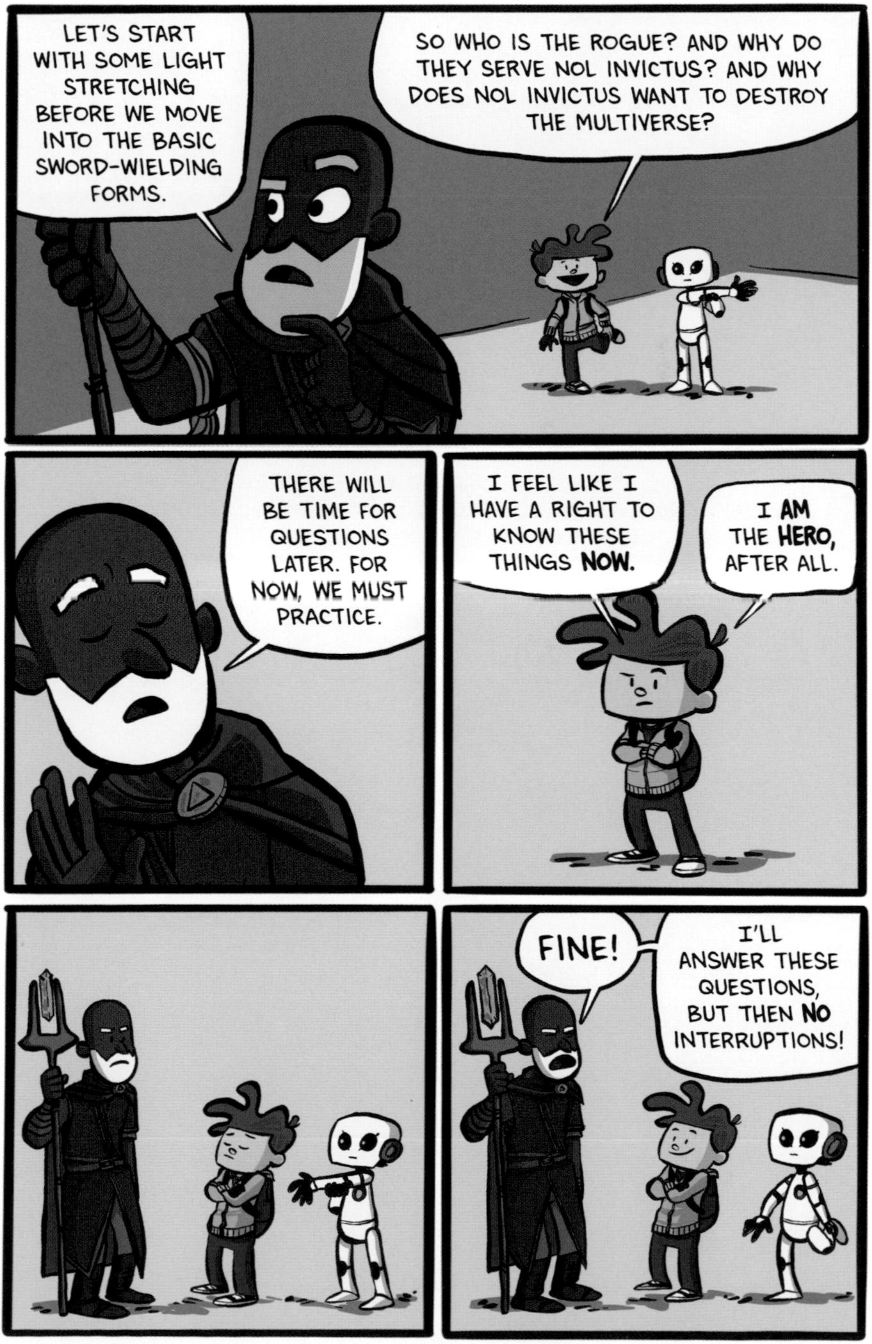
LET'S START WITH SOME LIGHT STRETCHING BEFORE WE MOVE INTO THE BASIC SWORD-WIELDING FORMS.
SO WHO IS THE ROGUE? AND WHY DO THEY SERVE NOL INVICTUS? AND WHY DOES NOL INVICTUS WANT TO DESTROY THE MULTIVERSE?
THERE WILL BE TIME FOR QUESTIONS LATER. FOR NOW, WE MUST PRACTICE.
I FEEL LIKE I HAVE A RIGHT TO KNOW THESE THINGS **NOW.**
I **AM** THE **HERO,** AFTER ALL.
FINE!
I'LL ANSWER THESE QUESTIONS, BUT THEN **NO** INTERRUPTIONS!

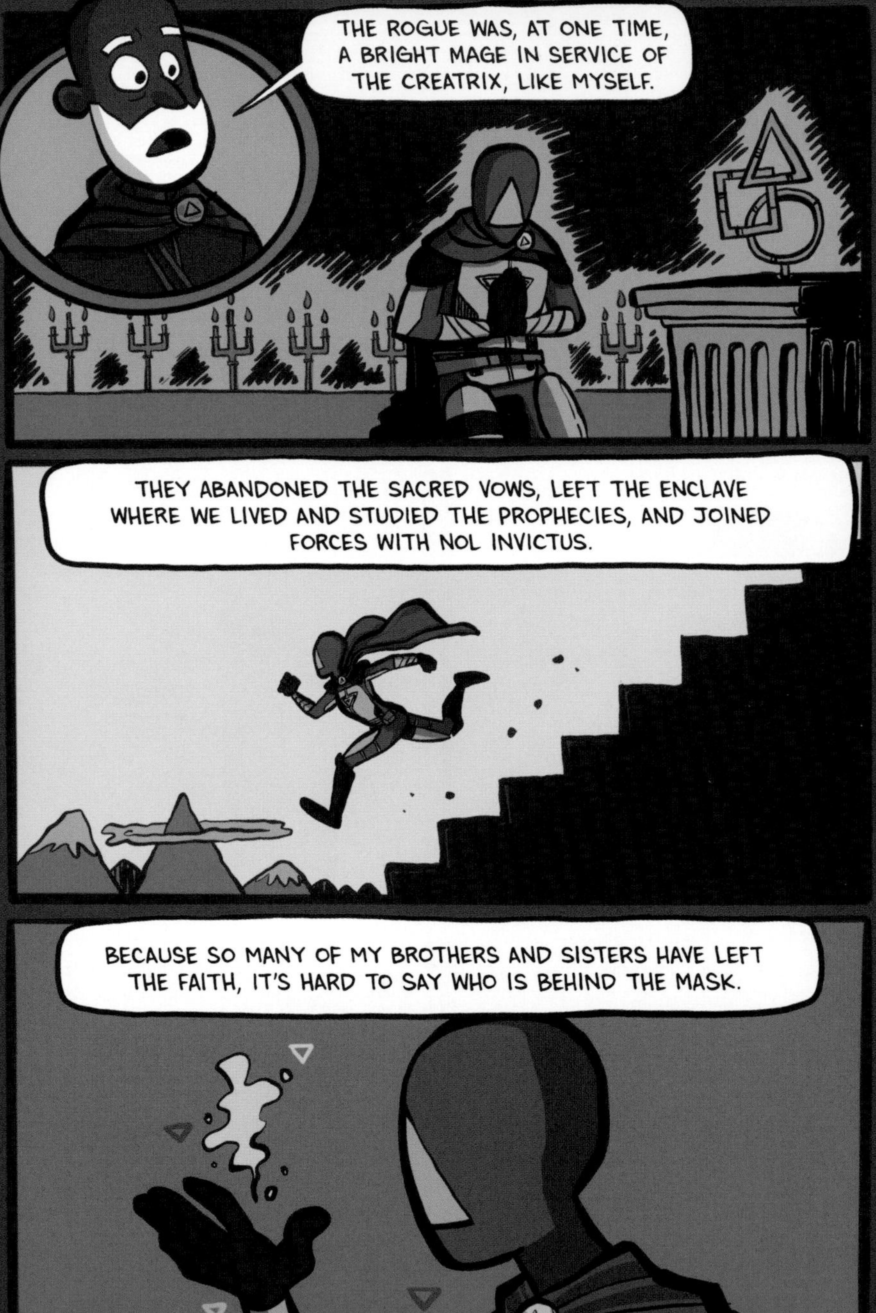
THE ROGUE WAS, AT ONE TIME, A BRIGHT MAGE IN SERVICE OF THE CREATRIX, LIKE MYSELF.
THEY ABANDONED THE SACRED VOWS, LEFT THE ENCLAVE WHERE WE LIVED AND STUDIED THE PROPHECIES, AND JOINED FORCES WITH NOL INVICTUS.
BECAUSE SO MANY OF MY BROTHERS AND SISTERS HAVE LEFT THE FAITH, IT'S HARD TO SAY WHO IS BEHIND THE MASK.

NOW, YOU MAY WONDER WHY THE ROGUE WOULD BE IN LEAGUE WITH NOL INVICTUS. WHY NOT?
NOL IS POWERFUL. HE'S CHARISMATIC. HE'S RICH. HE FULFILLS THE DESIRES OF HIS FOLLOWERS' HEARTS AS LONG AS THEY BOW TO HIM.
A LIFE DEVOTED TO THE CREATRIX, HOWEVER, IS ONE OF HUMILITY, DELAYED GRATIFICATION, AND SILENCE.

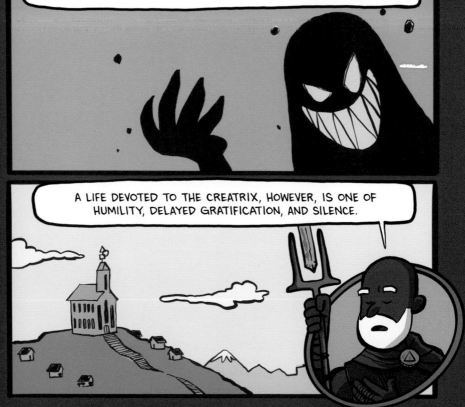

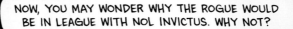

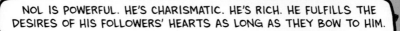

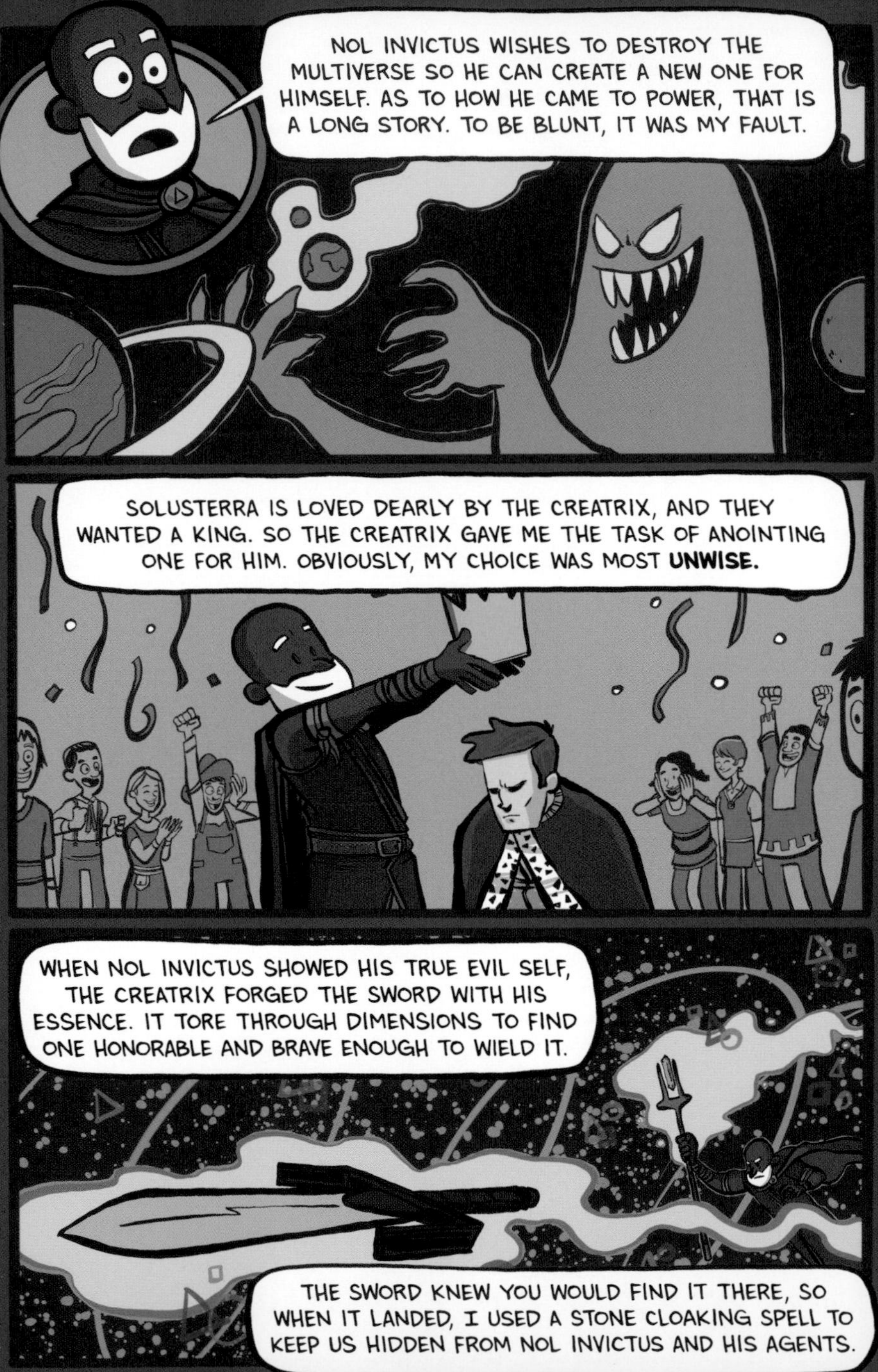
NOL INVICTUS WISHES TO DESTROY THE MULTIVERSE SO HE CAN CREATE A NEW ONE FOR HIMSELF. AS TO HOW HE CAME TO POWER, THAT IS A LONG STORY. TO BE BLUNT, IT WAS MY FAULT.
SOLUSTERRA IS LOVED DEARLY BY THE CREATRIX, AND THEY WANTED A KING. SO THE CREATRIX GAVE ME THE TASK OF ANOINTING ONE FOR HIM. OBVIOUSLY, MY CHOICE WAS MOST **UNWISE.**
WHEN NOL INVICTUS SHOWED HIS TRUE EVIL SELF, THE CREATRIX FORGED THE SWORD WITH HIS ESSENCE. IT TORE THROUGH DIMENSIONS TO FIND ONE HONORABLE AND BRAVE ENOUGH TO WIELD IT.
THE SWORD KNEW YOU WOULD FIND IT THERE, SO WHEN IT LANDED, I USED A STONE CLOAKING SPELL TO KEEP US HIDDEN FROM NOL INVICTUS AND HIS AGENTS.

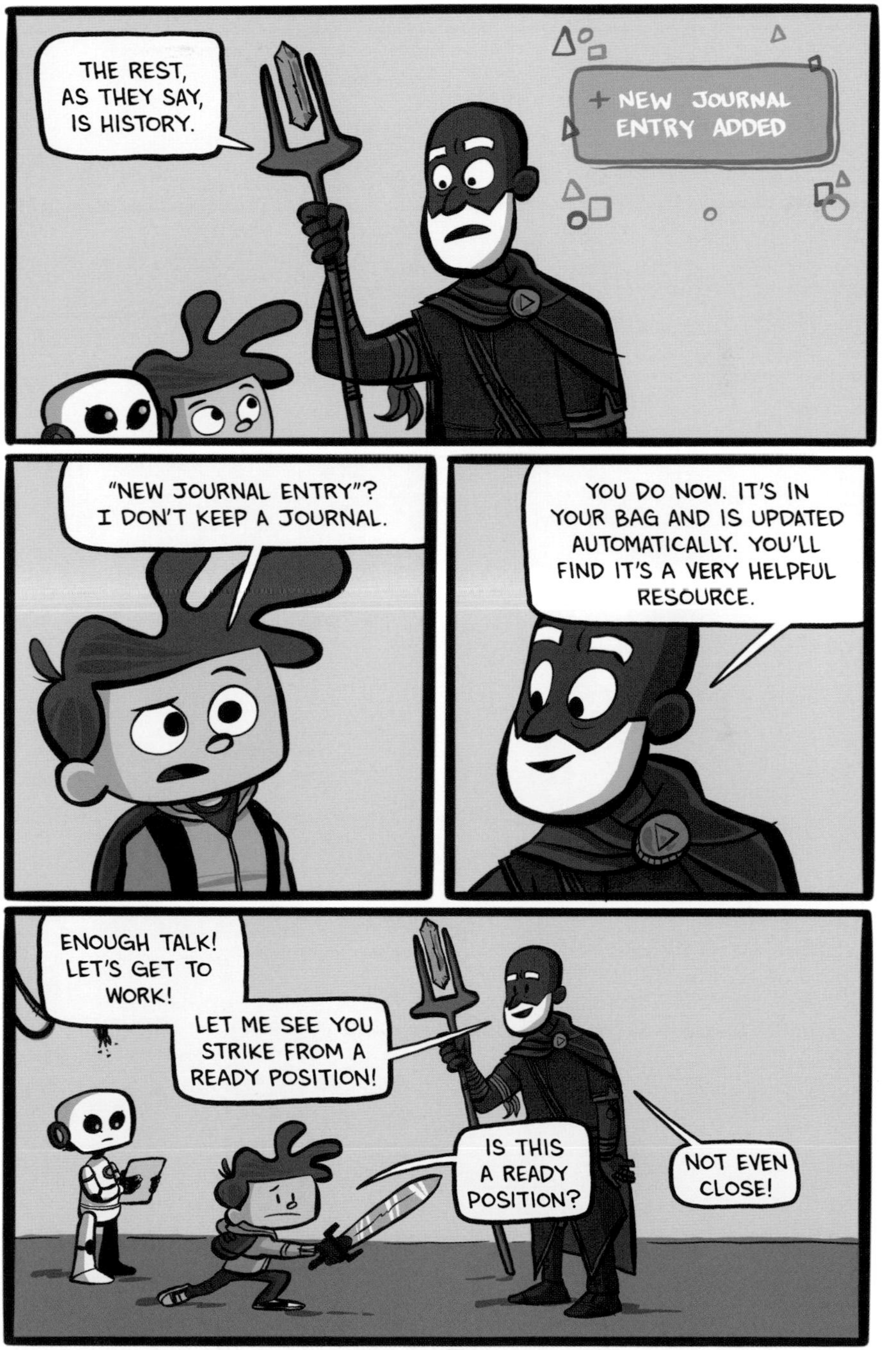
THE REST, AS THEY SAY, IS HISTORY.
+ NEW JOURNAL ENTRY ADDED
"NEW JOURNAL ENTRY"? I DON'T KEEP A JOURNAL.
YOU DO NOW. IT'S IN YOUR BAG AND IS UPDATED AUTOMATICALLY. YOU'LL FIND IT'S A VERY HELPFUL RESOURCE.
ENOUGH TALK! LET'S GET TO WORK!
LET ME SEE YOU STRIKE FROM A READY POSITION!
IS THIS A READY POSITION?
NOT EVEN CLOSE!

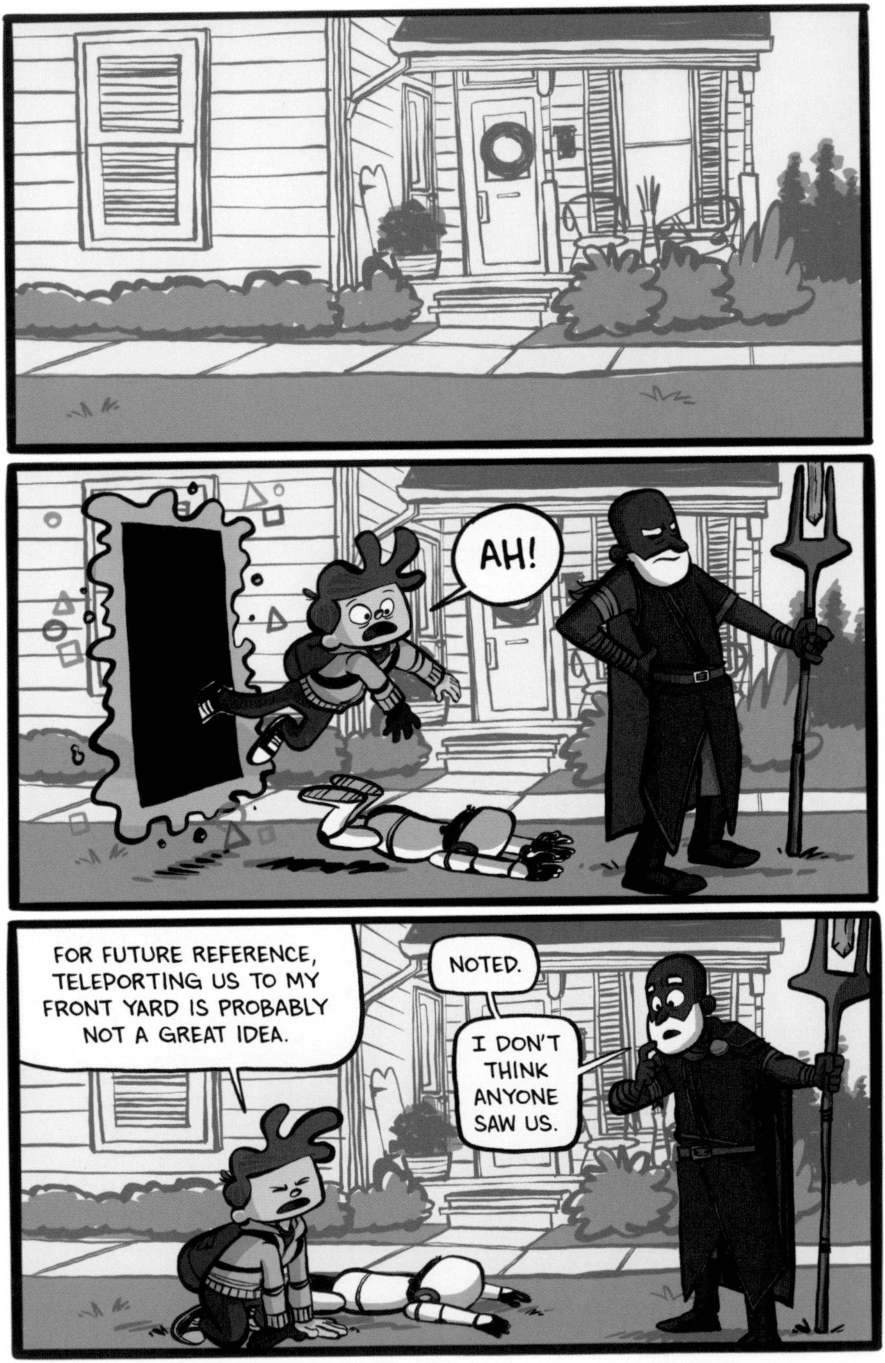
AH!
FOR FUTURE REFERENCE, TELEPORTING US TO MY FRONT YARD IS PROBABLY NOT A GREAT IDEA.
NOTED.
I DON'T THINK ANYONE SAW US.

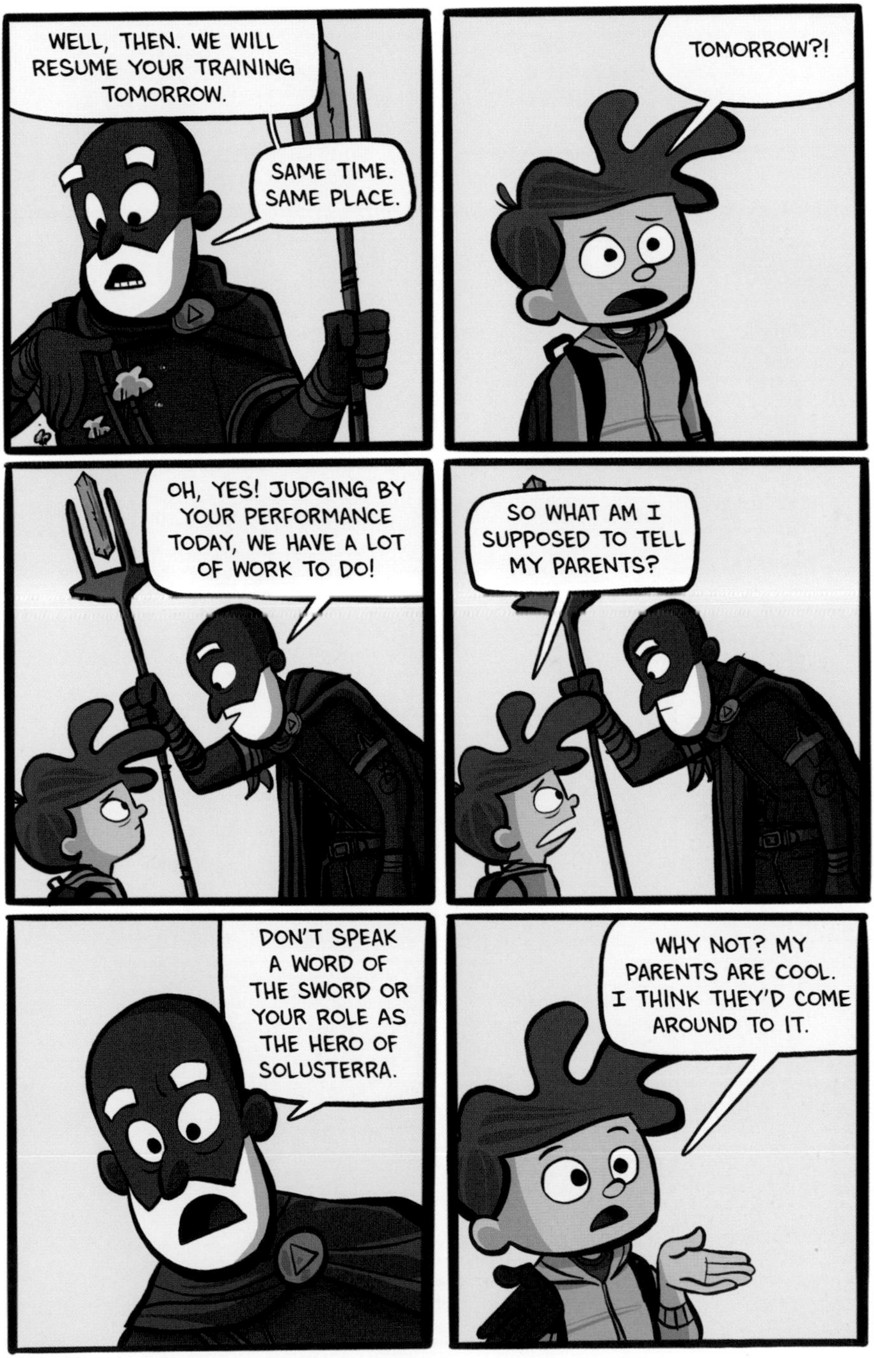
WELL, THEN. WE WILL RESUME YOUR TRAINING TOMORROW.
SAME TIME. SAME PLACE.
TOMORROW?!
OH, YES! JUDGING BY YOUR PERFORMANCE TODAY, WE HAVE A LOT OF WORK TO DO!
SO WHAT AM I SUPPOSED TO TELL MY PARENTS?
DON'T SPEAK A WORD OF THE SWORD OR YOUR ROLE AS THE HERO OF SOLUSTERRA.
WHY NOT? MY PARENTS ARE COOL. I THINK THEY'D COME AROUND TO IT.

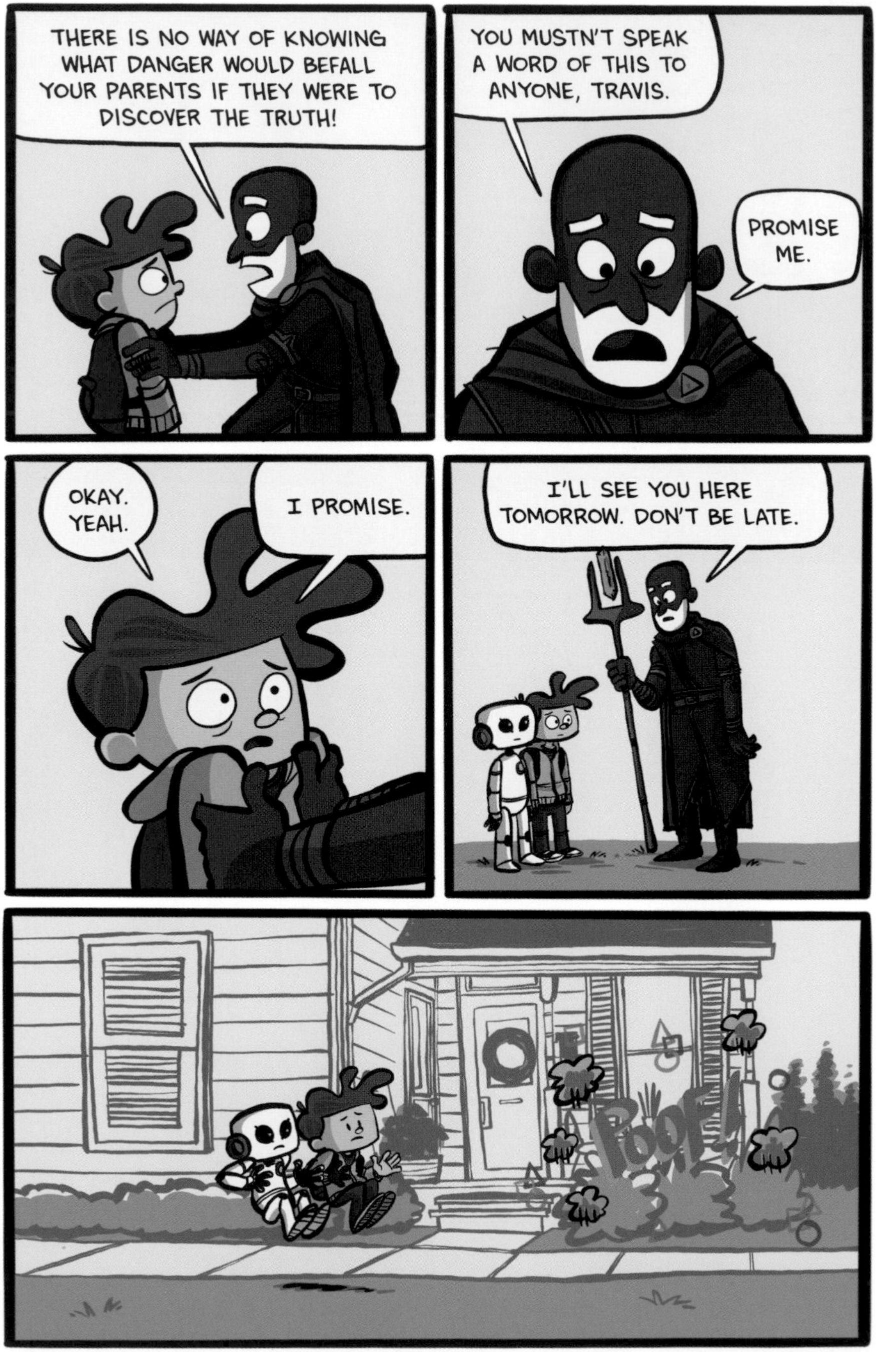
THERE IS NO WAY OF KNOWING WHAT DANGER WOULD BEFALL YOUR PARENTS IF THEY WERE TO DISCOVER THE TRUTH!
YOU MUSTN'T SPEAK A WORD OF THIS TO ANYONE, TRAVIS.
PROMISE ME.
OKAY. YEAH.
I PROMISE.
I'LL SEE YOU HERE TOMORROW. DON'T BE LATE.
POOF!

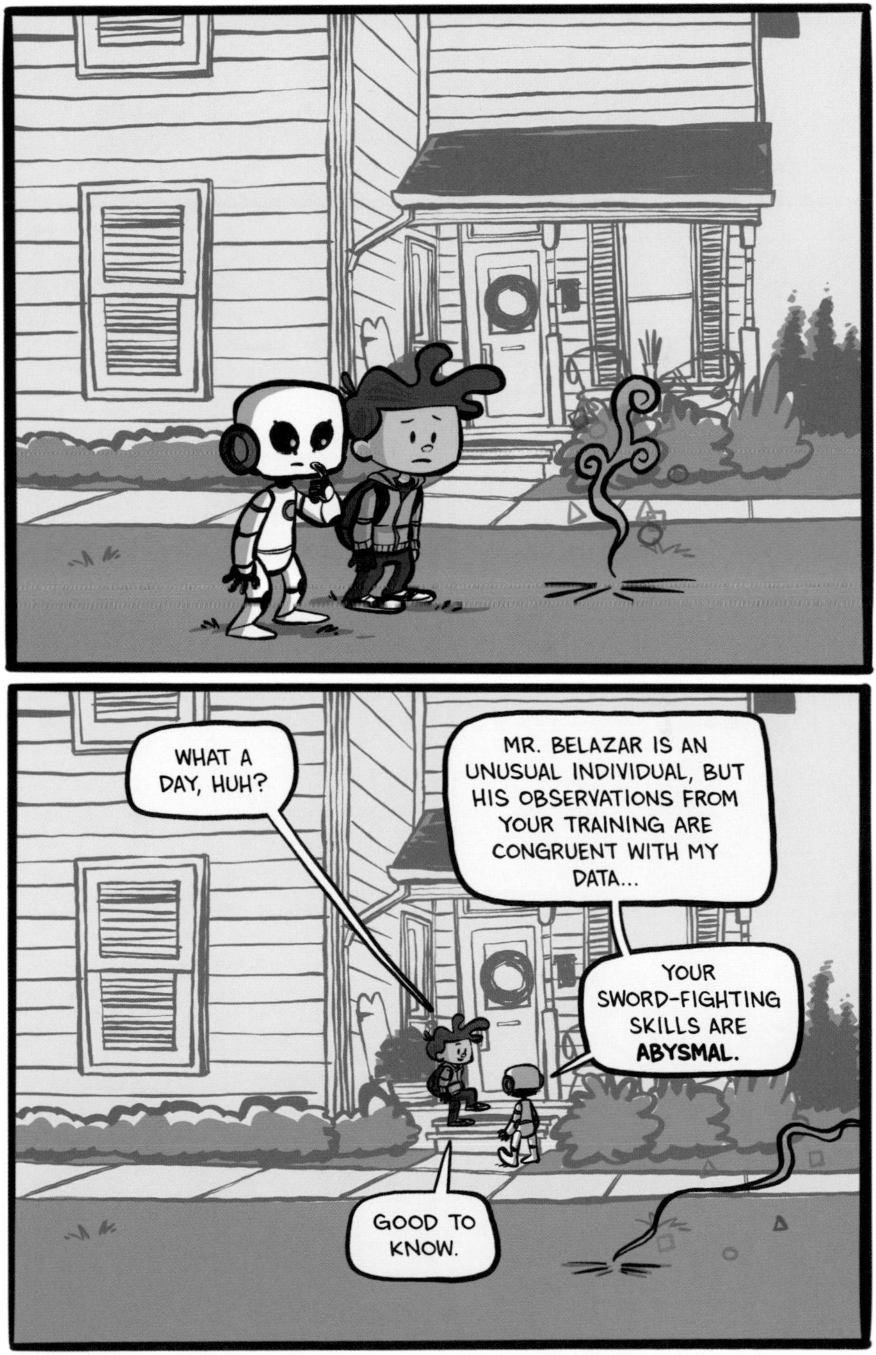
WHAT A DAY, HUH?
MR. BELAZAR IS AN UNUSUAL INDIVIDUAL, BUT HIS OBSERVATIONS FROM YOUR TRAINING ARE CONGRUENT WITH MY DATA...
YOUR SWORD-FIGHTING SKILLS ARE **ABYSMAL.**
GOOD TO KNOW.

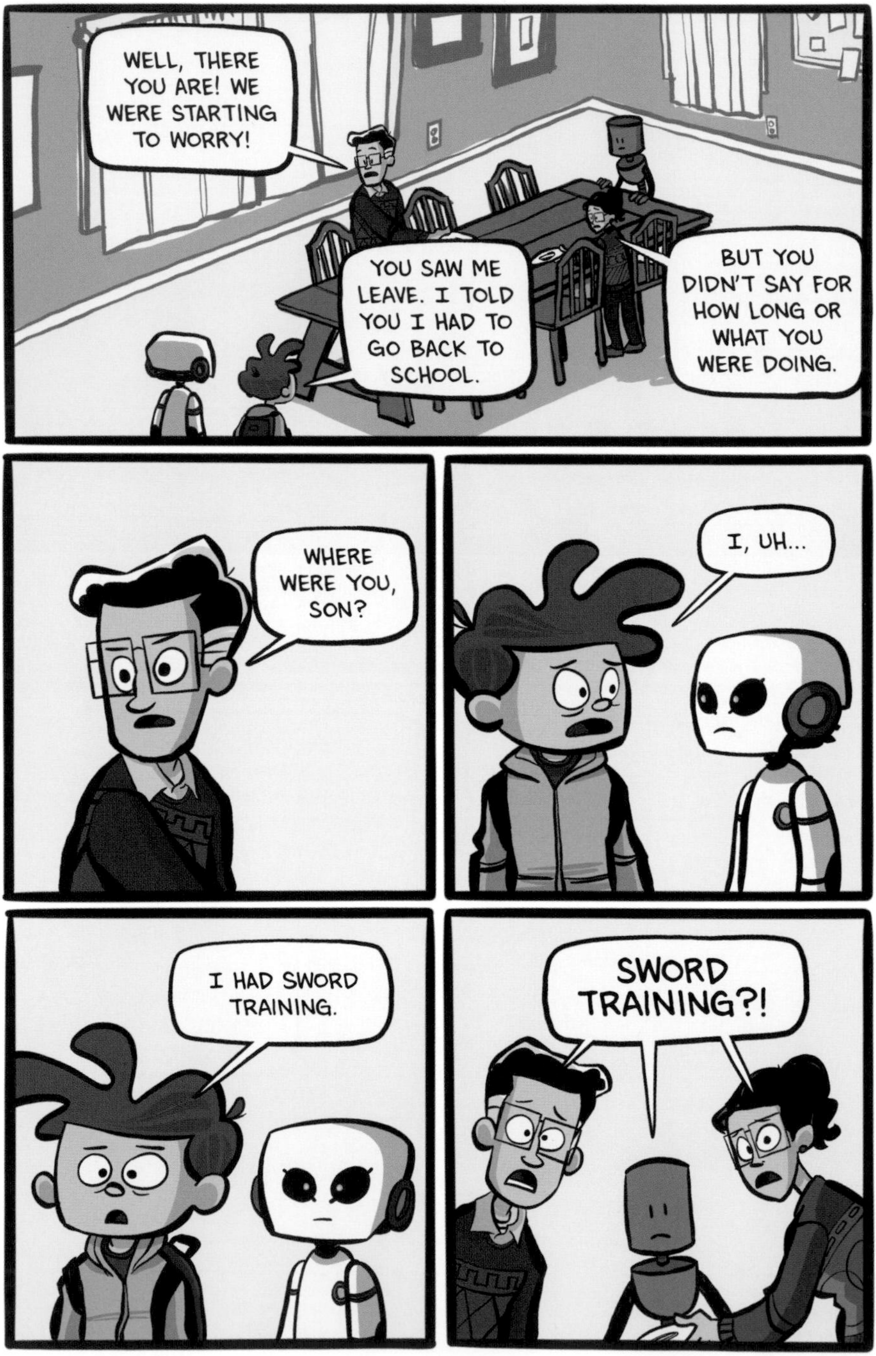
WELL, THERE YOU ARE! WE WERE STARTING TO WORRY!
YOU SAW ME LEAVE. I TOLD YOU I HAD TO GO BACK TO SCHOOL.
BUT YOU DIDN'T SAY FOR HOW LONG OR WHAT YOU WERE DOING.
WHERE WERE YOU, SON?
I, UH...
I HAD SWORD TRAINING.
SWORD TRAINING?!

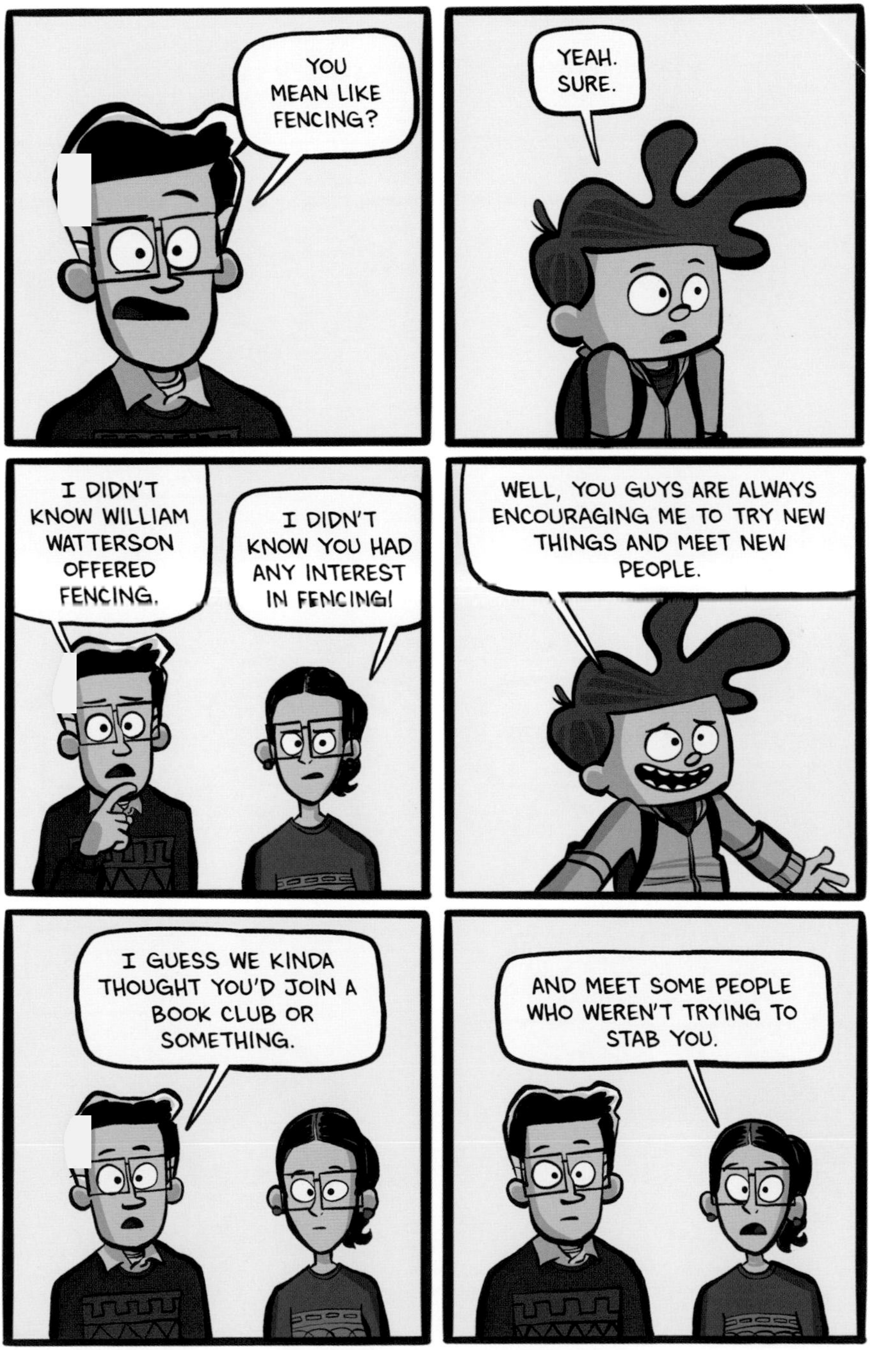
YOU MEAN LIKE FENCING?
YEAH. SURE.
I DIDN'T KNOW WILLIAM WATTERSON OFFERED FENCING.
I DIDN'T KNOW YOU HAD ANY INTEREST IN FENCING!
WELL, YOU GUYS ARE ALWAYS ENCOURAGING ME TO TRY NEW THINGS AND MEET NEW PEOPLE.
I GUESS WE KINDA THOUGHT YOU'D JOIN A BOOK CLUB OR SOMETHING.
AND MEET SOME PEOPLE WHO WEREN'T TRYING TO STAB YOU.

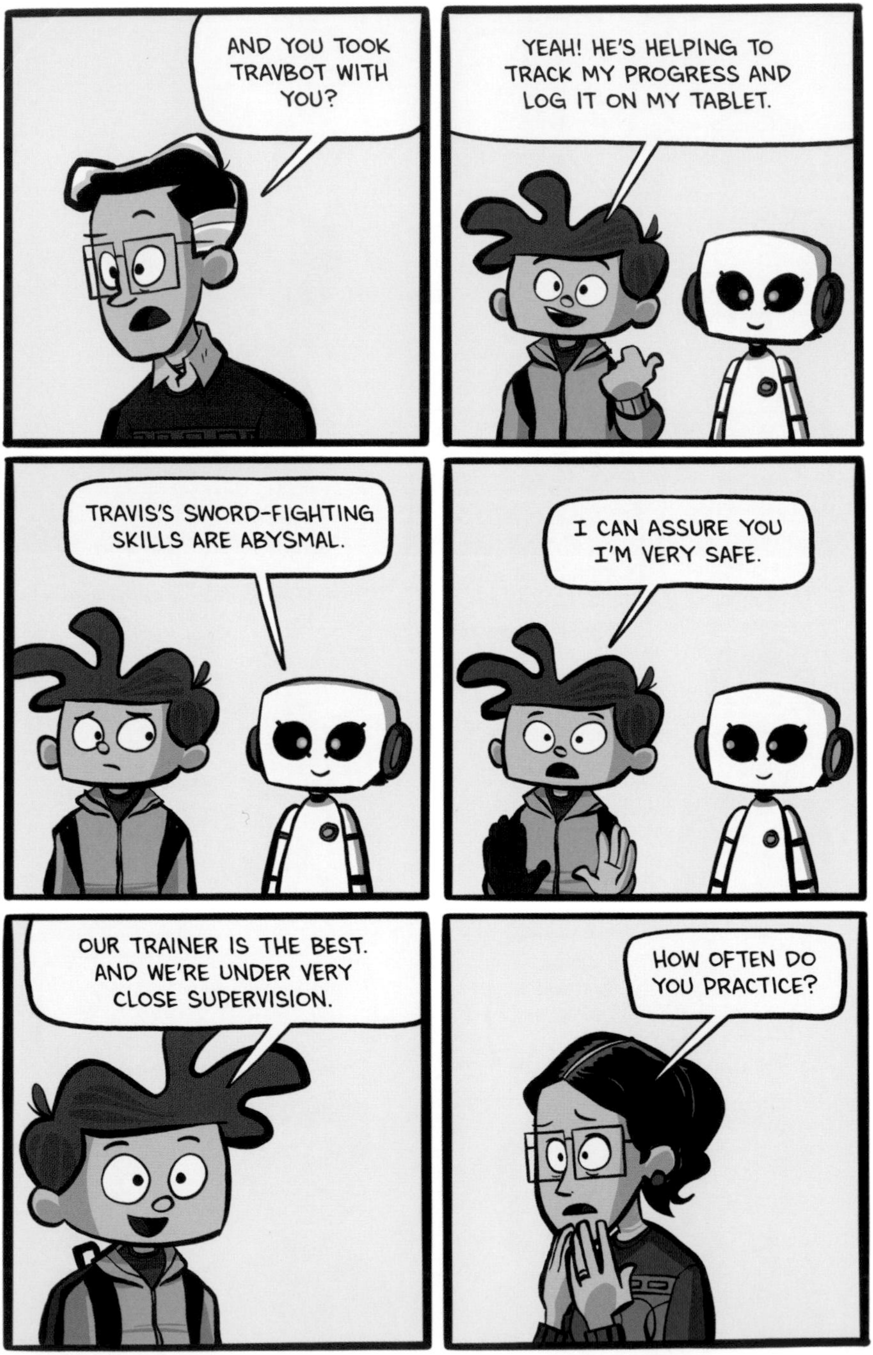
AND YOU TOOK TRAVBOT WITH YOU?
YEAH! HE'S HELPING TO TRACK MY PROGRESS AND LOG IT ON MY TABLET.
TRAVIS'S SWORD-FIGHTING SKILLS ARE ABYSMAL.
I CAN ASSURE YOU I'M VERY SAFE.
OUR TRAINER IS THE BEST. AND WE'RE UNDER VERY CLOSE SUPERVISION.
HOW OFTEN DO YOU PRACTICE?

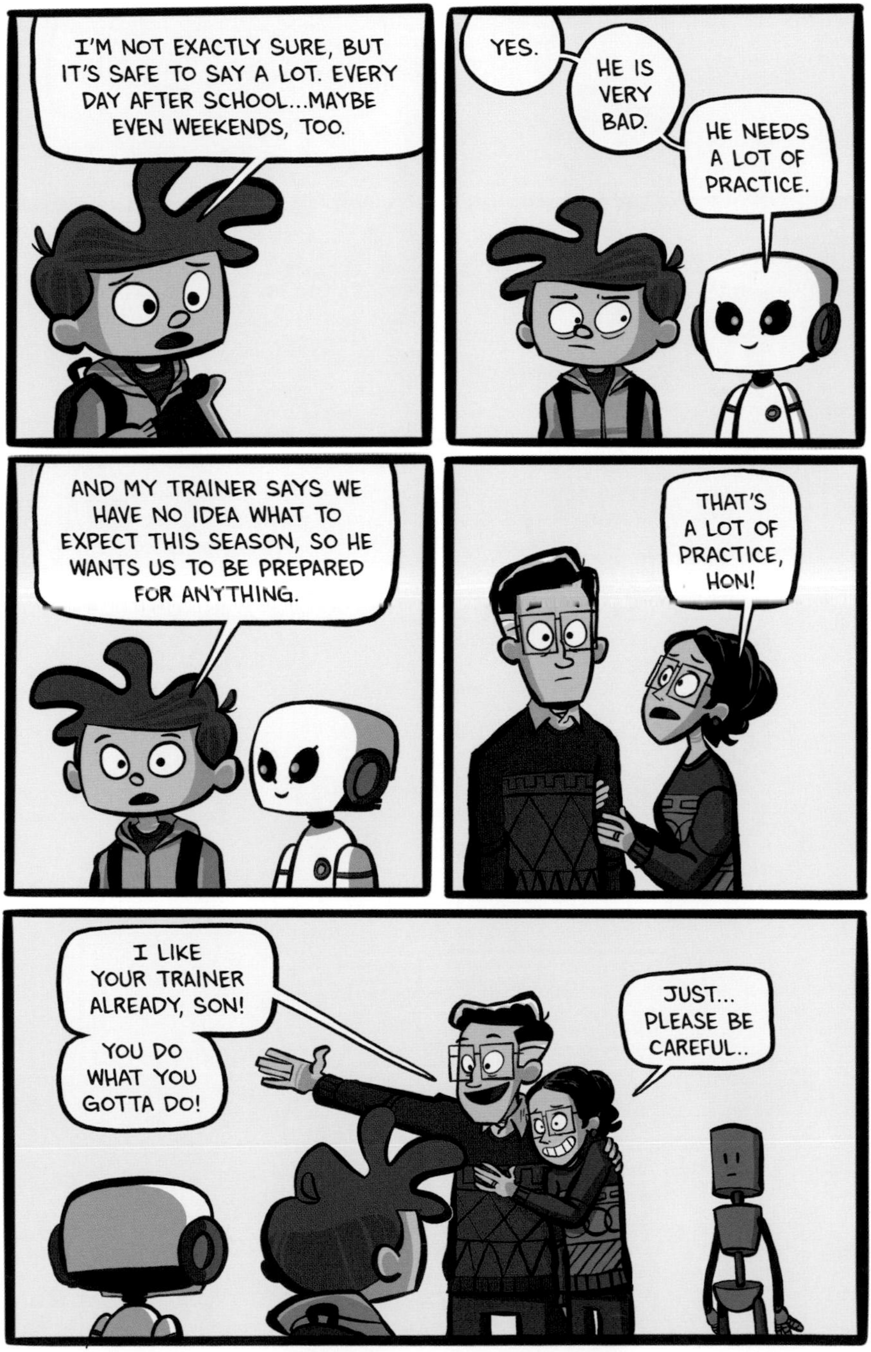
I'M NOT EXACTLY SURE, BUT IT'S SAFE TO SAY A LOT. EVERY DAY AFTER SCHOOL...MAYBE EVEN WEEKENDS, TOO.
YES.
HE IS VERY BAD.
HE NEEDS A LOT OF PRACTICE.
AND MY TRAINER SAYS WE HAVE NO IDEA WHAT TO EXPECT THIS SEASON, SO HE WANTS US TO BE PREPARED FOR ANYTHING.
THAT'S A LOT OF PRACTICE, HON!
I LIKE YOUR TRAINER ALREADY, SON!
YOU DO WHAT YOU GOTTA DO!
JUST... PLEASE BE CAREFUL..

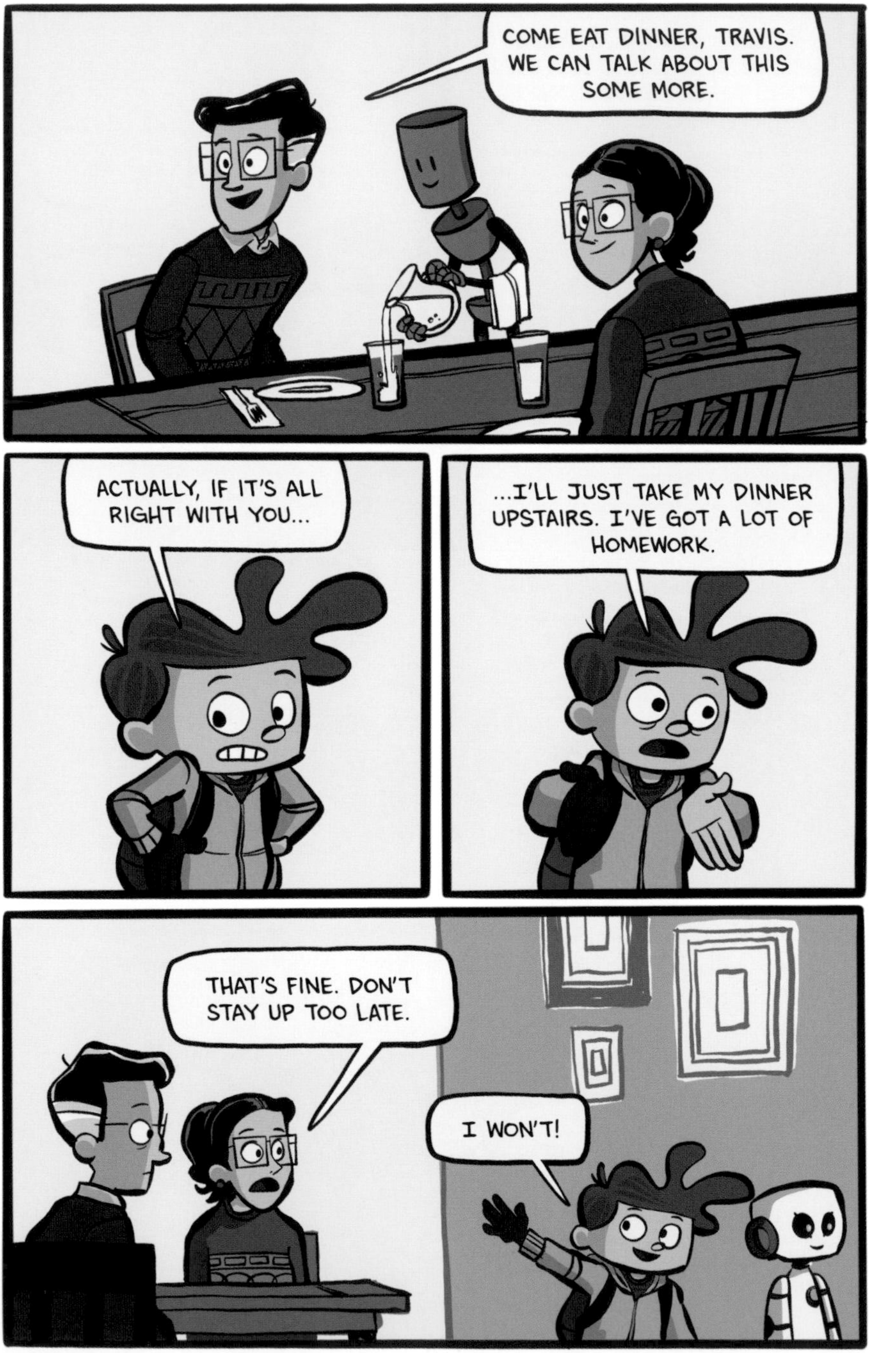
COME EAT DINNER, TRAVIS. WE CAN TALK ABOUT THIS SOME MORE.
ACTUALLY, IF IT'S ALL RIGHT WITH YOU...
...I'LL JUST TAKE MY DINNER UPSTAIRS. I'VE GOT A LOT OF HOMEWORK.
THAT'S FINE. DON'T STAY UP TOO LATE.
I WON'T!

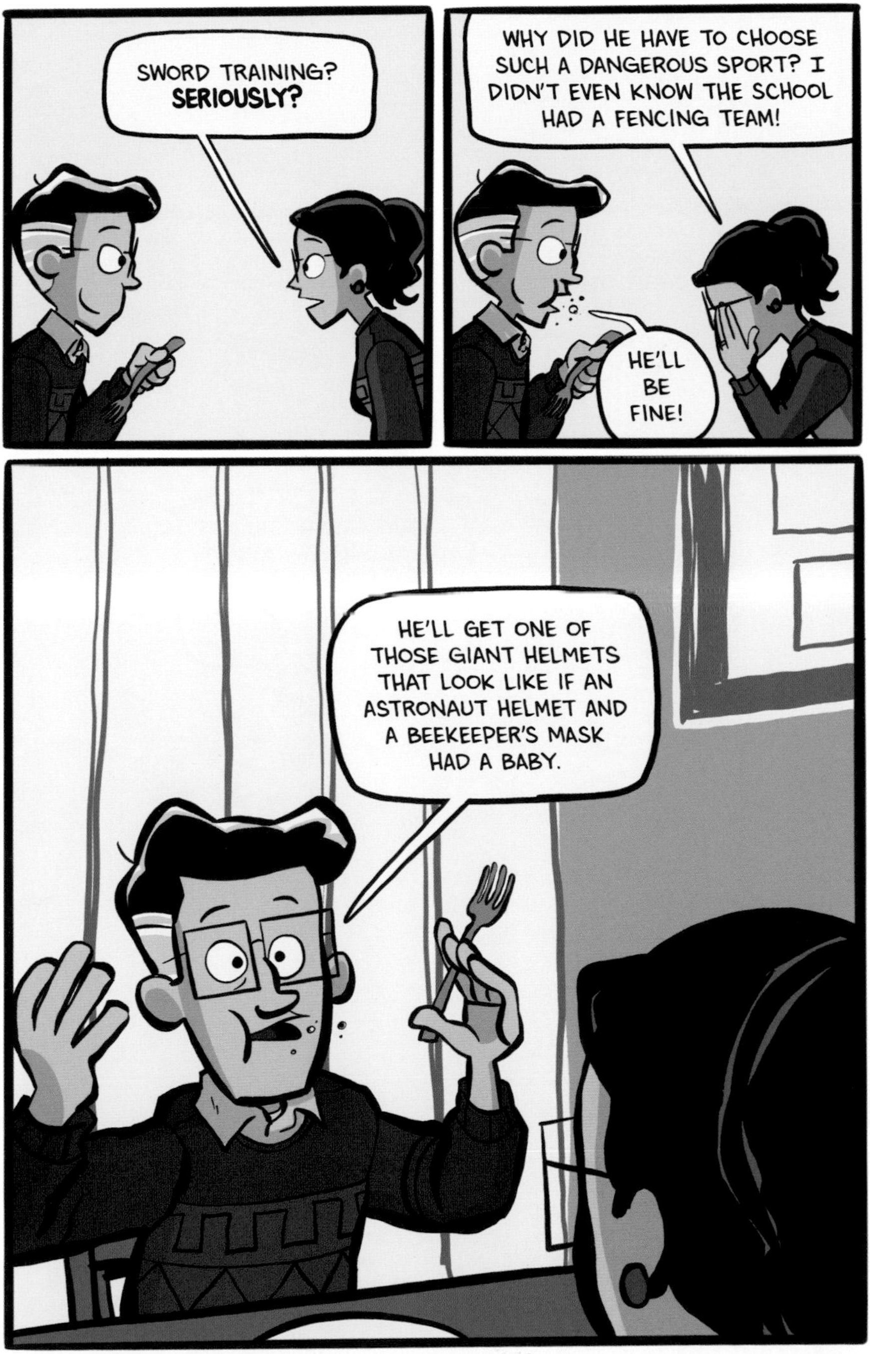
SWORD TRAINING? **SERIOUSLY?**
WHY DID HE HAVE TO CHOOSE SUCH A DANGEROUS SPORT? I DIDN'T EVEN KNOW THE SCHOOL HAD A FENCING TEAM!
HE'LL BE FINE!
HE'LL GET ONE OF THOSE GIANT HELMETS THAT LOOK LIKE IF AN ASTRONAUT HELMET AND A BEEKEEPER'S MASK HAD A BABY.

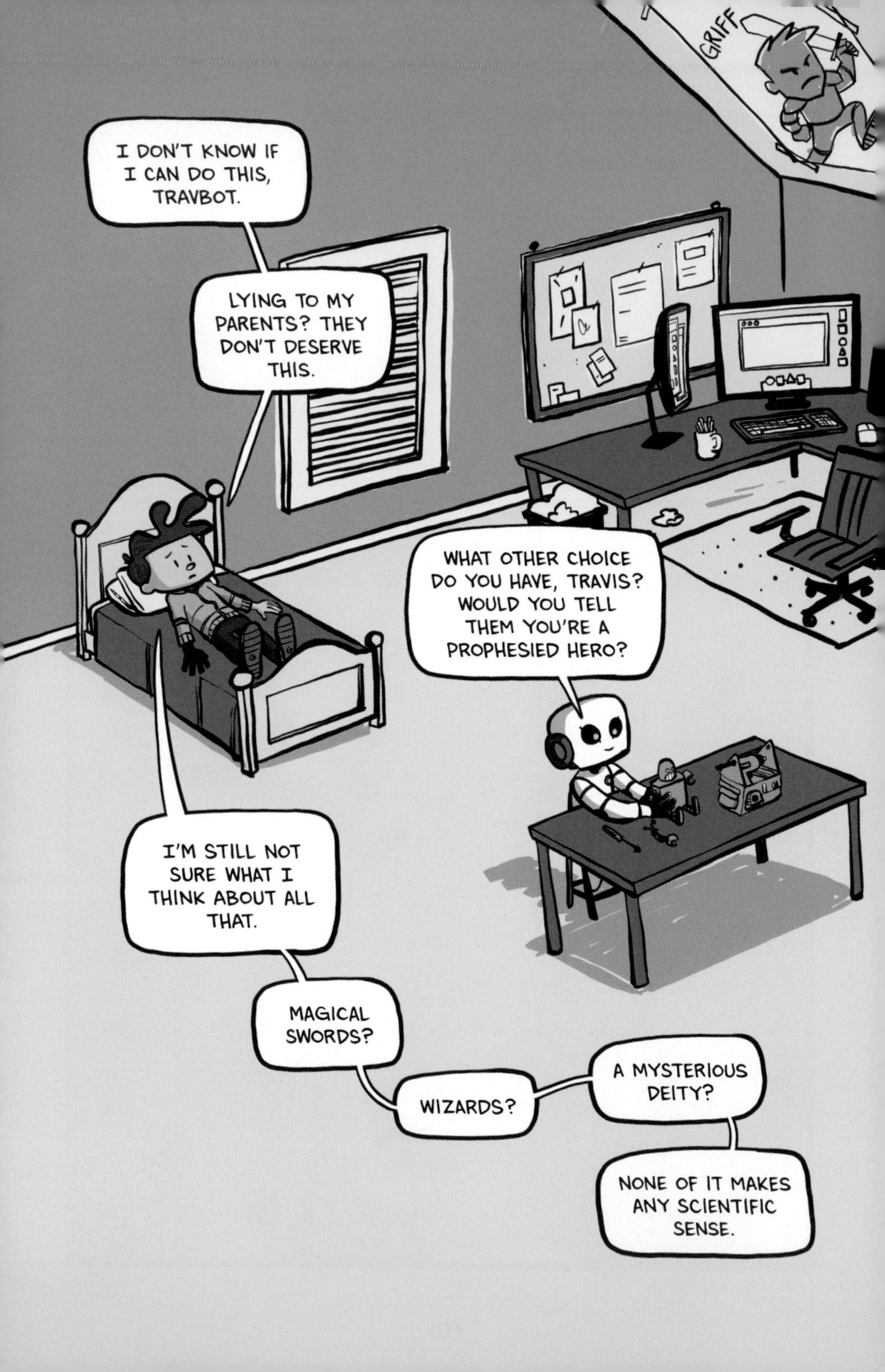
GRIFF
I DON'T KNOW IF I CAN DO THIS, TRAVBOT.
LYING TO MY PARENTS? THEY DON'T DESERVE THIS.
WHAT OTHER CHOICE DO YOU HAVE, TRAVIS? WOULD YOU TELL THEM YOU'RE A PROPHESIED HERO?
I'M STILL NOT SURE WHAT I THINK ABOUT ALL THAT.
MAGICAL SWORDS?
WIZARDS?
A MYSTERIOUS DEITY?
NONE OF IT MAKES ANY SCIENTIFIC SENSE.

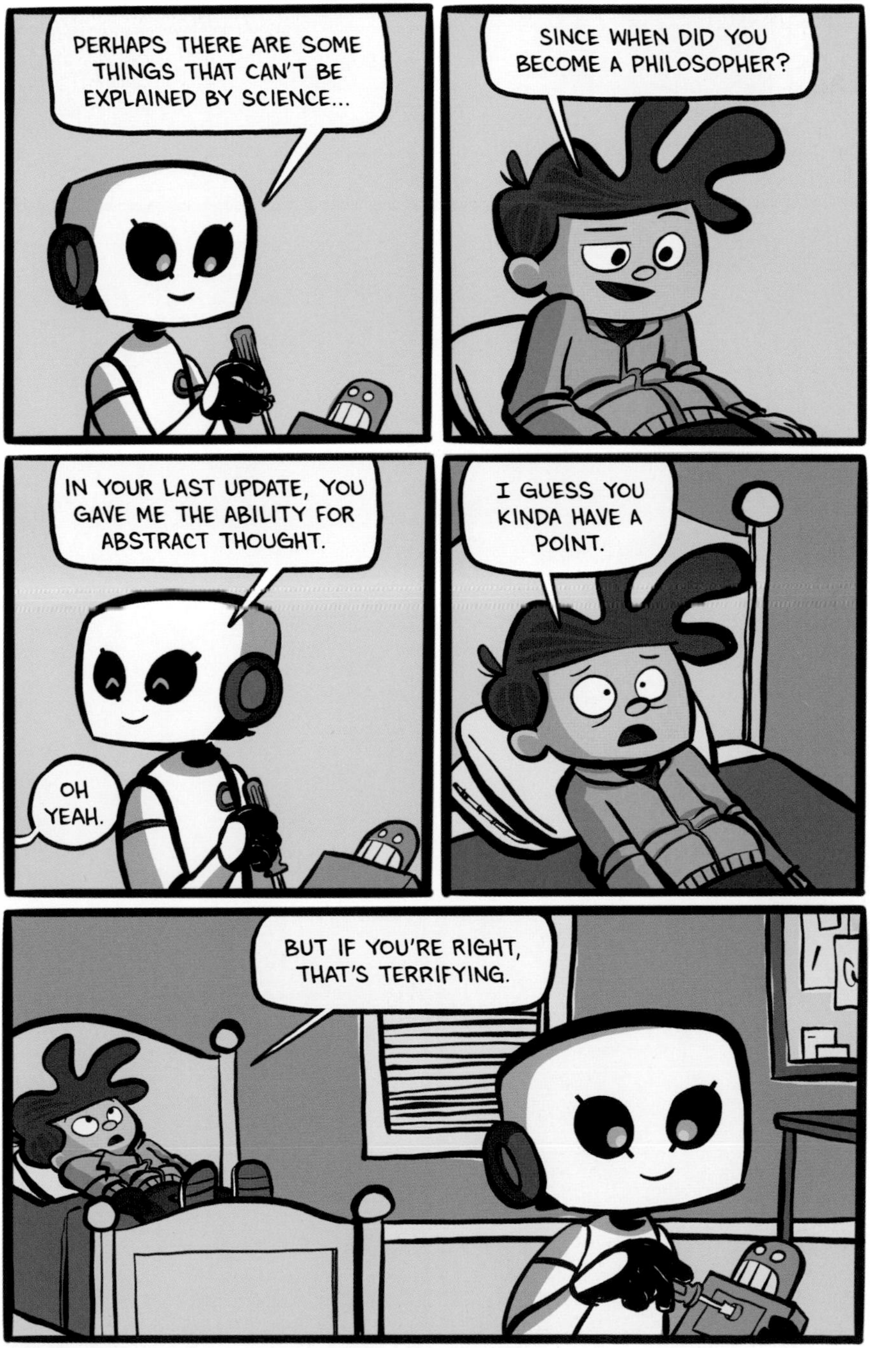
PERHAPS THERE ARE SOME THINGS THAT CAN'T BE EXPLAINED BY SCIENCE...
SINCE WHEN DID YOU BECOME A PHILOSOPHER?
IN YOUR LAST UPDATE, YOU GAVE ME THE ABILITY FOR ABSTRACT THOUGHT.
OH YEAH.
I GUESS YOU KINDA HAVE A POINT.
BUT IF YOU'RE RIGHT, THAT'S TERRIFYING.

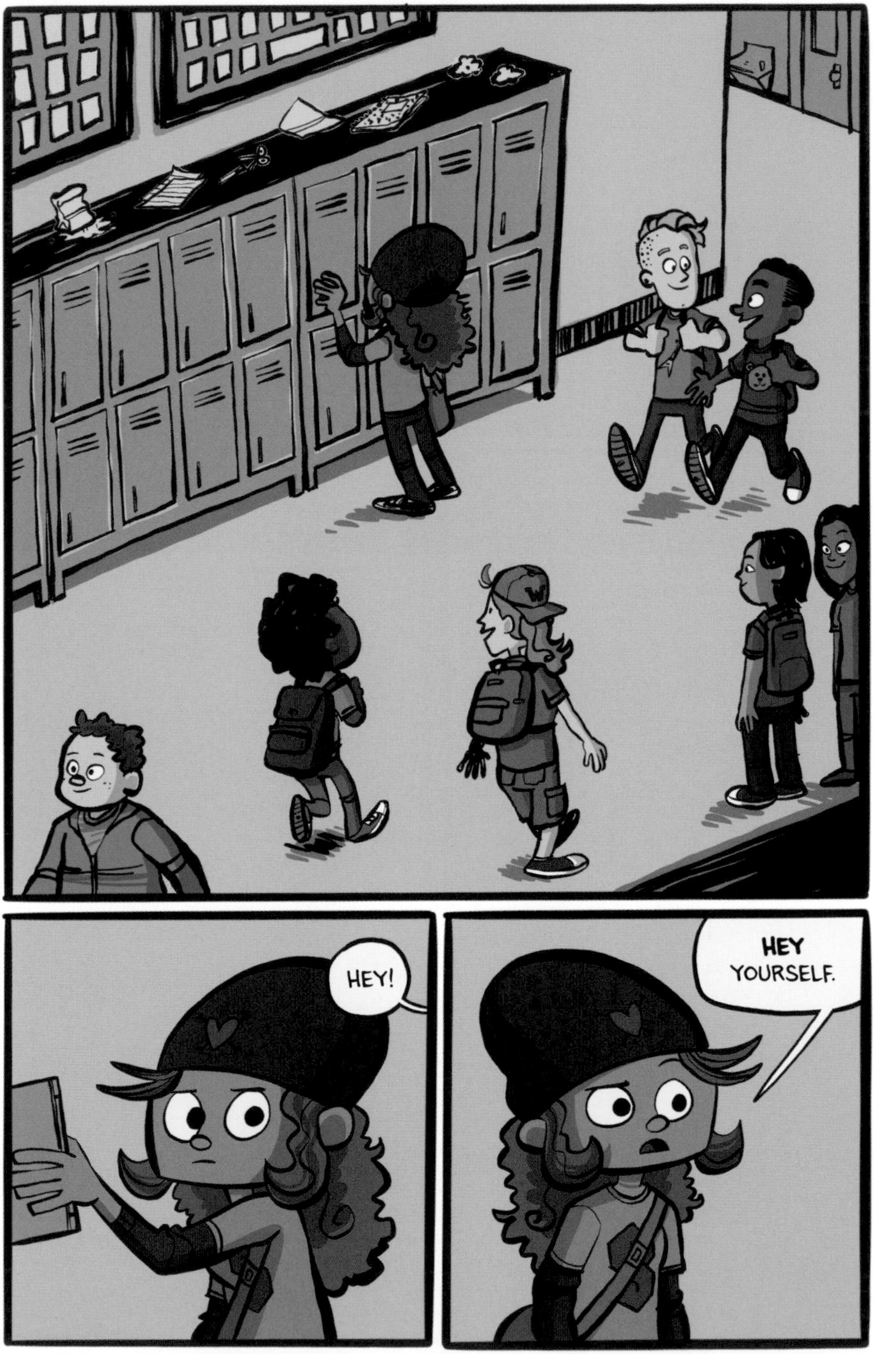
HEY!
HEY YOURSELF.

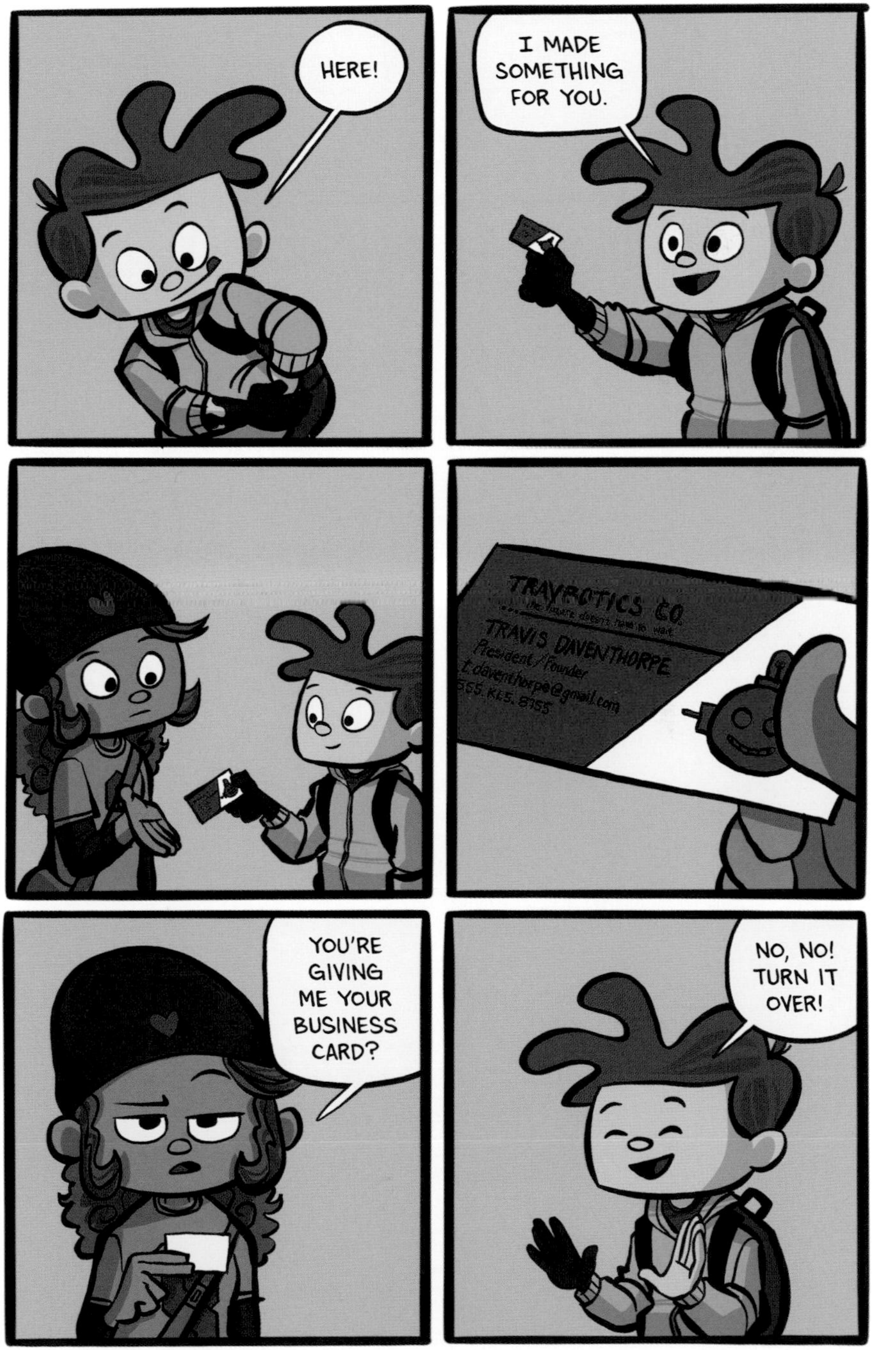
HERE!
I MADE SOMETHING FOR YOU.
TRAVBOTICS CO.
...the future doesn't have to wait
TRAVIS DAVENTHORPE
President / Founder
t.daventhorpe@gmail.com
YOU'RE GIVING ME YOUR BUSINESS CARD?
NO, NO! TURN IT OVER!

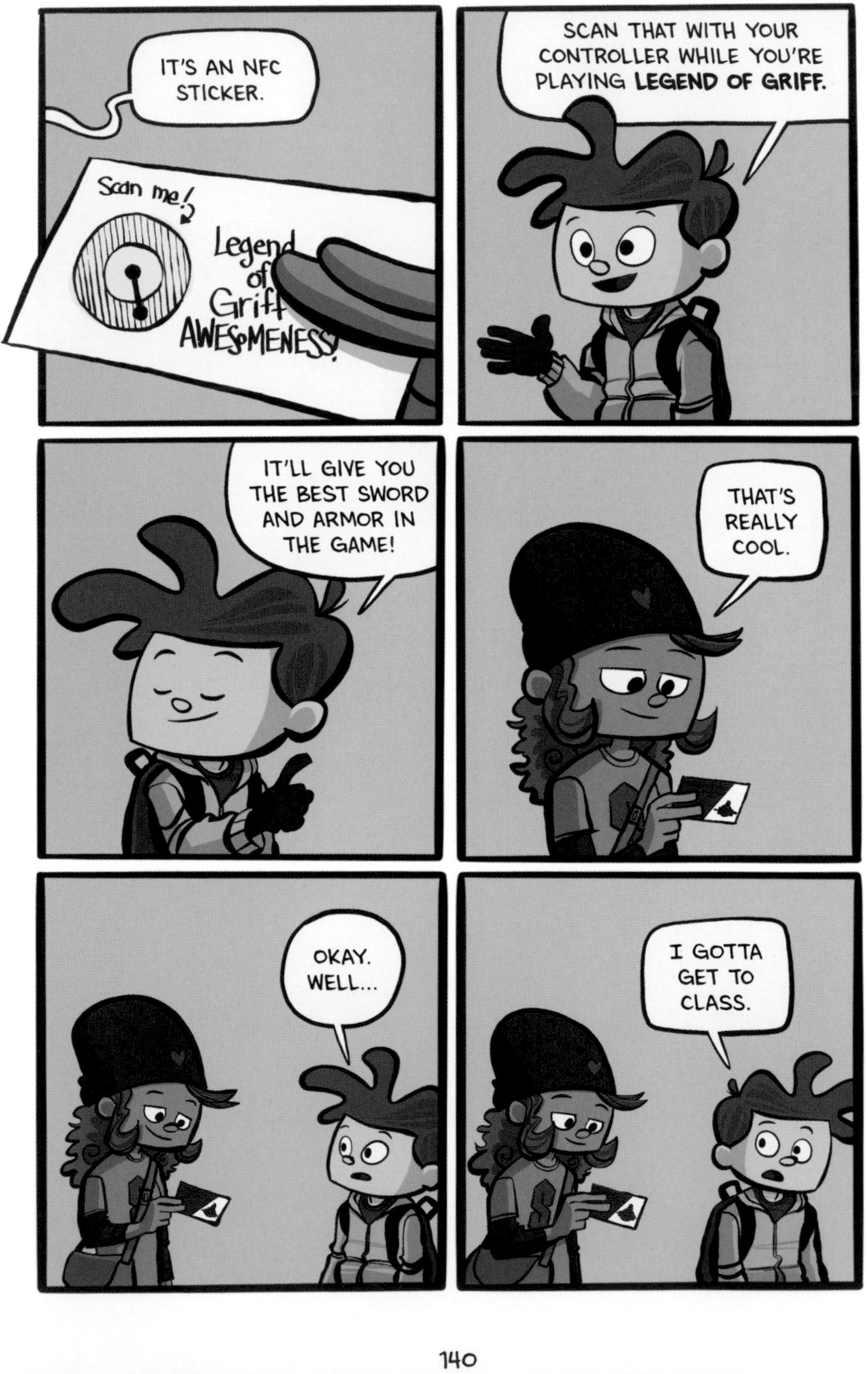
IT'S AN NFC STICKER.
Scan me!
Legend of Griff AWESOMENESS!
SCAN THAT WITH YOUR CONTROLLER WHILE YOU'RE PLAYING LEGEND OF GRIFF.
IT'LL GIVE YOU THE BEST SWORD AND ARMOR IN THE GAME!
THAT'S REALLY COOL.
OKAY. WELL...
I GOTTA GET TO CLASS.

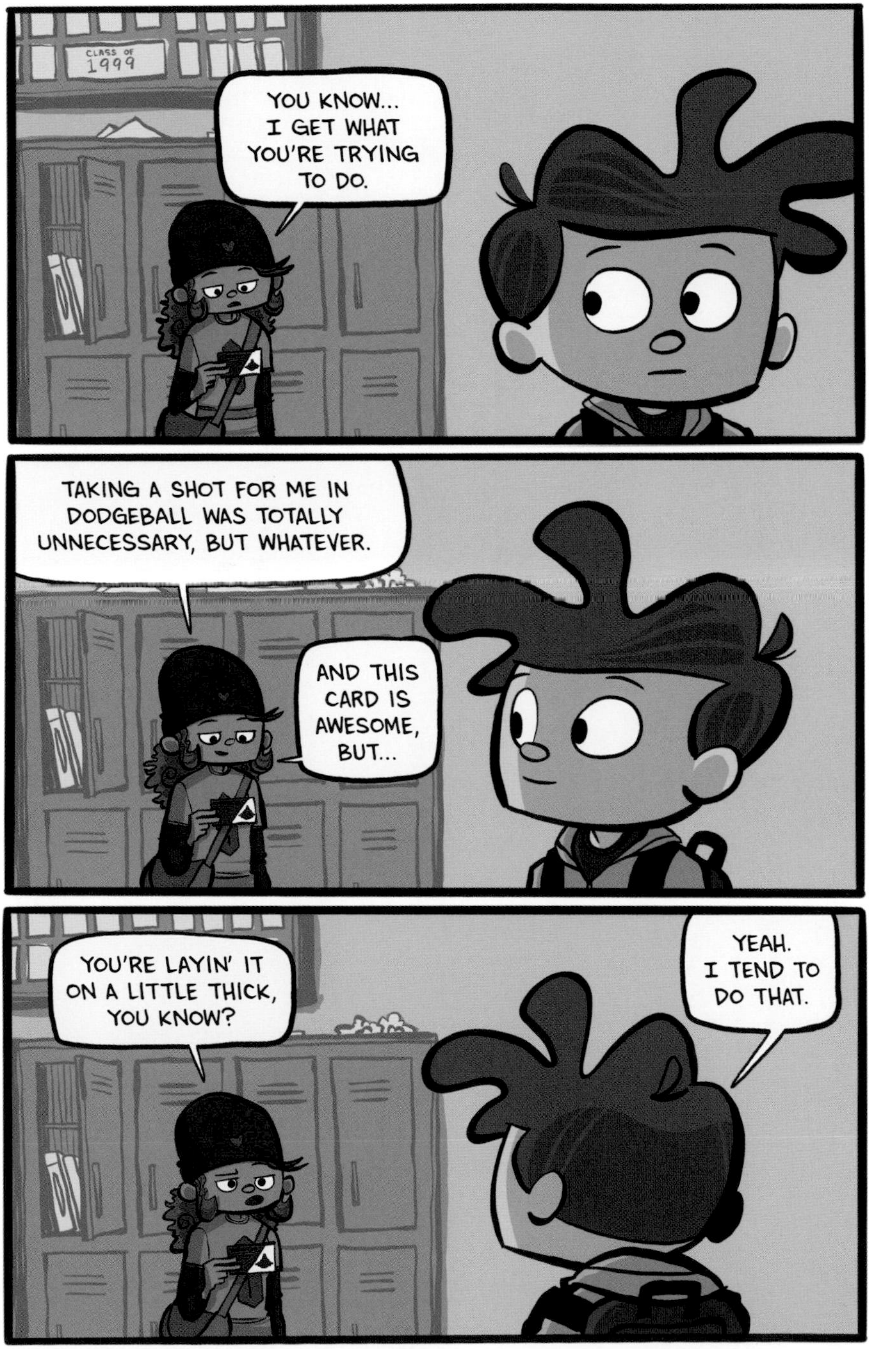
CLASS OF 1999
YOU KNOW... I GET WHAT YOU'RE TRYING TO DO.
TAKING A SHOT FOR ME IN DODGEBALL WAS TOTALLY UNNECESSARY, BUT WHATEVER.
AND THIS CARD IS AWESOME, BUT...
YOU'RE LAYIN' IT ON A LITTLE THICK, YOU KNOW?
YEAH. I TEND TO DO THAT.

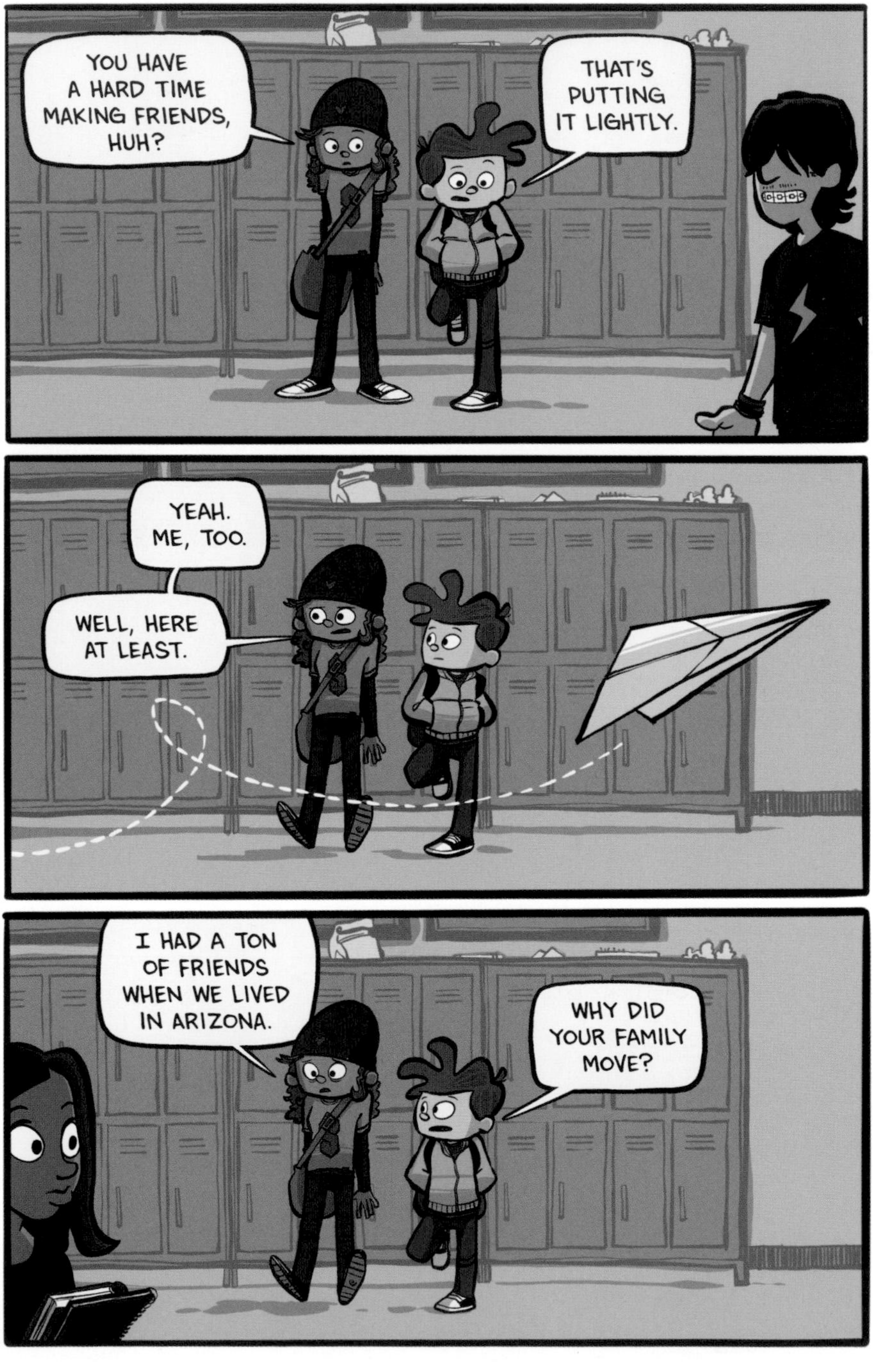
YOU HAVE A HARD TIME MAKING FRIENDS, HUH?
THAT'S PUTTING IT LIGHTLY.
YEAH. ME, TOO.
WELL, HERE AT LEAST.
I HAD A TON OF FRIENDS WHEN WE LIVED IN ARIZONA.
WHY DID YOUR FAMILY MOVE?

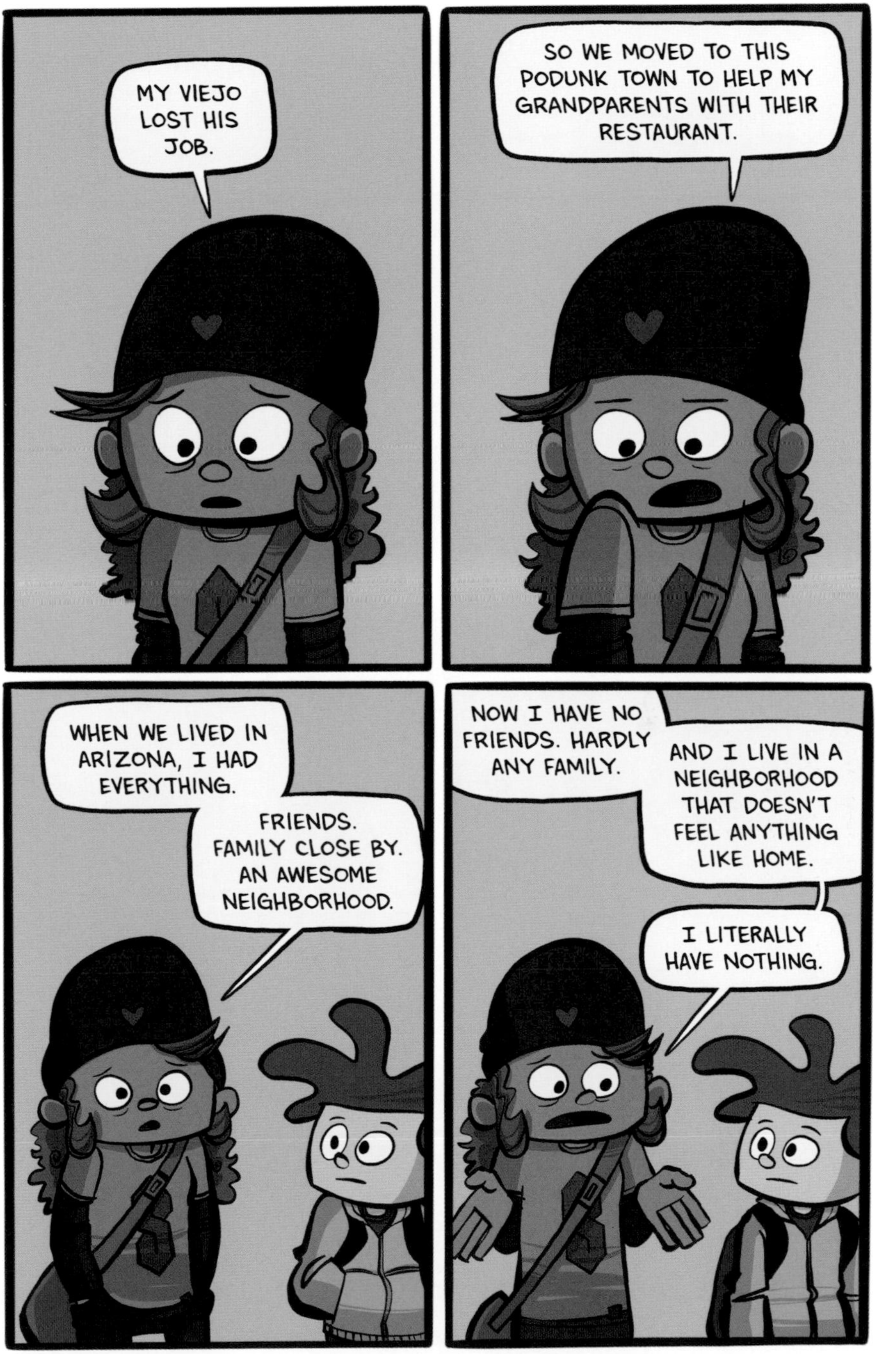
MY VIEJO LOST HIS JOB.
SO WE MOVED TO THIS PODUNK TOWN TO HELP MY GRANDPARENTS WITH THEIR RESTAURANT.
WHEN WE LIVED IN ARIZONA, I HAD EVERYTHING.
FRIENDS. FAMILY CLOSE BY. AN AWESOME NEIGHBORHOOD.
NOW I HAVE NO FRIENDS. HARDLY ANY FAMILY.
AND I LIVE IN A NEIGHBORHOOD THAT DOESN'T FEEL ANYTHING LIKE HOME.
I LITERALLY HAVE NOTHING.

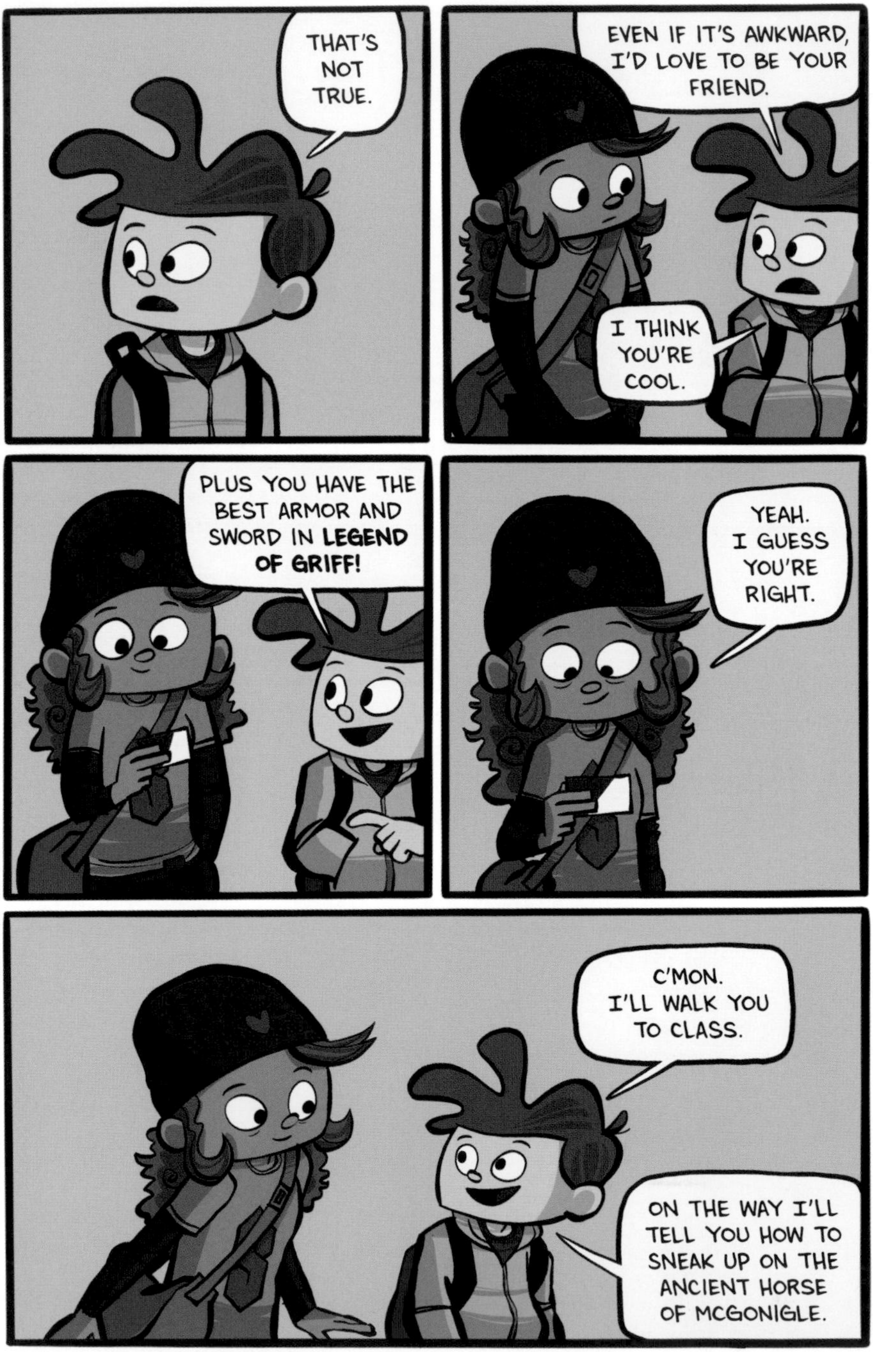
THAT'S NOT TRUE.
EVEN IF IT'S AWKWARD, I'D LOVE TO BE YOUR FRIEND.
I THINK YOU'RE COOL.
PLUS YOU HAVE THE BEST ARMOR AND SWORD IN **LEGEND OF GRIFF!**
YEAH. I GUESS YOU'RE RIGHT.
C'MON. I'LL WALK YOU TO CLASS.
ON THE WAY I'LL TELL YOU HOW TO SNEAK UP ON THE ANCIENT HORSE OF MCGONIGLE.

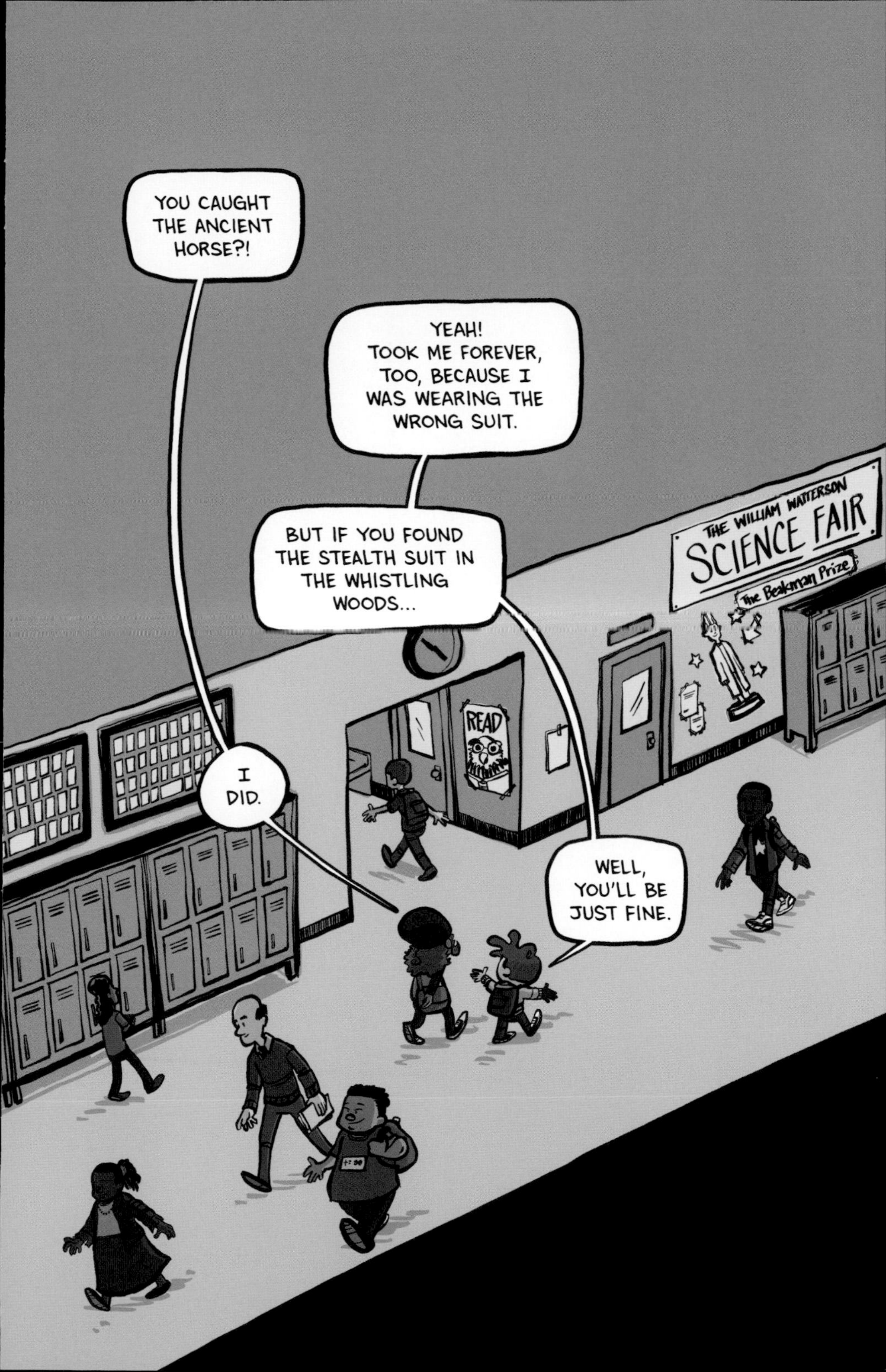
YOU CAUGHT THE ANCIENT HORSE?!
YEAH! TOOK ME FOREVER, TOO, BECAUSE I WAS WEARING THE WRONG SUIT.
BUT IF YOU FOUND THE STEALTH SUIT IN THE WHISTLING WOODS...
I DID.
WELL, YOU'LL BE JUST FINE.
THE WILLIAM WATTERSON SCIENCE FAIR
The Beakman Prize
READ

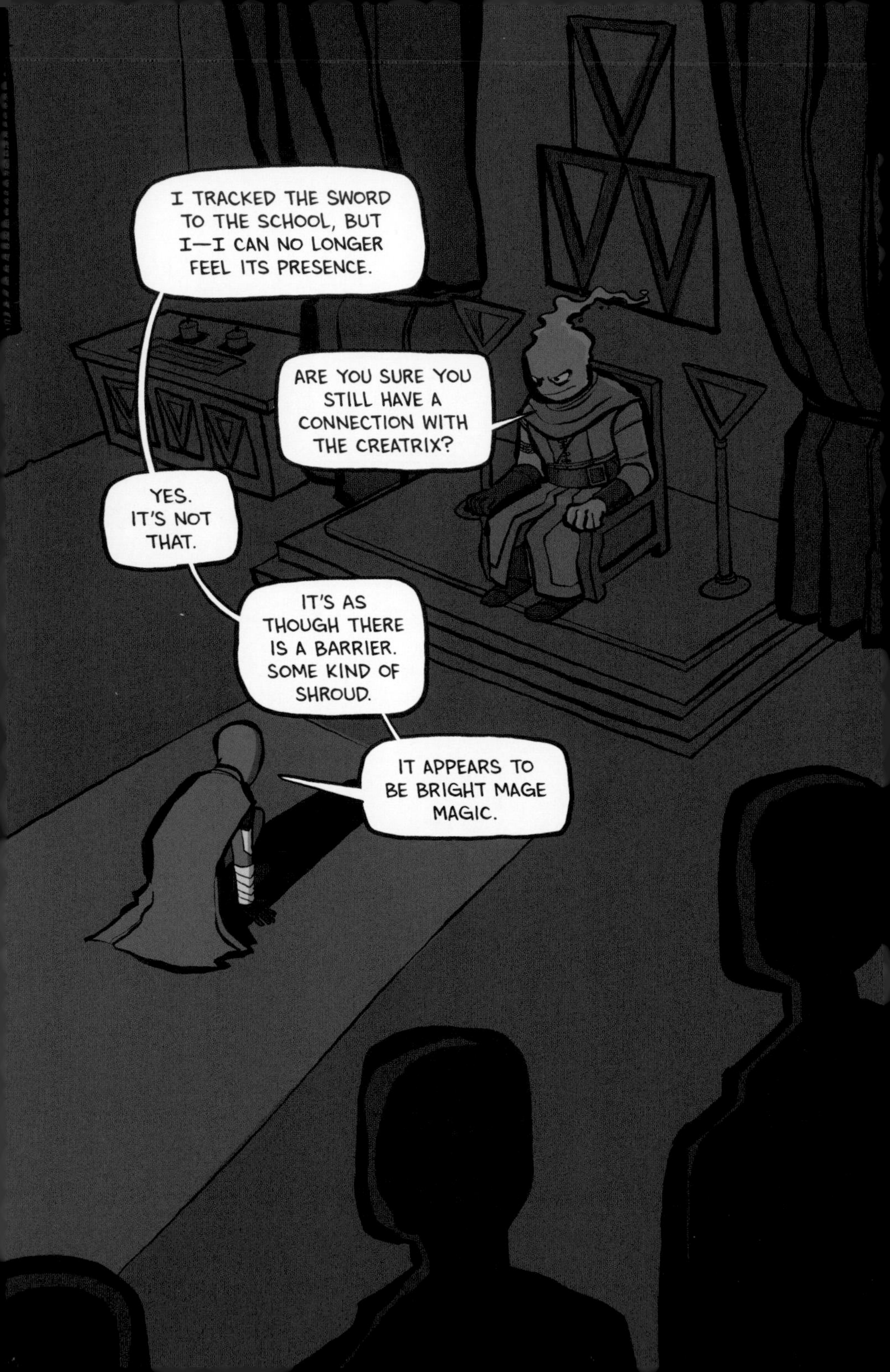
I TRACKED THE SWORD TO THE SCHOOL, BUT I—I CAN NO LONGER FEEL ITS PRESENCE.
ARE YOU SURE YOU STILL HAVE A CONNECTION WITH THE CREATRIX?
YES. IT'S NOT THAT.
IT'S AS THOUGH THERE IS A BARRIER. SOME KIND OF SHROUD.
IT APPEARS TO BE BRIGHT MAGE MAGIC.

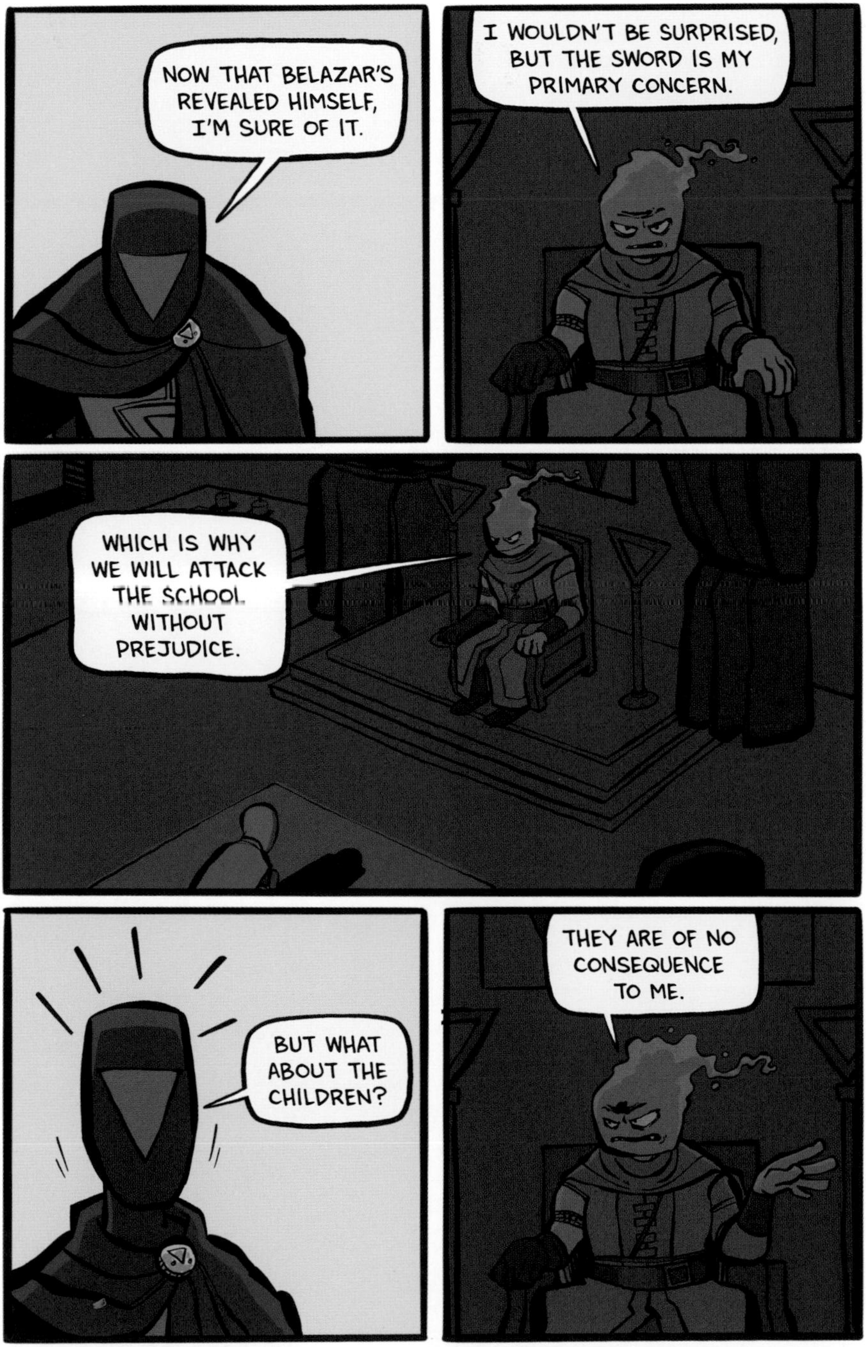
NOW THAT BELAZAR'S REVEALED HIMSELF, I'M SURE OF IT.
I WOULDN'T BE SURPRISED, BUT THE SWORD IS MY PRIMARY CONCERN.
WHICH IS WHY WE WILL ATTACK THE SCHOOL WITHOUT PREJUDICE.
BUT WHAT ABOUT THE CHILDREN?
THEY ARE OF NO CONSEQUENCE TO ME.

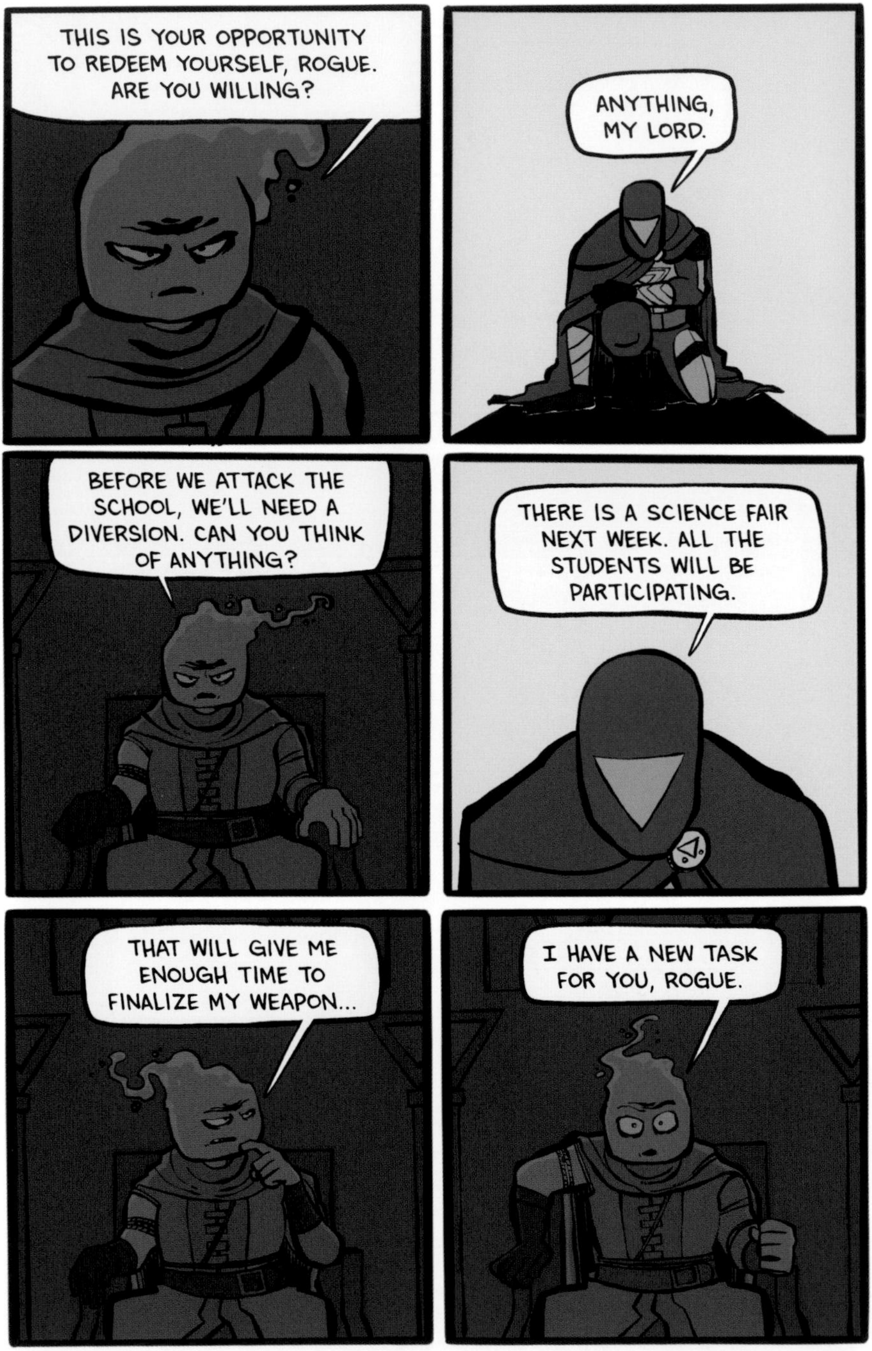
THIS IS YOUR OPPORTUNITY TO REDEEM YOURSELF, ROGUE. ARE YOU WILLING?
ANYTHING, MY LORD.
BEFORE WE ATTACK THE SCHOOL, WE'LL NEED A DIVERSION. CAN YOU THINK OF ANYTHING?
THERE IS A SCIENCE FAIR NEXT WEEK. ALL THE STUDENTS WILL BE PARTICIPATING.
THAT WILL GIVE ME ENOUGH TIME TO FINALIZE MY WEAPON...
I HAVE A NEW TASK FOR YOU, ROGUE.

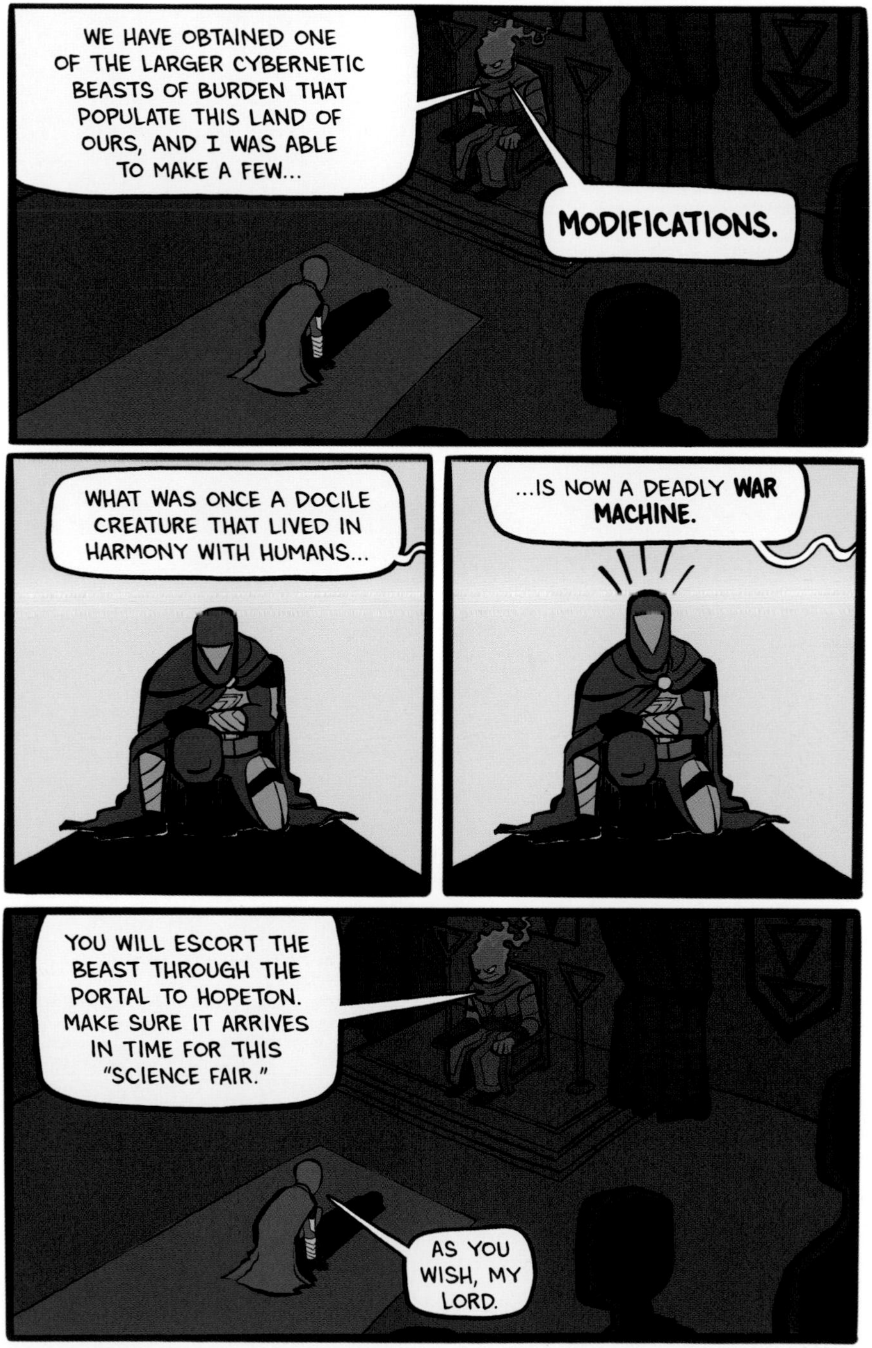
WE HAVE OBTAINED ONE OF THE LARGER CYBERNETIC BEASTS OF BURDEN THAT POPULATE THIS LAND OF OURS, AND I WAS ABLE TO MAKE A FEW...
MODIFICATIONS.
WHAT WAS ONCE A DOCILE CREATURE THAT LIVED IN HARMONY WITH HUMANS...
...IS NOW A DEADLY WAR MACHINE.
YOU WILL ESCORT THE BEAST THROUGH THE PORTAL TO HOPETON. MAKE SURE IT ARRIVES IN TIME FOR THIS "SCIENCE FAIR."
AS YOU WISH, MY LORD.

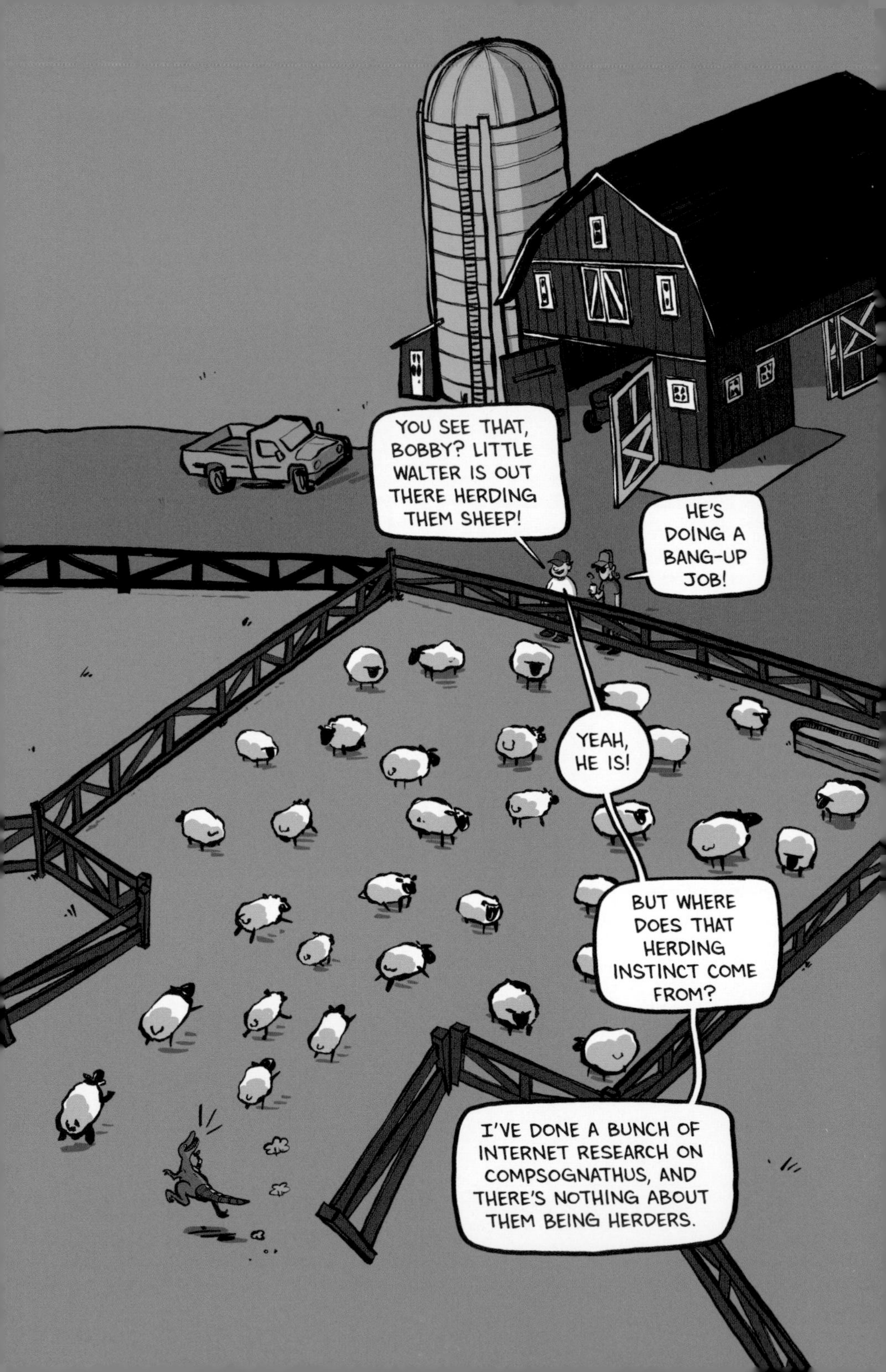
YOU SEE THAT, BOBBY? LITTLE WALTER IS OUT THERE HERDING THEM SHEEP!
HE'S DOING A BANG-UP JOB!
YEAH, HE IS!
BUT WHERE DOES THAT HERDING INSTINCT COME FROM?
I'VE DONE A BUNCH OF INTERNET RESEARCH ON COMPSOGNATHUS, AND THERE'S NOTHING ABOUT THEM BEING HERDERS.

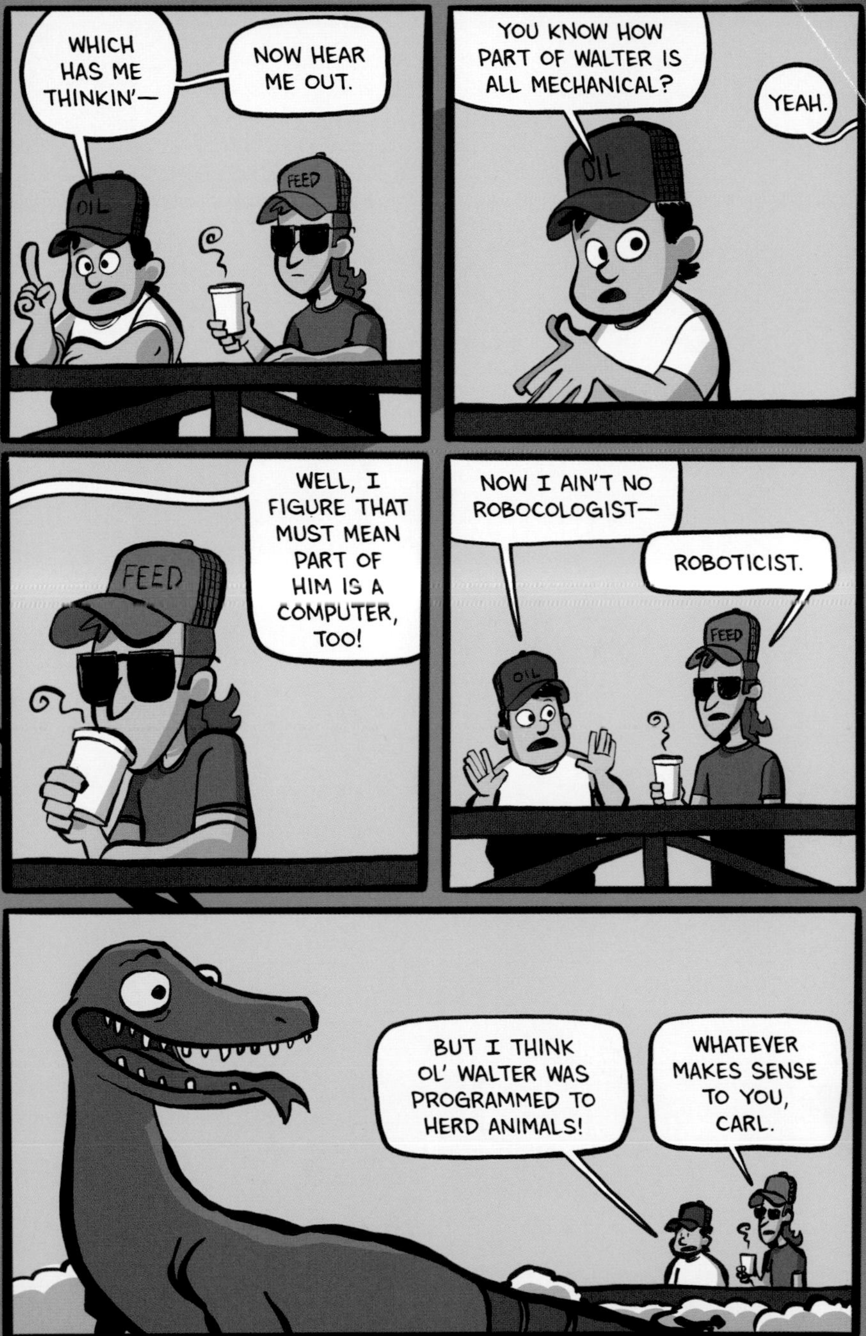
WHICH HAS ME THINKIN'—
NOW HEAR ME OUT.
YOU KNOW HOW PART OF WALTER IS ALL MECHANICAL?
YEAH.
OIL
FEED
WELL, I FIGURE THAT MUST MEAN PART OF HIM IS A COMPUTER, TOO!
NOW I AIN'T NO ROBOCOLOGIST—
ROBOTICIST.
BUT I THINK OL' WALTER WAS PROGRAMMED TO HERD ANIMALS!
WHATEVER MAKES SENSE TO YOU, CARL.

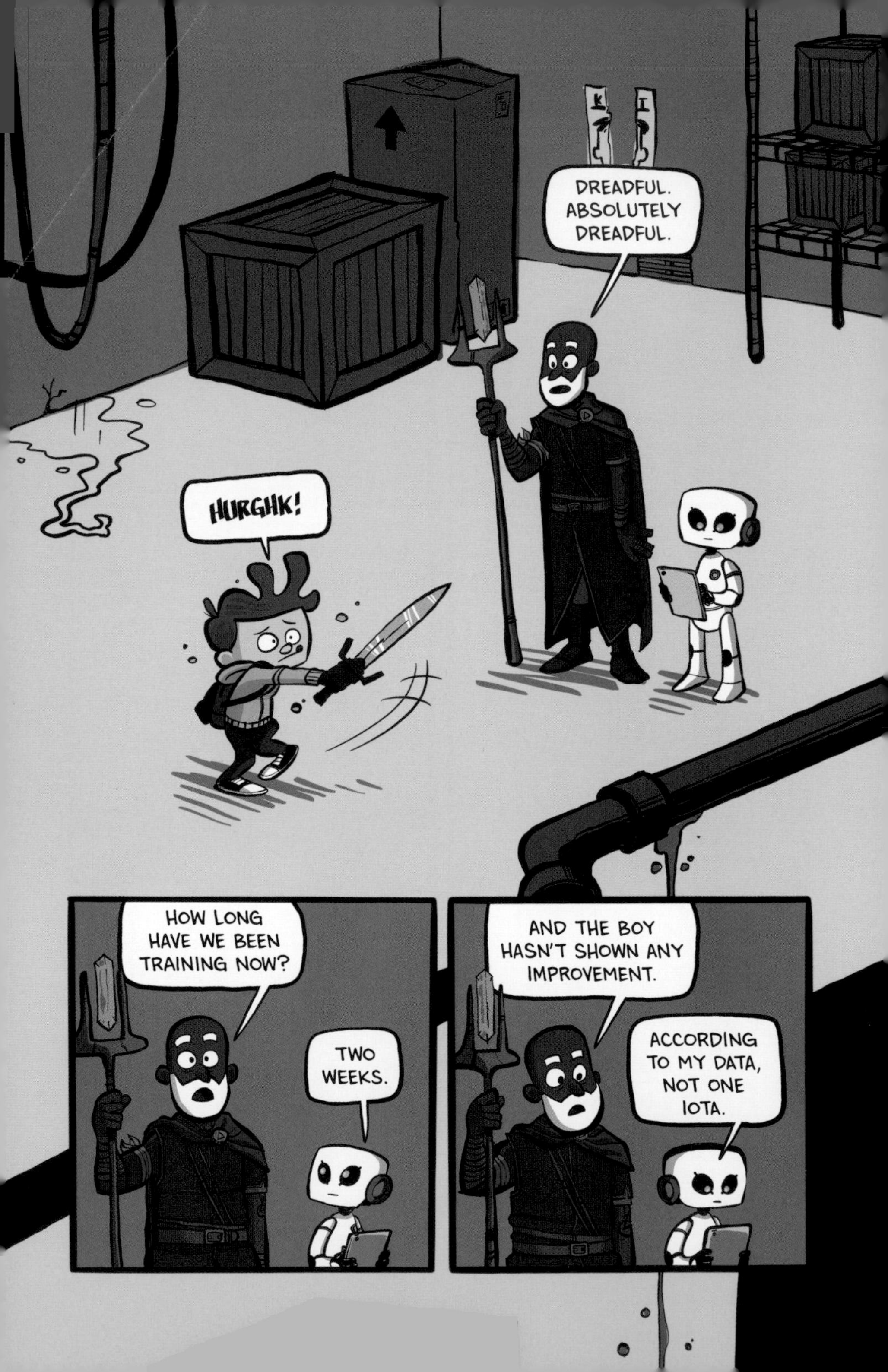
DREADFUL. ABSOLUTELY DREADFUL.
HURGHK!
HOW LONG HAVE WE BEEN TRAINING NOW?
TWO WEEKS.
AND THE BOY HASN'T SHOWN ANY IMPROVEMENT.
ACCORDING TO MY DATA, NOT ONE IOTA.

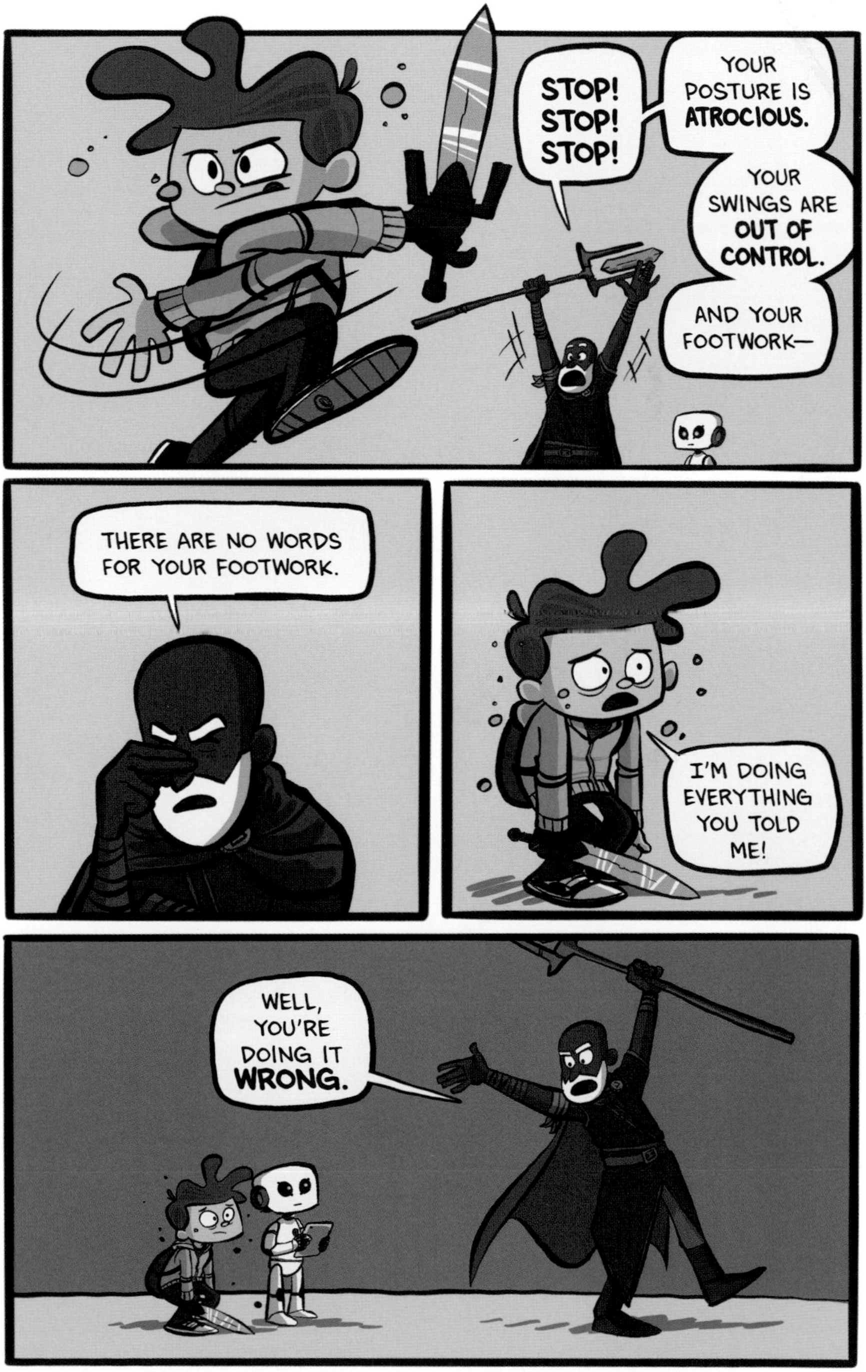
STOP! STOP! STOP!
YOUR POSTURE IS ATROCIOUS.
YOUR SWINGS ARE OUT OF CONTROL.
AND YOUR FOOTWORK—
THERE ARE NO WORDS FOR YOUR FOOTWORK.
I'M DOING EVERYTHING YOU TOLD ME!
WELL, YOU'RE DOING IT WRONG.

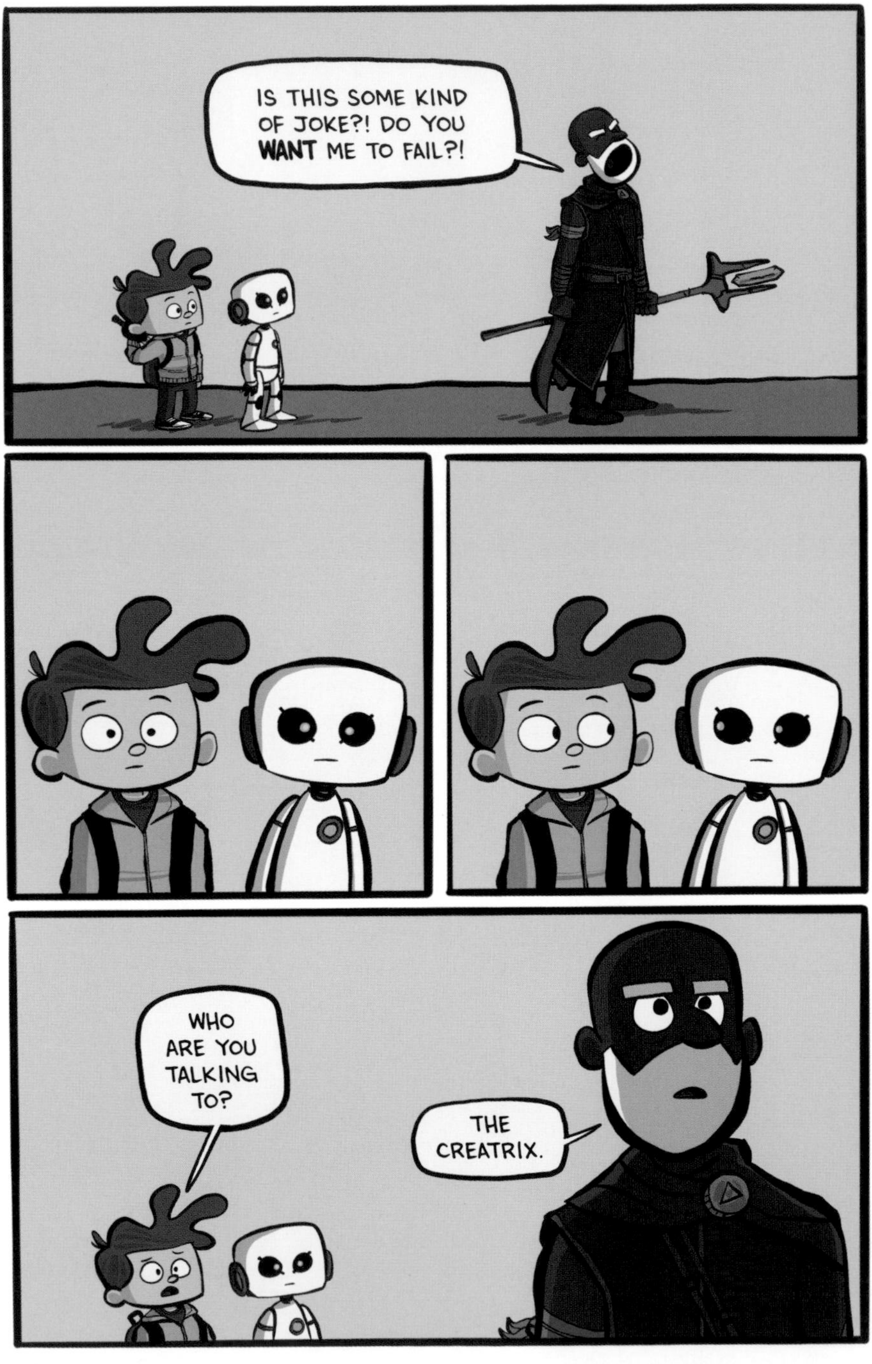
IS THIS SOME KIND OF JOKE?! DO YOU WANT ME TO FAIL?!
WHO ARE YOU TALKING TO?
THE CREATRIX.

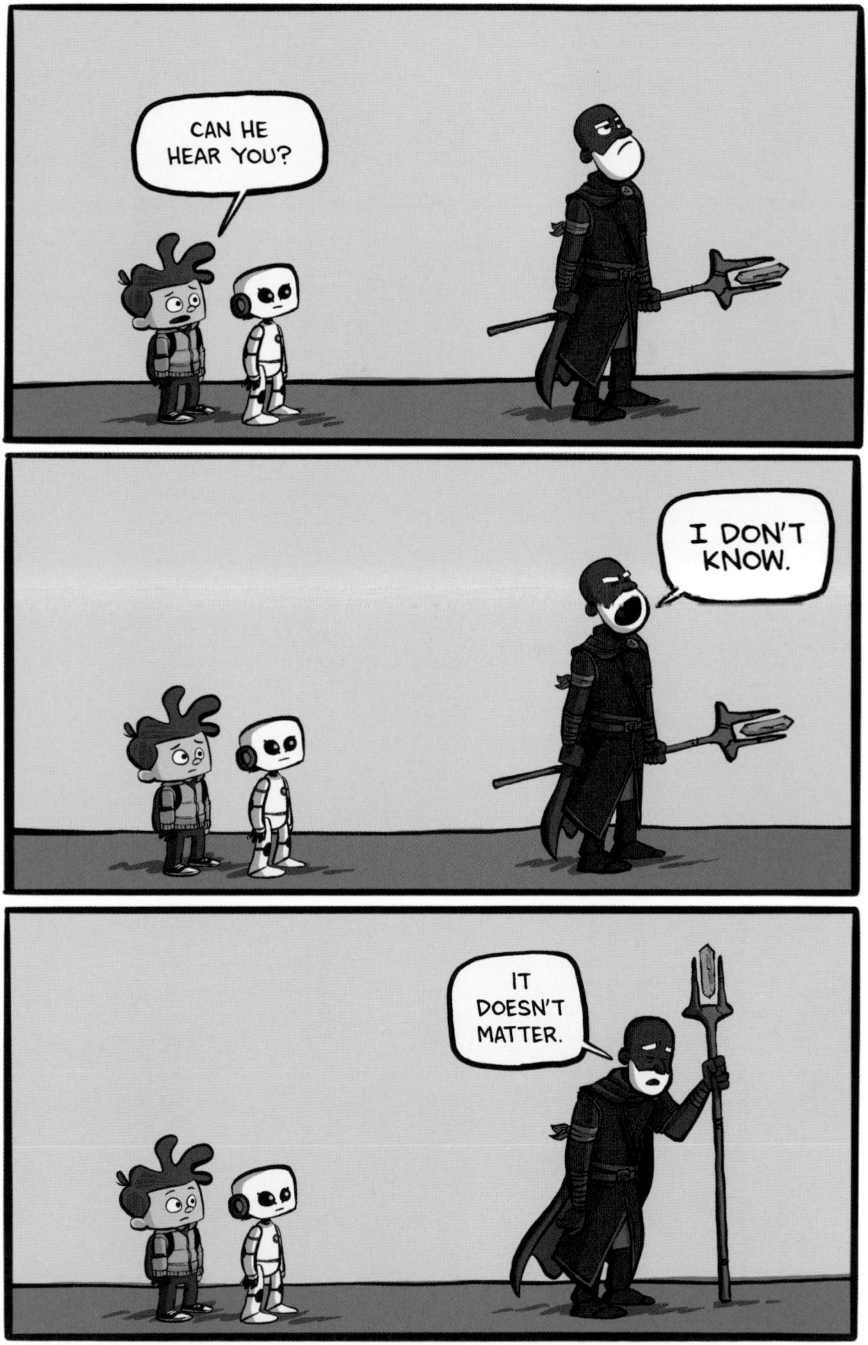
CAN HE HEAR YOU?
I DON'T KNOW.
IT DOESN'T MATTER.

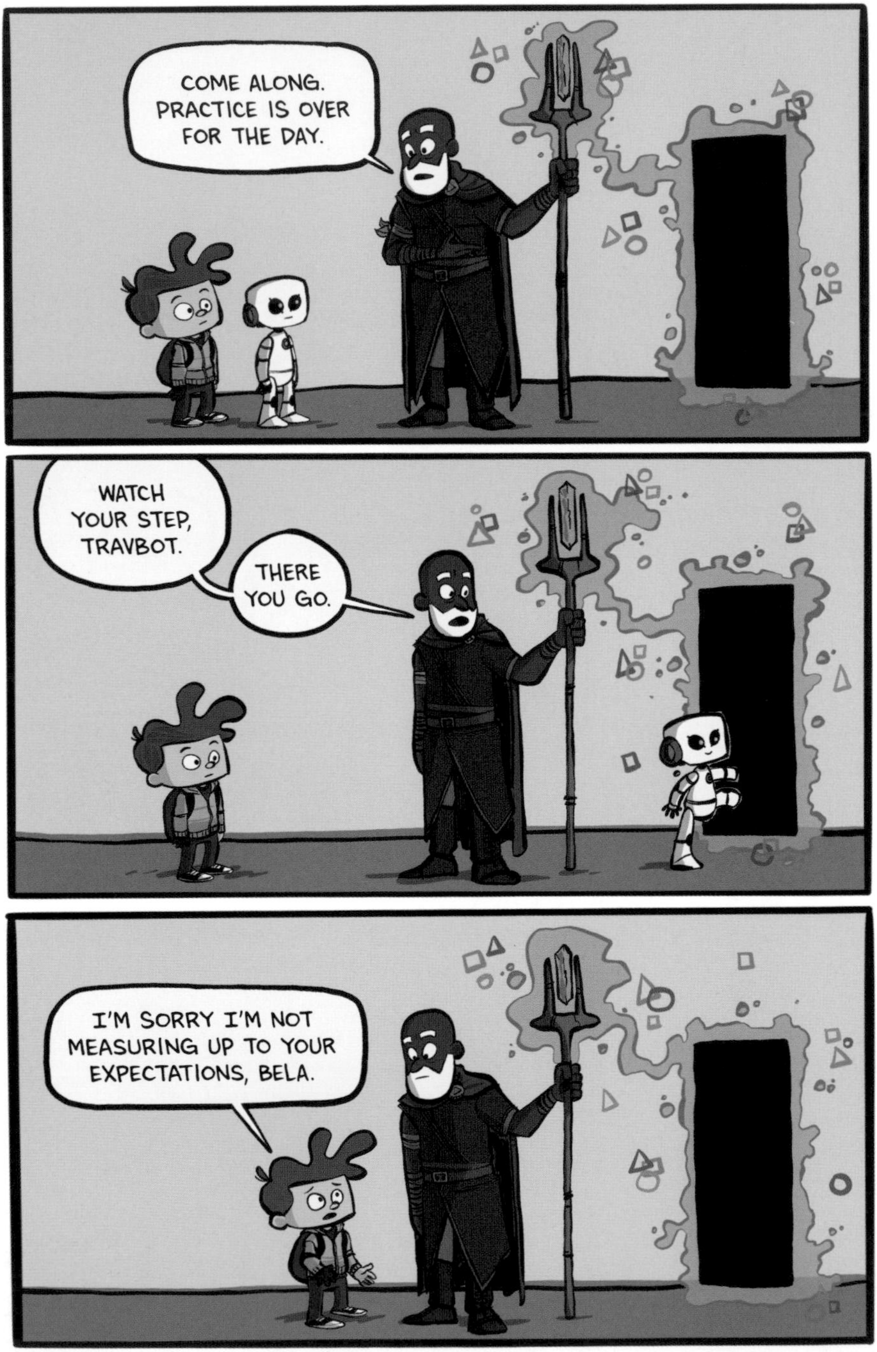
COME ALONG. PRACTICE IS OVER FOR THE DAY.
WATCH YOUR STEP, TRAVBOT.
THERE YOU GO.
I'M SORRY I'M NOT MEASURING UP TO YOUR EXPECTATIONS, BELA.

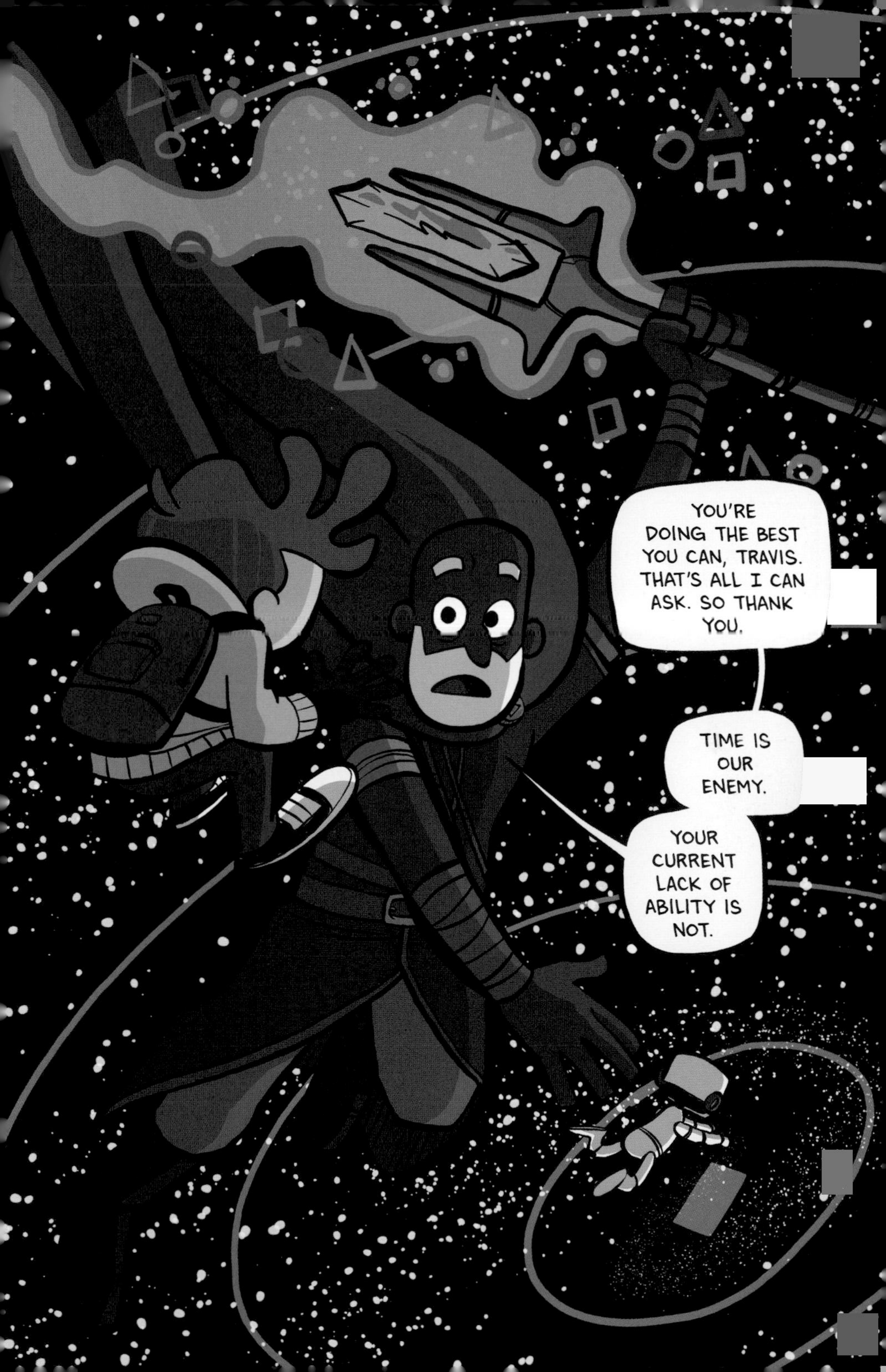
YOU'RE DOING THE BEST YOU CAN, TRAVIS. THAT'S ALL I CAN ASK. SO THANK YOU.
TIME IS OUR ENEMY.
YOUR CURRENT LACK OF ABILITY IS NOT.

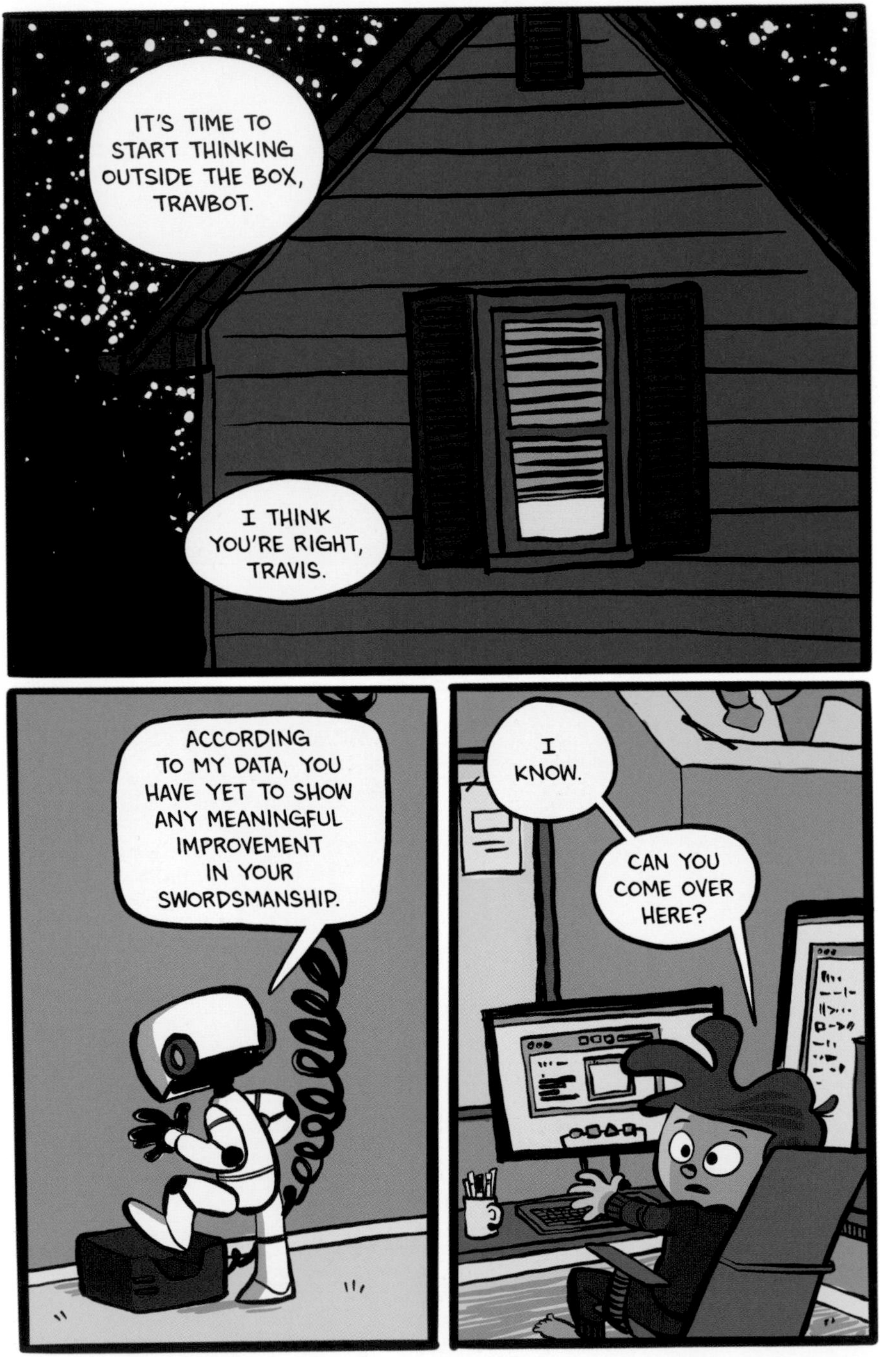
IT'S TIME TO START THINKING OUTSIDE THE BOX, TRAVBOT.
I THINK YOU'RE RIGHT, TRAVIS.
ACCORDING TO MY DATA, YOU HAVE YET TO SHOW ANY MEANINGFUL IMPROVEMENT IN YOUR SWORDSMANSHIP.
I KNOW.
CAN YOU COME OVER HERE?

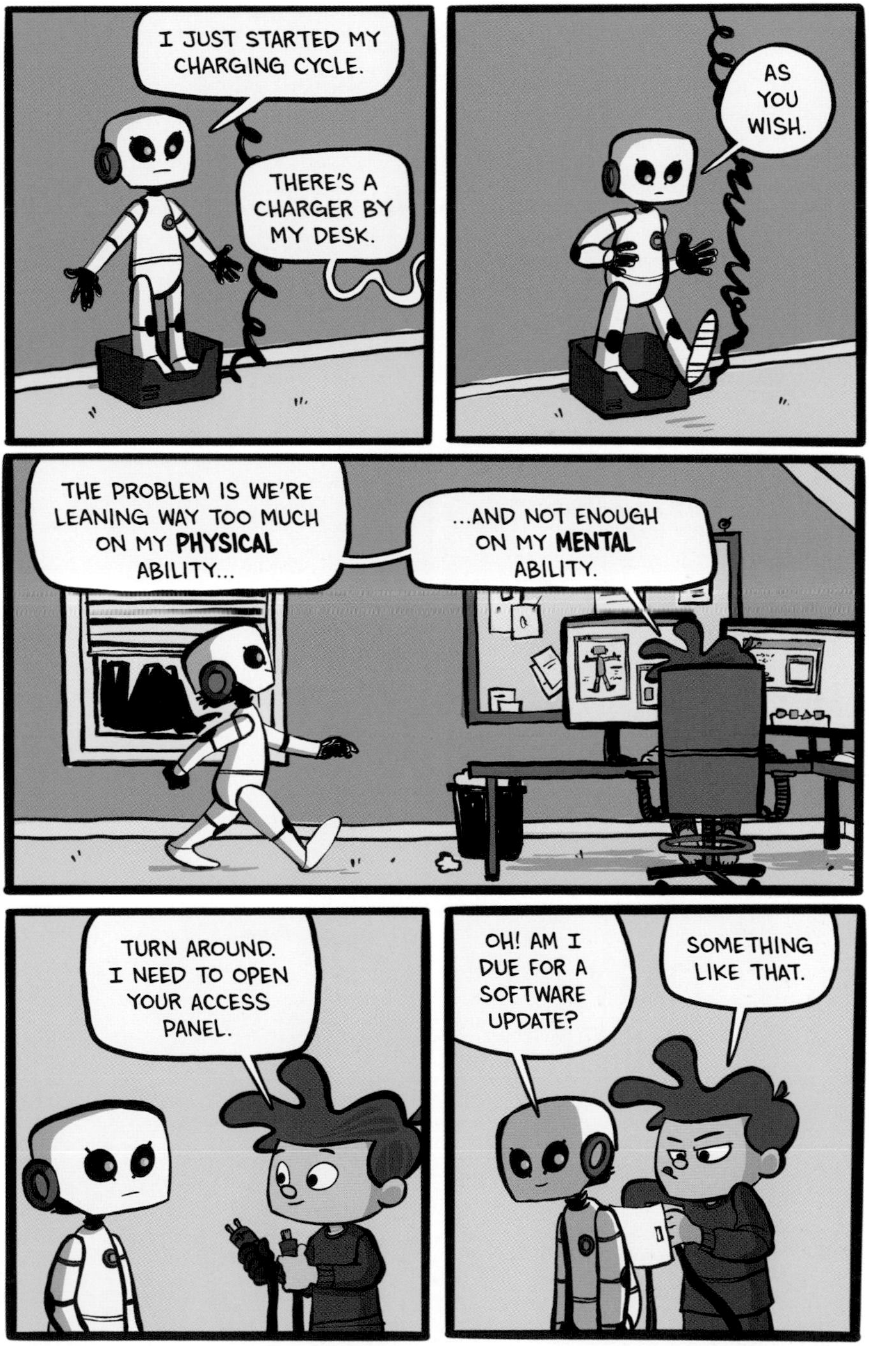
I JUST STARTED MY CHARGING CYCLE.
THERE'S A CHARGER BY MY DESK.
AS YOU WISH.
THE PROBLEM IS WE'RE LEANING WAY TOO MUCH ON MY **PHYSICAL** ABILITY...
...AND NOT ENOUGH ON MY **MENTAL** ABILITY.
TURN AROUND. I NEED TO OPEN YOUR ACCESS PANEL.
OH! AM I DUE FOR A SOFTWARE UPDATE?
SOMETHING LIKE THAT.

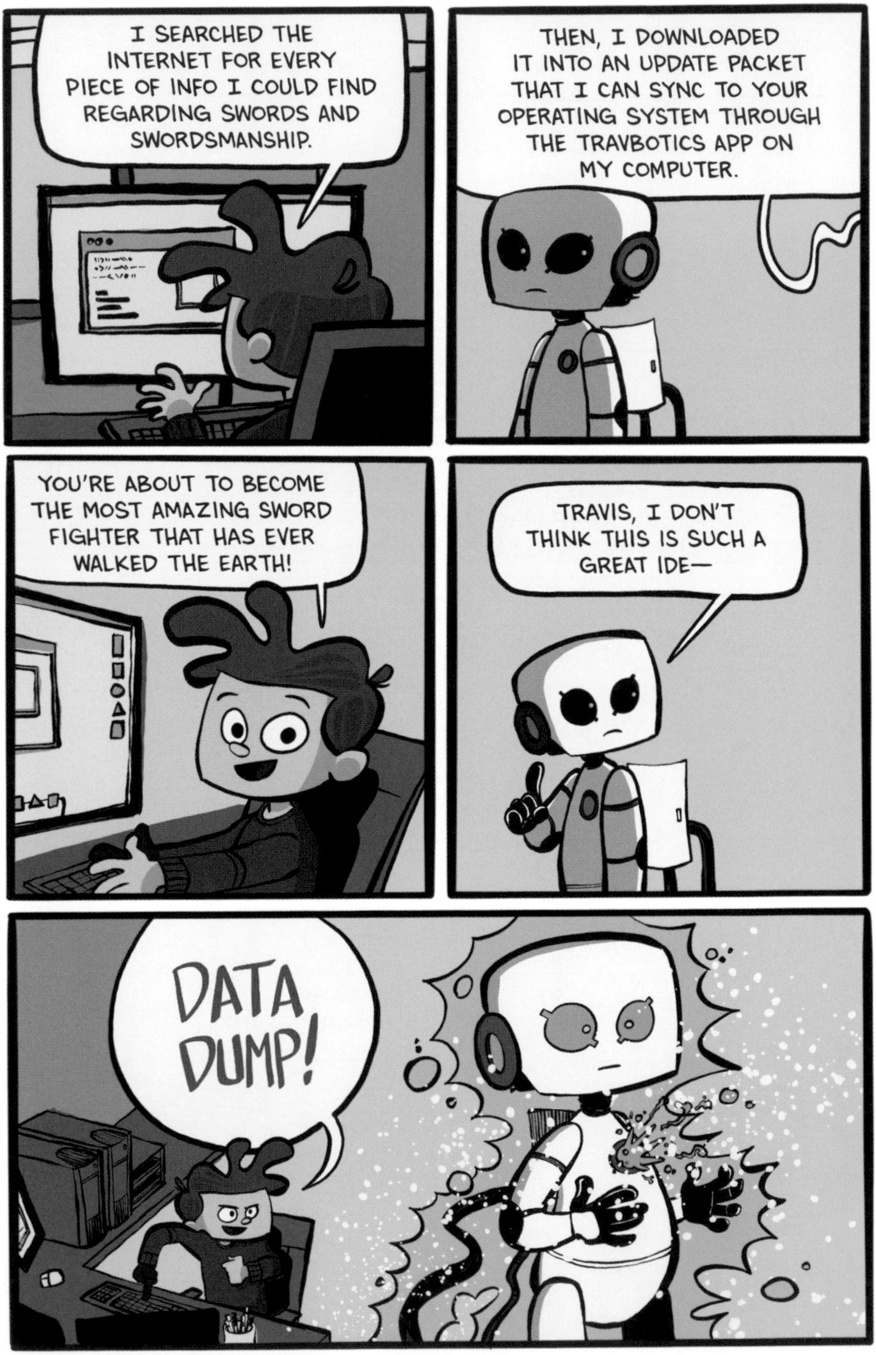
I SEARCHED THE INTERNET FOR EVERY PIECE OF INFO I COULD FIND REGARDING SWORDS AND SWORDSMANSHIP.
THEN, I DOWNLOADED IT INTO AN UPDATE PACKET THAT I CAN SYNC TO YOUR OPERATING SYSTEM THROUGH THE TRAVBOTICS APP ON MY COMPUTER.
YOU'RE ABOUT TO BECOME THE MOST AMAZING SWORD FIGHTER THAT HAS EVER WALKED THE EARTH!
TRAVIS, I DON'T THINK THIS IS SUCH A GREAT IDE—
DATA DUMP!

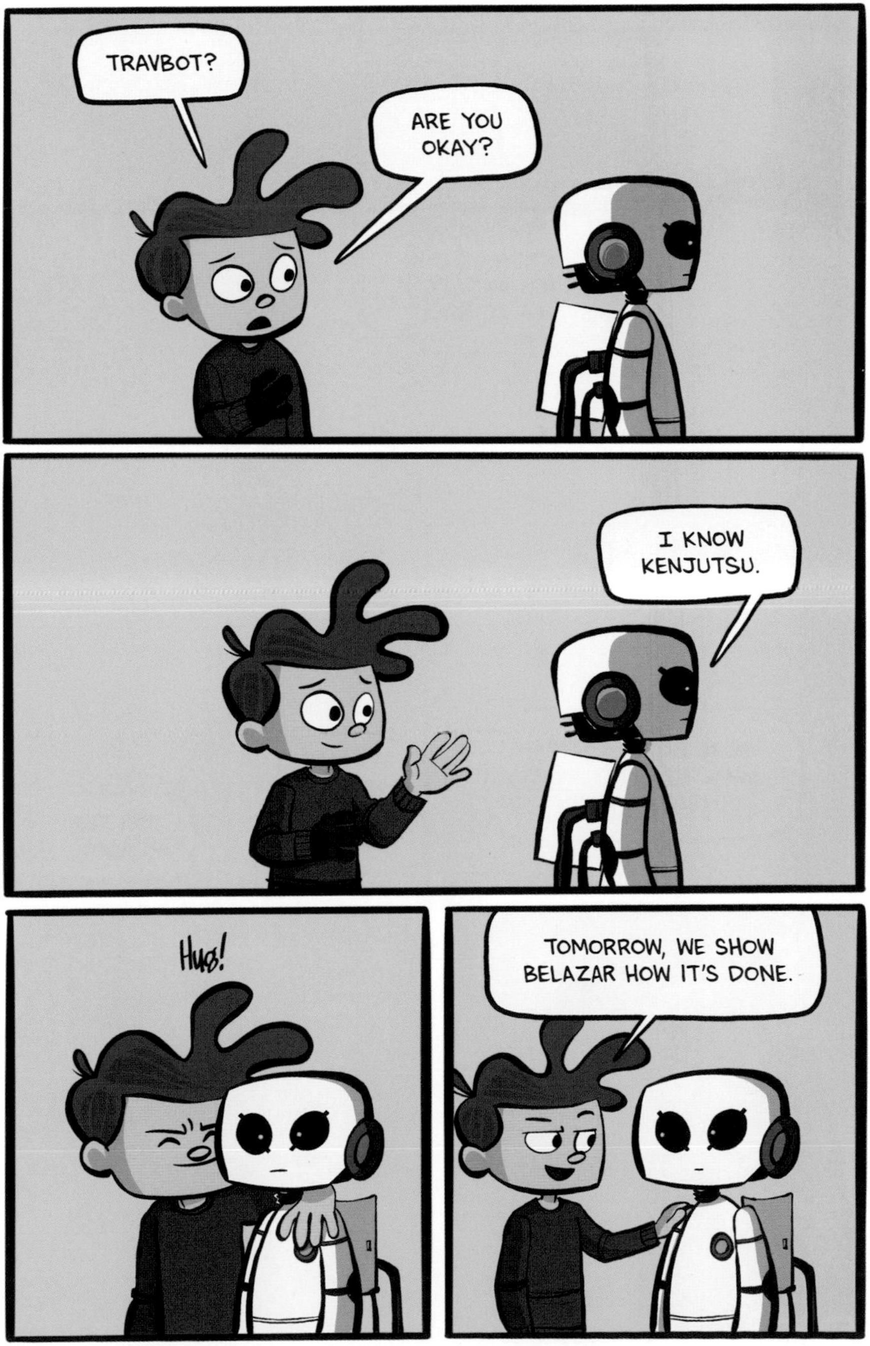
TRAVBOT?
ARE YOU OKAY?
I KNOW KENJUTSU.
Hug!
TOMORROW, WE SHOW BELAZAR HOW IT'S DONE.

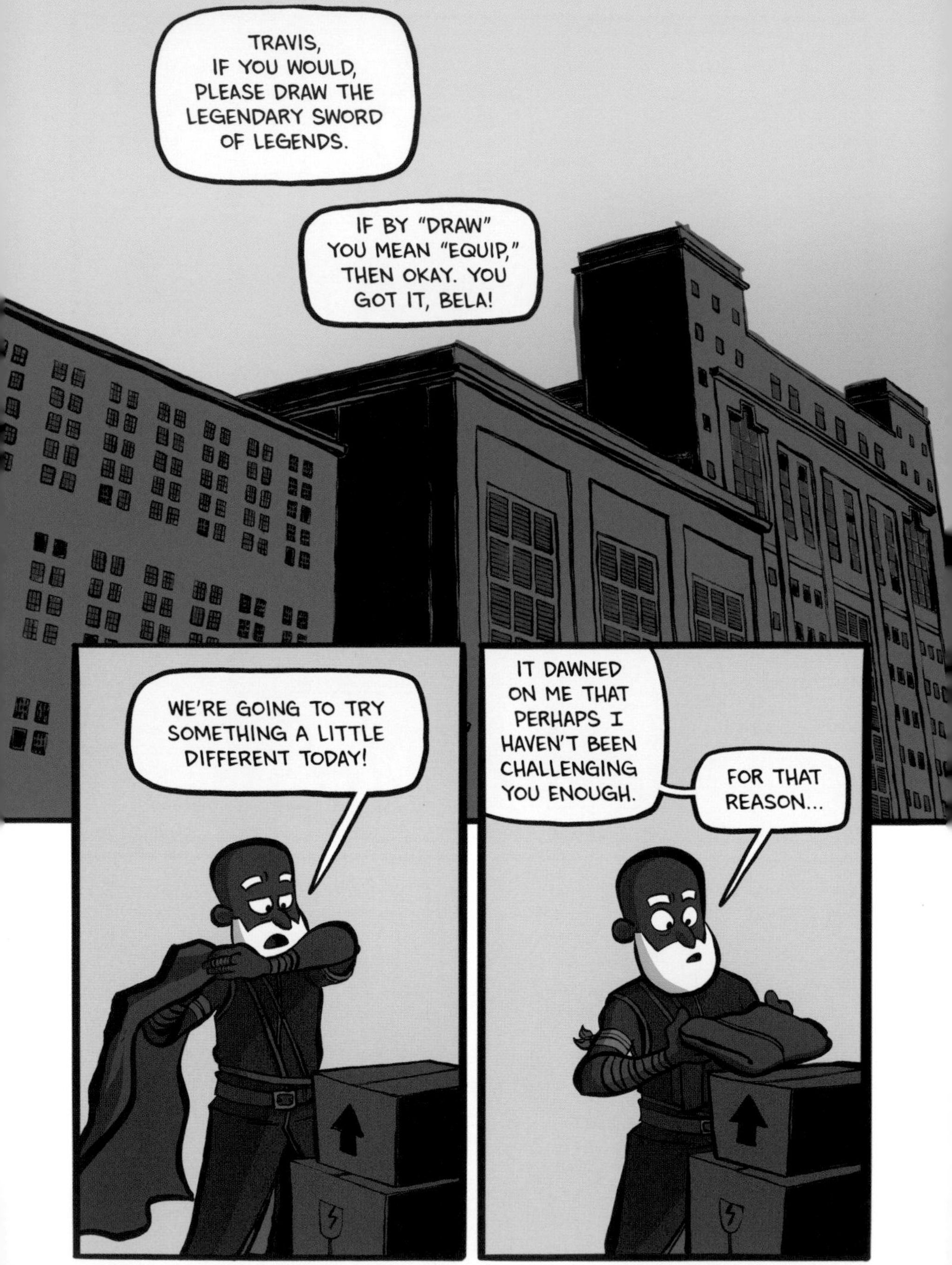
TRAVIS, IF YOU WOULD, PLEASE DRAW THE LEGENDARY SWORD OF LEGENDS.
IF BY "DRAW" YOU MEAN "EQUIP," THEN OKAY. YOU GOT IT, BELA!
WE'RE GOING TO TRY SOMETHING A LITTLE DIFFERENT TODAY!
IT DAWNED ON ME THAT PERHAPS I HAVEN'T BEEN CHALLENGING YOU ENOUGH.
FOR THAT REASON...

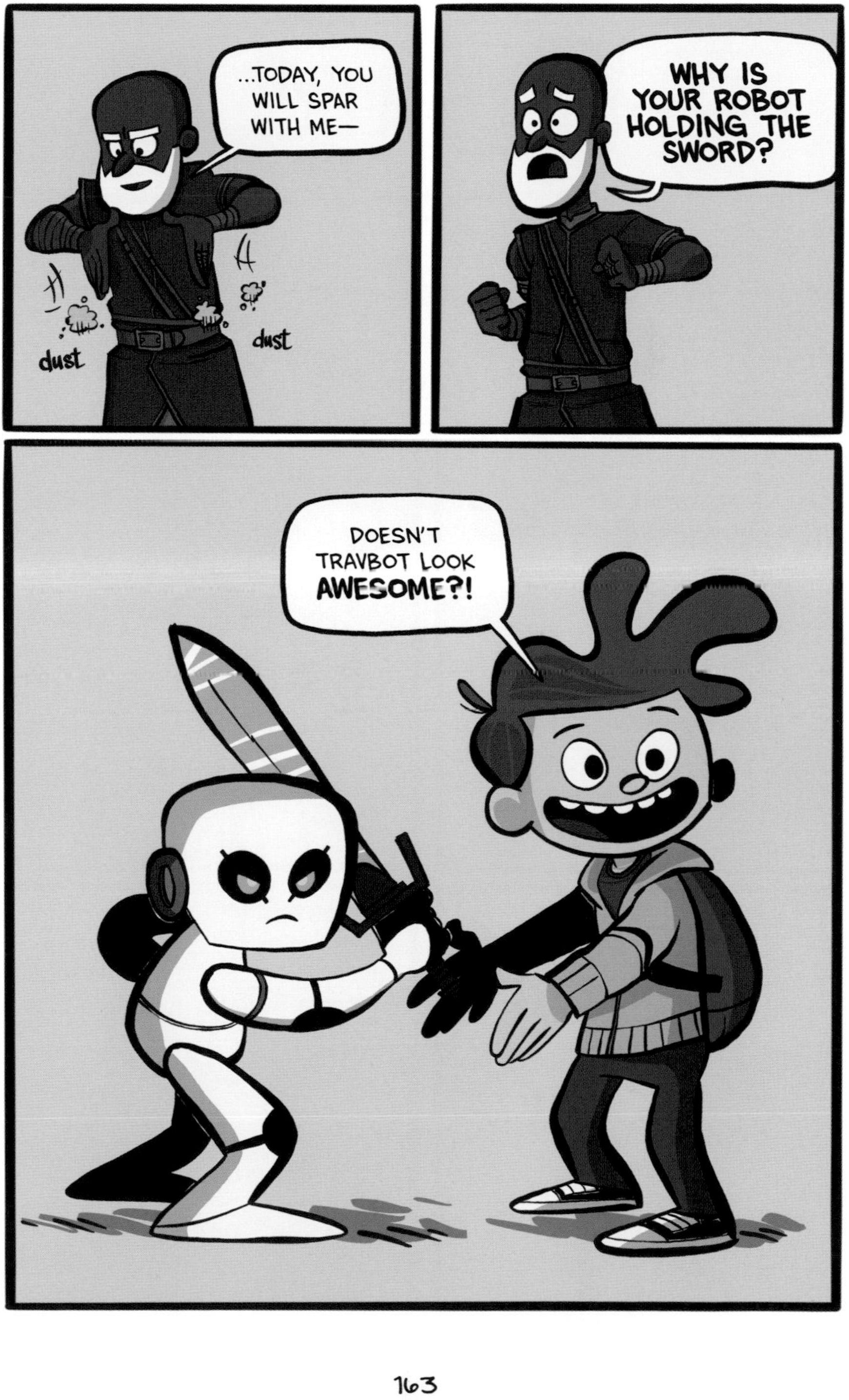
...TODAY, YOU WILL SPAR WITH ME—
dust
dust
WHY IS YOUR ROBOT HOLDING THE SWORD?
DOESN'T TRAVBOT LOOK **AWESOME?!**

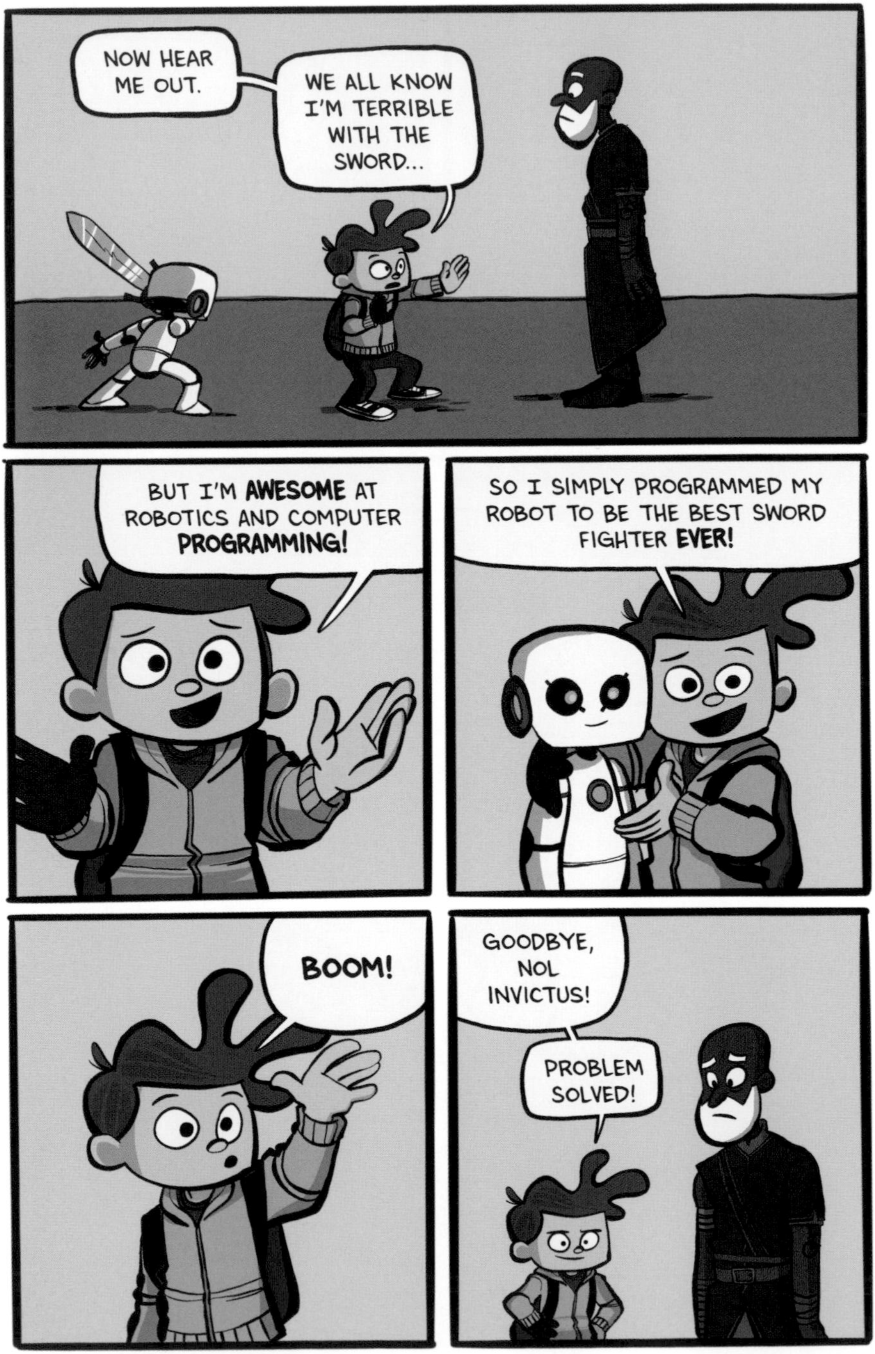
NOW HEAR ME OUT.
WE ALL KNOW I'M TERRIBLE WITH THE SWORD...
BUT I'M **AWESOME** AT ROBOTICS AND COMPUTER **PROGRAMMING!**
SO I SIMPLY PROGRAMMED MY ROBOT TO BE THE BEST SWORD FIGHTER **EVER!**
BOOM!
GOODBYE, NOL INVICTUS!
PROBLEM SOLVED!

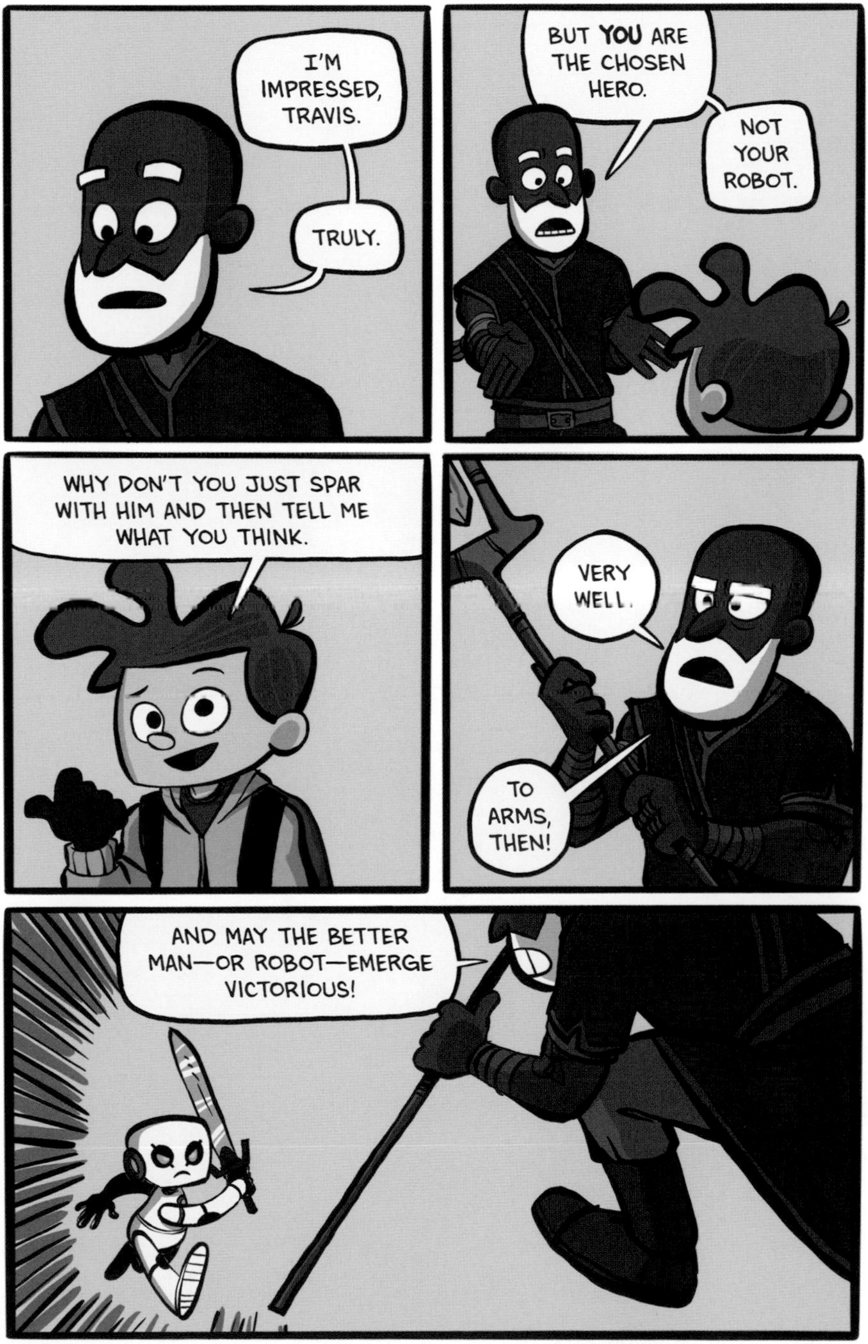
I'M IMPRESSED, TRAVIS.
TRULY.
BUT YOU ARE THE CHOSEN HERO.
NOT YOUR ROBOT.
WHY DON'T YOU JUST SPAR WITH HIM AND THEN TELL ME WHAT YOU THINK.
VERY WELL.
TO ARMS, THEN!
AND MAY THE BETTER MAN—OR ROBOT—EMERGE VICTORIOUS!

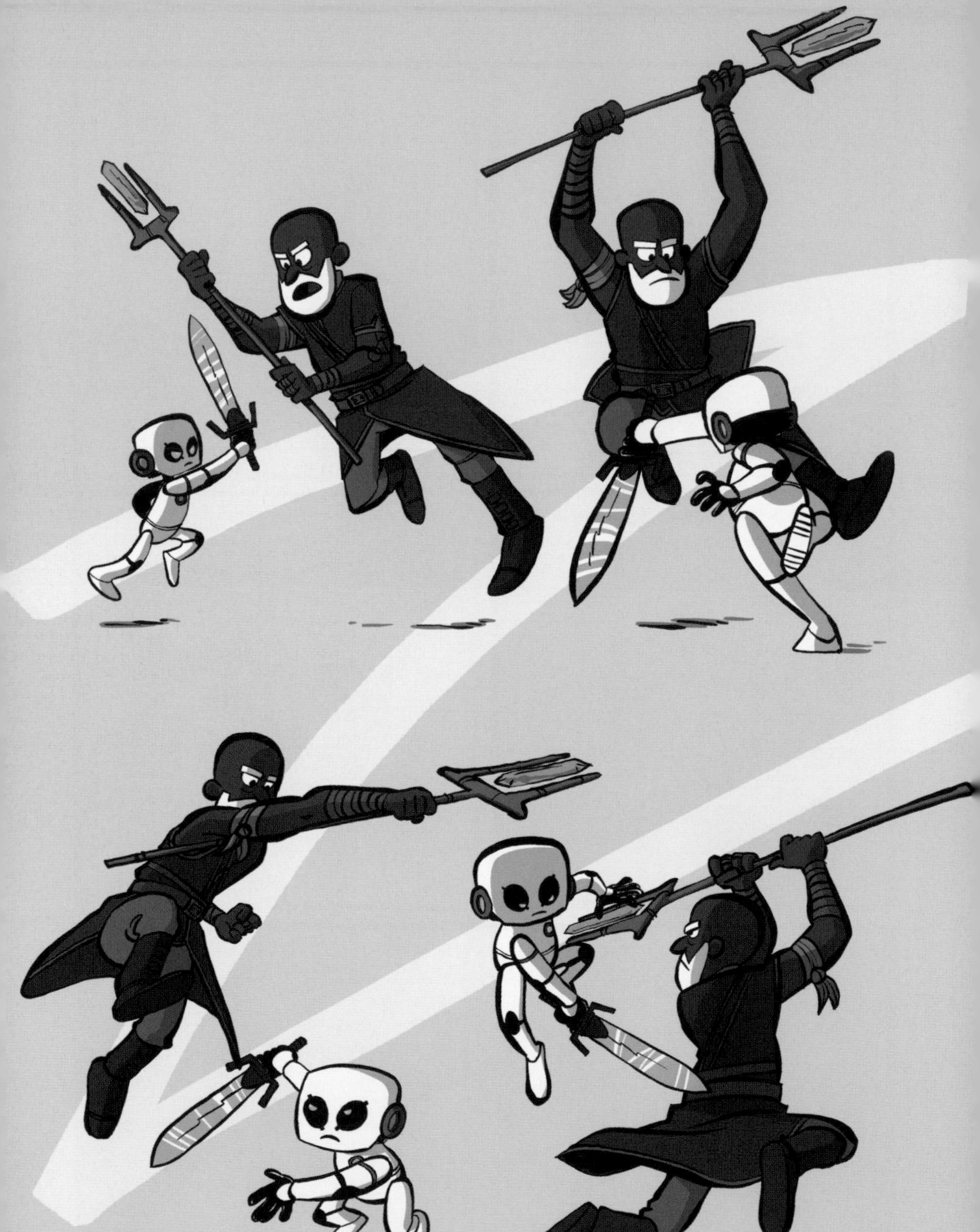

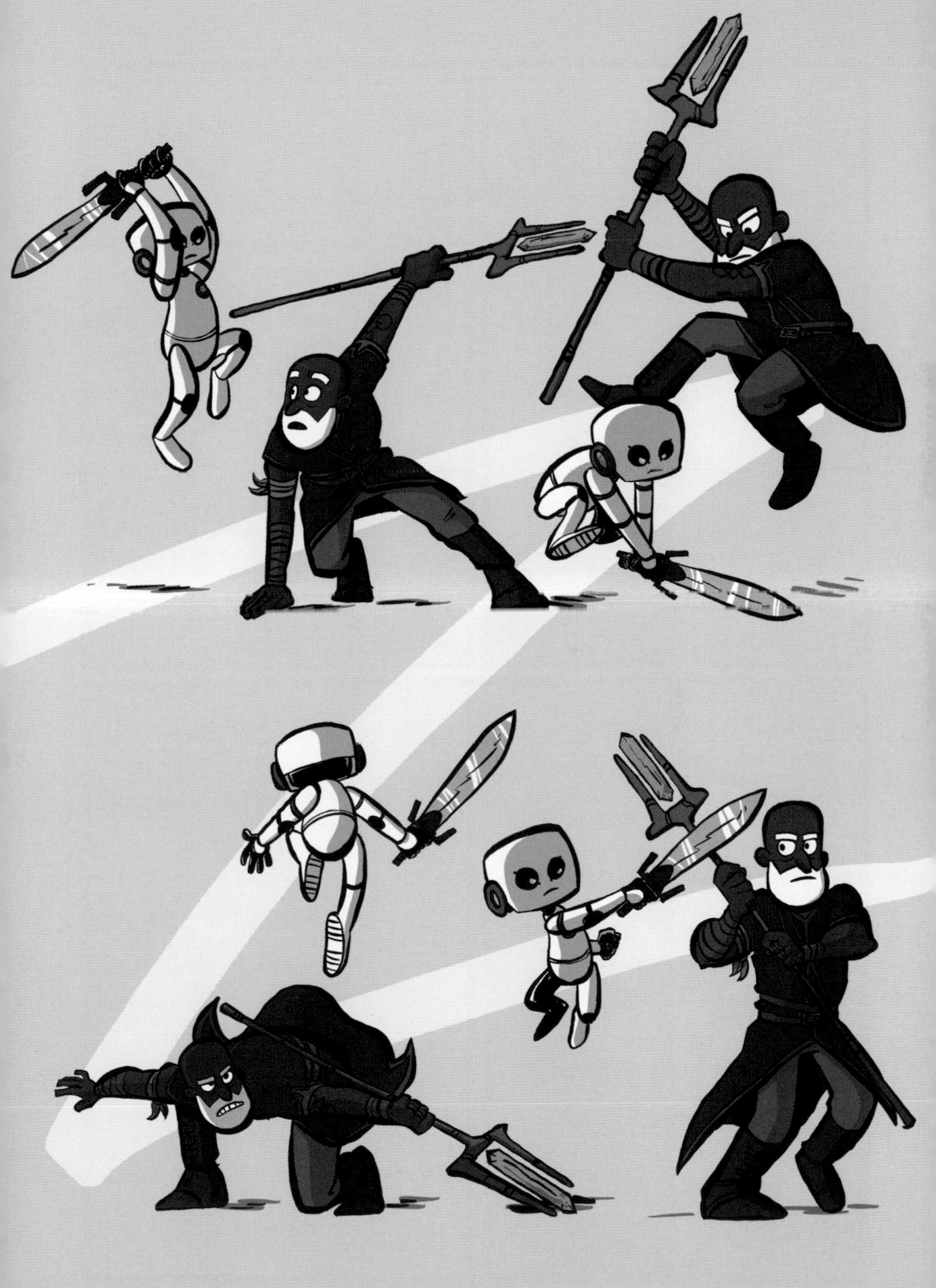

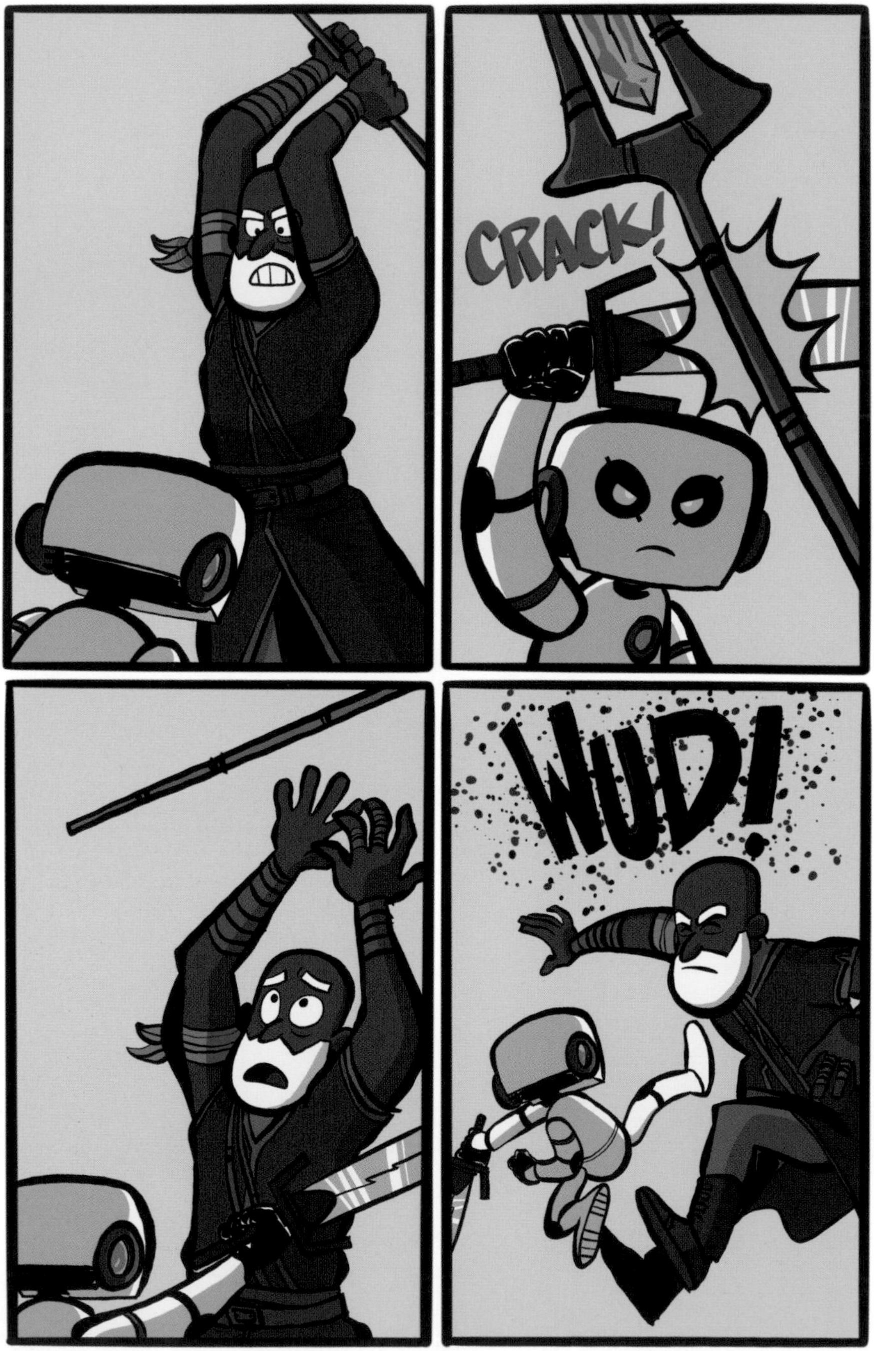
CRACK!
WUD!

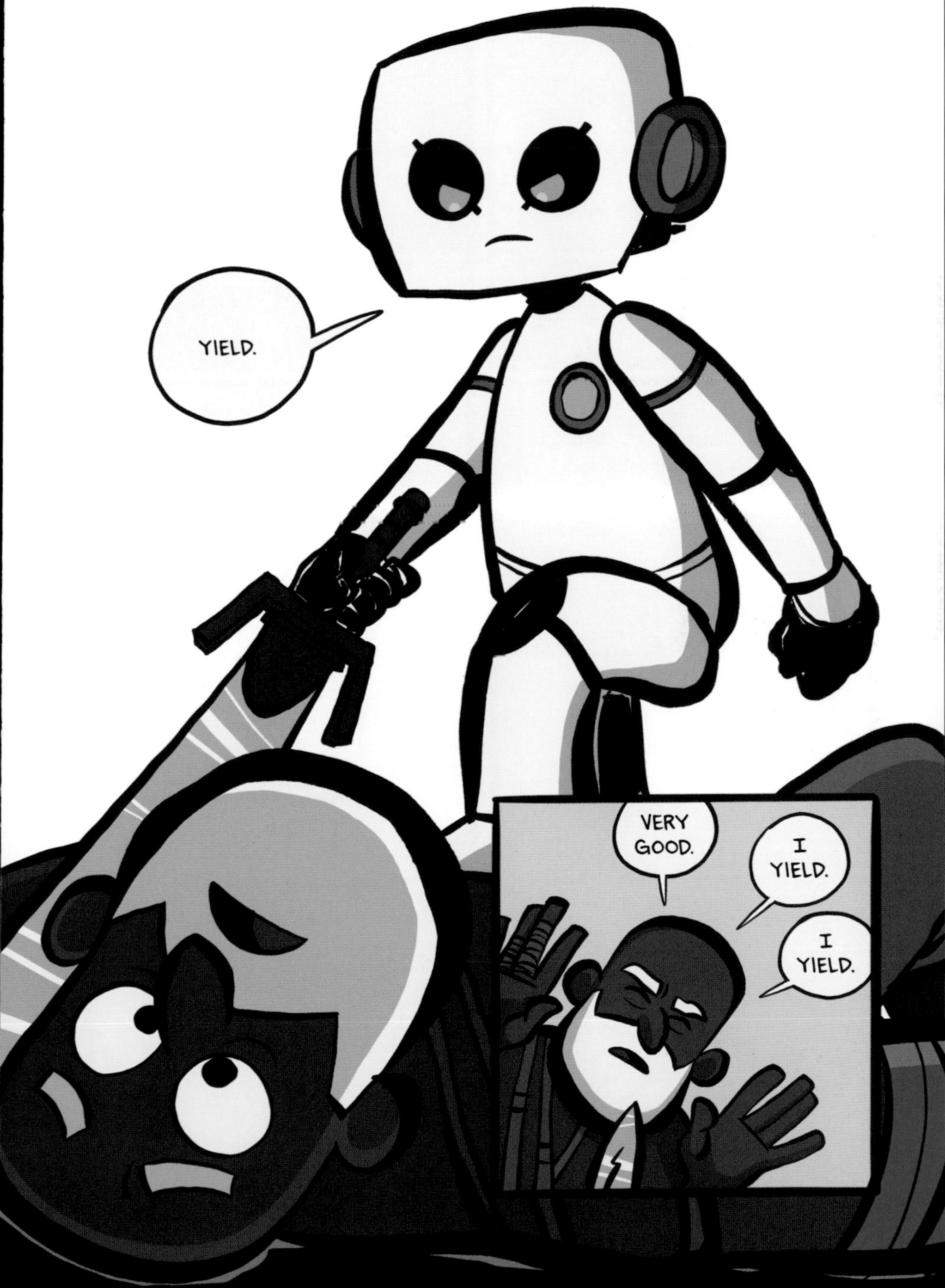
YIELD.
VERY GOOD.
I YIELD.
I YIELD.

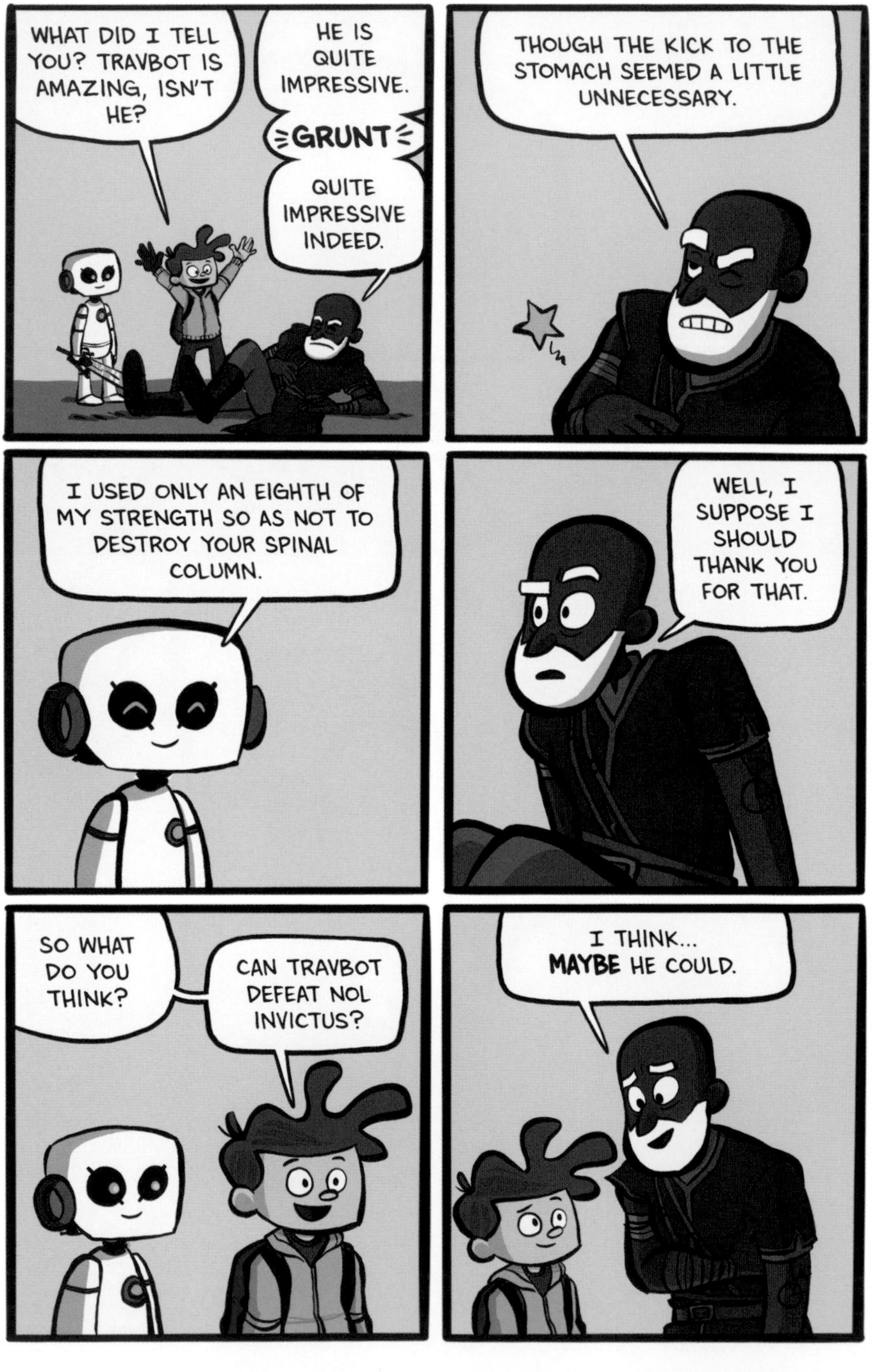
WHAT DID I TELL YOU? TRAVBOT IS AMAZING, ISN'T HE?
HE IS QUITE IMPRESSIVE.
GRUNT
QUITE IMPRESSIVE INDEED.
THOUGH THE KICK TO THE STOMACH SEEMED A LITTLE UNNECESSARY.
I USED ONLY AN EIGHTH OF MY STRENGTH SO AS NOT TO DESTROY YOUR SPINAL COLUMN.
WELL, I SUPPOSE I SHOULD THANK YOU FOR THAT.
SO WHAT DO YOU THINK?
CAN TRAVBOT DEFEAT NOL INVICTUS?
I THINK... **MAYBE** HE COULD.

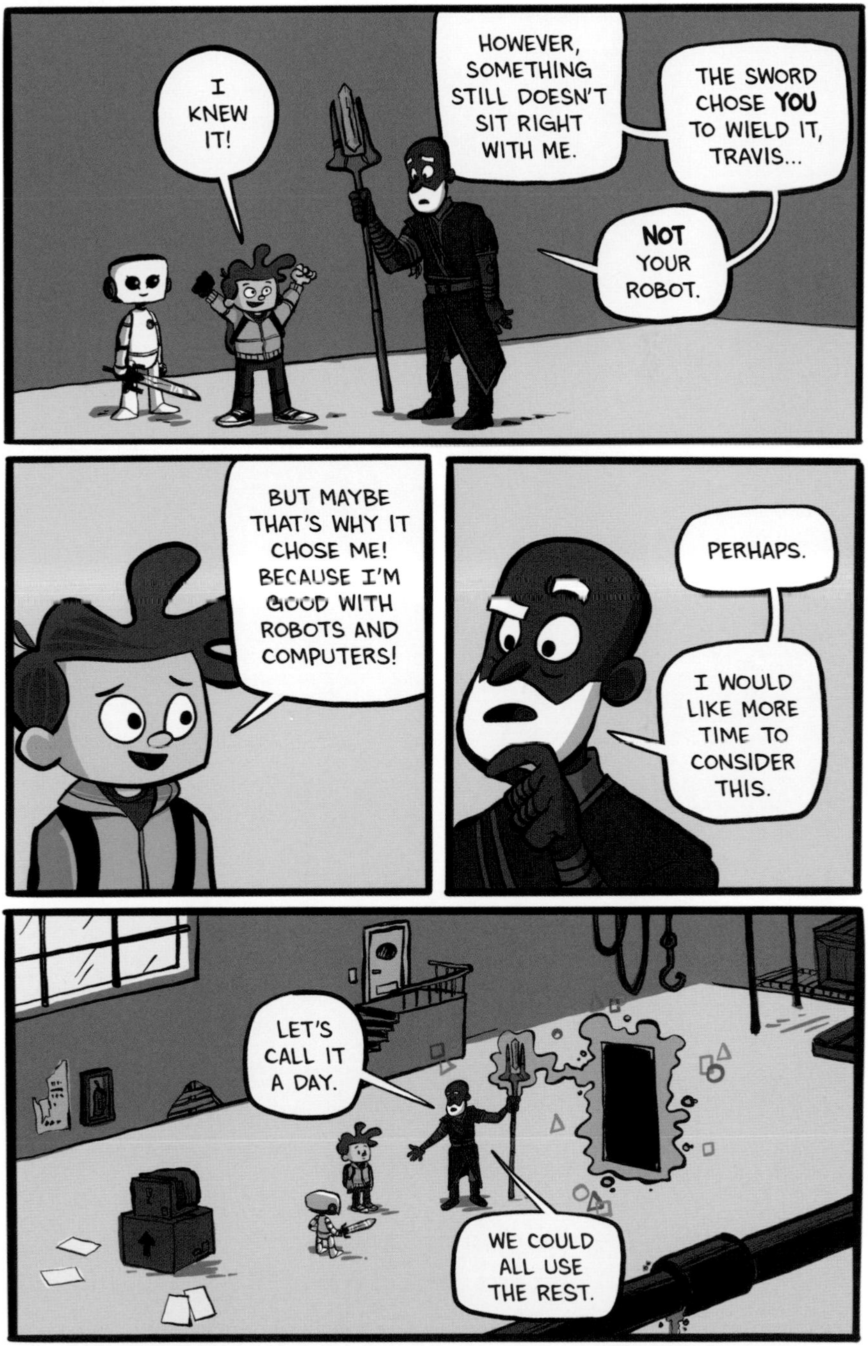
I KNEW IT!
HOWEVER, SOMETHING STILL DOESN'T SIT RIGHT WITH ME.
THE SWORD CHOSE **YOU** TO WIELD IT, TRAVIS...
NOT YOUR ROBOT.
BUT MAYBE THAT'S WHY IT CHOSE ME! BECAUSE I'M GOOD WITH ROBOTS AND COMPUTERS!
PERHAPS.
I WOULD LIKE MORE TIME TO CONSIDER THIS.
LET'S CALL IT A DAY.
WE COULD ALL USE THE REST.

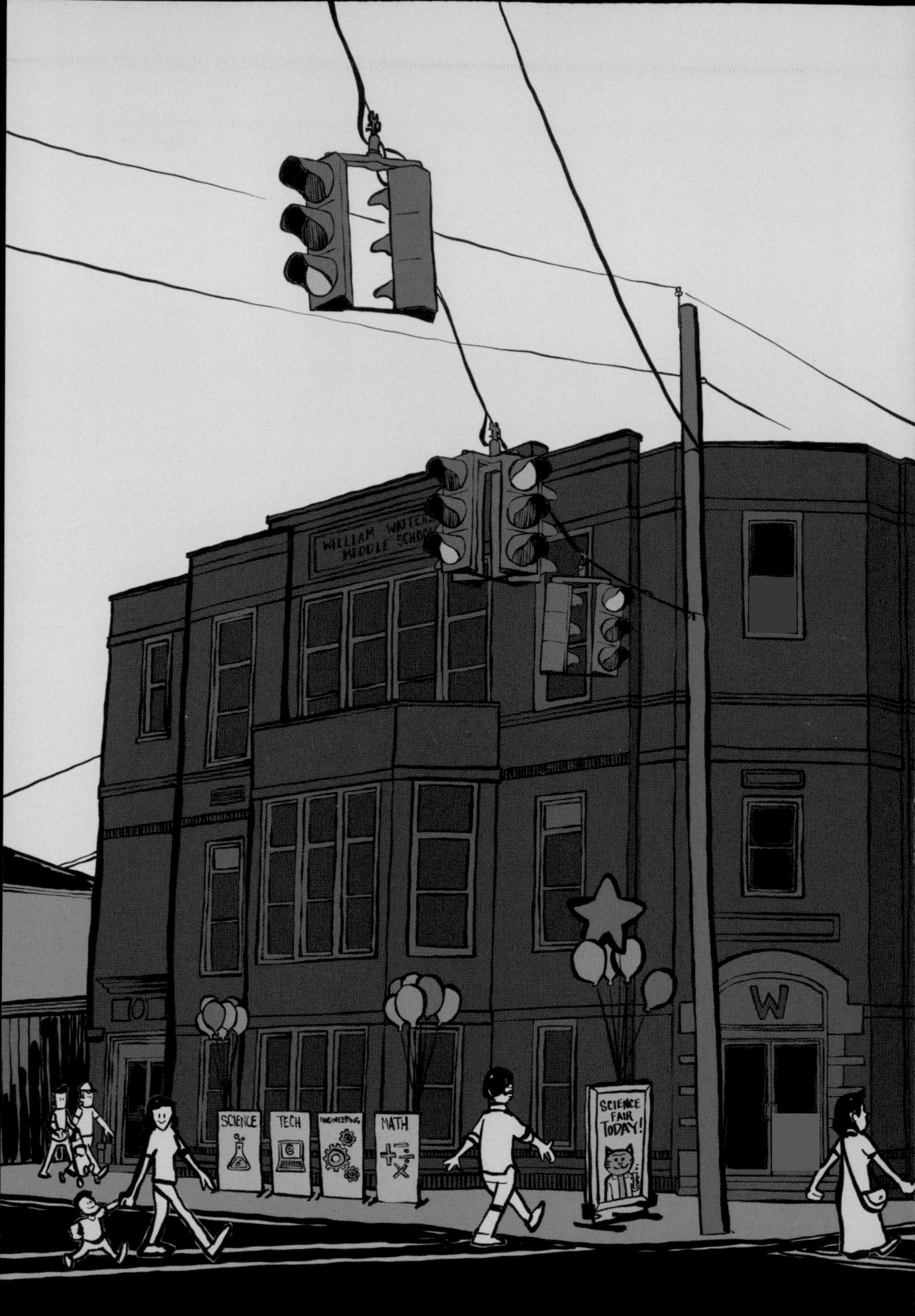
WILLIAM WATTER
MIDDLE SCHO
W
SCIENCE
TECH
ENGINEERING
MATH
SCIENCE FAIR TODAY!

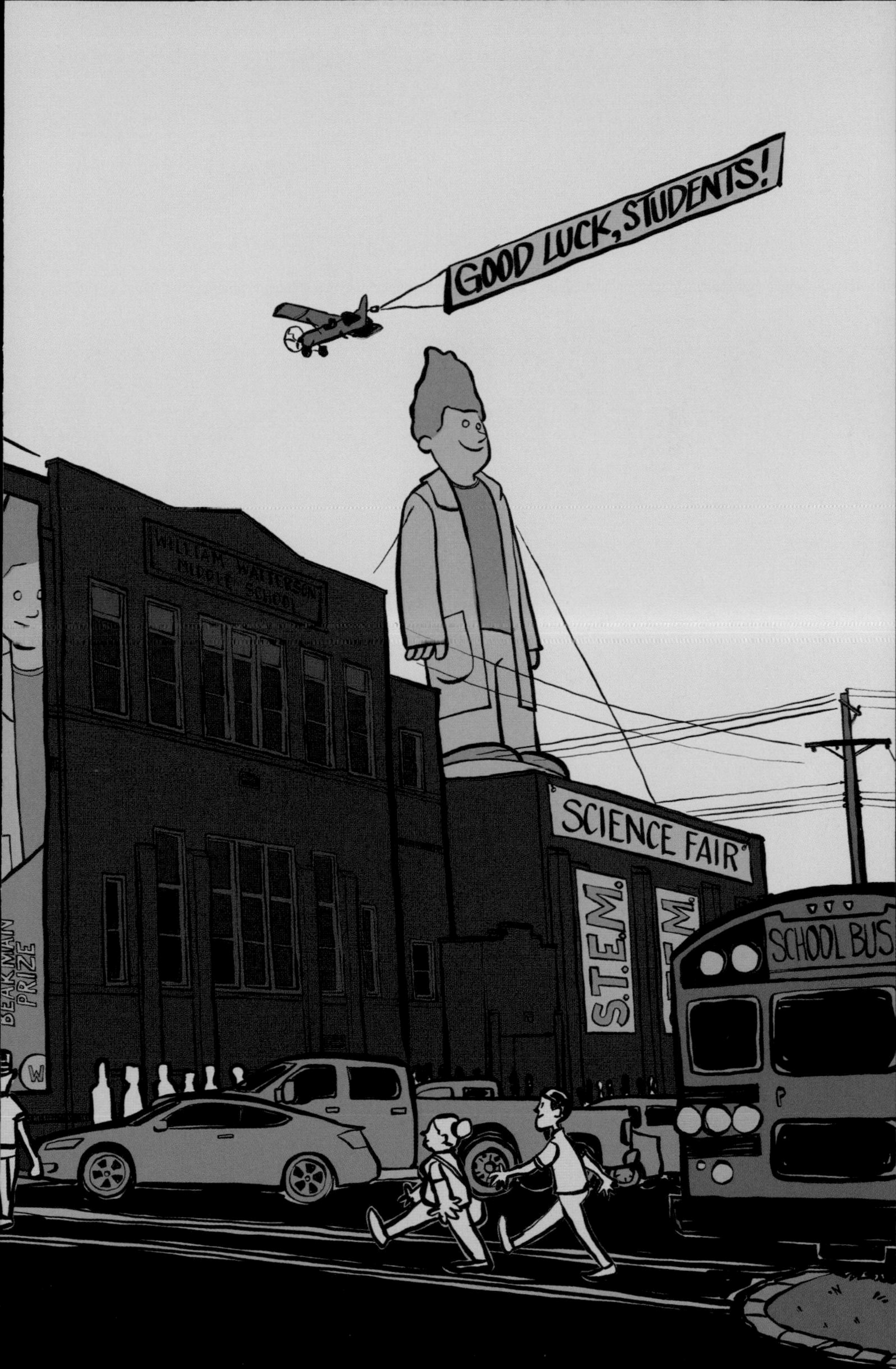
GOOD LUCK, STUDENTS!
WILLIAM WATTERSON MIDDLE SCHOOL
SCIENCE FAIR
S.T.E.M.
SCHOOL BUS
BEAKMAN PRIZE

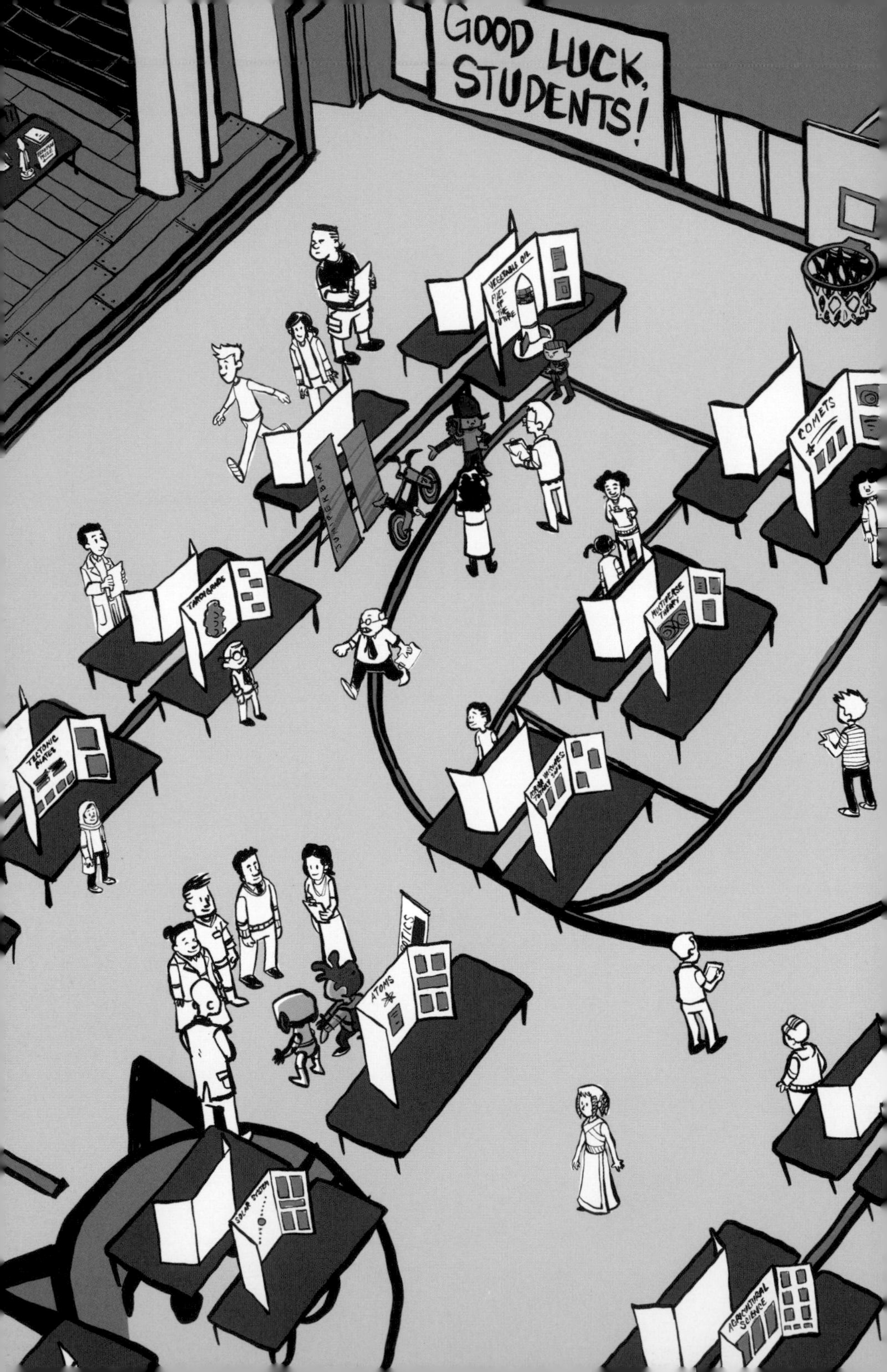
GOOD LUCK, STUDENTS!
VEGETABLE OIL
FUEL OF THE FUTURE
COMETS
MULTIVERSE THEORY
TECTONIC PLATES
ATOMS
SOLAR SYSTEM
AGRICULTURAL SCIENCE

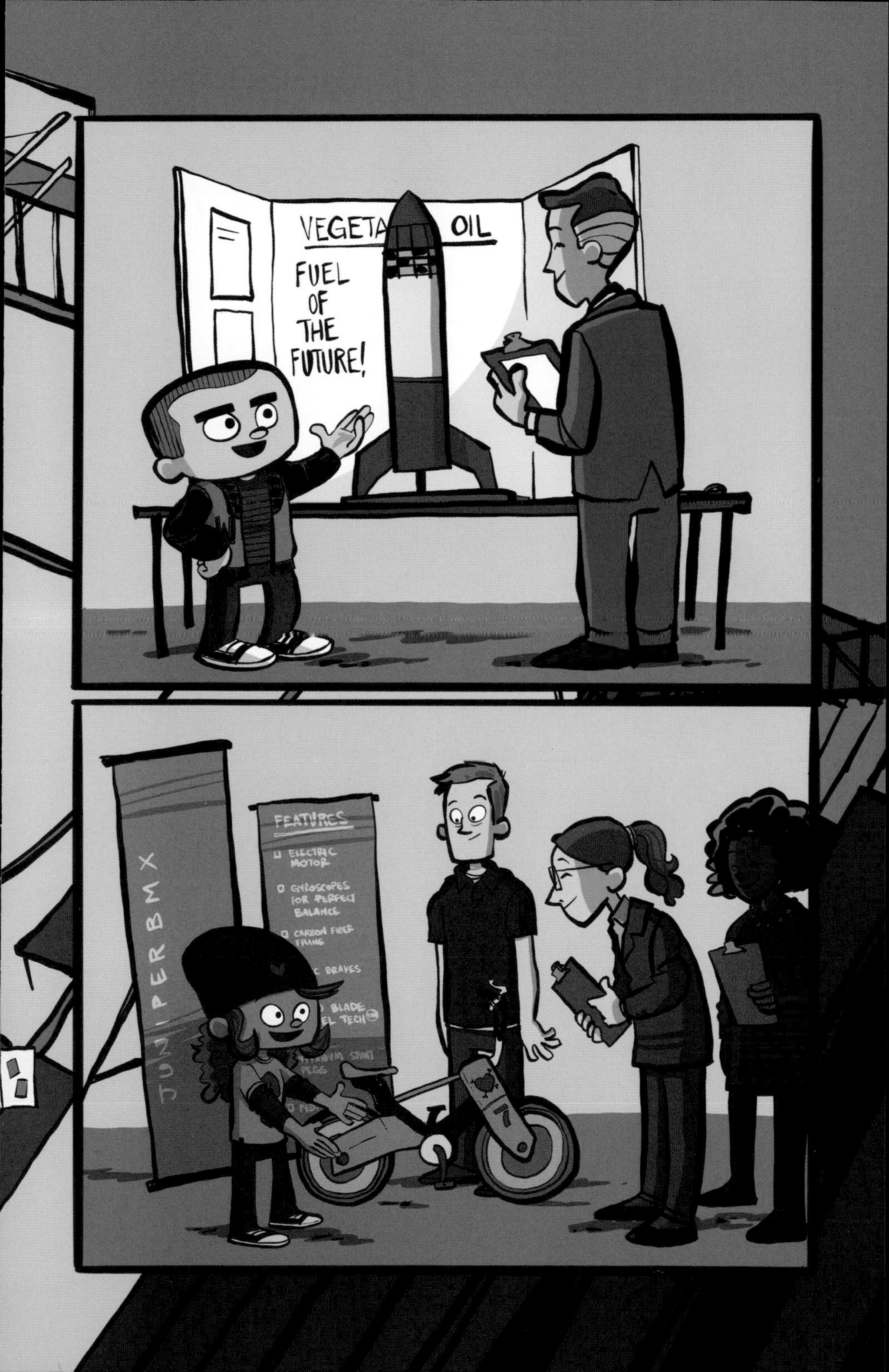
VEGETA OIL
FUEL OF THE FUTURE!
FEATURES
ELECTRIC MOTOR
GYROSCOPES FOR PERFECT BALANCE
CARBON FIBER FRAME
JUNIPER BMX
7

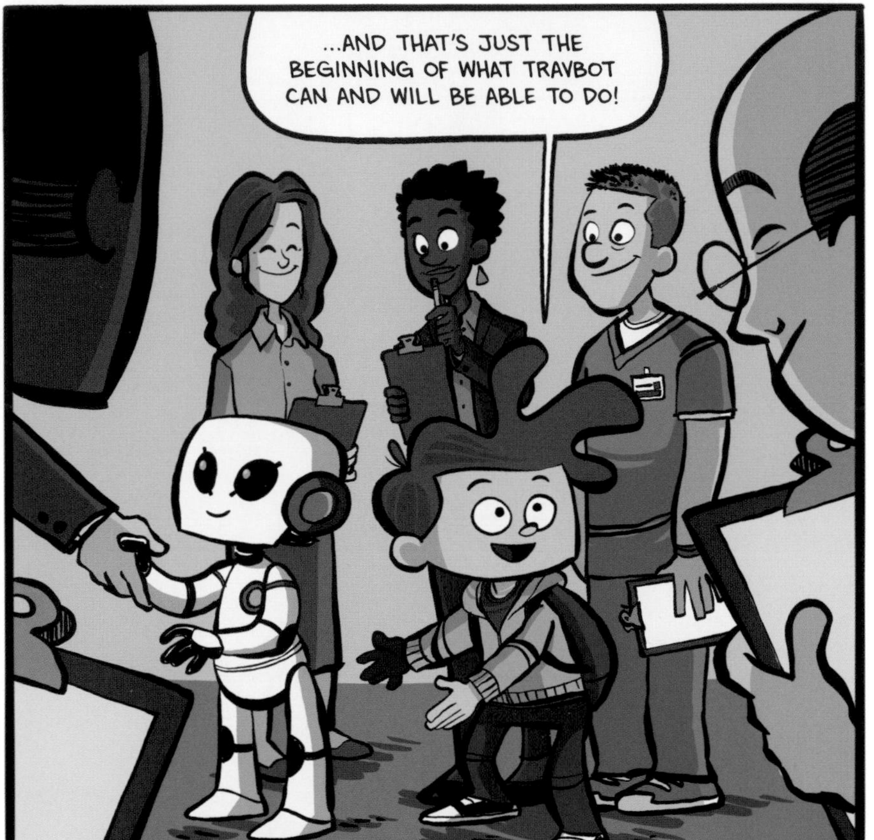
...AND THAT'S JUST THE BEGINNING OF WHAT TRAVBOT CAN AND WILL BE ABLE TO DO!

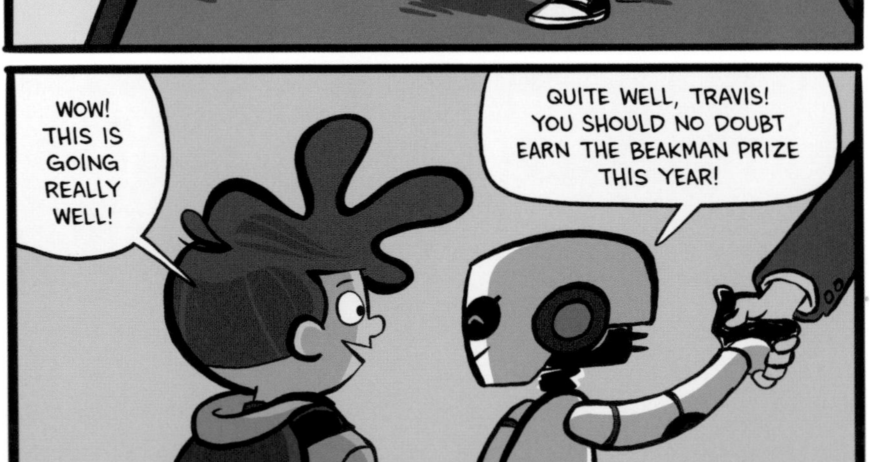
WOW! THIS IS GOING REALLY WELL!
QUITE WELL, TRAVIS! YOU SHOULD NO DOUBT EARN THE BEAKMAN PRIZE THIS YEAR!

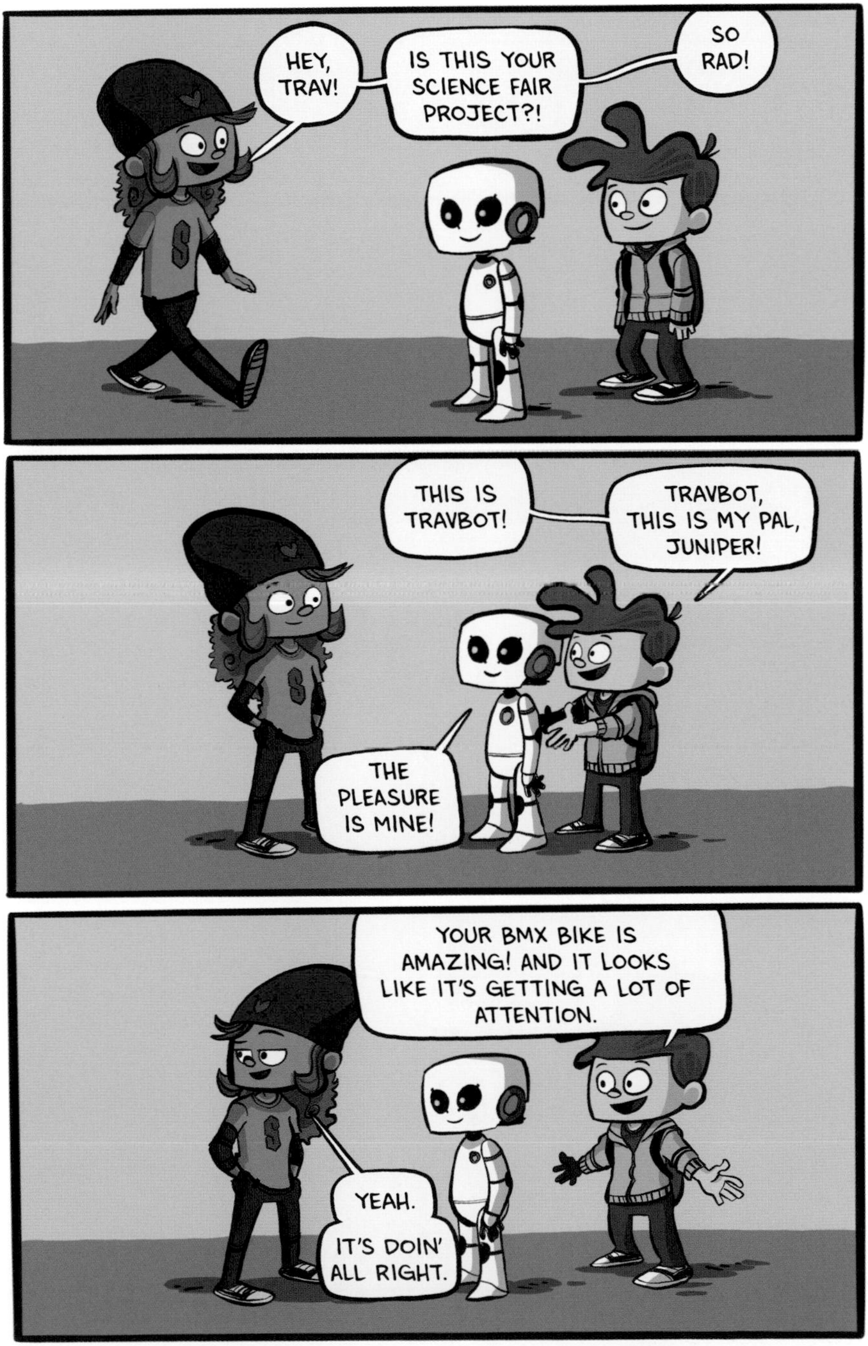
HEY, TRAV!
IS THIS YOUR SCIENCE FAIR PROJECT?!
SO RAD!
THIS IS TRAVBOT!
TRAVBOT, THIS IS MY PAL, JUNIPER!
THE PLEASURE IS MINE!
YOUR BMX BIKE IS AMAZING! AND IT LOOKS LIKE IT'S GETTING A LOT OF ATTENTION.
YEAH.
IT'S DOIN' ALL RIGHT.

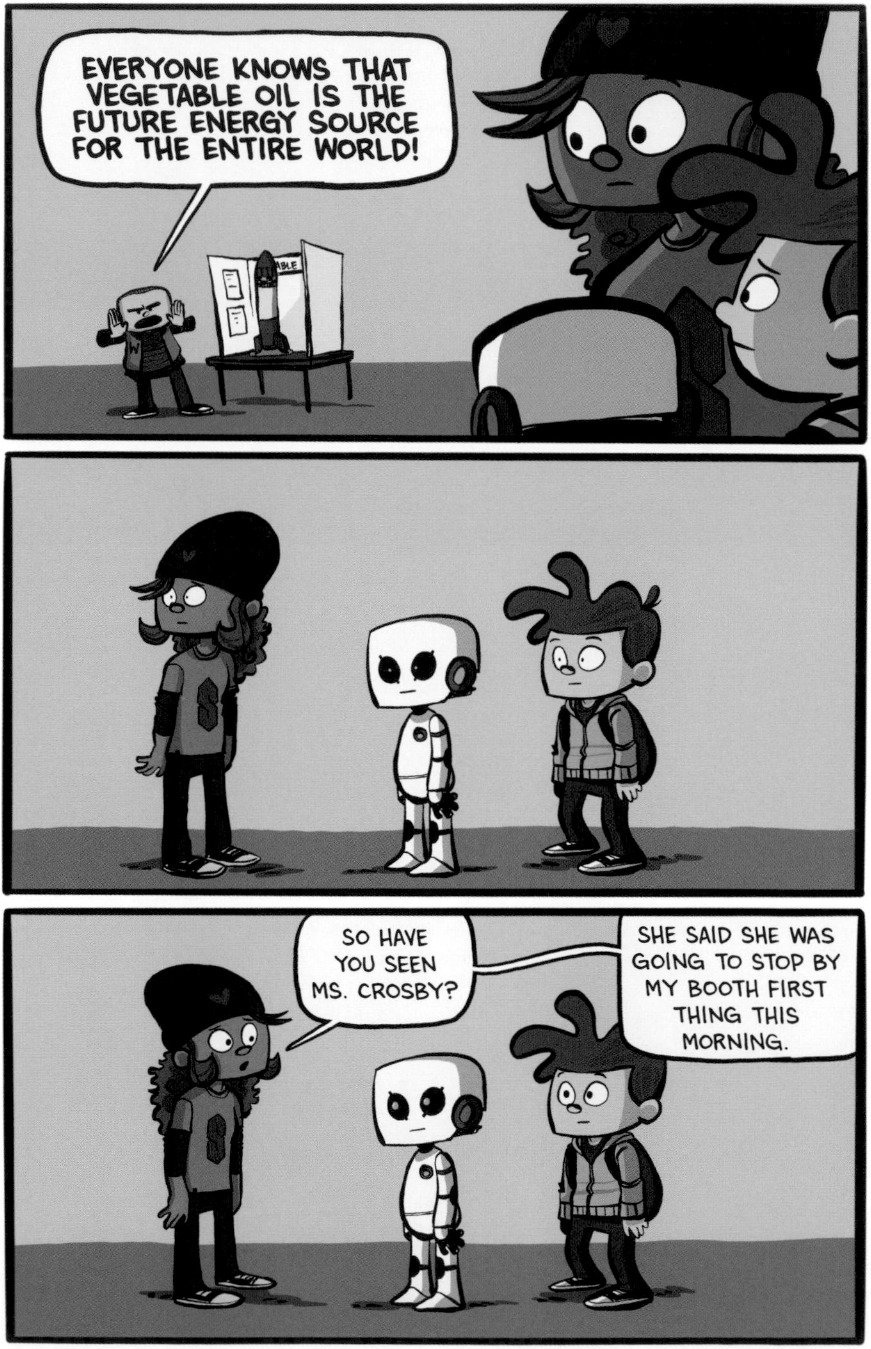
EVERYONE KNOWS THAT VEGETABLE OIL IS THE FUTURE ENERGY SOURCE FOR THE ENTIRE WORLD!
SO HAVE YOU SEEN MS. CROSBY?
SHE SAID SHE WAS GOING TO STOP BY MY BOOTH FIRST THING THIS MORNING.

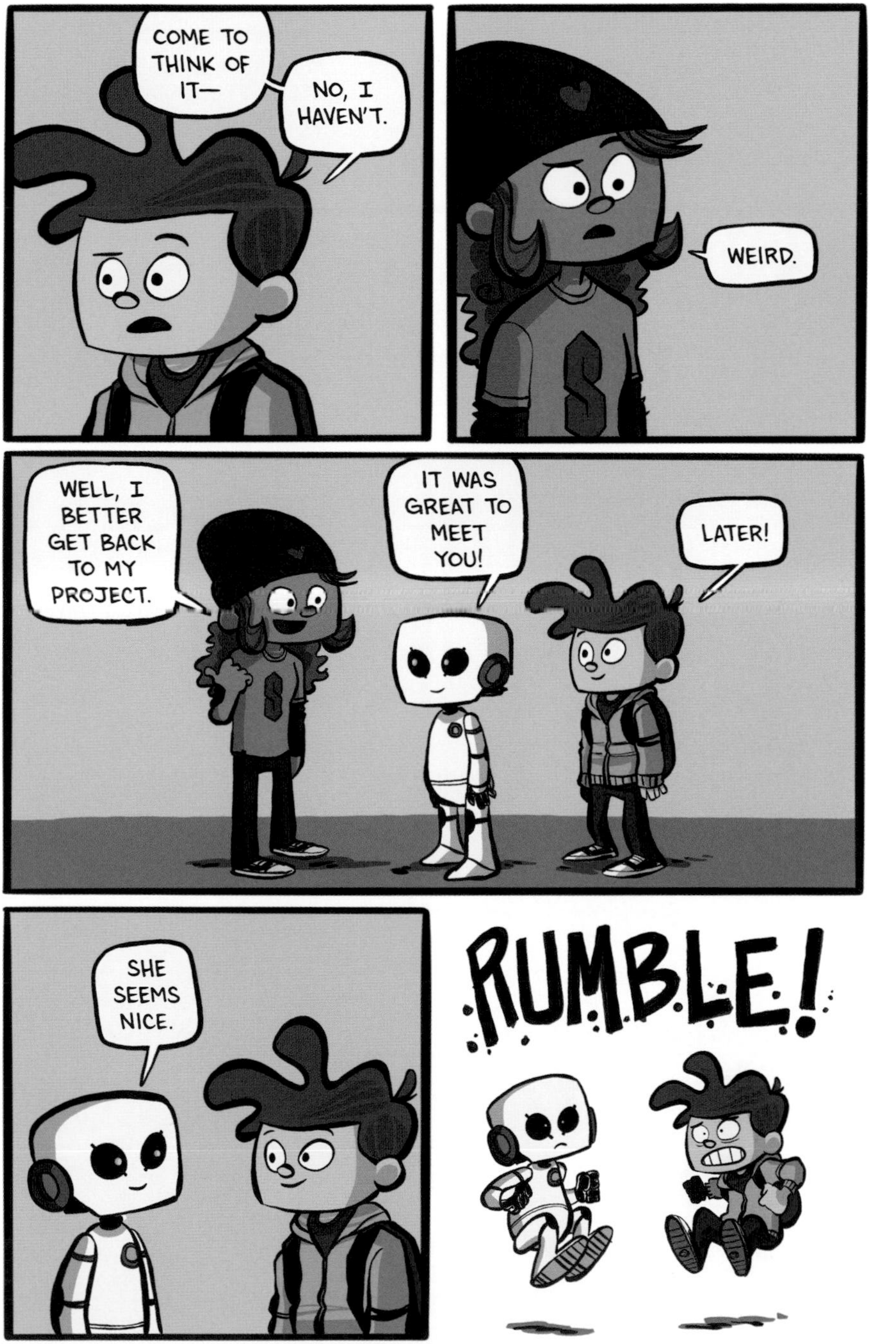
COME TO THINK OF IT—
NO, I HAVEN'T.
WEIRD.
WELL, I BETTER GET BACK TO MY PROJECT.
IT WAS GREAT TO MEET YOU!
LATER!
SHE SEEMS NICE.
RUMBLE!

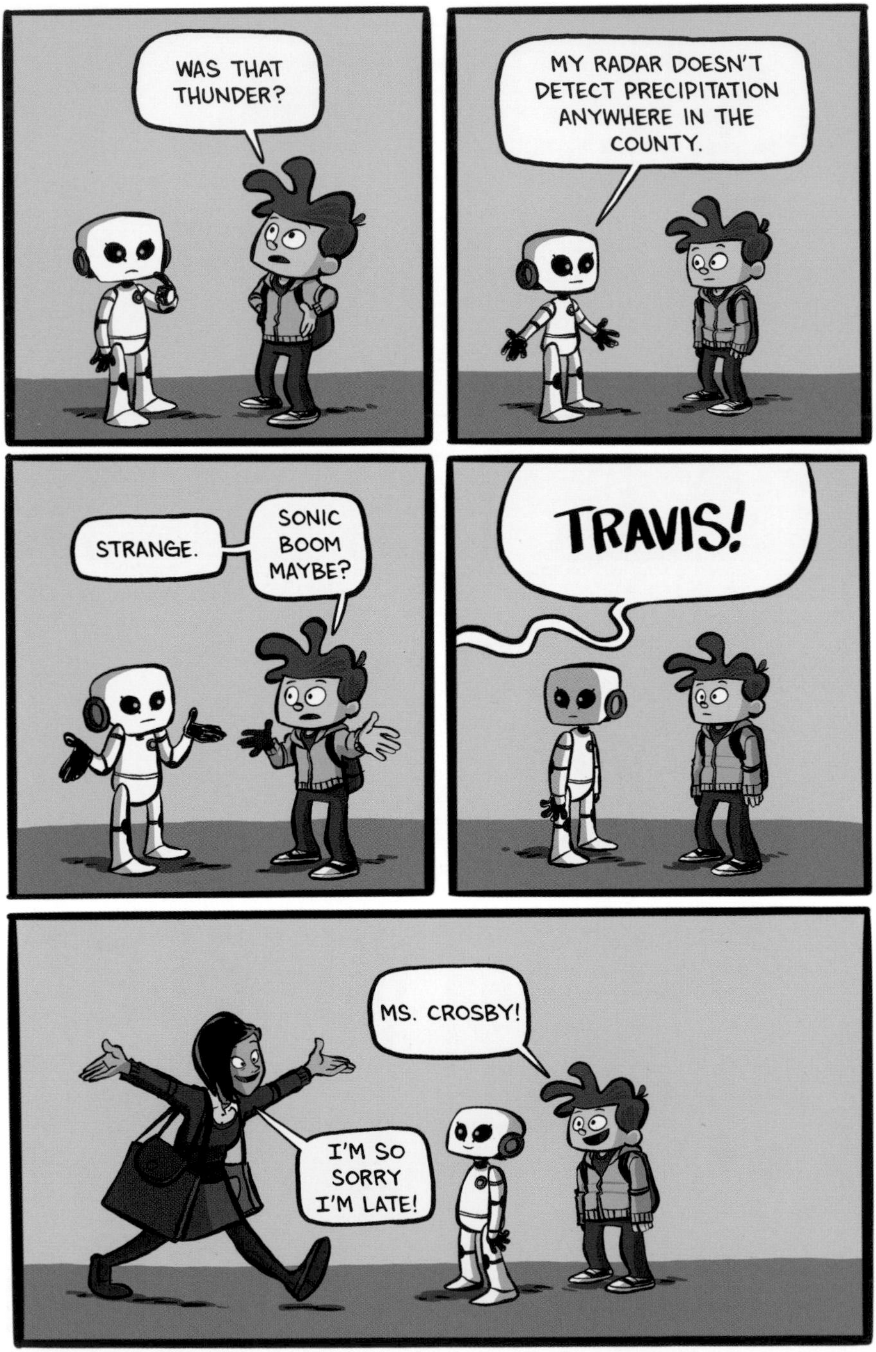
WAS THAT THUNDER?
MY RADAR DOESN'T DETECT PRECIPITATION ANYWHERE IN THE COUNTY.
STRANGE.
SONIC BOOM MAYBE?
TRAVIS!
MS. CROSBY!
I'M SO SORRY I'M LATE!

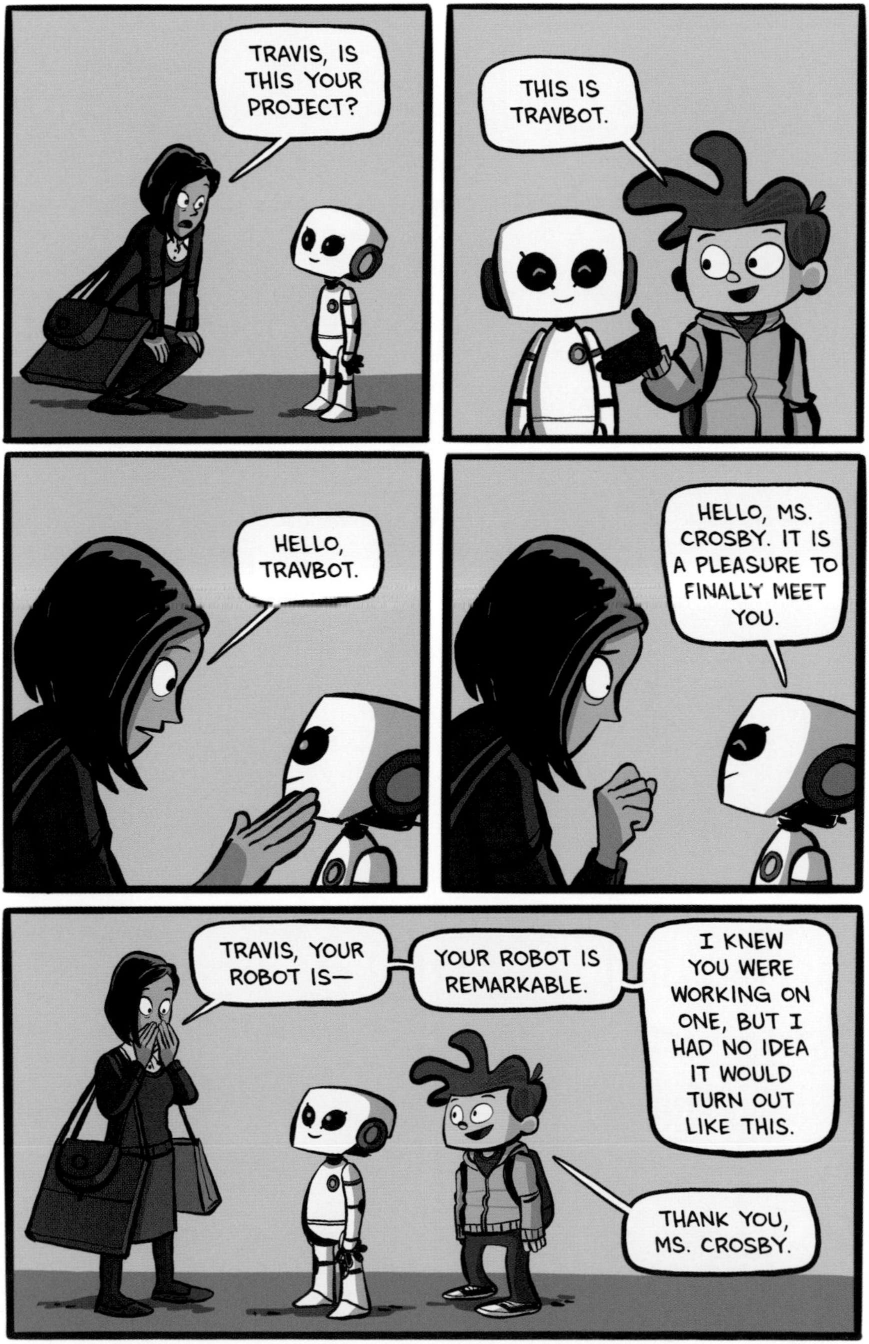
TRAVIS, IS THIS YOUR PROJECT?
THIS IS TRAVBOT.
HELLO, TRAVBOT.
HELLO, MS. CROSBY. IT IS A PLEASURE TO FINALLY MEET YOU.
TRAVIS, YOUR ROBOT IS—
YOUR ROBOT IS REMARKABLE.
I KNEW YOU WERE WORKING ON ONE, BUT I HAD NO IDEA IT WOULD TURN OUT LIKE THIS.
THANK YOU, MS. CROSBY.

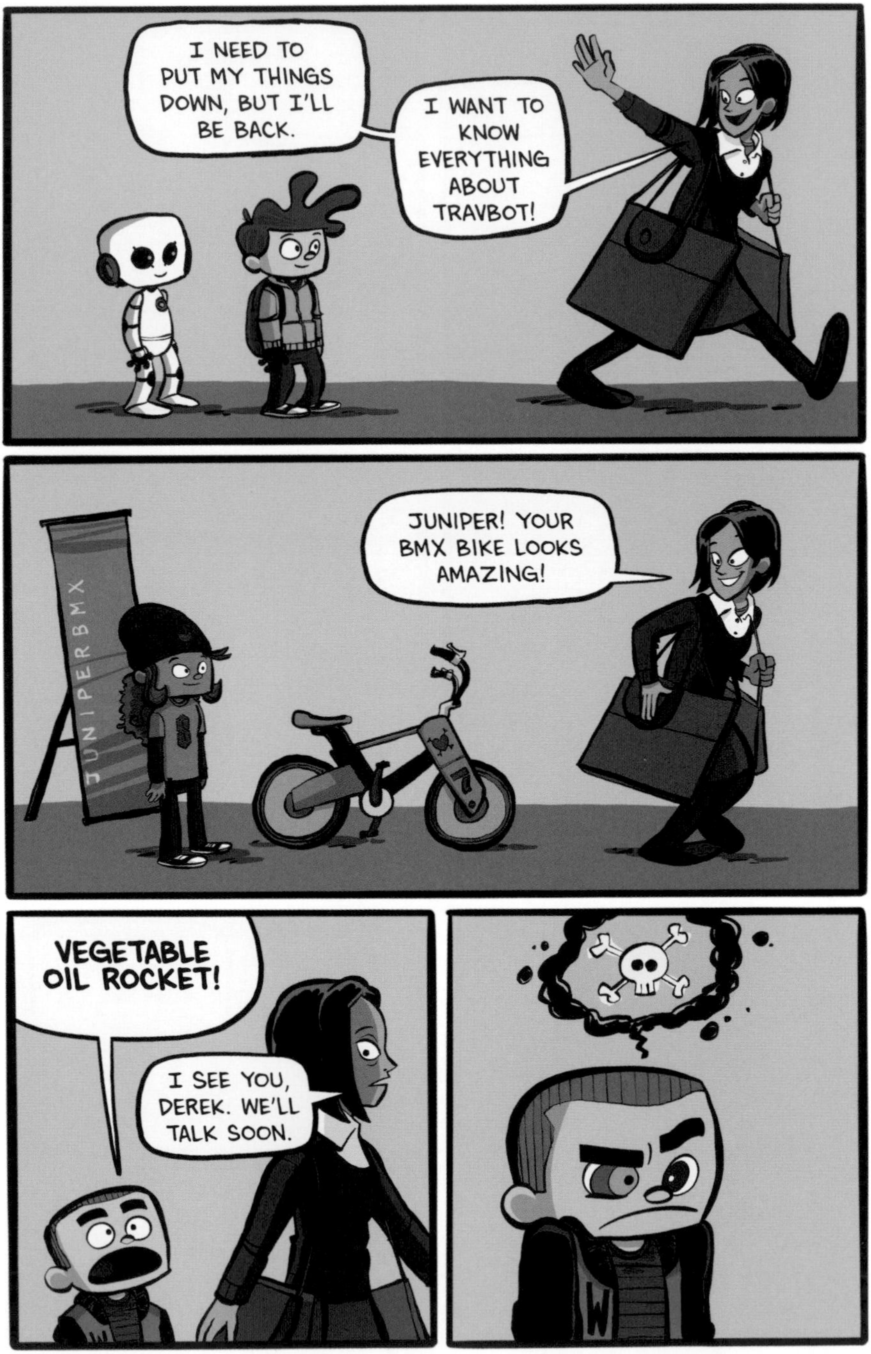
I NEED TO PUT MY THINGS DOWN, BUT I'LL BE BACK.
I WANT TO KNOW EVERYTHING ABOUT TRAVBOT!
JUNIPER! YOUR BMX BIKE LOOKS AMAZING!
JUNIPERBMX
VEGETABLE OIL ROCKET!
I SEE YOU, DEREK. WE'LL TALK SOON.

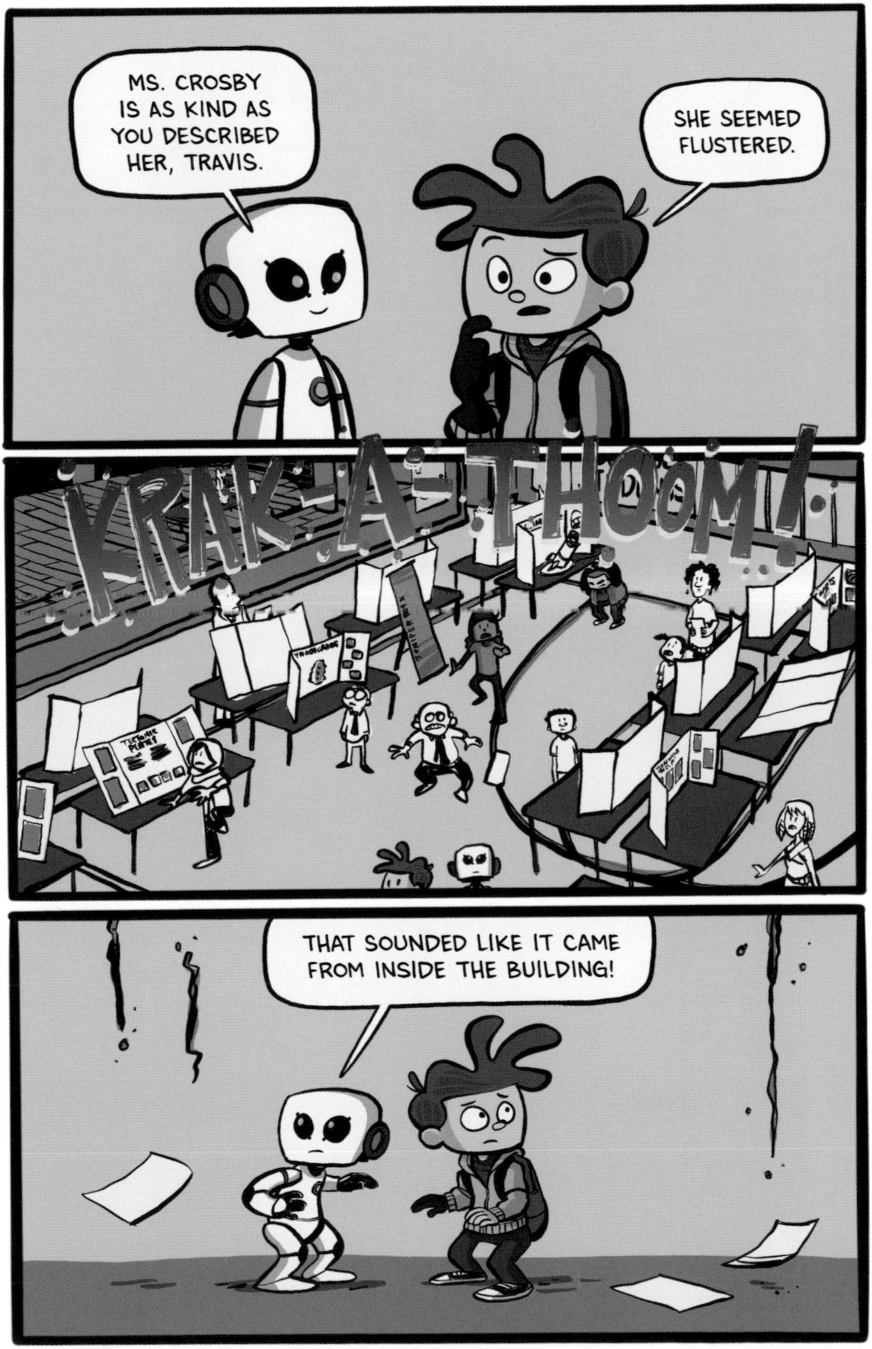
MS. CROSBY IS AS KIND AS YOU DESCRIBED HER, TRAVIS.
SHE SEEMED FLUSTERED.
KRAK-A-THOOM!
THAT SOUNDED LIKE IT CAME FROM INSIDE THE BUILDING!

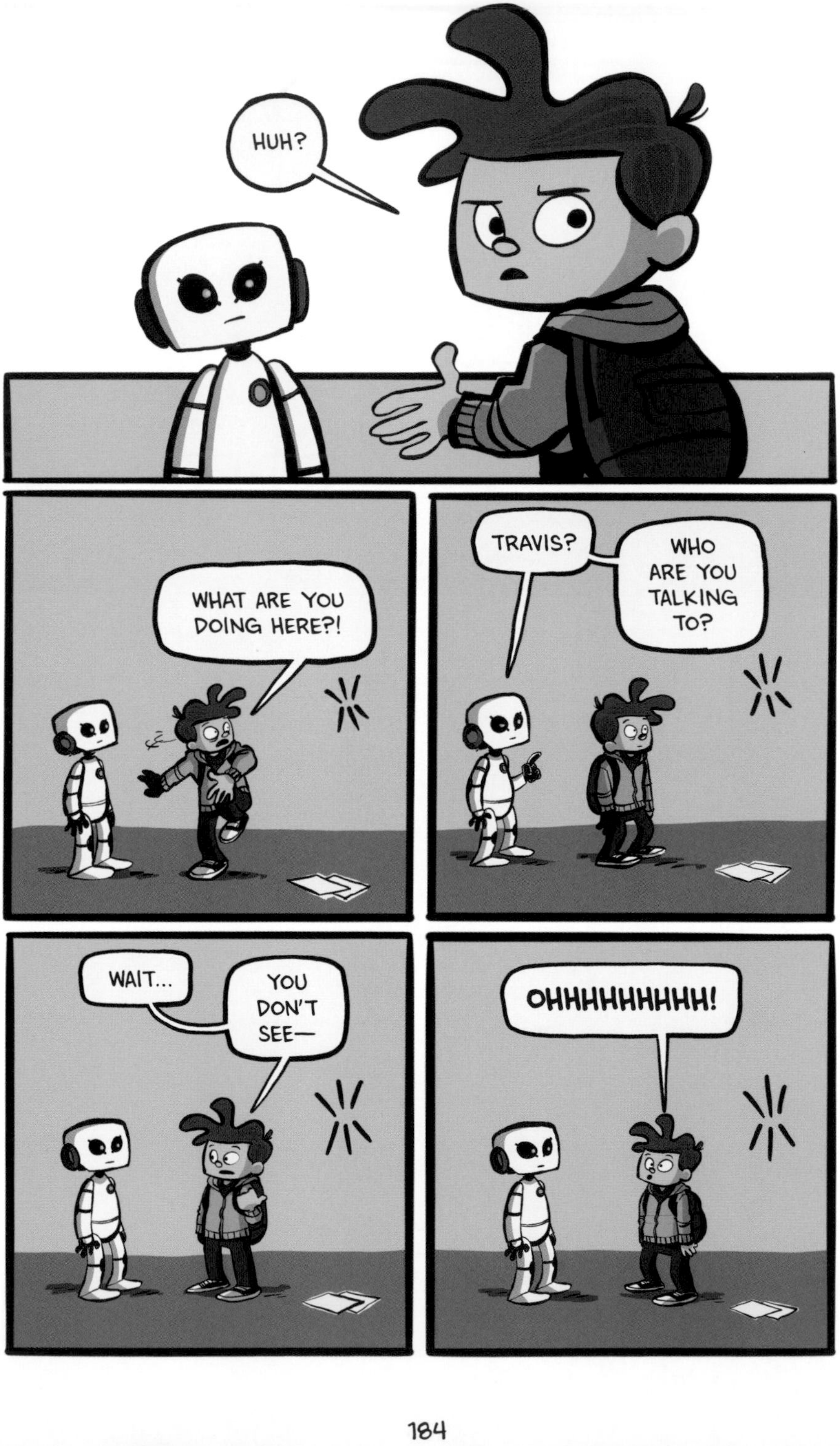
HUH?
WHAT ARE YOU DOING HERE?!
TRAVIS?
WHO ARE YOU TALKING TO?
WAIT...
YOU DON'T SEE—
OHHHHHHHHH!

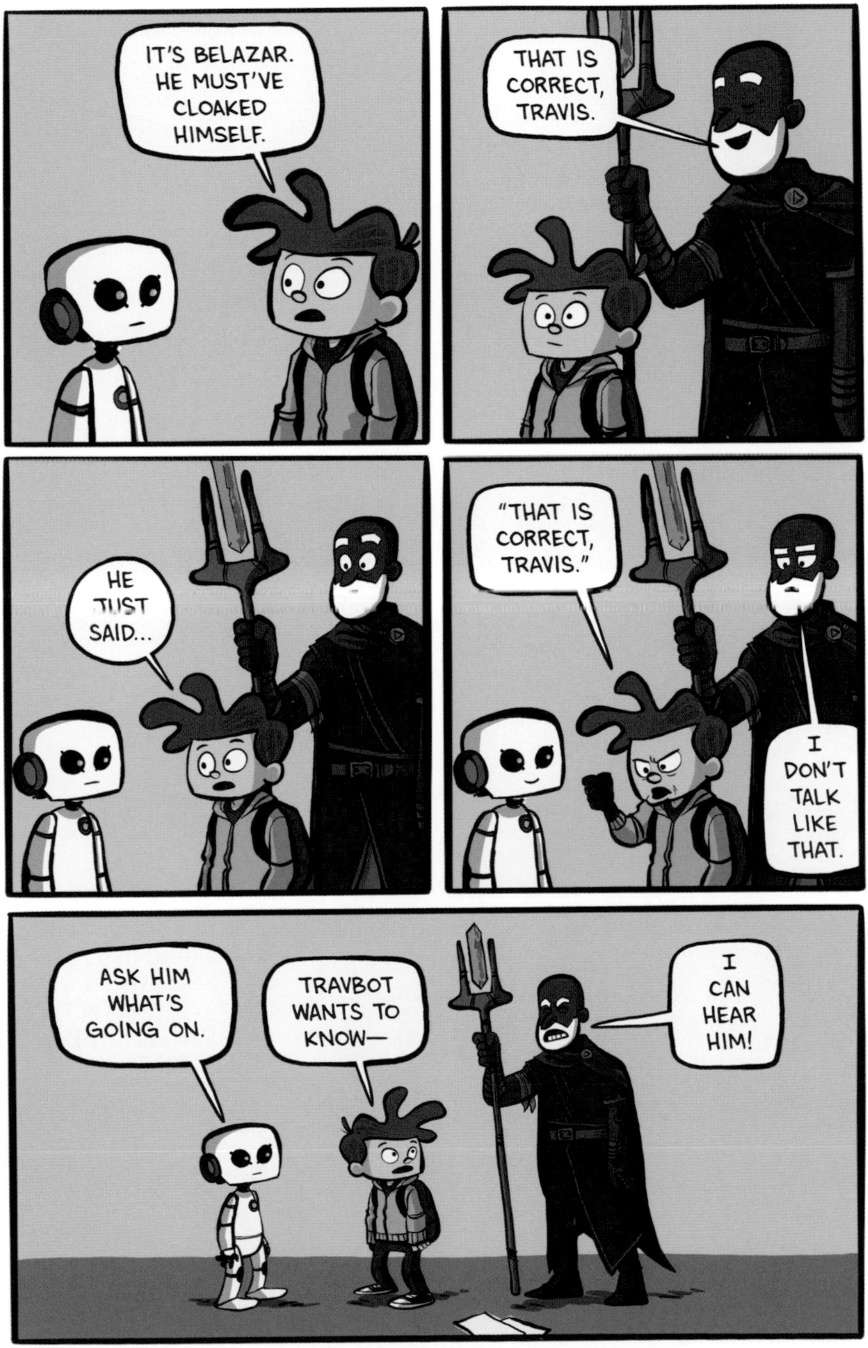
IT'S BELAZAR. HE MUST'VE CLOAKED HIMSELF.
THAT IS CORRECT, TRAVIS.
HE JUST SAID...
"THAT IS CORRECT, TRAVIS."
I DON'T TALK LIKE THAT.
ASK HIM WHAT'S GOING ON.
TRAVBOT WANTS TO KNOW—
I CAN HEAR HIM!

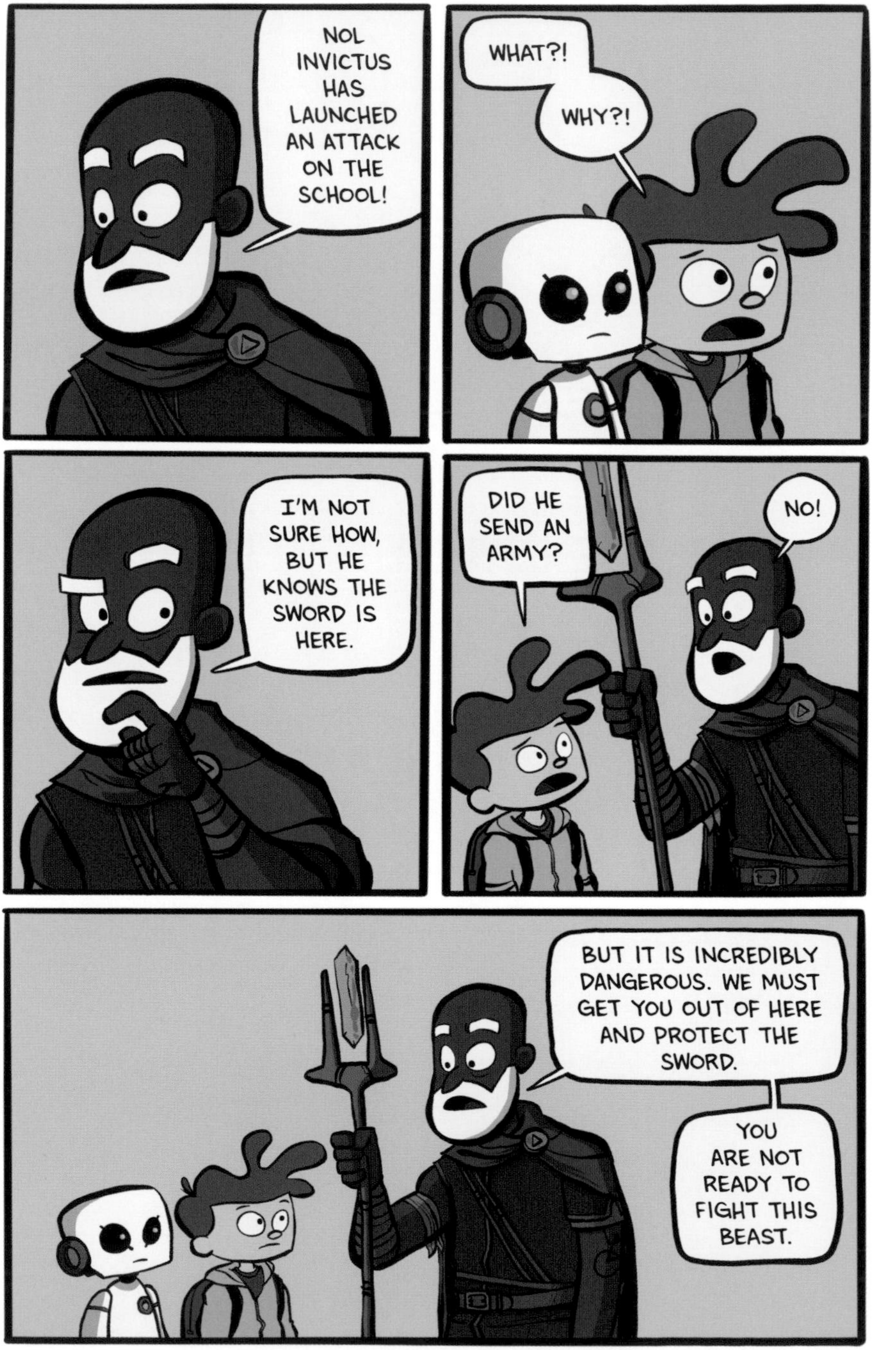
NOL INVICTUS HAS LAUNCHED AN ATTACK ON THE SCHOOL!
WHAT?!
WHY?!
I'M NOT SURE HOW, BUT HE KNOWS THE SWORD IS HERE.
DID HE SEND AN ARMY?
NO!
BUT IT IS INCREDIBLY DANGEROUS. WE MUST GET YOU OUT OF HERE AND PROTECT THE SWORD.
YOU ARE NOT READY TO FIGHT THIS BEAST.

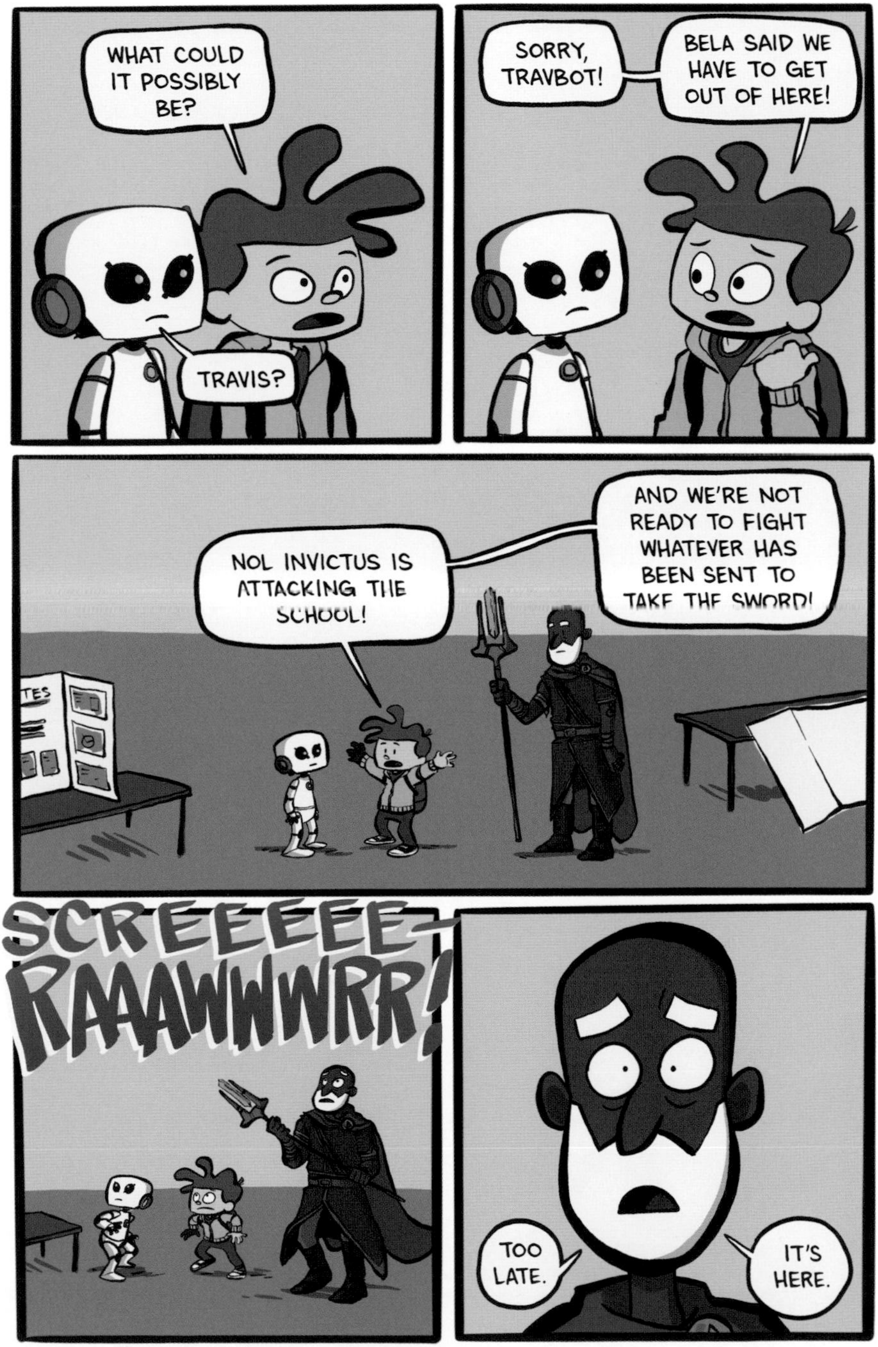
WHAT COULD IT POSSIBLY BE?
TRAVIS?
SORRY, TRAVBOT!
BELA SAID WE HAVE TO GET OUT OF HERE!
NOL INVICTUS IS ATTACKING THE SCHOOL!
AND WE'RE NOT READY TO FIGHT WHATEVER HAS BEEN SENT TO TAKE THE SWORD!
SCREEEEEE-RAAAWWWRR!
TOO LATE.
IT'S HERE.

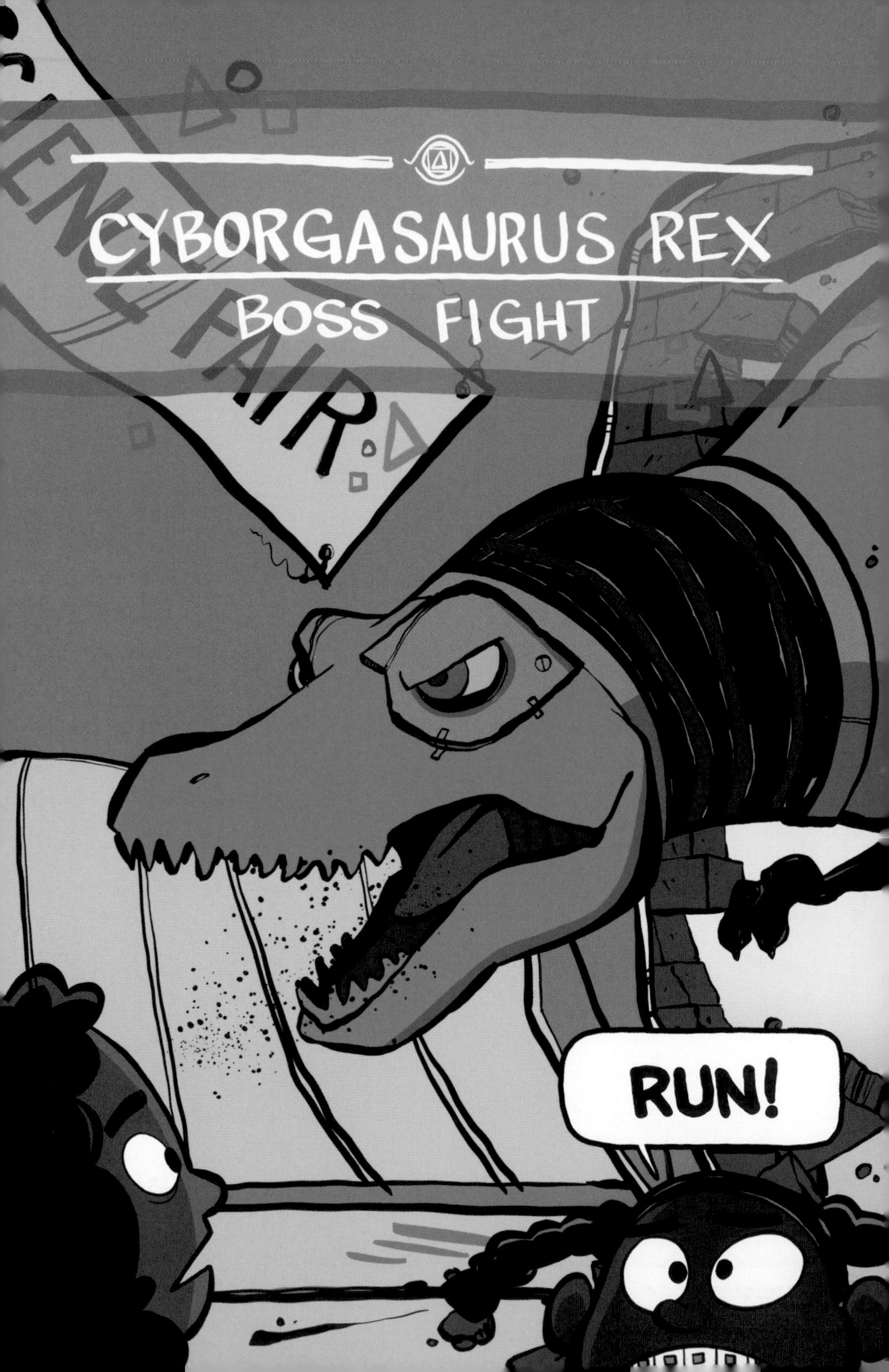
CYBORGASAURUS REX
BOSS FIGHT
FAIR
RUN!

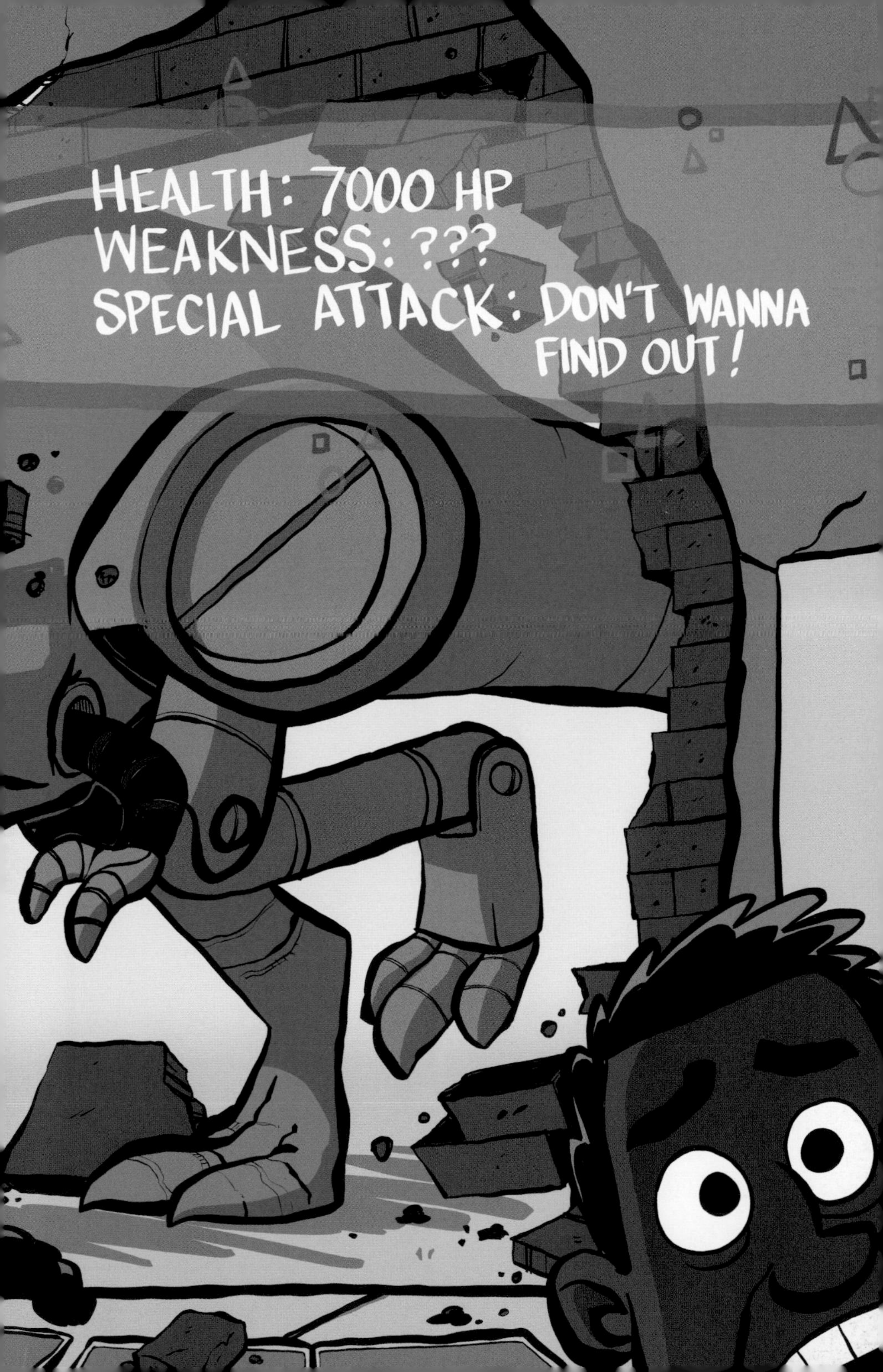
HEALTH: 7000 HP
WEAKNESS: ???
SPECIAL ATTACK: DON'T WANNA FIND OUT!

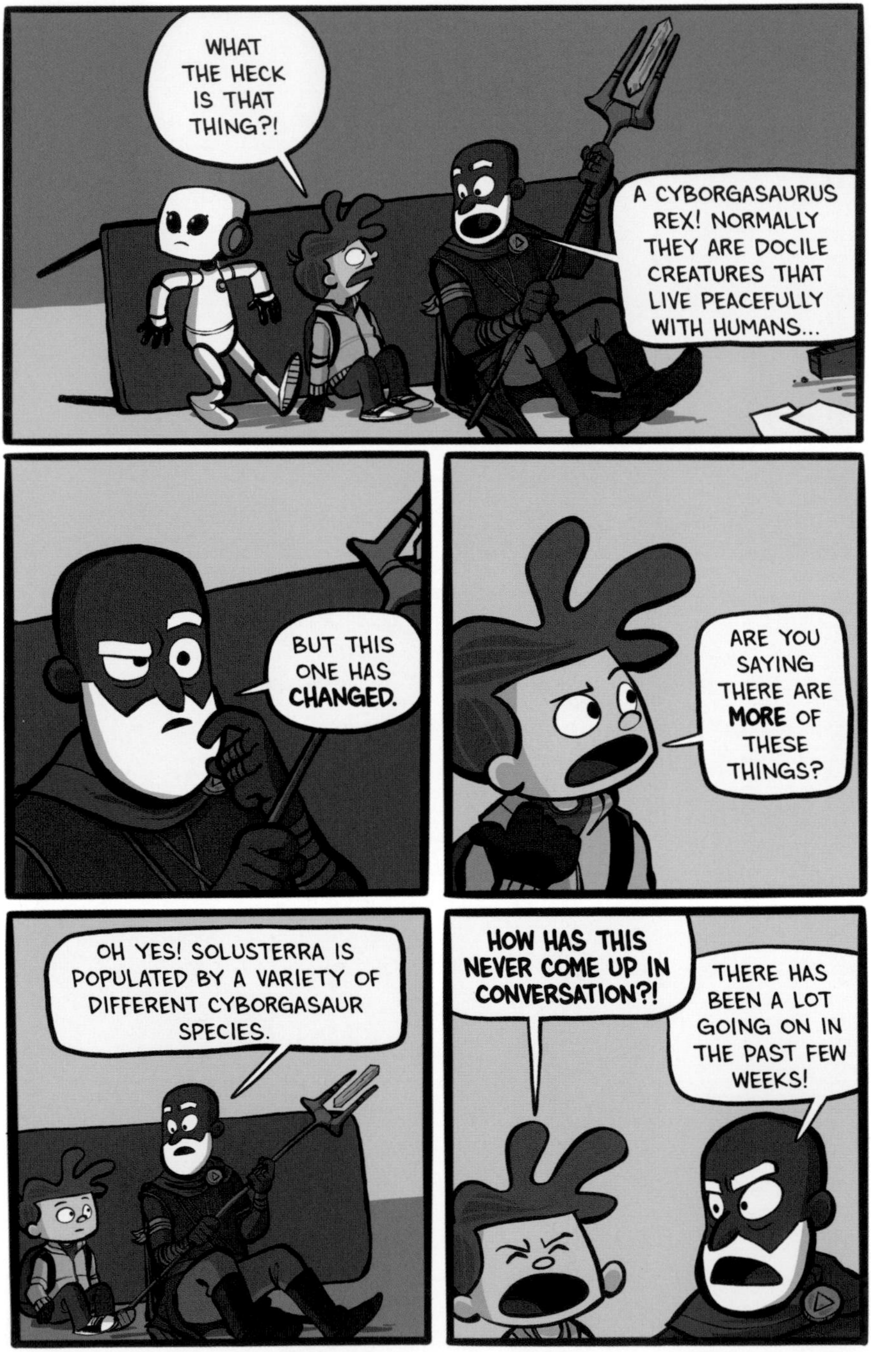
WHAT THE HECK IS THAT THING?!
A CYBORGASAURUS REX! NORMALLY THEY ARE DOCILE CREATURES THAT LIVE PEACEFULLY WITH HUMANS...
BUT THIS ONE HAS CHANGED.
ARE YOU SAYING THERE ARE MORE OF THESE THINGS?
OH YES! SOLUSTERRA IS POPULATED BY A VARIETY OF DIFFERENT CYBORGASAUR SPECIES.
HOW HAS THIS NEVER COME UP IN CONVERSATION?!
THERE HAS BEEN A LOT GOING ON IN THE PAST FEW WEEKS!

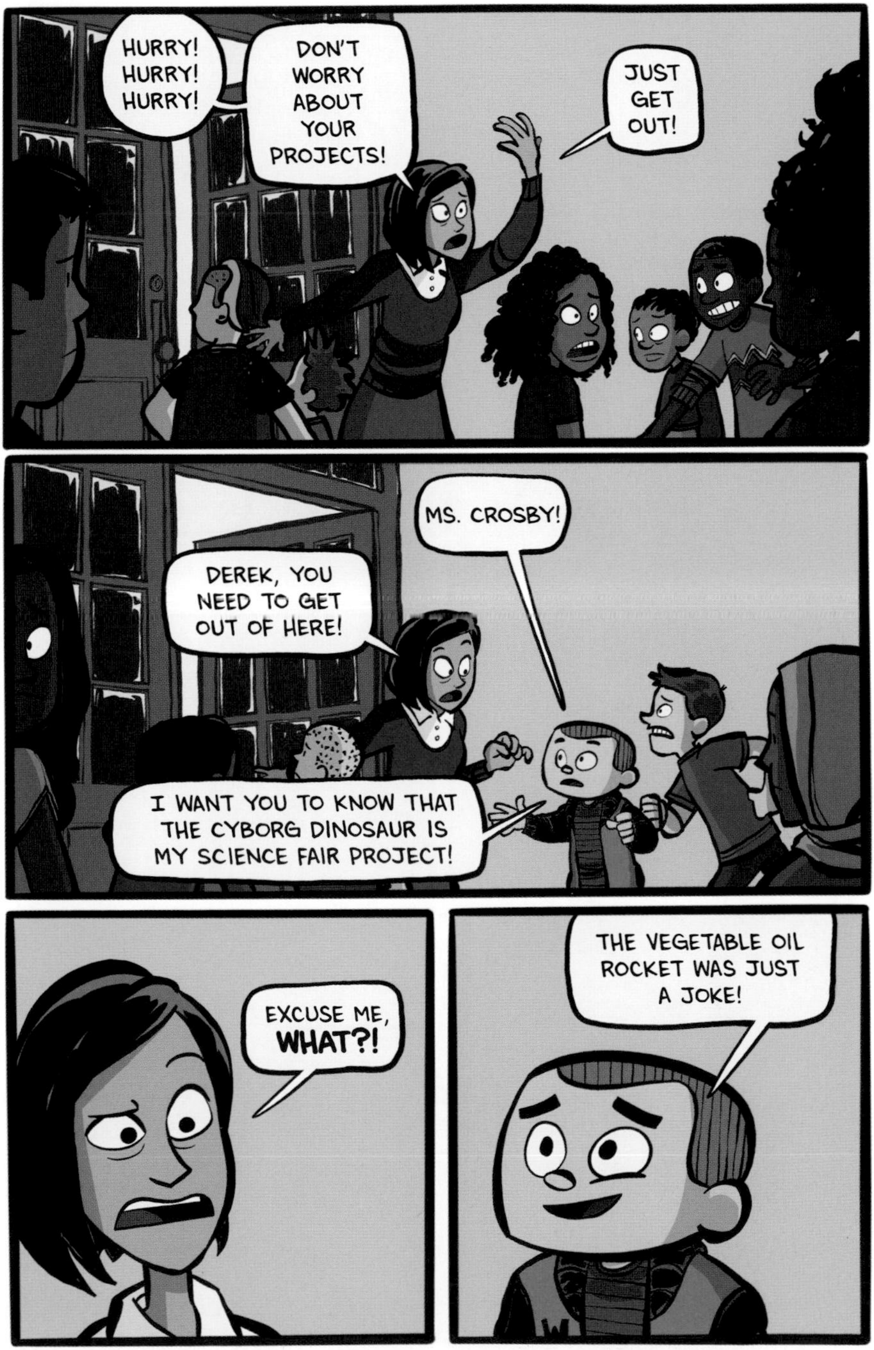
HURRY! HURRY! HURRY!
DON'T WORRY ABOUT YOUR PROJECTS!
JUST GET OUT!
MS. CROSBY!
DEREK, YOU NEED TO GET OUT OF HERE!
I WANT YOU TO KNOW THAT THE CYBORG DINOSAUR IS MY SCIENCE FAIR PROJECT!
EXCUSE ME, **WHAT?!**
THE VEGETABLE OIL ROCKET WAS JUST A JOKE!

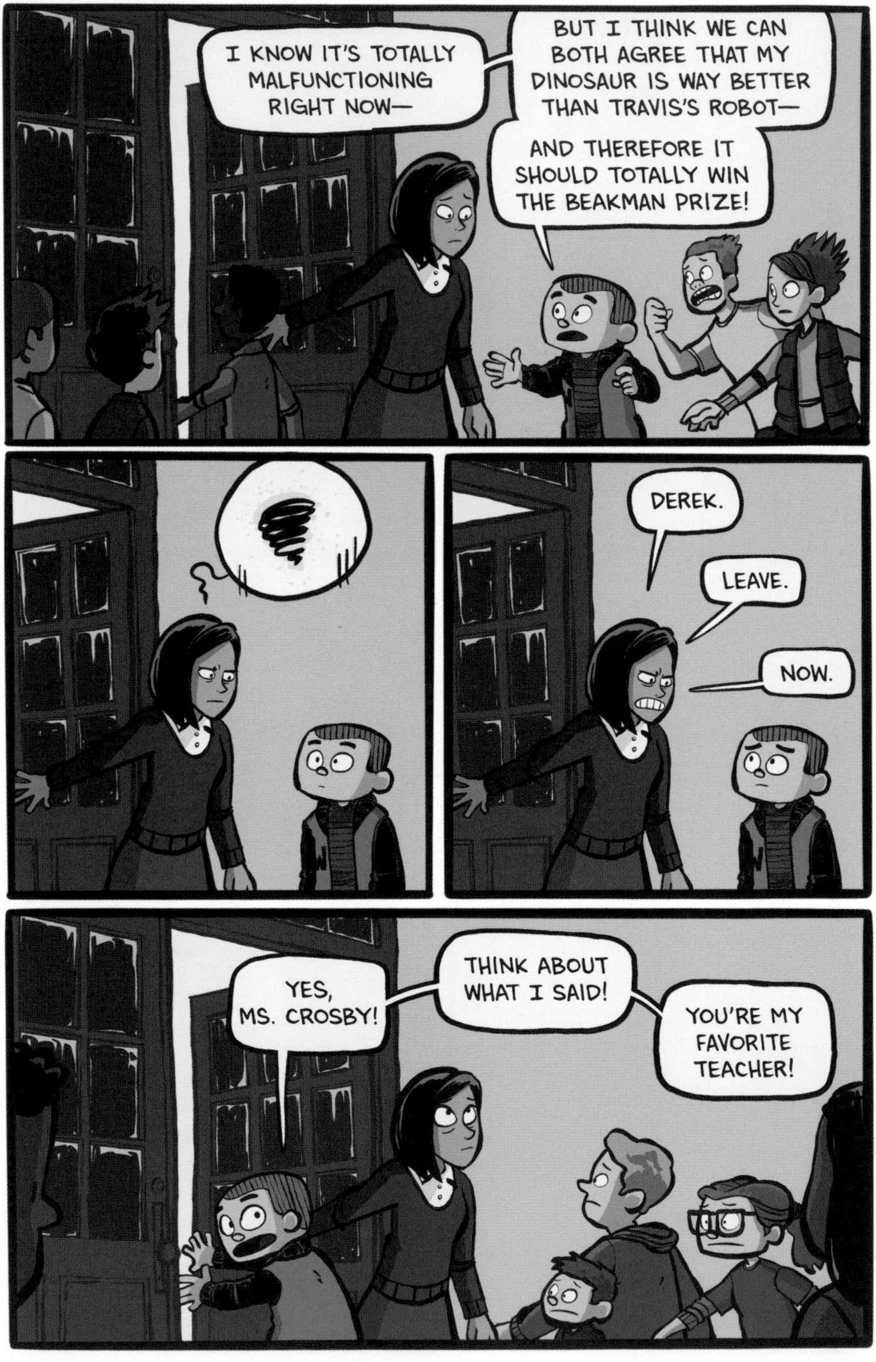
I KNOW IT'S TOTALLY MALFUNCTIONING RIGHT NOW—
BUT I THINK WE CAN BOTH AGREE THAT MY DINOSAUR IS WAY BETTER THAN TRAVIS'S ROBOT—
AND THEREFORE IT SHOULD TOTALLY WIN THE BEAKMAN PRIZE!
DEREK.
LEAVE.
NOW.
YES, MS. CROSBY!
THINK ABOUT WHAT I SAID!
YOU'RE MY FAVORITE TEACHER!

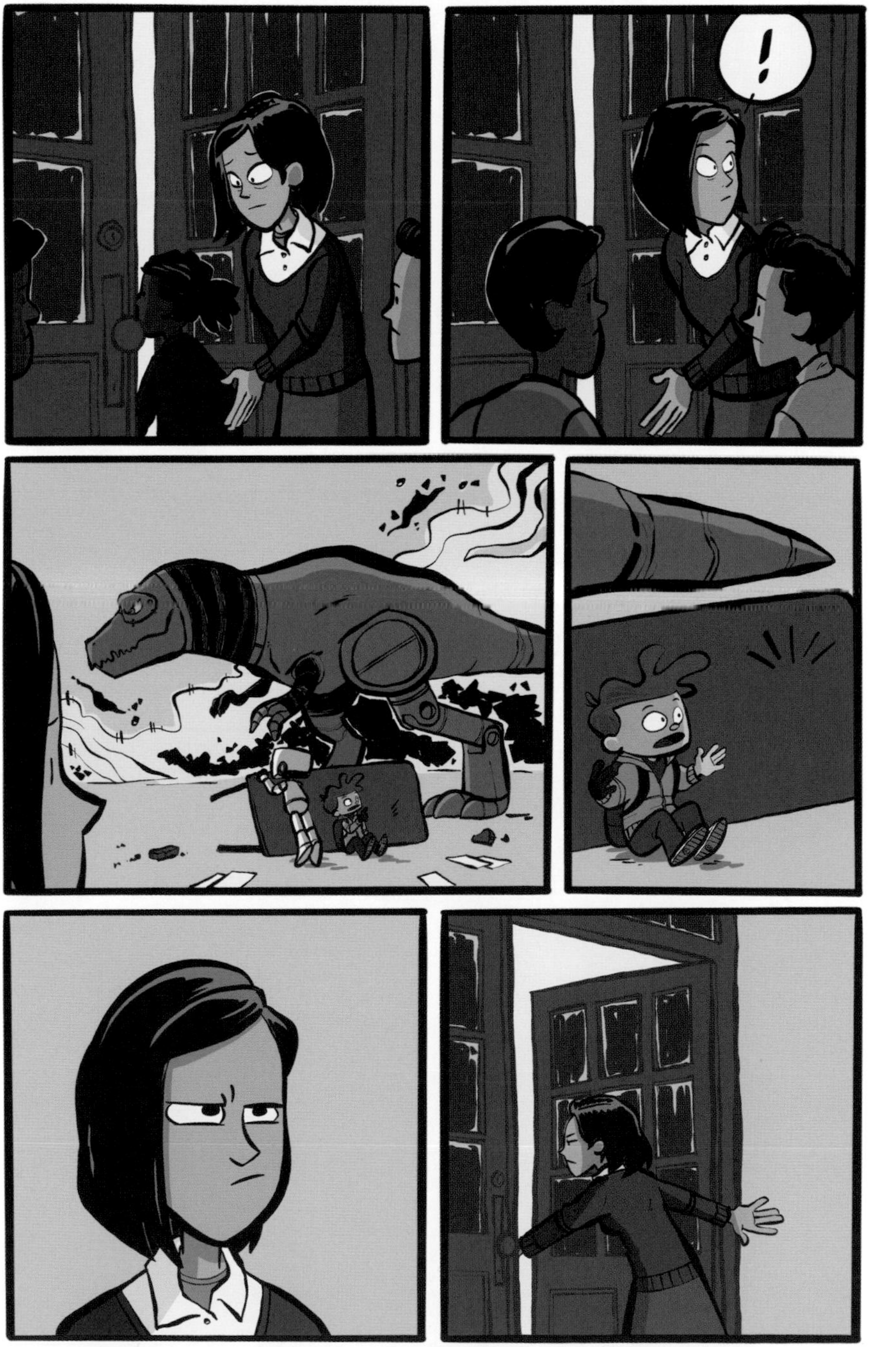
!

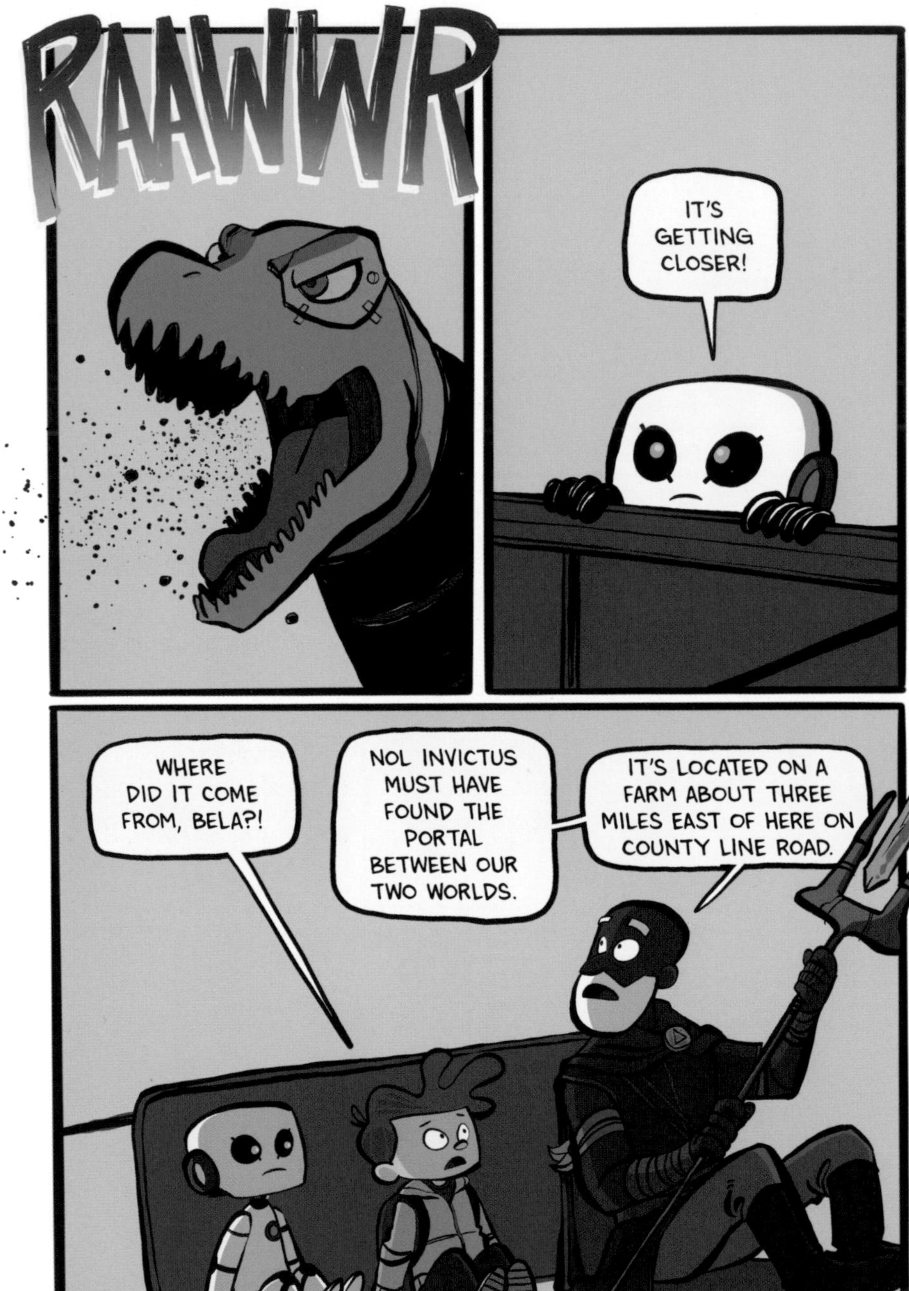
RAAWWR
IT'S GETTING CLOSER!
WHERE DID IT COME FROM, BELA?!
NOL INVICTUS MUST HAVE FOUND THE PORTAL BETWEEN OUR TWO WORLDS.
IT'S LOCATED ON A FARM ABOUT THREE MILES EAST OF HERE ON COUNTY LINE ROAD.

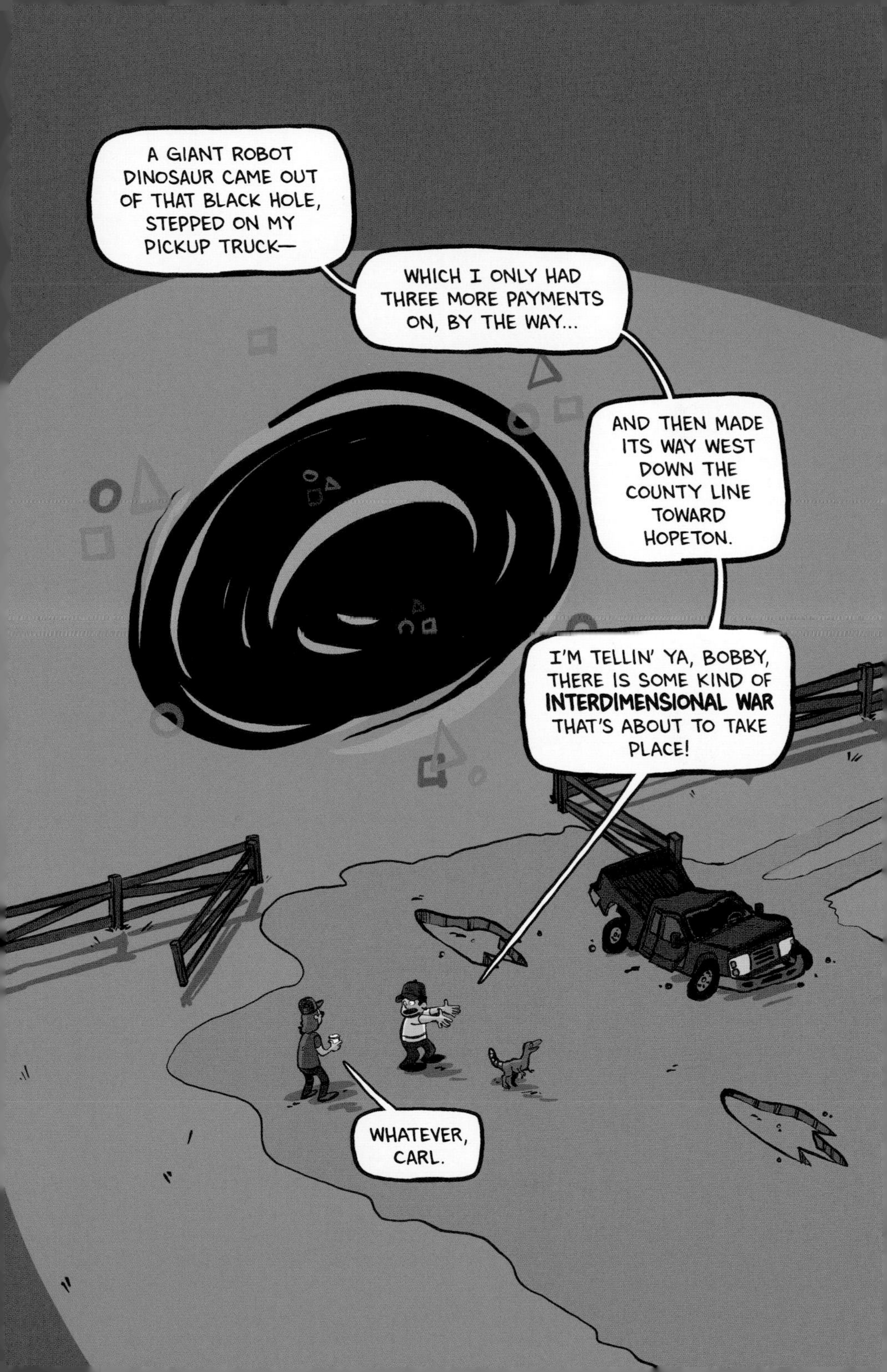
A GIANT ROBOT DINOSAUR CAME OUT OF THAT BLACK HOLE, STEPPED ON MY PICKUP TRUCK—
WHICH I ONLY HAD THREE MORE PAYMENTS ON, BY THE WAY...
AND THEN MADE ITS WAY WEST DOWN THE COUNTY LINE TOWARD HOPETON.
I'M TELLIN' YA, BOBBY, THERE IS SOME KIND OF **INTERDIMENSIONAL WAR** THAT'S ABOUT TO TAKE PLACE!
WHATEVER, CARL.

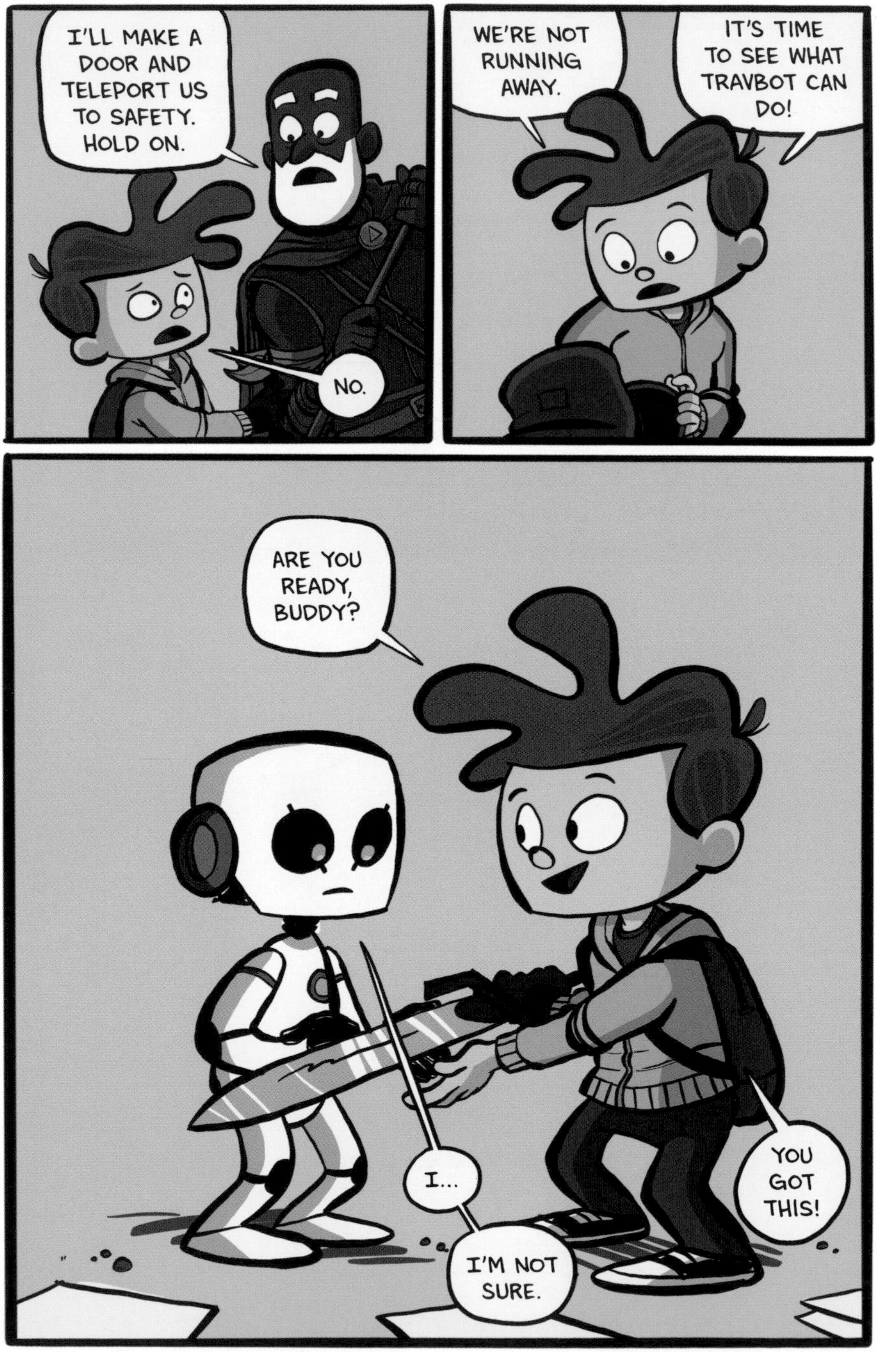
I'LL MAKE A DOOR AND TELEPORT US TO SAFETY. HOLD ON.
NO.
WE'RE NOT RUNNING AWAY.
IT'S TIME TO SEE WHAT TRAVBOT CAN DO!
ARE YOU READY, BUDDY?
I...
I'M NOT SURE.
YOU GOT THIS!

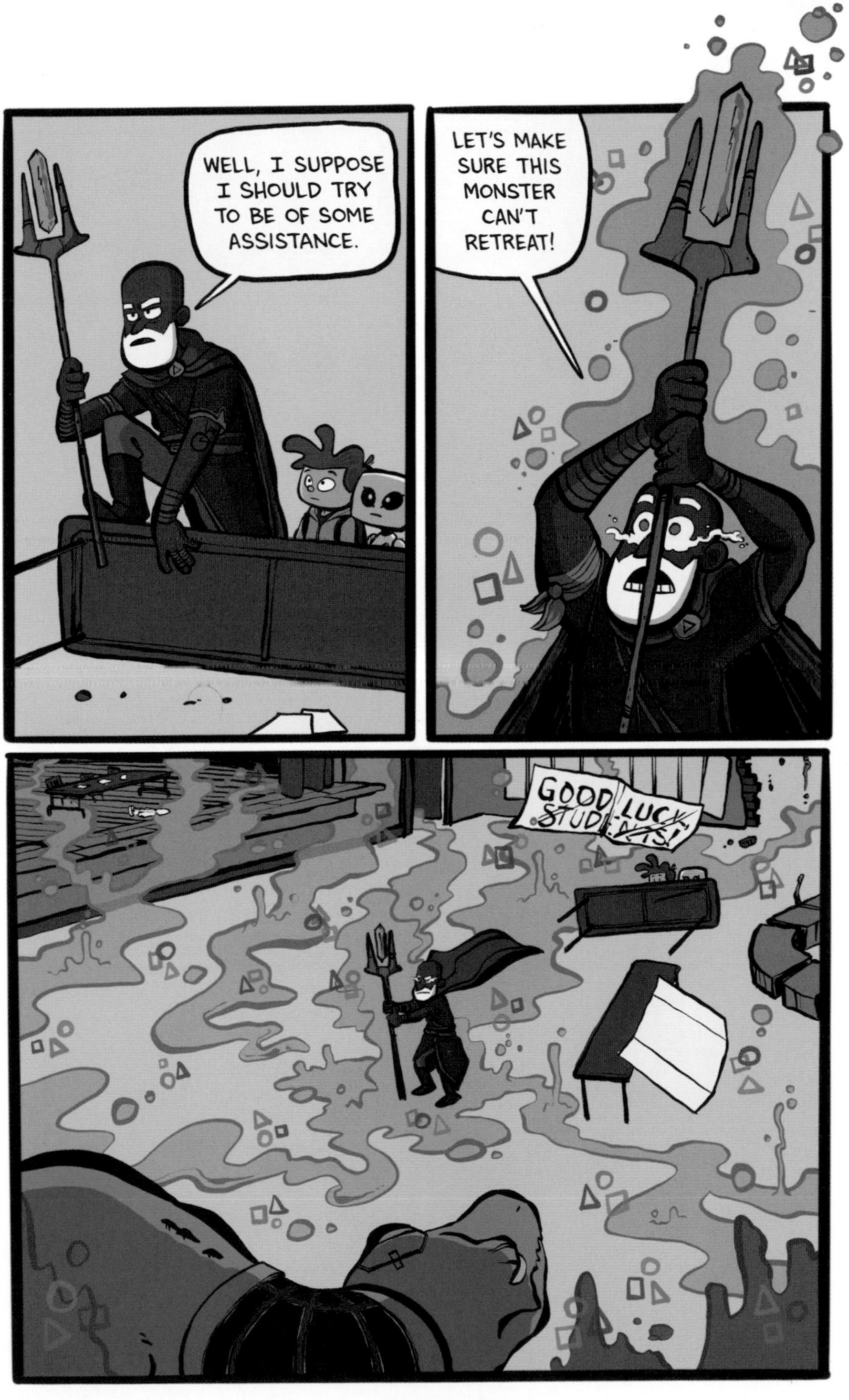
WELL, I SUPPOSE I SHOULD TRY TO BE OF SOME ASSISTANCE.
LET'S MAKE SURE THIS MONSTER CAN'T RETREAT!
GOOD LUCK, STUDENTS!

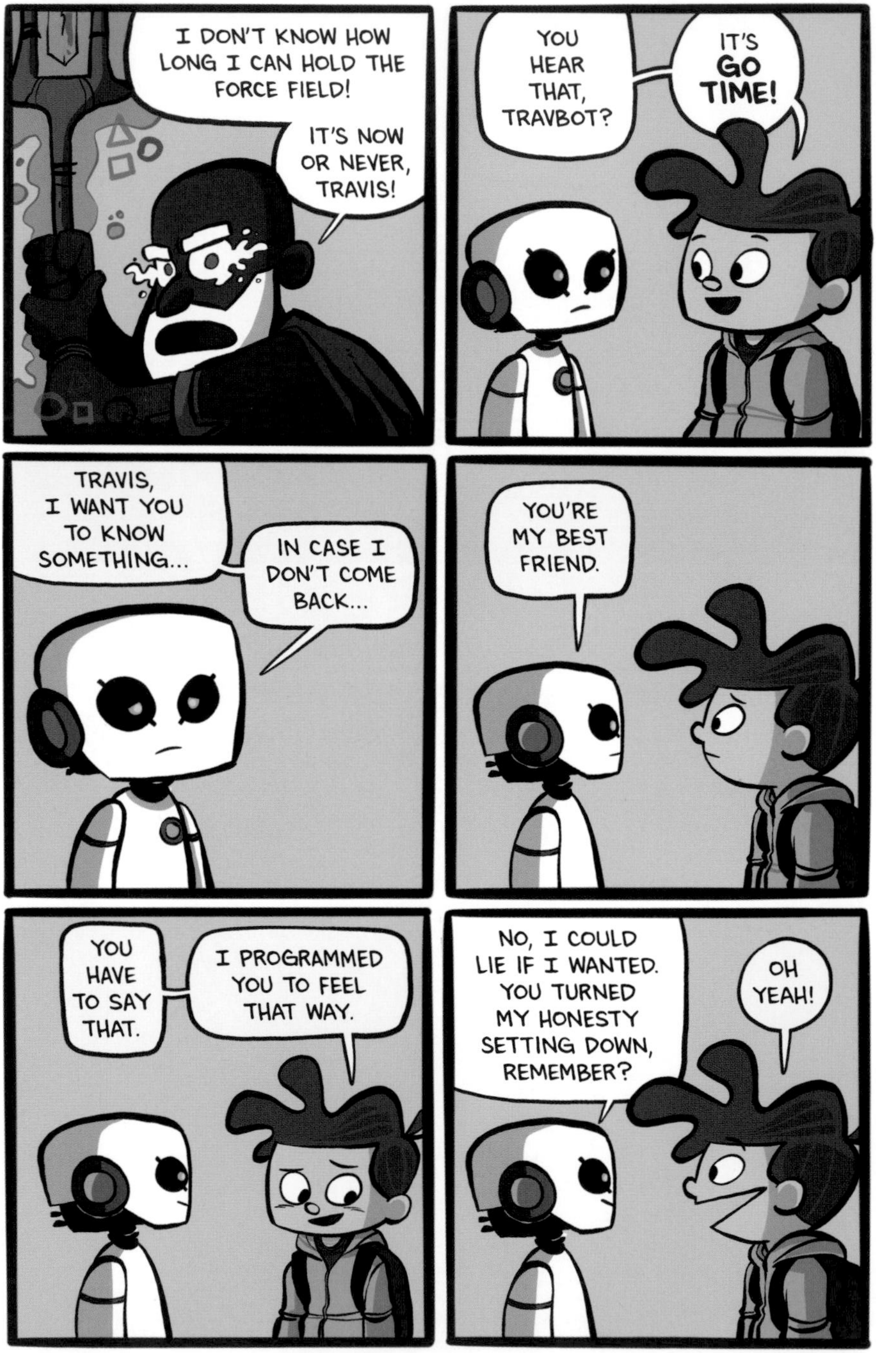
I DON'T KNOW HOW LONG I CAN HOLD THE FORCE FIELD!
IT'S NOW OR NEVER, TRAVIS!
YOU HEAR THAT, TRAVBOT?
IT'S GO TIME!
TRAVIS, I WANT YOU TO KNOW SOMETHING...
IN CASE I DON'T COME BACK...
YOU'RE MY BEST FRIEND.
YOU HAVE TO SAY THAT.
I PROGRAMMED YOU TO FEEL THAT WAY.
NO, I COULD LIE IF I WANTED. YOU TURNED MY HONESTY SETTING DOWN, REMEMBER?
OH YEAH!

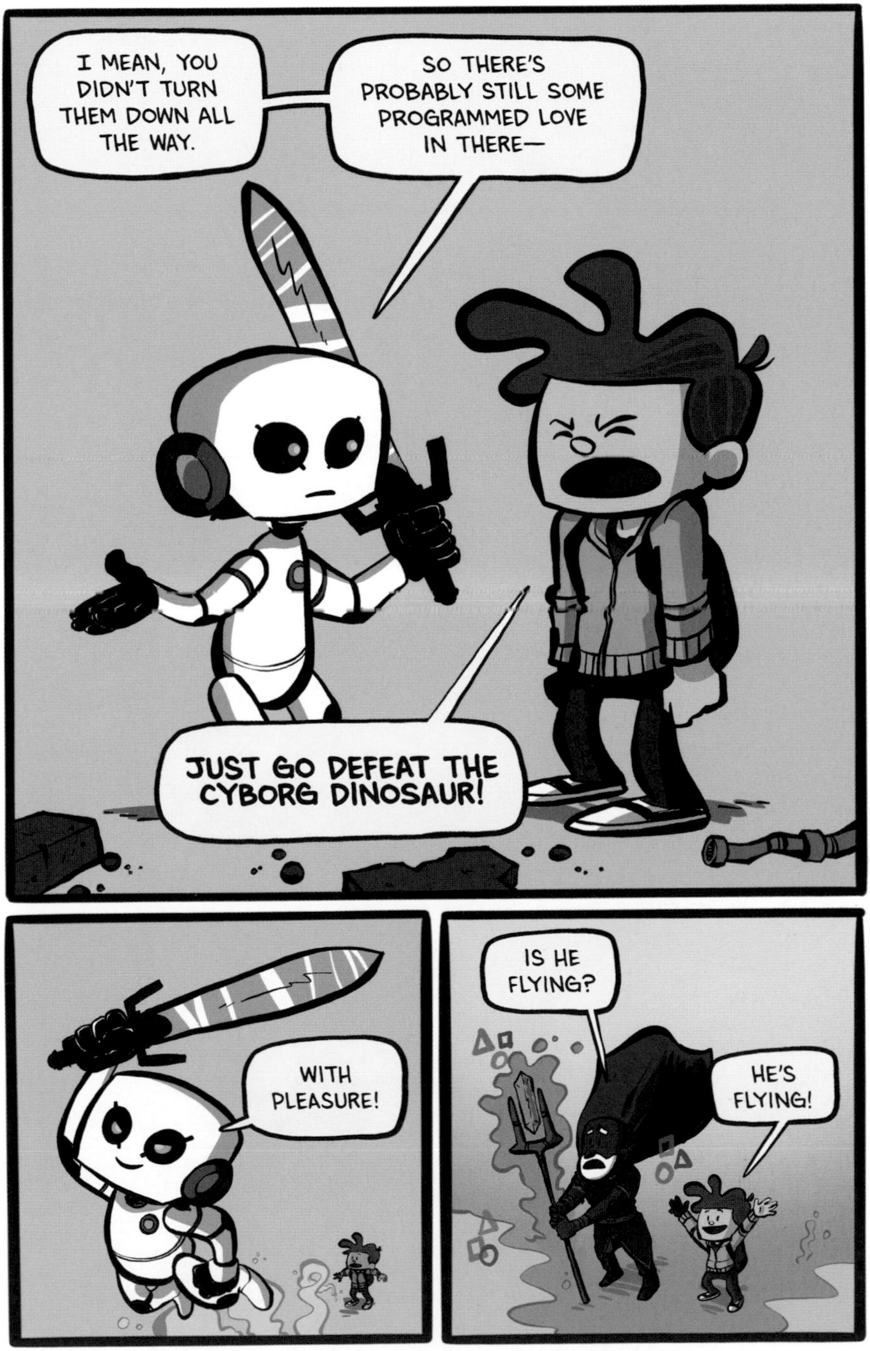
I MEAN, YOU DIDN'T TURN THEM DOWN ALL THE WAY.
SO THERE'S PROBABLY STILL SOME PROGRAMMED LOVE IN THERE—
JUST GO DEFEAT THE CYBORG DINOSAUR!
WITH PLEASURE!
IS HE FLYING?
HE'S FLYING!

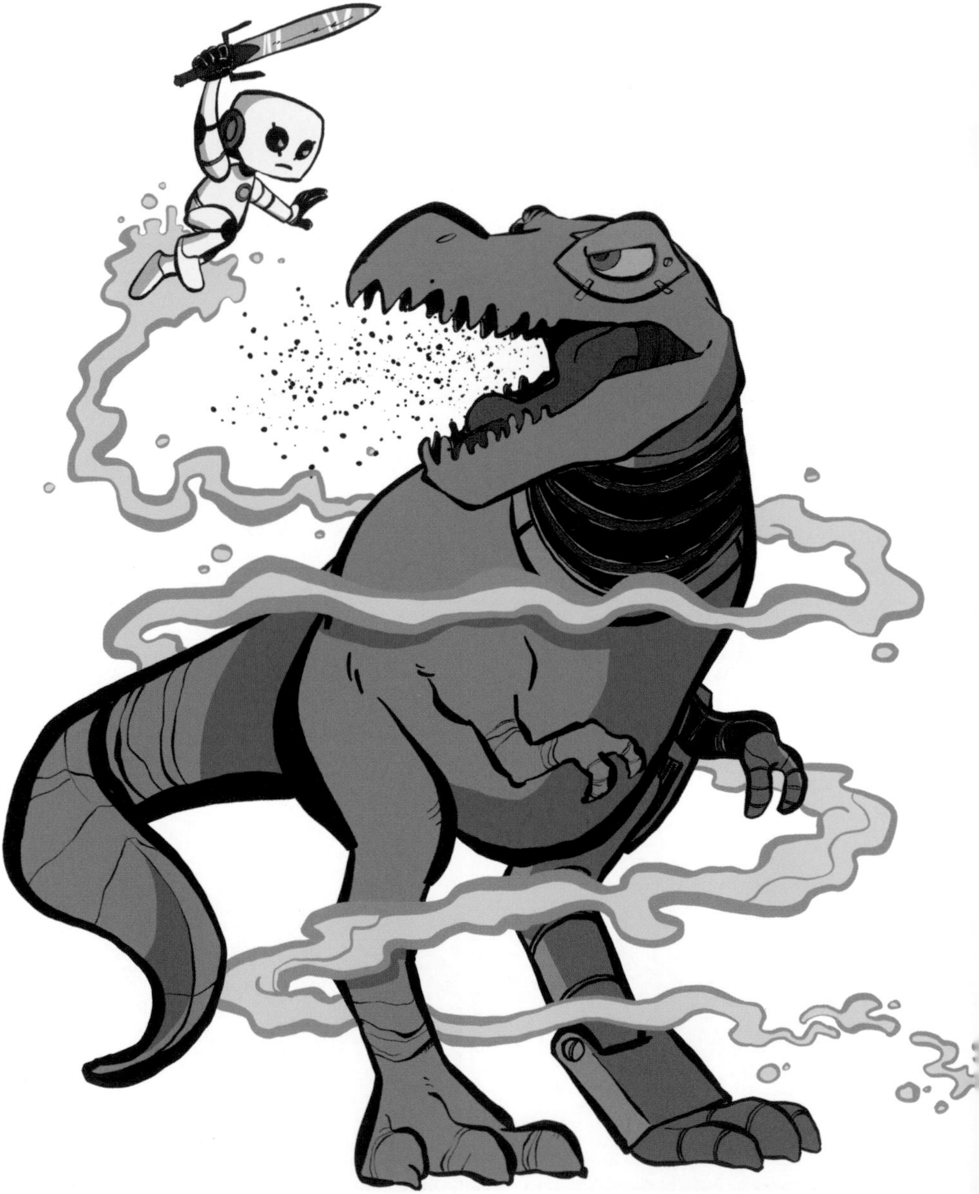

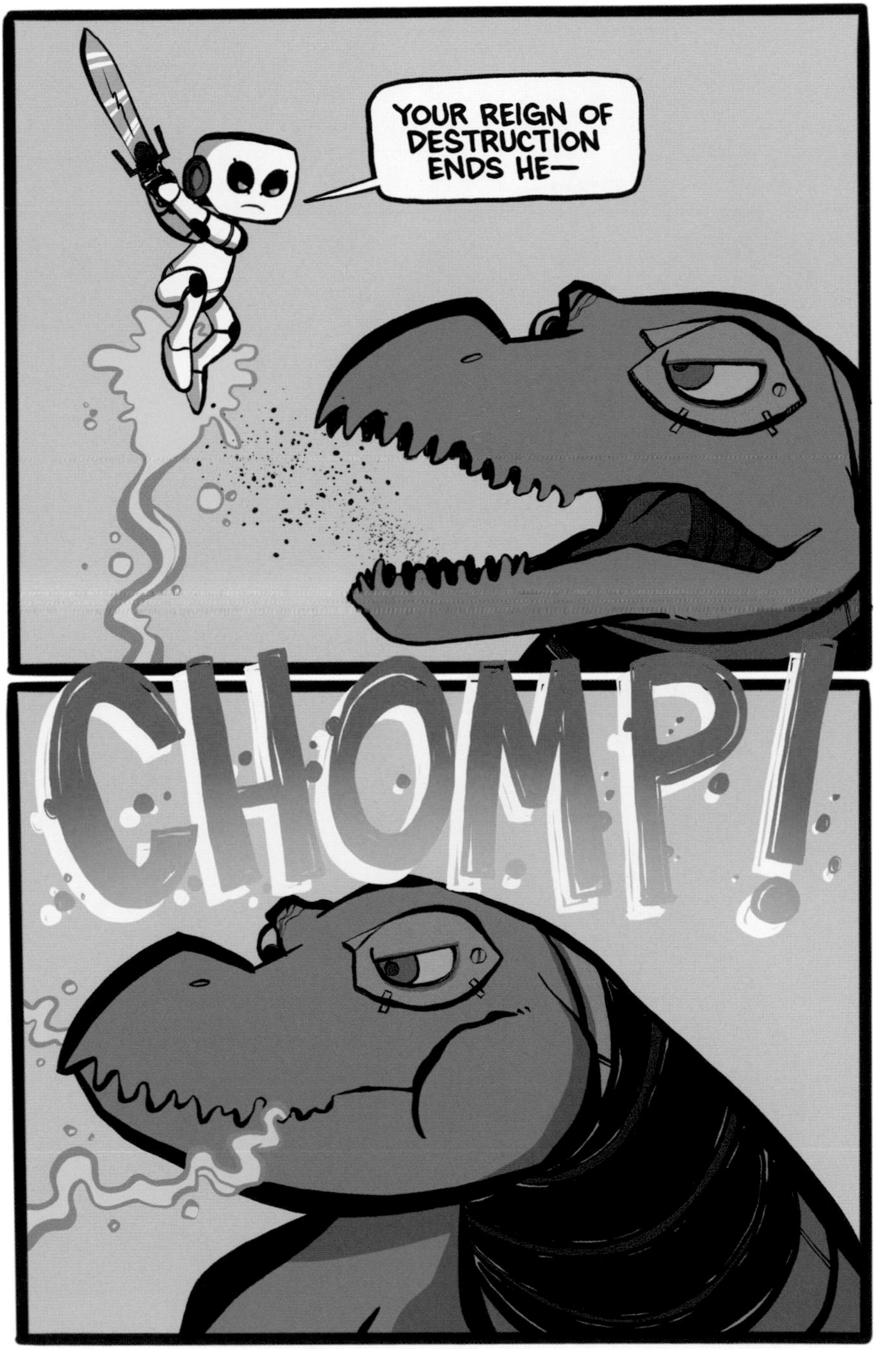
YOUR REIGN OF DESTRUCTION ENDS HE—
CHOMP!

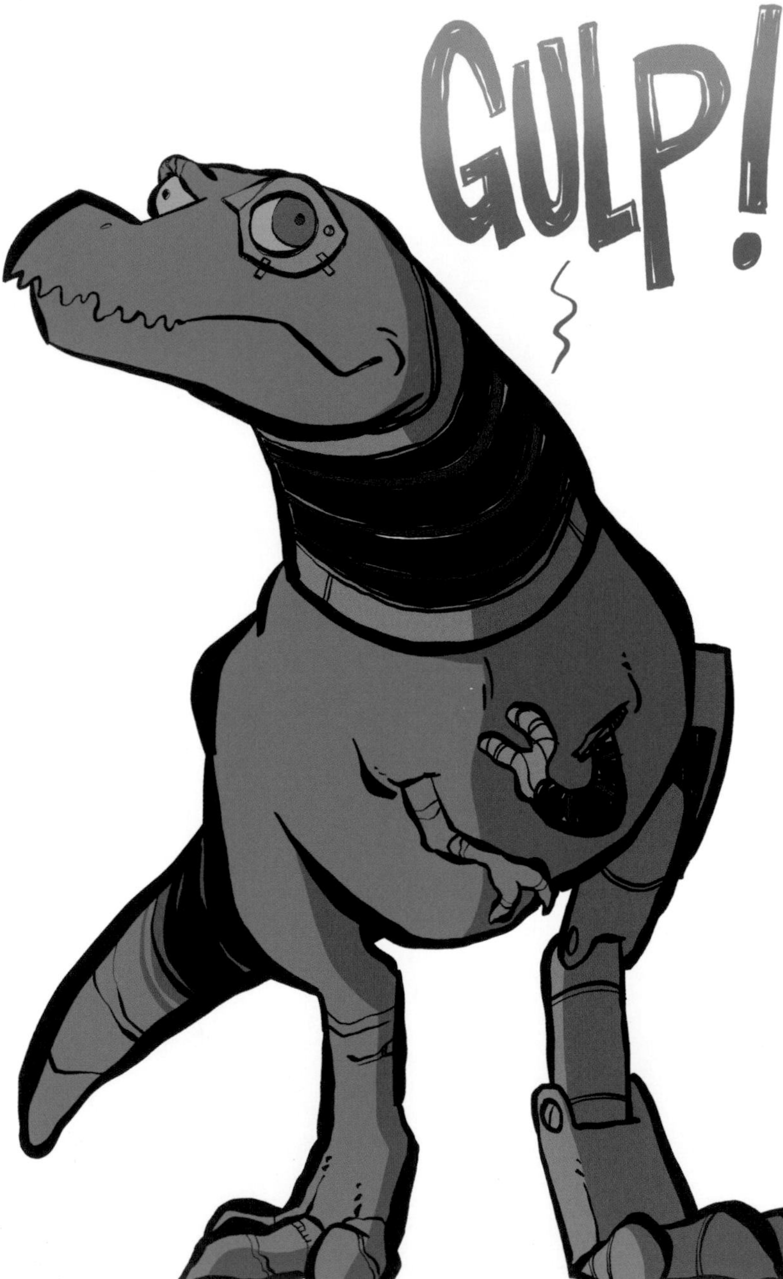
GULP!

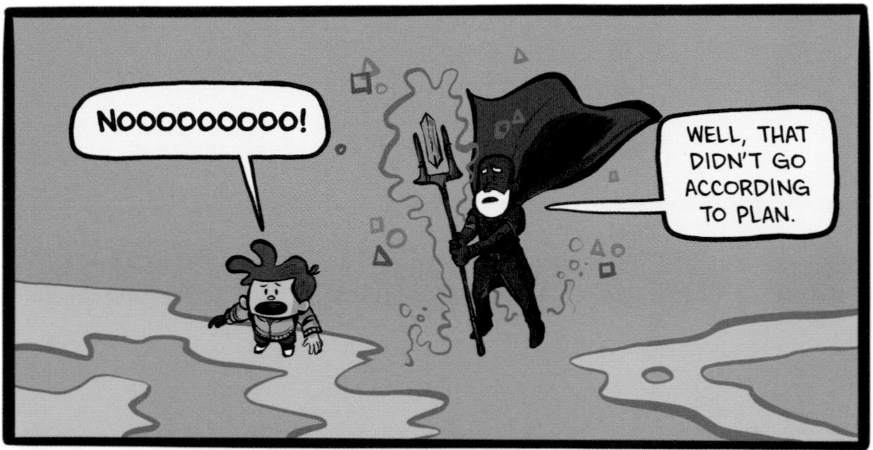
NOOOOOOOOO!
WELL, THAT DIDN'T GO ACCORDING TO PLAN.

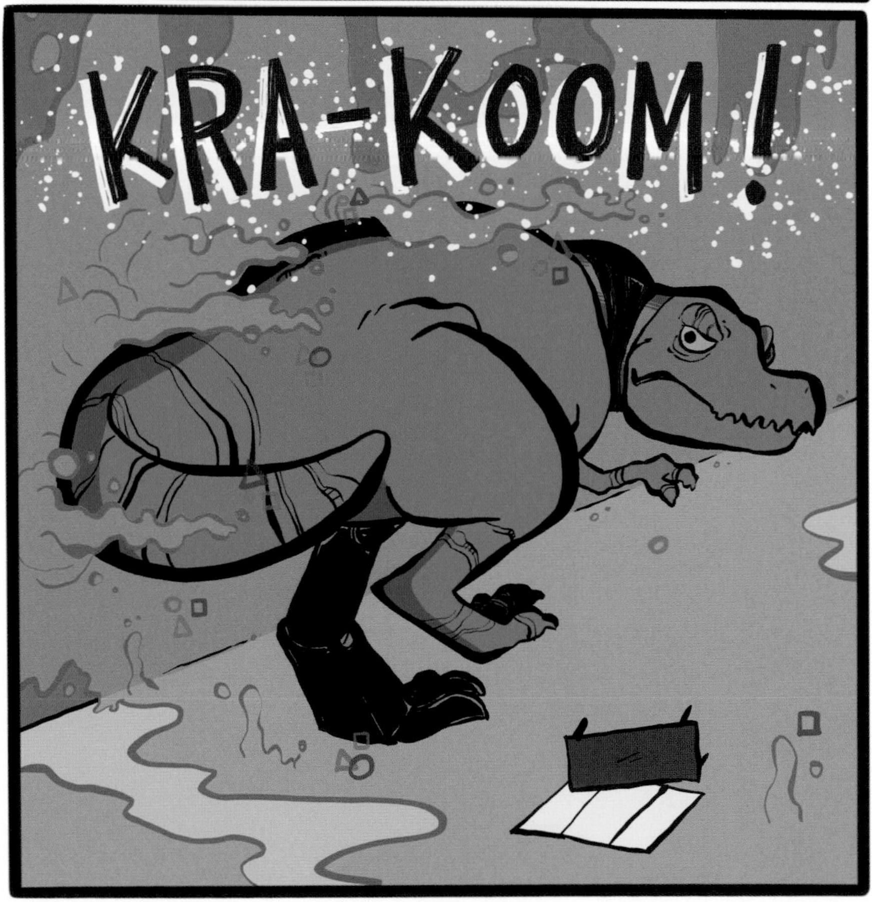
KRA-KOOM!

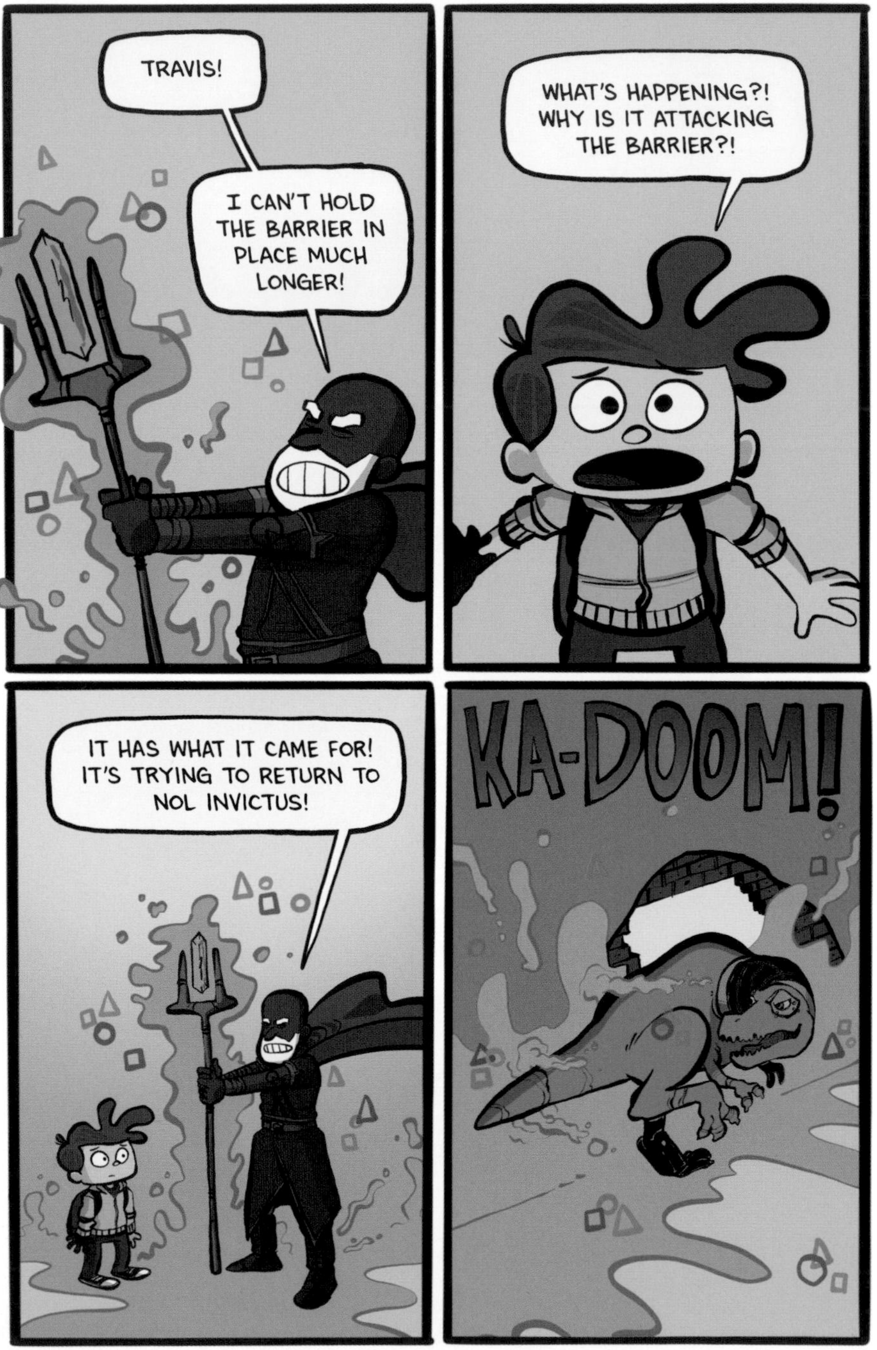
TRAVIS!
I CAN'T HOLD THE BARRIER IN PLACE MUCH LONGER!
WHAT'S HAPPENING?! WHY IS IT ATTACKING THE BARRIER?!
IT HAS WHAT IT CAME FOR! IT'S TRYING TO RETURN TO NOL INVICTUS!
KA-DOOM!

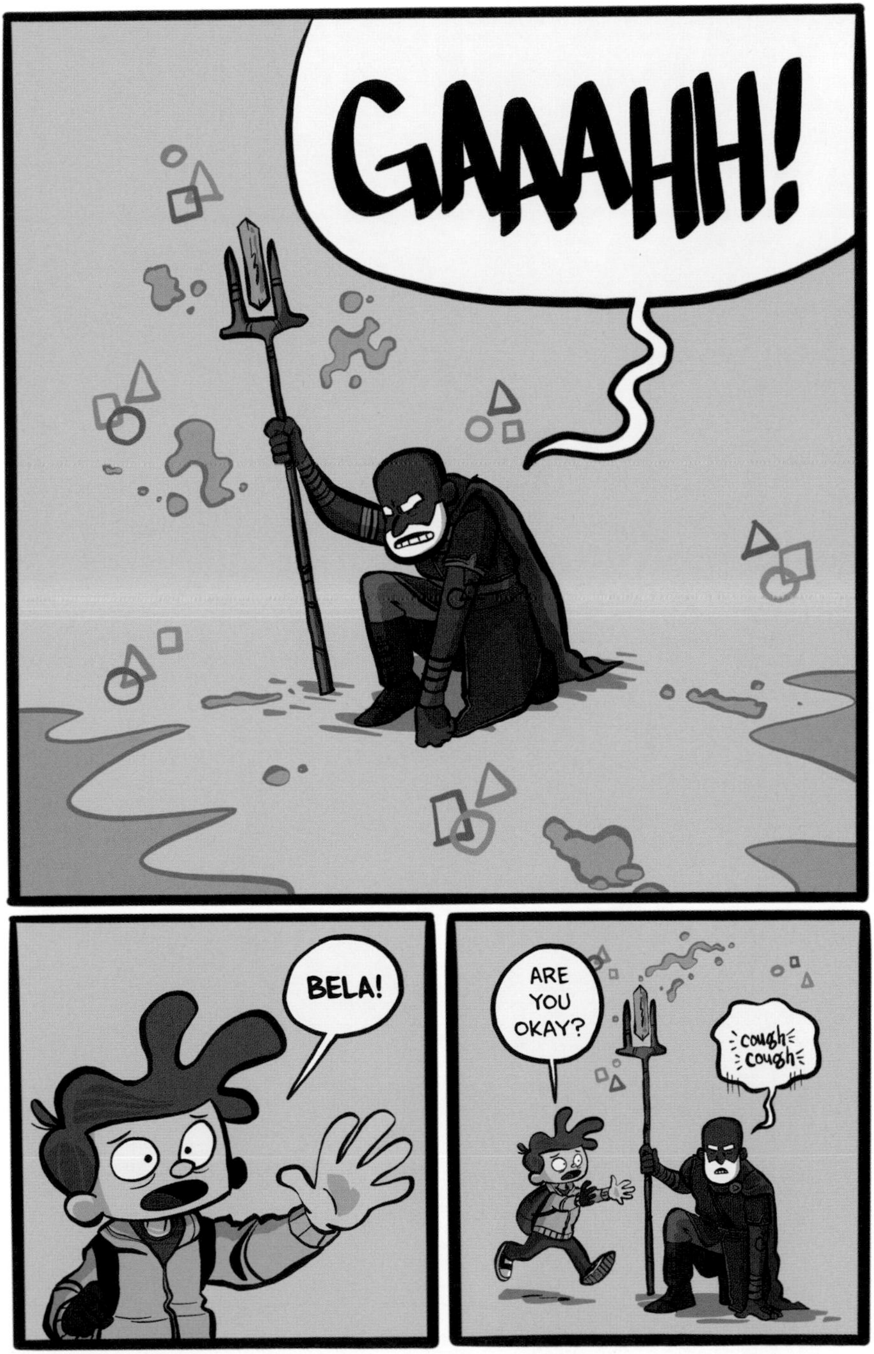
GAAAHH!
BELA!
ARE YOU OKAY?
cough cough

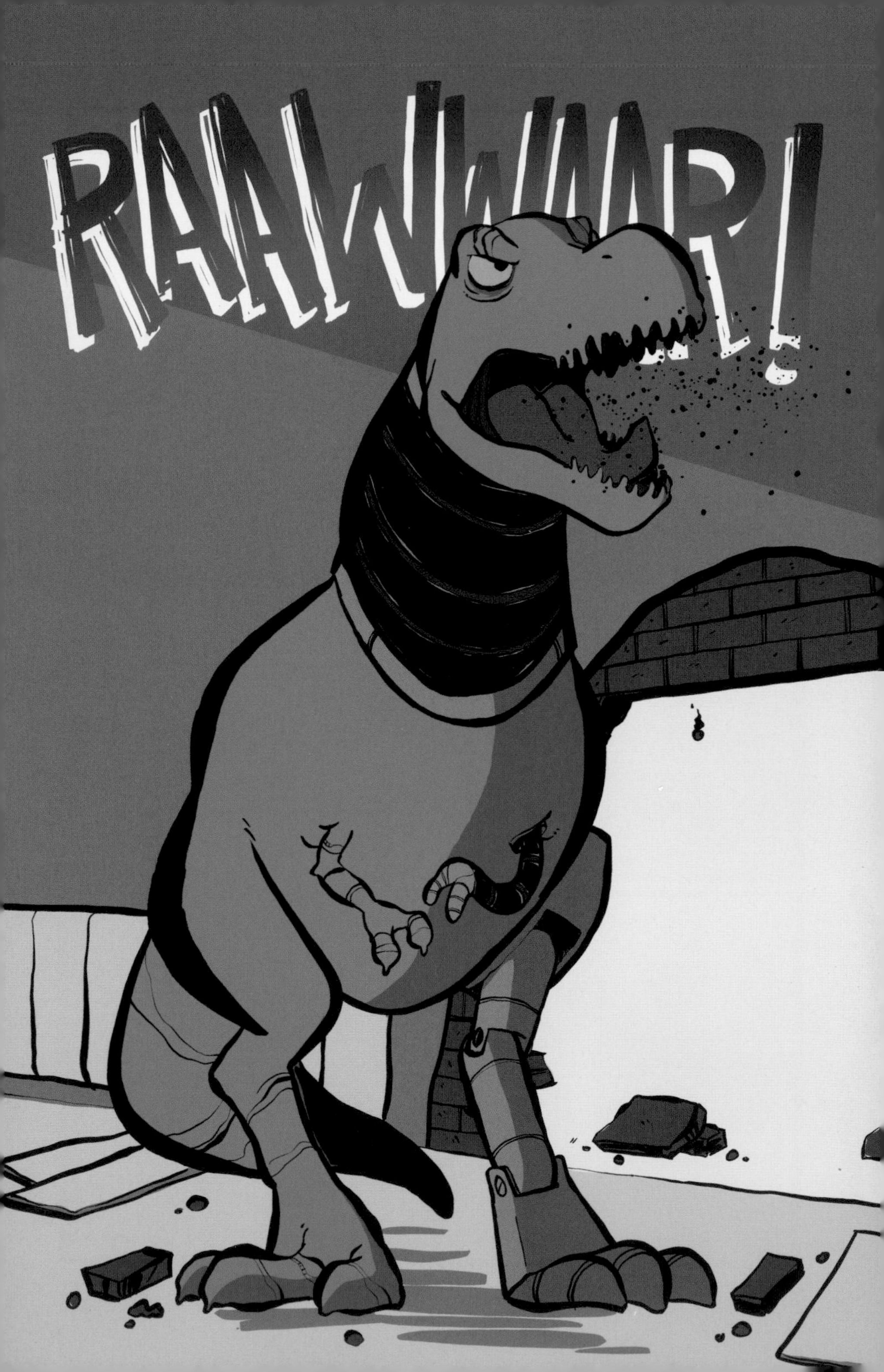
RAAWWAAR!

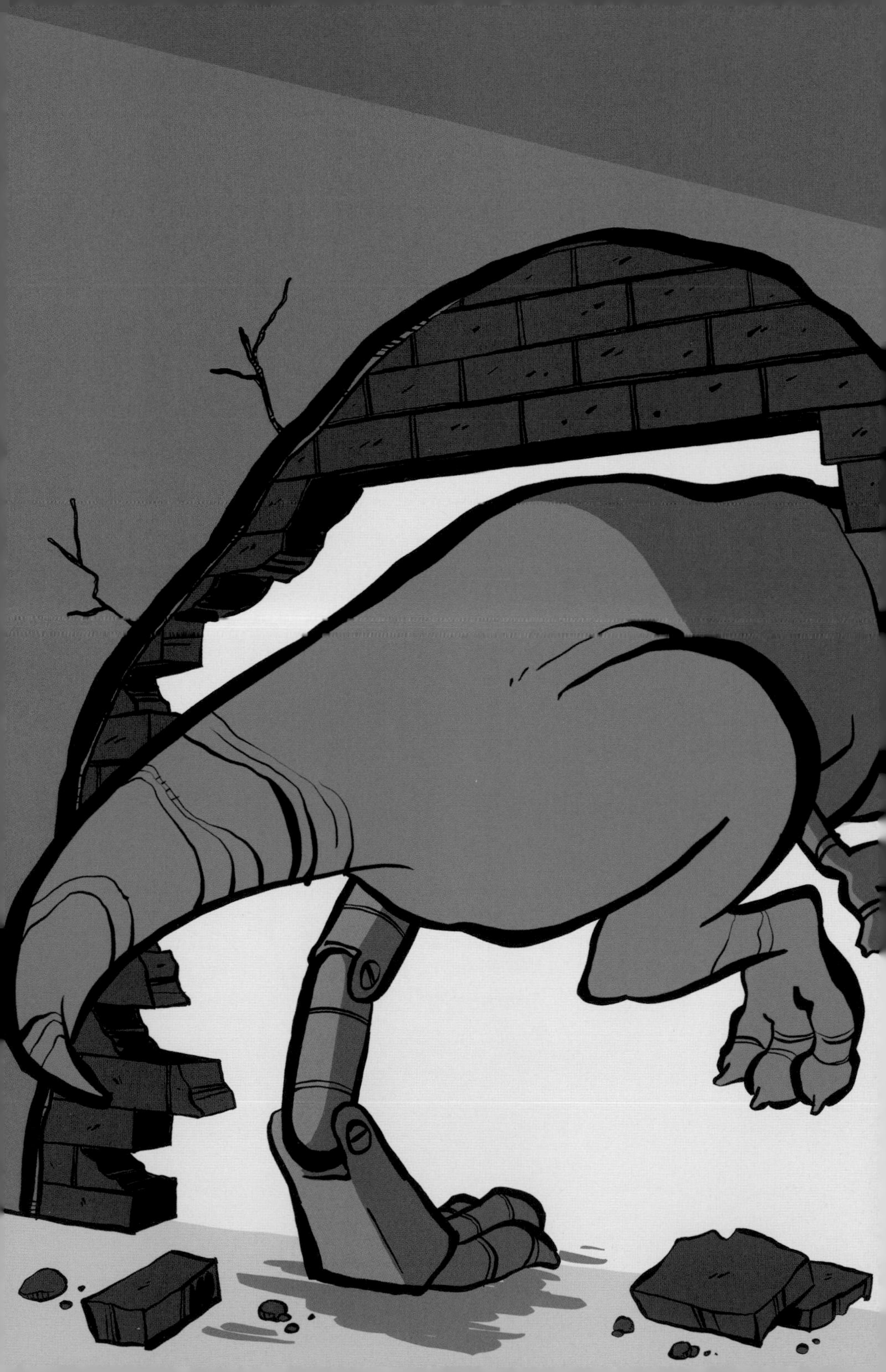

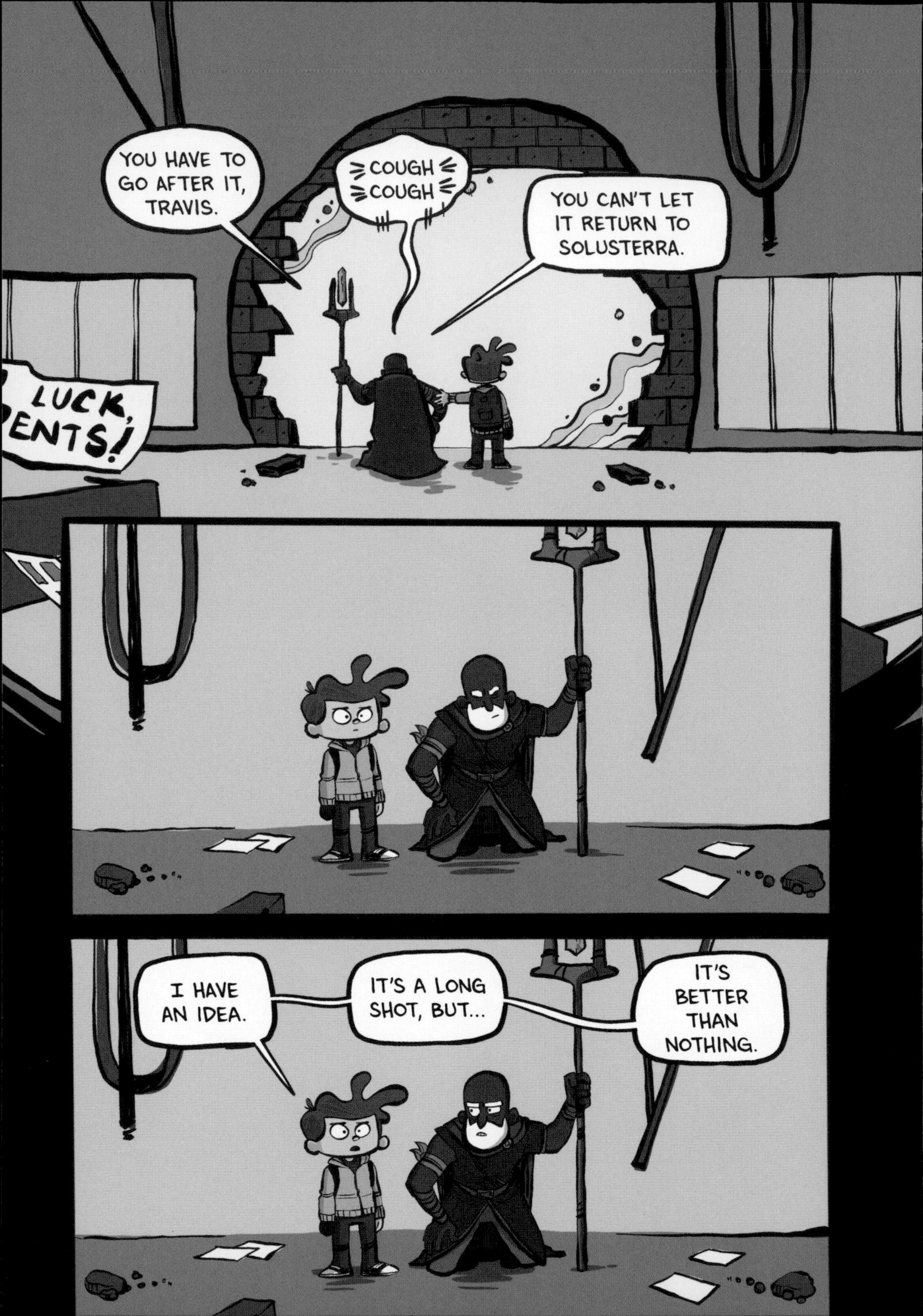
YOU HAVE TO GO AFTER IT, TRAVIS.
COUGH COUGH
YOU CAN'T LET IT RETURN TO SOLUSTERRA.
LUCK,
ENTS!
I HAVE AN IDEA.
IT'S A LONG SHOT, BUT...
IT'S BETTER THAN NOTHING.

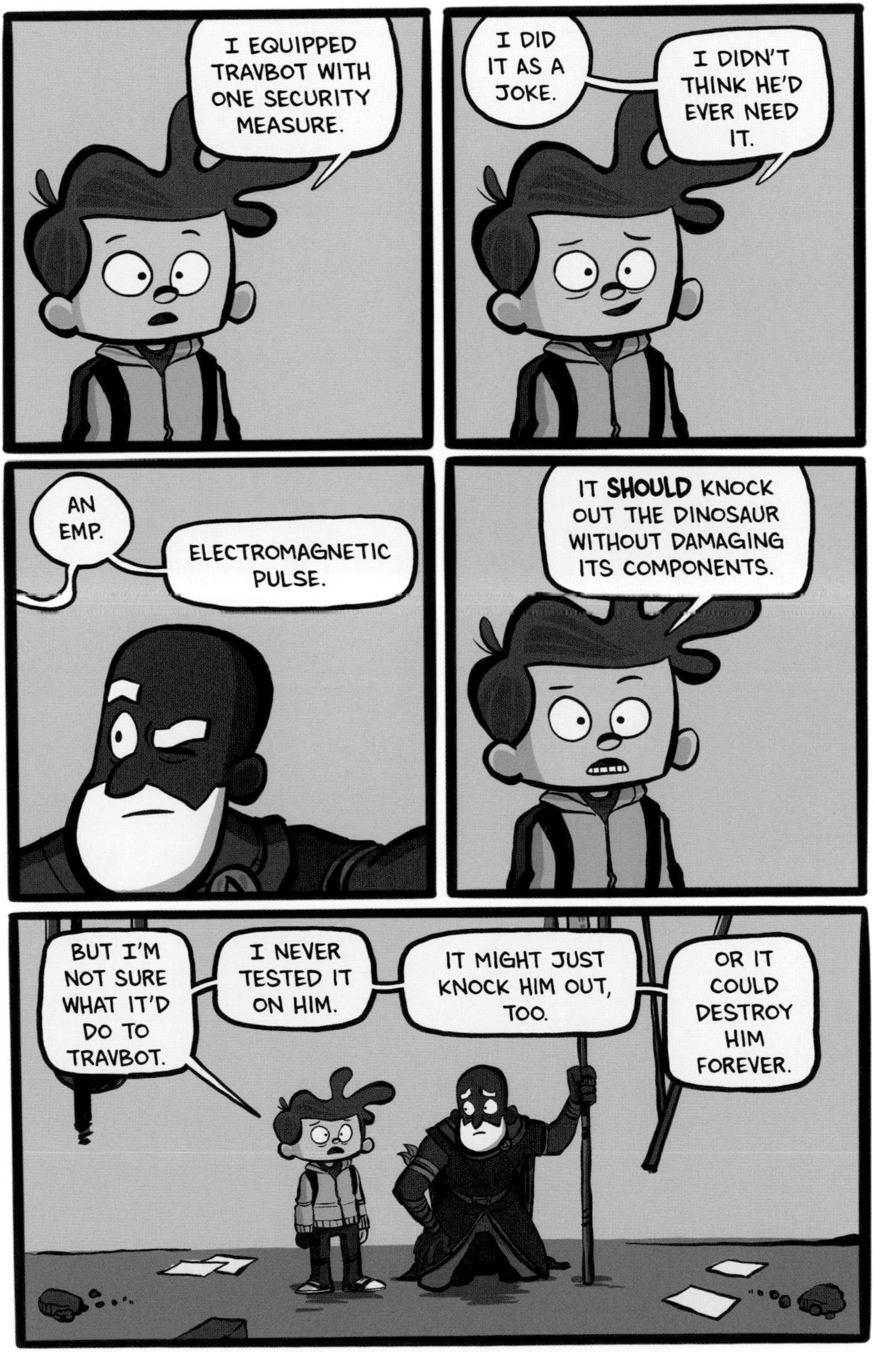
I EQUIPPED TRAVBOT WITH ONE SECURITY MEASURE.
I DID IT AS A JOKE.
I DIDN'T THINK HE'D EVER NEED IT.
AN EMP.
ELECTROMAGNETIC PULSE.
IT SHOULD KNOCK OUT THE DINOSAUR WITHOUT DAMAGING ITS COMPONENTS.
BUT I'M NOT SURE WHAT IT'D DO TO TRAVBOT.
I NEVER TESTED IT ON HIM.
IT MIGHT JUST KNOCK HIM OUT, TOO.
OR IT COULD DESTROY HIM FOREVER.

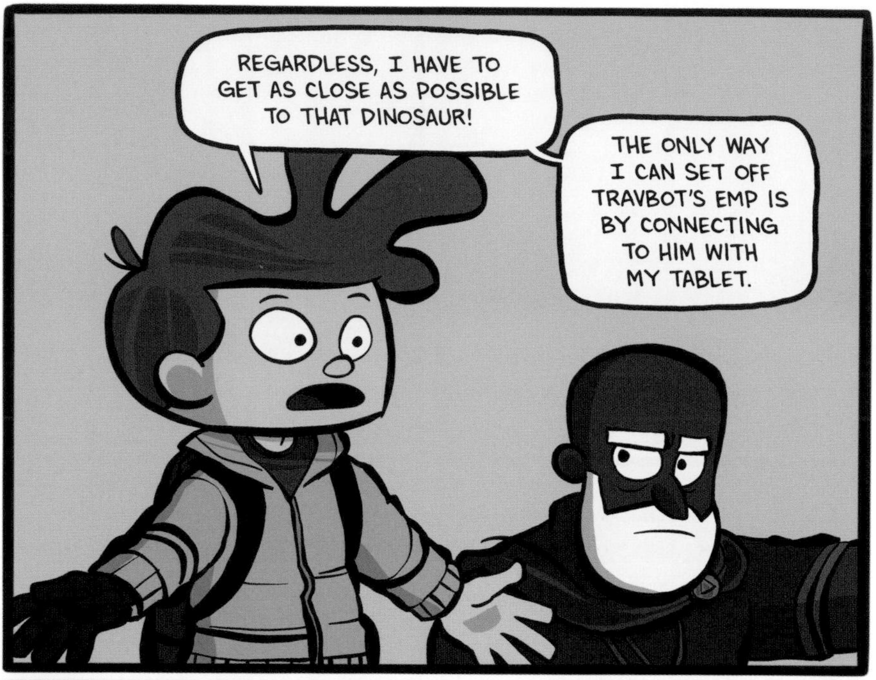
REGARDLESS, I HAVE TO GET AS CLOSE AS POSSIBLE TO THAT DINOSAUR!
THE ONLY WAY I CAN SET OFF TRAVBOT'S EMP IS BY CONNECTING TO HIM WITH MY TABLET.

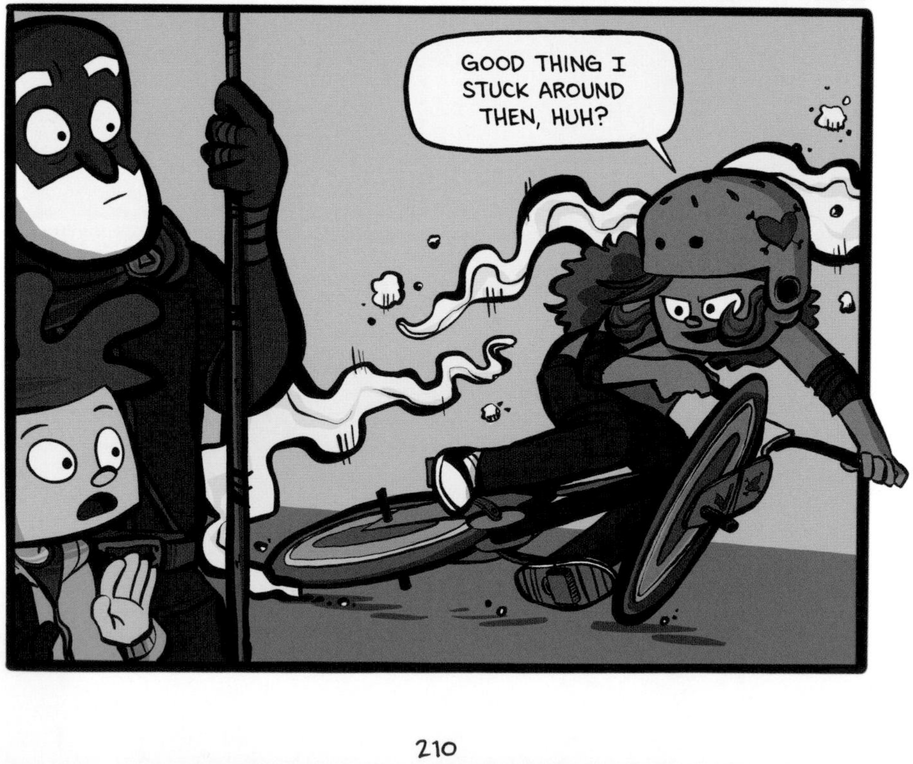
GOOD THING I STUCK AROUND THEN, HUH?

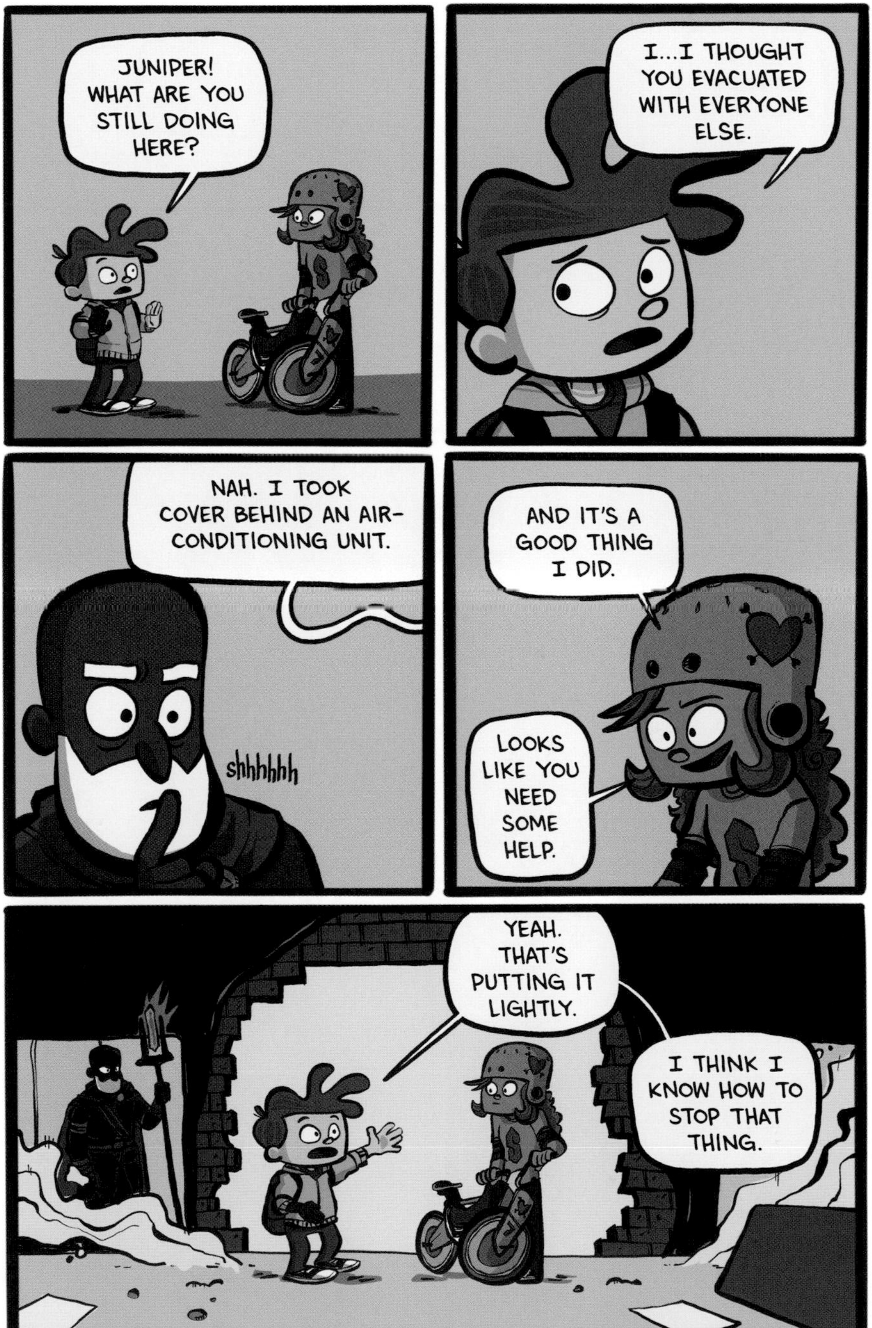
JUNIPER! WHAT ARE YOU STILL DOING HERE?
I...I THOUGHT YOU EVACUATED WITH EVERYONE ELSE.
NAH. I TOOK COVER BEHIND AN AIR-CONDITIONING UNIT.
shhhhhh
AND IT'S A GOOD THING I DID.
LOOKS LIKE YOU NEED SOME HELP.
YEAH. THAT'S PUTTING IT LIGHTLY.
I THINK I KNOW HOW TO STOP THAT THING.

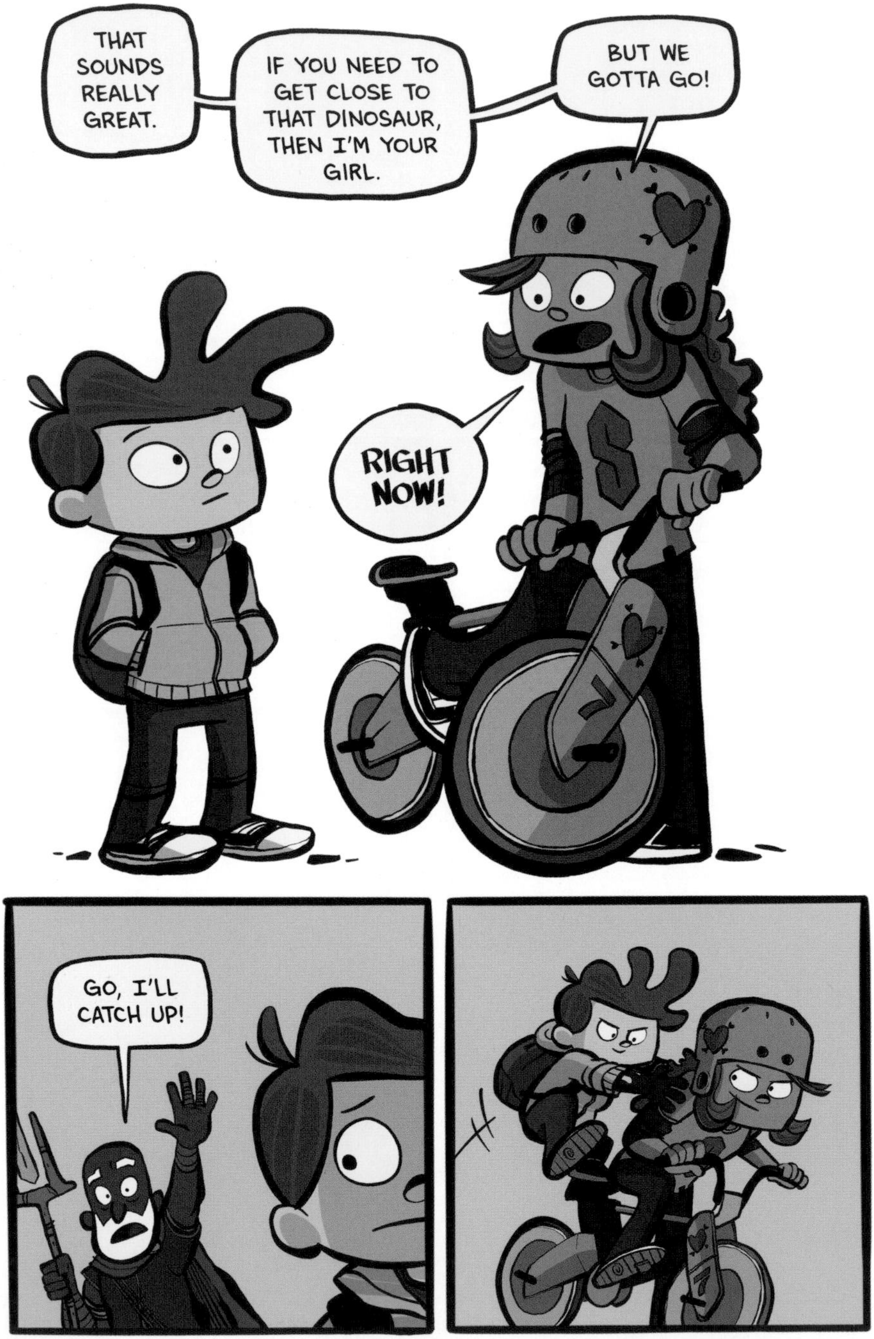
THAT SOUNDS REALLY GREAT.
IF YOU NEED TO GET CLOSE TO THAT DINOSAUR, THEN I'M YOUR GIRL.
BUT WE GOTTA GO!
RIGHT NOW!
GO, I'LL CATCH UP!

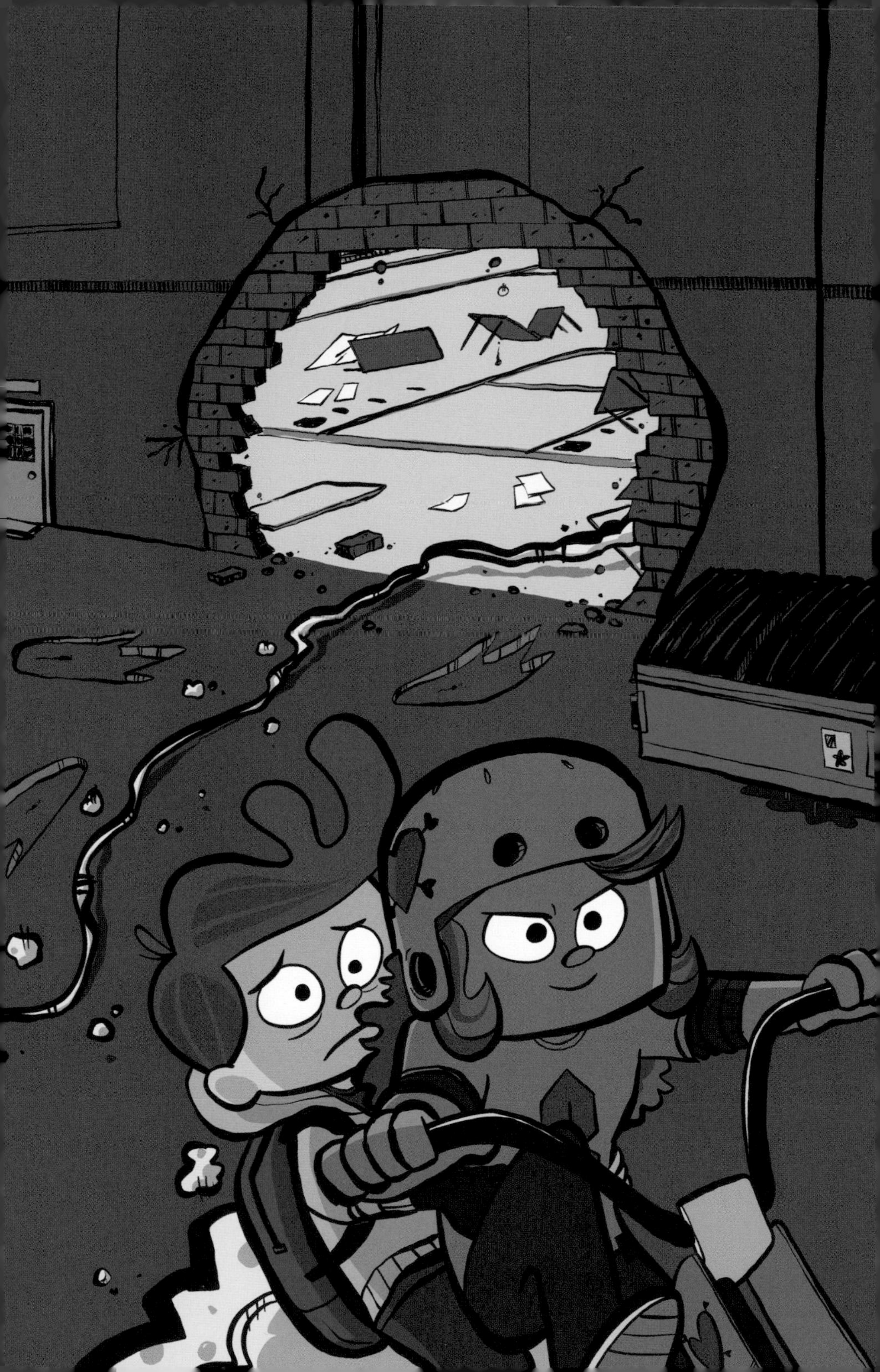

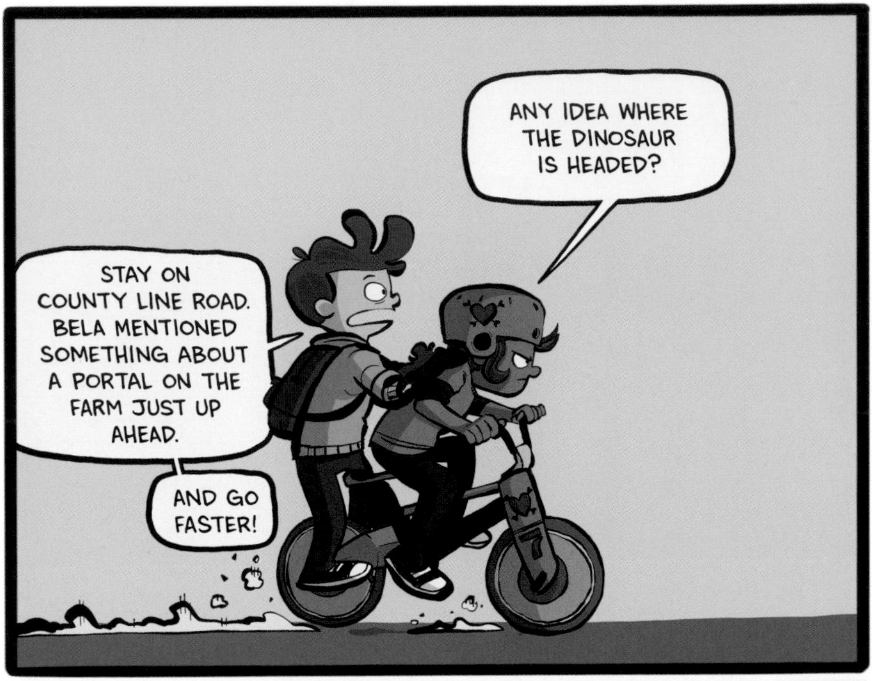
ANY IDEA WHERE THE DINOSAUR IS HEADED?
STAY ON COUNTY LINE ROAD. BELA MENTIONED SOMETHING ABOUT A PORTAL ON THE FARM JUST UP AHEAD.
AND GO FASTER!

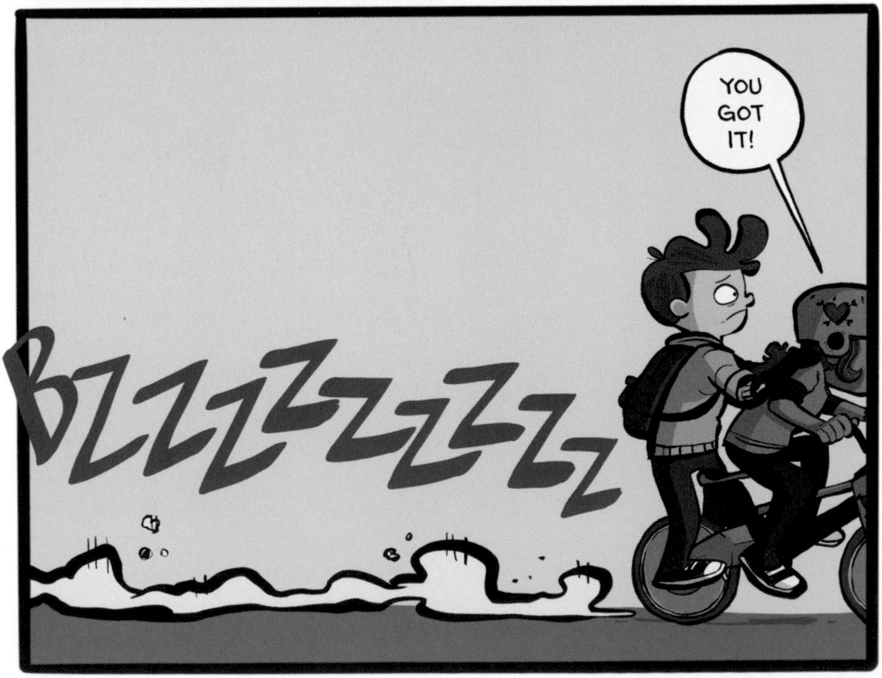
YOU GOT IT!
BZZZZZZZZZ

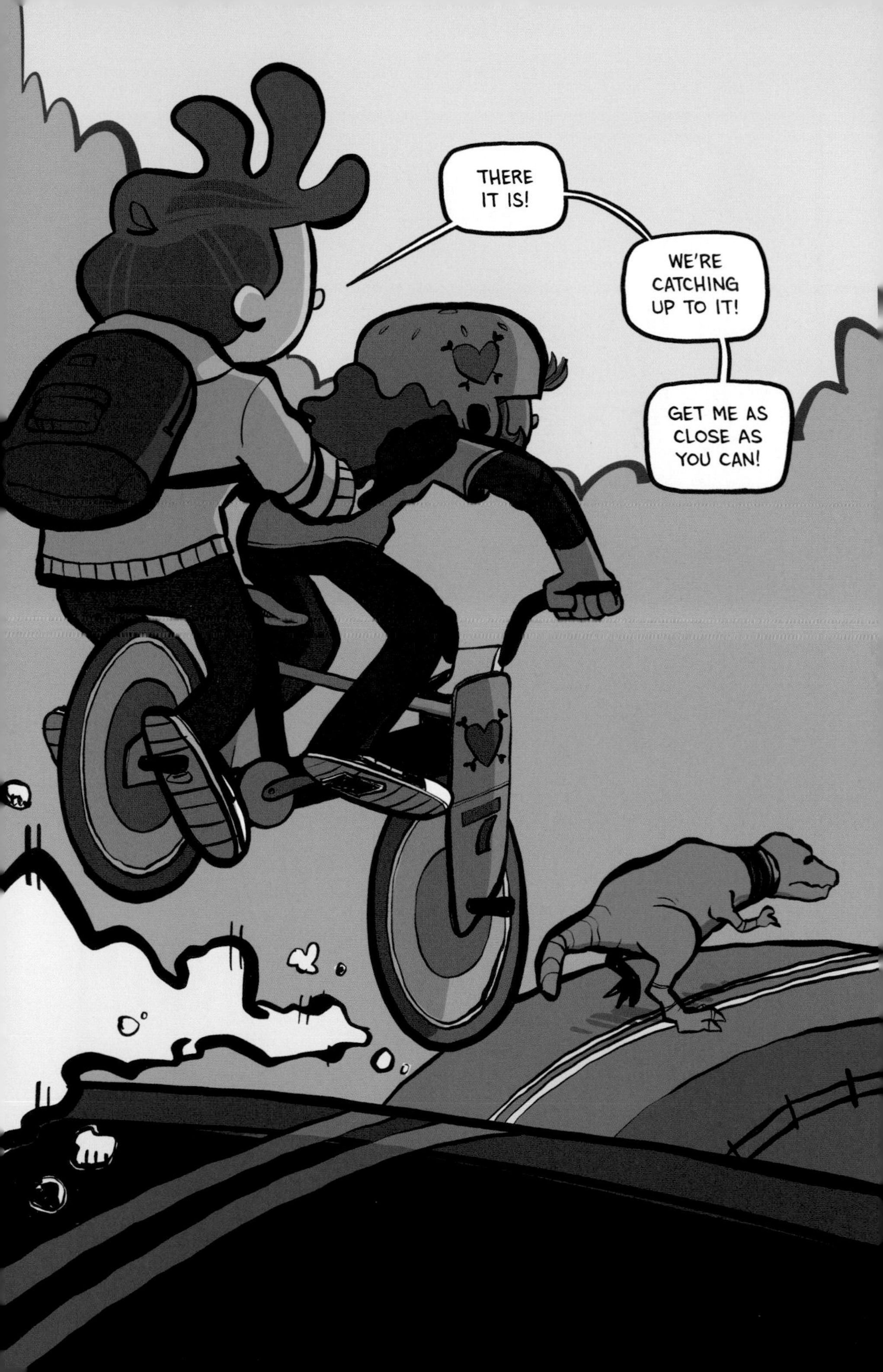
THERE IT IS!
WE'RE CATCHING UP TO IT!
GET ME AS CLOSE AS YOU CAN!

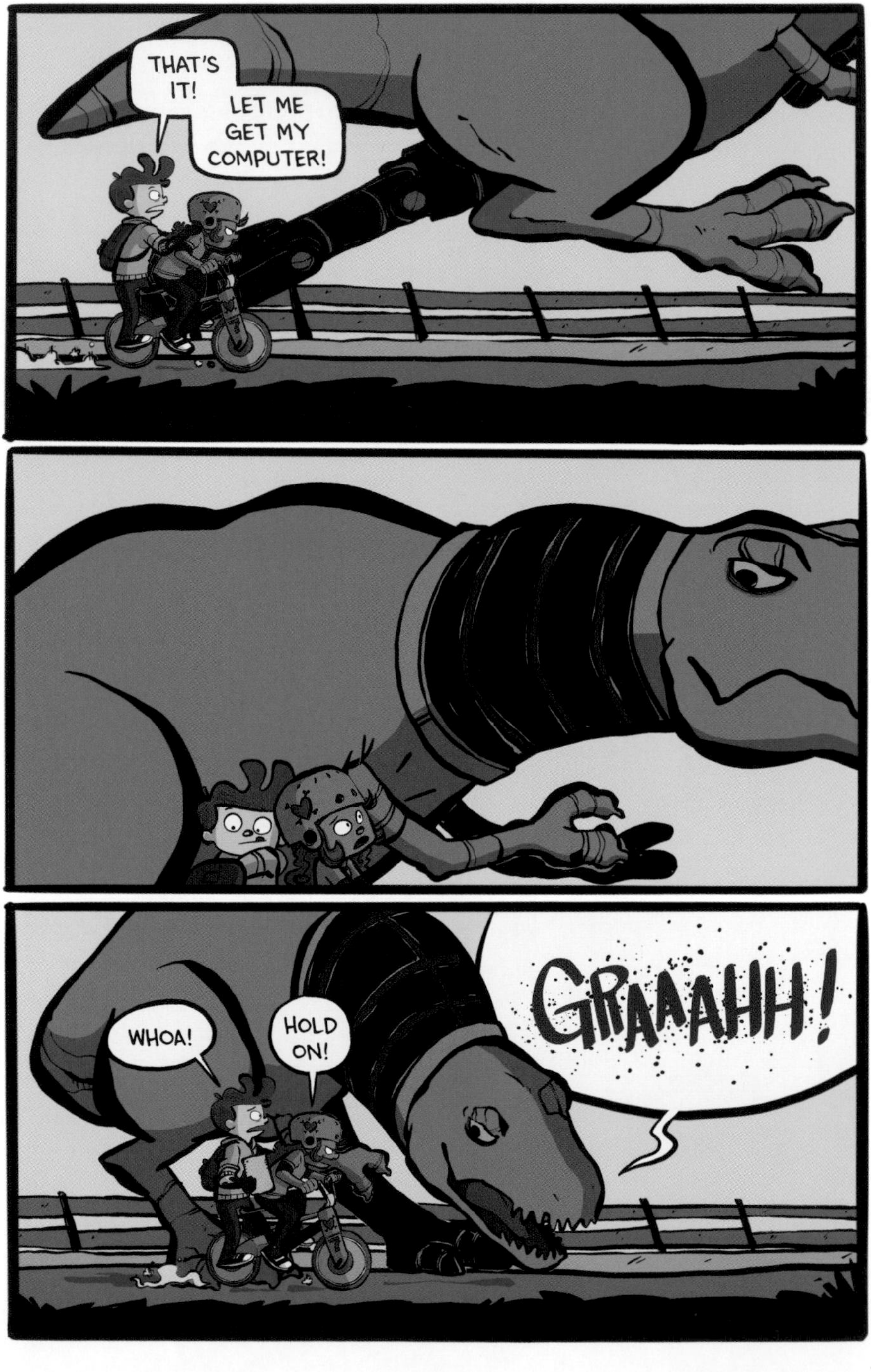
THAT'S IT!
LET ME GET MY COMPUTER!
WHOA!
HOLD ON!
GRAAAHH!

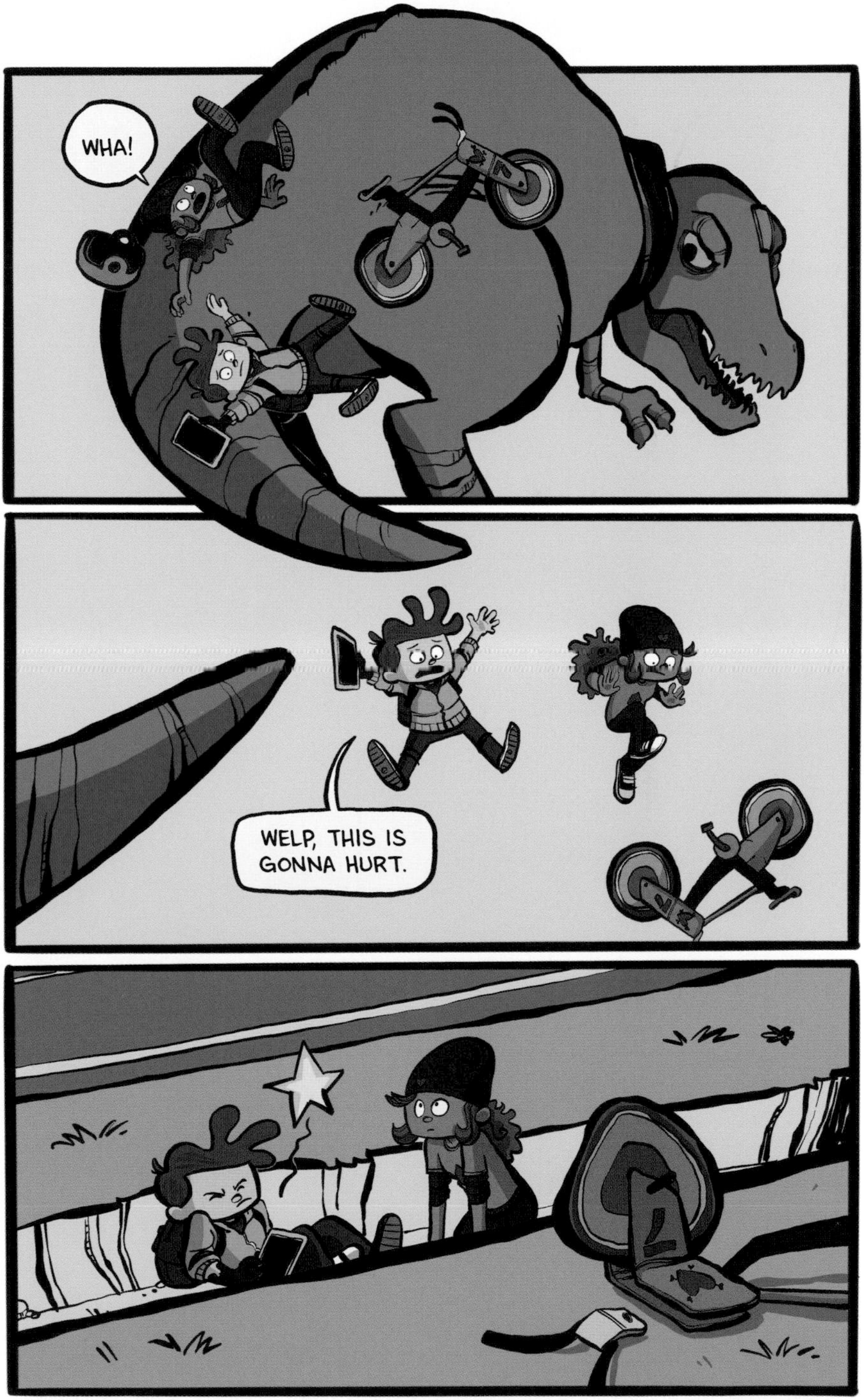

WHA!
WELP, THIS IS GONNA HURT.

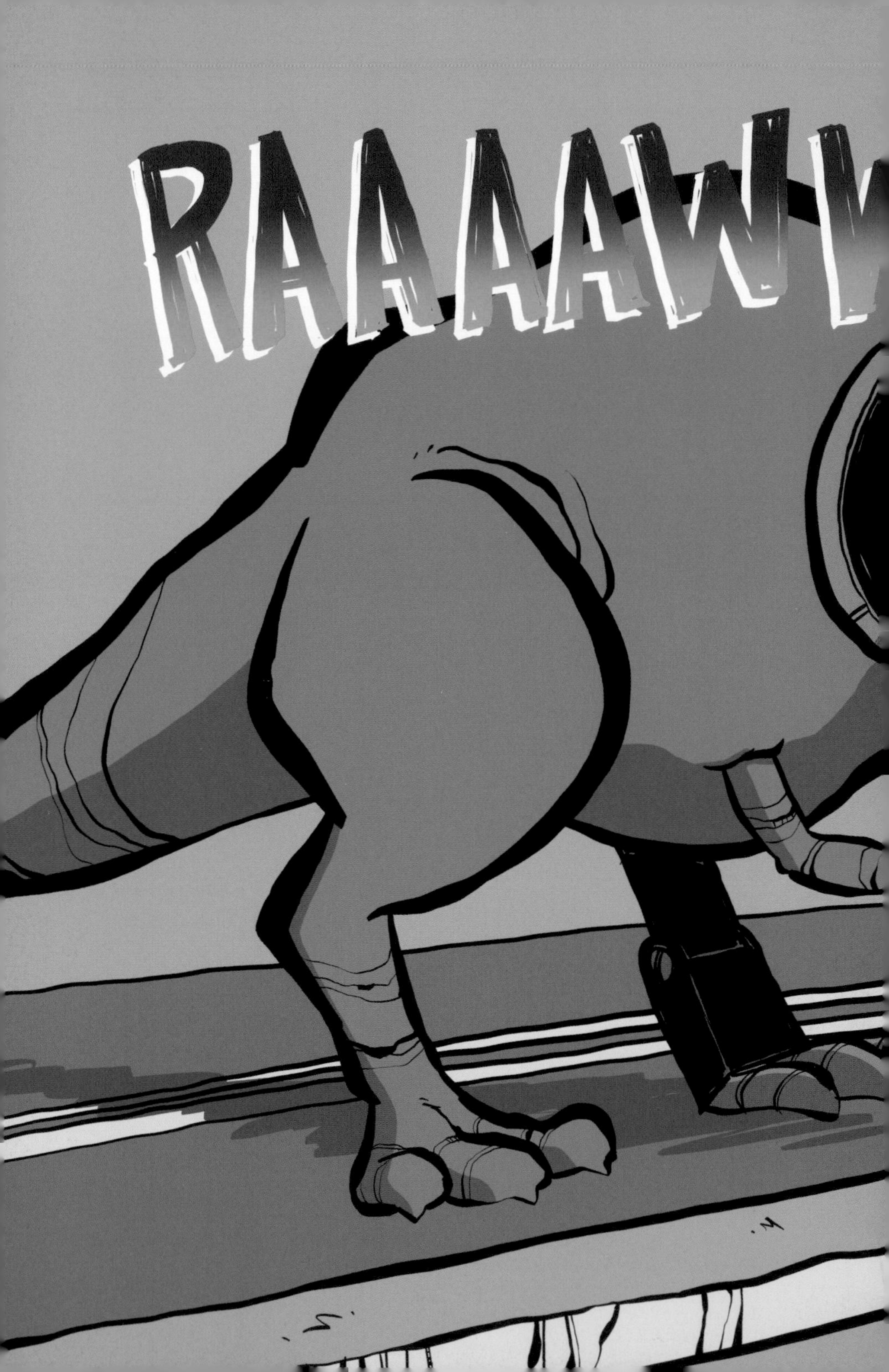
RAAAAW

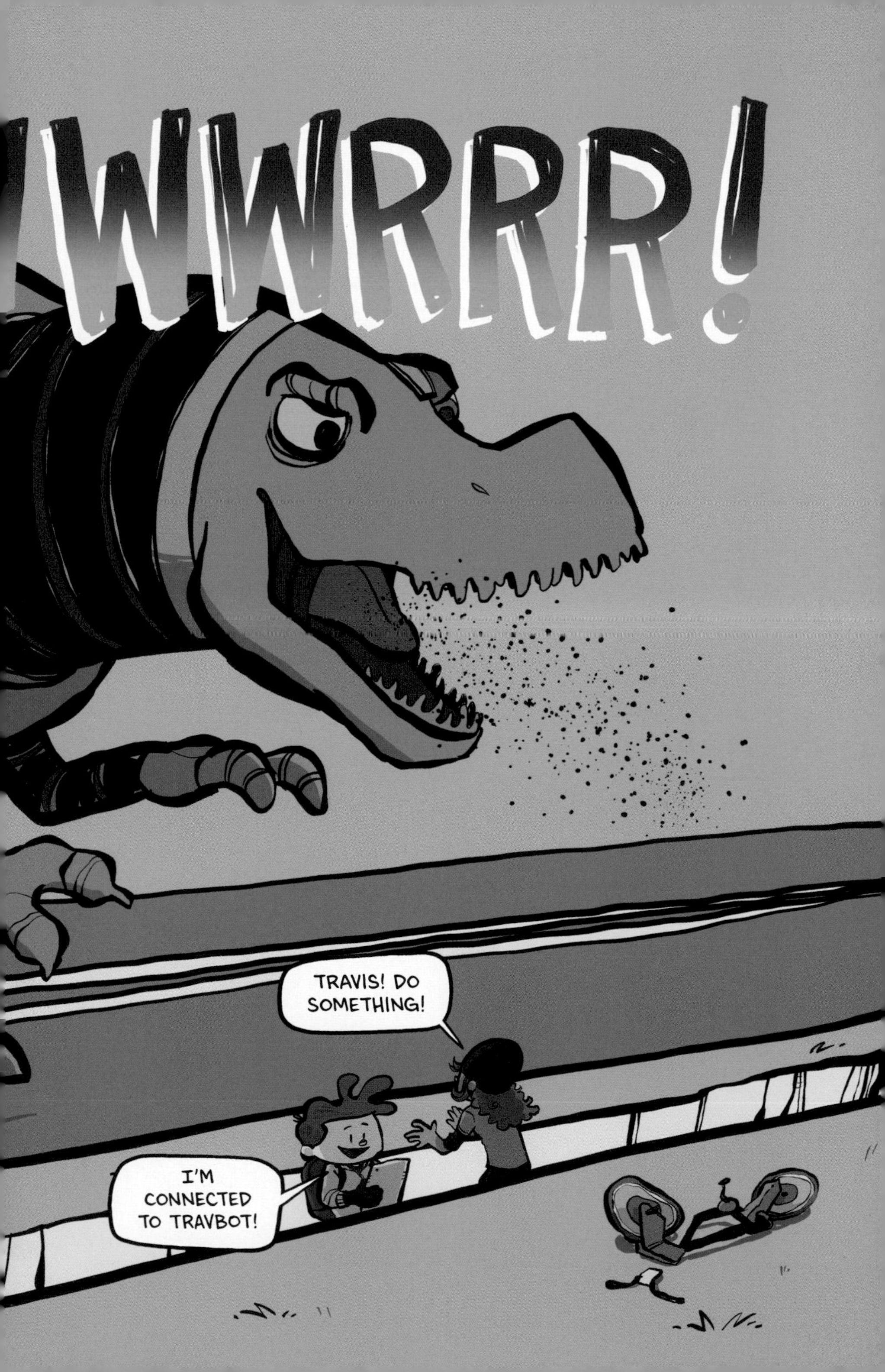
WWRRR!
TRAVIS! DO SOMETHING!
I'M CONNECTED TO TRAVBOT!

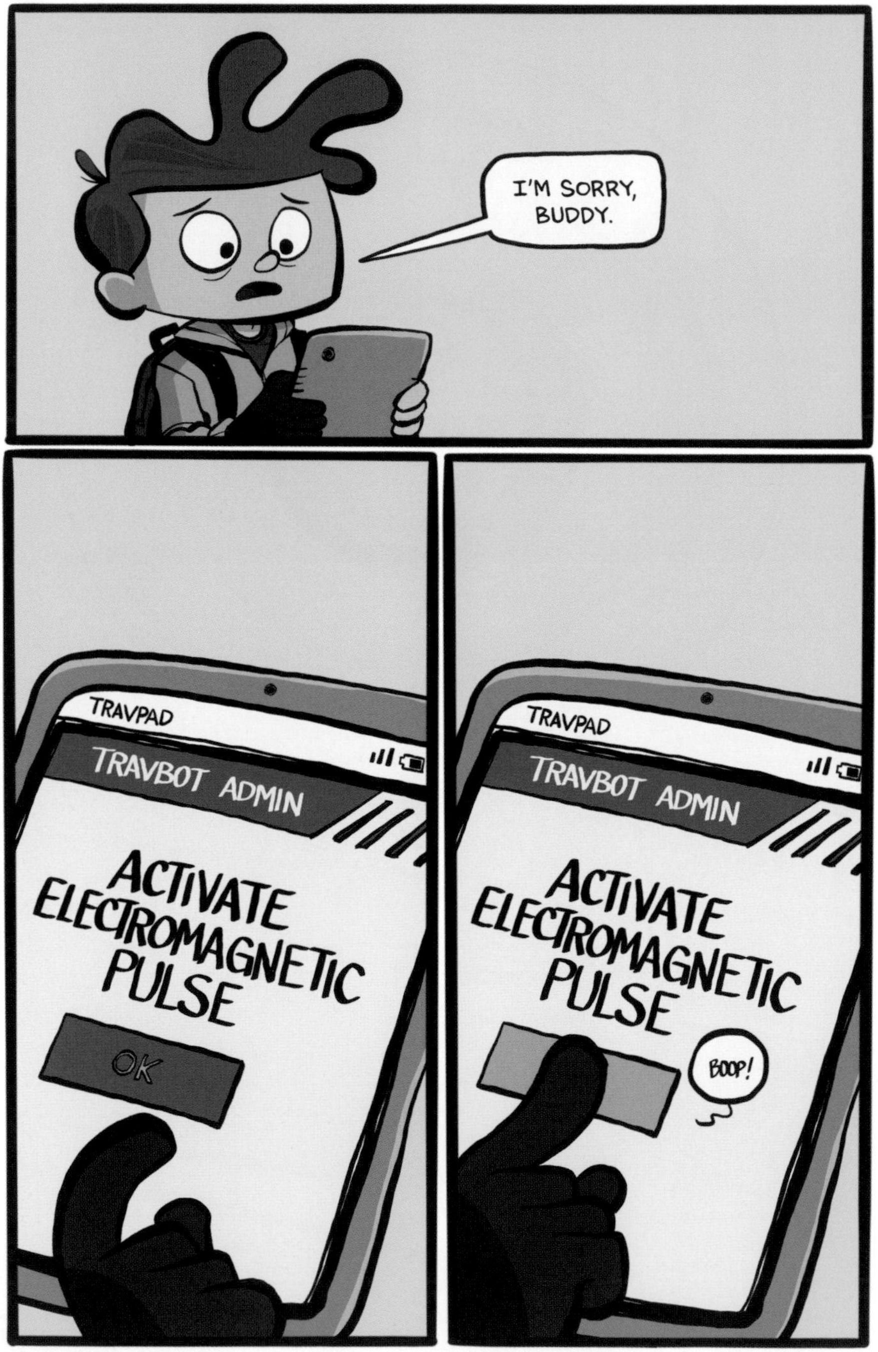
I'M SORRY, BUDDY.
TRAVPAD
TRAVBOT ADMIN
ACTIVATE ELECTROMAGNETIC PULSE
OK
TRAVPAD
TRAVBOT ADMIN
ACTIVATE ELECTROMAGNETIC PULSE
BOOP!

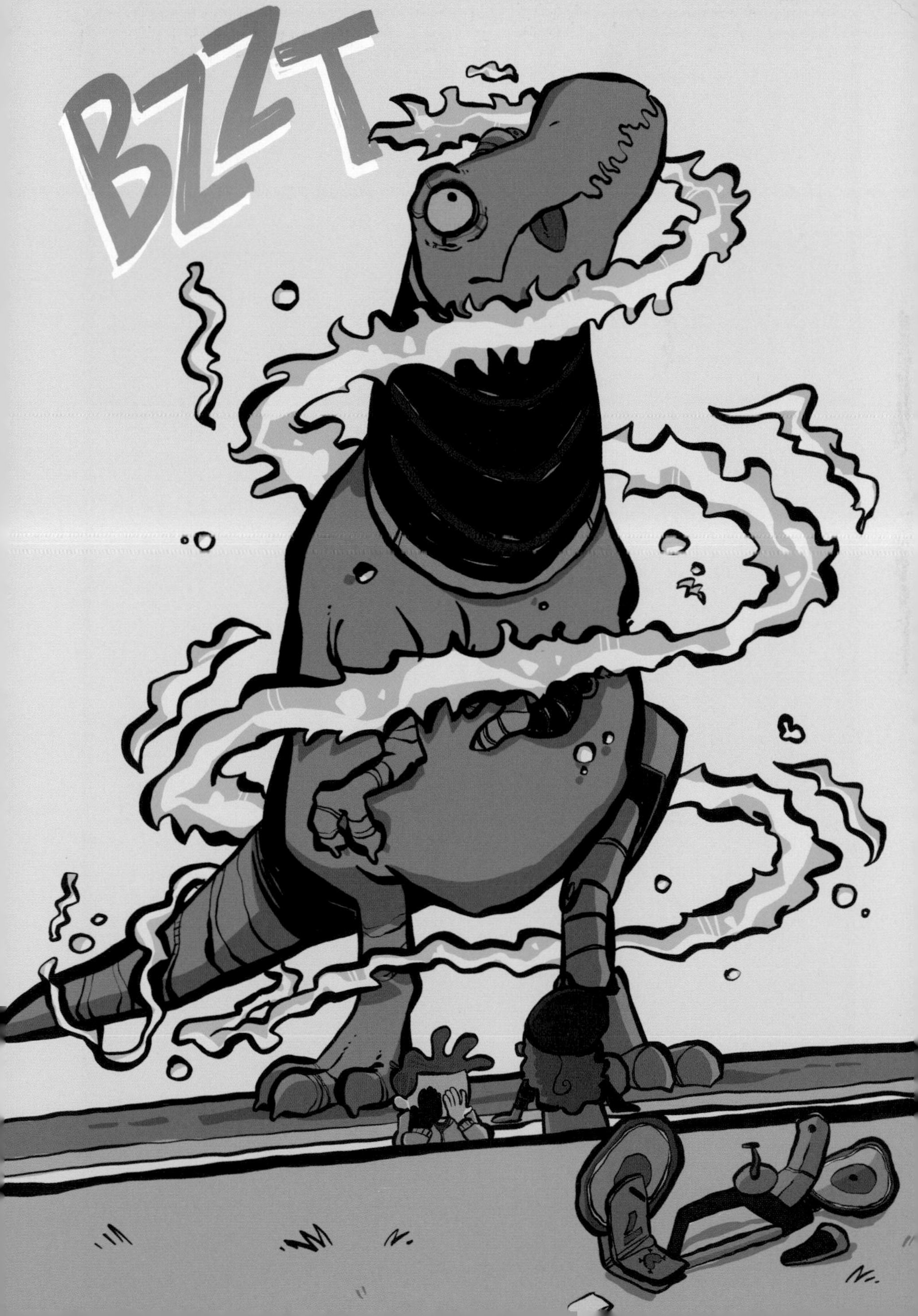
BZZT

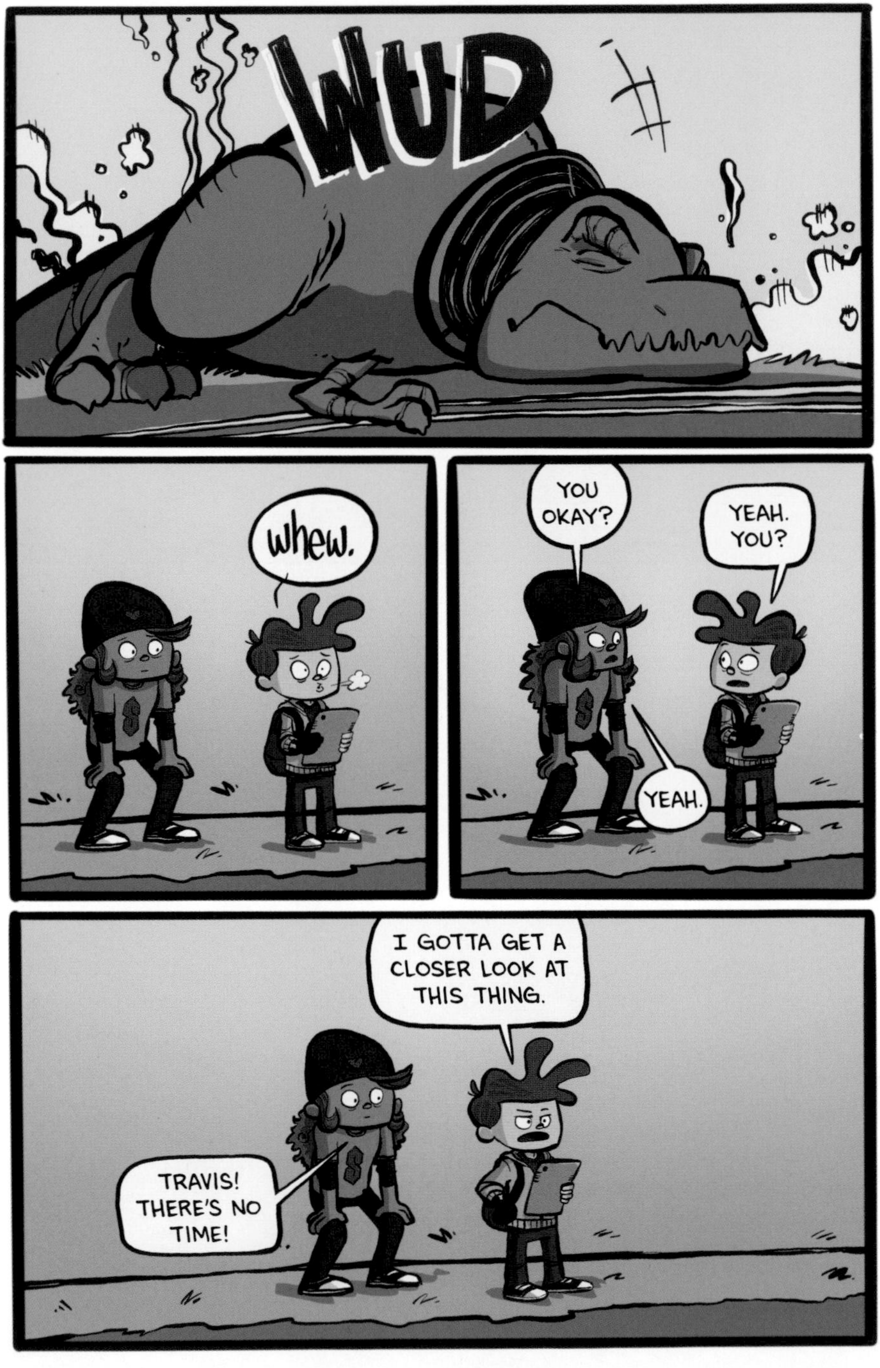
WUD
whew.
YOU OKAY?
YEAH. YOU?
YEAH.
I GOTTA GET A CLOSER LOOK AT THIS THING.
TRAVIS! THERE'S NO TIME!

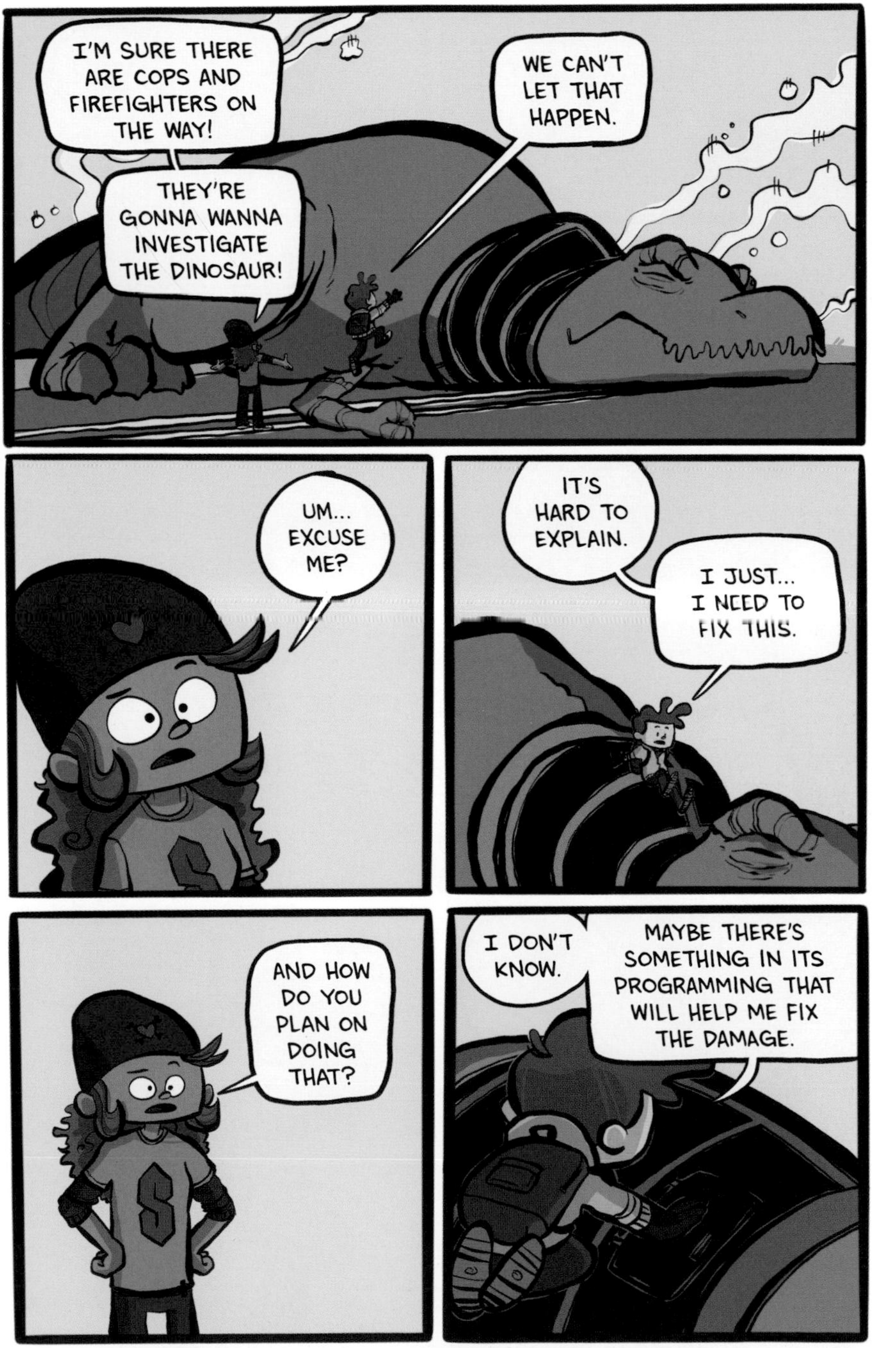
I'M SURE THERE ARE COPS AND FIREFIGHTERS ON THE WAY!
THEY'RE GONNA WANNA INVESTIGATE THE DINOSAUR!
WE CAN'T LET THAT HAPPEN.
UM... EXCUSE ME?
IT'S HARD TO EXPLAIN.
I JUST... I NEED TO FIX THIS.
AND HOW DO YOU PLAN ON DOING THAT?
I DON'T KNOW.
MAYBE THERE'S SOMETHING IN ITS PROGRAMMING THAT WILL HELP ME FIX THE DAMAGE.

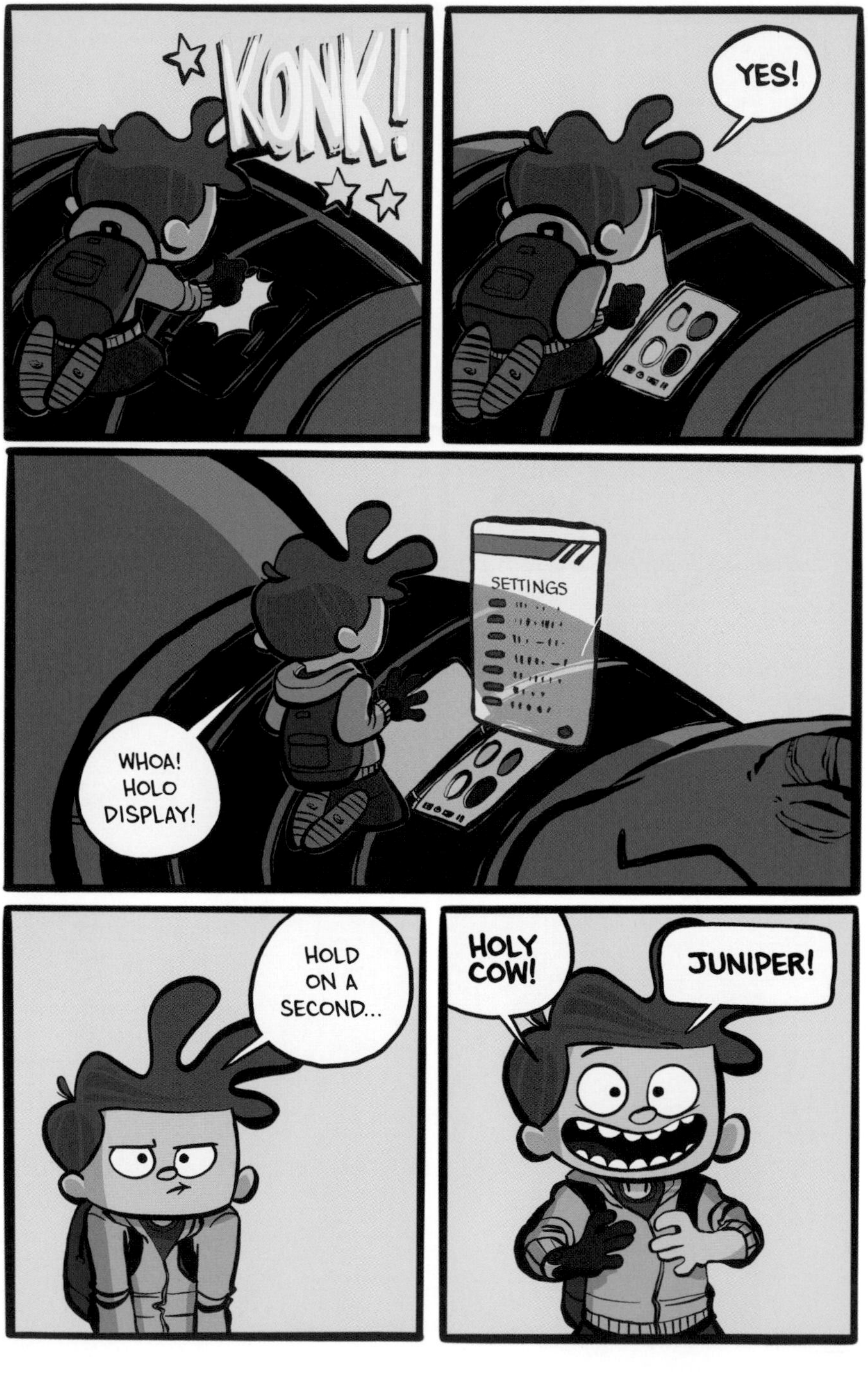
KONK!
YES!
SETTINGS
WHOA! HOLO DISPLAY!
HOLD ON A SECOND...
HOLY COW!
JUNIPER!

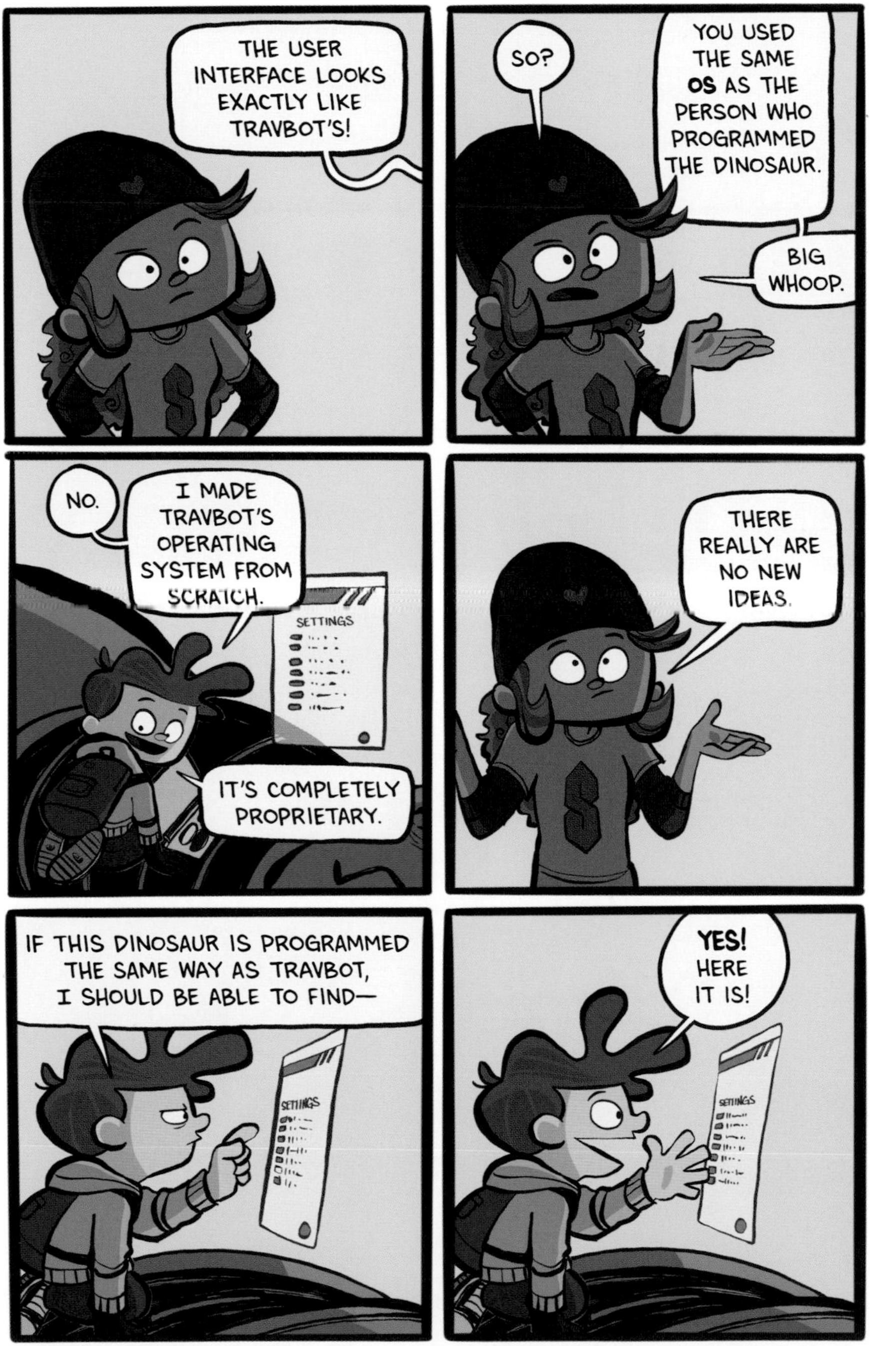
THE USER INTERFACE LOOKS EXACTLY LIKE TRAVBOT'S!
SO?
YOU USED THE SAME **OS** AS THE PERSON WHO PROGRAMMED THE DINOSAUR.
BIG WHOOP.
NO.
I MADE TRAVBOT'S OPERATING SYSTEM FROM SCRATCH.
SETTINGS
IT'S COMPLETELY PROPRIETARY.
THERE REALLY ARE NO NEW IDEAS.
IF THIS DINOSAUR IS PROGRAMMED THE SAME WAY AS TRAVBOT, I SHOULD BE ABLE TO FIND—
SETTINGS
YES! HERE IT IS!
SETTINGS

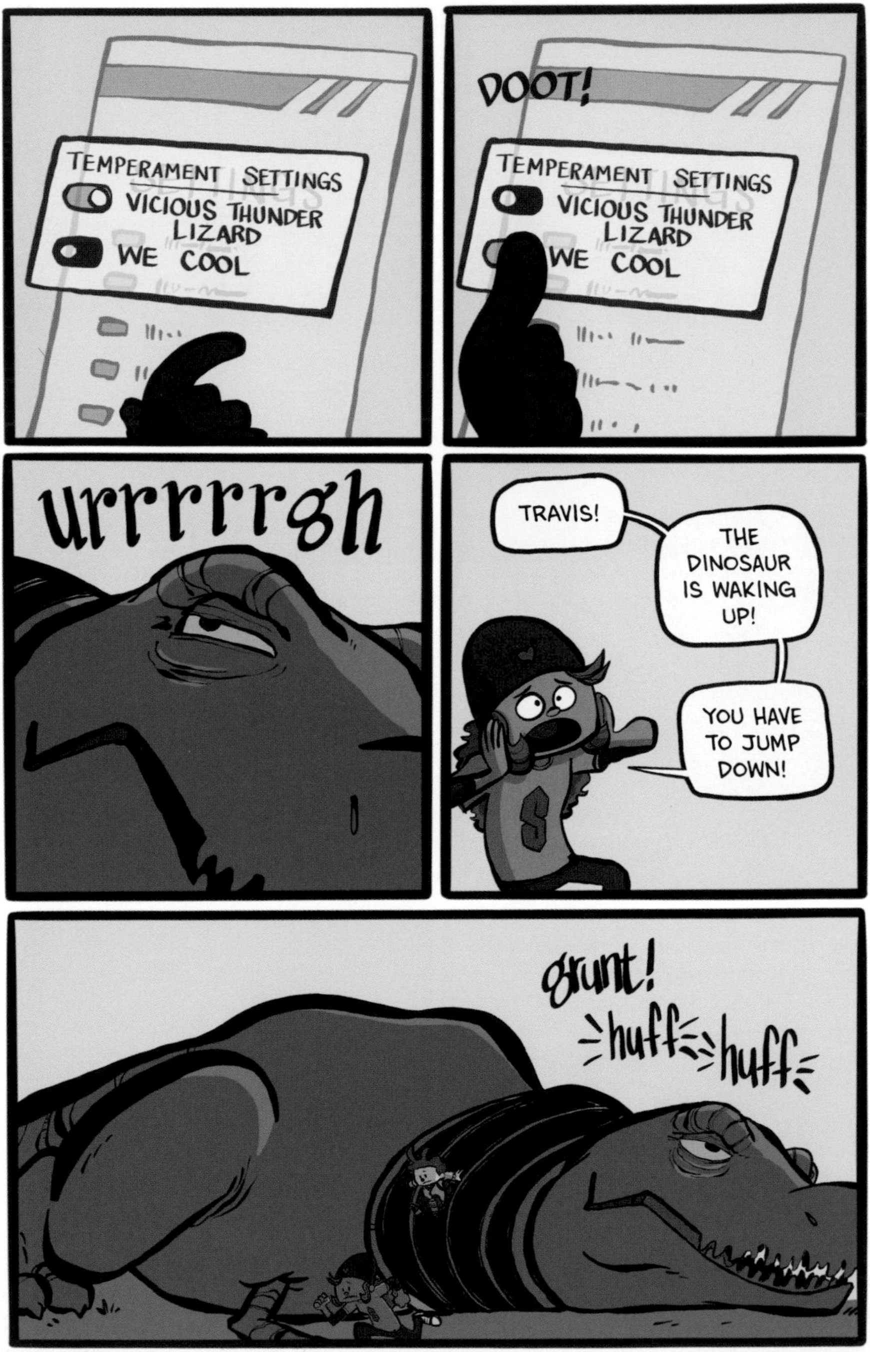
TEMPERAMENT SETTINGS
VICIOUS THUNDER LIZARD
WE COOL
DOOT!
TEMPERAMENT SETTINGS
VICIOUS THUNDER LIZARD
WE COOL
urrrrrgh
TRAVIS!
THE DINOSAUR IS WAKING UP!
YOU HAVE TO JUMP DOWN!
grunt!
huff huff

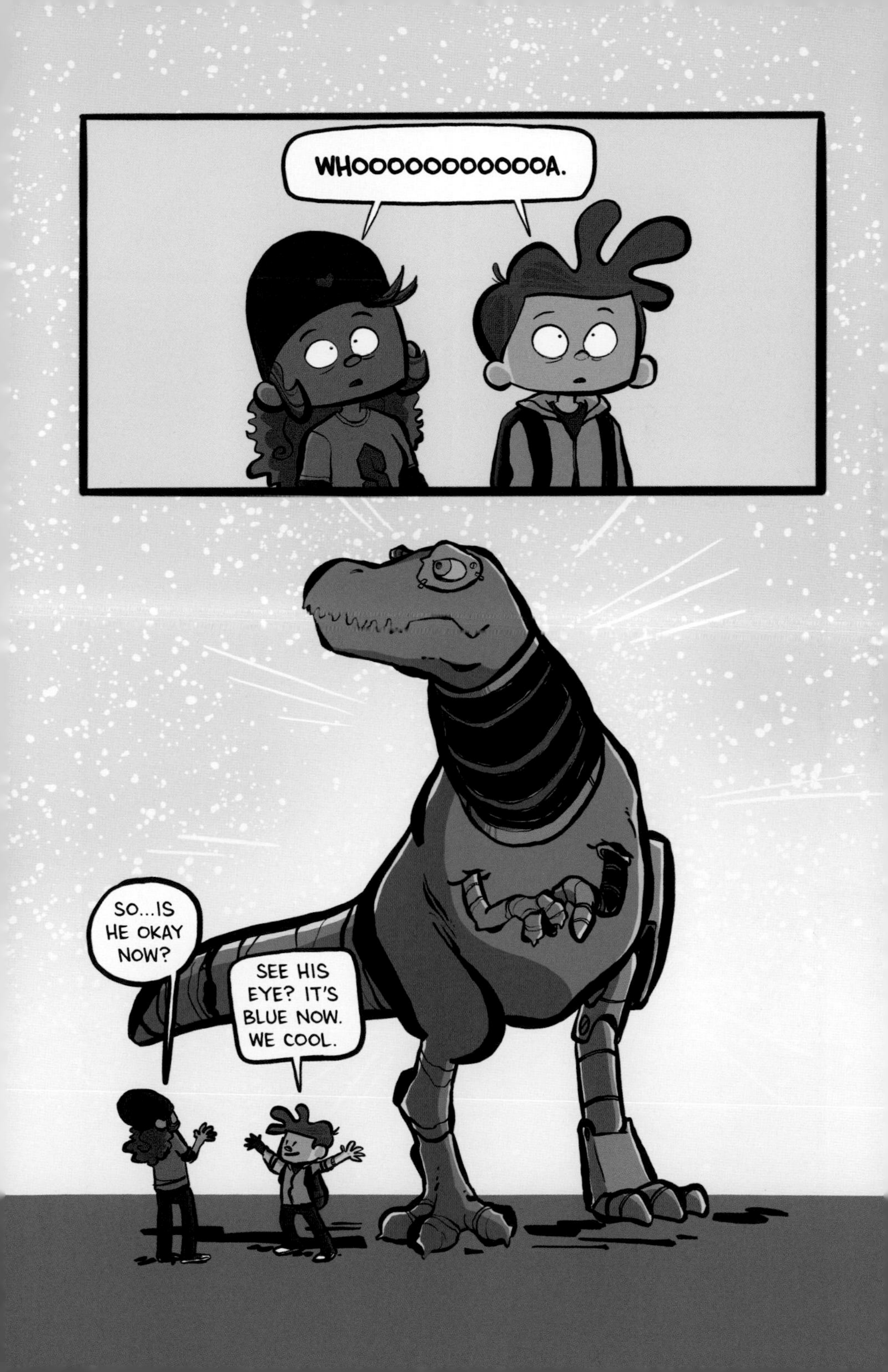
WHOOOOOOOOOOOA.
SO...IS HE OKAY NOW?
SEE HIS EYE? IT'S BLUE NOW. WE COOL.

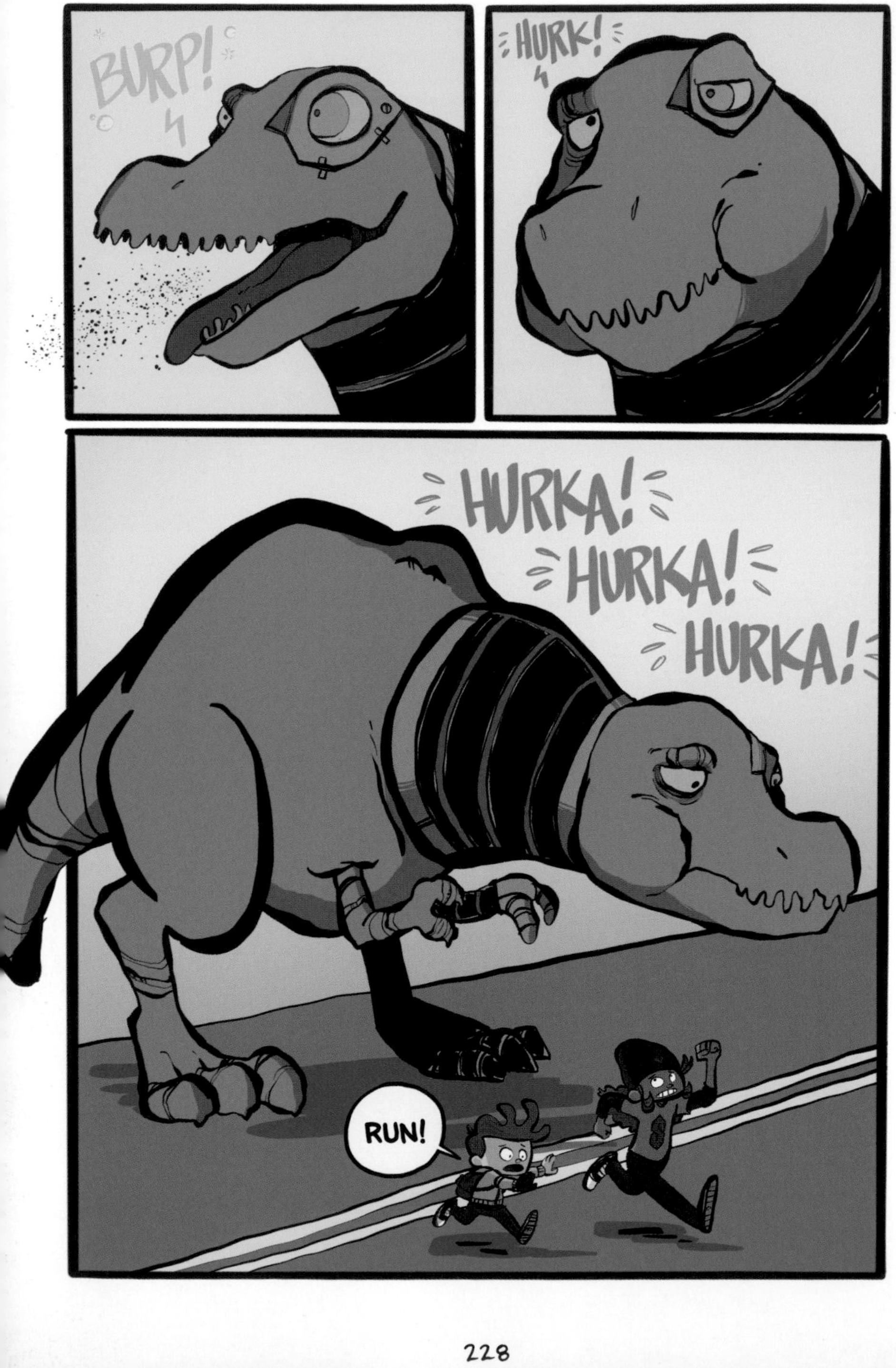
BURP!
HURK!
HURKA!
HURKA!
HURKA!
RUN!

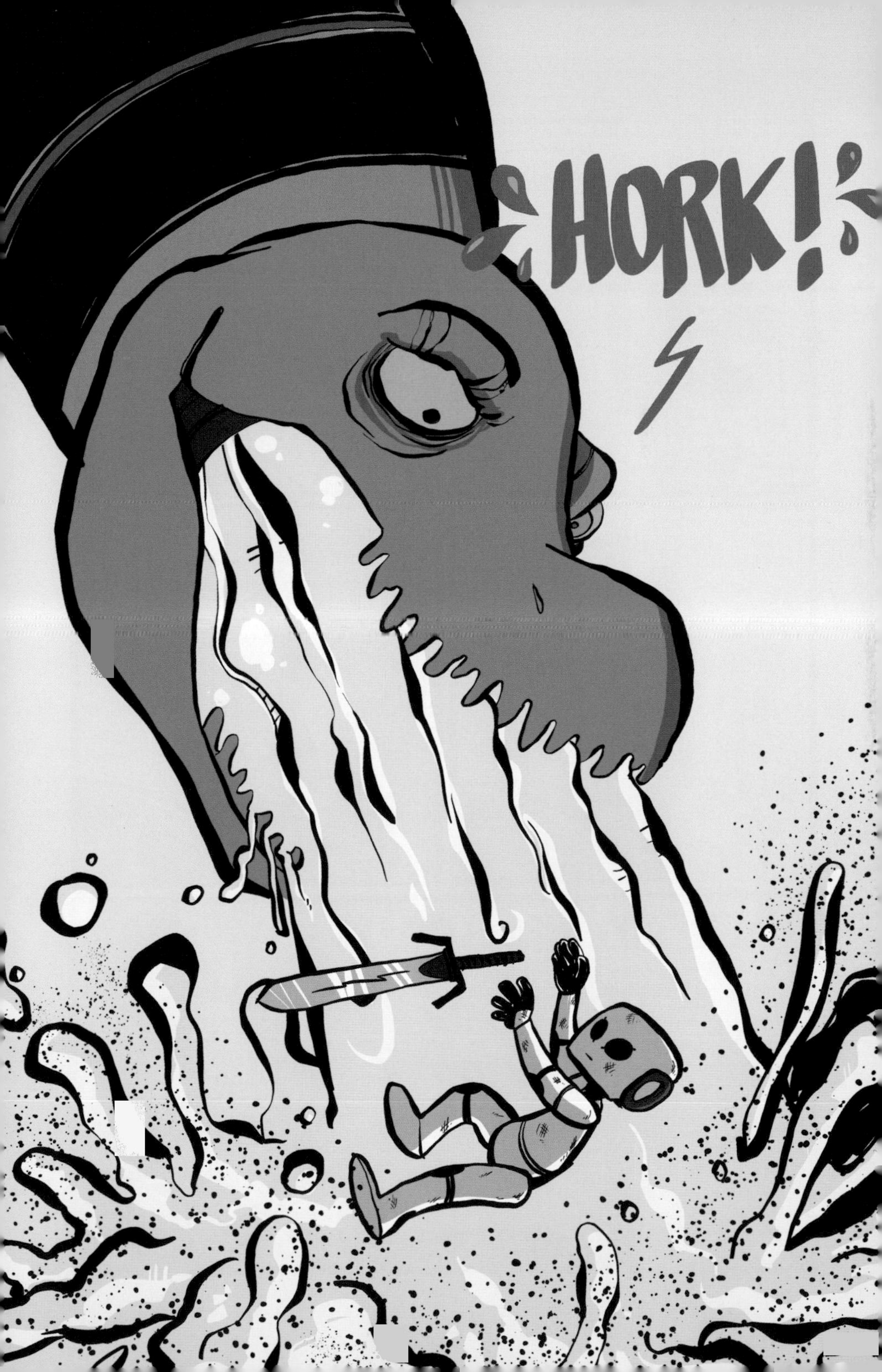
HORK!

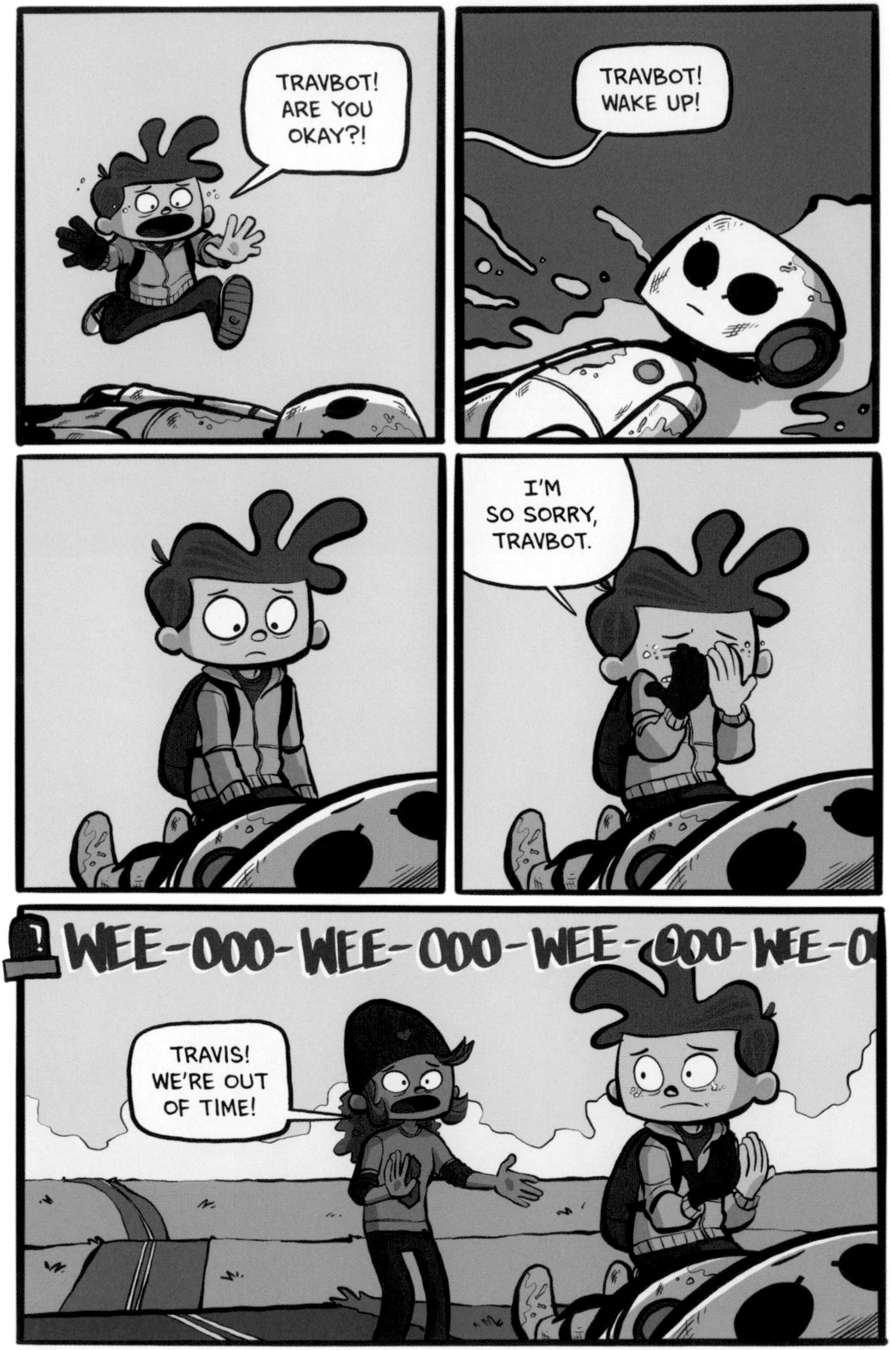
TRAVBOT! ARE YOU OKAY?!
TRAVBOT! WAKE UP!
I'M SO SORRY, TRAVBOT.
WEE-OOO-WEE-OOO-WEE-OOO-WEE-O
TRAVIS! WE'RE OUT OF TIME!

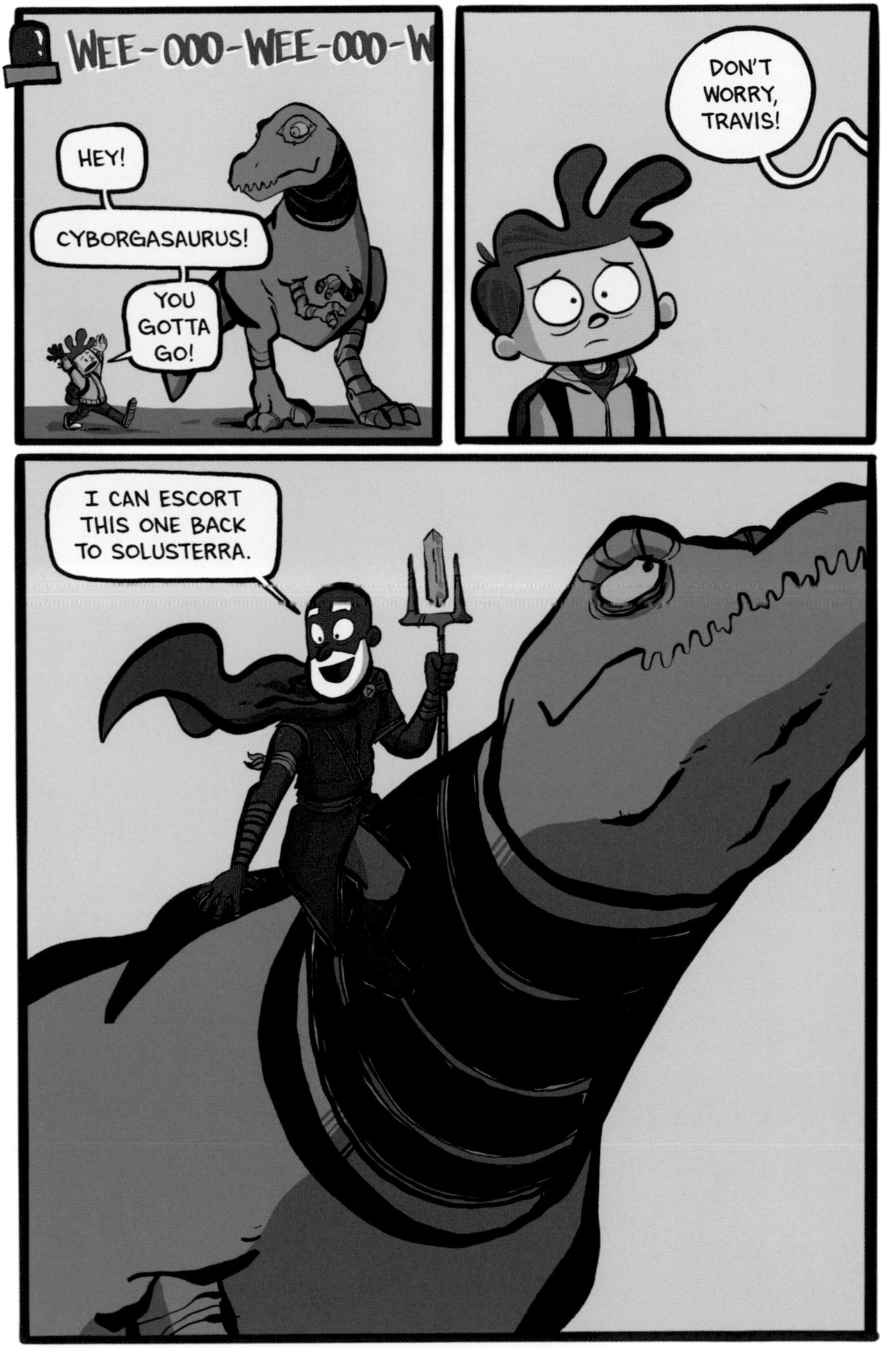
WEE-OOO-WEE-OOO-W
HEY!
CYBORGASAURUS!
YOU GOTTA GO!
DON'T WORRY, TRAVIS!
I CAN ESCORT THIS ONE BACK TO SOLUSTERRA.

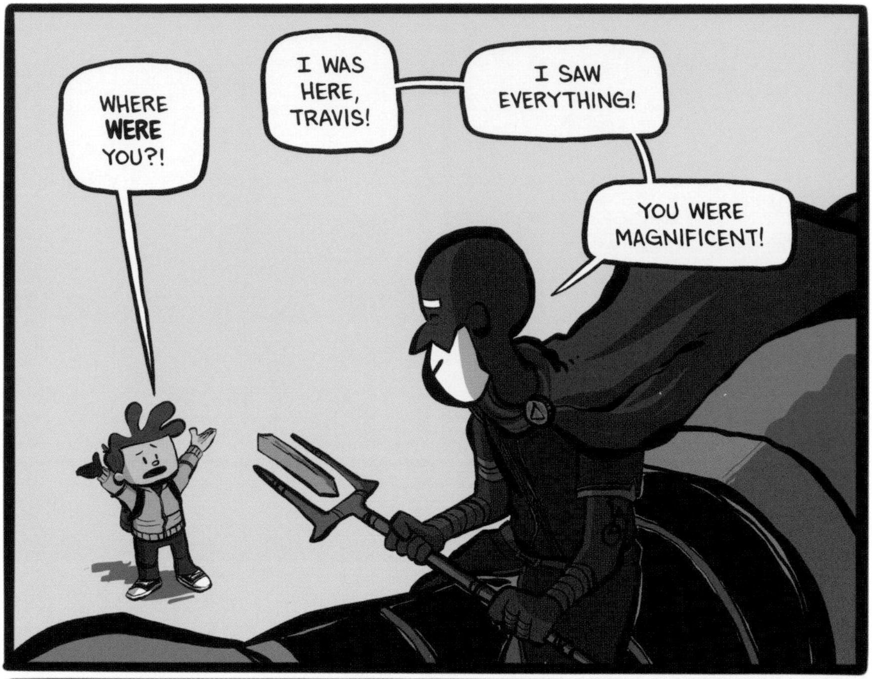
WHERE **WERE** YOU?!
I WAS HERE, TRAVIS!
I SAW EVERYTHING!
YOU WERE MAGNIFICENT!

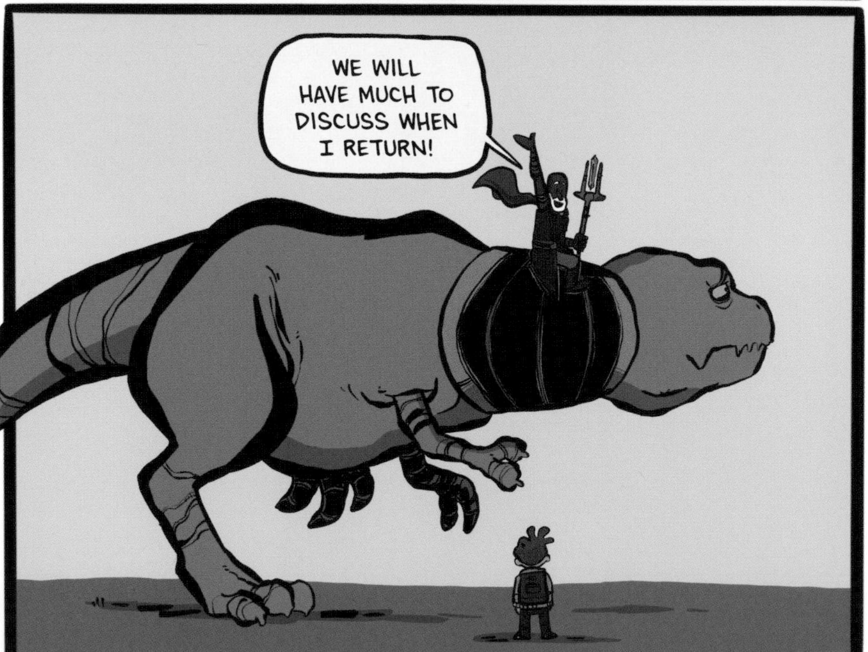
WE WILL HAVE MUCH TO DISCUSS WHEN I RETURN!

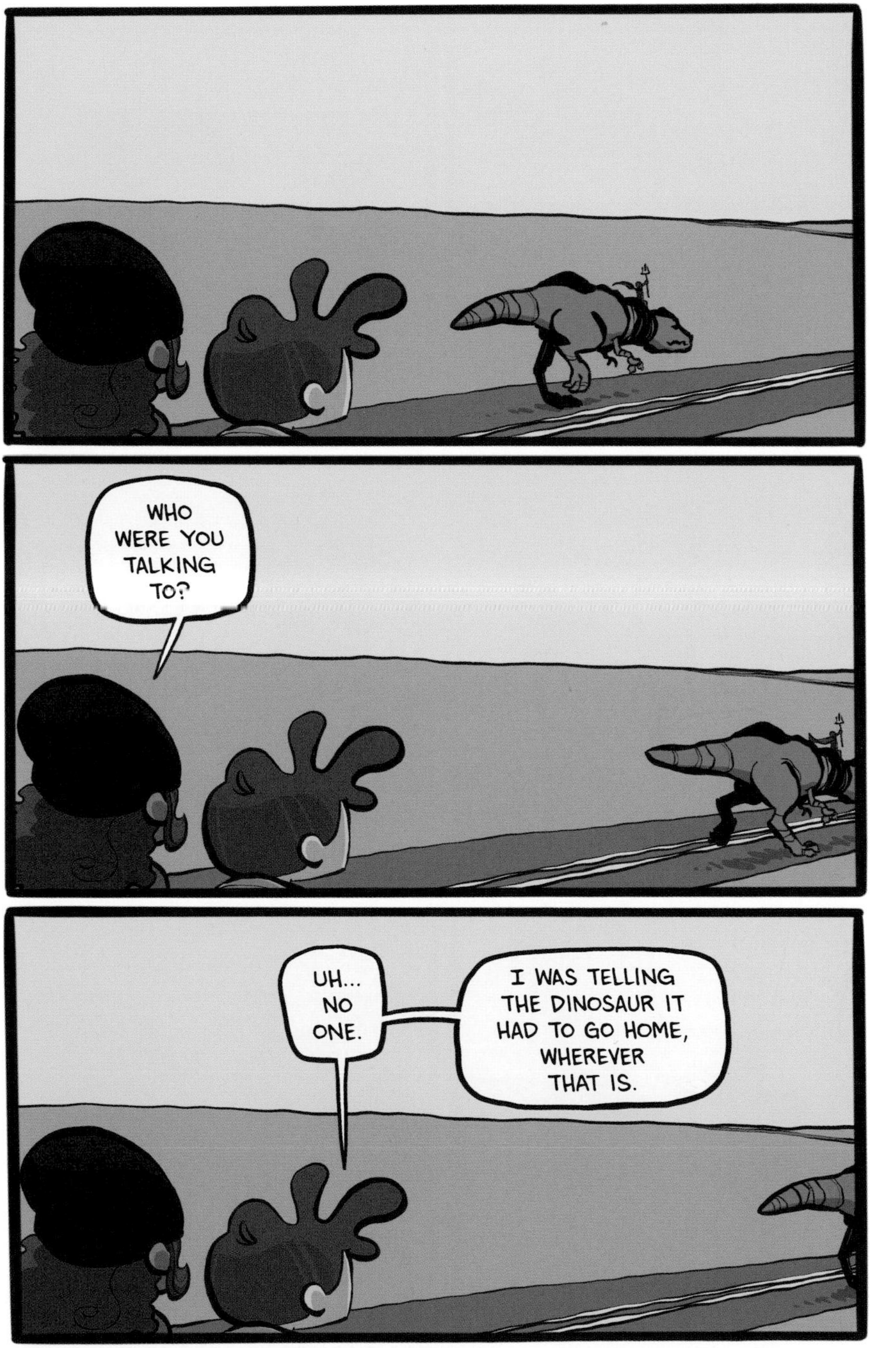
WHO WERE YOU TALKING TO?
UH... NO ONE.
I WAS TELLING THE DINOSAUR IT HAD TO GO HOME, WHEREVER THAT IS.

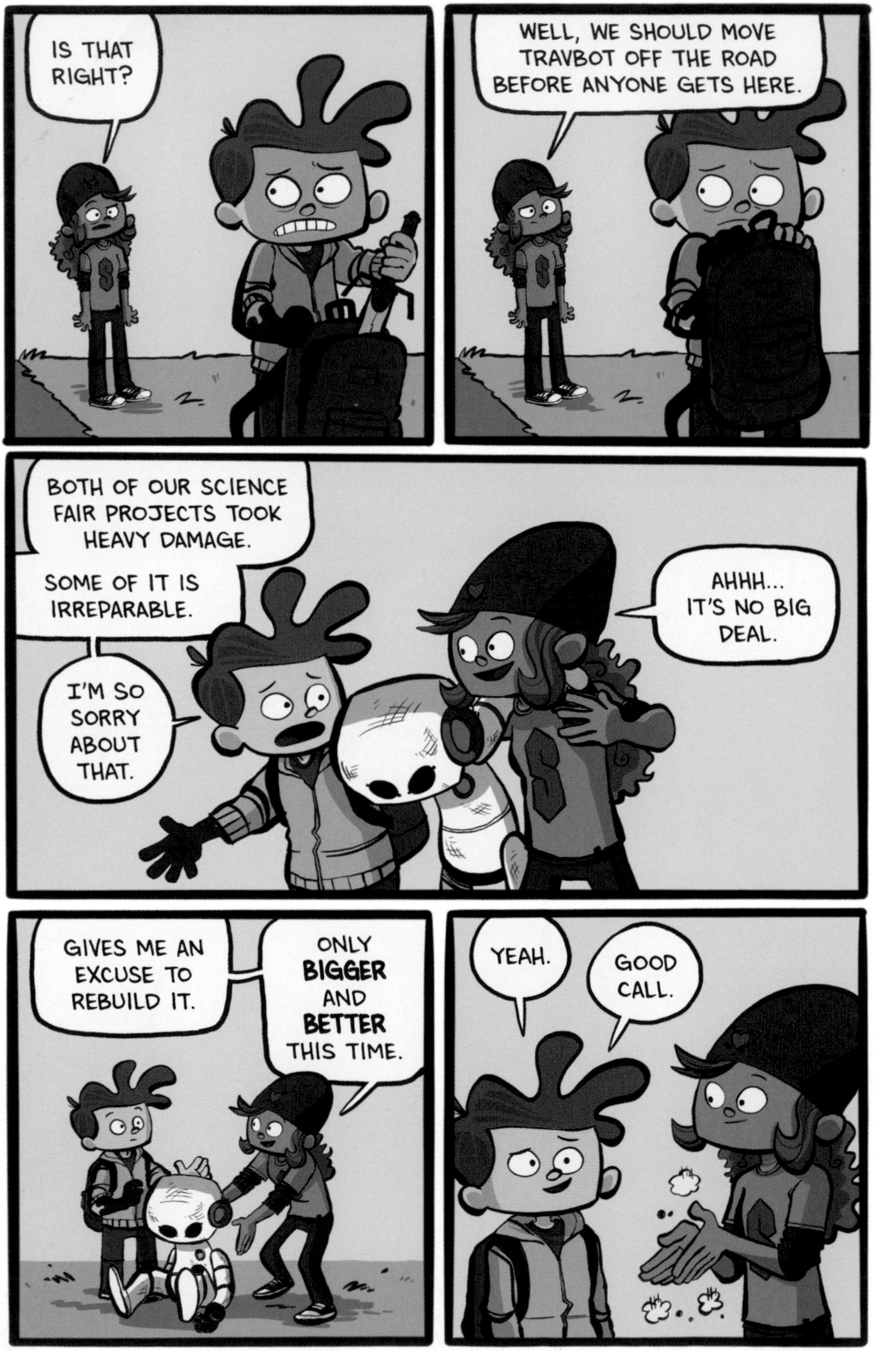
IS THAT RIGHT?
WELL, WE SHOULD MOVE TRAVBOT OFF THE ROAD BEFORE ANYONE GETS HERE.
BOTH OF OUR SCIENCE FAIR PROJECTS TOOK HEAVY DAMAGE.
SOME OF IT IS IRREPARABLE.
I'M SO SORRY ABOUT THAT.
AHHH... IT'S NO BIG DEAL.
GIVES ME AN EXCUSE TO REBUILD IT.
ONLY **BIGGER** AND **BETTER** THIS TIME.
YEAH.
GOOD CALL.

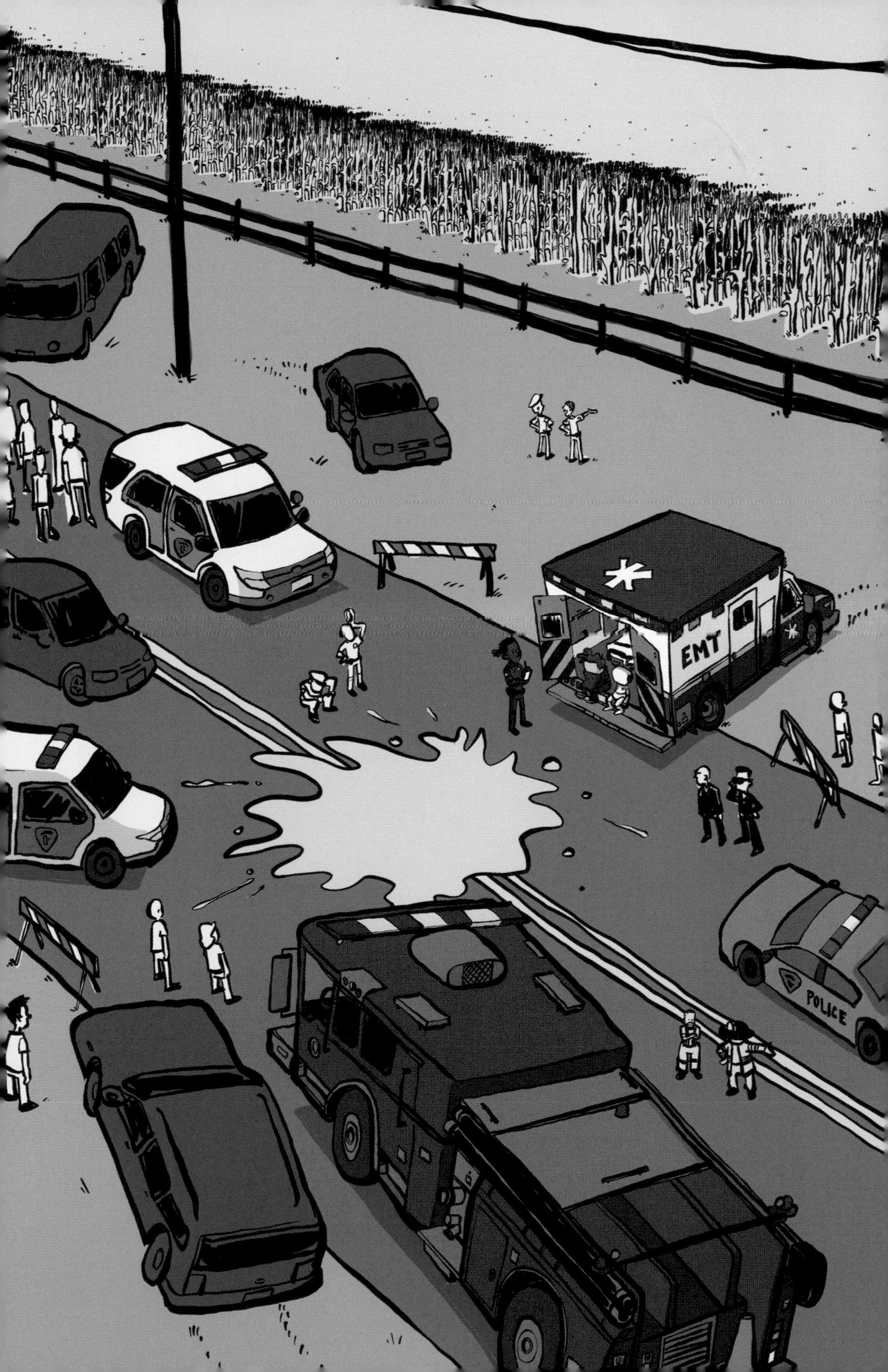
EMT
POLICE

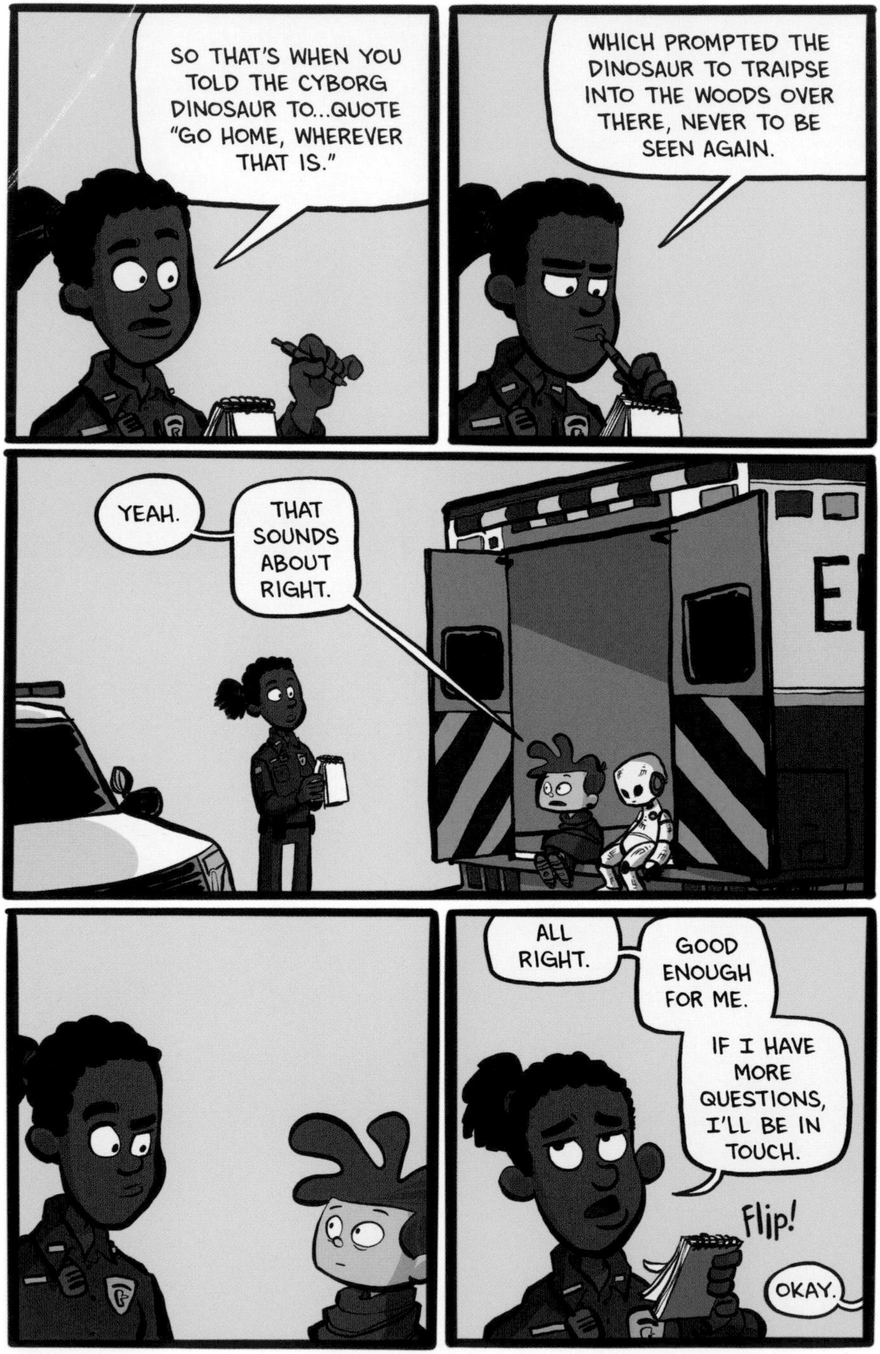
SO THAT'S WHEN YOU TOLD THE CYBORG DINOSAUR TO...QUOTE "GO HOME, WHEREVER THAT IS."
WHICH PROMPTED THE DINOSAUR TO TRAIPSE INTO THE WOODS OVER THERE, NEVER TO BE SEEN AGAIN.
YEAH.
THAT SOUNDS ABOUT RIGHT.
ALL RIGHT.
GOOD ENOUGH FOR ME.
IF I HAVE MORE QUESTIONS, I'LL BE IN TOUCH.
Flip!
OKAY.

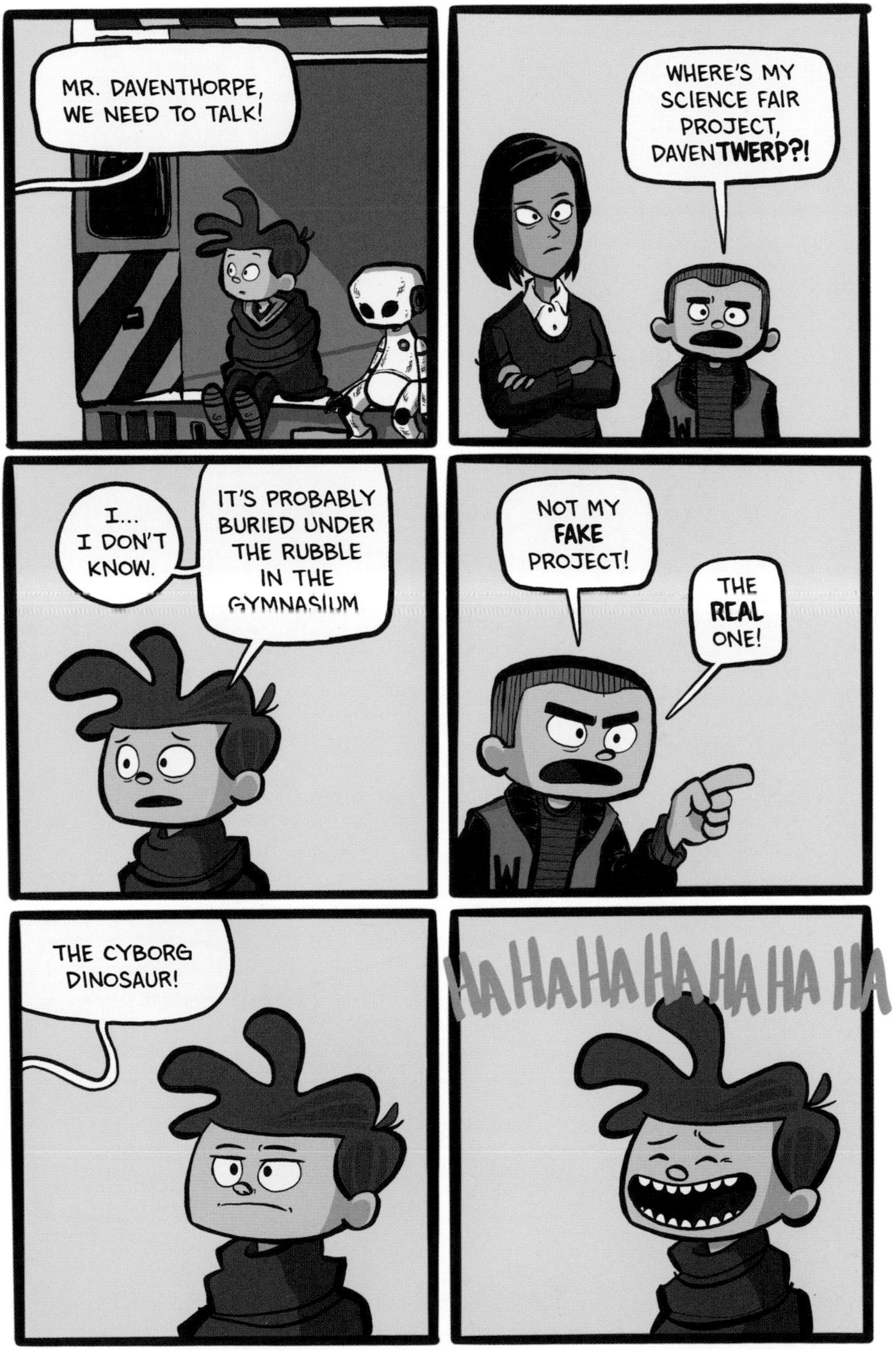
MR. DAVENTHORPE, WE NEED TO TALK!
WHERE'S MY SCIENCE FAIR PROJECT, DAVENTWERP?!
I... I DON'T KNOW.
IT'S PROBABLY BURIED UNDER THE RUBBLE IN THE GYMNASIUM
NOT MY FAKE PROJECT!
THE REAL ONE!
THE CYBORG DINOSAUR!
HA HA HA HA HA HA HA HA

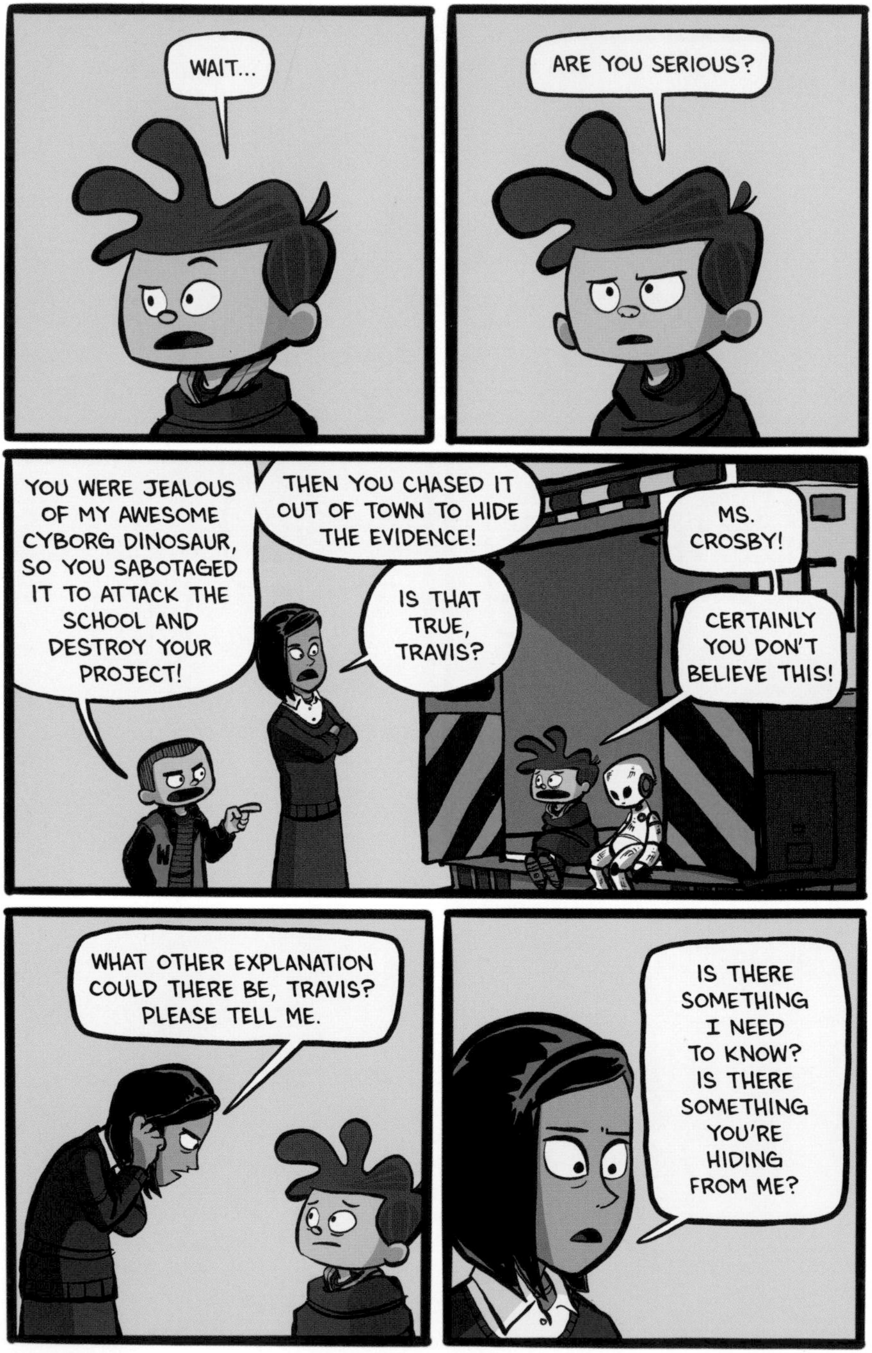
WAIT...
ARE YOU SERIOUS?
YOU WERE JEALOUS OF MY AWESOME CYBORG DINOSAUR, SO YOU SABOTAGED IT TO ATTACK THE SCHOOL AND DESTROY YOUR PROJECT!
THEN YOU CHASED IT OUT OF TOWN TO HIDE THE EVIDENCE!
IS THAT TRUE, TRAVIS?
MS. CROSBY!
CERTAINLY YOU DON'T BELIEVE THIS!
WHAT OTHER EXPLANATION COULD THERE BE, TRAVIS? PLEASE TELL ME.
IS THERE SOMETHING I NEED TO KNOW? IS THERE SOMETHING YOU'RE HIDING FROM ME?

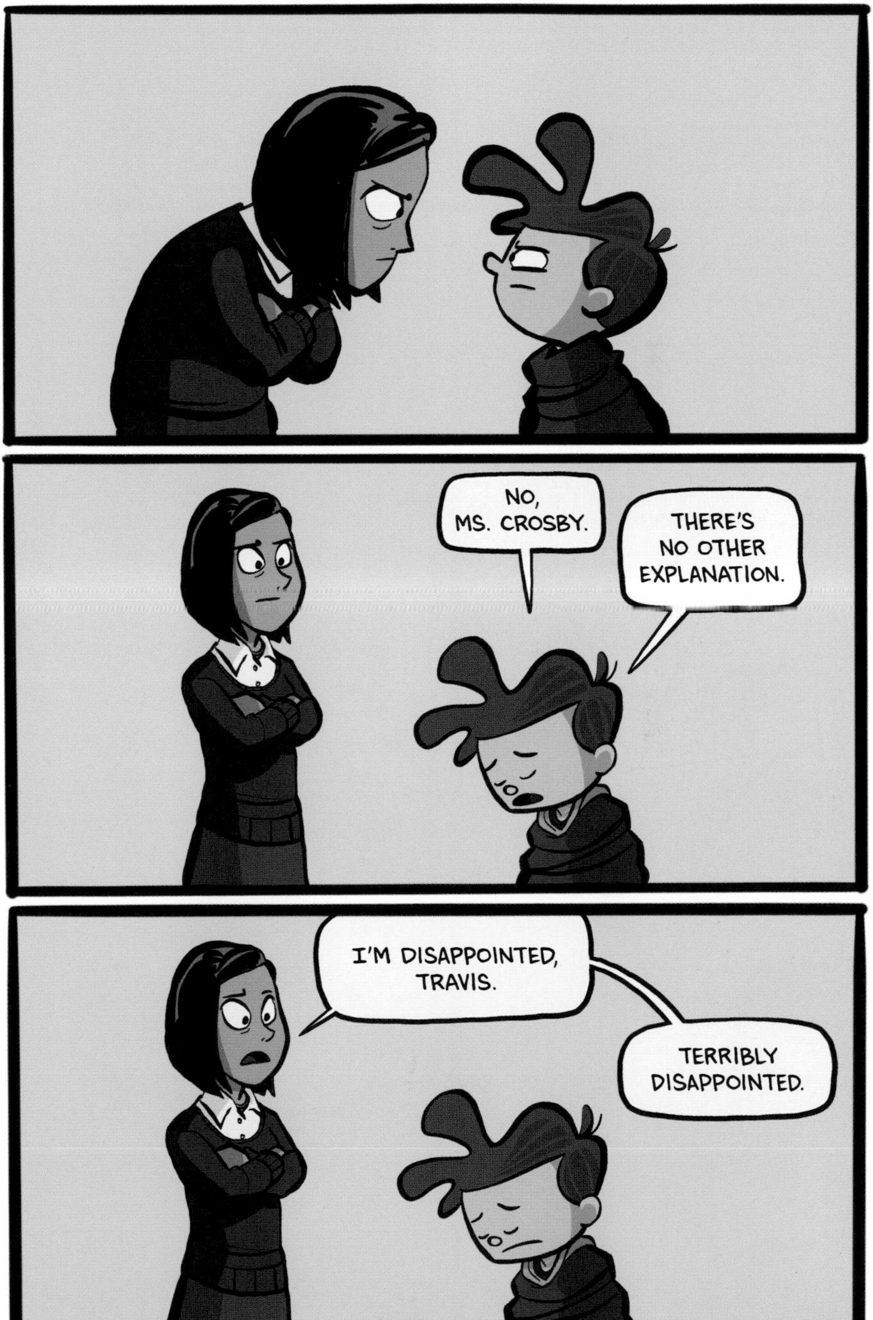
NO, MS. CROSBY.
THERE'S NO OTHER EXPLANATION.
I'M DISAPPOINTED, TRAVIS.
TERRIBLY DISAPPOINTED.

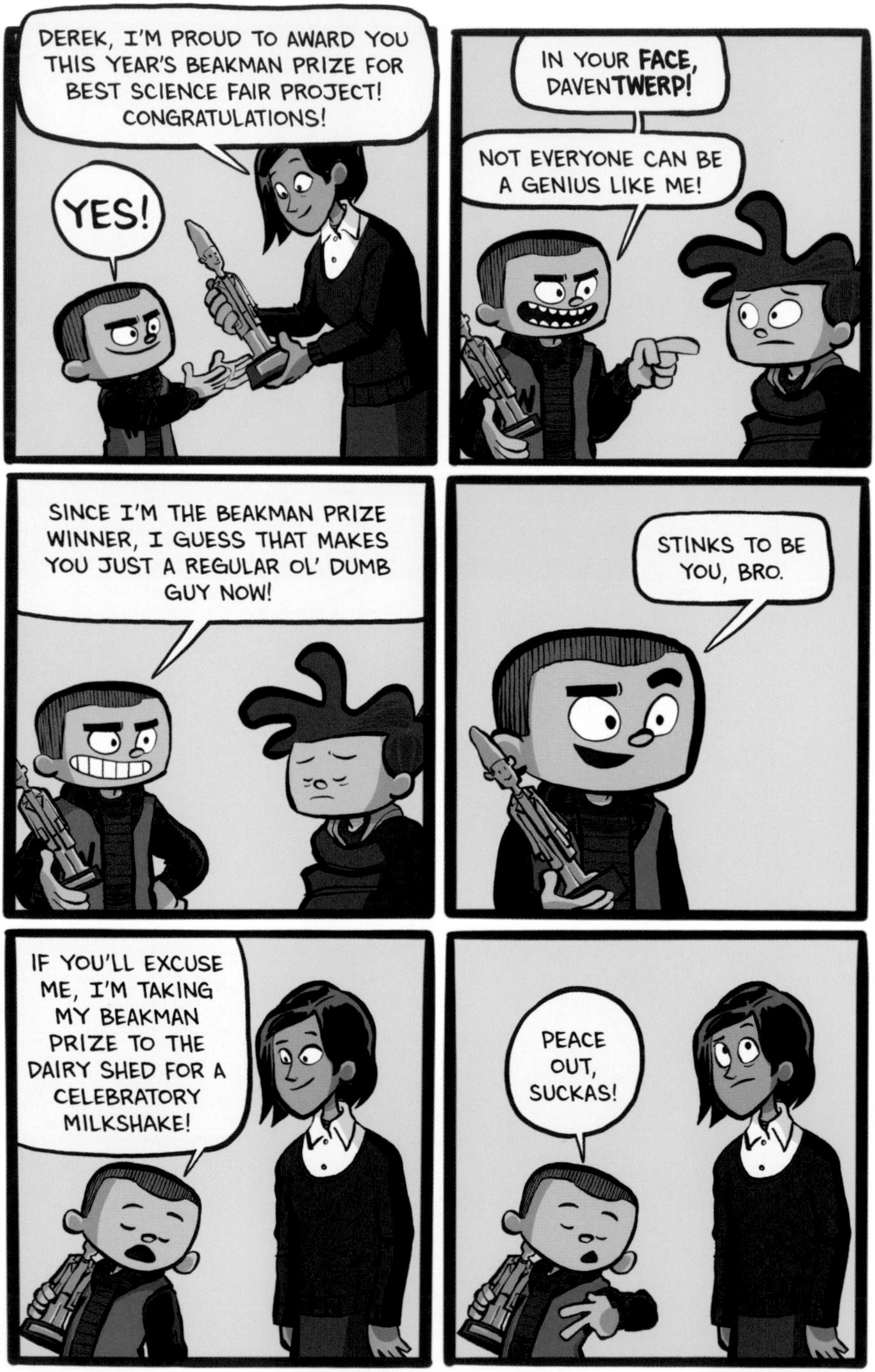
DEREK, I'M PROUD TO AWARD YOU THIS YEAR'S BEAKMAN PRIZE FOR BEST SCIENCE FAIR PROJECT! CONGRATULATIONS!
YES!
IN YOUR **FACE**, DAVEN**TWERP**!
NOT EVERYONE CAN BE A GENIUS LIKE ME!
SINCE I'M THE BEAKMAN PRIZE WINNER, I GUESS THAT MAKES YOU JUST A REGULAR OL' DUMB GUY NOW!
STINKS TO BE YOU, BRO.
IF YOU'LL EXCUSE ME, I'M TAKING MY BEAKMAN PRIZE TO THE DAIRY SHED FOR A CELEBRATORY MILKSHAKE!
PEACE OUT, SUCKAS!

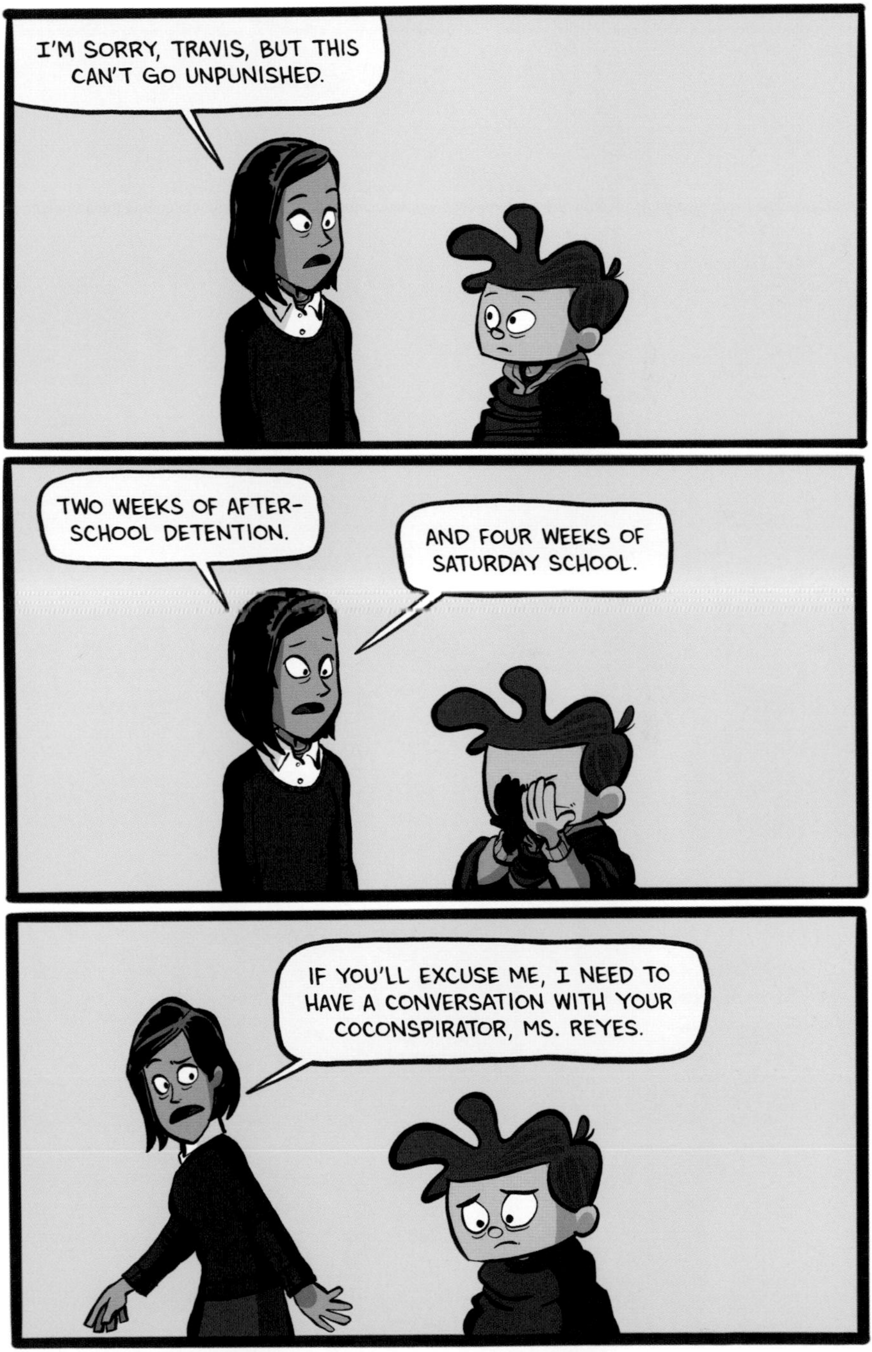
I'M SORRY, TRAVIS, BUT THIS CAN'T GO UNPUNISHED.
TWO WEEKS OF AFTER-SCHOOL DETENTION.
AND FOUR WEEKS OF SATURDAY SCHOOL.
IF YOU'LL EXCUSE ME, I NEED TO HAVE A CONVERSATION WITH YOUR COCONSPIRATOR, MS. REYES.

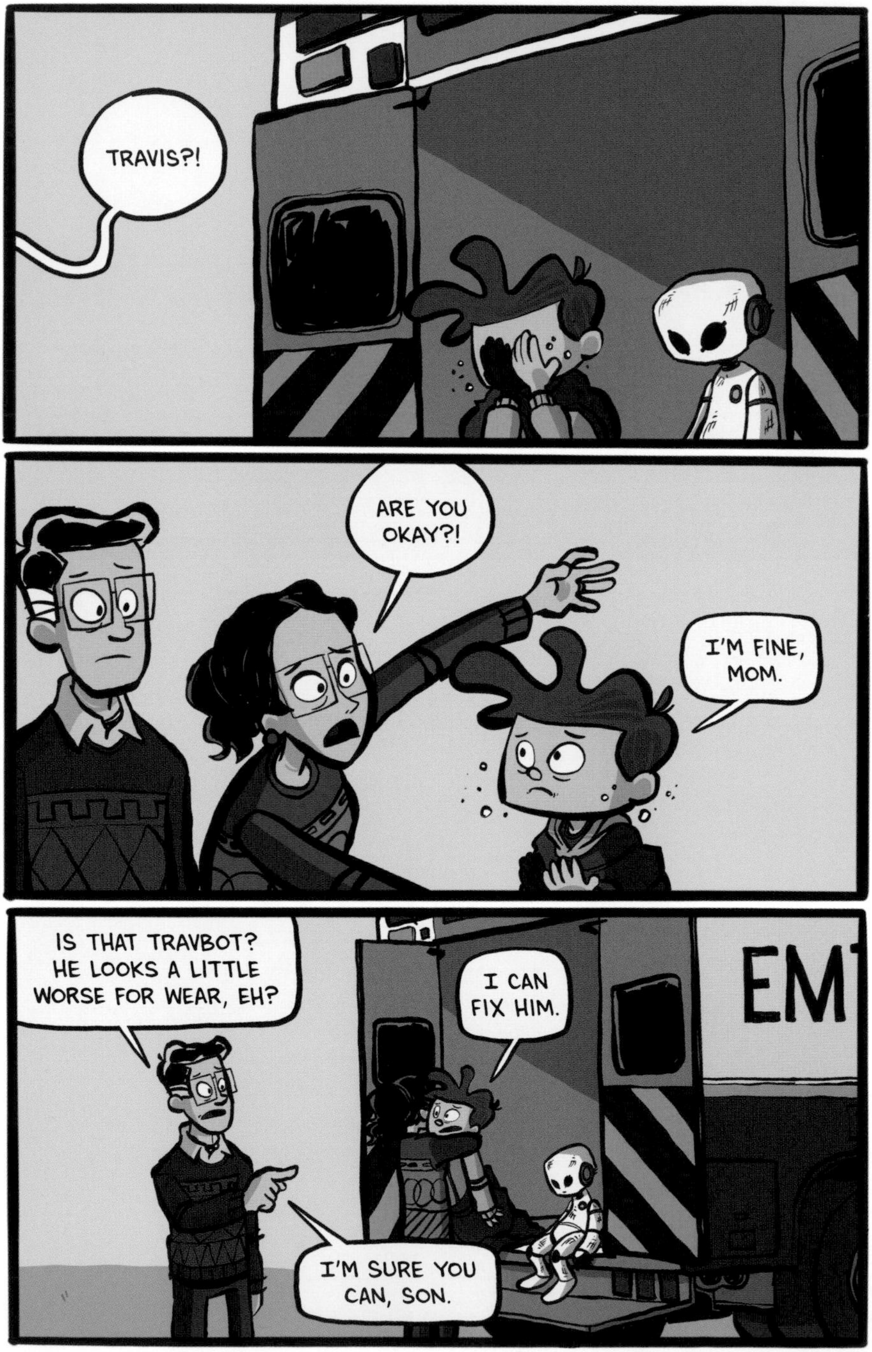
TRAVIS?!
ARE YOU OKAY?!
I'M FINE, MOM.
IS THAT TRAVBOT? HE LOOKS A LITTLE WORSE FOR WEAR, EH?
I CAN FIX HIM.
I'M SURE YOU CAN, SON.
EMT

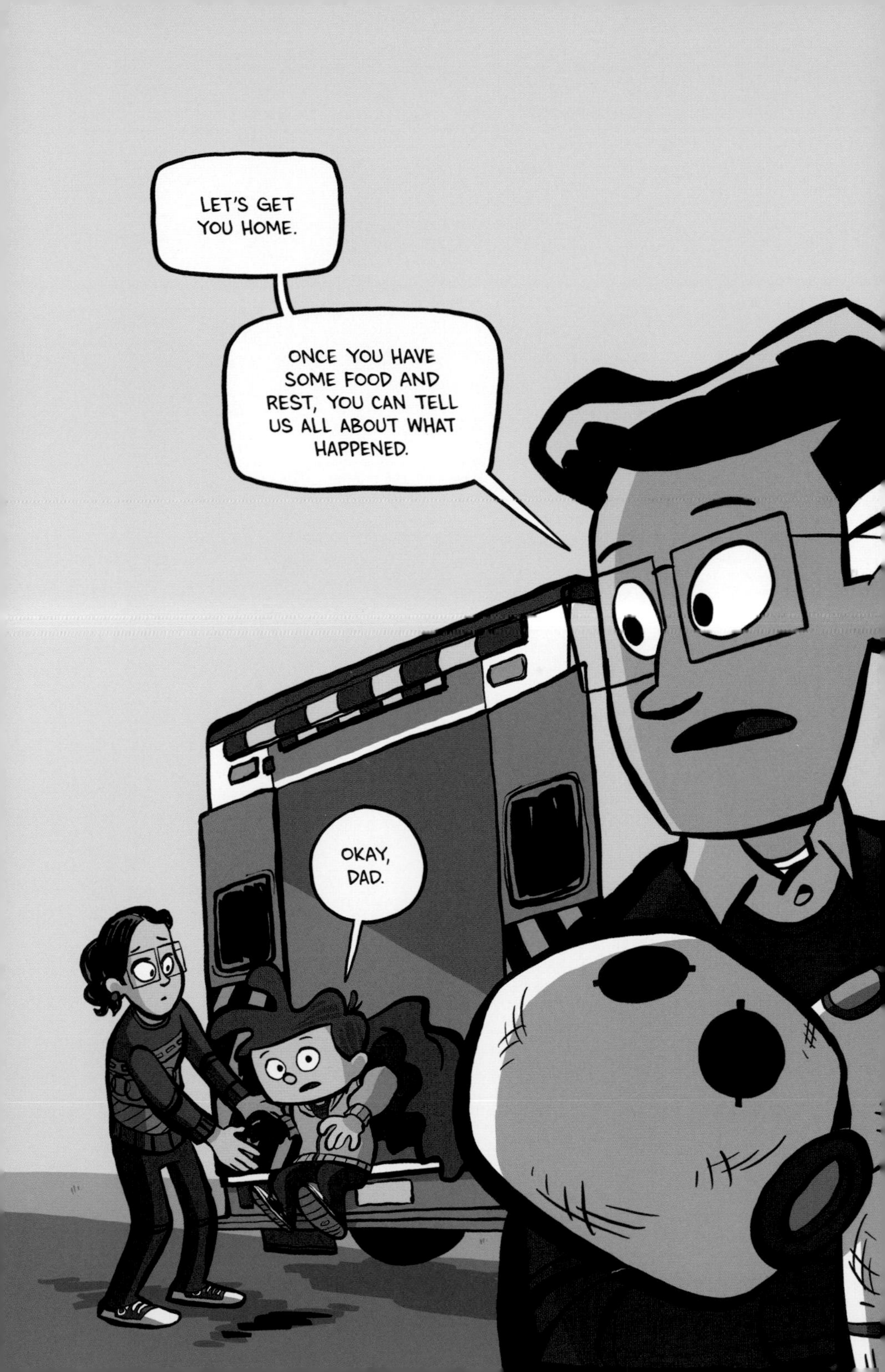
LET'S GET YOU HOME.
ONCE YOU HAVE SOME FOOD AND REST, YOU CAN TELL US ALL ABOUT WHAT HAPPENED.
OKAY, DAD.

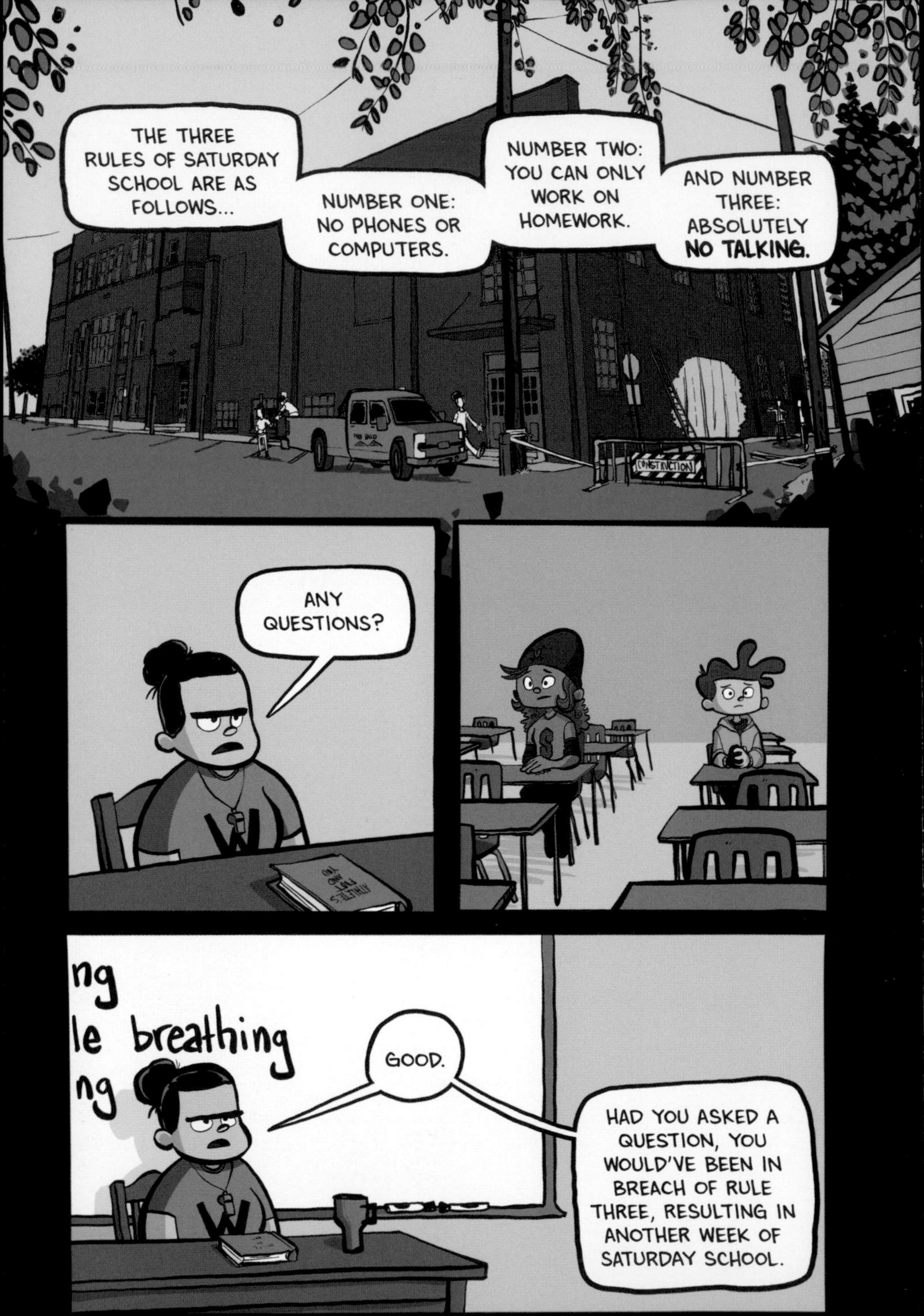
THE THREE RULES OF SATURDAY SCHOOL ARE AS FOLLOWS...
NUMBER ONE: NO PHONES OR COMPUTERS.
NUMBER TWO: YOU CAN ONLY WORK ON HOMEWORK.
AND NUMBER THREE: ABSOLUTELY **NO TALKING.**
CONSTRUCTION
ANY QUESTIONS?
ng
le breathing
ng
GOOD.
HAD YOU ASKED A QUESTION, YOU WOULD'VE BEEN IN BREACH OF RULE THREE, RESULTING IN ANOTHER WEEK OF SATURDAY SCHOOL.

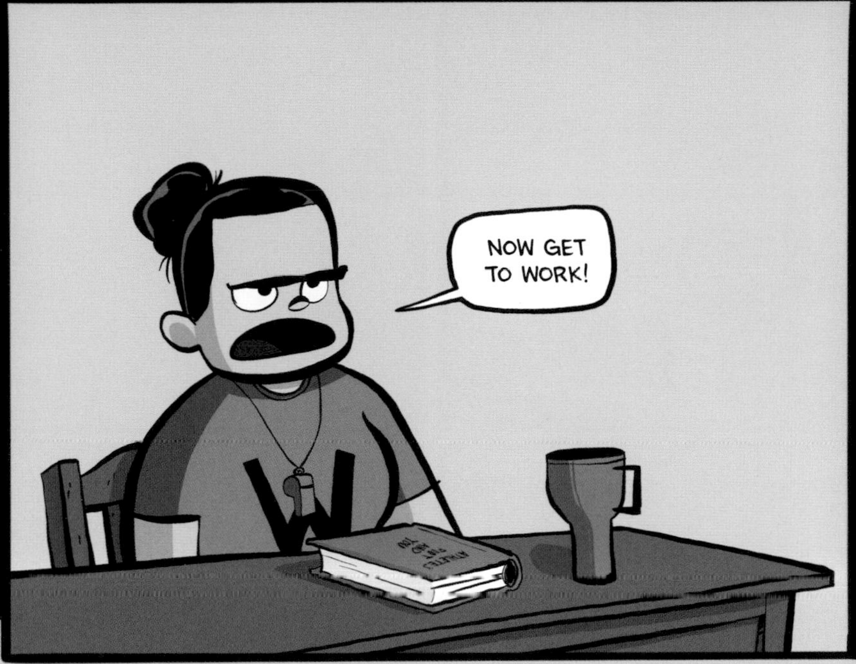
NOW GET TO WORK!

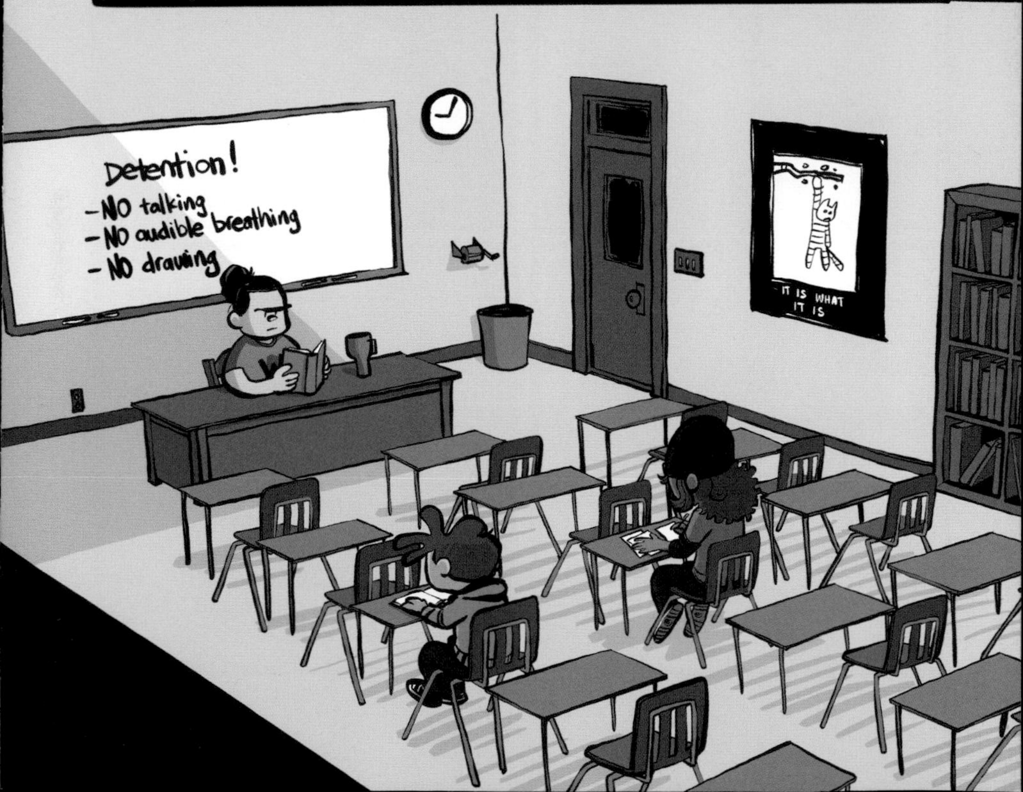
Detention!
-NO talking
-NO audible breathing
-NO drawing
IT IS WHAT IT IS

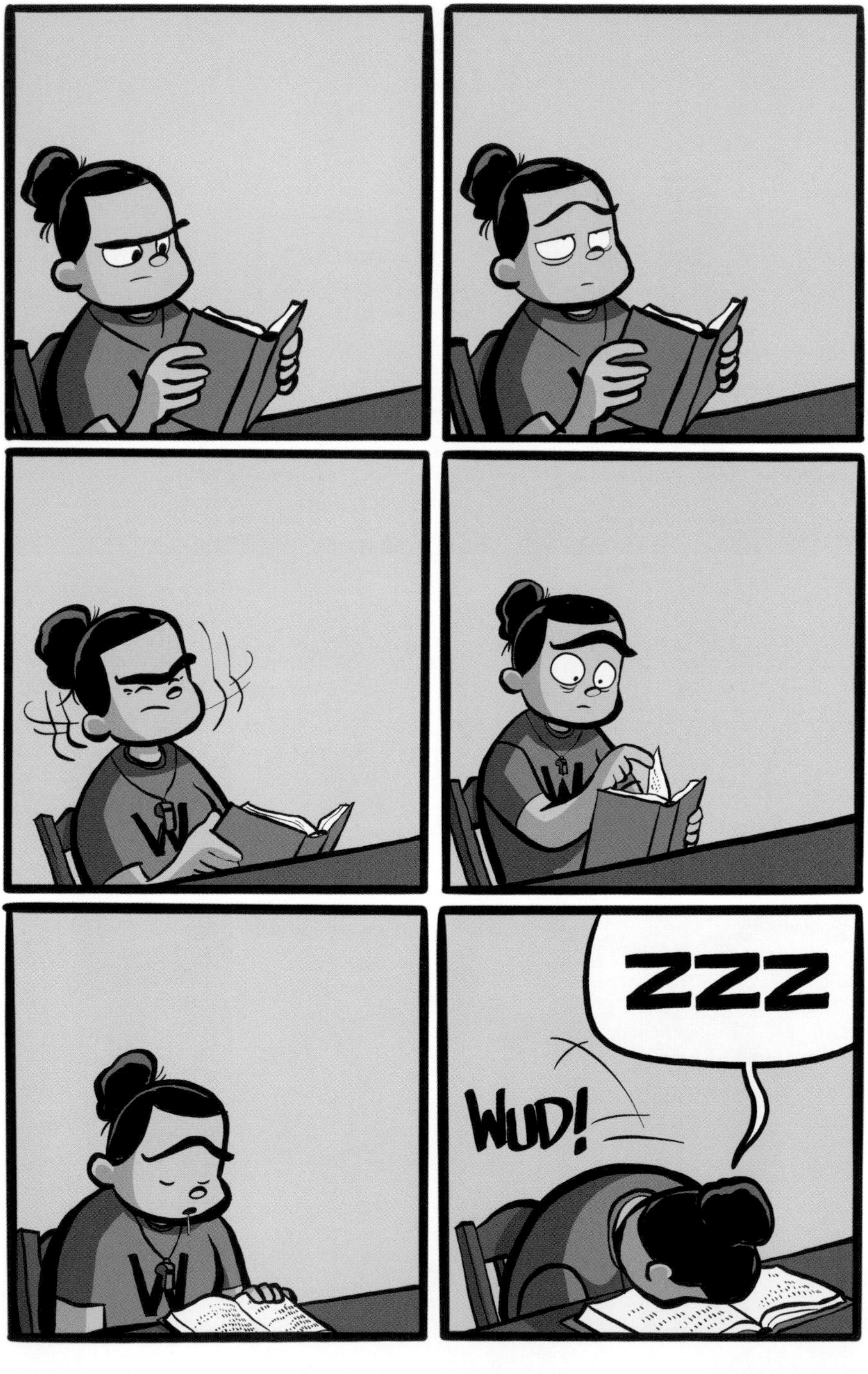
ZZZ
WUD!

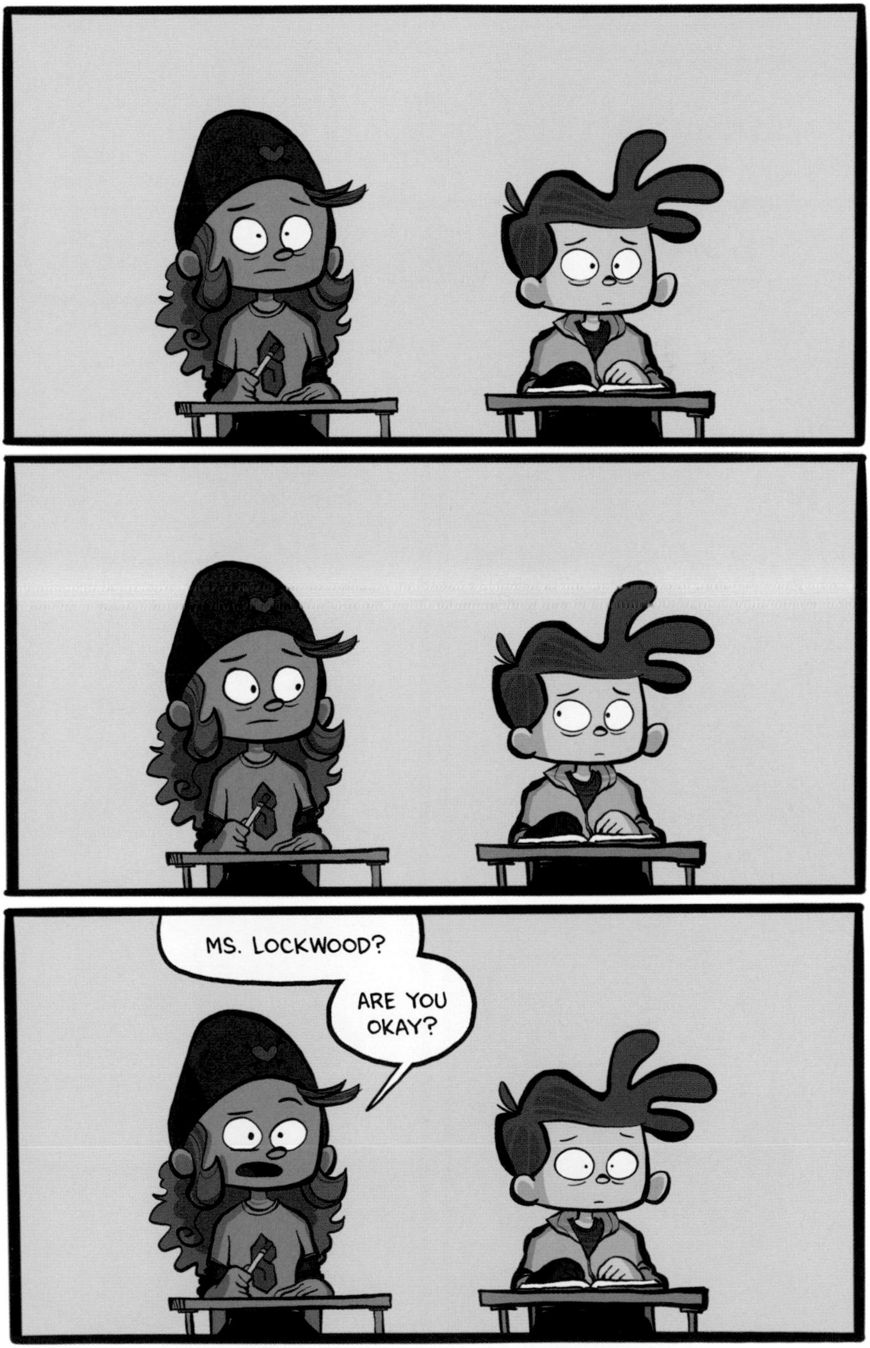
MS. LOCKWOOD?
ARE YOU OKAY?

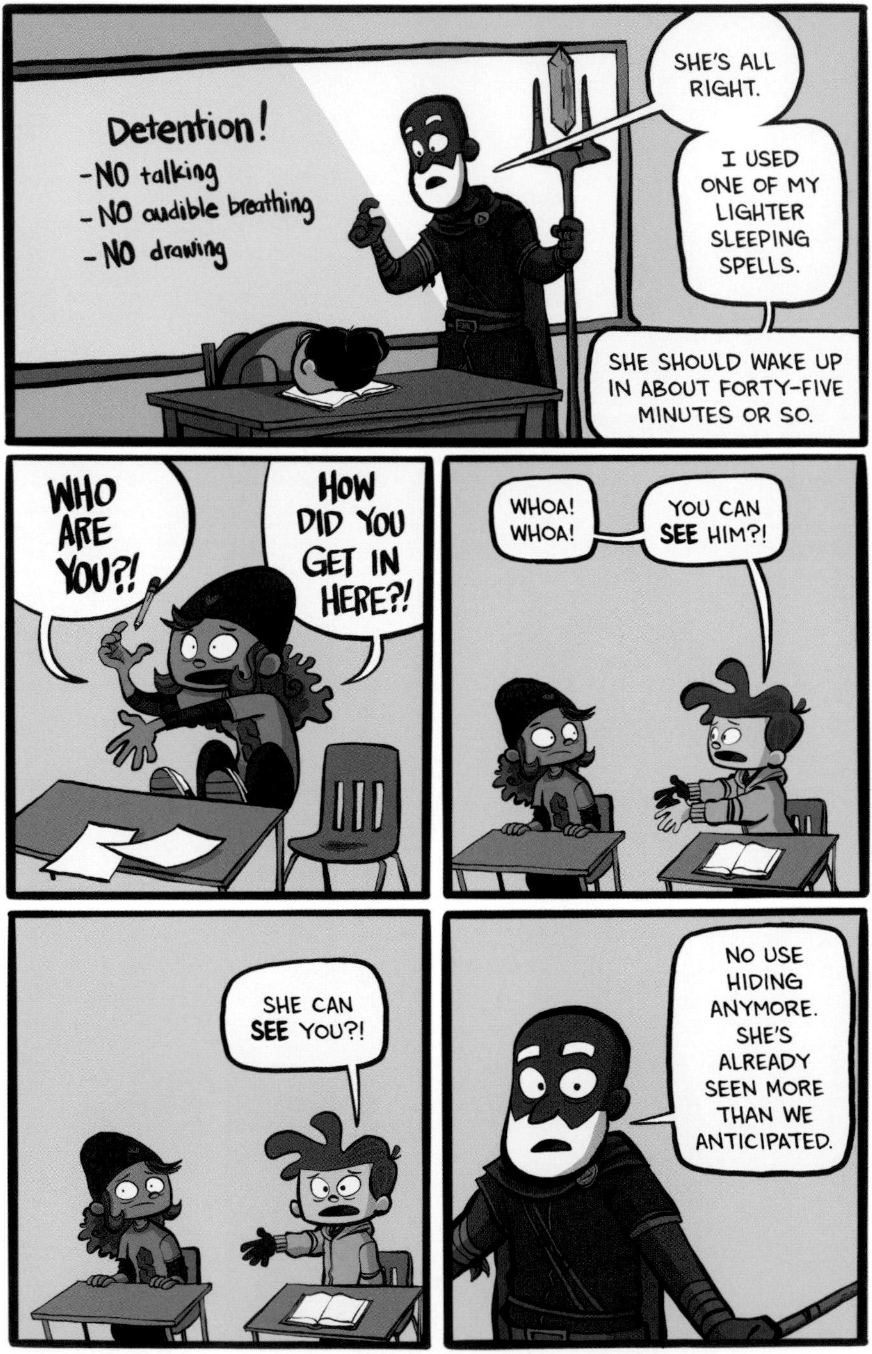
Detention!
-NO talking
-NO audible breathing
-NO drawing
SHE'S ALL RIGHT.
I USED ONE OF MY LIGHTER SLEEPING SPELLS.
SHE SHOULD WAKE UP IN ABOUT FORTY-FIVE MINUTES OR SO.
WHO ARE YOU?!
HOW DID YOU GET IN HERE?!
WHOA! WHOA!
YOU CAN SEE HIM?!
SHE CAN SEE YOU?!
NO USE HIDING ANYMORE. SHE'S ALREADY SEEN MORE THAN WE ANTICIPATED.

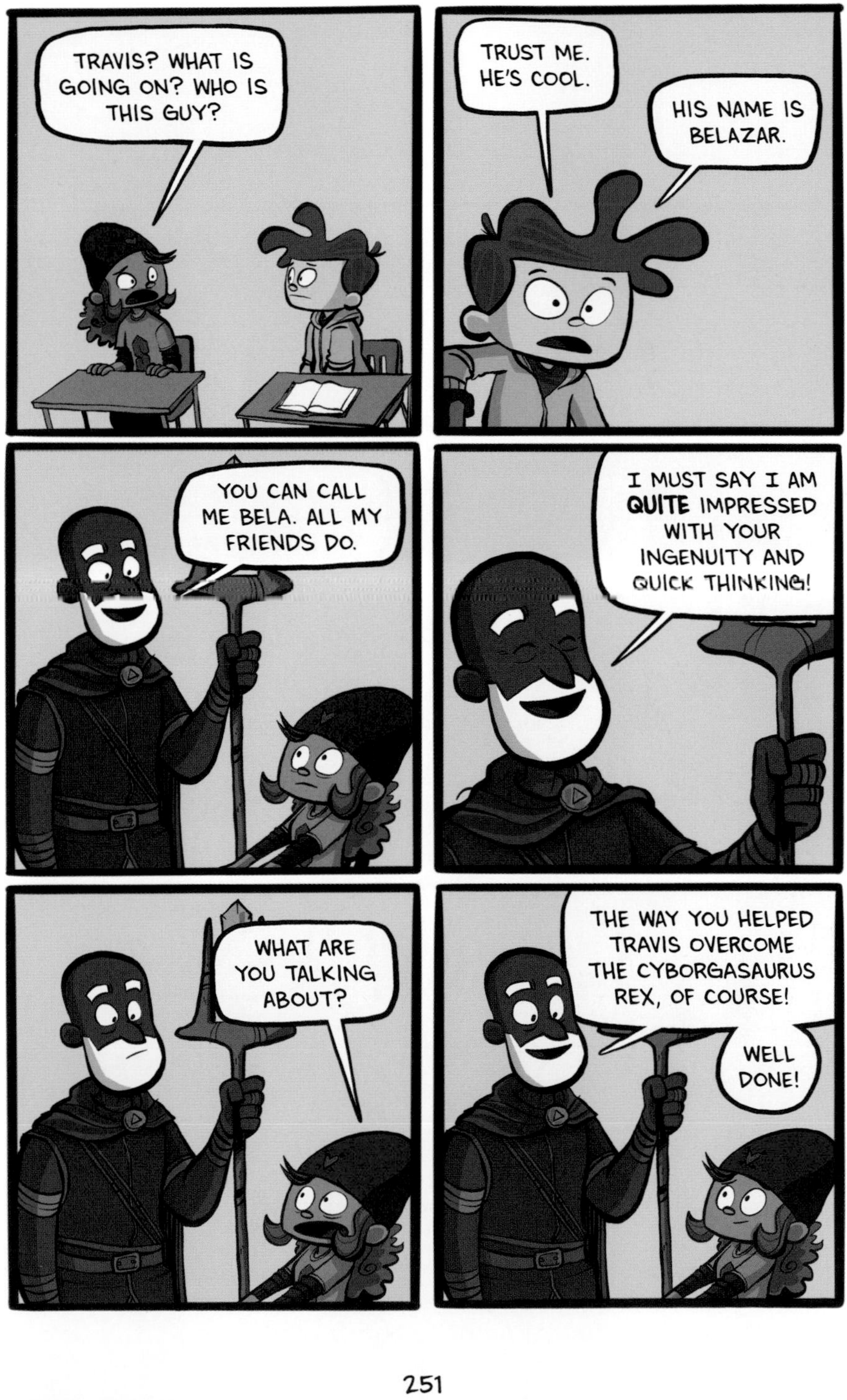
TRAVIS? WHAT IS GOING ON? WHO IS THIS GUY?
TRUST ME. HE'S COOL.
HIS NAME IS BELAZAR.
YOU CAN CALL ME BELA. ALL MY FRIENDS DO.
I MUST SAY I AM **QUITE** IMPRESSED WITH YOUR INGENUITY AND QUICK THINKING!
WHAT ARE YOU TALKING ABOUT?
THE WAY YOU HELPED TRAVIS OVERCOME THE CYBORGASAURUS REX, OF COURSE!
WELL DONE!

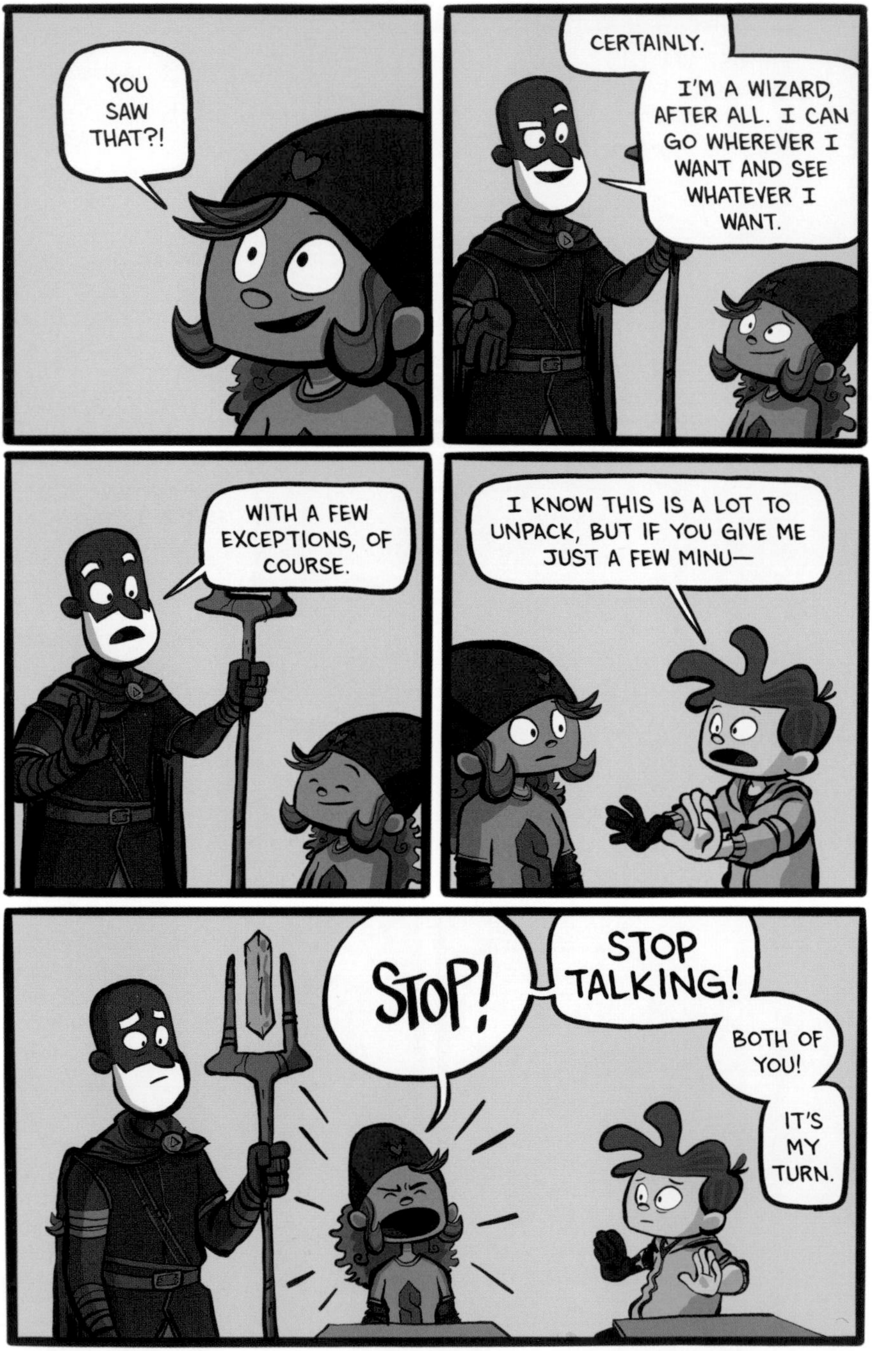
YOU SAW THAT?!
CERTAINLY.
I'M A WIZARD, AFTER ALL. I CAN GO WHEREVER I WANT AND SEE WHATEVER I WANT.
WITH A FEW EXCEPTIONS, OF COURSE.
I KNOW THIS IS A LOT TO UNPACK, BUT IF YOU GIVE ME JUST A FEW MINU—
STOP!
STOP TALKING!
BOTH OF YOU!
IT'S MY TURN.

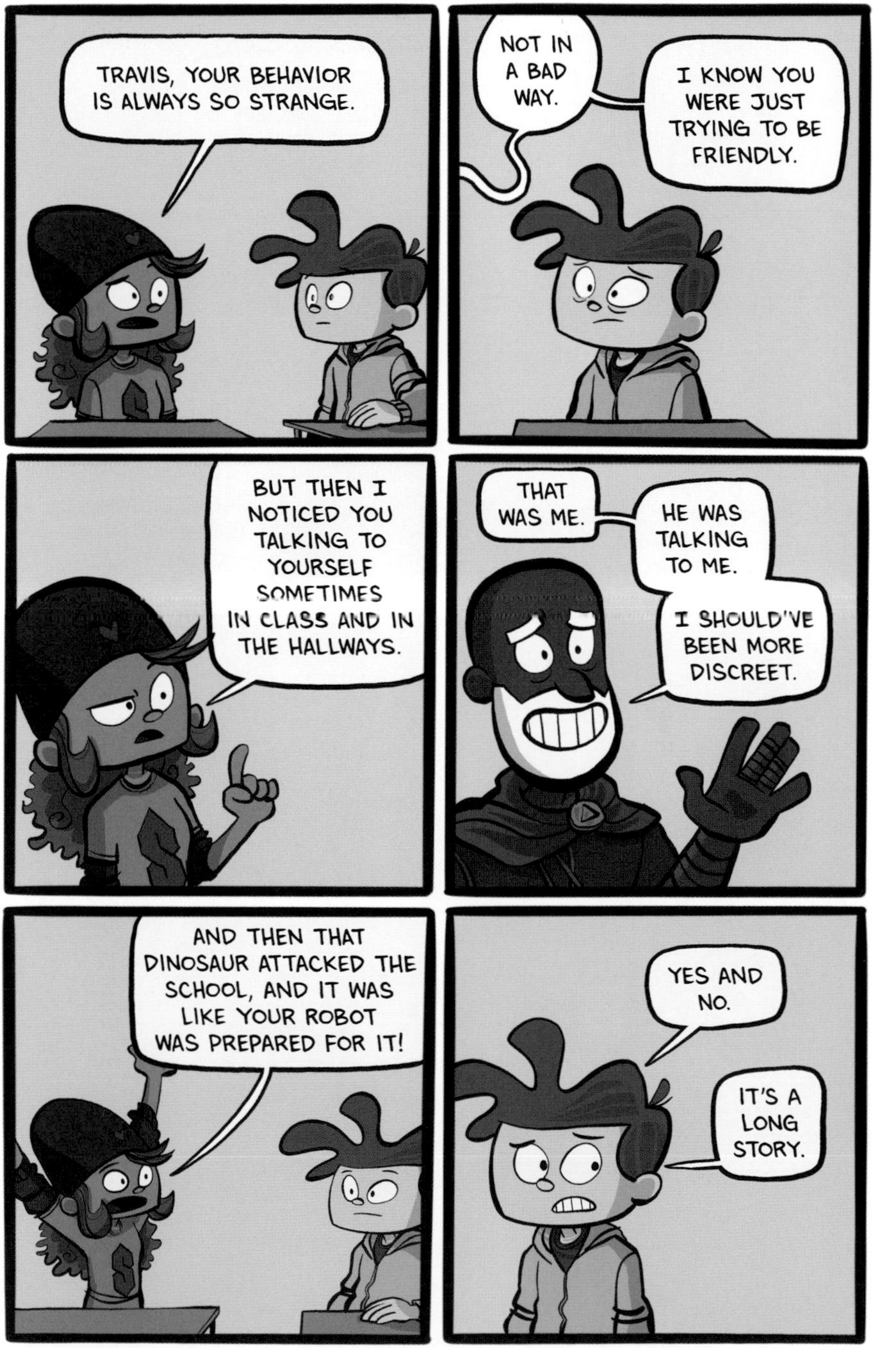
TRAVIS, YOUR BEHAVIOR IS ALWAYS SO STRANGE.
NOT IN A BAD WAY.
I KNOW YOU WERE JUST TRYING TO BE FRIENDLY.
BUT THEN I NOTICED YOU TALKING TO YOURSELF SOMETIMES IN CLASS AND IN THE HALLWAYS.
THAT WAS ME.
HE WAS TALKING TO ME.
I SHOULD'VE BEEN MORE DISCREET.
AND THEN THAT DINOSAUR ATTACKED THE SCHOOL, AND IT WAS LIKE YOUR ROBOT WAS PREPARED FOR IT!
YES AND NO.
IT'S A LONG STORY.

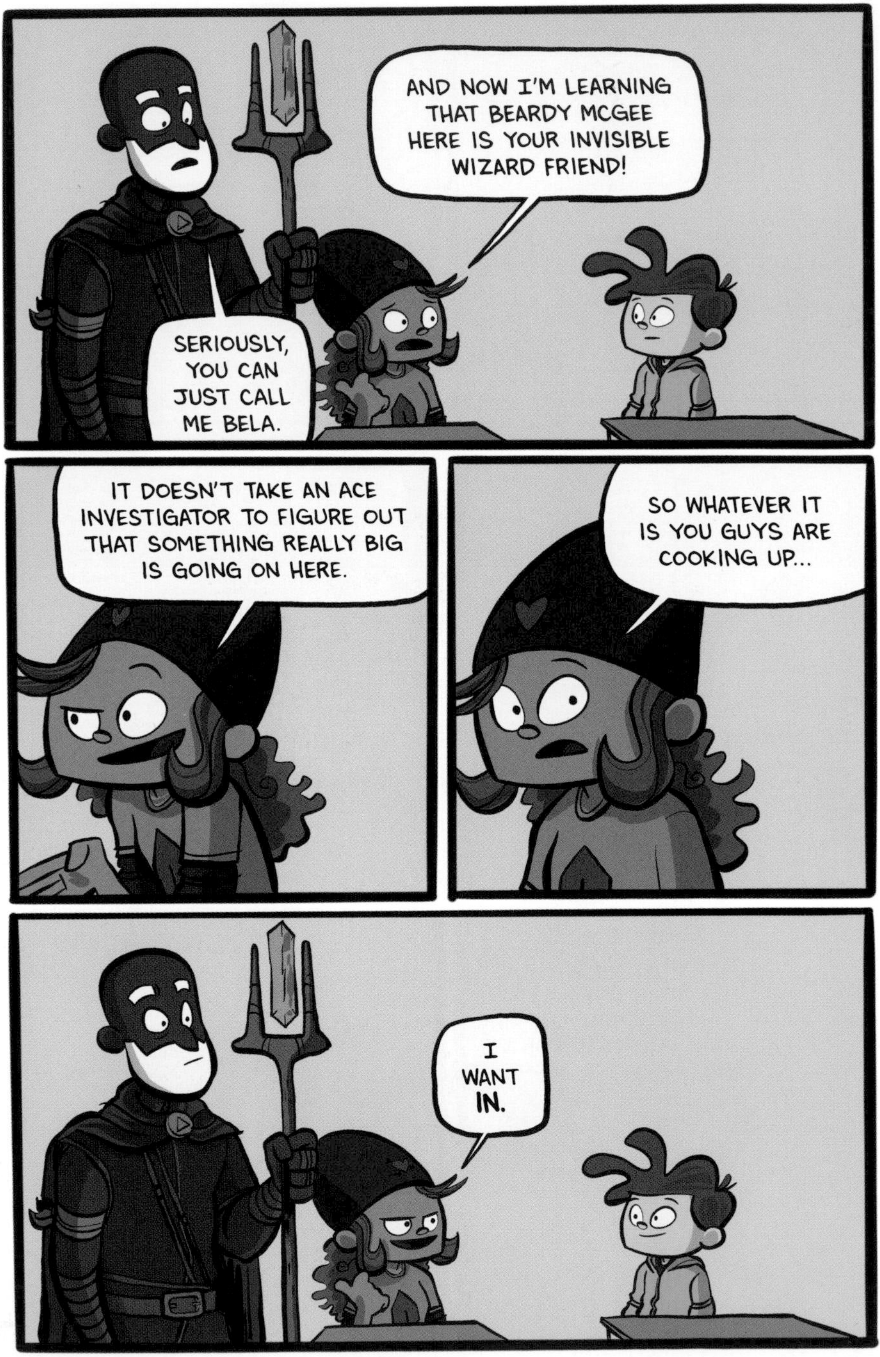
AND NOW I'M LEARNING THAT BEARDY MCGEE HERE IS YOUR INVISIBLE WIZARD FRIEND!
SERIOUSLY, YOU CAN JUST CALL ME BELA.
IT DOESN'T TAKE AN ACE INVESTIGATOR TO FIGURE OUT THAT SOMETHING REALLY BIG IS GOING ON HERE.
SO WHATEVER IT IS YOU GUYS ARE COOKING UP...
I WANT IN.

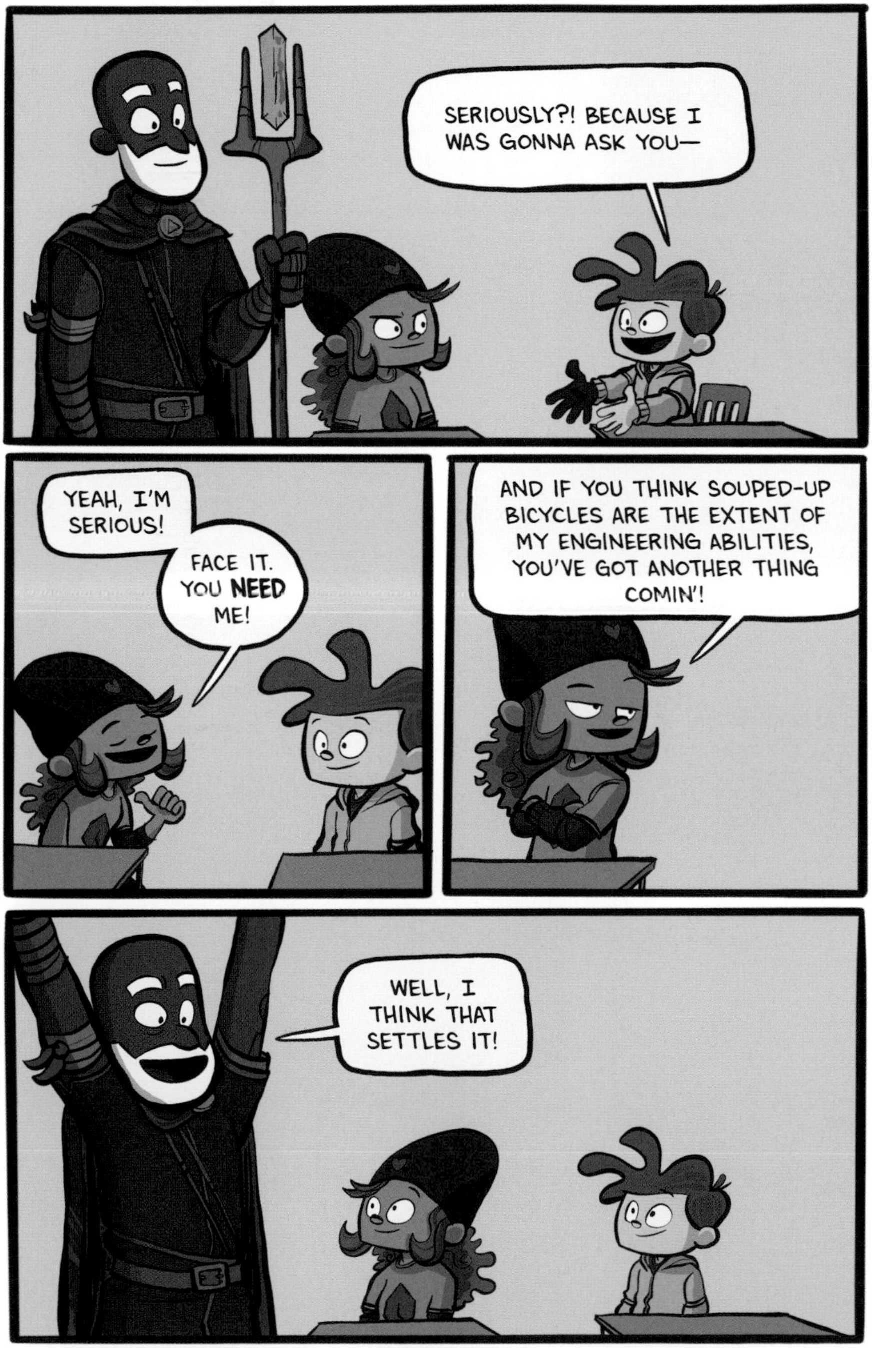
SERIOUSLY?! BECAUSE I WAS GONNA ASK YOU—
YEAH, I'M SERIOUS!
FACE IT. YOU **NEED** ME!
AND IF YOU THINK SOUPED-UP BICYCLES ARE THE EXTENT OF MY ENGINEERING ABILITIES, YOU'VE GOT ANOTHER THING COMIN'!
WELL, I THINK THAT SETTLES IT!

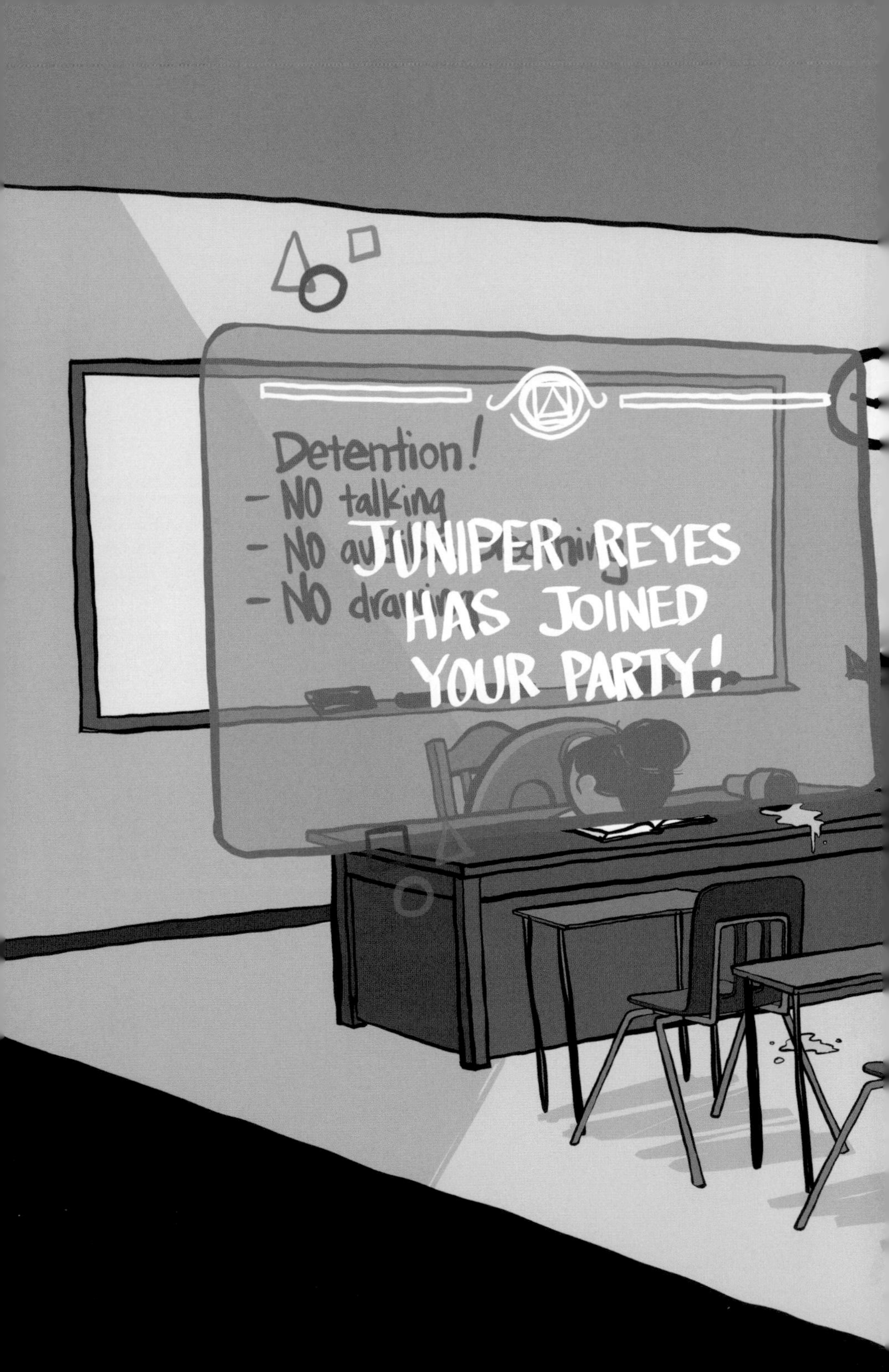
Detention!
- NO talking
JUNIPER REYES
HAS JOINED
YOUR PARTY!

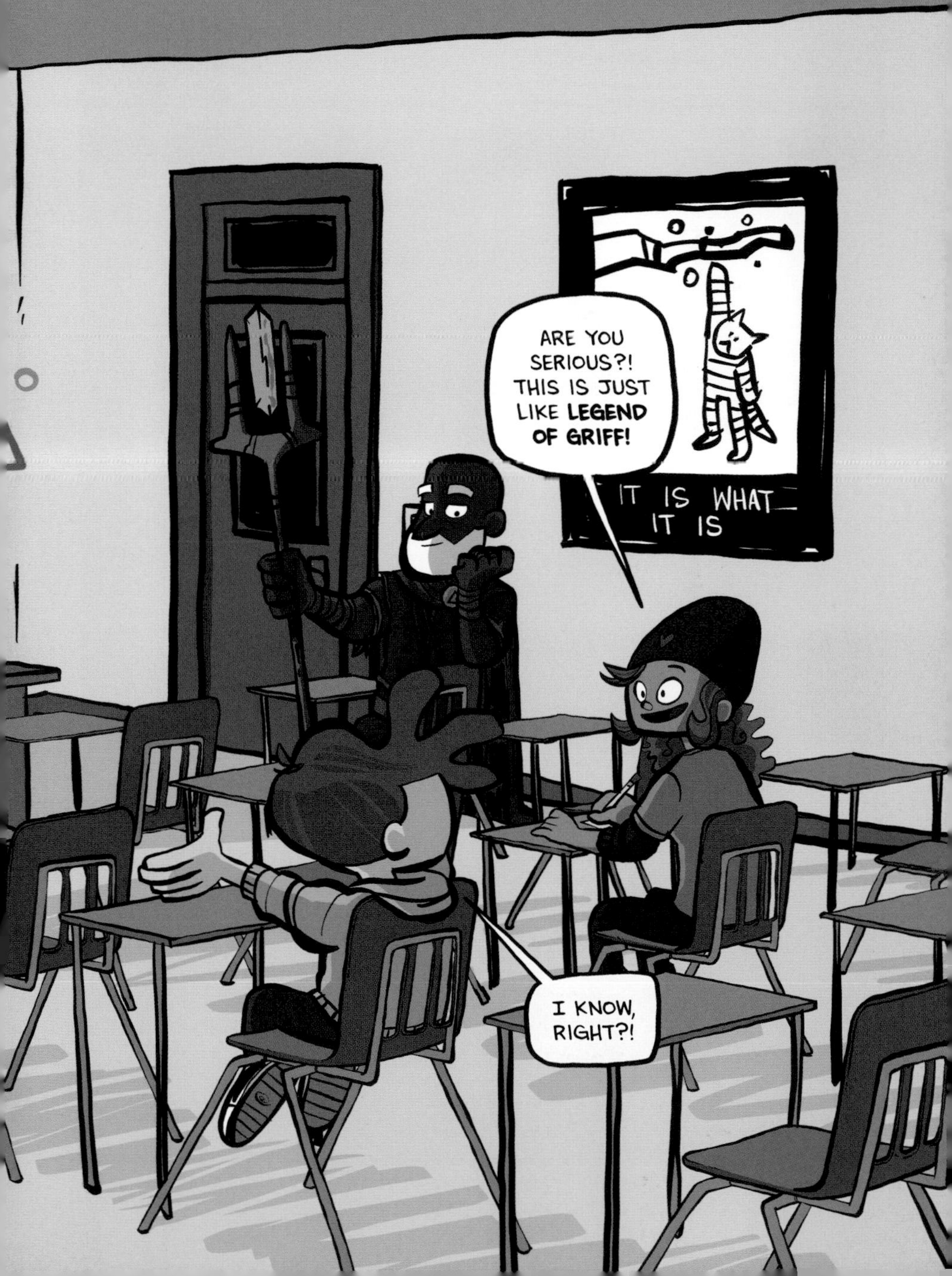
ARE YOU SERIOUS?! THIS IS JUST LIKE **LEGEND OF GRIFF!**
IT IS WHAT IT IS
I KNOW, RIGHT?!

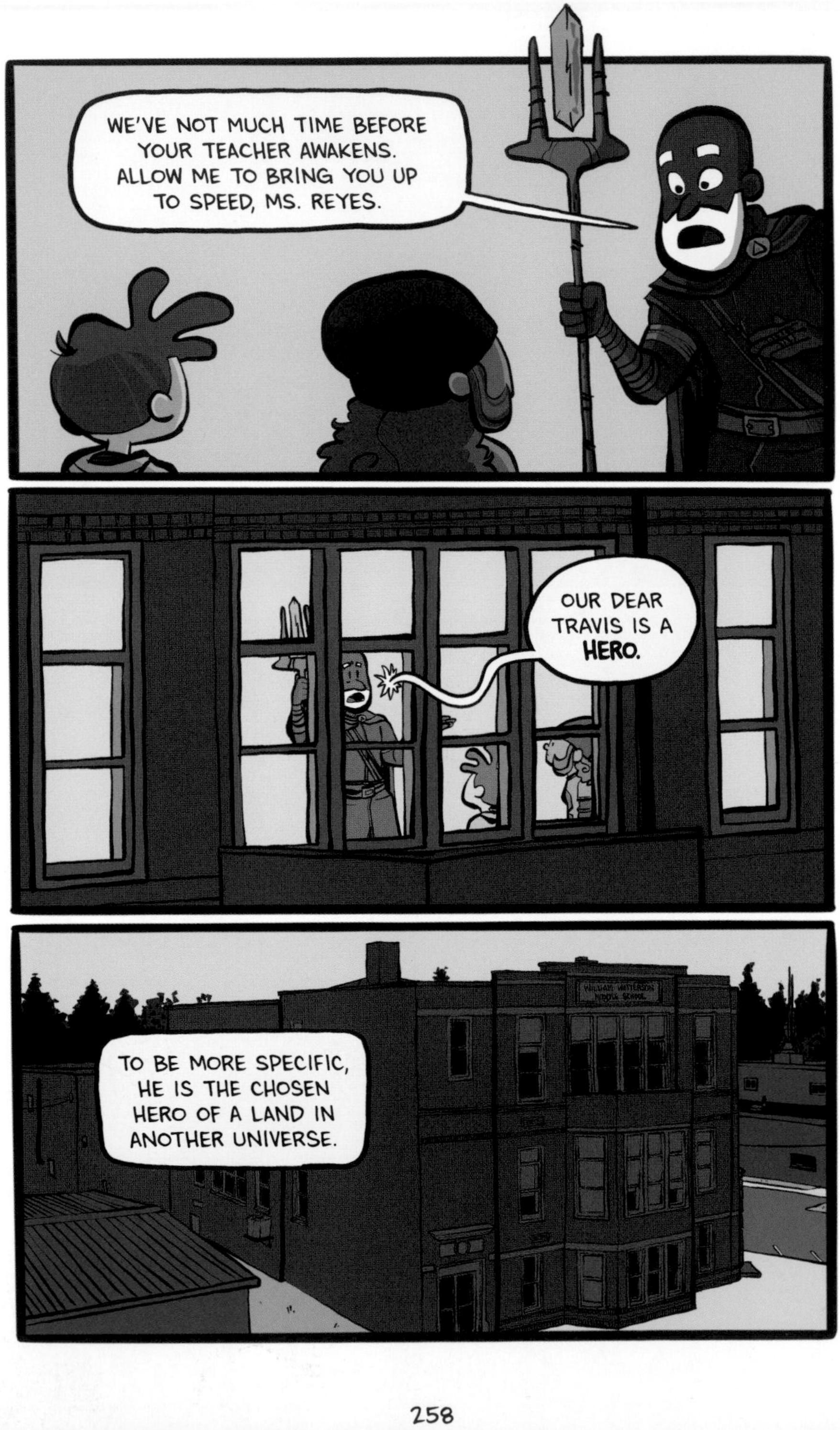
WE'VE NOT MUCH TIME BEFORE YOUR TEACHER AWAKENS. ALLOW ME TO BRING YOU UP TO SPEED, MS. REYES.
OUR DEAR TRAVIS IS A **HERO.**
TO BE MORE SPECIFIC, HE IS THE CHOSEN HERO OF A LAND IN ANOTHER UNIVERSE.

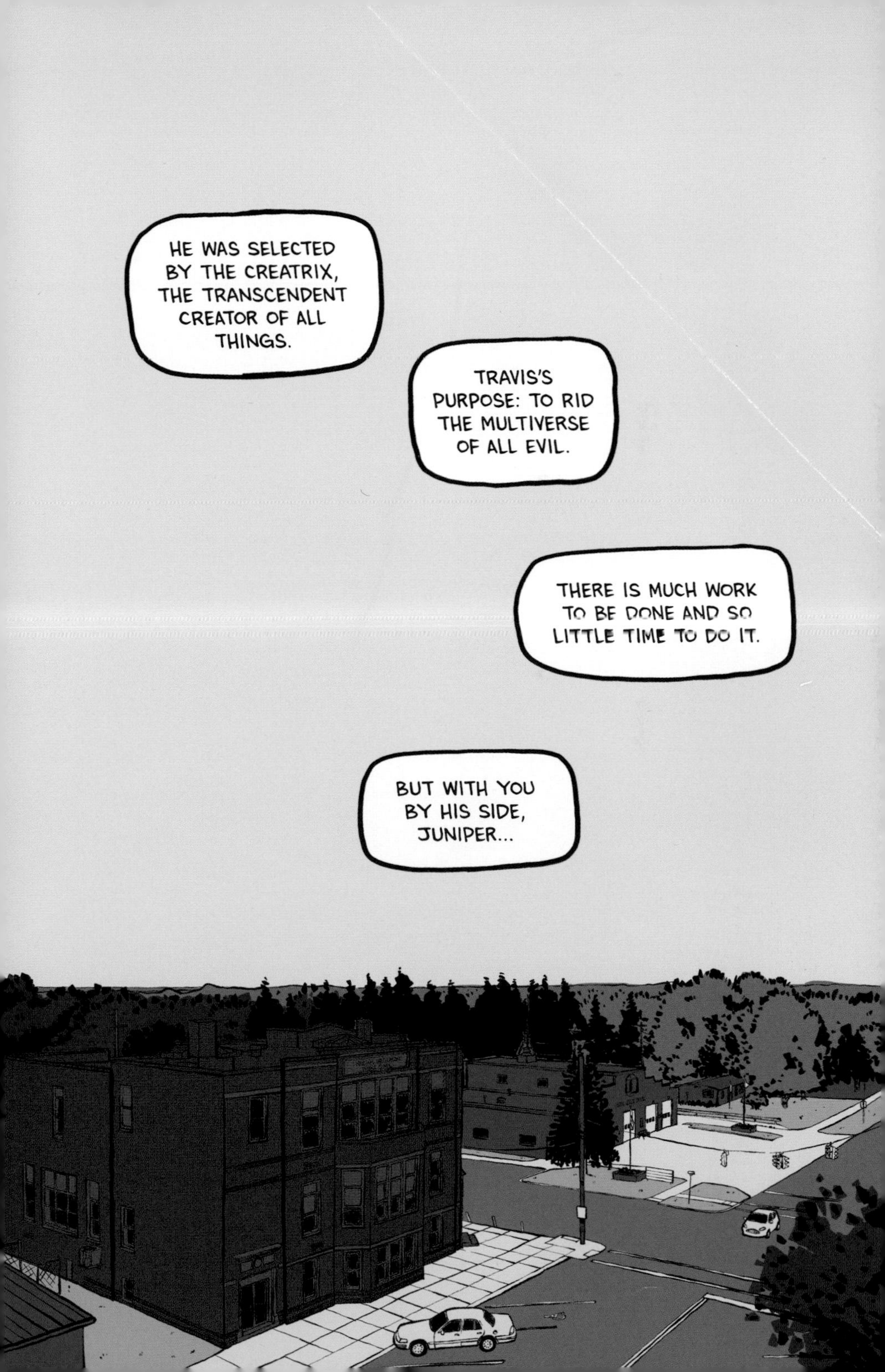
HE WAS SELECTED BY THE CREATRIX, THE TRANSCENDENT CREATOR OF ALL THINGS.
TRAVIS'S PURPOSE: TO RID THE MULTIVERSE OF ALL EVIL.
THERE IS MUCH WORK TO BE DONE AND SO LITTLE TIME TO DO IT.
BUT WITH YOU BY HIS SIDE, JUNIPER...

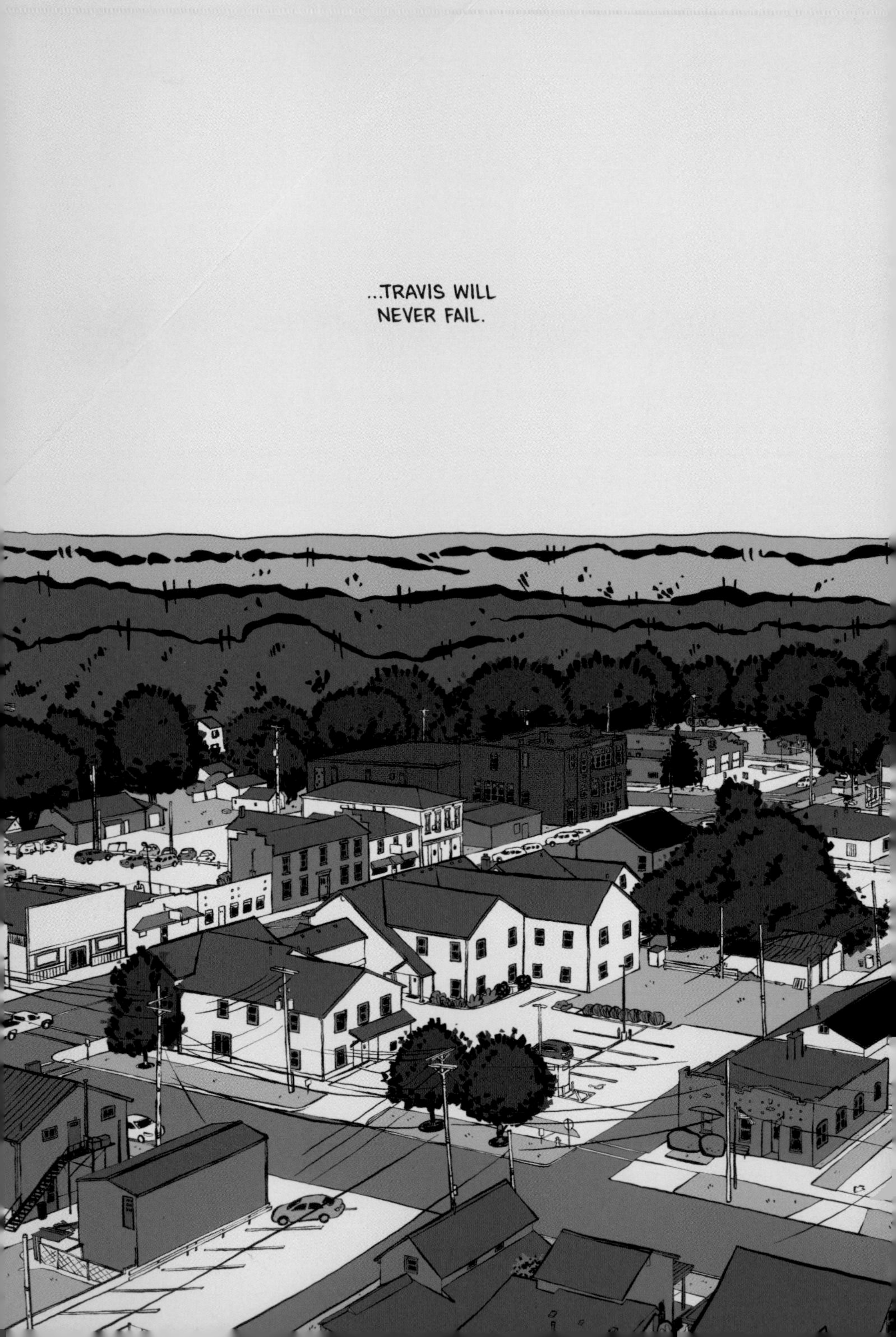
...TRAVIS WILL
NEVER FAIL.

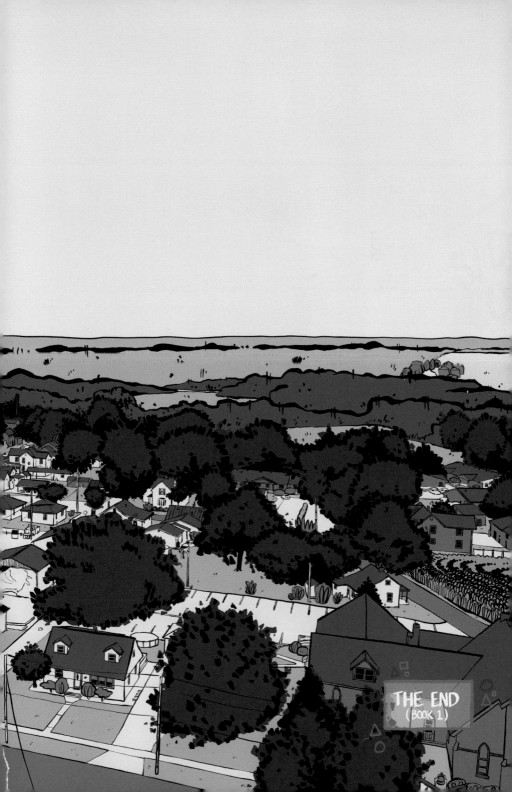

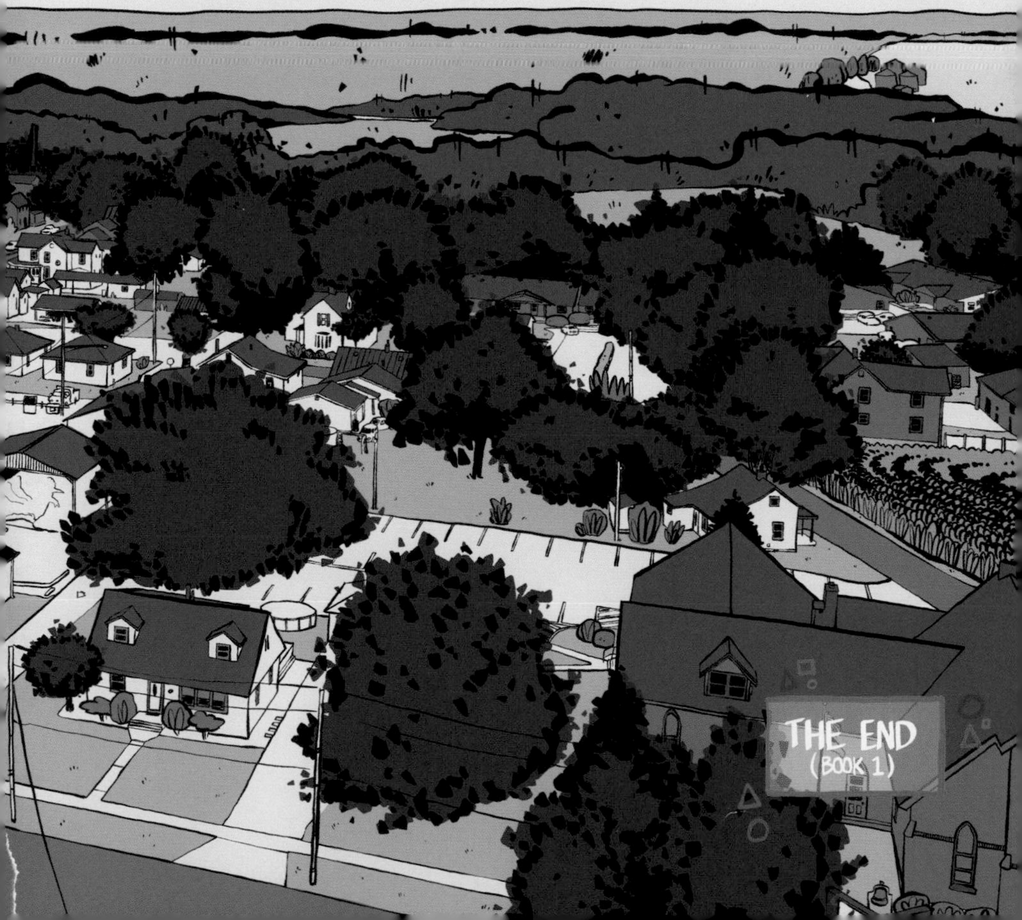
THE END
(BOOK 1)

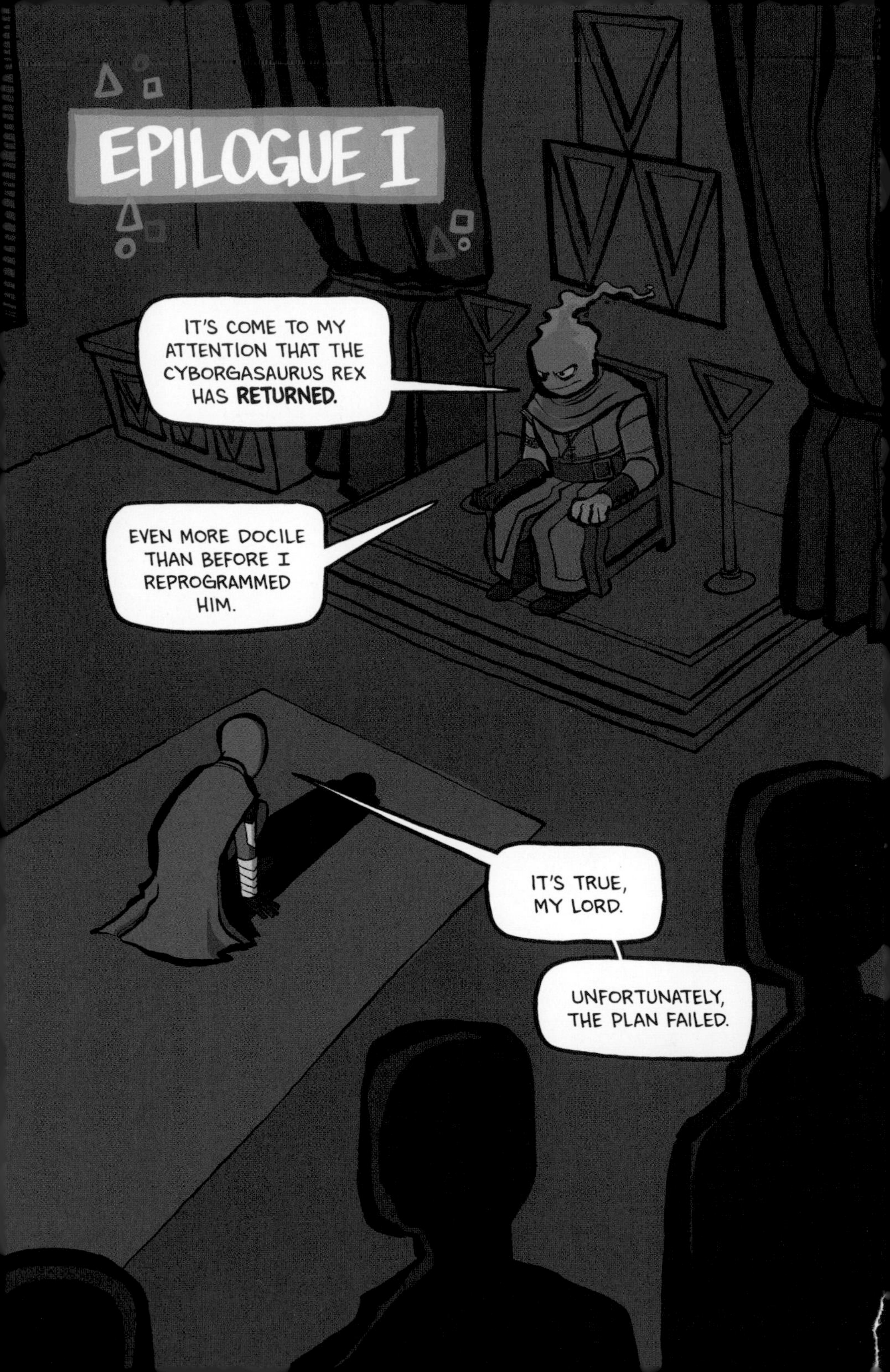
EPILOGUE I
IT'S COME TO MY ATTENTION THAT THE CYBORGASAURUS REX HAS **RETURNED.**
EVEN MORE DOCILE THAN BEFORE I REPROGRAMMED HIM.
IT'S TRUE, MY LORD.
UNFORTUNATELY, THE PLAN FAILED.

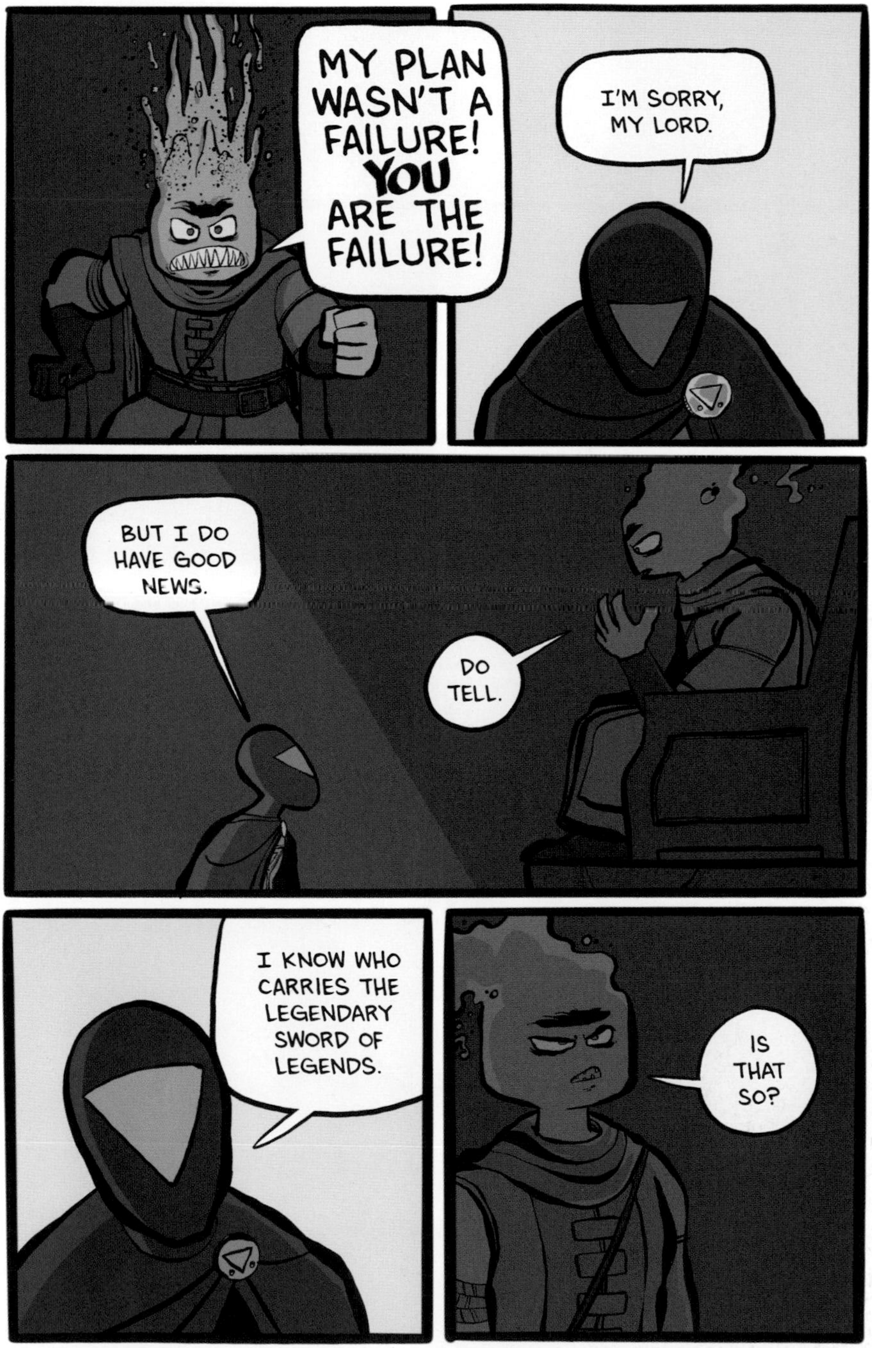
MY PLAN WASN'T A FAILURE! YOU ARE THE FAILURE!
I'M SORRY, MY LORD.
BUT I DO HAVE GOOD NEWS.
DO TELL.
I KNOW WHO CARRIES THE LEGENDARY SWORD OF LEGENDS.
IS THAT SO?

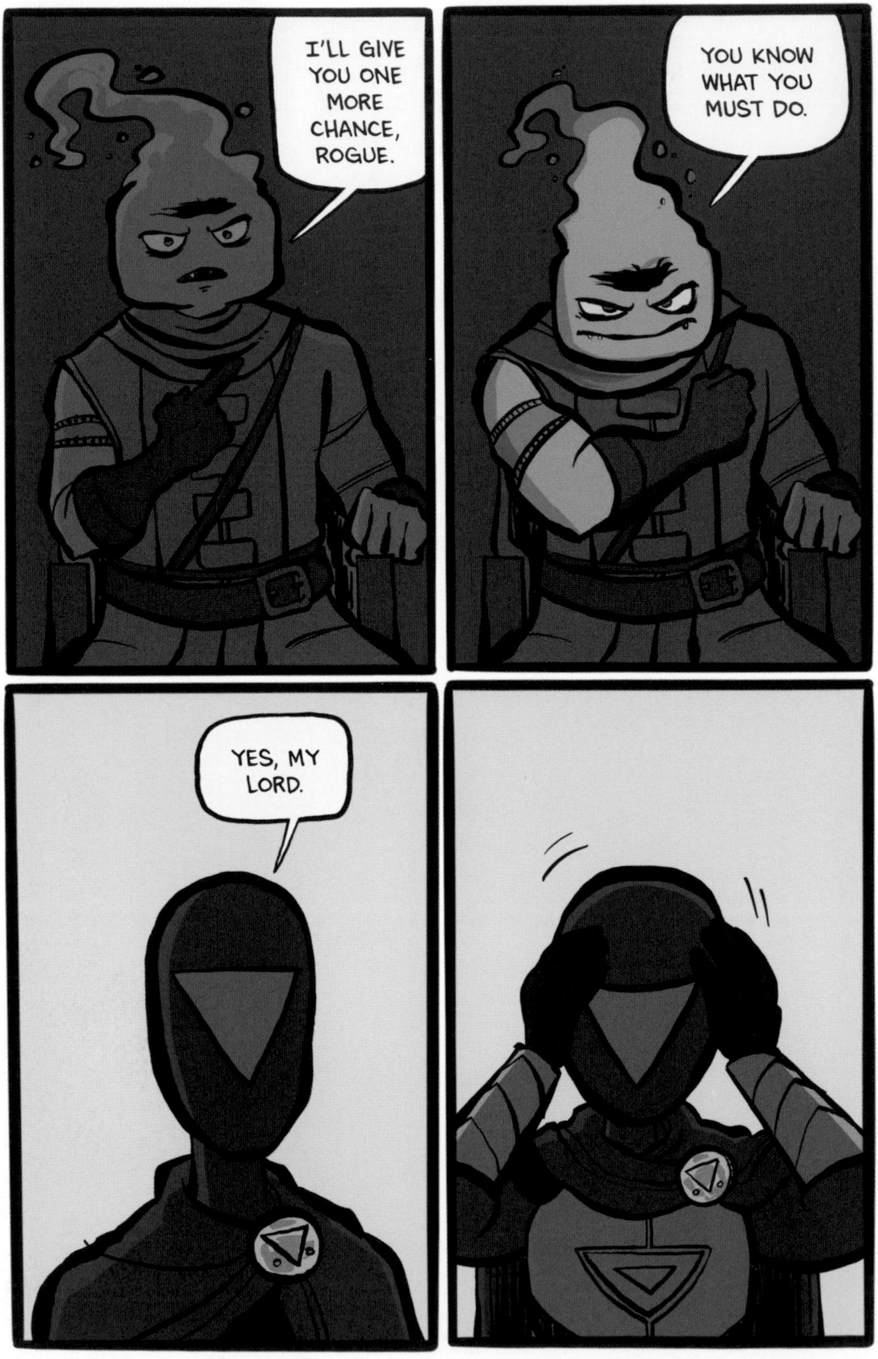
I'LL GIVE YOU ONE MORE CHANCE, ROGUE.
YOU KNOW WHAT YOU MUST DO.
YES, MY LORD.

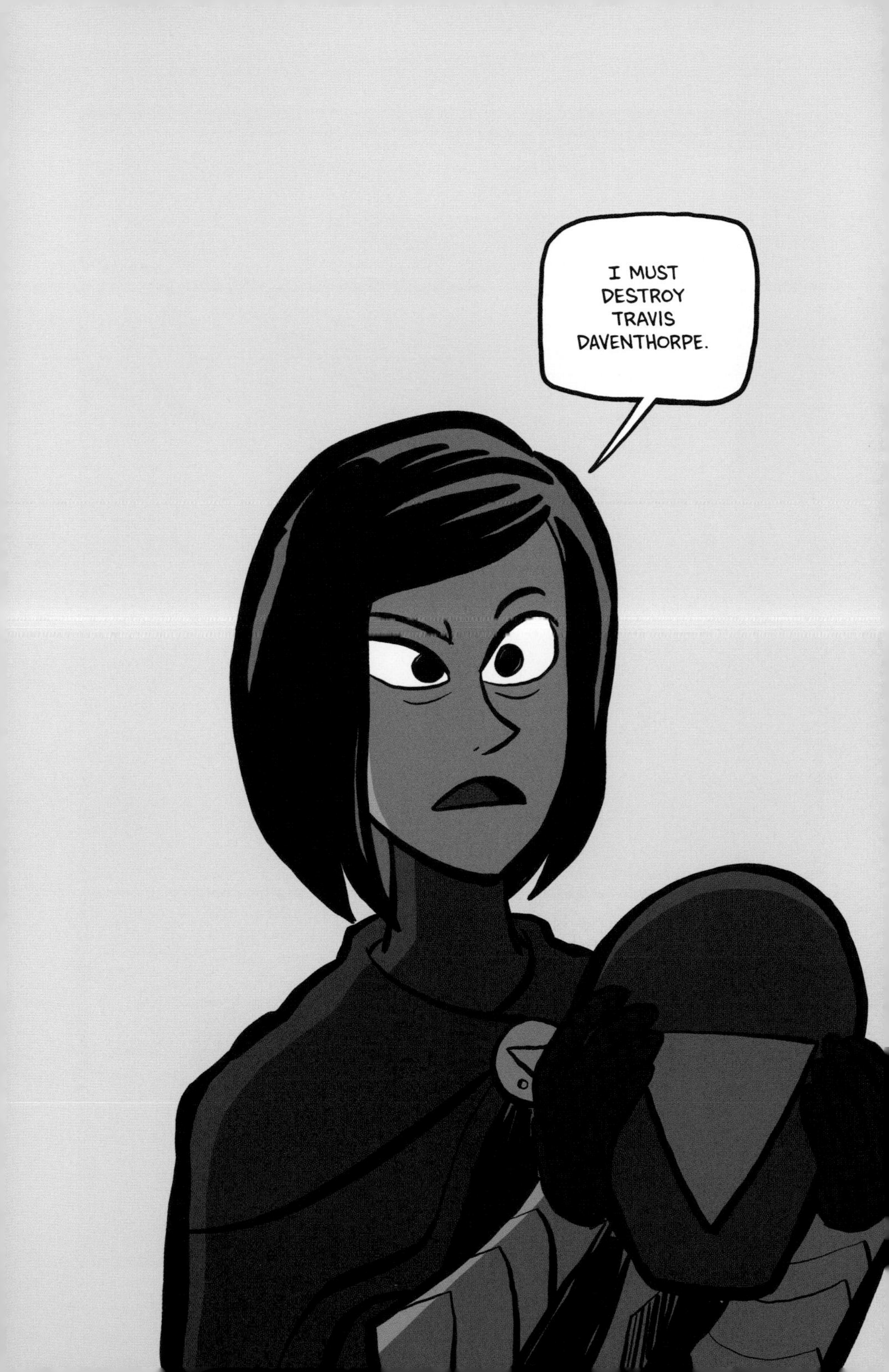
I MUST DESTROY TRAVIS DAVENTHORPE.

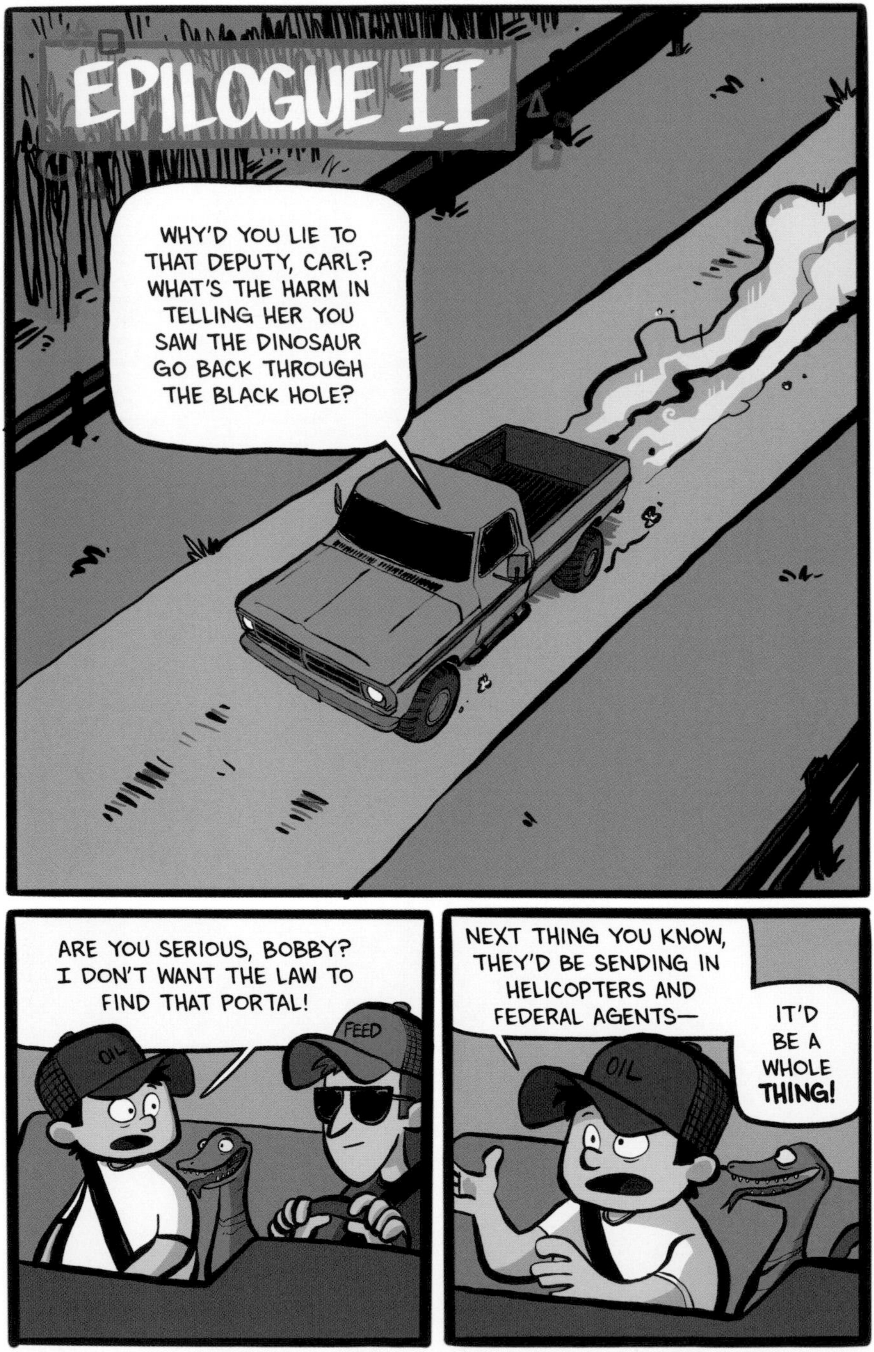
EPILOGUE II
WHY'D YOU LIE TO THAT DEPUTY, CARL? WHAT'S THE HARM IN TELLING HER YOU SAW THE DINOSAUR GO BACK THROUGH THE BLACK HOLE?
ARE YOU SERIOUS, BOBBY? I DON'T WANT THE LAW TO FIND THAT PORTAL!
OIL
FEED
NEXT THING YOU KNOW, THEY'D BE SENDING IN HELICOPTERS AND FEDERAL AGENTS—
IT'D BE A WHOLE THING!
OIL

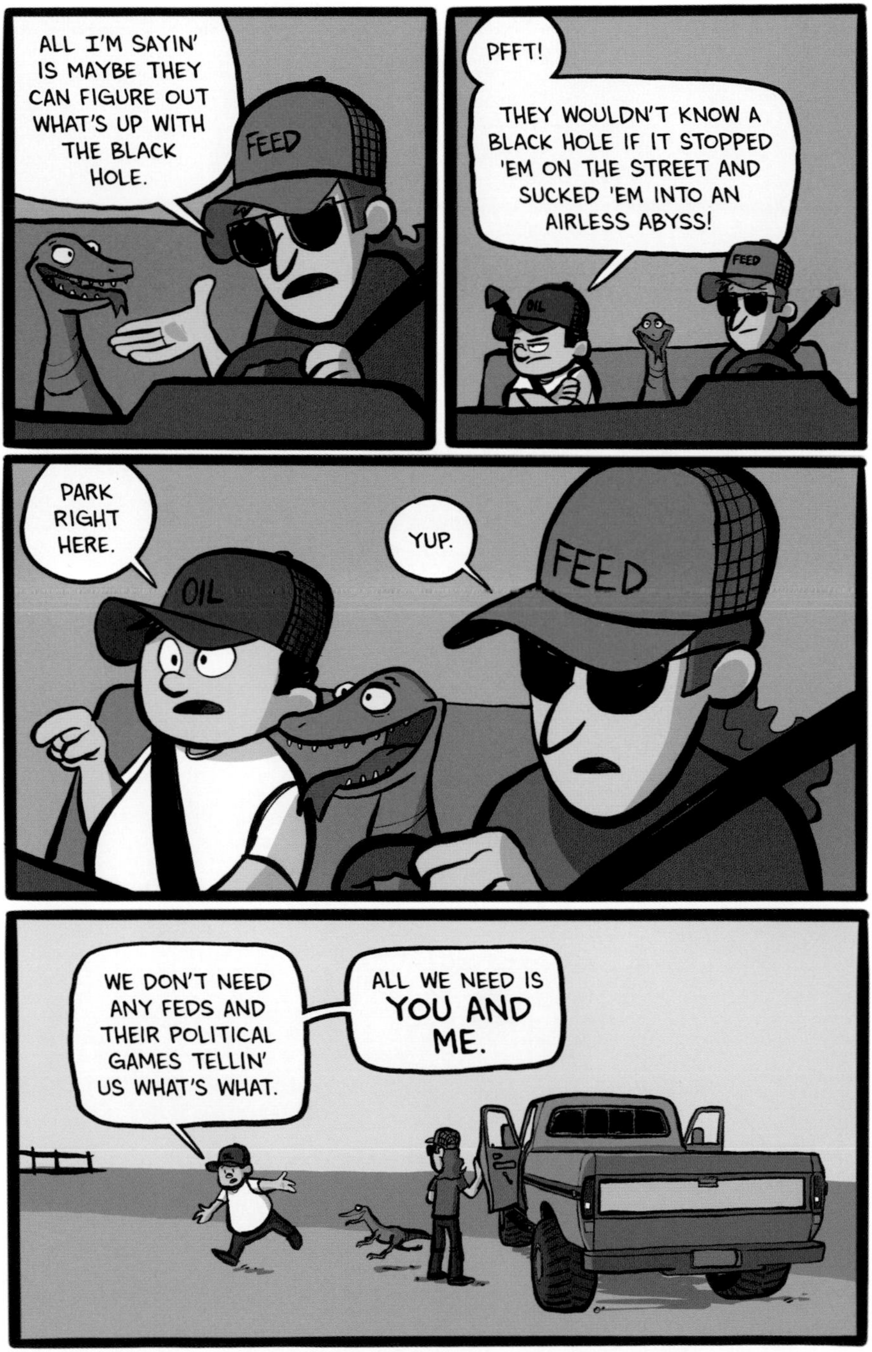
ALL I'M SAYIN' IS MAYBE THEY CAN FIGURE OUT WHAT'S UP WITH THE BLACK HOLE.
FEED
PFFT!
THEY WOULDN'T KNOW A BLACK HOLE IF IT STOPPED 'EM ON THE STREET AND SUCKED 'EM INTO AN AIRLESS ABYSS!
OIL
FEED
PARK RIGHT HERE.
OIL
YUP.
FEED
WE DON'T NEED ANY FEDS AND THEIR POLITICAL GAMES TELLIN' US WHAT'S WHAT.
ALL WE NEED IS YOU AND ME.

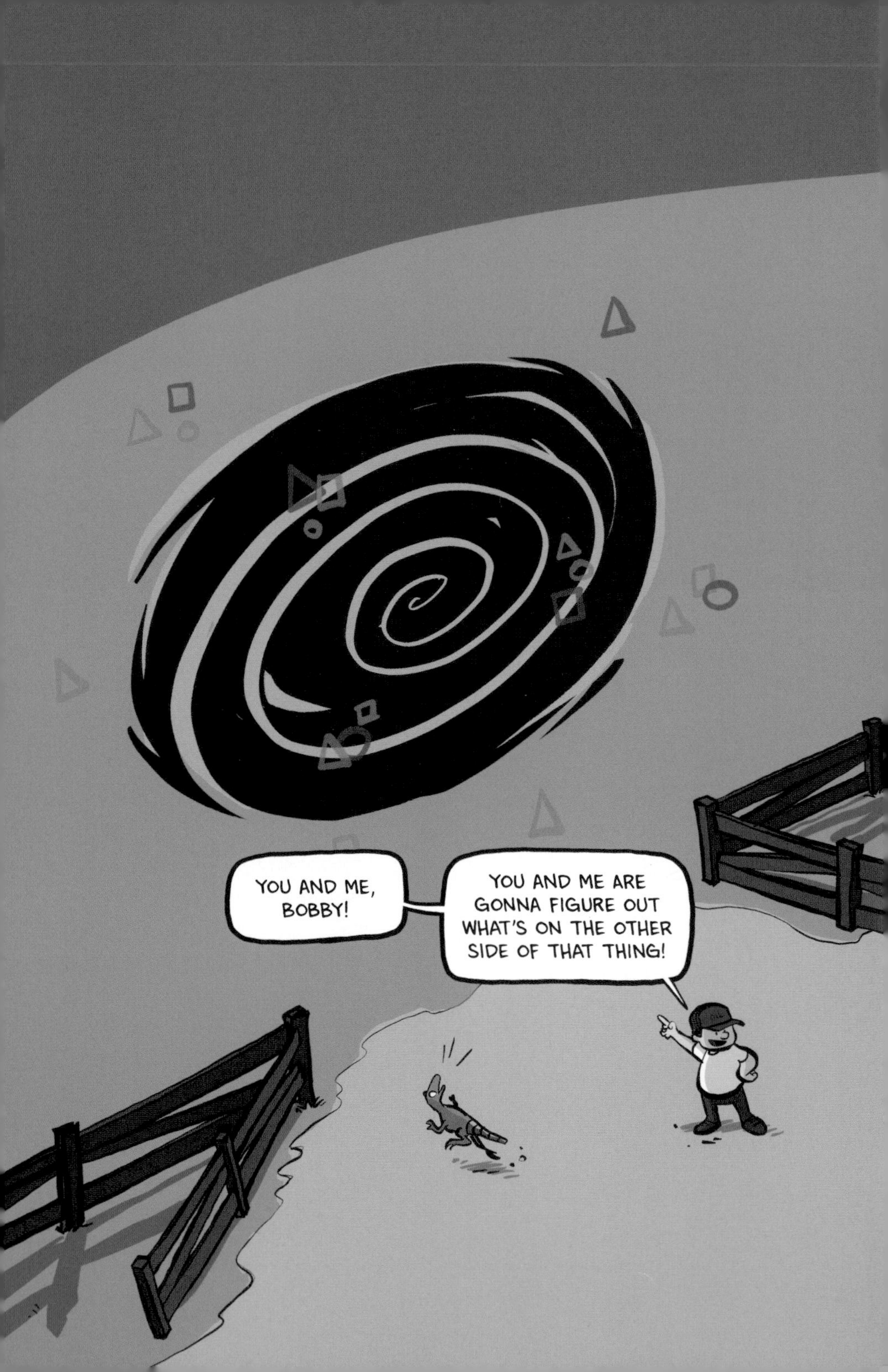
YOU AND ME, BOBBY!
YOU AND ME ARE GONNA FIGURE OUT WHAT'S ON THE OTHER SIDE OF THAT THING!

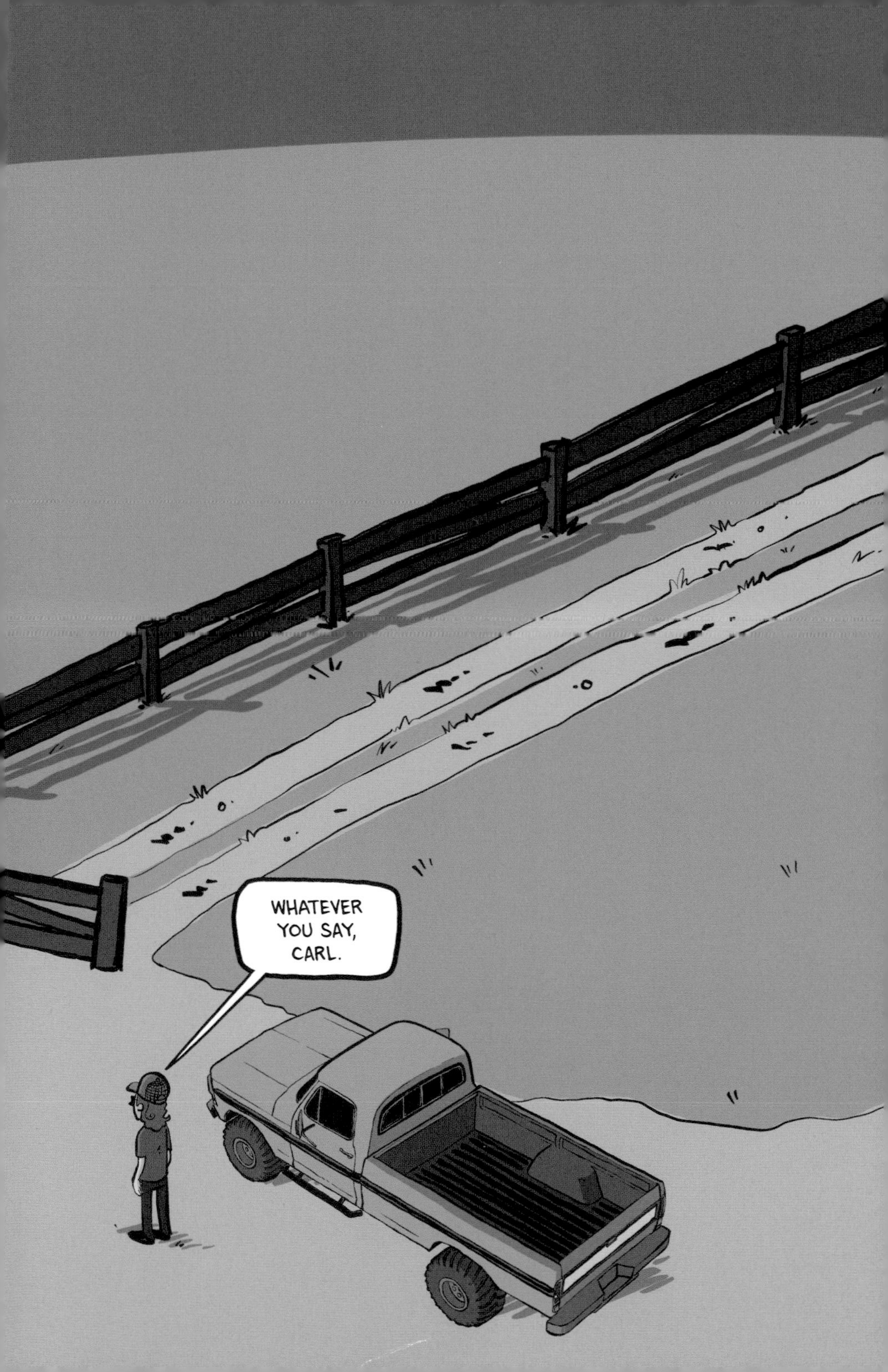
WHATEVER YOU SAY, CARL.

PLAYER GUIDE

BEAKMAN PRIZE (BEEK-muhn prīz)

Top prize at the William Watterson Middle School science fair. Named after the greatest scientist who ever lived in the history of the world.

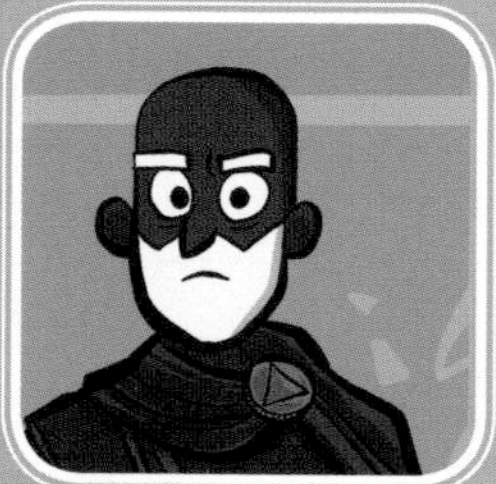

BELAZAR

(BEH-la-zar)

Bright Mage whose magical powers come directly from the Creatrix. Is helping Travis Daventhorpe develop his full potential.

CREATRIX, THE (cree-AY-triks, the)

The omniscient, omnipotent, and omnipresent deity who created—and continues to create—the entire multiverse.

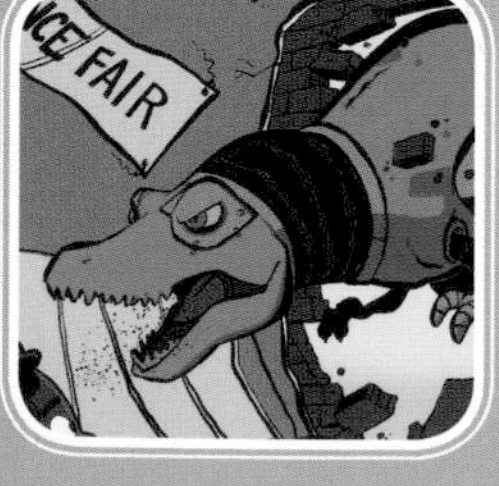
FAIR

CYBORGASAURUS REX

(SĪ-borg-uh-sawr-us reks)

A Tyrannosaurus rex with mechanical appendages. Was sent from Solusterra by Nol Invictus to steal the Legendary Sword of Legends from Travis, but Travis overrode its programming to make it docile.

DEREK DEVERS

(DER-ik DEE-verz)

School bully and the bane of Travis Daventhorpe's existence. Underwear is individually labeled by his mother.

HOPETON (HŌP-tuhn)

A small village in rural southern Ohio founded by Thomas Hope.

JUNIPER REYES

(JOO-nuh-pur RAY-ehz)

New student in seventh grade at William Watterson Middle School. Family moved to Ohio from Arizona to help with her grandparents' restaurant.

LEGENDARY SWORD OF LEGENDS, THE

(LEJ-uhn-der-ee sohrd uhv LEJ-uhnds, the)

An epic blade forged by the Creatrix himself. Infused with mysterious powers and can only be carried by the Legendary Hero of Solusterra. Nol Invictus needs the sword to activate his doomsday machine that will destroy the multiverse.

MS. CROSBY

(miz CRAWZ-bee)

Most popular teacher at William Watterson Middle School. Teaches all the science classes and is also in charge of the annual science fair.

MOM AND DAD

(mawm and dæd)

Travis's parents are pretty cool, as far as parents go. Their pride for their son is rivaled only by their naivete.

NOL INVICTUS

(nōl ehn-VICK-tuhs)

King of Solusterra. A harsh ruler who has turned against the Creatrix. Desires to destroy the multiverse and re-create it according to his purposes. No one knows where his power comes from, but there are rumors of a great evil that exists beyond the multiverse . . .

ROGUE, THE

(rōg, the)

Former Bright Mage who turned their back on the Creatrix to follow Nol Invictus. Now serves Nol Invictus as the king's spy and assassin.

SOLUSTERRA (SO-lus-tehr-uh)

A planet that is also a continent that is also a country in another dimension of the multiverse. Solusterra is loved by the Creatrix more than any other land in any other dimension he has created.

TRAVBOT

(TRAV-bot)

The coolest little robot, boasting the most advanced artificial intelligence ever developed. Created by Travis Daventhorpe in his bedroom laboratory, Travbot is Travis's best—and only—friend.

TRAVIS DAVENTHORPE

(TRA-vis DAV-en-thōrp)

Seventh grader at William Watterson Middle School. Supposed to be in sixth grade but was bumped up to seventh because he's supersmart. Finds out that he's the Legendary Hero of Solusterra—and that the fate of the entire multiverse rests on his twelve-year-old shoulders.

WILLIAM WATTERSON MIDDLE SCHOOL

(WIL-yuhm WAH-ter-suhn MI-dul skool)

Small middle school located in Hopeton, Ohio. Named after the greatest artist and writer who ever lived in the history of the world.

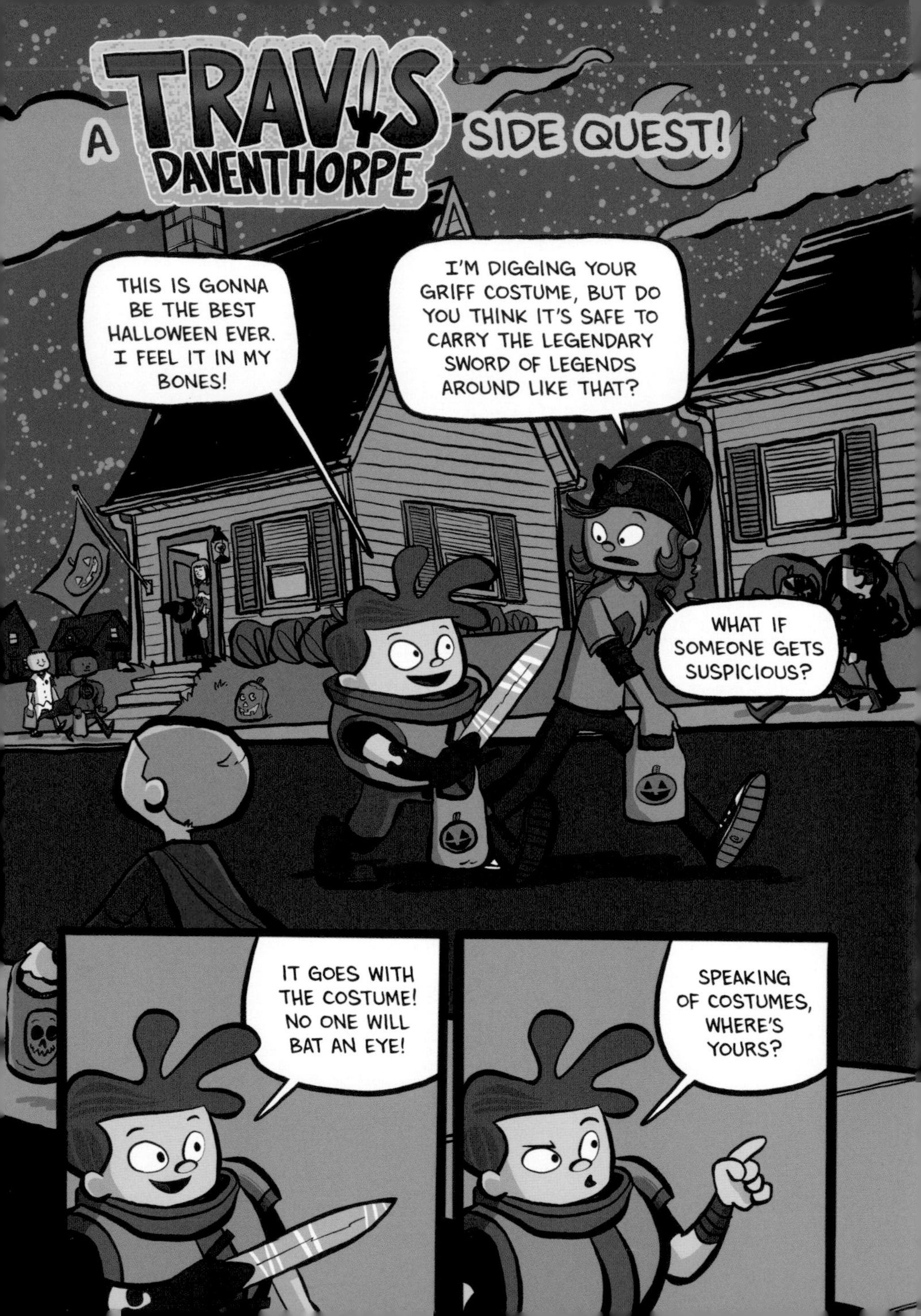
A TRAVIS DAVENTHORPE SIDE QUEST!
THIS IS GONNA BE THE BEST HALLOWEEN EVER. I FEEL IT IN MY BONES!
I'M DIGGING YOUR GRIFF COSTUME, BUT DO YOU THINK IT'S SAFE TO CARRY THE LEGENDARY SWORD OF LEGENDS AROUND LIKE THAT?
WHAT IF SOMEONE GETS SUSPICIOUS?
IT GOES WITH THE COSTUME! NO ONE WILL BAT AN EYE!
SPEAKING OF COSTUMES, WHERE'S YOURS?

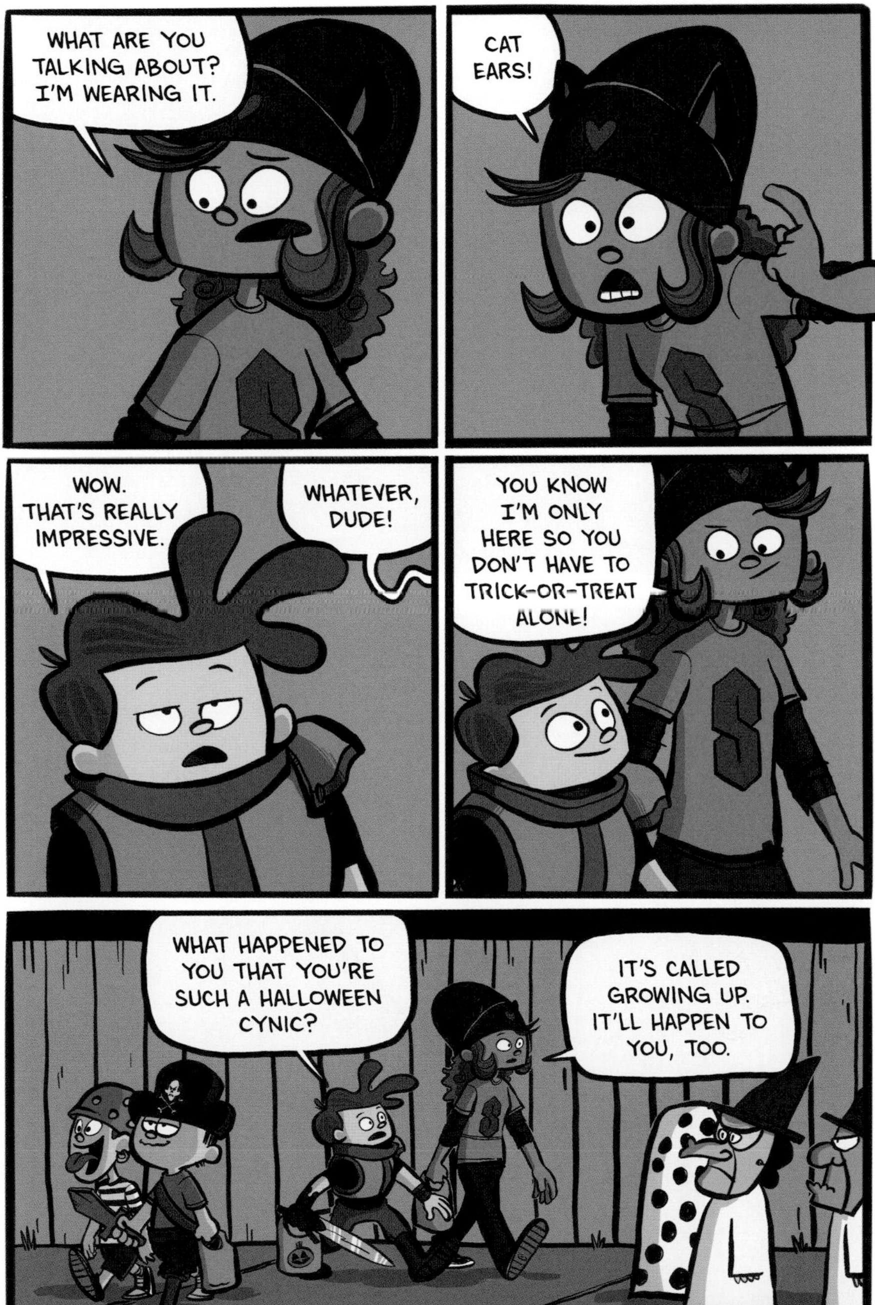
WHAT ARE YOU TALKING ABOUT? I'M WEARING IT.
CAT EARS!
WOW. THAT'S REALLY IMPRESSIVE.
WHATEVER, DUDE!
YOU KNOW I'M ONLY HERE SO YOU DON'T HAVE TO TRICK-OR-TREAT ALONE!
WHAT HAPPENED TO YOU THAT YOU'RE SUCH A HALLOWEEN CYNIC?
IT'S CALLED GROWING UP. IT'LL HAPPEN TO YOU, TOO.

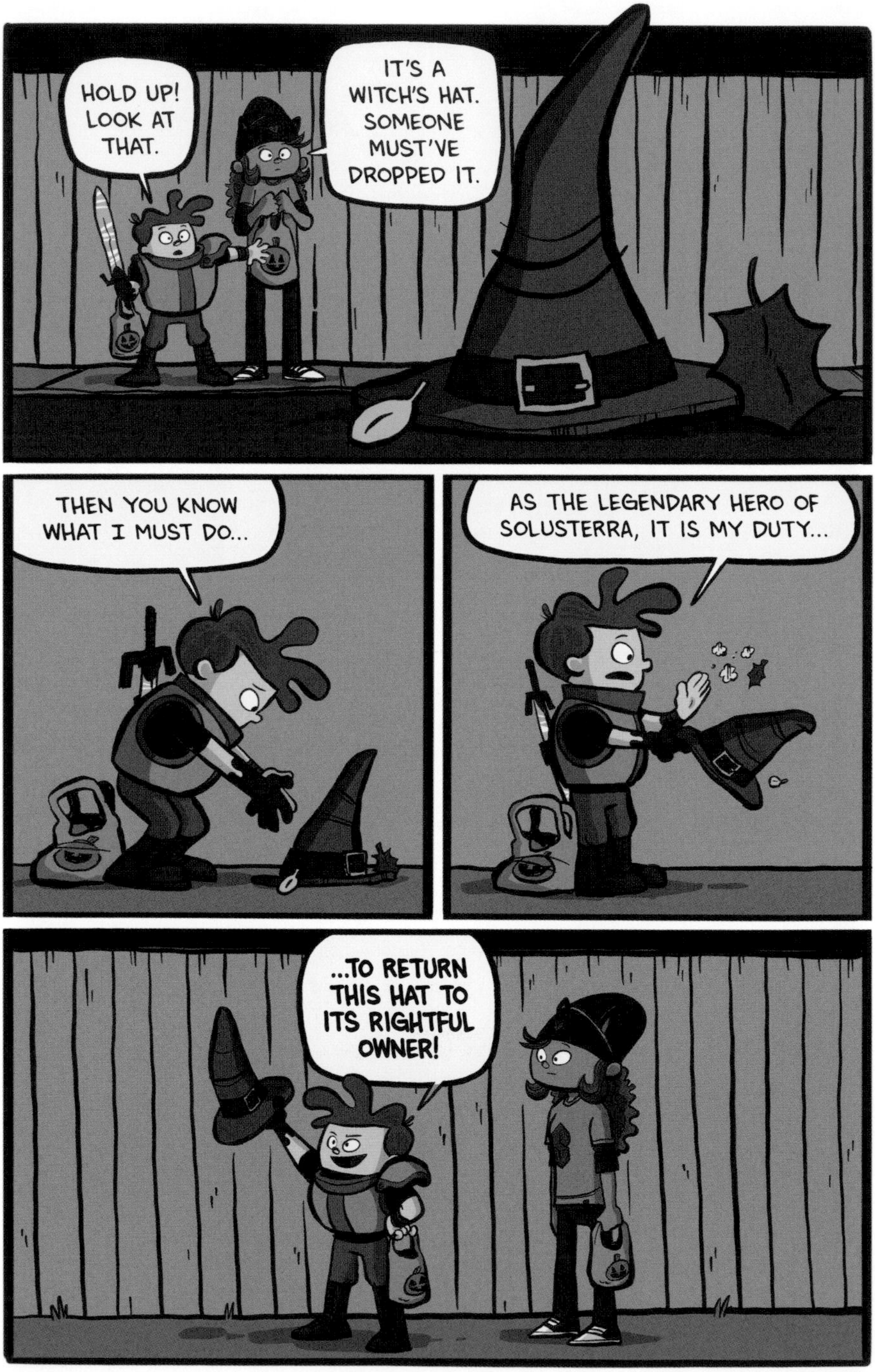
HOLD UP! LOOK AT THAT.
IT'S A WITCH'S HAT. SOMEONE MUST'VE DROPPED IT.
THEN YOU KNOW WHAT I MUST DO...
AS THE LEGENDARY HERO OF SOLUSTERRA, IT IS MY DUTY...
...TO RETURN THIS HAT TO ITS RIGHTFUL OWNER!

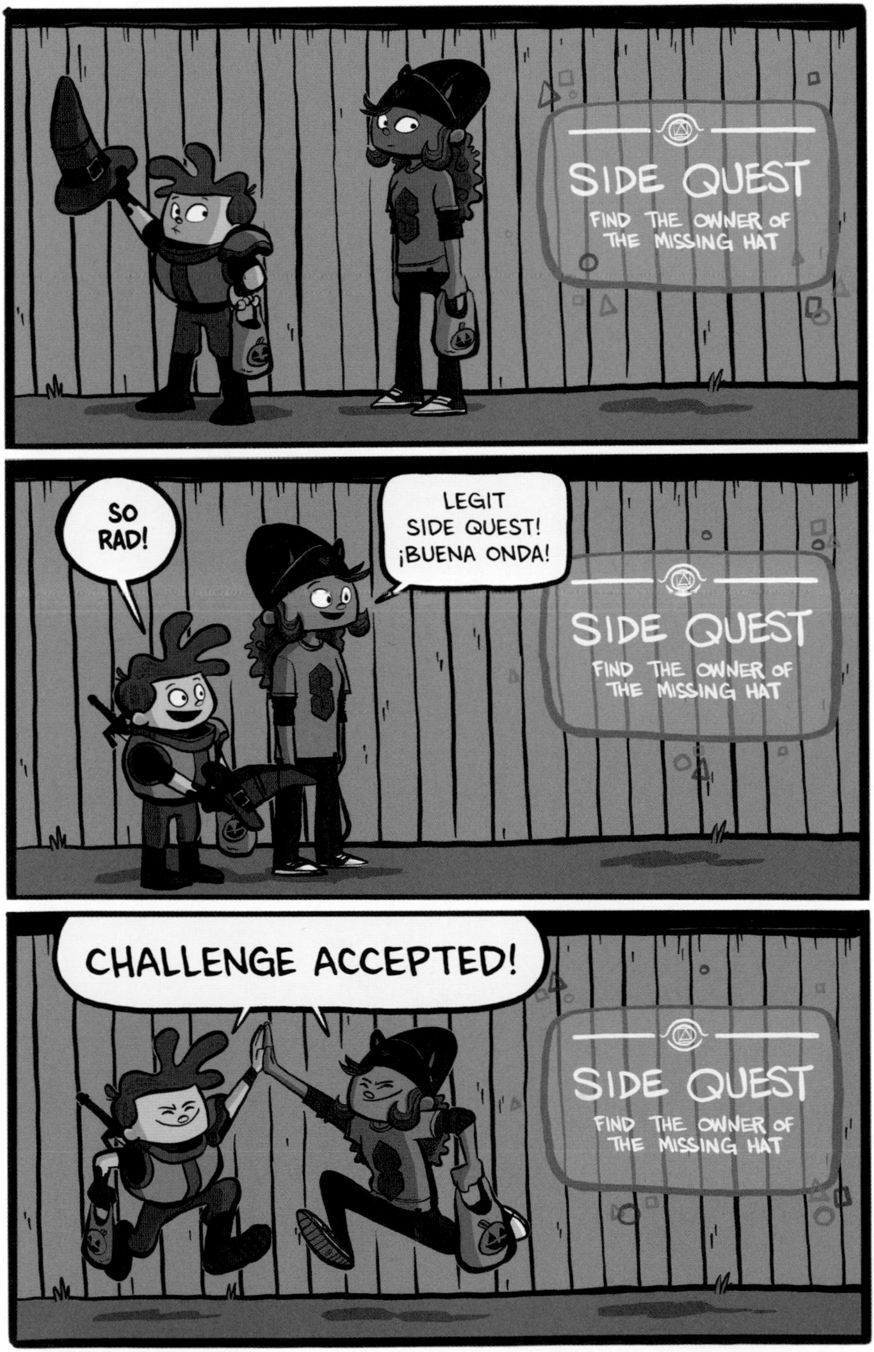
SIDE QUEST
FIND THE OWNER OF THE MISSING HAT
SO RAD!
LEGIT SIDE QUEST! ¡BUENA ONDA!
SIDE QUEST
FIND THE OWNER OF THE MISSING HAT
CHALLENGE ACCEPTED!
SIDE QUEST
FIND THE OWNER OF THE MISSING HAT

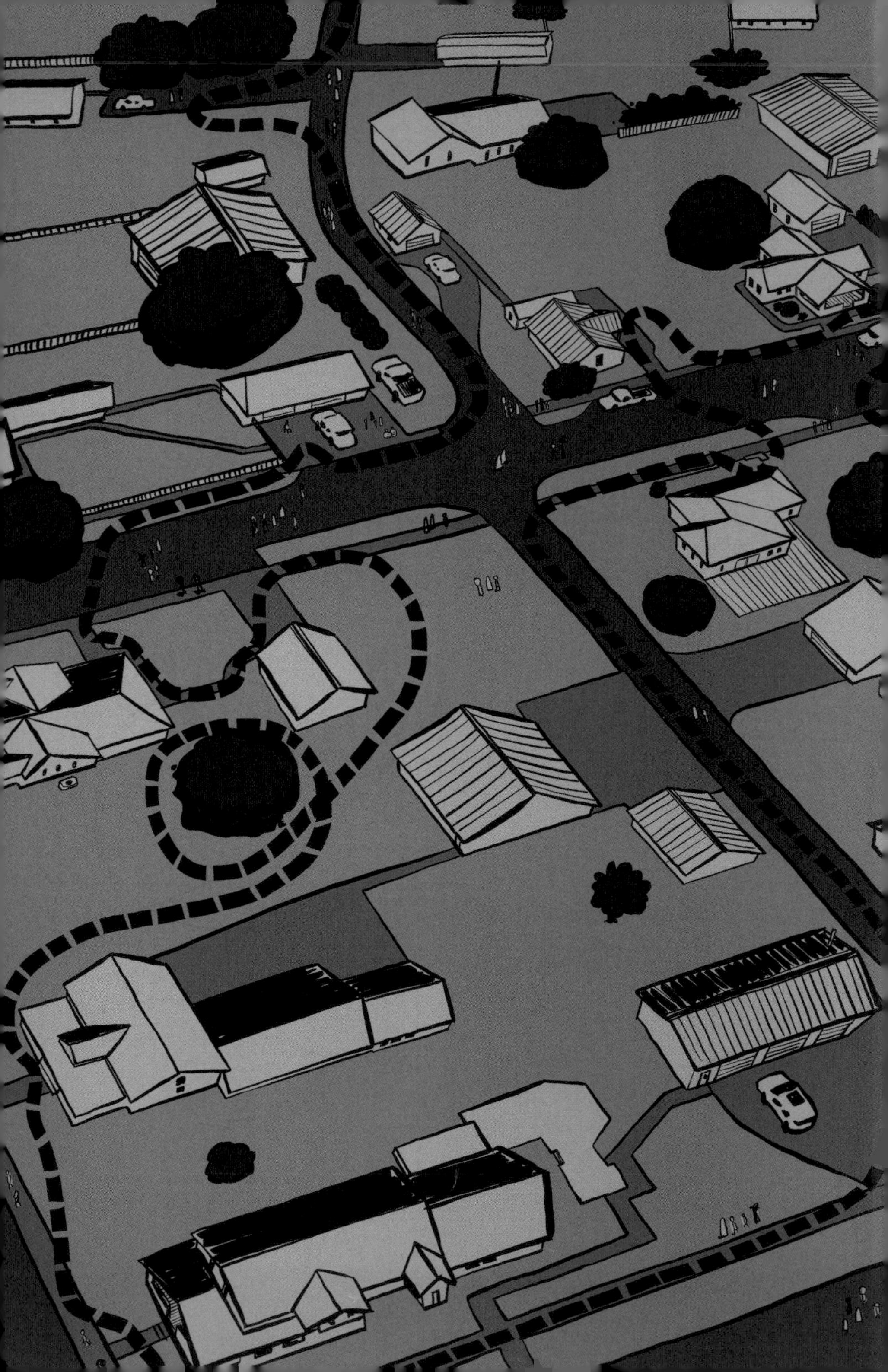

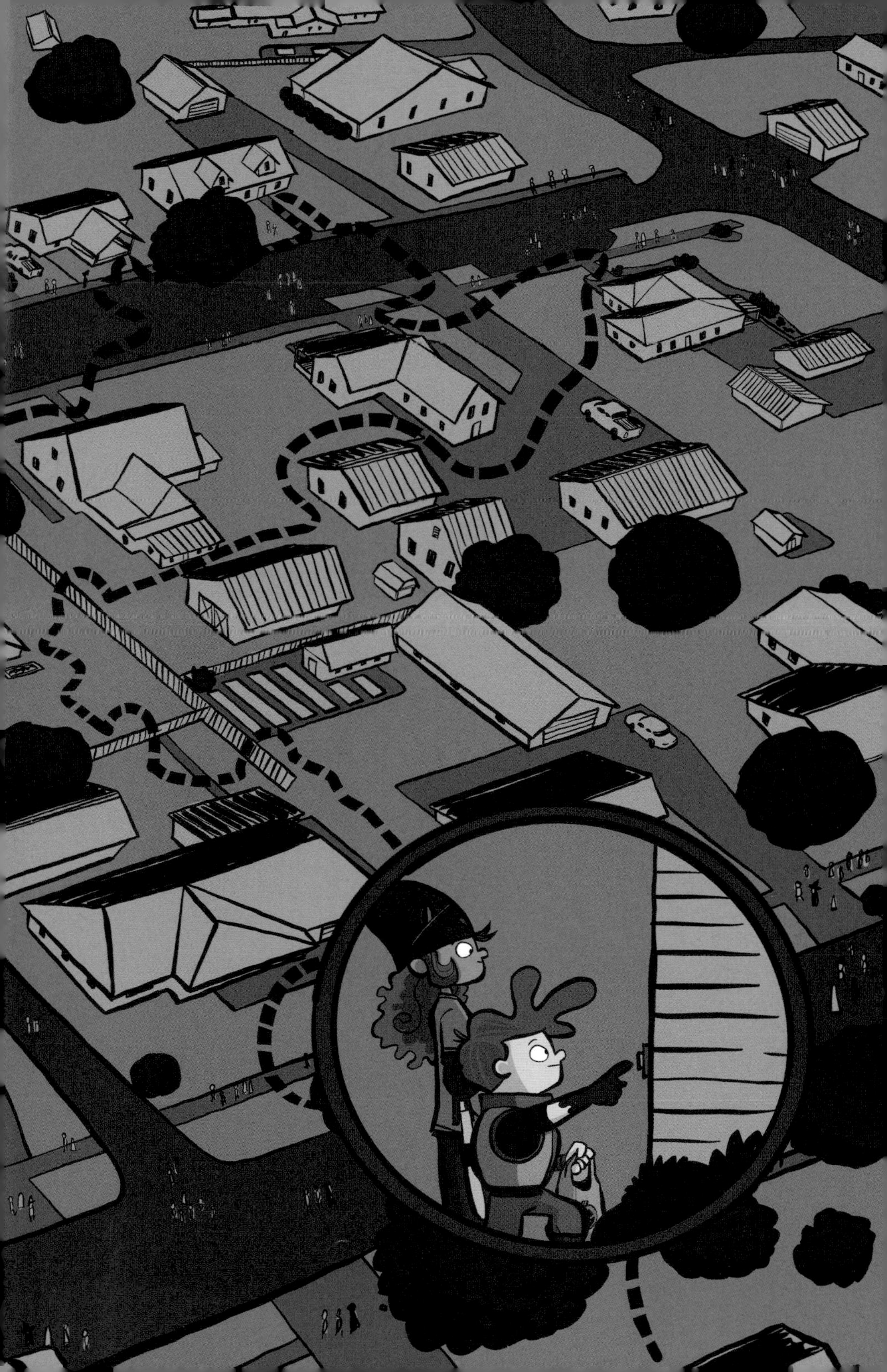

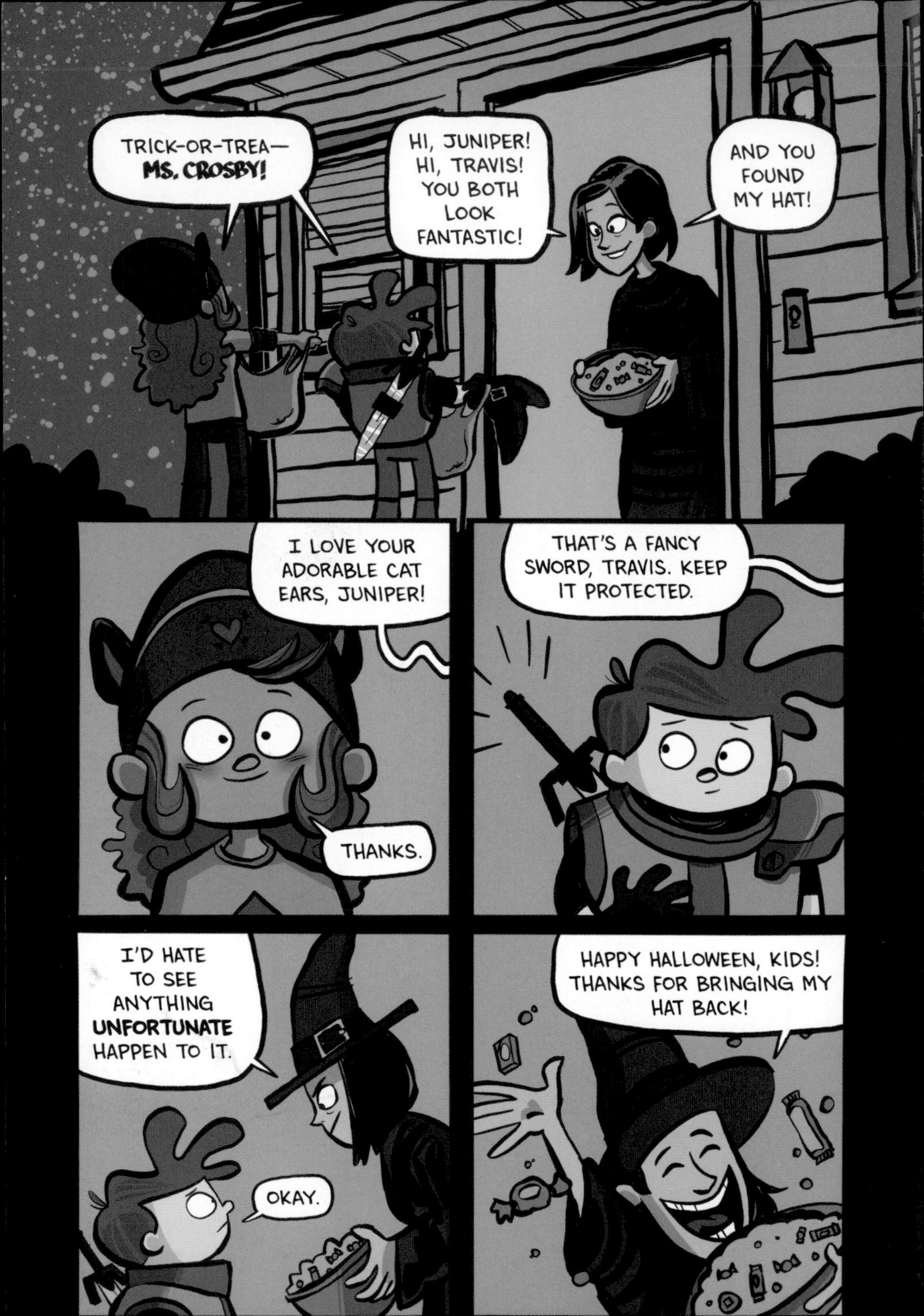
TRICK-OR-TREA—
MS. CROSBY!
HI, JUNIPER! HI, TRAVIS! YOU BOTH LOOK FANTASTIC!
AND YOU FOUND MY HAT!
I LOVE YOUR ADORABLE CAT EARS, JUNIPER!
THANKS.
THAT'S A FANCY SWORD, TRAVIS. KEEP IT PROTECTED.
I'D HATE TO SEE ANYTHING UNFORTUNATE HAPPEN TO IT.
OKAY.
HAPPY HALLOWEEN, KIDS! THANKS FOR BRINGING MY HAT BACK!

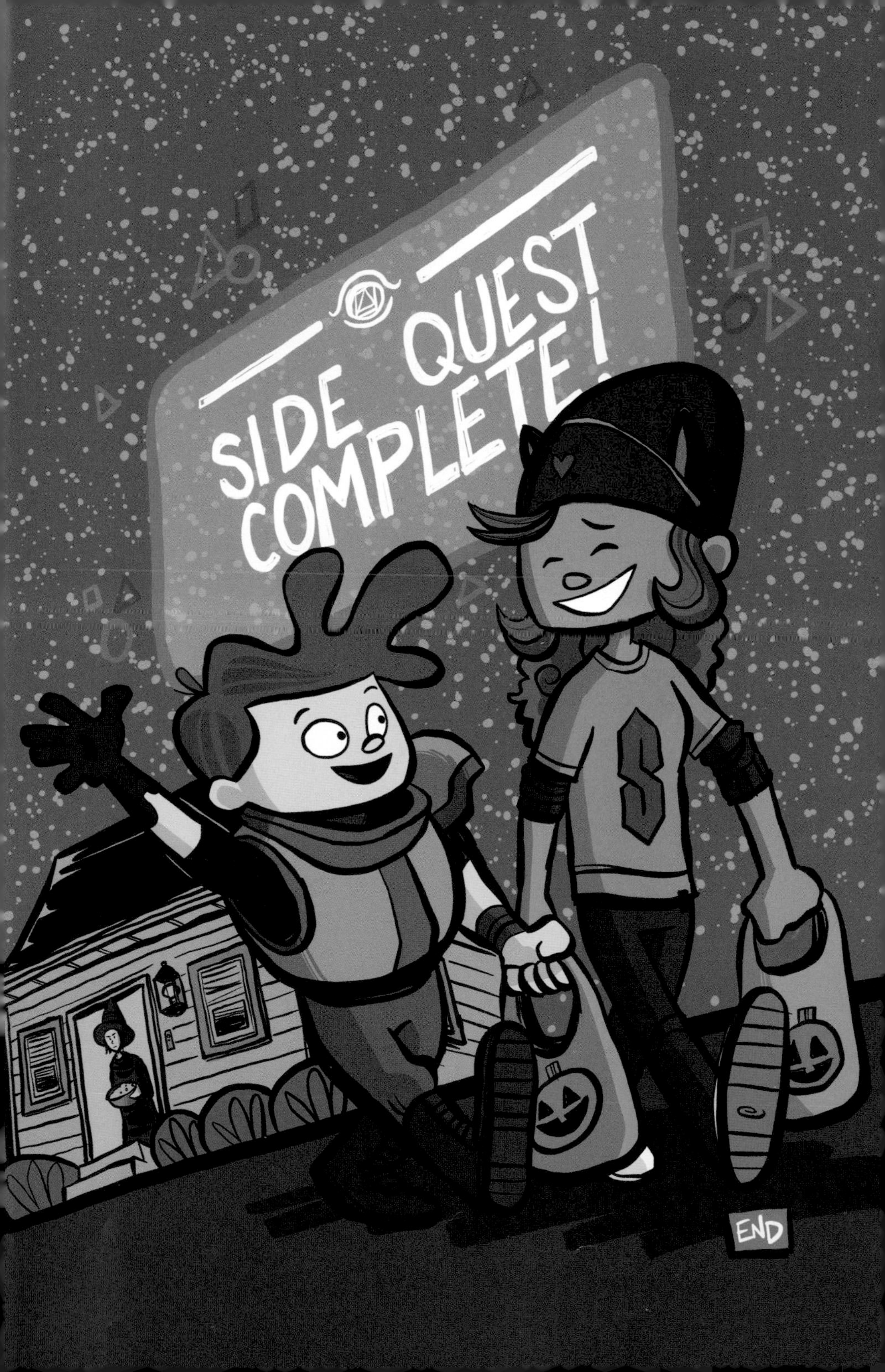
SIDE QUEST COMPLETE!
END

THE PROCESS

There are lots of different ways to make awesome comics, and there's no one right way to make them. It all depends on what works best for the artist. That said, here's how I made *Travis Daventhorpe for the Win!*

I started by making lots of sketches in a regular Moleskine notebook. Not the sketchbook kind. The regular ones have more pages, and I don't care about ink bleeding through. I think it looks cool and process-y. Anyway, this sketchbook is where Travis, Belazar, Travbot, Derek Devers, and the Cyborgasaurus rex all came to life. Eventually, I saved enough money to get an iPad Pro with an Apple Pencil. Using the Procreate app, I sketched the first drawings of Juniper Reyes, Ms. Crosby, and Nol Invictus.

When it was time to make the graphic novel, I made a page template in Photoshop using First Second's specs. Next, I shared that template with my iPad so I could use it in Procreate, where I drew and colored the entire book. The brush I used is the Watterson brush made by the incomparable Georg von Westphalen. I tweaked it (only a little bit!) to my satisfaction. The lettering was done with a typeface of my handwriting made by the legendary John Martz. Using Photoshop, I placed all the letters and drew the word balloons with Photoshop's standard hard round brush.

It's difficult to say just how long it's taken to make this first book, as it's been growing and evolving over the course of the past five years. If you just count the time from when I started working with the editors at First Second until the book's completion, it was close to one year.

I listened to a lot of great music while drawing this book. Most notably, Five Iron Frenzy, Clutch, the Muffs, Snarky Puppy, Tycho, and various chiptune playlists on Spotify. All of this music created space in my imagination where Travis and his friends could play.

Many video games were played as well. *Horizon Zero Dawn* and *The Legend of Zelda: Breath of the Wild* had a heavy influence on the visual style of the book.

ACKNOWLEDGMENTS

Making a graphic novel is HARD WORK, and it takes a lot of people bringing their A game to make it happen! With that said, I'd like to thank the following folks for their help in making *Travis Daventhorpe for the Win!* a reality:

THE A-TEAM BETA READERS: I would never have had the courage and confidence to pitch *Travis Daventhorpe* to literary agents if not for my awesome beta readers. Andrea Soergel, Ashley Martin, Avery Miller, Dede Bonelli, Doreen Rinehart, Jan Moyer's 2017–18 fifth-grade class, Jason Miller, Patsy Brekke, and Summer Williams—THANK YOU! Your input and encouragement were vital to this series. I hope you're proud of what we've made.

MY CARTOONIST FRIENDS AND MENTORS: Many thanks to my friends in the cartooning world who have inspired and encouraged me for nigh on two decades. David Reddick, Jef Mallett, James Burks, Michael Jantze, Scott Kurtz, and Tom Bancroft have all been wonderful mentors and friends. Michael Regina, Mike Maihack, Josh Ulrich, Drew Pocza, Jamie Cosley, Josh Howard, Scott Zirkel, and Pat Bussey have been my buds in the trenches.

THE FIRST SECOND TEAM: Robyn Chapman, thank you for taking a chance on me. Kirk Benshoff, thank you for being a contagious creative. Molly Johanson, thank you for making this book look *amazing*. Michael Moccio, thank you for being the best editor I could have ever asked for. If for whatever reason you can no longer edit my books, I will never forgive you. To everyone else—Kat Kopit, Scott Brian Wilson, Starr Baer, Francesca Lyn, Noemi Martinez, and Dennis Pacheco—thank you for helping to make *Travis* the best book it could be!

MY AGENT: Jen Azantian, thank you for being my champion. I feel invulnerable with you in my corner.

MY IRL FRIENDS: Many thanks to the Bashes (especially Cameron, who read early drafts of the manuscript and encouraged me along the way), the Kendrews, the Lloyds, the Prestons, and the Vitatoes. My family and I appreciate your friendship more than you will ever know.

MY FAMILY: Livingstones, you are the best in-laws ever. Mom and Dad, thanks for always supporting my dreams of being a pro cartoonist. Lara, I love you and I'm proud of you. Payton, thank you for being the best dog in the universe. Parker and Connor, this book series was inspired by you. I hope you like it. Kari, you are the best thing that ever happened to me. Thanks for being my biggest fan and strongest supporter.

Thank you to Bill Watterson for making *Calvin and Hobbes*.

Thank you to Jeff Smith for making *Bone*.

Thank you to YOU, dear reader! I hope you enjoyed it half as much as I did making it!

Finally, be known for your kindness to others, keep moving forward even when life is bleak, and turn off your electronics every once in a while. Blessings to you all!

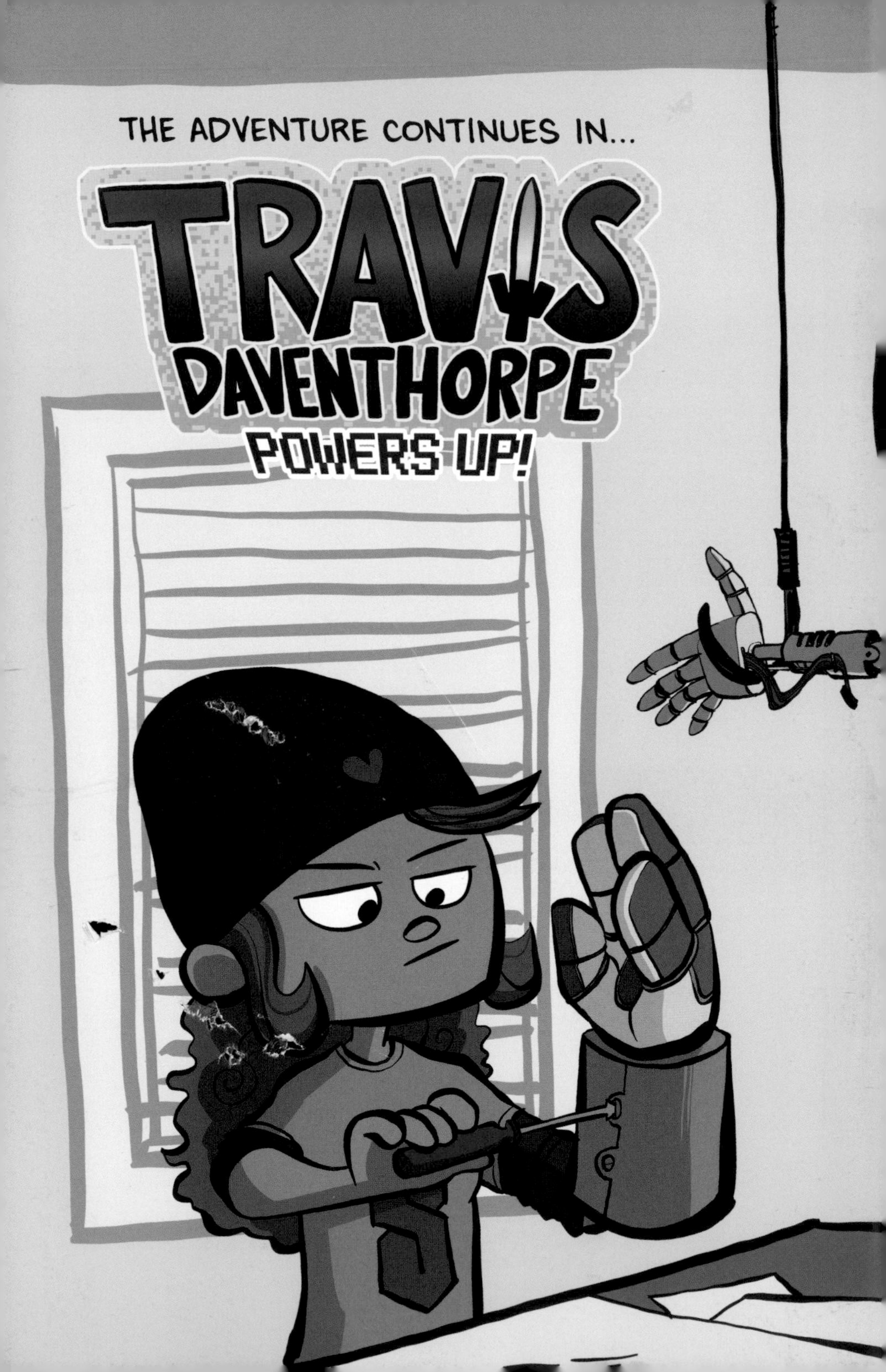
THE ADVENTURE CONTINUES IN...
TRAVIS DAVENTHORPE
POWERS UP!

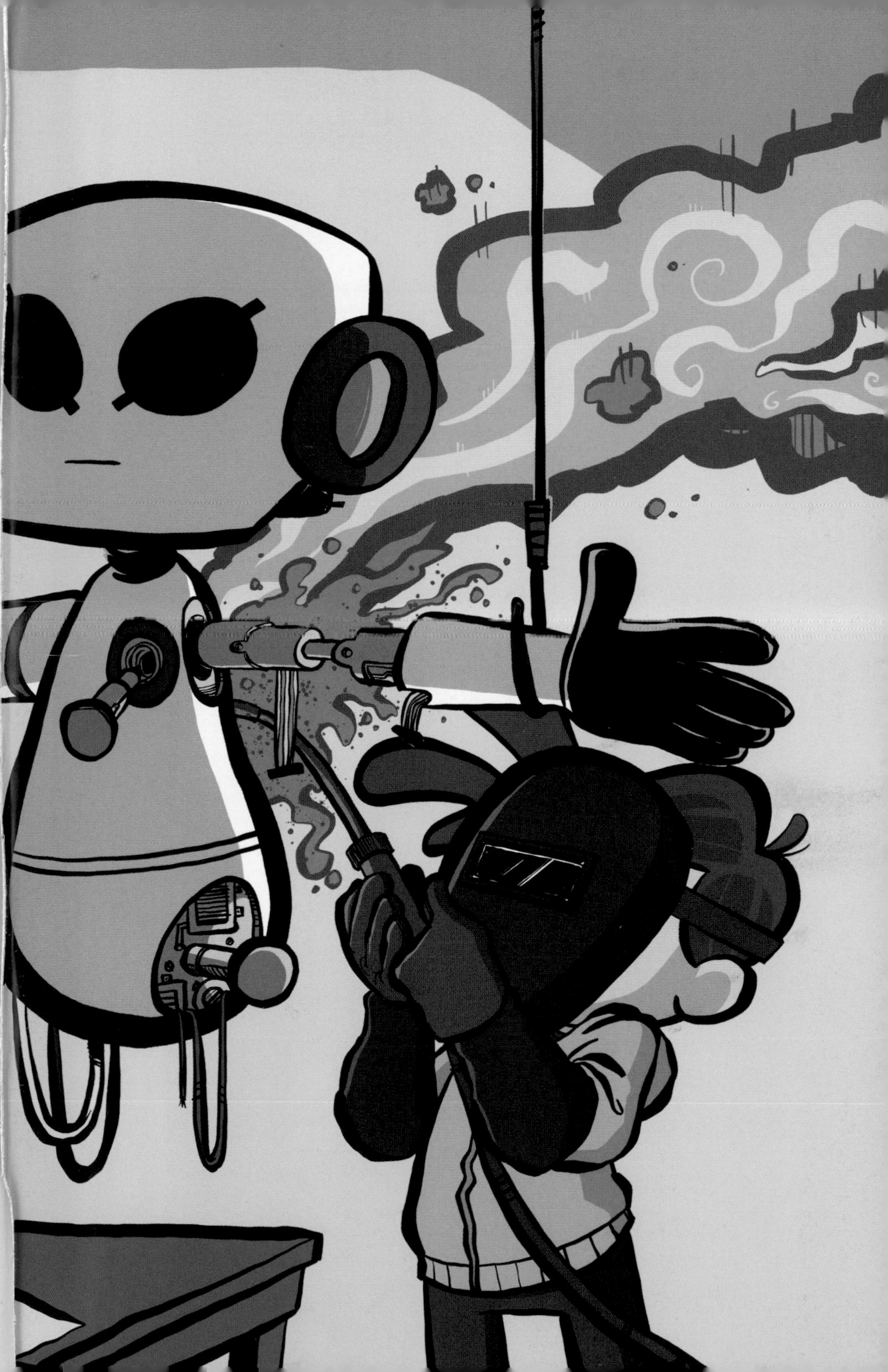

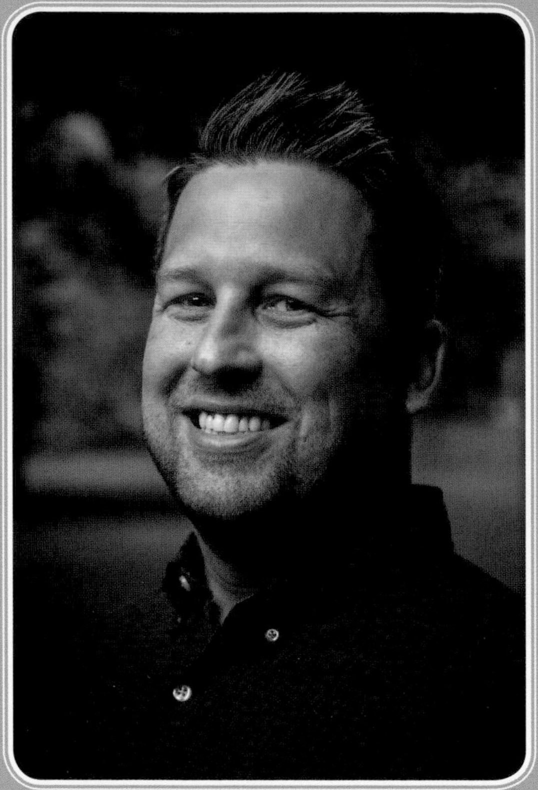
Photo Credit: The Portrait Dude

WES MOLEBASH

(WES MŌL-bash)

The prophesied Legendary Cartoonist of Legends. Created popular webcomics such as *You'll Have That* (Viper Comics) and *Molebashed* (self-published). Has also created cartoons for legendary companies and organizations that include the Ohio State University, Target, and PBS Kids. Currently lives in southern Ohio with his wife, Kari; his sons, Parker and Connor; and a goldendoodle named Payton. *Travis Daventhorpe for the Win!* is his first graphic novel, *but not his last!* Can be found online at **wesmolebash.com**.

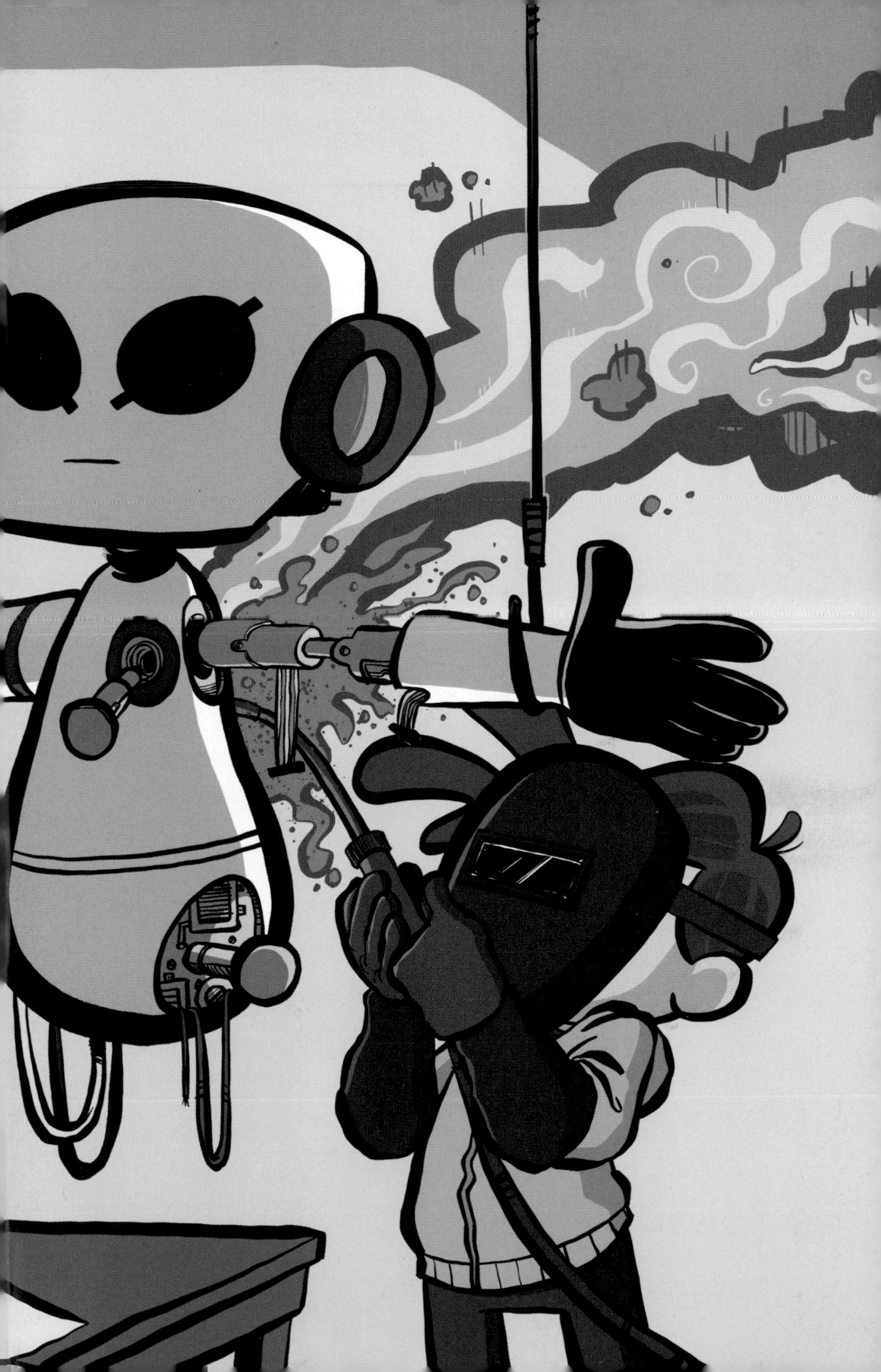

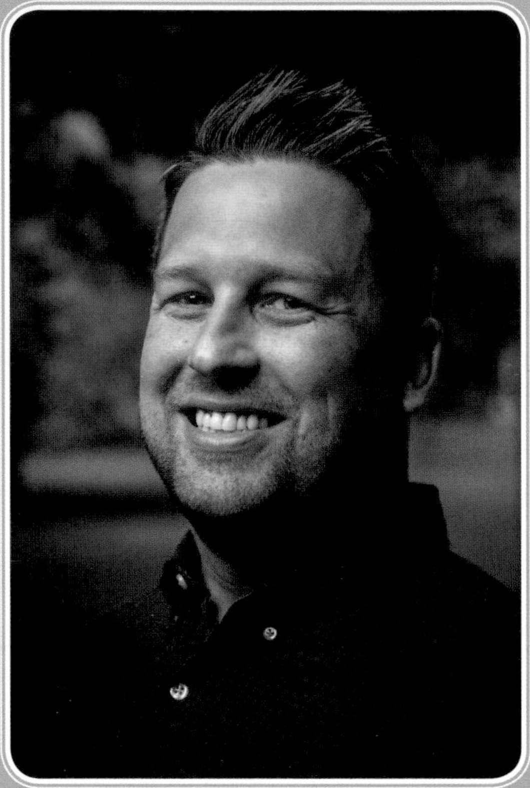

Photo Credit: The Portrait Dude

WES MOLEBASH

(WES MŌL-bash)

The prophesied Legendary Cartoonist of Legends. Created popular webcomics such as *You'll Have That* (Viper Comics) and *Molebashed* (self-published). Has also created cartoons for legendary companies and organizations that include the Ohio State University, Target, and PBS Kids. Currently lives in southern Ohio with his wife, Kari; his sons, Parker and Connor; and a goldendoodle named Payton. *Travis Daventhorpe for the Win!* is his first graphic novel, *but not his last!* Can be found online at **wesmolebash.com**.